1552

Eclipse
of the Crescent
Moon

A TALE OF THE SIEGE
OF EGER, 1552
by
GÉZA GÁRDONYI

Eclipse
of the
Crescent
Moon

CORVINA

Translated and with an Introduction
by
George F. Cushing

Title of the original: Egri csillagok (1901)

Cover and graphics by Győző Vida

Seventh edition

© English translation George F. Cushing, 1991

ISBN 963 13 5481 4

Published in 2005 by
Corvina Books, Budapest
Rákóczi út 16, Hungary 1072
E-mail: corvina@axelero.hu
www.corvinakiado.hu

CONTENTS

GÉZA GÁRDONYI AND *ECLIPSE OF THE CRESCENT MOON*

The historical records of the siege of Eger (Latin: *Agria*, German: *Erlau*) in 1552 contain all the ingredients of a good Victorian adventure-story for boys. The Hungarian defenders, including civilians, numbered about 2,000. They successfully held out unaided for thirty-nine days against a Turkish force at least twenty times as great which also had immense superiority in weapons. During their summer campaign that year two Turkish armies had captured thirty Hungarian fortresses with comparative ease; they now combined in a final attack on Eger to open a route northwards. Their task seemed simple. The fortress, as can still be seen, is awkwardly sited: only on the west and south does it dominate the landscape; hills rise directly above it on the other two sides, providing excellent gun-sites at very short range and commanding good views of the interior of the fortress. Turkish spies reported that Eger was in a weak condition and could be expected to capitulate quickly; a brief siege would therefore end a highly successful campaign. But the expected easy victory did not materialize, and the Turks withdrew in disgrace. The achievement of the defenders was remarkable by any standards. It was the first successful attempt to oppose the Turks in Hungary since the disastrous Battle of Mohács in 1526 had opened the way for their domination of the Danube Basin, something they were achieving with slow but inexorable determination. True, Miklós Jurisich and his 800 men had held a huge Turkish army at bay for twenty-five days at Kőszeg in 1532, but that encounter had ended with a feigned capitulation. Eger had an exceptional commander, István Dobó, who was not only a skilful tactician but a fine leader too. His co-commander István Mekcsey—the joint command was to ensure continuity should either be killed or seriously wounded

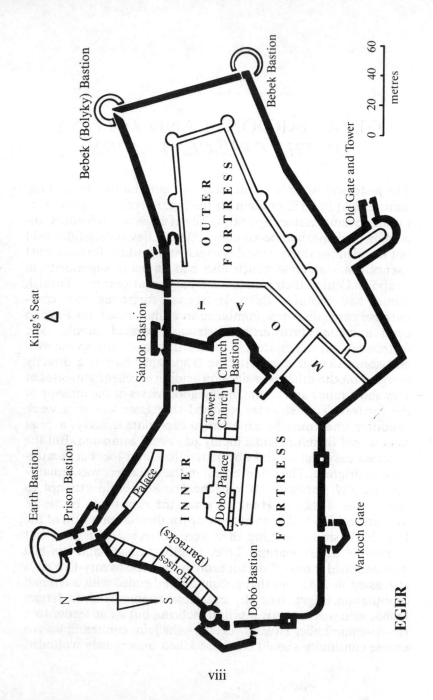

EGER

King's Seat

Bebek (Bolyky) Bastion

Bebek Bastion

Earth Bastion

Prison Bastion

Sándor Bastion

Church Bastion

Palace

Tower Church

Houses (Barracks)

Dobó Palace

Dobó Bastion

INNER FORTRESS

OUTER FORTRESS

MOAT

Old Gate and Tower

Varkoch Gate

metres

0   20   40   60

—was also a heroic figure. Many acts of personal heroism are recorded among both military and civilian defenders, the latter including the women who played a notable part in the final desperate stand. There was a traitor named Hegedűs, who was discovered and summarily executed, and there was a calamitous explosion that destroyed the gunpowder-store and caused extensive structural damage. Yet against all the odds the Hungarians survived to see their besiegers withdraw, defeated by a combination of circumstances: the unexpectedly resolute resistance of the defenders, the lack of adequate food supplies and the early onset of winter.

Among the Hungarian officers one name keeps recurring, that of Gergely Bornemissza, captain of a troop of 250 riflemen sent by the Archduke Maximilian in response to Dobó's request for reinforcements. Why he was chosen is a mystery, since another name appears in Dobó's letter alongside those of Pető and Zoltay who both took part in the defence of Eger. Bornemissza is called *deák*, in other words "scholar", an epithet given to educated laymen who were often employed as secretaries and clerks. But he won fame as an explosives expert. With great ingenuity he used the limited resources of the fortress to keep the Turks in continual fear of devices they had never before encountered. These ranged from simple straw rings dipped in pitch which were lighted and tossed on to the heads of the besiegers to delayed-action grenades and a huge wheel studded with broken rifle-barrels packed with gunpowder; this he rolled down a painstakingly constructed earth rampart into the advancing Turkish troops. He also destroyed a huge wooden siege-tower by tossing anything combustible into it as it was being built, then setting fire to the completed structure. There is no doubt that his fiendish cunning played a major role in the discomfiture of the Turks.

The records contained a story waiting to be told. The siege of Eger was commemorated often enough in story and verse: as early as 1554 the chronicler Sebestyén Tinódi had published two virtual eye-witness accounts of it, while in the nineteenth century the poet Mihály Vörösmarty had returned to the theme in his epic *Eger*, published in 1827. But it was the intriguing figure of Gergely Bornemissza that captured the imagination of the thirty-four year old writer Géza Gárdonyi when in 1897 he escaped from the turmoil of life in Budapest to an isolated house overlooking the ruins of the fortress. Two years later he began to publish *Eclipse of the Crescent Moon* (*Egri csillagok;* lit.: "Stars of Eger") in serial form in a Budapest daily newspaper. It rapidly became one of the most widely read novels in Hungarian and has remained a firm favourite. Generations have been captivated by its skilful blend of real history and imaginative fiction and have been fired by its patriotic and heroic fervour.

Eclipse of the Crescent Moon came as something of a surprise to readers acquainted with Gárdonyi's previous work. He was born Géza Ziegler in 1863, the second child of a skilled mechanic whose largely unsuccessful efforts to better his prospects kept him continually on the move. He and his growing family lived in sixteen places in twenty-three years. The young Géza's education was constantly interrupted and his poor memory served him ill in a system where so much learning by heart was demanded. His father, however, was a great reader and stimulated his son; he also imparted his own patriotic fervour with his memories of the revolution of 1848 in which he had played an exciting part and lost a fortune.

In 1878 Géza Ziegler entered the Teachers' Training College at Eger, not from any ambition to teach, but because his parents could no longer afford to keep him at secondary school. In the following year his father died, plunging the whole family into abject poverty. Géza bore this with stoical resignation, seeking solace in music, for he was a competent organist and later played various other instruments, and in writing. He published humorous sketches in student journals, based on his observation of country folk. Eger was a cathedral town and a place of pilgrimage, drawing huge crowds from all over Hungary; it offered plenty of opportunities for a youth with a quick eye and keen ear to gather material. It was here that he first adopted the name of Gárdonyi, after the village of Gárdony where he was baptized. He completed his course in 1881, and his diary for 23 September of that year records his "rules for life": moderation, silence, order, determination, satisfaction, use of time, sincerity, justice, innocence, cleanliness, calmness, chastity and humility.

x

These are hardly the virtues normally associated with an eighteen-year old, but testify to the hardships he had endured and to his acquaintance with the works of Benjamin Franklin, whose career seemed to him in many ways to resemble his own. For the young Gárdonyi was ambitious, though his future career at that stage was obscure.

He taught for only four years, in primary schools in small villages in Western Hungary. Though he enjoyed the challenge of teaching, he endured the humiliation of his lowly status and erratically-paid stipend with increasing discontent. He turned to writing once more, contributing to local papers, and started two novels which merely showed his indebtedness to the master of Hungarian romantic fiction, Mór Jókai. He also began to study foreign languages seriously, testing his new linguistic skill by attempting translations of Shakespeare and Victor Hugo. And all the time he continued his close observation of people, their oddities and eccentricities. These four years provided him with a wealth of material that he used to advantage in his later works.

Gárdonyi embarked on a journalistic career in 1885 in the town of Győr. At the same time he entered into an ill-advised marriage with a girl of 16 whose temperament and ambitions proved alien to his own. Although they had four children, they lived apart from 1892 and divorce-proceedings were initiated in 1907. Gárdonyi's mother supervised his household. His experience on a provincial paper served him well. He had to write everything from everyday reporting to theatre and music criticism and short stories. He soon developed a concise and graphic style that distinguished him from his contemporaries. Slowly his name became known in the Budapest daily press, a step rightly regarded as an important pointer to literary success, for journalism and imaginative writing were closely linked in Hungary. Meanwhile, with the memory of his teaching experiences fresh in his mind, he founded a new monthly journal *Tanítóbarát* (Teachers' Friend); it advocated radical reform of the educational system and improvement of the conditions of elementary-school teachers. It fulfilled a need and became popular, but demanded continual labour, since Gárdonyi wrote most of it himself. After two years he resigned from it. Since he depended entirely on his writing for his income, he was compelled to write popular romantic tales and humorous sketches that sold well; indeed a series of parodies of H. M. Stanley's explorations in Africa ran to fourteen editions. But in later life Gárdonyi repudiated almost all he had written at this time; he refused to allow republication and destroyed all the available copies. From Győr he moved to Szeged, then regarded as a stepping-stone to acceptance in Budapest, and the nursery of several well-known writers. There in 1890 he published at his own expense a collection of short stories and satires (*Figurák:* Figures) with an introduction by the established novelist Kálmán Mikszáth. Then in 1891 he finally made the move to Budapest where with the help of his friend Sándor Bródy he began to write for the opposition paper *Magyar Hírlap*. He became a successful parliamentary reporter, and in lighter vein began a series of dialect letters to the press, at first anonymously but later under his own name as readers demanded more. In 1894 he published a short novel *A lámpás* (The Lamp), based on his teaching experiences, a volume of verse, a series of sketches of members of parliament and two collections of short stories and articles. At last he had arrived; he was freed from the poverty that had beset him and his name became familiar in literary circles. Next he entered on a new venture, the translation of Dante's *Inferno*. It was published in 1896 and became popular, though it was not a particularly faithful version. Dante caught his imagination, and in his enthusiasm he designed a huge Dante panorama for the Millennial Exhibition of 1896. It proved a failure, and his creditors seized most of his possessions.

The celebrations of 1896 to mark a thousand years of the Hungarian occupation of the Danube Basin brought out in Gárdonyi all his radical and republican instincts. He deliberately refused to take part, instead making a lonely pilgrimage to the Transylvanian village where the poet Petőfi had disappeared during the revolution of 1848. In a remarkable essay based on considerable research, he suggested many of the conclusions about this episode which were worked out independently by András Dienes in 1958. He also had a wild idea of bringing a crowd of country folk to Budapest to demonstrate against the celebrations, but was dissuaded from this. Once again the analogy was with 1848, when the Diet was alarmed by the rumour that Petőfi was leading a mass of forty thousand peasants on Pest.

The strain of life in the capital taxed his health, which was never strong. He searched for a place not too far away where he could work in peace, and discovered it in the peasant house he bought and refurbished in Eger. From the windows he could look down on the ruined fortress; his son József describes how he would walk round the walls, picturing the siege of 1552 and taking special delight in the ingenious tricks of "Gergely the scholar". It was not long before he began to work in earnest, collecting material and reading sources in Hungarian, Latin, German and Turkish. He soon realized that his task was much bigger than he had expected, for "we have a false picture of the events of the Turkish–Hungarian period. If only someone could conjure up these characters so that we might see their eyes, hear their words and feel the beating of their hearts!" He continued to ponder whether it would be possible to write a novel "which would not use history merely as a backcloth but would serve as a light to illuminate the intriguing darkness of past centuries."

He had problems with his chosen hero. Gergely Bornemissza was virtually unknown until he appeared at Eger, but the few years he then had to live were recorded in detail; if Gárdonyi were to follow conventional practice, his novel would end in tragedy, for Gergely was executed in Constantinople at the hands of Ahmed Pasha, one of the unsuccessful Turkish commanders at Eger. So he described the sufferings of Hungarian prisoners in the Seven Towers before the siege proper, and merely hinted there at Gergely's fate (Part III, Chapter 12). As for Gergely's childhood, he sought in vain for clues, so decided to begin his story with Gergely and Eva already married; but this he found unsatisfactory, and for a time he gave up working on the book. Meanwhile he tested his capacity to set a tale convincingly in the Turkish–Hungarian period. *Dávidkáné* (Mrs. Dávidka), a short novel serialized in 1898, is a romantic story based on historical records of the town of Nagykőrös in the seventeenth century. Though it is a slight tale, it nevertheless shows Gárdonyi's eye for detail and attention to historical accuracy, two of the main features of *Eclipse of the Crescent Moon*. This was also the time when *Az én falum* (My Village), a cycle of short stories of village life, was first published. Later expanded, it has remained a firm favourite, not least because it is one of the earliest books to portray real peasants with individual characteristics.

Gárdonyi returned to the theme of the siege of Eger with further research in Vienna and then in Constantinople, where he immersed himself in the atmosphere of the city and witnessed a Shiite procession, duly recorded in Part III. He also gained entrance to the Seven Towers by making a sentry drunk, a scene likewise recalled in the novel. And he travelled by boat up the Golden Horn, carefully recording the scenery for the fine description of the city in the novel. It was an exhausting trip, but he returned with renewed vigour to his story. The first draft was complete at the end of October 1899, and the Budapest paper *Pesti Hírlap* began to publish it in instalments at Christmas of that year. It first appeared in book form in 1901 and won instant acclaim.

Eclipse of the Crescent Moon is a logical step in Gárdonyi's literary progress. It contains elements from all his previous experience. His past as a teacher is seen in didactic asides like the discovery of the potato, his reporter's keen eye in countless details, his care as a researcher in the notes he appends, his parliamentary experiences in such scenes as the one in which Isabella seeks advice from her counsellors, his love of music in the meticulous recording of the Shiite chant, his linguistic ability in the Turkish nicknames and his love of dramatic episode throughout the book. Many of the characters are modelled on friends and relations, for Gárdonyi kept a notebook in which he recorded their mannerisms. Dobó possesses the sternness of his father, while his mother appears as Mrs. Balogh. Gergely Bornemissza is based on his good friend Béla Horváth, a town councillor of Eger. András, the sixteenth-century mayor, is modelled on his nineteenth-century successor Dezső Jankovich. A fellow-student at the Teachers' Training College helped to bring Mekcsey to life, while the doughty fighters Zoltay and Pető are two contemporary writers, Viktor Rákosi and Lajos Pósa, who would have been surprised to discover themselves cast in these roles. Eva Cecey is modelled on Hermin Tima, the daughter of the schoolmaster in Devecser and Gárdonyi's first love. This is his successful method of achieving his object of bringing the period to life.

Yet Gárdonyi was not satisfied with his work; he introduced several revisions to make the novel tauter. Critics complained of its unevenness, and there is some justification in this charge. It falls into a series of episodes which certainly evoke the atmosphere of the period but do not always carry the action forward. The reason is to be sought in its patchwork composition, for Gárdonyi's diary reveals that he did not write it consecutively. And there is a basic unresolved problem, the creation of a convincing hero out of the unknown Gergely Bornemissza without detracting from the heroic figure of the well-known Dobó. At times Gárdonyi appears to play them off against each other. Moreover, the main characters do not develop: both Gergely and Dobó are presented from the beginning as heroic, and the same is true of Bálint Török. The traitor Hegedűs appears as a vacillating character when he is first introduced. But there are some convincing portraits like that of Yumurdjak. And the few women are good romantic figures: the indecisive queen, the noble Mrs. Balogh and the bold Éva Cecey, who is the fit and proper wife for a hero. It is rather the vivid action and colourful description that grip the reader, and here Gárdonyi is masterly. He knows the tradition of epic, and indeed borrows from it; his deliberately detailed description of the huge Turkish army in Part II and the scene in Part V where the defenders assemble in their finest array before the final struggle are reminiscent of Miklós Zrínyi's *Szigeti veszedelem* (The Siege of Sziget).

Gárdonyi's greatest achievement is to weave history with fiction so convincingly that generations of readers have come to regard his story as factual, as indeed much of it is. The only anachronism, and he could not have known this at the time, is that the underground passages were constructed when the fortress was rebuilt after the siege of 1552, as modern archaeological research has demonstrated. And the figure of Gergely Bornemissza remains mysterious. István Sugár's excellent biography (*Bornemissza Gergely deák élete,* Eger, 1984) establishes that he was a nobleman and probably a Lutheran, but where he studied to gain his title of "scholar" and, more important, where he acquired his expertise in explosives, are unknown. He was twice married (Eva Cecey is a fictional character). After the siege he was rewarded by both the monarch and the bishop, the owner of the fortress, with very large gifts of land, villages and houses. It was he who after the resignation of Dobó and Mekcsey reported personally to the king and returned to take over command of the fortress. His rebuilding operations were hampered by lack of funds and equipment, despite their urgency. The Turks, after all, had merely withdrawn; elsewhere in Hungary they were strengthening their grip, and a new attack had to be expected. (When it eventually came in 1596 the 7,000 defenders capitulated after little resistance. Sultan Mehmet III himself commanded the Turkish troops, and in his entourage was the English ambassador, Edward Barton, who wrote an account of it.) In 1554 Gergely Bornemissza received news of a marauding band of Turks near Eger and led a small force to drive them off. But the Turks, led by Veli Bey who figures in the novel, far outnumbered the Hungarians and captured them. Since theoretically an armistice was in force at the time, protests were made, but to no avail. Most of the captives were taken to Constantinople. It was at this time that Gergely Bornemissza made his will, one of the few documents known to be written by him; it reveals him as a rich and cultured man of great generosity who made specific provision for the poor in particular villages. He was imprisoned in the Seven Towers and urged to betray the weakest points of the fortress of Eger, as his letter to the ambassador Antal Verancsics reveals. It was Verancsics who first recorded his death. In a letter dated 15 October 1555 he wrote, "In the past few days Ahmed Pasha, shortly before his own death, had Gergely the scholar and a Croatian abominably put to death by hanging... As a soldier and a hero, it would have been much more honourable had he been dispatched by the sword." Such was Ahmed's revenge for his disgrace at Eger.

Gárdonyi wrote two more substantial historical novels at this time. The first, *Láthatatlan ember* (*Slave of the Huns,* Dent London, 1969) was published in 1901 and became his own favourite work. The second, *Isten rabjai* (Slaves of God, 1908), is based on the life of St. Margaret of Hungary. Both books reveal more of Gárdonyi's personal problems than does *Eclipse of the Crescent Moon*. He continued to experiment with various styles of writing till his death in 1922. He had asked for a simple burial, but the town of Eger would not allow its most famous resident to depart so unobtrusively and gave him a lavish funeral. His grave, marked by a single stone slab, is situated inside the fortress, an appropriate place for the writer who resurrected its past glory so vividly,

Gárdonyi was an extremely reserved individual, even to his own family. Yet an early poem, first published in his volume *Április* (April), 1894, is revealing; it is entitled *Történetem* (My Story):

The Lord went into the pottery.
"Today", he said, "I'll make a few animals;
I need an owl, a tiger, a lamb and a cricket."
And he settled down to work.
But because there happened to be too little clay
Some of the figures that should have been large turned out tiny.
"Oh!" he said, annoyed, "I'm having a bad day today
And I'm not in a good mood either."
And crushing together the four figures
He quickly created me out of them.

Here Gárdonyi characterized himself better than the critics who struggled to understand his complex character and fathom the variety and unevenness of his writing. In a brief portrait of him written in 1928 his younger fellow-writer Dezső Kosztolányi offered some excellent advice: "The one-time village schoolmaster is today the teacher of all Hungarians. Instead of theorizing and obscuring things with interpretations, let's begin to read Gárdonyi himself." Generations who have been captivated by *Eclipse of the Crescent Moon* in their youth would agree.

George Cushing

xvii

PART I

Where Do Hungarian Heroes Come From?

1

Two children, a boy and a girl, are bathing in the stream. Maybe it's not right for them to be bathing together, but they do not know that; the boy is not quite seven years old, the girl two years younger.

They were walking in the forest and came across a stream. The sun shone fiercely. In a hollow, the water widened into a pool the size of a cart. It attracted them.

At first they just dipped their feet into it, then they went in up to their knees. Gergely's little trousers got wet, so he threw them off. Then he pulled off his shirt as well. And all of a sudden both of them were splashing about with nothing on.

And they might well bathe; nobody could see them there. The road to Pécs was a long way off and the forest was endless. If anyone were to catch sight of them, there would be trouble. Never mind the little boy—he was no young gentleman,—but the little girl was a young lady, the daughter of the honourable Péter Cecey, and she had slipped out of the house without anyone seeing her.

Even without her clothes she is obviously a young lady of quality: she is plump as a pigeon and white as milk. As she splashes around in the water her two little blonde plaits bob about on her neck.

"Gergő," she says to the boy, "let's swim."

The thin little dark-haired boy she calls Gergő turns round. The little girl clasps his neck. Gergő strikes out for the bank, while the girl floats and kicks on the surface of the water.

But when they reach the bank, Gergő grasps the green clump of bulrushes and looks around anxiously.

"Oh, what's happened to the grey horse?"

He steps out of the water and runs here and there, peering among the trees. He examines the ground too for footprints.

"Wait for me, Evie," he shouts to the girl. "Wait for me, I'll be back soon!" And naked as he is, he dashes off, following the tracks towards the Pécs road.

3

A few minutes later he comes back on an old grey horse. On its head is a miserable halter made of twine. This had been tied to its feet, but the knot had come undone.

The boy silently strikes the horse with a bough of cornelian cherry. His face is pale with terror. He keeps glancing over his shoulder. When he arrives at the place where they have been bathing, he hangs on to the horse's neck, then slides down and jumps to the ground.

"Hide!" he whispers, shivering. "Hide! There's a Turk coming!"

With a couple of tugs he tethers the horse to a tree. He snatches his clothes from the ground. And the two little children run naked to a hawthorn bush. They hide, crouching on the dead leaves behind the bush.

In those times Turks were a common sight on the roads. And you, reader, who think that those two children were bathing this summer in the stream, are very much mistaken. Where are those two children now? And where are the Turk and all those people you will meet in this book, moving, acting, talking, laughing and crying? They are all dust and ashes.

So put aside this year's calendar, reader, and in your mind bring out the one for 1533. You are now living in May of that year, and you are under the rule of either King John Szapolyai or the Turks or Ferdinand I.

The little village from which the children come lies hidden in the Mecsek Hills. There are about thirty houses of cob and a large one of stone in all. The windows in every house, the large one too are of oilcloth. But otherwise they are thatched houses like those of today. The little village is encircled by trees with dense foliage, and its inhabitants think the Turks will never find the way there. How could they? The road is steep and there are no ruts in it. Nor is there a church tower. People live and die in the little hidden village like woodland insects.

The father of the boy Gergő had once been a smith in Pécs, but he had died. His mother had retired to Keresztesfalva with her father, a grey-haired old peasant who had once fought in the rebellion led by György Dózsa. For that reason, he had been given refuge by Cecey, the village squire.

The old man sometimes went down through the forest to Pécs

4

to beg. Even in winter they lived on what the old man managed to beg. From time to time scraps from the squire's house appeared on their table too.

That day the old man had returned from the town.

"Take the grey out to graze," he said to his grandson. "The poor thing hasn't had anything to eat since morning. And water it at the stream."

That was how Gergő had gone into the forest with the horse. On the way, as he passed the squire's house, little Eva had peeped out of the garden gate and begged him,

"Gergő, Gergő! Let me come too!"

Gergő dared not tell the young lady to stay at home. He got off the horse and took Eva wherever she wanted to go. Eva wanted to go where the butterflies went. The butterflies flitted into the forest, so they too ran in that direction. At last they caught sight of the stream and Gergő let the horse graze. That is how they came to the woodland stream and from there to the back of the hawthorn bush.

They crouch there. They tremble because of the Turk. And their fear is well-founded. A few minutes later the undergrowth crackles and suddenly a white Turkish cap with an ostrich-feather in it appears beneath the trees, together with a brown horse's head.

The Turk looks in all directions and turns his head this way and that. His glance rests on the grey horse. He is leading his own little chestnut.

Now they can see that the Turk is sharp-featured and dark-haired. Over his shoulder is a walnut-brown cloak. On his head a tall white cap. One of his eyes has a white cloth bandage. The other eye examines the grey horse tethered to the tree. The sneer on his face shows that he does not think much of it. But all the same he untethers it.

He would prefer to have the boy he had seen on the horse. Boys fetch a better price than horses. At the Constantinople slave-market they offer three times as much. But there is no sign of the boy anywhere.

The Turk looks behind several trees and peers up into the foliage too. Then he calls out in Hungarian, "Where are you, little boy? Come out, my little friend! I've some figs for you. Do come out!"

The boy does not appear.

"Come here! Don't be afraid, I won't hurt you! Come on out! If you don't, I'll take your horse away!"

And so saying he takes the reins of both horses in one hand and leads them away among the trees.

The two children listened, silent and pale, to the Turk. His offer of figs did not release them from their numb terror. At home they had far too often heard the curse "May the Turks carry you off!" and hair-raising tales about the Turks for them to venture out, however tempting the offer. But when the Turk said he would take the grey horse away, the boy Gergő stirred. He gazed at Evie as if he expected some advice from her, and he looked as if there was a thorn pricking his foot.

He's going off with the grey! What will they say at home if he goes back without the grey horse?

Little Eva did not respond to all these thoughts. She crouched beside him, deadly pale. Her big catlike eyes were moist with terror.

But the grey horse had gone. Gergő heard its footsteps. It had heavy, sluggish footsteps. The dry undergrowth crackled rhythmically beneath its feet. So the Turk really was taking it away!

"The grey..." stammers Gergő, his mouth drooping, ready to cry. And he raises his head.

The grey horse goes on. The forest undergrowth crackles under its feet.

And now Gergő forgets all about his fear. He jumps up and dashes, naked as he is, after the grey horse.

"Mister!" he calls, trembling, "Mister Turk!"

The Turk stops and gives a grin.

What an ugly man! He grins as if he is ready to bite.

"Mister, the grey..." stutters Gergő, crying. "The grey belongs to us..." And he stops about twenty paces away.

"Come on then, if it's yours," replies the Turk. "Here you are." And he throws the grey's reins out of his hand.

Now the boy only has eyes for the grey horse. As it starts to move sluggishly, he runs up to it and grabs the bridle.

At that instant he too is grabbed. The Turk's big strong

fingers twine round his feeble little bare arm and he is whisked up on to the other horse, the chestnut, and into its saddle.

Gergő whimpers.

"Shush!" says the Turk and pulls out his dagger.

But Gergő goes on to shout, "Evie! Evie!"

The Turk turns his head to where the boy does. His hand on the dagger.

Of course, when the other little naked child rises out of the grass he sticks the dagger back again and smiles.

"Come here, come on," he says, "I won't harm you." And he sets off with the two horses towards the little girl.

Gergő tries to get down from the horse. The Turk's hand comes down on his back with a great slap. So Gergő cries and stays sitting there, while the Turk leaves the two horses and runs after the little girl.

Poor little Eva tries hard to escape now, but her feet are tiny and the grass is tall. She falls down. Soon she is kicking and whimpering in the Turk's arms.

"Shush!" says the Turk, slapping her bottom. "Shush, or I'll eat you up if you don't keep quiet. Sh! Sh!"

The little girl falls silent. Only her heart pounds like that of a sparrow caught in someone's hand.

But as soon as they reach the horses she starts screaming again, "Daddy! Daddy!" For in her despair she thinks her cries can be heard at any distance.

The boy Gergő also cries. Twisting his fists in his eyes he cries, "I'm going home. I want to go home!"

"Shut up, you ragged little bastard!" the Turk snaps at him, "or I'll chop you in two!" And he waves his fist threateningly at Gergő.

The two children are silent. The little girl has almost fainted from terror. Gergő whimpers quietly as he sits on the chestnut.

And off they go.

They emerge from the forest. The boy Gergő sees a colourful horde of Turks in carts making its way along the road up the Mecsek Hills. *Akindjis* on horseback, *asabs* on foot, guerillas in varied uniforms. They straggle towards Pécs on nimble little horses.

The group in front of them escorts some ten loaded waggons

7

and carts. On the carts there are white bedclothes, cupboards, wooden beds, barrels, chairs, animal hides and sacks of corn in a confused jumble. Beside the carts tramp miserable captives with feet in chains and hands tied behind their backs.

Our janissary has three carts and seven prisoners. There are another five janissaries in baggy blue trousers, red boots and white caps—these adorned in front with a bone-spoon, except for one which has a wooden spoon; and there are three fur-capped *asab*s with long pikes. The one-eyed janissary's dust-covered white ostrich-feather flutters from the front of his cap almost half way down his back.

While he was away in the forest, the three carts had pulled aside off the road to let the others pass on their way home.

The janissaries greeted the two children and the grey horse with laughter.

What were they babbling about in Turkish? Gergő cannot understand them. Obviously they are talking about them and about the horse. They smile when they look at him and at Evie. When they look at the horse they wave as if they are chasing away a fly.

The Turk tosses the two children up on to the cart, on top of the bed-linen. A plump girl sits there, a captive with her legs in chains; he puts them in her charge. Then one of the janissaries unties a filthy sack and pulls out of it all sorts of clothes. They are all children's clothes. Among them are little skirts, little frieze-coats, jackets with metal buttons, caps, hats and little boots. The Turk selects two little shirts and a little frieze-coat and throws them up on to the cart.

"Put some clothes on them," says the one-eyed Turk to the plump girl.

The girl is about seventeen years old, a peasant girl. As she dresses the two children, she embraces them and kisses them. Her eyes are tearful.

"What's your name, my little angel?"

"Evie."

"And yours, my dear?"

"Gergő."

"Don't cry, dears. You'll be with me."

"But I want to go home," weeps Gergely.

8

"And so do I," weeps the little girl, "Home..."

The captive girl hugs them with both her hands.

"The good Lord will lead you home, so don't cry."

2

The village dogs snarled angrily as they leapt around a pilgrim with a white beard and a mop of hair. They would certainly have pulled his monk's habit off him if he had not boldly laid about him with his big stick that ended in a cross.

At first he walked in the middle of the road, but as the big shaggy dogs increased in number he carefully retreated to the angle of an L-shaped hedge and wielded his stick, waiting for someone to come out and release him from the siege.

But those who did come out at all the barking only had eyes for five Hungarian soldiers who galloped into the village. A light-haired warrior in a red cloak rode at their head. He had a crane's feather in his cap. Before him a rifle was slung across his saddle. From beneath his light, cherry-red jacket gleamed a shirt of mail. Behind him came four other soldiers. As they arrived in the village they turned their heads right and left as if each house in it were something miraculous. All five of them were perspiring from the heat.

In front of Cecey's gate there slumbered an ancient peasant with a pike, sitting on a projecting stone. At the sound of the horses he woke up, snorting. He quickly opened the other door in the gateway, and the horsemen trotted over the bridge into the yard.

Cecey was perched in the shade of the barn like an old eagle. Some of his serfs were shearing sheep there, shears in their hands, swords at their sides. Shirt, trousers, sandals and sword at one's side: that was the way of the world in Hungary at that time.

Cecey caught sight of the soldiers. He got up and walked over to meet them. The old man had a peculiar way of walking: one of his legs would not bend at the knee, the other would not bend at the ankle. How could they have bent, since both were of wood? And his right hand was missing too. The sleeve of his canvas jacket dangled empty from his wrist. His face seemed to be all beard; his shoulder-length hair was white and his beard grey.

The soldier with the crane-feather jumped from his horse and tossed the reins to one of the men. He hurried over to Cecey. "My name is István Dobó." And he clicked his heels.

He was a lanky, angular young man. His mouth was wider than normal—one of those stubborn, thin-lipped mouths that seem to be biting an invisible bit—and all his movements suggested strength; his legs seemed to be made of steel. His eyes were piercing, strong and grey.

Cecey stuck his hand behind his back. "Whose army are you serving in?" And his eyes blazed as if there were embers behind them.

"Now in Bálint Török's," replied Dobó.

"In other words, you're one of Ferdinand's men. Welcome, young friend!" And he offered him his hand. With one glance he sized up the horse, with the next his sword. "Which branch of the Dobó family do you come from?"

"The Ruszka branch, sir."

"Related to the Pálóczys."

"That's right."

"In other words you come from Upper Hungary. How do you come to be here? What wind blows you this way, lad?"

"We've just come from Palota, sir."

"From Móré's castle?"

"It's not his any longer."

"Whose then?"

"At the moment it's nobody's. Nor is it any longer a castle, just a heap of stones."

The wooden-legged old man stared. "Did you raze it?"

"To the ground."

"Thank God. Well, come into the shade, lad, here on the veranda. Hi, mother! We've got a visitor!" And once again he stared at Dobó. "You actually razed it to the ground?"

By now the stout little lady was busy on the veranda. With a servant she moved a table into the shade. The other servant had already opened the door of the wine-store.

"Pista Dobó," said Cecey, introducing the young man to his

10

wife, "a relative of the Pálóczys. Wine and something to eat for the soldiers."

Dobó took a red handkerchief from his jacket and wiped his face. "Before I sit down, sir," he said, examining Cecey's face, "I must ask you whether Móré's here. Because I'm looking for him."

"Here? Móré? The only place I want to see him is on the gallows."

Dobó went on wiping his face and neck. "Then we're on the wrong trail. I'd like a little water, please."

"Wait a moment. They're just getting the wine."

"I drink water when I'm thirsty, sir." And he picked up the big round pitcher and raised it to his lips. "If you'll allow me, I'll rest here till evening," he said, spluttering after his drink.

"But I'm not going to let you go for several days! Whatever are you thinking of?"

"Thank you. This is no time for merriment. I didn't sleep last night. We're going on tonight. But I'd be glad to take off my shirt of mail for a little. It's hot in weather like this, even if it's stitched full of holes."

While Dobó was undressing inside, the pilgrim also arrived at the gate.

"You've come from the Friar!" said Cecey, staring at him.

And his eyes once more glowed as if there were embers behind them.

"Yes," said the pilgrim with a smile, "How do you know?"

"I can tell from your beard. It's white with badger-grease."

"True."

"That tells me you've come a long way."

"That's also true."

"Well, nobody really sends me messages from a long way off except the Father Superior at Sajólád, who's a relative, may he be struck by lightning!"

"Oh, but he's not been Father Superior for a long time, sir. He's a friend of the king."

"I know that too, and may he and his master roast in hell! What's your name?"

"Imre Varsányi."

"How old are you?"

11

"Thirty."

"Right. Now let's see what news you've brought."

The pilgrim sat down on the ground and unpicked the lining of his cloak. "It's devilish hot in these parts," he muttered good-humouredly. "And the Turks are as thick as flies."

"We've got the Friar and your king to thank for that. Now where the devil have you sewn that letter?"

Varsányi finally pulled out a little letter with a red seal and offered it to him.

"Give this man something to eat and drink, and find him somewhere to sleep," said Cecey to his wife. And he broke the seal and unfolded the letter.

"That's the Friar's handwriting," he said, peering at the letter. "It's clear as print, but very tiny. I can't read it anyway. Send for the priest."

The pilgrim went and sat in the shade of the walnut-tree.

"I'm sure he wrote something good," he thought with satisfaction, "because he didn't urge me to hurry. Whenever he sends a letter with a big seal I've always got to make haste. This one's only got a little seal, so it's not a national matter." And with the quiet delight of a man who has reached his goal he took a swig from the wine-jug set in front of him.

The lady also took the letter in her hand. She looked at it below and above and examined the broken seal. She turned to the pilgrim. "Is Uncle George in good health?"

A servant put milk-cheese and bread before the pilgrim. He immediately searched for his knife. "He's never ill, madam."

By now the priest had also arrived, a bull-headed, broad-shouldered man with a grey beard. The stranger rose and wanted to kiss his hand. But the priest drew back.

"Are you a papist? Or a reformer?" And he grasped at the chin his silvery beard that reached half way down his chest.

"I'm a papist," replied the pilgrim.

Then the priest offered him his hand.

They went into the room. The priest went and stood by the window and read the Latin letter in Hungarian.

"My dear brother..."

The priest had an odd flat voice, as if the words were coming from his stomach. The consonants in his speech could only be guessed. But those who were used to it could understand what he was saying.

He went on,

"...*and dear Juliska. I desire that God may grant you all good health and a peaceful life. Furthermore, I am informed that in your part of the country either Móré or the Turks are daily laying waste the land, and that now only the serfs bound to the land remain in their places; whoever can do so is fleeing, some to Upper Hungary, others to the Austrians. So if you, my dear ones, are still alive and still there in Keresztes, save yourselves too. I have spoken with His Majesty to compensate you for your loss...*"

"Don't go on!" Cecey burst out. "Only a dog needs a dog's mercy!"

"Quiet, my dear," his wife restrained him. "George is wise. He knows that we won't accept anything from Szapolyai. Just listen to the rest of the letter."

The priest knitted his shaggy brows and went on reading:

"...*The king cannot give you back Sásod anyway, but there is a village not far from Nagyvárad...*"

"Stop, stop, Bálint!" Cecey lashed out, red with fury.

"There's something else to follow," replied the priest. And he went on reading:

"*But if your hatred for him is so deeply engrained...*"

"It is, it is!" cried Cecey and banged on the table. "Neither in this world nor the next! Or if there, well, there too only with arms!"

The priest continued to read:

"...*Here in Buda my own little house stands empty and we are moving to Nagyvárad soon. There's only a bowmaker living there in the basement. The three upper rooms are empty.*"

Cecey rose. "I don't want it! You bought it with Szapolyai's money, friar! May it fall down if I enter it!"

The priest shrugged. "How do you know he bought it with that? Suppose he inherited it?"

But Cecey was beyond listening to them. He stumped furiously out of the room and clattered his way along the veranda.

The pilgrim was eating there at the end of it, under the walnut-tree. He stopped in front of him, wrathful and haughty.

"Tell the Friar that I send my respects. What he wrote is the same as if he had written nothing."

"So there's no answer?"

"No." And on he plodded, out to the barn. He stumped up and down in the sunshine. From time to time he slashed to right and left with his stick as if he were driving away invisible dogs and murmured angrily,

"My head isn't made of wood yet!"

The peasants sheared the sheep all the more zealously. The dogs also retreated. Even the house seemed to have slipped lower down the bank.

The lady of the house stood with the priest in the porch. The priest was shrugging his shoulders.

"And even if it isn't inherited", he was saying, "it's something the Friar acquired with his work. He can give it to anyone he likes. So let him give it to Péter. In that case it'll be a Cecey house and not even the king himself can give orders there."

Dobó stepped out of the room. The lady introduced him to the priest and at the same time called Evie's name.

"Evie! Where are you, Evie?"

"She's playing in the garden," replied one of the servants.

Cecey also returned and snorted at the priest, "Hey, priest, you've changed your tune! You'll yet join John as his standard-bearer!"

"And you'll drop the name of Hungarian in your old age!" snarled the priest in return.

"You'll serve as a hangman!" screeched Cecey.

"And you as an Austrian!" retorted the enraged priest.

"Hangman!"

"Austrian!"

"Dog-catcher!"

"Traitor!"

By now the two old men were almost blue with rage as they roared at each other. Dobó waited for the moment when they would be dragged apart.

"Do stop wrangling, for heaven's sake!" he said uncomfortably, "or rather, save that for the Turks."

Cecey waved a hand. He flopped into a chair. "You don't understand, lad. Szapolyai had this priest's tongue and my right

14

hand cut off. So isn't he a fool to defend Szapolyai with the bit of tongue he's got left?"

"If he were only my enemy," replied the priest in a calm voice, "I'd have forgiven him long ago. But I still say, rather let him rule the Hungarians than the Austrian."

"But rather the Austrian than the Turks!" screamed Cecey once again.

Dobó interrupted them to prevent another clash between them.

"Neither of them's much good, that's true. We Upper Hungarians think we've got to wait and see whether the Austrians will raise a force against the Turks, and whether John will really betray the country to the Turks."

"He's sold it to them long ago, lad," Cecey said with a resigned wave of the hand.

"I don't think so," replied Dobó. "All he wanted was the crown, not the friendship of the Turks."

Meanwhile a dish of fried chicken was put on the table on the veranda. The expressions of the two old men relaxed.

They sat down to eat.

"Why, when I was as young as you are, lad," said Cecey, wagging his head, "— how old are you?"

"Thirty-one," replied Dobó. "Soon nobody's going to call me young, that's for sure."

"You're young until you get married. And it's high time you did."

"I haven't had the time so far," Dobó smiled. "Ever since I was a child I've always been in the wars."

"That's all right then. That's how Hungarians have lived since the beginning of the world. Do you think, maybe, that dancing made me lame in both legs? Why, my lad, I began with Kinizsi. King Matthias called me by my name. And then I ended with Dózsa, who, believe me, was a hero among heroes."

He took the brimming leaden cup and raised it to Dobó.

"May God favour the Hungarians, and you, my lad, especially. May He grant victory to your sword. And a pretty girl for your wife. Can you play chess?"

"No, I can't," replied Dobó, smiling at this sudden change of thought. And he drained his cup. It was good strong red wine.

He thought to himself, "Now I know what makes these two old men so angry."

"Well then, you'll never make a good military leader," said Cecey.

"Not if we were to fight oriental fashion, army against army. But we only fight like Hungarians, man against man. And that's something the chessboard doesn't teach."

"So you can play after all."

"No. I just happen to know the game."

"Well, when you learn to play, you'll judge it differently. A single hour of chess, my lad, contains all the problems of a real battle."

"So do you two always play chess here at home?"

"Us? Never. We quarrel enough without playing chess. We quarrel as soon as there's talk of politics. And, you see, we grew up together, lived together, fought together..."

"And we'll die together too," the priest finished the sentence, nodding.

And the two old men looked at each other amicably and touched their cups.

"But you must admit, Bálint, that the man who routed that fox Móré out of his castle did a fine job. And that was Ferdinand, of course." And he wiped his moustache.

"It wasn't only Ferdinand," responded Dobó. "It was the two kings together. The army was a joint one. They were fed up with his blackguardly tricks. The last thing he did was to turn over the graves."

"But all the same it was Ferdinand who fought better against him."

"No, John did more. Ferdinand merely instructed Bálint Török to aid John and sent fifty miners."

"To bring down the walls?"

"Yes. And there were some Turkish troops with us too."

"Under John's banner, of course."

"Yes, and the devil take such assistance! They always plunder on the way home."

"Those pigs of *akindjis*."

"Yes."

"And was it easy to deal with that castle?"

16

"I wouldn't say that, Mr. Cecey. It was built with tough walls. Neither army brought along any siege-guns. And what use are falconets?"

"I've been there," the priest said. "It's on rock, not palisaded. So they didn't surrender the castle?"

"No. We had to set the fifty miners to work on the rock. Their work was long and hard, I can tell you. The axes struck sparks on the stone, and the iron rods scarcely penetrated the rock an inch at each blow. But in the end even stone gives way to a lot of hands."

"Did you blow it up?"

"First of all we sent Móré a message that the mine was already full of gunpowder. Then he replied telling us to wait till morning. We waited. And what did that cunning fox do? He called the folk inside together and urged them to hold out firmly while he slipped out and ran for aid. "All right," they replied, "but what guarantee is there that you'll come back?" "Both my children will stay here," replied the rogue, "and all my gold and silver possessions. What more do you want?" And he slipped down a rope from the castle wall. He vanished. We couldn't see him, of course, in the darkness. When the sun rose and there was no sign of a white flag, no envoy, no opening of the gate, we set off the mines. Couldn't you hear it here? It was a mountain-shattering explosion. The walls fell down on the spot. And we went into the castle. Our soldiers were so furious that they slew all Móré's folk."

"His children too?"

"No, not them. We found them in a stone vault. They're a fine pair of little dark-haired boys. They've been with King John since then."

"So now you're searching for Móré?"

"I just made a detour this way with these four men of mine, because on the way we were talking with a watchman in whose wine-cellar he slept. He said he was coming in this direction, making for Pécs."

Mrs. Cecey turned round. "Magda," she said to the servant scrubbing in the yard, "where's Evie?"

"I haven't seen her," replied the servant-girl. "She was playing in the garden after lunch."

17

"Run along and look for her."

"That's my little daughter," smiled Cecey. "God's gift to me in my old age. You'll see what a little fairy she is."

"Haven't you a son, sir?"

Cecey shook his head, looking grave. "If I had a son, my lad, even this hand of mine would grow again like a lobster's claw."

But there was no sign of the child. Amidst all the conversation and reading of the letter everyone had forgotten about little Eva. The servant-girls certainly had no thought for her. They all found things to do in the yard. The soldiers twirled their moustaches. The girls fluttered their skirts. They were enjoying themselves, as if all the soldiers had come in search of brides to Cecey's house.

They were soon searching high and low around the house.

"Evie! Evie!"

They examined every bush, every place in the village where she played. Where was Aunt Kató? She looked after her. Maybe the old woman had gone off to sleep. Who'd seen Eva? Nobody. A little boy had talked with her at the back of the garden that afternoon. Who had gone that way that afternoon? Nobody but the boy Gergő. He'd taken his grandfather's horse out to graze. Well, where was Gergő then? He was nowhere to be found either. He must have gone with the horse into the forest. Oh, the rashness of the child! How many times had he been told not to go with the horse beyond the mulberry bushes!

They searched the forest around the village.

"Evie! Evie!"

Dobó and his men joined in too. They searched every tree, every bush, every dip and hollow and thicket around the village. Suppose she had fallen asleep somewhere?

"Evie! Evie!"

Gergely's mother joined in the search, weeping. They came across old Kató in the forest. She too had been looking for a long time. She had already shouted herself hoarse.

At last, towards evening, one of the servants gave a great shout.

"Here they are!"

"Thank God for that!"

"Their clothes are here."

18

Their clothes, yes, but only their clothes: the little cambric blouse, crimson boots, yellow taffeta skirt and the boy Gergő's shirt, trousers and hat. They had been bathing, that was plain. There were their footsteps in the soft sand on the bank of the stream. The bigger footprints, with the toes wide apart, were Gergő's, the smaller ones Eva's. They must surely have drowned somewhere in the water.

3

"My name's Margit. Just call me Auntie Margit," said the captive girl in the cart. "I'll tell you stories. I know a lot of stories. Where do you come from, dears?"

"The village", replied Gergő tearfully.

"The village", whimpered the little girl too.

"Which village?"

"That one, over there."

"But what's the name of the village?"

"Its name?"

"Yes, what's its name?"

"Its name? I don't know."

The girl who called herself Margit had a round face and a mouth pursed ready for kissing. There were a few freckles round her nose. She wore a necklace of blue glass beads. The Turks had seized her from an estate in Somogy.

She just shook her head at the children's replies. Secretly she tore some of the bedlinen in the cart and wound it round a wooden spoon to make a doll.

"This'll be Evie's doll. It's got a yellow head-scarf and a red skirt. We'll dress it, rock it, dance it and put it to sleep."

The cart and its captives went silently on.

Beside the cart there walked a broad-chested peasant lad and a pock-marked young gypsy. Both of them were barefoot. The gypsy was wearing a much-patched blue pair of trousers and a blue hussar's jacket. Sticking out of the inside pocket of his jacket was the filthy mouthpiece of a wooden pipe. On the other side of the cart hobbled a priest in a black gown and a peasant with tousled head and a big face. The peasant might have been about forty. The priest was younger. He was a tall, thin-faced man. He had neither beard nor moustache or even eyebrows. And he was red as beetroot. Only the pupils of his eyes were black. Only a few days ago the Turks had poured boiling water over him to make him hand over his church's treasures.

Treasures? His church had none.

So all of them, poor things, were captives. On their feet were chains, and their hands were also in irons, some in front, some behind. The lad was chained to the gypsy, the priest to the peasant. The lad had lined his chains with rags above his ankles.

The rags were already red.

"Do stop," he pleaded from time to time, looking over his shoulder, "and let me alter the position of my chains."

But the janissaries took no notice of him. They were gossiping to each other in Turkish, and at most their reply was just an angry glance.

Gergely's eyes were drawn to the lad. How big his hands were! And what a lot of buttons he had on his waistcoat! He was not afraid. If those hands had not been chained behind him, maybe all the Turks would have run away from him.

The lad was certainly not afraid. He raised his head and roared at the hunchbacked Turk riding beside him,

"May the lot of you burn in hellfire, you pagan wolves!"

"Gáspár, Gáspár!" Margit tried to calm him from the top of the cart. "Put up with it all in peace as long as you can. Look, the sun's beginning to go down; they always stop round about now."

As she wiped her eyes when she said this, the two children burst into tears.

"I want to go home," whimpered Gergely.

"To daddy!" wept little Eva.

The Turks did indeed halt. They got down from their horses and produced pitchers. They washed their hands, feet and faces. Then they knelt down in a straight line facing the east. They kissed the ground and prayed.

The captives watched them in silence.

The girl came down from the cart and tore a piece from the edge of her blouse. She wound it round the lad's leg and thus eased the chains away from it with kindly care.

20

"God bless you, Margit," sighed the lad.

"If we can, we'll put some plantains on it for the night, Gáspár." And her face dissolved into tears. She wept for a few minutes every hour, but immediately afterwards she sang to the children too. Because when she wept, they cried too.

· "Eh, but I am 'ungry!" the gypsy burst out as he sat beside them in the dust. "I've never 'ad such a long fast in all me life."

The driver, also a captive lad with his legs in chains, smiled at the gypsy's desire.

"I'm hungry too," he responded with a scornful glance at the Turks, "but this evening I'll cook such a paprika stew that it'll all be left for us."

"What? Be you the cook then?"

The driver raised his eyebrows at the familiarity of the tone, but all the same he replied, "Only in the evening. During the day these folk go robbing even for their lunch."

"May their eyes stick together! May their legs be racked with cramps at carnival-time! So 'ow long 'ave you been in service wi' them?"

"Three days."

"Isn't it possible to slip away somehow?"

"No. From these folk, never. Just see the kind of boots I'm wearing."

He pulled up his legs as he was sitting there. Thick, heavy chains clanked up with them.

"But suppose you don't do the cooking today?" the gypsy went on anxiously.

"I'm sure I shall. Yesterday I cooked them a meal that made them lick their lips afterwards like dogs."

"If only I could lick my lips now! But I don't even know if I've got a mouth, except when I speak now and again."

"They looted wine too at lunch-time. Here it is at the back of the cart."

"Don't give me that! The Turks don't drink!"

"Ah, but not one of them's a Turk when they see wine."

"Well then, today's me day," the gypsy brightened up. "I'll play 'em a tune that'll make 'em get up and dance."

When prayers were over, the one-eyed janissary did not set the carts on their way. From the top of the hill a town could be seen

21

down in the valley, veiled by the dusk. That was a haunt of Hungarians, a wasps' nest.

The Turks deliberated. Then the one-eyed janissary called over to the driver, "Follow me! Into the forest!"

And they took the carts and waggons a good way into the forest, about a quarter of an hour's drive.

Meanwhile the sun sank between the trees. Dusk covered the forest. The first star began to twinkle in the clear sky.

The Turks picketed the horses in a convenient clearing. The janissary released the priest's hands and shouted at him, "You build a fire!"

"I'm better at that!" said the gypsy eagerly. "Honourable Mister Turk, kiss yer 'ands and feet, let me lay a fire; that's me trade."

"Shut up!" the Turk belched at him.

They also called down three of the women captives to help make the fire. The women and the priest gathered brushwood and dry sticks beneath the nearby trees. With flint and steel they soon had a fire going.

They also released the driver from his seat.

"The same as yesterday," the one-eyed Turk commanded him.

The driver put a big iron pot full of water on the fire and when the priest and the gypsy had rapidly skinned the sheep, he chopped it up with a practised hand and dropped the pieces in. Onions followed and plenty of paprika. And doubtless he would have sliced potatoes into the broth too, except that in those days potatoes were rarer than pineapples. Even at aristocratic tables they were tasted as a speciality, and they had no proper name. They were called American apples or earth-apples.

Around the fire lay some twenty Turks of different kinds. When they had stopped, they had arranged the carts and waggons in a circle. The horses had been tethered outside the carts.

They drove the prisoners into a single group inside the circle. There were fourteen altogether; nine men and five women, and the two little children. They just collapsed on to the grass. Some of them went to sleep immediately.

Little Eva was asleep too, on top of the bed-linen. Her head rested on Margit's lap, and with her right hand she clasped her sorry little doll to her breast. Gergő lay·flat beside them. He rested his head in his hands and looked sleepily at the Turks. He thought it odd that the janissaries wore spoons in front of their white caps and that the caps were so soft that they drooped towards the back. The *asabs* were more blonde, slovenly, rough-faced men. Two of them had Hungarian boots on their feet, well-worn red boots.

The one-eyed janissary looked up at the children from time to time. He left them there on the cart with the girl.

The fire burned with tall flames. The Turks killed lambs, hens and geese. The captives busied themselves preparing the meal, and shortly meat was sizzling in the pots and pans, and legs of it were roasting on spits. One Turk undid a bag with beads of pastry in it.

An appetizing smell of food mingled with the forest air.

4

Hardly an hour had passed before András, the driver, received such a blow that his hat flew twelve feet into the air.

"May the seventh hell swallow you up!" roared the one-eyed janissary. "How much paprika did you put into the stew?" And squeezing his eye, he held his burnt tongue in the air.

The paprika stew went to the prisoners, to the great delight of the gypsy as well.

"Ah well, this is worth even two blows!"

The Turks themselves shared the drumsticks from the spit.

The barrels had already been tapped. The Turks drank the Hungarian wine from jugs and horns.

The gypsy got up. He wiped his mouth with his hand and his hand on his trousers, then twittered, "Honourable Mister Tummysack, kiss yer 'ands and feet, let me play a tune in honour of the respected company, for your enjoyment."

The one-eyed Turk addressed as Tummysack—his real name was Yumurdjak—turned round and looked scornfully at him.

"You mean you want to bring the Hungarians here with your cock-crowing?"

The gypsy slunk back undisturbed among the eaters and

dipped his wooden spoon into the pot once more. "Let'em 'ang yer when things is going best for yer!"

The Turks stuffed themselves and drank. Meanwhile they exchanged and shared their spoils. A grim-faced *akindji* with a drooping moustache took a little iron chest from the cart. They forced it open. Gold coins, rings and earrings poured out of it. They shared these out in the light of the fire. They admired the stones in one or two of the jewels.

Gergő was sleepy, but he could not take his eyes off his Turk. That bald head was a terrifying and strange sight to him. For when he took off his cap, the baldness of his head fused with the hairlessness of his face. And he had a peculiar laugh. When he laughed, you could see his gums.

He pulled a thick doeskin belt from under his jacket when they shared out the money. The belt was already stuffed full of coins. The Turk rose and went behind the carts to where the horses were grazing.

Gergő's eyes followed him. He saw the Turk pull a wooden peg out of the back of the saddle and pour the money into the pommel through a little hole.

The captives still went on eating. They were quite used to paprika. András the driver was almost jolly as he devoured the meat.

"And why aren't you eating?" the priest said to Gáspár.

The lad was sitting on the edge of the group, gazing grimly at nothing. "I don't want any," he replied casually.

A little while later he looked at the priest. "When you've finished eating, reverend, I'd like a word with you, if you'll hear me."

The priest put down his wooden spoon and clanked over to Gáspár. "Well, what is it, my son?"

The lad blinked. "I'd like you to hear my confession, if you will."

"Why?"

"So that I can go into the next world with a clear conscience."

"You're a long way from that, Gáspár."

"Not so far as you'd think."

He threw a dark glance towards the Turks and continued, "When the captives have finished eating, the Turk who captured me will come over here. He'll come and put the handcuffs on us. Well, I'm going to kill him."

"Don't do that, my son."

"But I am going to do it, reverend. When he comes here, I'll grab one of his knives and stab him. Right in the belly, the dog! So please hear my confession."

The priest just looked at him. "My son," he said calmly, "I can't absolve you. Because I'm a Lutheran."

"The new faith?"

"It's called the new faith, my son, but in reality it's the old true faith that Jesus of Nazareth left to us. We don't absolve, we just confess. For we believe that God sees our souls. But why should you destroy yourself? Look, here we're still on Hungarian soil, and Pécs is there below us. It's often happened that God has taken Hungarian captives out of the hands of the enemy."

"And if he doesn't?"

"The goodness of God may accompany us on our journey. More than one has found his life's good fortune on Turkish soil. He goes there in captive chains and there becomes a gentleman. Then he finds his way back. Come, my son, and eat."

The lad stared morosely at the Turks. "Damn the lot of them!" he muttered between his teeth.

The priest shook his head. "Why did you ask me over if you won't listen to me?"

At last the lad got up. He hobbled back among the others.

Most of the captives were young and strong. Among the women there was also a gypsy with gleaming eyes. Her hands and feet were reddened, gypsy-fashion, with Brazil wood, but she also had it on her hair.

She threw her head back from time to time, because her hair got into her eyes. And she often spoke in gypsy language to Sárközi, the pock-marked gypsy.

"Is she your wife, maybe?" asked the driver.

"No," replied the gypsy, "so far she's never been that."

"Well, what are you talking about in Gypsy?"

"This woman says that if you'll let 'er near the fire she'll tell our fortunes."

"The future's in the hands of God," said the priest sharply. "Don't get up to any tricks in his name."

25

Among the men there were two elderly ones. One of them was a silent, aristocratic looking man—grey-bearded and with a long, drooping moustache. From his dark skin he might have been either a gentleman or a gypsy. He refused to answer any questions. A long wound-scar showed red right across his face from his left ear. He shed a peculiar smell about him like the smell of spent gunpowder. The other was the round-faced peasant who was chained to the priest. His eyes are always wide-open, as if he were astonished, and he hangs his head as if it were much heavier than anyone else's. True, he had a large head.

As the prisoners went on eating the mutton-stew with paprika, they talked quietly. How could they free themselves from the Turks?

"No way," the peasant with the big head suddenly spoke out. He put down his spoon and wiped his mouth with his shirt-sleeve. "I ought to know. I've already suffered captivity once. I lost ten years of my life in it."

"Did they let you go home?"

"Of course not."

"Then how did you get free?"

"How? Why, for nothing. Under the protection of Jesus. They once brought me up to Belgrade. It was from there that I escaped. I swam across the Danube."

"And what was that captivity like?" asked a watery-eyed sixteen-year-old lad.

"Well, young chap, not many hens found their way out of this world on my account."

"Was your master a rich man?" came a voice from under the cart.

"The emperor himself!"

"The emperor? What were you when you served him?"

"Cleaner-in-chief."

"What sort of cleaner-in-chief? What did you clean?"

"His stables."

They had a little laugh. Then they became sad again.

"And how do they treat women?" asked a black-haired young woman.

The man shrugged his shoulders. "The young ones among you

26

will simply be women there too, except you'll be Turkish women. But mostly only servants."

"How do they treat them?"

"It all depends."

"Are they cruel?"

"Sometimes."

"They beat women, don't they, they beat women very much?"

The priest got up. "This means that you must know the route."

"If only I didn't know it!"

The priest put one of his legs on the hub of the wheel and by the light of the fire that reached them there screwed up his eyes to examine the broad, smooth iron band locked to his calf. There were tiny scratches on it, the jottings of some prisoner; the sufferings of a long journey in twenty words.

The priest read out the words. "From Belgrade it's one day to *Hisarlik*. Then *Baratina*."

"No," replied the man, "that's five stages away."

"In that case these five crosses represent five stages. So there are five stages. Then comes *Alopnitza.*"

The man nodded.

"Then *Nish.*"

"That's Serbia," sighed the man and clasped his knee. "That's where they begin to sow brass-pudding."

"Brass-pudding?" said one of the women in surprise.

The man did not reply.

The priest went on reading the scratches on the iron. "Next comes *Kuri-Kezme.*"

"That's where there are lots of scorpions."

"*Sárkövi.*"

"Three mills grind there. May the water dry up!"

"*Tsaribrod.*"

"That's where I got a great beating. Blood streamed from my nose and mouth. They scarred my head too."

"Why?" six voices asked in unison.

"Because I broke the iron on my leg, that's why."

"*Dragoman,*" the priest read on.

"That's Bulgaria," said the man. "From there we arrive in Sofia. There are lots of towers there. It's a big city. May it burn to ashes!"

27

The priest licked his finger and rubbed it over the iron.
"*Ihtiman.*"
"That's where a girl died, poor thing."
"*Kapiderven.*"
"There are mountains there. Snow covers the mountains even in summer."
"*Pozarki* or something."
"That's right, Pozarki, may the earth swallow it up! There we sleep in a sheep-fold. Rats run to and fro over us."
"*Filippe.*"
"That's another town. May it fall to the ground! And fall to the ground when everyone's inside at night!"
"*Kaladan.*"
"That's where they sold one of my mates. May the plague consume them!"
"*Uzunkova.*"
"Lots of orchards. A good place. A woman gave us two baskets of apples."
"*Harmanli.*"
"There a Turkish gentleman bought Antal Dávidka. Before that he'd bargained for me."
"*Mustafa-Pasha-Köprü.*"
"There's a good big stone bridge there. May it fall down!"
"*Adrianople.*"
"A stinking big city. That's where I saw an elifank."
The captives stared at him in surprise.
"What's that?"
"It's a great live animal," replied the peasant, "as big as this loaded cart here. But even bigger. It's got no hide, like a buffalo. And its nose is so big that it uses it like other animals their tail: when flies torture it, it rubs its back with it."
"*Gorlu.*"
"From there on we shall see the sea."
The captives sighed. Some of them buried their faces in their hands; others stared ahead, their eyes full of tears.
The scar-faced man who smelt of gunpowder broke the silence.
"Brothers," he said in a soft, rasping voice, "if you were able to free me, I could get you out of the hands of the Turks."

28

The prisoners looked at him.

The man glanced back at the Turks and went on even more softly, "I'm a gentleman. I've got a couple of castles; I've got soldiers and I've got money. And the only thing you have to do is to pretend to have a quarrel, make a row and squabble when I'm sitting over there by the fifth cart."

The peasant who had been in captivity shrugged his shoulders. "They'd beat us up and you too."

"What's your name, my son?" asked the priest.

"My name's Captive," replied the scar-faced man irritably. And he got up. He limped a few paces towards the Turk. Then he sat down and examined the firelit faces with his shifty eyes.

"He's no gentleman," one of the prisoners dismissed him. "He's a gypsy, or even a hangman."

Gergő shuddered at the word "hangman". His eyes were glued to him. His infant brain really believed him to be a gypsy hangman.

"If only there were some verbena," sighed Gáspár, the lad with the wounded leg who was sitting by the wheel.

The prisoners were sitting silently, lost in sad day-dreams.

"Verbena's a herb that makes chains fall off."

There was a stir among the janissaries; with a great roar of joy they gathered round a barrel. They had found sack in it. They rolled the barrel near to the fire and drank the wine, sipping it, smacking their lips and tossing it down their throats.

"Long live Hungary!" shouted Yumurdjak. And he raised his cup to the prisoners. "Long live Hungary, so that the Turk may drink as long as he lives!"

"How is it that you know Hungarian?" asked the scar-faced man who had just called himself Captive.

"What's that to do with you?" Yumurdjak laughed at him disdainfully.

By now the sky was moonlit and full of stars. Cockchafers were humming round the dewy leaves of the trees.

The captives were already lying to left and right in the grass, seeking liberation in their dreams. The priest was asleep too, his arm beneath his head. He must have been used to sleeping on a pillow. The gypsy slept on his back with his hands clasped on

29

his chest and his legs stretched out in a Y. All of them were fast asleep. Only Gáspár sighed once more in sleepy lamentation,
"I'll never see the fair city of Eger again!"

Gergő was also dozing now. He had fallen into slumber as he held his sunburnt, fine-featured little face in his hands. But his head had slipped lower to the edge of the quilt.

And he would have gone fast asleep, if his ear had not caught the name of Cecey. The gypsy hangman mentioned it in his husky voice, and his own Turk repeated it. They were talking beside the cart.

"Cecey's got it. I know for sure Cecey has it," said the gypsy hangman.

"Dózsa's treasure?"

"All of Dózsa's treasure. Well, all that he had with him."

"And what sort of treasure is it?"

"Gold chalices, gold cups. A big gold dish too. As big as the rising moon. Diamond and pearl bracelets, necklaces, pendants. All the sort of things you'd expect to find in a gentleman's treasury. That is, if they haven't melted down part of them into bars. But even then we'll find the bars at his house."

"Here, down in the forest?"

"Yes. That's why he withdrew from the world."

"Has he got arms too?"

"Beautiful silver-chased swords. Though I've only seen about five of those. And suits of armour. One fine light one belonged to King Louis. His loft is full up. And I know that in his room he has six or so iron chests. That's where his most valuable things may well be."

"Cecey... I've never heard that name."

"Because he doesn't fight any more. He was Dózsa's treasurer."

The Turk shook his head. "There are too few of us," he said, considering the matter. "We've got to wait here until tomorrow night. We've got to wait together for a good large company."

"Why so many men? If there are a lot of you, you'll have to share things out all the more. He's an old man now. And he has a wooden hand and legs."

"But he's got armed men there too."

"Of course he hasn't. Only serfs who plough and sow."

"When were you last there?"

"Maybe a year ago."

"A year's a long time. It would be better for a lot of us to go. If what you say is true, I'll set you free and indeed reward you. If it's not true, I'll have you hanged from Cecey's gate."

The Turk returned to the fire and presumably told the soldiers what the prisoner had said, because they listened with attention. Gergő's head grew heavy. He went off to sleep. But he had nothing but horrible dreams. In the end he dreamt that the Turks were rushing round their village with drawn swords; they seized his mother and plunged a knife into her breast.

He groaned and woke up.

Everywhere there was the darkness of night and the song of nightingales. A hundred, a thousand nightingales! It was as if all the nightingales in the world had come down in that forest to sing something to delight the dreams of the prisoners.

Gergő looked up into the sky. Broken clouds. A star or two shines through them in places. In one place the white sickle of the moon hangs through the cloud.

The fire under the tree was now covered in ash. Only in the middle of it did a fistful of embers still glow red. The janissaries were lying all around the fire in the grass.

Yumurdjak was lying there too. Under his head there was a kind of knapsack; beside him a cup or pot or even his cap— it was impossible to see properly in the dark.

Home, we've got to get home. That was Gergő's first thought. We're not allowed to. That was the second one.

He looked around. Nothing but folk asleep. Suppose he could slip through them. Well, he would have to, otherwise they would never get back to the village.

Little Eva was sleeping next to him. He whispered into her ear, "Evie!"

He shook her gently and whispered again, "Evie! Evie!"

Evie opened her eyes.

"Let's go home," whispered Gergő.

For an instant her mouth turned down, but she quickly recovered herself and sat up. She stared at Gergő like a little kitten seeing a stranger. Then her glance shifted to the doll in her lap and she picked it up, looking at it with a kittenish stare.

"Come on!" Gergő urged her. "But keep quiet!"

He climbed down the other side of the cart and lifted the little girl down too. An *asab* happened to be sitting there beside the cart, his lance in his lap and his head on the wheel-hub. His wooden canteen beside him.

He was so sound asleep that as far as he was concerned all the trees in the forest might have gone off—everything except the one cart against whose wheel he was resting.

Gergő took little Eva by the hand and dragged her after him. But he stopped when they caught sight of the horses.

"The grey horse..." he stuttered. "We've got to take the grey horse home too."

But the grey horse was tethered to the little Turkish horse. Gergő was able to undo the hobble somehow, but the two halters were beyond his ability.

"It's the very devil!" he grumbled at the knot.

He wept with rage and scratched his head. He tried again. Even with his teeth. But he got nowhere with this. In the end he grasped the grey horse and led it.

There was also a guard on the horses. But he too was asleep. He slept as he sat there with his back against a twisted tree. He was snoring with his mouth wide open. Gergő almost led the two horses over him.

The noise of the horses' hooves was lost in the grass. They moved like shadows. Nobody woke as they passed, either inside or outside the circle of carts.

When they reached a suitable tree-stump, Gergő stopped the grey horse and climbed on its back.

"You come and sit up here too," he said softly to the little girl.

Little Eva could not do it; the stump was high for her. Gergő had to get off again. He had to help little Eva first on to the stump and then on to the horse's back.

They sat next to each other on the grey horse. Gergely in front, Eva behind him. The little girl was still clutching the doll with the red skirt. They never thought that the little girl might sit in the saddle of the other horse. She might well have done so. The pommel of the saddle was so high that she could have sat there quite safely. But that horse did not belong to them. Eva held on to the boy's shoulders. The boy shook the reins and the

32

grey horse set off out of the wood, pulling the Turkish horse along with it.

They were soon out on the road. The grey horse knew its way then. It ambled lazily and sleepily along.

The road was dark. The moon lit it only dimly. The trees stood like giants beside the road. Gergő was not afraid of them. They were all Hungarian trees.

5

That night nobody slept in Cecey's house. They looked for the children until it grew dark. They left it to the next day at dawn before they searched the brook thoroughly. Only the soldiers retired to bed.

Father Bálint stayed at the Ceceys and tried to comfort the distraught couple.

The woman behaved as if she were mad. She kept weeping and fainting. "Oh my little pearl, my darling, my only little dear!"...

The wooden-legged man only shook his head at the priest's words of comfort and cried out bitterly, "There's no God!"

"There is!" retorted the priest.

"There isn't!" Cecey banged the table.

"There is!"

"There isn't!"

"What God gives he can also take away, and what he takes away he can also give back."

Tears welled into the eyes of the crippled old man. "He shouldn't take away what he's once given!"

It was only towards dawn that the priest left him to himself.

As he stepped out of the doorway, the pilgrim rose from his bed of matting at the end of the veranda.

"Reverend sir!" he said softly.

"What is it you want, brother?"

"They've not been drowned."

"Well?"

"They've been carried off by the Turks."

The priest almost fell against the wall. "How do you know?"

"When I too was looking for them with the other searchers

33

along the bank of the stream, I saw the print of a Turk's foot in a molehill."

"A Turkish footprint?"

"It was a footprint without a heel. Hungarians don't wear boots like that."

"But suppose it was a sandal?"

"Sandals don't have spurs. It was a Turk's footprint. And there's also the print of a Turkish horse there. You must know what a Turkish horseshoe looks like?"

"Then why didn't you say anything?"

"I thought it over and decided not to speak. Who knows where the Turks may have taken them? All the village would have scattered all over the place. And what good would that have done? There are lots of Turks and they're all armed."

The priest walked up and down with staring eyes. Once he went up to the door but came to a halt before he put his hand on the latch. And he went back again to the pilgrim.

"What are we to do?"

"Do what I'm doing: say nothing."

"It's dreadful, dreadful!"

"The Turks patrol the roads in all directions now. Where would they have gone? East? West? The result would only have been fighting and death."

"Would that they too had died!" the priest shook his head in grief.

"God knows where they were, even when we were looking all over the place for them."

The priest stood gloomily on the veranda. In the east the sky turned a pale rose colour. It was dawning.

Just then a great shout arose at the end of the village.

"Men and women, wake up! They've arrived!"

The priest pricked up his ears. What was this?

It was the watchman who was shouting, he realized that immediately. And he also heard the patter of his feet.

They've arrived? Who had arrived?

The footsteps drew nearer. There was a banging on the great gate.

"Let us in! Open up! The children have come back!"

34

The priest rushed into the house. "There is a God, Peter! Get up, for there is a God!"

The two children were waiting outside the gate. They were sitting on the grey horse, sleepy and pale.

6

The whole village crowded into the yard. Some of the women had only just thrown on skirts, and the men had no caps as they ran out at the shout. The boy Gergő was snatched from hand to hand and Eva was kissed by those who could reach her.

"Why, wherever did you get that fine Turkish horse?"

"I brought it along," said Gergely with a shrug.

"From this day Gergő is my son," said Cecey solemnly. And he put his hand on the boy's head. The boy's mother, barefoot and in a single underskirt, knelt at Cecey's feet.

Dobó looked in astonishment at the little peasant boy who had brought a horse from the Turks.

"Sir," he said to Cecey, "give me this boy. Let him come with me to Upper Hungary. I'll make a soldier out of him." And he lifted Gergő up.

"Would you like to be a soldier, my boy?"

"I should," replied the boy, with shining eyes.

"You've already got a horse; we'll get a sword too from the Turks."

"What, is that horse mine?"

Dobó's soldiers were making the little Turkish horse run in a clearing and praising it.

"Of course it's yours. You won it in war."

"It's yours," Cecey assured him, "saddle and bridle and all."

"In that case the money's also ours," said the boy proudly.

"What money do you mean?"

"The money that's inside the saddle."

They took off the fine velvet-pommelled saddle. They shook it. It rattled. They discovered how to open the pommel, and a shower of gold came pouring out of it.

"Why, whoever'd have thought it!" said Cecey in amazement, "now it's not I who'll receive you as my son, but you must adopt me as your father! Collect it, woman!" he shouted to the boy's mother.

The boy's mother watched with dazzled eyes as the gold coins rolled on to the ground. She thought she was dreaming.

"Are they mine?" she stuttered, looking now at Cecey, now at Dobó, now at the priest. "Mine?"

"Yes, they're yours," the priest nodded. "God gave them to your son."

The woman felt for her apron. She was not wearing it. A man offered her his cap. The woman collected up the gold with trembling hands.

Her son watched her. Suddenly he said, "Hide it well away, mother, because they'll be here tomorrow."

"Who'll be here?"

"The Turks."

"The Turks?"

The boy nodded. "I heard the Turk say so to the hangman."

"The hangman?"

"Yes, the gypsy hangman."

"That they're coming here?"

"Yes, they're coming here to take away the noble gentleman's treasure." And he pointed to Cecey.

"My treasure?" Cecey started back.

The boy blinked. "And they said there were six iron chests."

"This is serious," Dobó spoke up, "let's go into the room."

He took the boy by the hand and led him inside. They questioned him and drew out of him all that his child's mind had absorbed.

"A scar-faced man? Dark? What was his scar like?"

"A red furrow from his mouth to his ear."

Dobó leapt out of his chair. "It's Móré!"

"Why, who else could it be?" The rogue wants to escape, so he brings the Turks down on me."

"But does he know the way here?"

"He was here about six years ago. They turned everything upside down. They took away fifty-four forints of mine and my wife's little gold cross, and seven of my cows."

Dobó stumped angrily up and down the room. "How many men have you got, sir, that can take up arms?"

"Maybe forty all told, counting everyone in."

"That's not enough. What's the nearest place? Pécs, isn't it? But János Szerecsen's in charge there, and he's King John's man and our enemy."

"We must run away!" Cecey shakes his head. "Run and scatter in the forest, each for himself!"

"The whole village can't just run away like that! Abandon the village? Just for a pack of Turks? Never! When it's a question of defending ourselves against the Turks, Hungarians are Hungarians, whatever side they're on."

And he went out. "To horse!"

When he himself was in the saddle, he continued, "I'm going to see Szerecsen, brother Cecey. In the meantime start working. Drench every roof till they run with water. Let the folk in the village assemble all their possessions here in the yard. Pile stones here beside the gate and barrels to make a barricade. Put scythes, axes and pitchforks in the hands of the women too. I'll be back in two hours' time."

He looked at the dawn in the sky and galloped off with his soldiers.

7

The Cecey house was built with a stone wall enclosing some three acres. But the stone wall itself was scarcely the height of a man, and was beginning to crumble.

The whole village had been rounded up into the yard during the morning. Among the piles of bedlinen and bundles goats and pigs ran around, geese gobbled, ducks bobbed up and down and hens chased about. One man was sharpening swords, knives and scythes beside the barn. The priest had equipped himself with an immensely broad rusty sword; in the centre of the yard he brought it out, brandished it and thrust it back into its sheath, well-satisfied.

A few women were cooking food in vessels and pots in front of the kitchen.

Cecey had some six mouse-chewed bows and arrows up in the

loft. He distributed these among the old men who had fought with him in Dózsa's war.

Dobó returned about noon. He brought with him only thirty mercenaries or so, but the villagers greeted them with shouts of joy. He went the rounds of the yard. Here and there he had steps and platforms set up and stones collected. He barricaded half of the gateway. Then he called to the villagers who were armed, fifty-one of them in all, and grouped them in positions along the wall. He stationed himself with ten good riflemen on the platform of barrels beside the gate.

He despatched two trumpeters to the two entrances to the village. It was their job to herald the arrival of the enemy.

They did not have long to wait.

At about three o'clock in the afternoon the trumpet sounded at the eastern entrance to the village, and a few minutes later the soldiers with the trumpets could be heard returning at a gallop.

Cecey looked around. "Are we all here?"

Only Gergely's mother was still missing. The poor woman had been distracted by the gold. She kept digging and hiding it away. She dared not leave it at Cecey's house because she was afraid the Turks would take it away. Maybe she had even ventured out into the forest to hide her gold coins there.

"Close the gate!" ordered Dobó. "Bring more sacks, logs and stones. Leave just enough space for a horse and rider to get through."

The soldiers arrived.

"They're coming!" shouted one of them from a distance.

"Many of them?" asked Dobó.

"We only saw the first of them."

"Then get back," thundered Dobó, "and see how many are coming. You'll have plenty of time to run if they chase you."

The mercenary from Pécs reddened as he turned his horse and galloped back.

"Is that the kind of soldiers you are, then?" Dobó turned to the Pécs mercenaries.

"Certainly not," replied one of them, embarrassed. "That one's only just joined us. He was a tailor's apprentice. He's not been tested in battle yet."

A few minutes later the tailor came back again at a gallop,

with about fifteen red-capped *akindji*s on his tail. Now they really were chasing him.

"Let him in!" said Dobó.

And he beckoned to his riflemen, "Fire!"

The ten riflemen took aim. The shots cracked out. One of the janissaries among the Turks rolled from his horse and fell into the ditch. The rest started back. They turned round and galloped back.

The tailor thundered through the open gate.

"How many are they, then?" smiled Dobó.

"A thousand," panted the tailor, "maybe more."

Dobó waved his hand dismissively. "If there are only a hundred of them, then we shall be dancing today too."

"I said a thousand, sir."

"I heard you," replied Dobó. "If you saw a thousand, then there are only a hundred of them, if that."

Smoke billowed up from the end of the village. The *akindji*s were already setting fire to it.

Dobó shook his head. "Didn't you soak the roofs?"

"It's the hay and straw that are burning," said Cecey. And he drummed his sword on the top of the gate.

At that moment the one-eyed janissary appeared on the road. He had armour on. In his belt were daggers and pistols. On his left, also on horseback, was the Hungarian Gergő had called a gypsy hangman. Behind them was a band of *akindji*s, and at their side a few *asab*s were running along the houses with lighted brands in their hands.

"László Móré!" croaked Dobó, stamping his feet, "you disgrace to your country, you're destined for hell!"

The janissary looked in astonishment at the man riding beside him.

"Don't believe him," shouted Móré, turning pale. "He only wants to take you in."

The janissary pulled up his horse to join the group riding behind him.

"I recognize you too, Yumurdjak!" shouted Dobó. "Is this the honour of a Turk? Robbing those whom you were fighting alongside yesterday? You're a robber, a brigand, like your accomplice!"

39

The janissary looked up at him, but did not answer.

"Come on, then, come on!" shouted Dobó. "You fool, Móré! Here's my welcome!" And he aimed at him; he fired his rifle.

Yumurdjak sank down on his horse; he turned round and fell into the dust. The other rifles fired at virtually the same moment. The Turkish pistols returned the welcome.

Móré clutched at the janissary as he fell, but only managed to seize the dagger from his belt. The next instant he struck his horse's flanks with the flat of the blade. The steed gave a great leap and began to run. Móré flogged it as hard as he could.

"So much for the gold!" shouted Dobó to the Turks. They started back for a minute, but then dashed after Móré with angry shouts at a rapid gallop.

And as they rushed past the house, Dobó counted them.

"Ten... twenty... forty... fifty..."

He waited for a further minute, then jumped down from the platform.

"To horse, lads! There aren't even sixty of them!"

They leapt on their horses. Dobó called back to Cecey from the gate: "If the Turk in armour's still alive, lock him up! The villagers can beat the fire-raisers to death!" And he dashed out of the gate.

There were about five places in the village where the smoke was snaking to the sky. All of them rushed through the gate brandishing scythes and axes.

Cecey, the priest and a couple of serfs rushed out along the road. Yumurdjak was sitting up. He had only fainted. Dobó's bullet had dented his armour just above his heart.

"Bind him," said Cecey, "and take him back to the courtyard."

The Turk allowed his hands to be tied without a sound.

"Can you play chess?" Cecey roared at him.

The janissary nodded his head in the affirmative and said, "No."

As they were binding his hands there, the second Turk lifted his head out of the ditch.

"Carry on tying him up," said a lad, "while I strike this one dead."

"Stop," said Cecey.

He stumped over to the bloodstained janissary and holding his sword to his breast, asked, "Can you play chess?"

"*Kaplaman*," replied the Turk in a daze.

"Chess?"

"Chess, chess, mate?" asked the Turk with a groan.

"That's it! Mohamed give you a good kick! Take this one to the yard too; he's my prisoner!"

8

Dobó and his men did not return until dusk. With them they brought many cloaks, shirts of mail and all kinds of weapons. And a prisoner: Móré.

"Find a good hole for this wolf!" said Dobó jumping down from his horse.

Cecey almost leapt for joy. "How did you capture him?"

"The *akindji*s captured him for us. They had enough sense not to give him a young horse. They caught up with him easily. When they'd tied him up and nearly finished the job, we dealt with them!"

"Did you cut them all down?"

"As far as we could."

"Quick, bring out my best bullock!" shouted Cecey happily to his servants. "On a spit with it! But first bring wine! Roll that last barrel out of the cellar!"

"Not yet," said Dobó, gazing after Móré as he was escorted into the storehouse. "Where's that boy Gergő?"

"What do you want him for? He's over there on the veranda playing with my little girl. They're saying now that his mother has been killed."

"They did kill her, then?"

"Yes indeed. Some rascal came across her when they set fire to the village, and stabbed her. The boy doesn't know yet."

"And the gold?"

"The woman's lying in a corner of the room with her face on the ground. Doubtless that's where she dug in the coins."

Dobó muttered angrily. He turned to the boy. "Gergő! Gergő

41

Bornemissza! Come here, my little soldier! Get quickly on that good little horse of yours, my boy!"

"Where are you going?"

"For the prisoners, sir, of whom that boy was talking."

"Well, at least have a drop of wine. Wine, quickly!" he shouted to the servants. "Your Turk's alive, by the way. He's in the storehouse."

"Yumurdjak?"

"Devil knows what his name is. The one you shot down."

"That's the one. So he didn't die?"

"No. He only fainted. We brought in the other one too, from the ditch. I'm afraid he's not got long to live."

"You're afraid? Hang the wretch!"

"Oho! My prisoner!"

"Oh well, do whatever you like with him. But have that Yumurdjak brought out and give him a horse."

The soldiers drank great draughts of wine. They brought Yumurdjak out.

"Well, Yumurdjak," said Dobó, "was this what you wanted?"

"Me today, you tomorrow," replied the Turk sullenly.

And when he caught sight of his horse and the boy Gergő riding him, his jaw dropped in astonishment.

Dobó beckoned the boy to him and galloped out of the gate. Behind them the Turk was surrounded by soldiers.

"Do you know where we're going, Gergő?" asked Dobó.

"No, I don't," answered the boy.

"Now we're going for a sword."

"To the Turks?"

"Yes."

"For me?"

"Yes. Are you frightened?"

"No."

"That's the first thing, my boy—not to be afraid. The rest follows by itself."

They didn't speak a word.

The horses' hooves raised white clouds along the Mecsek carriage-road, and on the stony hillside the noise of the horsemen galloping sounded hard.

Like the rolling of a bell, Gergely kept hearing the words:

"The main thing is not to be afraid!"

9

They found the captives there in the forest. They were guarded by only six *asabs*.

As soon as the Hungarian soldiers appeared among the trees the captives jumped up and with shouts of joy rattled and dragged their chains.

"Hey, you curs and rogues!" screamed the gypsy.

The six *asabs* naturally fled in all directions. The Hungarians did not pursue them. They were concerned with the captives. They released them from their chains.

Dobó first of all offered his hand to the priest. "My name's István Dobó."

"And mine's Gábor Somogyi," replied the priest with tears in his eyes. "God bless you, István Dobó!"

The captives cried for joy. The women kissed the hands, the feet and the cloaks of their liberator. The gypsy turned cartwheels amid great shouts of joy.

"It's not me you have to thank," protested Dobó. "It was this little boy who has saved you." And he pointed to Gergő.

The boy, of course, was almost devoured, so many kisses and blessings did he receive. Ah well, he won't be kissed for a long time after this.

The plunder they obtained was fifteen loaded carts and all kinds of weapons. Before Dobó divided it, he asked the captives who had been the first to be taken prisoner. The young serf lad stepped forward and took off his cap.

"I was the first, sir."

"What's your name?"

"Gáspár Kocsis, at your service."

"Where do you come from?"

"Eger, sir."

"Where did they capture you?"

"Beneath Fejérvár, sir; we were carrying goods..."

"Do you know whose possessions these are in the carts?"

"I would, if we were where they picked them up. But those robbers collected them up from everywhere, sir."

Dobó turned to the Turk. "Tell me, Yumurdjak."

43

"We picked them up where Allah permitted us to do so. What belongs to the unbelievers is ours. We take whatever we find."

"In that case just spread everything out. I'll divide it among you."

In one cart there was a heap of weapons of all kinds. That too was a shoddy collection of plunder, most of it from Móré's castle. But amongst it there appeared a small light sword in a cherry-red velvet sheath; it probably belonged to some aristocratic boy.

Dobó picked it up.

"Gergely Bornemissza, come here! Take this sword. It's yours. Be a faithful soldier to your homeland and a devout servant of God. Blessing and good fortune be upon your weapon."

He fastened the sword round the boy's waist and kissed the little soldier on the forehead.

The little boy received the distinction with awe. He almost turned pale at it. Perhaps a breath of what was to come passed over his spirit for an instant; he felt not only that the sword had been bound to him, but also that he had been bound to the sword.

Dobó left for the captives what the soldiers did not need. Every prisoner got a cart, a horse and arms. For the soldiers certainly did not snap up the thin peasant-horses harnessed to the carts.

The gypsy uttered great shouts of joy. He jumped around the horse and cart that he had been allotted. But very soon he hurried back to the pile of arms. He snatched up all the rusty and worthless weapons left there by the soldiers and got himself up in them. Turkish-fashion, he tied a band round his waist and stuck all kinds of knives and daggers in it so that he looked like a hedgehog.

A shoddy Turkish shield woven of maize-stalks was also lying there. He put it on his arm. He tied two great rusty spurs to his bare legs and put a helmet on his head. He had enough sense to leave his hat on underneath it. Then he picked up a long pike from the ground and lurched towards the Turk with solemn steps as if he were walking on eggshells.

"Well, Tummysack," he said, tickling him under the nose with his pike, "'ow are you now, you Turkish blockhead?"

As everyone burst out laughing at this, Dobó said sharply to the gypsy, "Stop bragging, there! Where do you come from?" The gypsy immediately crumpled into a state of servility.

"Everywhere, kiss yer 'ands and feet, where they play music."

"Can you mend rifles?"

"Of course, Mister Soldier. I can mend the worst rifle so that it's better than new."

"In that case, make your way immediately to Szigetvár, to Bálint Török's establishment. You'll be on to a good thing there."

The skinny little gypsy woman begged Dobó to let her tell fortunes.

"Me wife," said the gypsy, "is so good at telling the future that not a word she says is wrong. Why, this morning she said that we were going to be set free."

The women confirmed that she had indeed said this.

"She did say so," Gáspár added, "but we didn't believe her."

"That's the trouble; they never believe 'er," gesticulated the gypsy. "Now maybe, you blockhead, you'll believe 'er."

By now the gypsy woman was sitting by the fire. She scraped the embers together and sprinkled tiny black seeds on them.

"Datura stramonium," said the priest contemptuously.

From the embers a blue column of smoke arose. The gypsy woman sat on a stone and held her face in the smoke.

The soldiers and the ex-prisoners stood round her inquisitively.

"Your hand..." the gypsy woman said after a few minutes to Dobó. Dobó held it out to her.

"Right then, let's see what you know."

The gypsy woman looked up into the sky, showing the whites of her eyes as she did so, and spoke with trembling lips.

"I see red and black birds... They're flying after each other... Ten... fifteen... seventeen... eighteen..."

"Those are my years," smiled Dobó.

"That's right," the gypsy rejoiced.

"With the eighteenth bird there's an angel in flight. It flies

45

down to you and remains with you. It puts a bandage round your brow. Its name is Sara."

"In other words, Sara will be my wife. A fine old bachelor I shall be before I find Sara!"

"Before that you may be noble, honourable and titled," the gypsy comforted him.

The woman went on, "The nineteenth bird is red. It brings with it a dark cloud with lightning. On the earth three great pillars have fallen."

"Buda? Temesvár? Fehérvár?" asked Dobó reflectively.

"Yes, that's right, noble, honourable..."

"And the fourth one is in flames now, but you'll sustain it, though fire falls on your head and hands like hail."

"Szolnok? Eger?"

"Eger, Eger it is, honourable, noble Mister Soldier."

"The twentieth bird is gold-coloured. It is dressed in the rays of the sun. On its head is a crown. A diamond from that crown falls into your lap."

"That's a good sign."

"Aye, a great big lot of good, noble, honourable..."

"Then once again red and black birds are flying after each other... But there's darkness to follow... I can't see anything more... I can hear the sound of chains rattling... And your sighs..."

She shuddered and let go of Dobó's hand.

"That means I shall die in prison," said Dobó with a shiver.

"What nonsense you're prophesying now!" the gypsy turned on her. "Not a word of it's true, honourable Mister Soldier."

"There's no sense in it," said the priest dismissively.

Now the gypsy woman had taken Gergely's hand. She held her face in the smoke, listened and once again looked up at the sky.

"A dove will accompany you through your life... A white dove, only with pink wings. But you're surrounded by fire. Even from your hands wheels of fire set forth... Then the dove is left all alone and seeks you sadly till her death..."

She was silent for a moment. Her face was distorted by spasms of horror. She let go of the boy's hand, and holding her palms to the sky too, stammered, "Two stars rise into the sky. One

from prison. The other on the seashore... They shine for ever..."
And reeling with horror, she hid her eyes in her hands.

"Stupid nonsense!" said Dobó dismissively. "Pour some water over that woman!"

"Water for the idiot!" croaked the gypsy, "'ow dare yer forecast such nonsense for yer benefactors!"

And he himself snatched up a bucket and splashed the water over the woman's head.

The prisoners laughed. Dobó took Gergely's hand and said farewell to the captives.

"Honourable, noble Mister Soldier! What shall we do with this murderous brigand?" the gypsy shouted after Dobó. And he pointed at the Turk.

"Hang him!" said Dobó over his shoulder.

He set Gergő in the saddle and turned to his horse.

10

"Now you cur of a Turk," roared Gáspár Kocsis, "now it's your turn!"

"Rope!" shouted András the driver. "There's a lasso over there."

"You're going to die!" screamed the gypsy, rolling his eyes with rage.

"You wounded my leg with those irons!" fulminated Gáspár.

"You killed my father!" a woman shouted at him.

"You drove away our cows and wrecked our house!"

And the Turk was surrounded by a frenzy of angry faces and fists. He was shoved and pushed under an old beech-tree by the irate mob.

At their head stood the large-headed peasant who had been in captivity; he held his sword in his hand.

"What! Finish him off straight away? First light a fire under his feet!"

"Fire under his feet!" they all shouted. "Let's burn the infernal creature alive!"

The women were already breaking sticks, and a fire was lit beneath the tree.

"People!" said the priest at that stage, "if you waste time here now with a hanging, another marauding Turkish band may come along, and we may all fall into captivity again."

The angry crowd suddenly calmed down and glanced round. The priest was leaning on a Turkish lance with a bone hilt. He continued, "You know what this man did to me. Which of you has more right to deal with this wild animal?"

There was no reply to his question. Almost all of them were there when they bound the priest to a bench and poured boiling water over him to make him confess where he had hidden the church treasure.

"Just go on with the soldiers," went on the priest. "Go under their protection as far as you can, then scatter along roads that nobody uses as far as possible. God bless you and lead you all home." And he spread out his arms in blessing.

They gave up building the fire. One after another they jumped on to the horse and cart they had been given.

"Gee up!"

The gypsy got up too and called to the woman, "Follow me, Beske!"

Gáspár tied his cart to Margit's. They sat side by side.

"Torture him well and truly!" he called back to the priest.

"Don't be stingy with the fire!" croaked one of the women.

And off they went in line. The last one to go was the driver, the one the Turks had forced to do the cooking.

"Devil take the rogue, I'm not leaving here until I've returned that blow!" he said. And so he did.

The priest remained alone with the Turk.

11

Gergely thought he must be dreaming. As he galloped beside Dobó on the nimble little Turkish horse, he wondered how he had become involved in this great distinction.

He looked now at the horse, now at the fine sword. He stroked the horse and drew out the sword from time to time. If they happened to meet a Turk and Dobó said to him, "Strike him,

Gergő!", it was certain that Gergő would have slaughtered not one, but a whole army!

They turned north on the Mecsek highroad.

Darkness was falling now. The sky was covered with little scaly clouds and as the sun began to gild the sky, it looked as though the whole of the heavens had turned into golden scales.

As they trotted down the road, Dobó's horse suddenly halted as if its front legs had become rooted to the ground. It raised its head. It snorted and pawed the ground restlessly.

Dobó glanced backwards. He shook his head. "My horse smells a Turk. Let's stop."

When they set out he had sent two soldiers on ahead. They waited for them. A few minutes later both of them came back at a gallop.

"Down in the valley there's a Turkish troop coming along the highroad," one of them reported to Dobó.

"They're in marching order," added the other.

"Are they far away?" asked Dobó.

"A good way off. It'll take a good two hours for them to get here."

"How many are there?"

"Two hundred or so."

"Are they coming along the highroad?"

"Yes, on the highroad."

"Have they got captives too?"

"Yes, captives and a lot of carts."

"Oh the brigands! They must be Kászon's rearguard. All the same, we'll attack them."

The highroad winds in broad curves up the Mecsek Hills. Dobó spied out for his troop a place where a rock jutted out over a bend in the road. That was a good place to hide and surprise the Turks.

"Are there enough of us?" asked a blonde, freckled young soldier, the first glance at whom would have revealed that he was brought up in cotton-wool.

"Quite enough, Gyurka," smiled Dobó over his shoulder. "When a blessing falls on them so suddenly, there's no time for counting our heads. It would be dark by then. And even if we can't cut them all down, well, it'll be enough if we can make

49

them scatter. Then they'll be able to deal with them separately in the villages."

It was then that the former prisoners appeared in a long line of carts at a bend in the road.

Dobó was annoyed. "It was no use my telling them not to go along the highroad."

He sent a soldier to meet them and tell them to turn and make for Pécs; from there they could go east or west, but not to north or south.

They could see the soldier reach them. The line of carts halted, then they turned one by one and the whole line went back.

Dobó looked at Gergely. "What the devil am I going to do with this boy?" he muttered irritably.

12

The priest remained alone with the Turk.

The Turk stood by the oak tree and stared at the grass. The priest, resting on his lance, stood ten paces in front of him. The rattle of the carts could be heard for a time, then they were enveloped by the silence of the forest.

Then the Turk raised his face. "Before you kill me," he stammered pallidly, "listen to what I have to say. The belt round my waist is full of gold. For so great a prize, you can at least bury me."

The priest did not respond. He just looked expressionlessly at the Turk.

"Once you have hanged me," continued Yumurdjak, "dig my grave here under the tree and place me in it sitting. Turn my face towards Mecca. Towards the east. You can do that for my money." He said no more. He waited for the priest to speak, and then the rope.

"Yumurdjak," the priest broke his silence, "I heard you say yesterday that your mother was Hungarian."

"She was," replied the Turk, his face brightening.

"So you're half Hungarian?"

"Yes."

"Did the Turks seize you when you were an infant?"
"You've guessed right, sir."
"Where from?"
The Turk shrugged and simply stared. "I've forgotten now."
"How old were you?"
"I was very small."
"Do you remember your father?"
"No."
"Nor what your name was?"
"Nor that either."
"Can't you remember any name from your childhood?"
"No."
"It's strange that you haven't forgotten the language."
"There were lots of Hungarian boys at the janissary-depot."
"Didn't you know a boy from Lak? He was called Imre, Imre Somogyi."
"Off the cuff..."
"He was a round-headed, sturdy little boy with black eyes when he was captured, and scarcely five years old. On his left breast there was a cloverleaf-shaped birthmark like mine."

The priest pulled his shirt aside, and there between his shoulder and nipple could be seen three round marks grouped together like a cloverleaf.

"I know that boy," said the Turk. "I often saw that mark when we were washing. But now he has a different name, Ahmet or Kubat, some Turkish name like that."

"Weren't you together then?"

"Sometimes we were, sometimes not. He's fighting in Persia now."

The priest gazed rigidly at the Turk. "You're lying!"

The Turk stared at his boots, his red boots tied with leather laces, as if he were wondering when and how the left one had split open on top of his foot...

"You scoundrel!" said the priest contemptuously. "You really deserve to be killed."

The Turk fell to his knees. "Oh sir! Have pity and spare me! Take all I have and make me your slave! No dog will be as faithful to you as I shall be!"

51

"The only question is whether you're a man or a wild beast. If I let you go, who'll guarantee that you won't kill and plunder my poor people again?"

"May Allah flay me with all his whips if I ever take arms in my hands again!"

The priest shook his head.

The Turk went on: "I swear it to you on the most fearful oath a Turk may utter."

The priest folded his arms and looked straight into the eyes of his captive. "Yumurdjak, here on the threshold of death you fall on your knees and argue with me and think I'm a fool. Or do you imagine I don't know what the Koran says about an oath sworn to an infidel?"

Sweat broke out on the Turk's brow. "Well then, sir, say something. Say whatever you like, and it shall be done."

The priest rested his chin in his hands and pondered.

"Every Turk carries some amulet," he said at last, "an amulet that protects him in battle and assists him when his fortunes are good."

The Turk's head fell.

"I don't want your money," said the priest. "I wish to have that amulet of yours."

"Reach under my waistcoat," murmured the Turk. "It's hanging round my neck."

He raised his head. The priest did indeed find the amulet there, sewn into a little silk pouch. He broke it off the golden chain and put it in his pocket. Then he stepped behind the Turk and cut through the rope that knotted together his legs, hands and arms.

The Turk shook the bonds from his two hands and suddenly turned round. His eyes flashed at Father Gábor with the yellow burning glance of a tiger.

But the priest already had the lance pointed at him, and smiled. "Come, come, Yumurdjak! Look out, don't spear your nose on it!"

In his fury Yumurdjak seemed to breathe fire as he backed away from the priest. When he was about twenty paces away from him he shouted derisively, "Know who it was you had in your clutches, you stupid infidel! I am the son of the famous

52

Mohamed Yahya-Pasha-Oglu! For me you might have got gold by the sack!"

The priest made no reply. With a disdainful glance he threw his lance into his cart.

13

The sun was just sinking on the horizon when Father Gábor mounted his cart. He too turned along the highroad.

He could still see the end of the line of carts carrying his fellow-captives as they went down to Pécs, but he thought that they were only a section of them, and that the rest had gone northwards.

He knew the road home. Nor was there any other highroad in those parts; it went from Pécs through Kaposvár to Székesfehérvár and from there to Buda. But he was only to go as far as Lak on it, to Pál Bakics's castle. There a narrow little cart-track turns off towards the Balaton. There was his village below a grove of poplars. How his flock would rejoice and marvel at him when they saw that he had escaped!

He got down and fixed the wheel-drag. He patted the heads of the two horses contentedly, then got up again and set off down the slope.

But Dobó's detachment was blocking the road.

"Why did you turn back?" asked one of the soldiers, when he recognized him as one of the captives.

The priest did not understand the question.

"The Turks are coming," explained the soldier, "and we're watching for them here. So just turn round and hurry to Pécs like the rest."

"Wait a minute, Father!" called Dobó. And he galloped over to him. "Which is your village?"

"Kishida," answered the priest.

"Near the Balaton?"

"Yes."

"I'd like you to take this little boy with you and, as soon as it's possible, send him for me to Bálint Török at Szigetvár."

"Gladly," replied the priest.

"I'm worried in case he comes to some harm," explained

Dobó. "Here we're going to scare off a fairly large band of Turks, and, you see, any one of them might wound him."

Gergő looked doubtfully at Dobó. "My mother will be looking for me..."

"No, she won't, my boy. She knows already where you're going!"

The priest turned the cart around.

"Are you going to ride in the cart?" he asked Gergő. "Or are you going to stay on your horse?"

"On my horse," responded the boy, still looking at Dobó.

For even if he was ready for a bloody conflict, he felt secure beside Dobó. That there would be slaughter? The Turk wasn't human, just a wild beast laying waste the country. Even with the heart of a child, he already hated them.

"God bless you, my little soldier," said Dobó in farewell. "I know you'd like to be with us in battle, but you haven't even got any boots yet. So just go along with the priest, and we'll meet in a few days' time."

The priest released the drag and brought the whip down between the two horses.

Gergő trotted sadly after the cart.

14

Darkness had fallen by the time the cart passed the castle of Pécs. They did not stop there. The priest wanted them to be at home the next morning. They had to go right round the Mecsek Hills.

Towards midnight the moon shone out. They could make a good pace along the narrow earth cart-track.

By now Gergő always rode ahead, calling back to the priest when they reached a doubtful bridge.

It was round about midnight when a building looking like an inn loomed white before them.

"Have a look inside, my boy," said the priest. "See whether it's an inn or something else. We'll feed the horses here."

Gergő rode into the courtyard and returned after a few minutes.

"It's an empty house," he reported. "Not even the door's shut."

"Well, we'll feed them all the same."

Then a shaggy little white dog came out and barked at them. Nobody else appeared.

The priest jumped down from the cart and went round the house. "Hello there! Is there anyone at home?" he called through the door and windows.

The house was in darkness. There was no answer. On the threshold was the wreckage of a small cupboard. The Turks must have been there.

The priest shook his head.

"First of all let's take a look at the well, Gergely, because my skin's still burning."

He let down the bucket and drew up water. Then he began to rummage in his cart. There was everything there: bedlinen, corn, a chest, a carved chair, a cask of wine and full sacks. One of the sacks was soft. He undid it. What he sought he found there: linen. He soaked a cloth with water and undressed to the waist. He poulticed his body with it.

Gergő dismounted too. He led his horse to the trough and watered it.

The priest tugged a bundle of hay from under the seat and threw it to the horses. There was also a knapsack there. He felt bread in it.

"Are you hungry, my boy?"

"I certainly am," replied the child. And he smiled shyly.

The priest drew out his sword, but before he cut the bread with it, he raised his face to heaven.

"Blessed be thy name, Lord!" he called in a warm and thankful voice. "Thou hast freed us from our chains and given us our daily bread."

The sky was clear and starry. The pale glow of the half-moon shone gently from the middle of the sky upon their dinner.

They sat on the rim of the well and had their food there. From time to time the priest threw a bit to the dog, while Gergő broke his loaf into two and gave half of it to his horse.

Then in the distance a soft patter of hooves could be heard. The two eaters pricked up their ears. Their jaws stopped moving.

"Someone on horseback's coming this way," said the priest.

"Just one," added Gergely. And they went on eating.

The patter gradually turned into thundering on the dry car-track. A few minutes later the rider himself arrived.

He reined in his horse in front of the inn and stepped into the courtyard. It was obvious that he was a Hungarian. There was no cap on his head, but he had plenty of hair, so he was Hungarian. He stopped and stared.

"Mübarek olsun!" he called to the priest in a hoarse voice. He thought he was a Turk, seeing the wet white cloth on his head.

"I'm Hungarian," replied the priest. And he rose. He had recognized Móré.

Gergely also recognized him. He shuddered.

"Who is there here?" asked Móré, dismounting from his steaming steed. "Where's the host?"

"There's nobody here except for this little boy and me," replied the priest. "The house is empty."

"I must have a horse! A fresh horse!"

The priest shrugged. "You're hardly likely to find one here."

"My journey's urgent. I've no money. We're Christians. Give me your horse."

He sized up the two horses. The third, Gergely's, was grazing in the shadow. It was a small horse and looked puny. Móré did not wait for a reply; he simply untied the near horse from the shaft.

"Oho!" said the priest, "at least tell me why you're in such a hurry."

"Dobó has routed the Turks. He freed us too."

"Where's he going?"

"We left him on the highroad."

Móré said nothing more. He hurled himself on to the peasant horse and galloped on his way.

"Well," muttered the priest, "he doesn't take long to bargain over horses."

When he moved, he felt something slip out of his pocket. He picked it up and stared at it. Then when he felt it, it occurred to him that it was the Turk's talisman. There was something hard in the little silk pouch. He split it open with his sword, and a ring rolled out of it.

56

The stone in the ring was unusually large, a square black stone, either dark-coloured garnet or obsidian; it was impossible to tell in the moonlight. But on it there could clearly be seen a moon in some pale yellow stone, and round it five tiny diamond stars. And inside the pouch too there was something sparkling —Turkish script sewn in silver thread.

The priest knew Turkish, but not Turkish script. He put it back into his pocket and glanced at Gergő to tell him it was time to start. The little boy was already fast asleep on the sack full of linen.

15

How joyfully and splendidly the sun sheds its light from the sky! But around Lake Balaton it cannot see anything but blackened house-roofs, dead bodies scattered all around and trampled crops. If the sun were the face of God, not rays, but tears would fall on the earth!

The priest already knew that his village had been ravaged. Even so, when they reached the hill-top and the soot-blackened, roofless tower loomed up beyond the trees in the garden his eyes became moist.

He did not urge the horses on; they just ambled at their own pace. And step by step the destroyed village opened up before them. Nowhere a complete roof, nowhere a whole gate. In the yards bits of furniture, barrel-staves, heaps of flour, dead men and lifeless horses, pigs and dogs.

And nowhere anyone alive. Only a dog or two which had slunk off during the raid and returned after it was over, and a few fowls which had been able to fly away from the robbers' hands.

The priest got down from the cart and took off his cap.

"Take off your cap too, my boy," he said to Gergely. "This is a village of the dead, not of the living."

Leading their horses, they went further into the village. A peasant with a shock of grey hair lay across the road. He was still holding a pitchfork in his dead hand.

The priest shook his head. "Poor old András!" He took the

57

dead man's hand and dragged him out of the way, so that the horses could get past him.

Another young peasant, his back broken, dangled his dead head over the fence into the street. He seemed to be gazing at his own blood, which had dripped from his head and turned black there. His pig was grazing behind him in the yard which was covered in mattress-feathers. The Turks do not touch pigs. And a naked baby boy lay there too nearby, beside the gate. A wound gaped in his little breast.

The stench of soot and dead bodies was everywhere; and this wild scene of murder was simply because a young farmer defending his wife had stuck a pitchfork into a piper who was a favourite of the Turks.

"Nobody's to remain alive here!" the frenzied Turks had shouted.

The priest took his horse's bridle and led it. He looked no longer to right or left; he just gazed at the road, where the dust gleamed yellow in the sunlight.

At last they arrived at the priest's house.

That had no roof either. The charred black rafters, forming great letter As, projected through the layer of ash that had been the roof, and above the window overlooking the street the wall was black with the traces of fire. They had set fire to the house when they doused him with boiling water to make him give up the church treasures.

The bench was still standing in the middle of the yard. Around it were the fragments of the big walnut chest, books, a scatter of corn, trampled house-plants, chair-legs, bits of crockery. And beside the broken-legged table an old lady in black lay on her back, her arms outstretched. And there was a black pool of blood round her. That was the priest's mother.

"We've arrived home," said the priest, turning his tear-drenched face to Gergely. "We've arrived home."

16

They buried the dead for two days almost without a break. The priest took off the side of the cart and carried three or four bodies to the cemetery with each trip.

Gergő always went in front of the cart. At his side was the sword Dobó had given him, in his hand the funeral cross. The priest, now singing, now praying, led the horses.

Out there he covered the bodies with rush-matting to prevent the crows or ravens from getting at them and then went back.

On the morning of the third day a peasant woman and a child turned up in the village. They had been hiding in the reeds by Lake Balaton. And that evening two men returned home, furtively, cautiously and ever on the alert.

Then they dug the graves; the priest dug with them too. Only when they had cleared away the dead bodies did the priest begin to put his own dwelling in order as far as possible. There were three rooms in the house, but all the ceilings had come down in the fire.

First of all the room on the street side was roofed over with planks by the priest, to shelter them from rain. Then he tacked together a cupboard and made Gergely bring the books lying round in the courtyard and put them in it.

After all the sadness of their previous labours, Gergely enjoyed carrying the books. He had a look at one or two of them to see whether there were any pictures in them. There were five with illustrations. In one were all kinds of insects, while another was full of drawings of flowers. Altogether the priest's library contained about thirty volumes bound in parchment.

The woman tidied the kitchen and cooked for them. She cooked pease pudding without meat and brown soup with eggs in it. Two dishes of food for a whole village!

After lunch the priest looked out into his garden. "I wonder whether they've spared my bees? Come along, Gergő."

He took Gergely into the garden, where there was what looked like a little chapel containing his beehives. The Turks had smashed down its door, but since they had not seen anything inside except a bench, a little fireplace, a trestle-table and some tall glass bottles, they had not destroyed anything there.

The bottles were for chemical experiments. The priest was astonished to see that they were undamaged.

Just then a woman came through the garden-gate. She carried a dead baby in her apron—a little boy about a year old. Her face was red with weeping.

"It's my little János..." she said, bursting into tears.

"We'll bury him," replied the priest. And he put on his cap. Gergely picked up the cross and led the way.

"I hid him," lamented the woman. "I was so scared I hid him in the grain-pit among the linen. By then they'd killed Jancsi next door. I thought I couldn't hide if he cried. I hid behind the hen-coop. But they fell on me and chased me and I ran away. That night I wanted to come back, but then I met another band of pagans. They searched the whole reed-bed; God knows who they carried off and who they killed. By the time I could get back here I found my little János like this. Oh God, oh God! Why have you taken him from me?"

"Don't ask God," the priest reproved her. "God knows what he is doing, but you don't."

"But why was he born then, if he had to die like that!"

"We don't know why we're born; nor do we know why we die. Don't say any more about God."

They dug the little grave. Gergő helped with his hoe.

The mother undid her apron and put the child into the ground wrapped in it. "Just a minute!" she wept, choking, "just a minute!"

She picked grass and flowers. These she scattered on her child. Meanwhile she wept and cried, "Oh why must I give you to the earth! Never again will you hug me with your little arms! Never again will you call me mummy! Oh how those red roses have faded on your dear little face! I'll never be able to stroke your lovely flaxen hair again!"

And she turned to the priest.

"What lovely eyes he had! What lovely brown eyes, weren't they? How he looked, how prettily he looked! Oh, my dearest child, you'll never look at me again, never!"

Meanwhile the priest shovelled earth into the grave and made a mound above it, patting it down with the spade. Then he broke a strong branch from an elder tree on the edge of the cemetery, a cross-shaped branch. He stuck it at the head of the mound.

"Oh God has taken you away from me!" wept the mother. "Why does he need you more than I do?" And she embraced the little mound.

"Because he can look after him better than you," said the priest, rather annoyed. He knocked the soil from the hoe and threw it over his shoulder. He went on in a kindlier tone, "Some go on ahead and await those who still have work to do on the Earth. Sometimes the child goes ahead, sometimes the parent. But the Creator has so arranged it that there shall be someone to welcome them when they arrive beyond the stars. Come along."

But the woman stayed there.

17

Next day they mounted their horses and set off southwards to Szigetvár. It was a hot and cloudless day. In all the ravaged villages they were burying the dead and repairing the roofs. In some of the villages only one or two old people were wandering about, as in theirs. The Turks had driven away the inhabitants.

When they reached the reed-thickets of Szigetvár, the priest looked up. "They're at home, thank God."

Gergely realized he was talking about Bálint Török. He was surprised.

"How do you know?"

"Can you see the flag?"

"That one on the tower?"

"Yes."

"It's red and blue."

"They're the master's colours. That means he's at home."

They entered the reed-thicket and rode side by side on their way. In front of them the water of the Almás brook broadened into a big lake and glistened. In the middle of the water the projecting bastion in the brown walls of the ramparts proudly contemplated its reflection in the water. Great gaggles of geese gleamed white on all sides in the water.

The priest spoke once again.

"Has it struck you, my boy, that Dobó went into battle with a very small force? He might well have remained there."

"In the battle?"

"Yes."

Gergely had not thought anything like that. To him Dobó was invincible; Gergely would not have been surprised if he had attacked the Turkish force all alone.

"If he's died," said the priest, "I'll adopt you as my son."

He galloped on to the first wooden bridge, built on high piles, that led across the water to the outer fortress. On the water and even under the bridge there were hosts of ducks and geese. They clattered through the new town and once again reached a wooden bridge, a short one. This gave entrance to the old town. In front of the twin-towered church three fruit-sellers were sitting, and all three of them were selling cherries. One of them was just measuring some into the apron of a barefooted little girl. The doors of the church had been secured with iron.

Then there followed yet another bridge, but this one was long and wide, and the water beneath it was deep.

"Now we're coming to the inner fortress," said the priest, "And high time too." And he carefully wiped his face with his handkerchief.

The gate of the fortress was wide open, and from inside a loud clatter of hooves could be heard. In the spacious courtyard they glimpsed a man in armour galloping madly in a cloud of dust, and then a second one dashing towards him. It looked like two bronze statues sitting on two living horses. One was new and silvery, the other was discoloured, in places rusty, as if it had been lying around till now in some storehouse. Otherwise only the two helmets were different; one was smooth and round, the other had a silvery bear's head gleaming on top of it. The horses' chests were also covered in armour.

"That's the master," said the priest respectfully, "That one with the bear's head."

The two horsemen dashed at each other with pikes, and as they clashed the two horses reared against each other. But the two pikes slithered along the armour.

62

"Clubs!" thundered the man in the bear-headed helmet as the horses backed away from each other.

It was impossible to see either of their faces. For they were wearing helmets that covered their faces too.

At the shout a page dressed in red and blue ran from the doorway and offered two similar bronze-headed clubs and two iron shields to the contestants.

They once again backed away from each other. White foam was hanging from the mouth of the smooth-helmeted rider's horse. They rushed at each other in the middle of the courtyard.

The smooth-helmeted one struck first. The other raised his shield above his head. It clanged like a cracked bell. But from beneath the shield his hand shot out with the club; he struck his opponent so hard on the head that his helmet was dented.

Then the man with the dented helmet pulled back his horse and threw away his weapon. The man in the bear-headed helmet took off his helmet and laughed.

He was a full-faced, dark-haired man. His long dense black moustache was pressed flat against his cheeks from the pressure of the helmet, and one side of it curled up to his eyebrows, the other down to his neck.

"Master Bálint," said the priest to the boy in a respectful tone. "Take off your cap if he looks this way."

But Bálint Török did not look in their direction. He was gazing at his opponent, from whose head the servants had pulled the helmet.

That rider, as soon as they had managed to get the helmet off his head, a difficult task, first of all spat three teeth on to the gravel of the courtyard and then swore in Turkish.

From the doorway some eight Turkish captives emerged. They helped him to extricate himself from the armour. And he too was just a Turkish captive like the others.

"Now then, which of you still has any inclination for a fight?" shouted Bálint Török, prancing round on his horse. "The reward for anyone who can beat me is freedom!"

A red-waistcoated, muscular Turk with a wispy beard stood forward.

"Maybe I'll be more lucky today."

He donned the heavy armour. His comrades strapped the iron

plates together behind his back. They pressed an iron helmet on his head and a set of greaves on his legs. For the Turk had big legs. Then they helped him on to his horse with a crane. They put a broadsword into his hand.

"You're a fool, Ahmed!" called Bálint Török merrily. "A broadsword doesn't go with armour."

"It's the only thing I'm used to," replied the captive. "If you won't dare to take me on like this, I'm not going to try anything else."

They talked in Turkish. The priest explained what they were saying to Gergő.

Master Bálint buckled his helmet on again. He simply brandished a light pike as he galloped around the courtyard. "Go!" he shouted and dashed for the centre.

Gergő trembled.

The Turk bent forward in the saddle. Holding the broadsword in both hands, he dashed at Master Bálint. "Allah!"

When they met, he rose and prepared to deliver a terrific blow.

Master Bálint aimed his pike at the Turk's waist. His pike slipped and fell out of his hand. Nevertheless he caught the Turk's fearsome blow with his shield. And at that instant he grabbed the Turk's arm and twisted him off his horse.

The Turk fell sideways into the arena and a cloud of dust billowed round him.

"That's enough," laughed Bálint Török, raising his visor. "If I'm at home tomorrow, you can fight with me again." And he shook with laughter.

"It's not fair!" shouted the Turk as he stumbled to his feet with his arm dislocated.

"Why not?" asked Master Bálint.

"It's not proper for a knight to pull his opponent down with his hand."

"Why, you're not a knight, you dog of a pagan! I'm certainly not taking any lessons in chivalry from you lot! Common thieves!"

The Turk sulked in silence.

"You surely don't imagine it's a chivalrous tournament simply because I offer you a challenge," continued Bálint Török, shouting. "Devil take all his ragamuffins and spike them!" And he took his right foot out of the stirrup to dismount.

"Sir!" called a thin, grey-bearded prisoner in a plaintive voice, "I'd like to have another bout with you today."

Those standing in the courtyard broke into laughter.

"Of course, now you think I'm tired out. All the same, you shall have your pleasure."

And he pushed his helmet back on to his head; it had just been in his lap.

"How many times have you fought with me, Parrot?"

"This is the seventeenth time," answered the parrot-nosed Turkish prisoner in a miserable voice.

Bálint Török took off his helmet and threw it aside. "Well then, I'll give up so much of my strength to your advantage... Let's see!"

The difference in strength between them was striking. Master Bálint was a well-built man in the prime of life, all muscle and mobility. The Turk was about fifty, with no muscles and a crooked back.

They fought with pikes. At the very first clash Master Bálint hurled the Turk so hard out of the saddle that he turned a somersault in the air and dropped into the dust.

The servants, pages and prisoners all laughed.

Master Bálint threw off his shield and gloves of mail, and jumped from his horse for the pages to liberate him from the rest of his armour. Parrot got to his feet.

"Sir!" he wept, turning his bloodstained face towards Bálint Török, "please let me go home! My wife and son have been waiting for me at home for two years now!"

"Why didn't you stay at home too, you pagan!" replied Bálint Török angrily. He always flared up if the prisoners pleaded for mercy.

"Sir," pleaded the prisoner, wringing his hands, "have compassion on me! I've a lovely little son with black eyes! I haven't seen him for two years." And he crawled on his knees up to Master Bálint and knelt before him in the dust. "Have pity on me, sir!"

Master Bálint wiped his face with a cloth. Sweat was pouring from him. "If only every wretched Turk were here in chains,

65

together with your emperor!" he panted. "Thieves, murderers and brigands! Not even humans, but beasts!" And he went on his way.

The Turk picked up a handful of dust from the ground and threw it towards Master Bálint.

"Then may Allah strike you dead, you rotten-hearted giaour! May you grow old in chains! May you leave a widow and orphans before you die! May Allah teach you to weep three times over what I weep before he casts your soul into hell!" And as he uttered this curse, tears poured from his eyes and turned to blood as they coursed down his smashed face.

The servants dragged off the pagan, now foaming with anger, and took him to the well. They poured water on him from the bucket.

Bálint Török was used to such scenes by now. They angered him. But neither fair words nor curses unlocked the chains in his fortress. After all, every prisoner in every age and place weeps for liberty, one silently, the next aloud. Since his childhood he had lived among such captives' entreaties, and in that age too prisoners counted as assets in the internal economy. Some were redeemed for money and others exchanged for Hungarian prisoners. So how could anyone possibly imagine letting an enemy prisoner go scot-free?

He held his back and arms so that the pages could brush them. Then, twirling the ends of his moustache with an angry flush, he walked over to the priest.

"Welcome, Father, welcome!" and he offered his hand. "I heard that they'd boiled you like a lobster. At least you'll grow some new skin."

"Sir," answered the priest, holding his cap in his hand, "my skin's the least of my troubles. A greater one is that they've slaughtered my flock; they've also killed my poor mother."

"Devil take them all!" raged Bálint Török with a backward glance. "One curses me for not setting him free, another tries to teach me what chivalry is. I go out to fight with a pike and he charges me with a broadsword like an executioner's. To him that's a joust. But when I drag him down, he still has the upper hand. Dogs and crows devour him!"

Angrily he gave a hitch to his trousers and was as red as the

66

bear which pranced in the coat of arms above his gate. Then he looked at the boy.

"Why, is that him?" he smiled in astonishment.

"Get down quickly," said the priest to Gergő. "Take off your cap."

The little barefooted boy with a sword immediately lay flat on the saddle and slipped down from the horse. He stood in front of Bálint Török.

"Is this the horse you captured?" asked Bálint Török.

"Yes, it is," replied the boy proudly.

Bálint Török took him by the hand and led him off to his wife so quickly that Father Gábor could hardly keep up with them.

His wife was a little blonde creature with a white face and double chin. She was sitting in the garden of the inner fortress beside a table made of a millstone. She was sealing preserves in mugs and pots. A cassocked priest with white hands, the parish priest of the castle, was at work with her. Nearby two little boys were playing, one five years old, the other three.

"Kata, my dear, just look here!" called Bálint Török, "Here's Dobó's page! This little puppy!"

Gergő kissed hands.

The little blue-eyed, double-chinned lady who had come from German stock looked at him with a smile of surprise. Then she bent down and kissed him on the face.

"This one?" The priest also stared at him. "Why, he's still a suckling."

"Yes, indeed. He sucks Turkish blood," replied the lord of the fortress.

"Are you hungry, my little warrior?" asked the lady.

"Yes, I am," replied Gergő, "but first I'd like to go to Mr. Dobó!"

"Oho, my boy, that's not possible," said Master Bálint, his face becoming serious. "Your master's in bed..."

He turned to Father Gábor.

"Haven't you heard? He attacked two hundred Turks with a force of fifty. One Turk hurled his lance so hard into his thigh that its point ended up in the wood of the saddle."

Gergő listened to the conversation wide-eyed. He was upset that he had not been beside Dobó. He would have struck that Turk hard.

67

"Go along and play with the young gentlemen," said the parish priest.

The two little black-haired boys by now were staring at Gergő from beside their mother's skirt.

"Now, whatever are you afraid of?" she said to them. "He's a Hungarian boy. He likes you." Then she said to Gergely, "The elder one here's Jancsi and the younger one's Feri."

"Come along," said Gergő amicably, "and I'll show you my sword."

The three boys quickly made friends.

"And what about you, Father," said Bálint Török, sitting down on the bench. "What are you doing now without a church?"

Father Gábor shrugged. "Well... I'll just live there somehow, like a hermit, if there's no other way."

Bálint Török twirled his moustache as he pondered. "Do you know Turkish?"

"Yes."

"And German?"

"I was a student for two years on German soil."

"Well, I've an idea, father. Leave there and come over here to Szigetvár. Or rather, not to Szigetvár but to Somogyvár, because we're moving there in a few days. So come there. My wife has a papist priest, so why shouldn't I have one belonging to the new faith? And then it'll only be a year or two before the boys grow up and I'll put you in charge of their education."

The parish priest's eyes grew wide. "Sir, what about me?"

"Well, you can teach them too. You can teach them Latin, and he'll teach them Turkish. Believe me, my good sir, the Turkish language is just as necessary to salvation as Latin!" He looked towards his boys, who were chasing each other and Gergely round the apple tree. All three of them were red and laughing.

"I'll take over that boy from Dobó," smiled Bálint Török, "maybe he'll do as a third instructor. And perhaps he'll be a better teacher then the two of you put together."

PART II

The Fall of Buda

King John has died. His son is still a baby. The nation is without a leader. Now the country is like those coats of arms in which griffins, angrily poised to strike each other, reach for the crown hovering between them.

There is confusion of thought within the nation. Nobody knows whether to fear the rule of the pagan Turk more than that of the Christian Austrian.

The Austrian King Ferdinand despatches his ancient senile general Roggendorf to Buda. The Turkish emperor sets out in person to hoist the crescent flag over the Hungarian royal palace.

And the chronicles write the year 1541.

1

One moonlit night in August two horsemen were trotting up the hill on the Mecsek highroad. One was a thin, clean-shaven man in a black cloak who must have been a priest. The other was a long-haired young gentleman not yet sixteen years old.

A tall mounted servant trailed along the road behind them. Perhaps he was so tall because instead of a saddle he had two bulging sacks to sit on. And on his back there was a big leather bag, the equivalent of a modern knapsack. Out of it protruded three objects like handles. One of them glinted from time to time; it was a long-barrelled rifle.

A vast wild pear tree loomed up beside the road—maybe as ancient as the road itself. There they turned off the road with their horses. The priest surveyed the tree.

"Is this the one, then?"

"Yes," replied the young man. "In my childhood an owl nested in it. Since then the hollow in it must have widened; one man, possibly even two, can get inside it."

He stood on the saddle and clambered up into the wild pear

tree. With a single swing he appeared at the top of it. He prodded with his sword at the decaying trunk. Nothing flew out of it.

He let himself down inside it.

"There's room for both of us!" he called merrily. "We can even sit in it too!" He climbed out and jumped down on to the grass.

The priest threw off his cloak. "Then let's get down to work!"

It was Father Gábor. And the young student was Gergely Bornemissza.

Eight years have passed since we last saw them. The priest has not changed much, except that his eyebrows have grown again. He has shaved off his moustache and beard. And he has become a little thinner.

The boy has changed all the more. The eight years have matured him; he is almost an adult. But only in build. His face is indeterminate, neither good-looking nor ugly, just like that of any normal fifteen-year-old boy. The long wavy hair that reached his shoulders was fashionable for men at that time.

The servant took two spades out of his sack and also a mattock. One of the spades the priest picked up, the other went to the young man.

They began to dig in the middle of the highroad.

The servant put down the two sacks and returned to the horses. He took off their bridles and hobbled them. They could graze at will on the good dewy grass of the forest.

Then he too got to work. He laid out all the contents of the leather bag: bread, a wine-bottle and arms. He scraped into the bag the gravelly earth turned up by the two spades, and scattered it in the ditch by the side of the road. When he returned he carried big, heavy stones to the hole. Before an hour had passed the two men were up to their waist in the hole.

"That's enough," said the priest. "János, bring the sacks over here now."

The servant dragged the two sacks over.

"Don't put the rifle on to the wet grass!" commanded the priest. Then he went on, "Take that mattock. Cut a trench from the hole as far as that wild pear tree. Here on the road the trench is to be four feet deep; it can be half that on the grass. Take up the grass in such a way that we can replace it. We mustn't let our work be visible."

While the servant was digging the trench, the two gentlemen lowered the two sacks into the hole.

In the sacks was gunpowder, sewn into skins. They pressed them down and fetched big stones to cover them, filling the spaces between them with small stones and earth.

Meanwhile the servant dug the trench to the tree and lined it with stones. The fuse lay along the trench. They covered it right the way along with oilcloth and flat stones to prevent it getting soaked if it rained.

"Well now," said the servant joyfully, "I know what's going to happen here."

"What then, János?"

"Someone's going to fly up to the heavens here."

"And who do you think it'll be?"

"Who? Why, that's an easy one. Tomorrow the Turkish emperor's coming this way."

"Today," responded the priest, glancing at the dawn breaking in the sky. And he wiped his perspiring face with his handkerchief.

When the rising sun illuminated the highroad there was no trace of either hole or trench. The priest threw aside the mattock. "Now, János my lad, get on your horse and go up to the top of the Mecsek. Keep going until you find a spot where you can look right along the road."

"I understand, sir."

"The student and I will lie down twenty or thirty paces behind the tree. And you watch for when the Turks come. As soon as you see the first horseman, gallop back and wake us up."

They found a good grassy spot in the forest. There they spread out their cloaks and both fell asleep straight away.

2

Towards noon the servant returned at a swift gallop from the top of the hill.

"They're coming!" he shouted from a good way off. "There's

an enormous great army pouring along! Thousands and thousands of camels and carts! A few horsemen have already come on ahead along the highroad."

The priest turned to the student. "In that case we can go to your second father's for lunch."

"To Mr. Cecey's?"

"Yes."

The student looked questioningly at the priest. So did the servant.

The priest smiled. "We've come a day too early. Don't you see? These are the camp-pitchers. They go on ahead and drive in the tent-poles and erect the tents, so that by the time the army reaches Mohács the sleeping-quarters and evening meal will be all ready for it."

"Then let's go to Mr. Cecey's," said the student joyfully.

They dismounted at the stream and had a good wash. The student picked a posy of wild flowers.

"Who's that for, Gergő?"

"It's for my wife," smiled Gergő.

"Your wife?"

"Well, that's what we call it. Little Eva Cecey, she's going to be my wife. We were children together; then when her father adopted me, every time I visited them I had to kiss her."

"I hope you were glad to do that."

"Indeed I was. Her face is like a white carnation."

"But that doesn't mean that you should regard her as your wife."

"The old priest told me that they'd promised their daughter to me. According to Cecey's will, I'm to have the village and the girl too."

"Which means that the old priest gave away a secret."

"No. He just warned me to make myself worthy of such a fortune."

"But will you be happy with that girl?"

The boy gave a smile.

"Just have a look at her, master. Once you see her, you won't ask me again whether I'll be happy with her."

The horse pranced beneath the student and ran a few paces ahead. When he had pulled up his horse, he said, "That girl's like a little white cat!"

74

The priest smiled and shrugged his shoulders.

They reached a thicket and had to dismount. Gergely led the way. He knew that this thicket hid the village.

When they plunged down into the valley, the women ran from the houses.

"Gergő! It's Gergő!" they shouted joyfully.

Gergely waved his cap right and left. "Good day, Aunt Juci! Good day, Mistress Panni!"

"The master and his family aren't at home!" called one of the women.

Gergely was crestfallen. He pulled up his horse. "What was that you said?"

"They've gone away. They've moved."

"Where to?"

"To Buda."

Gergely was stupefied. "All of them?"

Vain and childish hope! He thought the reply would be, "No, the young lady's stayed here."

But it was predictable that the reply would simply be, "All of them, as I said. Even the priest went with them too."

"When?"

"After St. George's Day."

"But there must be someone in the house."

"Just the Turk."

Disappointed, Gergely turned to the priest. "They've gone to Buda. Friar George gave them a house there a long time ago. But I don't understand why they didn't tell me; after all I was here at carnival time."

"Then where are we going to have lunch?"

"The Turk's here."

"What Turk?"

"Cecey's Turk, Tulip. He does everything here. But here we are at the cemetery. Let me just go inside for a moment."

Behind the house could be seen a cemetery surrounded by lilac bushes. It was no bigger than the site of a house. There were nothing but wooden crosses, and the wood was rough. Not one of them had a name on it.

He handed his horse to the servant and himself went inside. He stopped before a brown wooden cross that had sunk well into the ground. He laid the wild flowers on the grave and knelt down.

The priest also dismounted. He went and knelt by the boy and raised his face to heaven. He prayed aloud.

"Lord of the living and the dead, God who dwellest in heaven, give quiet rest to the mother whose ashes lie here and a happy life to the orphan boy who kneels here. Amen."

He embraced the boy and gave him a kiss.

The Cecey house was almost opposite the cemetery. By now the gate was wide open and a dumpy little red-faced woman was looking with a smile at the newcomers.

"Good day, Mrs. Tulip," the student greeted her. "And where's that husband of yours?" For it was Tulip's job to open the gate.

"He's drunk," responded the woman with annoyance.

"Drunk?"

"He's always drunk, is that one. Wherever I hide the key of the cellar, he always finds it. Today I put it under the mangle, and he even found it there."

"Well then, stop hiding it. If he can have a drink when he wants, he'll not drink so much."

"Oh but he will. He drinks like a fish. All he does is drink and sing. Curse him, he doesn't want to do any work."

And indeed in the shade of the mulberry tree there sat a dark-skinned peasant. Beneath him was a rush mat, in front of him a green enamelled pitcher. So far he wasn't sufficiently drunk for the pitcher to be taken away from him. He was drinking there with his son, a little barefoot six-year-old child with eyes as black as his father's, except that his father's eyes always seemed to be smiling at some secret mischief.

This Turk had been pardoned by Cecey because he said he could play chess. Afterwards it became clear that there was no point in playing chess with him, but that he could be put to any kind of work around the house. He was particularly good at cooking. His father had served as a cook in the house of some pasha. The women grew fond of him when he showed them how to cook pilaf, *börek*, *mahallebi* and sherbets, and they fooled around with him a great deal. And Cecey became fond of him when the Turk carved him a wooden hand, one that even had

76

fingers on it. If he pulled a glove over it, nobody would have said that his hand was made of wood. First of all the old man tried out his bow with it. He had a bow as big as he was brought down from the loft. He was able to bend it with the wooden hand. That was when the old man made him a general factotum.

At about that time one of the Hungarian wives had lost her husband, so the Turk became friendly with her, and finally married her. Of course he was christened first. He became as good a Hungarian as if he had been born one.

When he caught sight of the student and the priest, he rose and crossed his hands on his breast in Turkish fashion. He also tried to bow, but realized that this would have ended with him falling on his nose, so he expressed his respects with a stagger forwards.

"Eh, Tulip," said Gergely with a shake of the head, "we're still fond of the bottle, are we?"

"Got to drink," replied Tulip seriously, but with a mischievous twinkle in his eye. "Got to make up for twenty-five years of being a Turk and not drinking."

"But if you're drunk, how are you going to cook lunch for us?"

"My wife'll do the cooking," and he jerked his thumb in the direction of the woman. "She can cook curds with noodles too. Good to eat!"

"But we'd like pilaf."

"She can do that too; she knows how."

"So where's the master, then?"

"In Buda. There was a letter. Master went. Got a house. Beautiful young lady sits in the house like a rose in a little garden."

The student turned to the priest.

"What'll happen to them if the Turks somehow occupy the fortress?"

"Oho!" replied the priest. "The whole country will fall before the fortress of Buda. But no enemy's ever occupied the fortress of Buda yet!"

And seeing Gergely still looking disbelievingly at him, he continued, "The nation protects the country, God himself protects the fortress of Buda."

77

Tulip opened the doors. Out of the rooms came the stale smell of lavender. He opened the windows too.

The priest stepped inside. His glance rested on the portraits hanging on the wall.

"This one's Cecey, I suppose?" he said pointing to the portrait of a man in a helmet.

"Yes," replied Gergely. "Except that now he's not so dark-haired. He's white."

"And who's this lady with a squint?"

"That's his wife. I don't know whether she had a squint when that was painted. She hasn't now."

"She must be a sour woman."

"No, she's rather sweet. And now I just call her mother."

The boy felt himself at home, so drew up a chair for the priest and showed off the shoddy old furniture with a happy face.

"Look, master, this is where Evie usually sits when she's sewing. She puts her feet on this footstool. In this window she watches the sun go down and then her head casts a shadow on the wall. She drew this picture. A weeping willow and a grave. I painted the butterflies in it. And then, you see, this is how she sits here on this seat. She rests on her elbow like this and smiles so mischievously, oh how mischievously!, that you've never seen anything like it!"

"All right, all right," responded the priest wearily, "but now just go and hurry up the lunch."

3

That night they went to bed late.

The priest said he had some letters to write, so he did not sleep in the same room as the student. The student also took paper and a quill with his tallow candle. First of all he drew a beautiful forget-me-not on the paper, then he wrote to his little kitten how he had been surprised by the empty house, and why hadn't they told him they were moving away? If they had written to him, then surely that letter must have gone astray. For at that time there was no post in the land of Hungary. Only the great magnates could correspond with each other. Anyone wanting to send a letter from Buda to Öreglak had also to find someone to take it.

Then the student was overcome by sleep. He stretched out on the wolfskin-covered bench and slept. And maybe he would have slept until the sun was high in the morning, had not a cow mooed beneath his window at dawn. This was unusual for him. Neither at Somogyvár, nor at Szigetvár, nor at any other castle belonging to Bálint Török had cows mooed under his window. He was always woken up by manservants at the same time as Master Bálint's boys, and by the time they had breakfasted the priest was waiting for them in the garden with his book.

The student sat up and rubbed his eyes. It occurred to him that today's lesson was something special: the Turkish emperor had to be hurled up into paradise.

He rose and knocked on the door of the next room.

"Master! It's daybreak! Time to go!"

No response. The room was dark.

The student opened one of the shutters and the window made of oilcloth.

The priest's bed was empty.

On the table a few letters glowed white. Gergely stared.

"What's all this?" he muttered. "The bed hasn't been slept in. It's still made up."

He rushed out of the room. In the yard Mrs. Tulip, in a single underskirt and barefoot, was driving her pig outside.

"Mrs. Tulip! Where's the priest?"

"He went off at midnight, when the moon was up."

"Did János go with him too?"

"No. He's still here. The priest went off by himself, on foot."

The student went back to the room in some confusion. He already had some idea of what the priest intended to do. He hurried straight to the table. Among the letters lying there, one was open. The salutation was written in strong, thick script:

My dear boy Gergely,

This one was for him. He stepped over to the window with it. The ink was apparently damp on the paper. Gergely read:

It is your idea and to your credit if today that crowned savage beast flies to hell. But your idea also has its dangers. Leave those to me, my boy.

You live surrounded by love and are young. Your ingenuity, knowledge and bravery can become a great asset to the nation.

Beside my letter you will find a pouch with a Turkish ring in it. That is my only treasure. I intended the one I love most to have it. It is yours, my boy.

And let my library be yours too. Read there once the clouds have dispersed from the Hungarian sky. Hungarian hands must hold swords now, not books.

Give my arms to Bálint Török, my collection of stones to János and the collection of flowers to Feri. Let them each choose a book of mine to remember me by, and tell them to be brave patriots like their father; they must never be followers of the pagan Turks, but strive with you to restore the national monarchy. Incidentally I am writing to them as well, and what I write to all three of you is to remain my spirit, divided into three.

You were asleep when I left, my boy. I gave you a kiss.

Father Gábor

Gergely was rigid as he gazed at the letter.

Death? A fifteen-year-old boy has not yet learnt the meaning of this word. He only thinks of the spectacle of a Turkish emperor being blown to bits amid smoke and flame and flying into the skies before his very eyes.

He thrust the pouch with the ring in it into his pocket, the letter too, and went outside. He hurried across the yard to the Tulips.

"Tulip," he said to the man stretched out under the eaves, and went on in Turkish, "have you still got your Turkish clothes?"

"No," replied Tulip, "the wife made two waistcoats out of them, one for her and one for the boy."

"Haven't you got your turban either?"

"The wife made an undershirt out of that. It was fine linen."

The student showed his vexation as he walked up and down beneath the eaves.

"What shall I do then? Give me some advice. Today the

80

Turkish army's passing by here along the highroad. The emperor's coming too. I'd like to see the emperor."

"The emperor?"

"Yes."

"Well, you can do that, young sir."

Gergely's eyes shone.

"Really? How?"

"There's a rock beside the highroad. Or rather not one, but two, opposite each other. You can climb to the top of it, hide your head in foliage and see the army as it goes past."

"In that case, Tulip, get dressed quickly and come with me. Your wife can put up some food in a knapsack. You can bring a bottle as well."

That word suddenly brought Tulip to life. He flung on his clothes and cheerily called towards the barn.

"Juliska my love, come here quick, my darling!"

The woman was feeding the hens. She threw them the remains of the feed and turned round.

"What do you want?"

"The bottle, my pearl," laughed Tulip, raising his eyebrows, "the bottle, my emerald."

"Thunder and lightning! Up to now you've only taken to it in the afternoon. Are you going to start at dawn now?"

"Now, now, my lamb, my Turkish delight, it's not for me, it's for the young master."

"But he doesn't drink wine."

"That's true, I don't," said Gergely with a smile, "but we've got to go out and we may be gone till evening. I don't want Tulip to get thirsty."

"Go out? Where are you going, young master?"

"We're going to have a look at the Turkish army, Aunt Juli. Today they're crossing the Mecsek Hills."

The woman was taken aback. "The Turkish army? My dear young sir, don't go!"

"Oh but we are going. I've got to see it."

"My dear young master, what terrible danger you'll run into! What are you thinking of?"

"Come down to brass tacks!" said Gergely impatiently. "What we asked you for wasn't advice but wine!" And as he stamped his foot too, the woman ran into the house. But she quickly returned. Her face was sullen. "I don't mind about you; you can go where you like, young sir. I can't give you orders. But Tulip shan't go with you. I can give him orders."

"Not so," replied Tulip.

"You're staying right here at home, understand?"

"Tulip has to come with me," said Gergely impatiently. "Your servant can carry the food. Why, what's the point of having a servant? It's his job to serve you."

The servant János thought the same. He was already prepared, with a full knapsack, and had watered the horses.

Tulip sensed the woman's worry and rebelled. "Well, I *am* going, my dear, so there! Strike me blind if I don't! In any case you'll only let me have wine if I go down on my knees for it. You're not a good wife."

The woman turned pale. "The Turks'll carry you off if they catch sight of you."

"So what?"

"You mean you'd abandon these two lovely children and me too? Oh my God!"

"But you won't let me have wine. And you beat me too last Thursday."

"I'll give you as much as you want, my dearest, if only you'll not leave me. Don't leave me, dear!..."

By now she was whimpering.

"Very well, then. Just don't forget what you have vowed to do in front of the young master. I'm only going to accompany him and I'll return. But make sure there's something for me to drink!"

"From now on there always will be."

"If you'll let me drink in peace, I shan't get drunk. The only reason I'm always getting drunk is because I'm thinking that tomorrow you won't let me have any wine."

The woman became a little calmer at this. She prepared the food. All the same she was weeping as she accompanied her husband to the gate and she looked so worried as she watched them go that Tulip swelled with joy.

*

82

János went with them to the thicket. There they dismounted. János led the three horses back to the village, while they continued on foot.

The rock by the roadside is still there to this day. It is about five times the height of a man. From its top there is a view right down the road to the wild pear tree where the priest was already in hiding.

The Turk pulled an armful of leafy branches from the trees and so encircled the rock with leaves that the two of them could see everything from up there without anyone down below suspecting that men were hidden there.

"Let's put some foliage over there too," said Gergely, "on the north side."

"Why?"

"So when the sultan's gone past us, we can turn round and watch him go."

Then the sun rose. The forest was covered in dew. Blackbirds trilled. Pigeons cooed. In the distance the first horsemen raised a cloud of dust as they came from the direction of Pécs.

The road could be seen stretching in the cloud of dust as far as the city itself. At last a paprika-red banner appeared in the cloud in front of them, then two, then five and then more and more of them. Beneath and after the banners came soldiers in high turbans on Arab steeds. The horses were so tiny that some soldiers' feet almost touched the ground.

"Those are the *gurebas*," Tulip explained. "They are always the first to come. They're not real Turks."

"What are they then?"

"Arabs, Persians, Egyptians, a mixture of all kinds of riff-raff."

That was obvious. They were wearing a mixture of clothes. One had an enormous brass plume on his head, and his nose was missing. He had already been in Hungary.

The second regiment following them carried a green-striped white banner. Their faces were tanned and they wore blue baggy trousers. Their faces showed that they had eaten and drunk well that night.

"Those are the *ulufedjis*," said Tulip. "Mercenaries, military policemen. They also look after the war-treasury. Can you see

83

that fat-bellied man with the smashed forehead? With big brass buttons on his chest...?"

"Yes."

"His name's Turna. That means 'crane'. But I'd sooner call him 'pig'."

"Why?"

"I once saw him eating a hedgehog."

And Tulip turned his head and spat.

A regiment with a yellow banner galloped along in their wake. Their weapons shone brighter. The horse of one of the agas sported a silver-studded breast-ornament.

"Those are the *silahtar*s," said Tulip. "They're also mercenaries. Hey, you bandits and gallows-birds! I served with you for two years!" And he laughed.

Next came the *spahi*s with their bows and arrows and red flags, their officers in armour; with broad curving swords at their side. Then the Tatars with their pointed caps. A mass of fat faces, leather jerkins and wooden saddles.

"A thousand... two thousand... five thousand... ten thousand," counted Gergely.

"You'll never count them," said Tulip with a dismissive wave, "there are probably something like twenty thousand of them."

"Well, they're ugly, bony-cheeked people."

"The Turks detest them too. They eat horses' heads."

"Horses' heads?"

"Well, they don't get one each, but they're certain to put one in the centre of the table."

"Boiled or roast?"

"It would be something if they were at least boiled or roasted, but they eat them raw. And these dogs have no mercy even for newly-born babes. You see, they take out a man's spleen."

"Don't say such horrible things!"

"But that's how it is. You see, they think that if they rub their horse's palate with human spleen it will gain new energy, however tired it is."

Gergely withdrew his head in disgust from among the foliage.

"I'm not watching them," he said. "They're not human."

Tulip, however, went on watching them.

"Here comes the *nisandji bey*," he said a quarter of an hour

84

later. "He's the one who inscribes the name of the *padishah* on papers that have his seal."

Gergely looked down. All he saw was a pike-headed stately Turk with a long moustache sitting plumply on his little steed among the soldiers.

Next came the *defterdar*, an elderly crook-backed Arab, the Turkish Minister of Finance. Following him in another group of soldiers was the *kazai asker* in a long yellow robe and a tall white cap. He was the chief judge-advocate. The *cheshnidjis*, or stewards and butlers came next, then the court bodyguard. They glittered with gold.

And now the Turkish bands were playing. Amid all the braying of trumpets and the clash of tambourines the varied colours of numerous army corps appeared and went past—the court hunters, whose horses' manes were coloured red, while they themselves carried falcons on their arms.

After the huntsmen came the imperial stud. Prancing, fiery steeds, some already saddled. *Solak*s and janissaries led the horses.

After the horsemen tall horsetailed banners fluttered over the road. Three hundred *kapudjis*, all of them in identical white caps embroidered with gold. At home they were the sultan's palace guards.

Through the clouds of dust the long line of janissaries gleamed white along the road. Their backward-drooping white caps soon became mingled with the officers' red caps and the blue broadcloth uniforms they wore. Their caps were decorated with a spoon in front.

"Is the sultan still a long way off?" asked Gergely.

"Oh yes, he must still be some way off," replied Tulip. "There are at least ten thousand janissaries. Then come the *chavishes* and all sorts of court dignitaries."

"In that case let's move back a bit and have a bite to eat."

On the south side the rock hid them from the army. On the road which sloped down to the north they could see the countless host descending into the valley.

"We might even have a nap too," declared Tulip. And he opened his knapsack. Out of it rattled a chain.

"Why, whatever's that?" asked Gergely in surprise.

85

Tulip raised his eyebrows and laughed. "It's a good friend to me. Without it I never step outside the village."

And since the student looked at him in puzzlement, he went on, "That's my chain. Every time I go out of the village, I fasten one end of it to my leg. You see, then I've no need to fear the Turks. Because the Turks, instead of capturing me, will set me free. And at night I can release myself from it. And it would be a good thing for me to fasten it on now. Here's the key. Put it in your pocket. If we get into trouble, we'll admit that we're from Bálint Török's household; me a prisoner, you a clerk. Master Bálint's on the side of the Turks, so they won't be too hard on us. Then that night I'll release you and we can escape back home."

"What a clever one you are!"

"Indeed I am! I can even outwit my wife when I'm sober. And she's a very clever woman. If only she hadn't such a big tongue!"

Out of the depths of the knapsack came freshly-baked brown bread, ham and bacon, and a few green paprikas. The student got to work on the ham. Tulip took the bacon in his hand and sprinkled it with thick layers of salt and paprika.

"If only the army could see this!" he said, motioning sideways with his head.

"Why so?"

"The Turks drink wine," smiled Tulip, "but they detest bacon as much as we Hungarians detest rat-meat."

Gergely laughed.

"But if they knew," continued Tulip raising his eyebrows, "what heavenly food bacon with paprika is... Though I'm of the opinion that Mohamed never tasted bacon with paprika."

"Then it's better to be Hungarian than Turkish."

"Everyone who's not a Hungarian is a fool!"

He parted his silky black moustache and took a pull from the bottle. He offered it to the student too. Gergely shook his head.

"Later, maybe." He reached into his pocket and pulled out the pouch. "Do you know this ring, Tulip?"

"No, but I can see that it's worth a marble palace. What's that tiny thing? A diamond?"

"Yes."

"Then it's good to look at. I've often heard that looking at a diamond clears the eyes."

"Well, can you read this writing?"

"Of course. I was a janissary too, but they threw me out because once in Nish I ate bacon. We learnt to read in the janissary-school. But only reading the Koran."

And he read, "*Ila mashallah la hakk ve la kuvvet il a billah el ali el azim.* That means 'What God wishes: there is no justice and strength outside the exalted and powerful God.' " And he nodded in agreement, "And so it is. If God hadn't wished it, I couldn't have become Hungarian."

They pondered in silence. Then Tulip spoke up. "You'll soon catch sight of the sultan. What a fine man! His people are a motley lot, but he himself only dresses up when there's a festival or when he receives guests. After the sultan comes a huge forest of golden banners, mainly horsetails. The inner dignitaries of the court also follow him, the *chucadar,* the chief steward; the *tülbendar,* the apparitor; the *rikabdar,* the holder of the stirrups; then the twelve inner pashas: the *chamashir pasha* in charge of the linen, the *berber pasha,* the barber, the *ibriktar pasha* who superintends the ablutions, the *peshkirdji pasha* who holds the towels, the *sherbetchi pasha* who holds the goblet, the *sofradji pasha,* the butler..."

"Oh, stop it, Tulip!"

"Just let me mention the *tirmukdji pasha* who cuts the sultan's most gracious finger-nails."

"Well, he doesn't make a very good job of it. What troops come next?"

"A hundred trumpeters. They each have their trumpet hanging by a golden chain from their shoulder. After the trumpeters two hundred kettle-drummers, two hundred with rattles, a hundred with tambourines and pipes."

"The sultan must have a good ear if he has to listen to that row all day."

"Well, it is a hellish noise. They only stop when they have a rest. But the Turks need it, especially in battle. If there's no music, the Turk won't fight."

"And is it true that the janissaries are recruited and trained from among Christian boys?"

"More than half of them. Though I'm not sure. It's certainly true that the captured boys make the best janissaries. They've got neither father nor mother. They know it's glory for them if they die in battle."

"What comes after the band?"

"A host of riff-raff. Then rope-dancers, jugglers, quacks, traders who watch out for plunder and sell little things. You'll also see a lot of water-carriers too. There are at least five hundred camels in the rear. They carry goatskins, but the water's usually tepid."

"And is that the lot?"

"Oh no. There are about a hundred caravans of gypsies to follow, and dogs. They live on the refuse. But they won't get here until tomorrow or the day after."

"And then?"

Tulip shrugged. "Vultures."

"Bearded vultures?"

"All sorts: bearded ones, ravens, crows. Every army's followed by a black army in the sky. Sometimes there are more of them than there are of men."

The noonday sun shone warmly. The student took off his jacket. They leaned once again on the edge of the rock among the branches and watched the procession of white-capped janissaries passing beneath them. Tulip named quite a number of them.

"That dark one there was with me at school. In his breast there's a stab-wound, a hole so big that a child's fist would go into it. That one who's sweating and took off his turban for a minute killed at least a hundred men in the Persian war. There isn't a scratch on him, unless he's received one since. That thin scraggy man's a marvellous dagger-thrower. He can hurl his dagger into the breast of an enemy at twenty-five paces. His name's Chapkin. Incidentally there are lots like him. At the janissary-school there's a hillock covered with grass. That's where they teach how to throw a dagger. There are some who manage to reach two thousand times a day."

"What about that Saracen?"

"Why, if it isn't old Keshkin! You're still alive, then! He's a devilish good swimmer. He grips his sword in his mouth and swims over a river like that, however wide it is."

"Oh well, Hungarians do that too."

"Maybe. But he never gets tired. And he fetches coins from under the water too. The sultan once had a good time with him on the bank of the Danube. He threw gold coins into the water and lots of men dived in after them, but he brought up the most. Look there! That's old Kalen! That man with big limbs and a trumpet of a nose. Do you see that brown broadsword at his side? It weighs twenty-five pounds! In the battle at Belgrade he hit a Hungarian so hard a blow with it that not only was the Hungarian's head sliced off, but his horse's too... And both of them were in armour."

"Of course the Hungarian got off his horse then to pick up his head."

"Oh well, I didn't see it myself, I only heard about it," Tulip excused himself.

All of a sudden he gave a start. "Am I dreaming? Yumurdjak!..."

And indeed the tense-faced one-eyed Arab janissary was trotting towards them on a small piebald steed with a strong chest. His clothes were more ornate than those of the others. An enormous ostrich feather fluttered from his long white cap.

"It is him, by Jove!" said Gergely in wonder.

"But they said the priest had hanged him!"

"That was what I was told too."

"Didn't the priest say anything about it?"

"No."

"Well, I don't understand it," said the thunderstruck Tulip. And he gazed after the janissary.

Then their astonished eyes met, as if each expected an explanation from the other. They fell silent. About five minutes later the student spoke.

"Tell me honestly, Tulip, don't you ever want to join them again?"

Tulip shook his head.

"It's better to sit than to walk."

"All the same..."

"My wife's a good woman, and I wouldn't give up my children for all the treasure of Stamboul. The younger's a very fine boy. And the older one's so clever that the chief mufti hasn't a better brain. The other day he asked me why horses don't have horns."

"The devil only knows!" laughed Gergely.

Then they stopped talking. The student's expression grew more and more serious as he watched the endless stream of janissaries on the hilly road. The air had already turned into a sea of dust. As the sound of each band faded out in the winding valley, the continuous rattle of weapons and clatter of horses seemed to drug their senses.

The student suddenly jerked up his head. "Tulip! All these men haven't come for nothing!"

"Well, no, they never do."

"They intend to occupy Buda!"

"Possibly," replied Tulip, unmoved.

The student stared at him with a face drained of colour. "And if the sultan happens to die on the way there?"

"He won't die."

"But all the same..."

Tulip shrugged. "He always has his sons with him."

"In other words, he's a seven-headed dragon."

"What do you mean?"

"How long will it take them to get to Buda, what do you think?"

Tulip raised his shoulders. Gergely watched him worriedly.

"All the same, what do you think?"

"If it rains, they'll rest for two or three days, maybe even for a whole week."

"But suppose it doesn't rain?"

"If it's too hot they'll rest too."

The student distractedly scratched the back of his neck. "Then I can get there before they do."

"What's that you're saying?"

"That if they're advancing on Buda, then I've either got to bring the Ceceys back or go and be with them there."

The braying of a new band drowned their conversation. The long procession of janissaries at last came to an end, and a magnificent host with ostrich feathers and yellow banners followed them. A dignified elderly giant of a man towered above them. His face was red with the heat. Two long red horsetails were borne in front of him and their poles glittered with gold. Gergely shuddered as if ice had been thrust down his neck.

"That's the sultan!"

"Of course it isn't," said Tulip scornfully. "That's only the janissary-aga. And all those dressed-up men around him are all *yaya-bashi*s."

"And what the devil are *yaya-bashi*s?"

"Janissary-officers."

Next came a glittering troop in a forest of gilded halberds. Two young men with calm faces were riding in their midst. Both of them on grey horses.

"The sultan's sons," explained Tulip respectfully. "Mohamed and Selim."

But he soon shrugged his shoulders. "May the djinns carry them off!"

The two sons of the sultan were dark-haired young men. They did not resemble each other, but their affection for each other was obvious.

"Look! There goes Yaya-oglu Mohamed!"

"The famous pasha?"

"Yes."

A dignified-looking grey-bearded pasha trailed after the two sons of the sultan. Before him they carried seven horsetail banners. On his head was a mound of white turbans.

"That," said Tulip, "is Yumurdjak's father."

"Never!"

"Oh yes it is. His second son Arslan Bey went past us a little while ago."

"Then what sort of a name is Yumurdjak?"

"A nickname," smiled Tulip. And he broke off a blade of grass. He chewed it in his boredom.

A troop in terrifyingly tall turbans followed; they were armed with silver and gold clubs. The student was seized with a fit of trembling. He sensed that the sultan was next to come.

"All-powerful God of the Hungarians!" he prayed. "Be with us!"

All the gold and silver weapons and glittering robes rose and

91

fell before his eyes. He even covered his eyes with his two hands and kept them there for a minute to be able to see better.

Tulip nudged him. "Just look!" and his voice trembled, "Here he comes..."

"Which one?"

"The one with the dervish whirling in front of him."

A horseman were riding alone in a simple grey robe. In front of him a dervish whirled mechanically at an even speed. On his head the dervish wore a tall camel-hide cap about two feet high. His two hands were wide apart. One pointed upwards, the other down. His skirt spread out like a bell with his whirling.

"A whirling dervish," explained Tulip.

"It's a wonder neither he nor the horse gets dizzy."

"Both of them are used to it."

The horse indeed always had a free path. Another six white-skirted dervishes walked on each side ready to relieve the one who was whirling.

"Those seven dervishes whirl like that before the sultan all the way from Constantinople to Buda," shouted Tulip into the student's ear. For there was no other way to communicate in the noise of the trumpets, pipes, drums and cymbals.

The sultan was riding a splendid little Arab steed. Behind him two half-naked Saracens protected their master from the blazing heat of the sun with two six-foot long peacock-feather sunshades. In any case the air in the bend of the valley was stuffy, and His Majesty breathed in the same dust as the most ragged of his soldiers, and his face too was just as red.

As he reached the foot of the rock, it could be seen that he was wearing a red satin pelisse and baggy trousers to match. His turban was green. His face was thin and hollow. Beneath his long, thin, drooping nose was a thin grey moustache. His chin was hidden by a curly grey beard cut short. His eyes protruded like marbles.

Just as Gergely was going to take a better look at him, there was a sudden boom, an explosion that rocked heaven and earth... The rock trembled beneath them...

The horses started back... The sultan jerked on to the neck of his retreating steed... The music stopped... Wild confusion... Dust and bits of stone... limbs... weapons... drops of blood all fall like rain from the sky... Turmoil and shouts rise from the host in the valley...

"It's all over with us!" cried Gergely, clashing his hands together. And he fixed his terrified eyes on the valley.

From the valley a dark column of smoke rose up to the clouds. The air grew heavy with the stench of gunpowder.

"What's happened?" asked Tulip in terror.

Gergely's head drooped.

"What's happened? Why, the janissary-aga isn't the sultan!"

4

The explosion was followed by a minute of stunned silence. Every man, every horse seemed to have turned to stone. The music, the braying of the trumpets, the tumult, the clatter of hooves and clashing of weapons suddenly stopped. The whole universe seemed suddenly to have turned deaf at that moment.

But the next minute the cries and curses of thousands and thousands swelled up in a great hurricane of sound. The army milled around like an anthill that has been disturbed. But everyone pressed forward to where the column of flame had shot up.

That place was covered with the bodies of dead and wounded.

Those further away were also in confusion. They did not know whether it was an ancient gun belonging to some hidden army that had gone off, or whether a gunpowder-cart had exploded on the road. The janissaries, however, knew that a mine had been deliberately exploded among them. They scattered into the forest like wasps from a nest that had been disturbed.

They searched for the enemy. But all they found in the forest was the priest, then the student and Tulip.

Two janissaries gripped the priest by his arms as if they were holding some corpse on its legs. His eyes were closed. His clothes looked as if they had been sprinkled with bran. These were the splinters of wood from the tree. The explosion had blown the tree down and thrown him out of the hollow trunk.

The sultan ordered the three captives to be brought before him. He dismounted from his horse. The soldiers set a big copper drum on the ground as a seat. One of the staff officers spread his own blue silk kaftan over it as a carpet.

The sultan, however, did not sit down. He looked at Tulip. "Who are you?"

He recognized him as a Turkish prisoner by his face and by the chain.

"I'm a prisoner," replied Tulip on his knees. "You can see that, father of all true believers: here's the chain on my leg. I am a janissary, and my name is Tulip; I am the dust of Your Majesty's Feet."

"And this whelp?"

The student just stood there confused at his situation, and stared at the hazel-eyed man with his painted face and nose of a sheep, the master of millions of folk, who a moment or so ago should have flown up to the paradise of the Turks.

"The adopted son of Bálint Török," replied Tulip humbly.

"The dog of Enying?"

"Yes, your Majesty."

The sultan looked at the priest. "And this man?"

The priest was held up by two janissaries. His head drooped. Blood dripped from his mouth right down his breast. It was impossible to tell whether he had fainted or had died.

Tulip gazed at the priest.

One of the staff officers grasped the priest's hair from behind and pulled his head round so that Tulip could get a better view.

The blood dripped from the chin of the half-dead man. His breast heaved.

"I don't know the accursed man," replied Tulip.

"Doesn't the student know him either?"

Gergely shook his head.

The sultan glanced at the boy, then turned again to Tulip. "What explosion was that?"

"Your Majesty," responded Tulip, "the student and I were collecting mushrooms here. We heard the music. We hurried over here. I, the unworthy dust of your feet, just waited for you to pass by, then I would have called out for you to set me free."

"That means that you know nothing."

"No, may I find salvation in the paradise of true believers."

"Set him free," commanded the sultan. "Put the chain on the whelp's leg."

94

Then he looked at the priest.

"Let the doctors take care of this dog. I want us to get a confession from him."

The sultan remounted his horse. His sons joined him, and they rode off accompanied by *bostandjis* and pashas to the place of the explosion.

While they were putting his leg in chains, the student saw them laying the priest face upwards on the ground and splashing water from a leather bag on to his face and breast. They washed the blood from him.

A grave Turk in an ash-coloured kaftan pulled up the priest's eyelids from time to time and watched him attentively.

Meanwhile they locked the chain on the student's leg and escorted him over to the prisoners.

The boy was pale and simply stared ahead like a wax doll.

A quarter of an hour later Tulip turned up there too. He was dressed in blue like the janissaries. On his head was a backward-drooping white cap, on his feet red boots.

He shook his fist at the student and roared angrily into his face, "Now I've got you in my hands, *ibn el-haram!* [Son of sin]" And he pushed away the janissary at Gergely's side.

"He's my prisoner! Up to now I was his prisoner; now he's mine. Allah is just and powerful."

The janissary nodded at him and let Tulip go up to Gergely. The boy gazed at Tulip with a pale face. Had Tulip really changed sides?

5

Gergely fetched up at the back with a group of weary and dusty child-captives. They were accompanied on each side by a line of janissaries. Behind them rumbled the gun-carriages. One of the guns was of enormous size: fifty pairs of oxen pulled it along. It was escorted by a host of *topchis* in short red cloaks. Behind them was a crowd of camels carrying great loads.

The burning heat of the sun tortured the army and captives alike. Even the dust of the road was hot. One eight-year-old boy whined every ten paces, "Water! Give me some water!..."

Gergely said sadly to Tulip, "Give him some."

"There isn't any," replied Tulip in Hungarian, in tones that suggested they were talking in Cecey's yard, "the flask got left behind."

"There you are, my boy, there isn't any," said Gergely over his shoulder to the boy. "We'd gladly give you some if there were any. So just put up with it till evening as best you can."

He held the chain first in one hand, then in the other to be able to walk, but the weight of the chain gradually grew. At sundown he felt as if he were carrying a couple of hundredweight.

By then the herd of children was sitting on the guns and camels. The *topchi*s picked them up because they kept falling down with weariness.

"Have we still far to go to where we rest?" Gergely asked the ragged soldier on his right. He opened his eyes wide when he heard Gergely talking Turkish.

"Yok." [No.]

The Turk was a young giant with a round face. He wore a torn leather jerkin from which his arms protruded naked. What arms! Other men would have been glad to have them as thighs. His weapons were two long daggers stuck in the dirty red sash he wore as a belt round his waist. One had a deer-bone as a handle, the other a yellow leg-bone of an ox; even the knob at the end of them was as Nature had created it. But his main weapon was a long rusty-headed pike which he carried on his shoulder. He was one of the volunteers, only there for the booty. He took orders from everyone, but as far as obeying them was concerned, he would only obey so long as his knapsack was not full. Well, he had a good large knapsack, and it was very flat. It flopped down his back, and it was obviously home-made. It still had hair on the ox-hide and a brand-mark on it. The brand depicted a hand-sized circle divided into four. And a detestable stench of leather and sweat exuded from the man.

"Are you Turkish?" he asked.

"No," replied the student proudly. "I don't belong to any nation that goes around stealing."

The giant either did not take in the insulting remark or was insensitive. He walked on at an even pace.

The student looked him up and down, and his glance became

fixed on his gigantic sandals. In front they had worn into a hole.
The white dust of the highroad entered there and always shot
out of the hole at the back.

"Can you read?" the Turk asked again after a quarter of an
hour or so.

"Yes, I can," replied Gergely.

"And can you write too?"

"Yes, that too."

"And you don't want to be a Turk?"

"No."

The Turk shook his head. "That's a pity."

"Why?"

"Soliman pasha was a Hungarian too. He was able to write
and read. Now he's a pasha."

"And he's fighting against his native country."

"He's fighting for the true faith."

"If the true faith to him is what that prophet of yours
proclaimed, then let him fight somewhere else."

"He fights where Allah wishes."

After this they spoke no more.

The giant, lost in thought, continued to shoot the dust out of
his sandals.

6

It grew dark. Stars began to appear in the sky. As the road
wound up a hill, the darkness of the countryside seemed to
become part of the sky, a sky studded with red stars, out of
which on the eastern side five huge red stars shine out amongst
the others, almost touching each other.

"We're there," said the giant. And he scratched his side contentedly.

But they still went on for a quarter of an hour across plough-
land, pastures, hills and fallow land.

Each group found its place without searching for it, and every
man his own tent. The camp-fires were red stars, beside which
mutton flavoured with onion was steaming. The five huge red
stars consisted of the four wax torches of enormous size blazing

in front of the sultan's towering tent and the large golden ball with a crescent moon on the top of the tent glittering in the light of the torches.

At the end of a field of sunflowers, the *topchi bashi* blew his whistle twice. They stopped.

The tents were set up there in a U formation. The captives were escorted into the centre of the U. The giant sniffed in the direction of the sunflowers and went among them to pick the seeds. The student collapsed on to the grass.

The soldiers came and went and shouted all around them. The camels grunted in chorus. Some Turks undid their bundles, others thronged round the cooking-pot. The whole camp was a seething mass of activity.

Gergely looked for Tulip, but he only caught sight of him for a moment as a janissary was talking to him. Tulip shrugged his shoulders and then went with the janissary beside a beetroot-red tent. Presumably they had assigned him a place among the janissaries in one of the tents.

But suppose the only reason why Tulip had to go away was because he wanted to be on guard over the captives! Then in that case both of them would remain prisoners in everlasting uncertainty. This thought weighed like lead on Gergely's breast.

All the guards were changed. It was the soldiers who had pitched the tents who took over. All unknown men, who would have nothing to do with him.

By this time the water-carrying camels had also appeared in the camp.

"*Sudju! Sudju!*" the cries of the water-carriers could be heard in all directions. And the soldiers drank the Danube water from earthenware pots, horns, caps and lead cups.

Gergely too was thirsty. He made a dent in the crown of his cap and held it out under the goatskin offered by the Turkish camel-driver.

The water was tepid and not very clean, but all the same he drank greedily. Then he thought of the boy who had kept asking for water on the road. He looked around. He saw some of the guns in the darkness. Near them he also saw oxen grazing. Topchis were sitting and lying beside the guns. He could not see the child.

So he drank the rest of the water and waved his cap to and fro. He put it back on his head.

"We drink better water than this at home, don't we?" he said to the new guard, a long-necked, smooth-faced *asab*.

Maybe he was trying to win his friendship.

"Shut up!" roared the guard in reply, "and lie down, you little cur!" And he threatened him with his lance and went on his way.

Gergely began to feel his chains even more uncomfortable. He was almost glad to catch sight of Yumurdjak. He was organizing the changing of the guards, and carried an unsheathed sword in his hand.

"Yumurdjak!" he called to him, as if he were welcoming an old acquaintance. For he wanted to escape from the torture of loneliness.

The Turk looked round to see who was addressing him. Someone among the captives? He blinked at Gergely in astonishment. "Who are you?"

The boy rose. "I'm a captive," he replied, suddenly losing his courage, "I only wanted to ask er... how is it that you're alive."

"Why shouldn't I be alive?" replied the Turk with a shrug. "Why indeed shouldn't I be alive?"

As he sheathed his sword again, it could be seen that his left hand was injured. The fingers looked as if he had once taken a pinch of salt and had never been able to separate them again. And he too exuded that detestable stench of sweat like the giant.

"I heard they'd hanged you."

"Me?"

"Yes, you. Nine years ago; it was a priest in the Mecsek Hills."

At the word "priest" the Turk opened his eyes still wider.

"Where's that priest? What do you know about him? Where does he live?" And he grabbed the student by the breast.

"Do you want to do him some harm, then?" stuttered the student.

"Of course not," replied the Turk in a milder tone. "I'd rather like to thank him for not harming me." And he put his hand on the student's shoulder.

"Where is that priest?"

"You mean you didn't thank him at the time?" asked Gergely.

"It all happened so suddenly," Yumurdjak spread his hands; "I didn't even think then of thanking him. I thought he was joking."

"So instead of hanging you he let you go?"

"Yes, like a Christian. I didn't understand that at the time. Since then I've heard that the Christian religion demands forgiveness."

"Well, would you like to do him some good?"

"Yes, I would. I don't like owing anyone money or kindness."

"Well, the priest is here too," said the student with confidence.

"What? Here in the camp?"

"Yes, here in the camp. A prisoner of the sultan. They accuse him of setting off that explosion in the Mecsek."

Yumurdjak staggered backwards. His eyes glittered like those of a snake rearing to strike its prey.

"How come that you know the priest?"

"We live near to each other," replied the student cautiously.

"Did the priest ever show you a ring?"

"He might have done."

"A Turkish ring. There's a moon on it, and stars."

The student shook his head. "He may have shown others something like that, but not me." And he thrust his hand into his pocket.

Yumurdjak scratched his shoulder. The big ostrich-feather waved backwards and forwards on his cap. He turned round and walked away. The guards saluted him in turn. Later only the movement of the guards' lances showed which way he was going.

Gergely was left to himself again. He sat down again on the grass. They brought the captives soup in a pot, and with it clumsy wooden spoons. The Turk who brought it scratched himself there while they ate, and when a captive spoke in a whisper to his neighbour, he kicked him away.

Gergely also tasted the soup. It was made with flour, and had no salt or fat in it. The normal morning and evening meal for captives in the camp.

He put down his spoon and turned away from those who were eating. The captives too gradually stopped eating and lay down; they were soon asleep.

100

Only Gergely remained awake. His eyes filled with tears, and they rolled down his cheeks.

The moon was a pike and a half's height above the horizon now, and it lit up the gilded and horse-tailed knobs on the tops of the tents, the tips of the lances and the guns.

Every time the long-necked guard walked past him, he gave him a glance. Gergely was annoyed by these glances. He was almost relieved when he saw once again the mighty shoulders of the giant Turk approaching them.

He was chewing a plateful of sunflower seeds just as a pig does. He was neither a guard nor a regular soldier; he could loaf about wherever he pleased.

"The advance party broke them all down before we got here," he complained to the long-necked guard. "I've had a job to find this plateful."

"Or the infidels have stored them away," replied the guard sullenly. "For these people, if they smell a Turk, will pick the lot, even if they're not ripe." And he went on his way among the prisoners. Sometimes he stopped to scratch his thigh or his side.

The giant ate the seeds from the sunflower and then bit into the stalk. He spat it out.

"Didn't they give you anything to eat?" asked Gergely.

"Not up to now," replied the Turk. "They feed the janissaries first. This is the first time I've been in the army."

"What were you before?"

"A drover. An elephant-drover. In Teheran."

"What's your name?"

"Hassan."

Another janissary was sitting beside them on the grass. He was holding a piece of boiled mutton on the bone, cutting the meat from it with his knife. He spoke out now.

"We simply call him Hayvan. Because he's an idiot."

"Why's he an idiot?" asked the student.

"Because," replied the janissary, tossing the bone over his shoulder, "he's always dreaming that he's the janissary aga."

The student also lay full length on the grass and put his arm under his head. He was tired, but only his eyes were closed. His brain was working on the problem of liberation. He was not pleased to see Hayvan return and squat down beside him, still chewing. He had been given a meat-bone from one of the pots.

"Infidel," said Hayvan, nudging the student's knee, "if you're hungry, I'll fetch you one too."

"No, thank you," replied the student. "I'm not hungry."

"You haven't eaten since we captured you."

"I tell you I'm not hungry."

The giant obviously found it strange that someone was not hungry. He shook his head. "I'm always hungry." And he went on chewing.

The student lay back on his arm in order to get away from the smell of Hayvan, and stared at the moon. The moon was rising in an orange glow to the east above the tents. The head of a guard about thirty paces away half covered it. He was like a spectral bishop in a big mitre, and the lance in his hand seemed like the handle of the moon.

"Don't go to sleep," said Hayvan softly. "I've got something to say to you."

"There's time for that tomorrow."

"No. I'd like to tell you today."

"Well then, get on with it."

"Wait a bit, till the moon gets brighter."

There was a sudden movement on one side of the area where they had been herded, and six new shadows appeared from among the armed shadows of the guards.

They were new prisoners. Five men and a woman. The men looked like gentry. A large black veil covered the head and shoulders of the woman. It was impossible to see her face because she was crying.

"Oh God! Oh God!"

"Let me go and see the sultan!" shouted one of the men in Hungarian, growling like a bear. "I'm not Austrian! Damn the Austrians! You mustn't lay hands on me! The Turks aren't enemies of the Hungarians now. How dare you touch me?"

But the soldiers did not understand what he was saying. When he stopped, they pushed him on.

Near Gergely there was a clearing big enough to turn a cart in it. They settled the new arrivals there. The Hungarian saw that nobody would listen to him, so he just swore to himself.

"May the pagan pigs have no God! They keep on saying they're friends of the Hungarians! Friends be damned! The man who first believed them was a fool! And the one who invited them in! May they be swept from the face of the earth together with their bandit of an emperor!"

Meanwhile the woman had been taken from them away to the oxen and buffaloes which pulled the guns. Her shrieks were in vain; they just pulled her along. The other four men sat silent on the grass. They were Austrian soldiers. One of them wore armour of metal that gleamed on his breast. There was nothing on his head but a tousled mop of hair.

Gergely turned to the Hungarian. "It's true, isn't it," he asked, "that these Austrians escaped from below Buda?"

"Very probably," answered the Hungarian reluctantly. "I only met up with them here in the vineyard. Is there any water here? I'm thirsty."

It was then that Gergely saw that the gruff-voiced Hungarian was a thin little man with a full beard, and that he was sitting in his shirt sleeves among the others.

"That's not likely now," replied Gergely. "How did you come to be taken prisoner?"

"I was hiding from them in a cellar, may they be eaten by worms! Maybe the fools thought I was a spy. The devil I am! I'm an honest cobbler. I'm only too glad not to see any Turks, never mind follow them around. Filthy curs!"

"Have you come from Buda, maybe?"

"Yes, I have. If only I'd stayed at home!"

"Do you know old Cecey in Buda?"

"The one with the wooden leg? Of course I do. One of his hands is wood too."

"What's the old chap doing?"

"What's he doing? Fighting!"

"Fighting?"

"I'll say he is. He had himself strapped to a horse, then galloped off with Master Bálint against the Austrians."

"One-handed?"

"One-handed. He charged the Austrians like a young lad. When they came back, I saw them; Master Bálint had him at his side and took him off to see the Queen."

"Bálint Török?"

"Yes. He's another of those reared on dragon's milk. He came back from the fight each day covered with blood up to his shoulders. But if only they'd attack these pagans too!"

"And did the old man come to any harm?"

"Oh yes," the cobbler laughed. "They chopped off his wooden hand in battle."

"Do you know his daughter?" asked the student shyly.

"Of course I know her. Two weeks ago I made her a pair of boots. They were of yellow leather, with fine gold decorations on the ankle. That's what young ladies of quality are wearing now, at any rate those who can afford them."

"A pretty girl, isn't she?"

The cobbler shrugged his shoulders. "She's neat."

He was silent for a minute and pulled at his moustache.

"God desert these pagans!" he said, suddenly changing his tone. "They might at least give me back my fur jacket! I don't mind about my shirt. They pulled it off me; never mind that. But my jacket..."

"When did you leave Buda?" the student went on with his questions.

"I escaped three days ago. But if only I hadn't! It couldn't have been worse than this. Though the Turks are dogs! At Belgrade too they promised not to harm anyone, yet they slaughtered all the folk in the citadel, didn't they?"

"You surely don't think that Buda will fall into the hands of the Turks?"

"Certainly I do."

"Why, what makes you so certain?"

"Every night in the church Turkish souls have been saying mass for a week now or longer."

"What? What on earth are you saying?"

"At midnight every night there are lights in the Church of Our

104

Lady, and then you can hear all the 'illallahs' from the Turks singing and shouting to their god."

"That's impossible, old chap."

"I swear it's true. Why, wasn't it the same at Belgrade? There too they heard Turkish singing in the church every night and a week later the fortress fell to the Turks."

Gergely shuddered. "Oh, that's just one of those superstitions."

"Whatever it is, I myself have seen it and heard it. Otherwise I shouldn't have left the castle."

"You mean that's why you escaped?"

"Of course. I sent my family to Sopron to their grandmother before the Austrian attack. I couldn't go with them because I'd got a good business. You see, when the gentry come up to Buda, the first thing they do is have new shoes made for them. I made some for Bálint Török too, and for Master Werbőczy as well. And as for Perényi!"

The cobbler was unable to finish what he wanted to say because Hayvan grabbed him by the collar of his waistcoat and lifted him up like a cat. He tossed him about ten paces away from the student. The cobbler fell into the grass with a groan. Hayvan settled down where he had been sitting.

"You said you could read and write, so I'll show you something."

He wiped all his ten fingers on his trousers and pulled the white oxhide sack round from his back. Again he wiped his fingers on the oxhide, and then pulled out of the sack a bundle of crumpled bits of parchment.

"Look here," he said. "I found these under the robe of a dead dervish. He'd been killed by some wound. The wound was on his back. They'd either stabbed him or shot him. But that's by the way. He'd also got money on him: thirty-six gold coins. I've got that too in my knapsack. Well, if you'll tell me what these papers have written on them, I'll give you a gold piece. But if you won't, I'll give you such a blow on the face that you'll die instantly."

The moon was shining brightly. Everyone around them was asleep. Even the cobbler was curled up on the grass and was probably asleep too.

The student unfolded the bundle of papers. They were about the size of a hand, and on them were all kinds of drawings with four, five and six sides to them.

"I can't see very well," said the student. "The writing's very small."

The Turk got up and fetched a blazing branch as thick as his arm from the fire. He held it there.

The student looked carefully and grimly at the writing and the drawings. The heat of the fire flamed into his face, but he scarcely felt it. Then he raised his head.

"Have you shown anyone these documents yet?"

"Oh yes, but they couldn't read what was in them."

The flaming branch subsided. The Turk put it down.

"I don't want your money," continued the student. "Nor am I afraid of your fist. For I am the prisoner of the sultan. If you hit me, you'll account for that to the sultan. But if you want me to explain this writing to you, I can ask you for something too."

"What?"

"This writing's worth a lot to you, because it comes from a holy dervish. It's a lucky chance in a thousand that you've shown it to me, because any Turk would take it away from you. But I'll explain it to you on one condition: that you'll go and see that priest who caused the explosion at midday, or if he didn't, they found him there."

"It must have been him."

"Well, it's all the same. You'll go and see whether he's alive or dead."

The Turk grasped his chin and looked thoughtfully at Gergely.

"And while you're gone I'll look through all these papers of yours," the student continued encouragingly. "Now there's no need of a torch. The moon's bright enough."

And he returned to a careful study of the drawings.

They were drawings of fortresses in Hungary. They were done with a lead point. In places there were erasures. On one of the drawings the marks X and O stood out. At the bottom of the paper there was an explanatory note in Latin: *X marks the weakest point of the fortress, O a place suitable for mining.* In some places the O mark had an arrow-shaped line from it, in others it was missing.

106

The student shook his head sorrowfully. He was holding the sketches of some spy in his hand. Drawings of more than thirty fortresses in Hungary.

What was he to do? Steal them? That was impossible. Burn them? The Turk would strangle him.

He held the papers in his hand, pale with excitement. Then he reached into the pocket of his jacket and took out a piece of lead. He rubbed out all the Xs and Os on the sketches and in the same script put them elsewhere. That was all he could do.

Since the Turk had still not returned, he examined the last sketch at length. This was a drawing of the fortress at Eger, looking like a frog with every leg cut short. The reason it caught his attention was that he saw on it four underground passages, among them rooms and a square reservoir. What a strange construction! Those who had built them seemed to have reckoned on continuing the battle underground, and if they did not succeed there, in escaping from the fortress in four different directions, while their pursuers would be drowned in the reservoir.

He glanced up to see whether the Turk was coming back.

He was. He was coming past the guns like a tall giant shadow. With his left hand he was scratching under his right arm.

Gergely quickly screwed that one sketch into a ball and stuck it into the pocket of his jerkin. He opened a hole in the pocket with his finger and pushed it through. Then he bent once again over the drawings spread over his knees.

"The priest's still alive," said the Turk as he squatted down, "but they say he won't last till morning."

"Did you see him?"

"Yes, I did. All the doctors are sitting there around the tent. The priest is lying on a bed with pillows, and he's snorting like a dying horse."

Gergely covered his face with his hands.

The Turk stared at him like a tiger catching sight of its prey. "You're his accomplice!"

"And what if I am? I've got your fortune in my hands."

The Turk blinked. Suddenly he brightened up. "Does that paper bring good fortune?"

"Not the paper, but its secret. But only for a Turk." And he offered it back to him.

107

"All right, just speak," whispered the giant with hungry eyes. "I've done what you asked me to do."

"But you've got to set me free as well."

"Oho!"

"This secret's worth more than that to you."

"I'll find it out from someone else."

"A Turk would take it from you. A Christian? When will you ever come across another Christian who knows Latin as well as Turkish, and to whom you can do such a favour that he will give you the key to your fortune in exchange?"

The Turk grabbed the student by the throat. "I'll strangle you if you won't tell me!"

"I'll tell the whole world that you've got in your possession the blessing of a holy man."

He could say no more. The Turk's fingers closed round his neck like an iron clamp. His breath was stifled.

But the Turk did not want to stifle him. What use would it be for him to stifle the student? He might stifle his own fortune at the same time. And Hayvan had not set off to war to get his head knocked in. He wanted to be a gentleman, like every ordinary soldier.

He relaxed his fingers on the student's neck.

"All right then," he said grimly. "I can easily beat you to death if you get me into trouble. How do you think I can set you free?"

The student could not answer immediately. He had to get back his breath after that fierce pressure.

"First of all," he panted, "you'll saw the chains off my leg."

The giant smiled scornfully. He looked round and stretched a great red hand down for one of the chains. He broke it in two places. The chains subsided into the grass with a gentle clinking.

"What next?" he went on with burning eyes.

"You'll get a *spahi* cap and cloak for me."

"That's difficult."

"You can take them from one of those who are asleep."

The Turk scratched his neck.

"And that's not all," continued the student. "You've got to get me a horse and some kind of weapon. It doesn't matter what; anything'll do."

108

"If I can't find one, I'll give you one of my daggers, this smaller one."

"I'll accept that."

The Turk looked round. Men were asleep everywhere; only the sentries walked up and down with noiseless footsteps. The long-necked one was standing about twenty paces away. His lance was fixed firmly in the ground. He was leaning on it.

"Wait," said the giant.

He got up and shuffled off. He disappeared among the tents.

8

Gergely rolled over in the grass as if he were asleep too. But he did not let himself go off to sleep, however tired he felt. He kept looking at the sky with one eye, watching the moon to see whether it would meet up with that long raft-shaped cloud that was slowly and lazily spreading in the middle of the sky. (If it did, welcome darkness would cover the land.) With the other eye he examined that thin-necked surly janissary who was standing like a bald-headed eagle in captivity. He must surely have been sleeping upright. Weary soldiers can sleep even when they are standing.

It was a mild night. The air throbbed with the gentle snores of a hundred thousand men. The earth itself seemed to be murmuring with a deep monotonous murmur, like a cat purring. Only from time to time there could be heard a dog barking, a sentry reporting and the gentle crunching of the horses as they grazed.

Gergely gradually became sleepy too. He was exhausted by weariness and worry. (Men condemned to death always sleep the night before they are executed.) But he did not wish to sleep. He almost welcomed the gnat that kept circling his nose. It had a thin hum, but in the end he flicked it away and continued the fight against the drowsy air of sleep that weighed heavy on the camp. He struggled, but in the end he closed his eyes.

And suddenly he saw that he was where he had started out: in the schoolroom of the old castle of Somogyvár, with the two sons of Bálint Török. They were sitting at the table, the big unvarnished oak table. Opposite him Father Gábor was bent over a large book bound in parchment. To the left was the window, through whose round leaded lights the sun was shining, casting its rays on the corner of the table. On the wall were two large maps. One depicted Hungary, the other the three continents. (At that time scholars had not yet mapped out the land of Columbus; there was merely a rumour that the Portuguese had discovered a hitherto unknown continent. But nobody knew how much truth there was in it. And even Columbus had not yet even dreamt of Australia.)

On the map of Hungary the fortresses were shown as tent-shaped figures, and the forests had their trees sketched in them. These were good maps. They could easily be understood even by those who could not read. And at that time even among the titled nobility there were many who could neither read nor write. And why should they? It was the job of the clerk to write if anything needed writing, and if a letter arrived, to read it to his master.

The priest raised his head and spoke: "From today we're not going to study syntax or geography or history or botany, but only the Turkish language and German. And only so much of chemistry as is necessary to know for the manufacture of gunpowder."

Jancsi Török stuck his goose-quill pen into the inkstand. "It would be a waste of time, master. After all, we can already talk with any of the Turkish captives. And my father's turned his back on the Austrians."

The little Feri, who was ten years old, threw back his shoulder-length hazel-brown hair with a light toss of his head and interrupted. "And why chemistry? My father's got enough gunpowder to last as long as the world does."

"Oho, young man," smiled the priest. "You can't even read decently. Why, yesterday you read Cicero as Kikero."

The dashing figure of Bálint Török appeared in the middle of the room. He was wearing the blue velvet dolman that King John had left to him when he died, and at his waist was the light curving sword that he only wore for special occasions.

"A visitor's come," he said to the priest. "Put on your best clothes, boys, and come down to the courtyard."

In the yard there was a big iron-waggon from Vienna. Beside it was an Austrian with his servant. Gleaming suits of armour were being unloaded from the waggon and handed out to the Turkish captives. They hung these on posts in the courtyard. Beside the waggon stood four distinguished gentlemen together with Bálint Török. He introduced his sons to them. One was a small dark youth with a short nose and fiery eyes. He picked up the little Feri Török and gave him a kiss.

"Do you still know who I am?"

"Yes, you're Uncle Miklós," replied the boy.

"And my other name?"

Feri looked thoughtfully at Uncle Miklós's soft black beard. János spoke instead. "It's Zirinyi."

"Not Zirinyi," his father corrected him. "It's Zrínyi."

All this had once taken place. Sometimes we dream again what is past, and no changes are made in the dream. And as the events of that day continued to unroll, so Gergely's dream went on.

When the six breastplates had been set up on the poles, the gentlemen produced rifles and shot at them. One of them was pierced by the bullet. It was given back to the trader from Vienna. They bought the others which were merely dented by the shots and divided them up between them.

Meanwhile it grew dark. They sat down to dinner. Mrs. Török sat at the head of the table and Master Bálint at the foot of it. During the meal the guests questioned the boys about how much they knew. The Bible and the catechism were particular themes for their questions. For a time Bálint Török smiled in silence as he listened to the innocent questions, then he shook his head.

"What? Do you think that my sons study only the catechism? Jancsi, tell us how cannon are cast."

"What size, father?"

"A hundred-pounder, for heaven's sake!"

"For a hundred-pounder," the boy began, standing up, "you need ninety pounds of bronze and ten pounds of lead. But if necessary you can make cannon out of bells and then there's no need to use any lead. When you've got the materials together, you dig a hole as deep as you want the gun to be long. Then first of all you've got to make a core-rod out of sticky and pure clay. Mix tow in with the clay, and run an iron rod through the centre."

"What's the point of the iron rod?" asked Master Bálint.

"To keep the clay upright; otherwise it would collapse or bend."

Then, fixing his intelligent eyes on his father, he went on, "The clay has to be moulded hard, and the tow added to the mixture in proper quantities. Sometimes it has to be done for two whole days without a break. When it is ready, it is placed in the hole and measured carefully to see that it stands upright. Then the gunfounder makes a similar outer covering of purified and kneaded clay, building it up carefully round the clay core. There has to be a gap of five inches all round, but if there's plenty of bronze, the barrel can be thicker. When this is ready too, they surround the clay with stones and iron props; on each side they fill a vessel with ten cords of wood and pile the brass on top of it. And then..."

"You've forgotten something."

"The lead," interrupted Feri with sharp eyes.

"But I was just going to say that," retorted the boy. "Pieces of lead are mixed with it. Then they keep a fire going day and night until the bronze starts to melt."

"You haven't told us how big the furnace has to be," his young brother interrupted again.

"Well, a big thick one. Anyone with brains must know that."

The guests laughed. Then Jancsi resumed his seat, blushing.

"Just a minute," he muttered, his eyes flashing at his brother. "We'll settle this later."

"All right then," their father said. "If you don't know, then your brother can tell us. What still has to be done, Feri?"

"What's still to be done?" replied the small boy with a shrug. "Well, the gun's got to be taken out of the ground when it's cool."

"Of course it has," said Jancsi triumphantly. "So what about the filing? And the polishing? And the three test firings?"

Feri blushed. And the two boys would have fought each other there and then at the table if the guests had not pulled them apart and covered them with kisses.

112

"The best of all is," laughed Bálint Török, "that they've both forgotten the touch-hole."

Then the conversation at the table turned to all kinds of military matters, the Turks and the Austrians. They also spoke to Gergely.

"He's going to be an excellent chap," said Bálint Török, smiling at Gergely as if he were praising one of his horses. "His brain's as sharp as a needle; only his arms are still on the weak side."

"Oh," said Zrínyi with a dismissive gesture, "the main thing isn't strength in the arms, but strength in the heart: bravery. One hound has hunted a hundred rabbits."

The dinner came to an end. Only the silver goblets remained on the table.

"Now boys, say good-bye to the guests and go back to your mother," said Bálint Török.

"Why, isn't Uncle Sebők going to sing?" asked young Feri.

At this a gentle little man with a hairy face made a movement at the table. He looked towards Master Bálint.

"Oh yes, my good Tinódi," said Zrínyi, glancing warmly at him, "sing us something good."

Sebestyén Tinódi got up and walked over to the corner of the room. He took down a lyre from its hook.

"All right then," said the boys' father, "you can listen to one song all the way through, but then we'll sound the retreat."

Tinódi pushed his chair back and ran his fingers over the five strings of the lyre.

"What shall I sing about?"

"Give us the latest song, the one you composed last week."

"The one about Mohács?"

"Yes, unless my guests want something else."

"No, no," said the guests. "Let's hear the latest one."

The room grew silent. The servants snuffed out the remains of the wax candles on the table and retired to the corner by the door. Tinódi once more ran his fingers over the lyre. He took a pull at the silver goblet in front of him and began his song in a deep, gentle bass voice:

Of Hungary I sing now, and her plight,
The blood-soaked field of Mohács, woeful sight,
Where perished myriads of the nation's might,
The young king too, in lamentable fight.

There was a peculiar strain in his singing. His song was more
of a narration than singing. Sometimes he would sing a complete
line, then he would speak the next, leaving the melody to the
lyre. Sometimes he sang only the very last part of the final line.
While he was singing he stared straight ahead, and his performance indicated that he seemed to be alone in the room and was
singing to himself.

But his simple poems, as Father Gábor had once observed,
though appearing rough and inartistic when read, sounded
beautiful and moving on his lips. Words took on a different
meaning when he sang them. If he said "mourning", then all
turned dark before the eyes of the audience; if he said "battle",
they could see the fighting and killing; if he said "God", they
all sensed the light of God around their heads.

Even the first stanza made the guests cover their eyes with
their hands as they leant on the table, and the tears welled from
Bálint Török's eyes. He had fought at Mohács at the side of the
king, among his bodyguard. There were still four thousand
soldiers alive who had witnessed that battle, and Hungary was
overwhelmed by a sense of impotence and desertion. A mourn-
ing-veil seemed to be fluttering over the whole country.

Tinódi sang the story of the whole battle, and his audience
listened with sad attention. Their eyes lit up at the heroic scenes;
they wept to hear the familiar names. At last Tinódi arrived at
the final stanza, and his epic was more of a sigh than singing:

By Mohács there's desert waste untilled —
The biggest graveyard in the world, that field
Where an entire nation's blood was spilled;
Maybe they'll never rise, so God has willed!

Zrínyi struck his sword. "But they will rise!" And he leapt
up. He raised his right hand.
"A sacred oath, gentlemen, that we'll devote all the thoughts

114

of our life to the resurrection of our country. That we'll not sleep on soft beds as long as the Turk can call a single foot of the soil of Hungary his own!"

"And what about the Austrian?" Bálint Török leant back in his chair with a bitter expression. "Are twenty-four thousand Hungarians to die again just for the Austrians to lord it over us? Devil take them! A hundred times rather the honest pagan than the deceitful Austrian puffed up with lies!"

"Your father-in-law's an Austrian," retorted Zrínyi, flaring up. "The Austrians are at least Christians."

An old man fluttered his hands to calm him.

"In the first place, I'm not Austrian. Nor is the Danube Austrian when it reaches Hungarian soil. The proper course is for the Hungarians not to be allowed to fight for at least fifty years. We've got to increase our population before we fight."

"Thank you!" said Zrínyi, banging the table, "I don't want to lie in my bed for fifty years." And with that he rose from the table and his sword clattered.

At the clatter Gergely opened his eyes and saw to his astonishment that he was not sitting at Bálint Török's table, but lying down beneath a starry sky; it was not Zrínyi standing in front of him, but a broad-shouldered Turk.

It was Hayvan. He had touched his leg to wake him. "Here are the clothes." He threw a cloak and turban in front of the student. "We'll get hold of a horse on our way."

The student threw on the *spahi* cloak and pulled the tall turban over his head. Both were rather large, but the student was more delighted with them than if he had been given the best Hungarian clothes of velvet and silk.

The giant bent down and with a couple of cracks broke the other chain from the student's leg. Then he led the way towards the north.

The student found the cloak too long. He had to hold it up round his waist. He walked with rapid steps beside the giant.

Within the tents and in front of them everyone was sleeping. Sentries were standing in front of one or two of the tents with brass knobs and horse-tails on them, but they too were asleep. The camp seemed to go on for ever. The whole world was a mass of tents, it seemed.

115

Then in one place there was a mass of camels. The tents were few there; men were sprawling on the grass everywhere, fast asleep. Hayvan stopped outside a tent patched with pieces of blue canvas.

"Old man!" he shouted inside. "Wake up!"

A little old man emerged from the tent. His head was bald, his beard long and white. He stepped outside barefoot, in a shirt down to his knees.

"What's the matter?" he asked, eyes wide with terror. "Oh, it's you, Hayvan."

"Yes, it's me. A week ago I made you an offer for this grey horse." And he pointed to a big ungainly horse grazing among the camels. "Will you let me have it?"

"Is that why you've woken me up? Twenty kurush, that's what I said."

The Turk dug the silver coins out of his belt. First he counted them into one hand, then into the other, finally counting them again into the trader's hand.

"I'll want spurs as well," said the student in Turkish while the trader was untethering the horse.

"You'll throw in a pair of spurs as well," said Hayvan.

"Tomorrow will do."

"No. Now, this instant."

The trader went into the tent. There he fished around, rattling things in the dark. Then he brought out some rusty spurs.

9

At that very same time Yumurdjak was wandering among the tents where the sick lay.

"Which is the prisoner who today wanted to blow His Majesty the Sultan to paradise?" he asked one of the sentries.

The sentry pointed to a square white tent.

In front of the tent five elderly men in white turbans and black kaftans were squatting round the fire. They were the sultan's doctors. All five of them were grave and sad-looking.

Yumurdjak stopped in front of the sentry on guard there.

"Can I speak to the prisoner?"

"Ask the doctors," replied the sentry respectfully.

Yumurdjak bowed to the doctors. They too inclined their heads.

"Effendis, if possible I'd like to speak with the prisoner; if you'll give me permission, I'll be able to do something good for the Padishah.

One of them shrugged. From the movement of his hand he might have indicated "It's impossible". Or else, "Go inside the tent." Yumurdjak took the second interpretation.

The curtain of the tent was drawn aside. Inside a large oil-lamp was burning. The priest lay on his back on the bed, his eyes half-open.

"Infidel," said the Turk, stepping up to him, "do you recognize me?" And his voice trembled.

The priest did not reply. He lay motionless on his back. The light illuminated the tip of his nose.

"I am that Yumurdjak who was once entrusted to you for hanging. You set me free at the cost of my amulet."

The priest did not reply. His eyelashes did not stir.

"Now you're a prisoner," the Turk went on, "and there's nothing more certain than that they'll behead you."

Even at this the priest said nothing.

"I've come for the amulet," went on the Turk humbly. "To you it means nothing. For me it contains all my power. Since it's not been with me, I've had bad luck in everything. I had a house on the shore of the Bosphorus, a lovely little palace. I bought it to spend my old age there. The house was burnt to ashes. The treasures in it were stolen. My arm was pierced through in one battle. Look at my left hand; maybe it's permanently maimed." And he showed the red scar which must have been about three months old.

The priest was silent and motionless. The very darkness round him seemed to be silent.

"Infidel," said the Turk in tones softened to the verge of tears, "you're a good man. I've often thought about you, and I've always come to the conclusion that your goodness of heart was unparalleled. Give me back my amulet!"

The priest made no answer. Only the lamp spluttered; maybe a fly had touched its flame.

117

"I'll do everything you desire," the Turk continued after a pause. "I'll even try to save you from the hand of the executioner. My father's a powerful pasha. Arslan Bey is my brother. While there's life, there's hope. Just tell me where my amulet is."

The priest remained silent.

"My amulet!" The Turk ground his teeth. And he seized the priest's shoulder. "My amulet!"

And since the priest's head was hanging down, he dragged him up to a sitting position.

Then the priest's jaw dropped. With glazed eyes and mouth wide open, he gazed into nothingness.

10

When they had got beyond the furthest sentry, Hayvan stopped.

"There we are," he said. "I've done what you asked me to do. Now tell me about that secret fortune I'm carrying around with me."

"It's Cabbala," replied the student mysteriously.

"Cabbala?" repeated the Turk with a growl. And he frowned as if trying to penetrate the meaning of a word which was obscure to him.

"If you look at it more closely," said the student, resting his shoulder on the saddle, "you'll see that each paper contains the drawing of a star. The holy dervish wrote a prayer round every good star.—You promised a yataghan too."

The Turk offered both his yataghans to the student. "Choose!"

The student chose the smaller one and stuck it in his belt.

"These pictures," he went on, "are meant for you to carry round about your body. Cut each of them into seven pieces and sew them into the lining of your clothes. Put them inside the lining of your turban too. Bullets will not touch the parts covered by this sacred parchment."

The Turk's eyes gleamed. "Is that certain?"

"The holy dervish says so. You must have heard before of heroes whom bullets couldn't harm."

118

"Of course."

"Well, don't give any of them to anyone either for money or for fine words. And don't show them to anybody either, or they'll take them from you, steal them or entice them from you."

"Oho! I've got my wits about me."

"But that isn't all. One of the papers says that you mustn't touch children or women either with your hands or with weapons until you're a great man. Just concentrate on being a soldier."

"I will."

"For there's a great rank in store for you. You're going to be the beylerbey of Hungary."

The Turk's mouth fell open in astonishment. *Beylerbey?*

"Well not tomorrow morning, that's for certain, but in time, when your courage is well-known. And then it also says here that you must live according to the words of the Koran. Be persistent in prayer and in ritual washing. And don't do evil to anyone who does good to you."

The great dim-witted man gazed with devotion at the student.

"I've often dreamt," he stammered, "that I'm going to be a gentleman. With a marble palace and a silken kaftan. And surrounded by lots of wives. Yes, I've dreamt that. So in seven pieces?"

"Yes. It doesn't matter if they're not all the same size. It depends which part of your body you want to protect most."

The Turk stared ahead in happy contemplation.

"Well," he said, raising his head, "if I become a gentleman, I'll engage you as my secretary."

Gergely bit his lip to stop himself from laughing.

"Up you get, my friend," said Hayvan warmly. And he held the horse while the student mounted.

The student reached into his pocket. "Look here, Hayvan, here's a ring. You know it's usual for Hungarians not to accept anything for nothing."

Hayvan took the ring and stared at it.

The student went on, "You gave me freedom and a horse, and I'll pay you with this ring. May Allah aid you, baldhead!" And he struck the horse.

Hayvan grabbed the bridle. "Stop a moment! This is a Turkish ring, isn't it?"

"Yes."

"Where did you get it?"

"What's that to do with you? If you really want to know, it belonged to a janissary."

For a moment Hayvan stared stupidly ahead, then he offered back the ring. "I don't want it. You've repaid me sufficiently for your freedom and the horse."

And he slipped the ring back into the student's pocket.

*

Gergely went off in a southerly direction, so that if he were pursued they would chase him that way and not along the Buda road.

The moon was descending towards the west among the clouds. In the east the dawn was breaking.

At one point the broad highroad was crossed by a narrow lane. Gergely caught sight of a rider galloping fast along this lane. If they both continued at the same speed, they must meet at the crossroads. Gergely first reined in his horse to slow down, but when the other rider also slowed down, he again continued at a gallop. At that rate he would reach there a hundred paces or so sooner. He kept his eye on the other horseman. In the increasing light of the morning he saw to his astonishment that it was a janissary in a tall turban approaching him.

He gave the reins a tug and stopped. So did the other rider.

"The devil!" he muttered "that Turk will yet capture me!"

And his breath failed in his terror.

But at that moment István Dobó's words sounded like a tolling bell in his heart: "The main thing is not to be afraid!".

He had not seen Dobó since his childhood. Since Bálint Török had abandoned Ferdinand and taken King John's side, Dobó had not visited Szigetvár or Somogyvár or Ozora. All the same, Gergely remembered him with gratitude, and that one sentence of his had stayed in his head: "The main thing, my boy, is not to be afraid!"

The Turk set off again on his little horse. He too used his spurs. So be it: they would meet at the crossroads. Maybe it wasn't him that the Turk was pursuing. He would call "Good morning!" to him and gallop on his way.

120

Except that the road on which the Turk was coming would be just right to take him northwards. They would have to meet. And suppose the Turk were to produce a weapon?

Gergely had never yet fought anyone. At Bálint Török's court both Father Gábor and Bálint Török himself had taught him to fence and every day he had battled with the Turkish prisoners. But that was only a game. They were in armour from head to foot and could hardly have done much harm to each other even with an axe. If only he had a pike or a sword like the janissary! But this miserable yataghan...

"The main thing is not to be afraid!" said the voice inside him again. So he continued to gallop along the road without changing direction.

The Turk, however, did not gallop. He halted.

Gergely in a sudden burst of courage turned into the road on which the Turk was standing and almost shouted for joy when he saw the Turk turn round and back away from him.

That could only be Tulip!

"Tulip!" shouted the student.

At the shout the Turk whipped up his horse even more and dashed along the narrow cart-track.

The little horse ran well, but the road was full of puddles and the earth there was clay. The Turk leapt over a ditch to turn aside into a field. The horse slipped. The Turk rolled over on the ground. By the time the student reached him, he was on his feet again and holding his pike in his hand.

"Tulip!" laughed the student. "Don't be a fool!"

"Well, of all things!" said Tulip, ill at ease. "Is it really you, young master?"

"You're a fine soldier, aren't you?" laughed Gergely. And he jumped from his horse.

"I thought I was being chased," said Tulip in embarrassment. "How did you manage to escape, then?"

"I used my brains, Tulip. I waited for a bit for you to free me."

"It was impossible," Tulip excused himself. "The prisoners were all kept in the middle of the camp, and there were so many guards all over the place that I myself could hardly slip through them." He gave his horse a tug and scratched his head. "May crows devour this horse! How ever shall I get back home on it?

121

And then these clothes too... They'll beat me to death on the way."

"Go on in shirt-sleeves. You can wear the trousers."

"I'll do that. Aren't you coming with me?"

"No."

"What then?"

"I'm going to Buda."

"Then you'll fall into Turkish hands again."

"I'll get there before they do. And if there is any trouble, my master's already there. He's a powerful man. He could even be king, if he wanted."

Tulip mounted his horse again. Gergely held out his hand. "My greetings to those at home."

"Thank you," replied Tulip. "I too send my greetings to the master. Don't tell him that you found me drunk. I drink the servants' wine."

"All right, Tulip. God bless you!" And he too remounted his horse.

Tulip turned round once again. "And what about the priest?"

The student's eyes filled with tears. "Poor man, he's ill. I couldn't talk to him."

He wanted to say something else, but either his tears prevented him or he thought better of it. He gave the reins a shake and set off towards the east.

*

The student spent the daylight hours in the forest. He slept. Only in the evening did he dare to set out in a wide detour in the direction of Buda, as far as he could judge.

The sun was rising when he arrived at the great plain that extends south of the Gellért Hill. There he threw away his turban and tied the cloak over the saddle-tree. The fields were pearly with dew. Gergely got off his horse. He stripped to the waist, collected the dew in both hands and washed away the dust of the previous two days.

He felt refreshed after his wash. Meanwhile the horse grazed. Warmed by the first rays of the sun, they hurried on their way along the highroad.

Now there were traces of the battle for Buda all over the road.

Broken pikes, bits of gun-carriages, dented shoulder-pieces, dead horses, armour, swords and black-painted, pot-shaped rotten old Austrian helmets lay around in all directions. And corpses still unburied.

Round one blackthorn-bush lay five Austrians. Two were sprawling on their backs, one curled up and two with heads shot to pieces. Three might have been killed by bullets. Two might have dragged themselves there mortally wounded and breathed their last there.

An oppressive stench filled the air.

As the rider approached crows flew up from the dead bodies and circled a few feet above the grass. They settled further away to continue their feast.

The sound of a trumpet made Gergely raise his head from this dismal scene. A red-clothed company of riders came down from Buda at a slow pace. They were led by about five dignitaries in gala dress. Behind them came a long line of infantry in uniform of dark blue. Among those in front Gergely spied a priest in a white cowl.

"That must be the famous Friar George," he thought. "It can't be anyone else."

And his heart beat faster. From his early childhood onwards he had heard so much talk of Friar George! To him he was greater than the king himself.

Beside the Friar rode a horseman in a red velvet pelisse studded with jewels that sparkled afar off. Gergely recognized Bálint Török.

Should he run away?

That might arouse suspicion. Bálint Török would send a rider after him and he would be dragged like a criminal before his beloved master.

Was he to tell him what had happened to the priest?

If he did, Bálint Török would banish him from his sight. After all, it was he who had called in the Turks against the Austrians. Was he to hear now that his own household wanted to destroy the Turks?

Gergely's head was in a whirl. He hated telling lies. He regarded it as dishonourable to lie to the very man who had brought him up. So he just stood there at the side of the road, his head

123

bare and his face red. Then he dismounted and held his horse by the bridle.

Whatever must be, must be!

The horse was hungry. When it saw that there was nothing for it to do it started to bite the grass. God bless that horse! And particularly its hunger! How good it was now to pull it to left and right and circle round with it as if it were stubborn! What luck that during this he could turn his back on the gentlemen who were deep in conversation!

Now they were clattering past, now they were talking. The old horse had to turn now left, now right; sometimes the horse ran round its master, and sometimes the master ran round the horse. And who the devil would have thought that the wind was also useful? A little breeze from the east raises a veil of yellow dust from the road, and all that can be seen is a young lad struggling on the grass with an ungainly grey horse. The Austrians must surely have left it behind unclaimed. Much joy may he have of it!

Gergely breathed a sigh of relief when he saw that the gentlemen had their backs to him and nobody had called out, "Gergely, my boy!"

He jumped on the horse once more, first flattening himself on its back, but then he threw his leg over. He turned to face the procession.

It was then that he saw that the infantrymen in dark-blue uniform were all in chains. Their clothes were in rags, their hair muddy, their faces pale. There were no old men among them, but very many were wounded. The face of one tall ragged prisoner was just a swollen red and blue wound; only one eye could be seen in the wrecked face.

Could it have been Bálint Török, he wondered, who had struck him on the nose?

11

That was when Gergely saw Buda for the first time. All those towers, the high walls, the royal garden with its trees and greenery sloping down on the Pest side—all these astounded him.

124

So this was where King Matthias had lived! And King Louis! And does his own little Eva live here and see all this?

At the gate a halberdier stood on guard, but he did not even glance at Gergely. It was rather strange to him that nobody greeted him, but he thought this was as it should be. He stared up at the palace courtyard and the great red marble basin in the centre of it. Then he stopped in St. George's Square. A group of cannon on big wheels caught his attention. Smoke-blackened, unwieldy cannon. Their muddy wheels betrayed that they had been captured from the Austrians, perhaps only yesterday.

"Good day," he said to the soldier guarding them, "they're Austrian plunder, aren't they?"

"Yes," replied the soldier proudly.

He was a dark-haired man with a full face and a twisted moustache, and looked as if he were for ever blowing on his porridge.

Gergely again stared at the big cannon. Three of them were so large that it would have taken more than twenty oxen to move them. And all the guns still reeked of gunpowder.

"Sir," said Gergely once again. "Do you know old Cecey, the one with the wooden hand?"

"Of course I know him."

"Where does he live?"

"Down there," and he nodded towards the north, "in St. John's Street."

"Oh, but I don't know the streets round here."

"Well just carry straight on, lad, and ask. He lives in a little green house. Above the gate there hangs a bow. A bowmaker lives there."

"Sagittarius?"

"Yes."

Gergely took another glance at the cannon, then ambled off on the grey horse.

*

After a lot of enquiries and directions he finally discovered St. John's Street and a little two-storeyed house there painted green.

Only five little windows could be seen in the house. Three on the first floor and two on the ground floor. The entrance gate

125

in the middle was only the size of a room-door. Above it hung the great red tin bow.

The Ceceys lived on the upper floor, and as Gergely opened the door, he found the old man in a morning robe and slippers, beating on the side of the cupboard with a long-handled fly-whisk.

"Take that, you dog!" he said, making it crack like a rifle-shot. Then as he heard footsteps, he went on, "There's no braver creature in the world! I keep hitting and beating them here in each other's sight, but instead of escaping they even settle on my beard. Take that!" And he swished the fly-whisk in the air.

"My dear father," smiled Gergely, "good morning!"

Cecey turned round, surprised. And Gergely too was surprised to see how the old man's beard seemed to have slipped down his face a couple of inches. At home it had reached up to his eyes. But now Gergely realized that the old man had shaved the upper part of his face. He looked much younger.

"Why, if it isn't Gergely!" Cecey stared at him. "Is it really you, my boy?"

Gergely himself thought it remarkable that he was there, but all the same he waited for them to embrace him and kiss him as they had done at home in Keresztes.

When she heard voices, the lady came out of the next room. She too was taken aback and stared like her husband.

"How did you get here?" she asked. "What brought you here, my boy?"

And she did indeed give him a kiss and stroked his hair.

But earlier she would have given him a warmer kiss, he thought. This was just the shadow of a fleeting thought to Gergely, more of a feeling than a thought.

"The only reason I've come," replied Gergely, "is to get you to return to Keresztes."

"Oho!" said the old man. But he seemed to be saying, "That's even more stupid."

The lady too looked at the boy with such a pitying glance that she might have been gazing at a half-wit whose simple brain had thought out such a silly plan.

"Are you hungry, dear?" she asked, resting her hand on the boy's shoulder. "Maybe you haven't slept either?"

126

Gergely nodded yes and no. He kept glancing towards the open door as he stared at the chessboard on the table.

"You're expecting to see Evie, aren't you?" smiled the lady with a glance at her husband. "She isn't at home. Nor does she come home. She's with the queen, and can only get away very rarely. And even then she comes in a carriage with one of the court postilions, so she does!"

Then a hissing sound could be heard, and she clasped her hands. "Good heavens! The milk's boiling over!"

Gergely waited for Cecey to continue talking about Eva, but the old man simply sat there blinking and said nothing.

"What about the priest?" asked Gergely with a heavy heart.

"He's out at a funeral," replied Cecey with a bored expression. "He joined a number of friars to bury some corpses."

"Austrians?"

"Of course, Austrians. Since we've been at war, he goes out every day to bury. And it's worth while burying Austrians!"

"And haven't they fired at him?"

"They wear white. They don't shoot at them."

"Well, I saw a lot of unburied bodies."

"I'll believe you, young man; we slaughtered quite a lot."

The words "young man" again made Gergely uneasy. But he could not bear it any longer, and steered the conversation to Eva.

"Is she with the queen now?"

"Yes," replied the old man. He got up and stumped the length of the room. Meanwhile his face took on a serious and dignified expression. Then he plunged into an explanation of how Friar George had taken off little Eva one day and introduced her to the queen in the royal garden. The baby prince suddenly smiled at Eva and stretched out his hands to her. Eva was quick to react; she took him in her lap like the peasant women at home, and rocked him in the air with no sign of respect at all. She even said to him, "You silly little boy." From that day onwards the queen liked to have her around, and now she would not even let her go home to sleep.

At first Gergely listened with interest, but then his eyes began to sparkle. He found it rather odd that Cecey should assume such a dignified expression and look at him so coldly. At last he grew grave once again.

"Well, what's the matter with you?" barked the old man. "What makes you look so stupid?"

"I'm tired," replied Gergely. And he could hardly restrain his tears.

For by then he had realized that little Eva would never become his wife.

12

So what had been happening in Buda?

The Austrians would have liked to occupy it. The queen would have allowed this, but the Hungarian aristocracy were by no means happy at the thought of Austrians being quartered in the palace of King Matthias. Let the King of Hungary be a Hungarian!

So they called the Turks to their aid and defended it in the meantime. By the time the Turkish advance troops had arrived, the numbers of Austrians had dwindled. And by the time the sultan himself came on the scene with his vast army, Roggendorf's troops were scattered.

The Friar—for that was the name they gave to the famous George Martinuzzi—took four hundred Austrians in chains with him to greet the sultan.

He was accompanied by Bálint Török and the elderly Péter Petrovich too.

The sultan halted at Cserepes with his army; that was a stage away from Buda. He received the gentlemen graciously in his silken tent with its towers and porch. He already knew of all three by name. Of the Friar he knew that the Hungarian nation thought through his brain. And he knew of Bálint Török from the time when he wanted to hoist the crescent flag in the city of Vienna. That was when Master Bálint had massacred Kason pasha and his army, and the Turks called him a fiery devil.

His interpreter had advised the sultan in advance that old Petrovich was a relative of the baby king, and that it was he who in 1514 had brought György Dózsa off his horse and captured him.

The three men were ushered into the tent. All three of them bowed. Then as the sultan stepped up to them and offered his hand, the Friar also stepped forward and kissed the sultan's hand. Old Petrovich also kissed it. Instead of doing this, Bálint Török bowed again and gazed proudly, though with a pale face, at the sultan.

What an insult! The Friar was chilled to the marrow. If he had known about this, he would never have urged Master Bálint to join them.

The sultan did not bat an eyelid. He raised the hand he had offered for a kiss a little higher and placed it on Bálint Török's shoulder. He embraced him.

All this happened in such a natural Hungarian way, as if it could not have been otherwise.

Inside the tent the two young sons of the sultan stood behind their father. They shook hands affably with the Hungarians. Presumably they had been instructed in advance how to behave. Then they went back behind their father and fixed their eyes on Bálint Török.

And he was somebody to look at! What a dignified, fine Hungarian he was! As he stood there in his red satin robe with slashed sleeves, every other dignitary paled beside him.

The sultan's ancient sheep's eyes also turned more frequently to Bálint Török than to the constantly bowing figure of the Friar, who in a devious Latin oration reported that the Austrian peril had now been averted and that the Hungarian nation was happy to feel the shelter of the wings of such a powerful protector.

The interpreter was Suleyman pasha, a thin and sickly old man who as a growing lad had left Hungarian soil for the Turks and spoke both languages perfectly. He translated the Friar's oration sentence by sentence.

The sultan kept nodding. Then as he ended the speech with a deep bow, the sultan gave a smile.

"You have spoken well. I came here because King John was my friend. The fate of his people is not that of a foreign nation to me. Peace must return to the country. From now on the Hungarian nation can sleep in peace: my sword shall stand guard over it for all time."

The Friar bowed with an expression of joy. Old Petrovich

wiped a tear from his eye. Only Bálint Török gazed ahead with a clouded brow.

"Now let's see what sort of folk you had to fight," said the sultan.

He mounted his horse and rode slowly through the ranks of captives, accompanied by the Hungarians. The captives stood and knelt in two long lines in the sand near to the Danube.

The Friar rode on the sultan's right, Suleyman pasha on the left. Sometimes, however, the sultan turned and spoke over his shoulder to Petrovich, or Bálint Török or his sons.

The long line of prisoners bowed to the sultan. One or two of them raised their chained hands to him in a plea for mercy.

"Wretched mercenary folk!" said the sultan in Turkish. "But strongly-built, all the same."

"There were stronger ones too," said Bálint Török in Hungarian, as the sultan turned to him. "There were a few hundred of them, but they're not here."

And as the sultan looked questioningly at him, Master Bálint added calmly, "They were the ones I slew."

They returned to the tent. The sultan did not enter it, so they brought out an armchair. But they did not bring chairs for the delegation or for the sultan's sons.

"What shall we do with the prisoners, Your Majesty?" asked Amhat pasha.

"Cut off their heads," replied the sultan as indifferently as if he had said "Brush my kaftan."

He sat in the chair outside his tent on a gold-embroidered cushion. Behind him stood two servants with peacock-feather fans, not as a display of pomp, but really because of the flies. It was getting towards the end of August and myriads of flies travelled with the army.

Beside the sultan stood his two sons. In front of him the Hungarian gentlemen, holding their fur caps.

The sultan mused for a moment, then turned to Bálint Török: "Some priest or other was taken captive on the way. He came from your county. Do you know him, by chance?"

Török understood the sultan perfectly, but all the same he listened to the interpreter.

He replied in Hungarian too: "I don't know all the priests in

130

my county. On my estates there are several hundred of different faiths. But it's possible that I may know that particular captive."

"Bring him here," commanded the sultan. And arching his eyebrows, he stared ahead with boredom.

The noise of the executions rose from the bank of the Danube. Shouts and cries for mercy all mixed with the noises of the camp.

Then two men hastily brought along a human figure covered by a sheet. They laid him on the ground before the sultan and pulled the sheet aside from his head.

"Do you know him?" asked the sultan, looking sideways at Bálint Török.

"Of course I do," replied Bálint Török with emotion. "Why, that's my chaplain!"

And he looked round those who were there, as if seeking an explanation. But the faces of the Turkish dignitaries were cold. All he met were glacial stares from black eyes.

"Something had happened to him," went on the sultan. "He was a sick man when he was brought to my camp. Bury him decently," he said, turning to the servants, "in accordance with the rites of the Christian faith."

Then they brought round cooling drinks in silver cups on a silver tray. The drink was made of orange-juice and rose-water and was iced and fragrant.

With a gracious smile the sultan offered the first one to Bálint Török.

13

The Ceceys made up a bed for Gergely in a little room overlooking the yard. It was not so much the bed that the boy found comforting as the fact that he could be alone with his grief.

He was not at all surprised that the queen had fallen in love with his own little Eva. In his opinion there was no more lovable creature in the whole wide world. But all the same it pained him deeply that the Ceceys were so proud of her. Little Eva had risen to the royal court where only princes and the great men of the country circulated. How was a little nobody like him, with no house or coat-of-arms or even a dog, to gain access to her now?

He slumped on to the worn bearskin-covered bench and rested his tearful face on his arm.

Misery has one good property: it sends one off to sleep and gives comfort with all kinds of pleasant dreams.

Gergely slept a good half day on the bearskin and woke up afterwards with a smile. He looked in surprise at the wall of the little room and the picture of St. Imre with his twisted leg that hung there, then grew serious. He cupped his face in his hands and rested his elbows on his knees. The events of the last two days swam through his head in a black whirl. The huge Turkish camp, his capture, the death of the priest, the escape, the castle of Buda, the flight of his own little wife, the change in his foster-parents—all these things mixed in the whirling thoughts in his head. Then he thought of the horse, the old grey one. Had they given it anything to eat and drink? How was he to amble back home on it to Somogyvár? What was he to answer if he was asked where his master was? Who would teach them from now on? Presumably Sebestyén Tinódi, the fine lutenist with the maimed hand.

He rose and gave himself a shake, as if to release himself from the bonds of a bad dream. He went through to the Ceceys.

"Mother," he said to the lady, "I only came to give you news of the Turkish peril. I'm going back now."

The lady was sitting at the window, edging some white linen with gold thread. In those days women wore gold-embroidered collars. She was sewing it for her daughter.

"What's the hurry?" she said in surprise. "We haven't had a chat yet. My husband isn't in. Maybe he'd like to talk to you as well. Have you been to see Master Bálint yet?"

Gergely blinked. "No. I'm not going to see him either. I left the house so quickly that I didn't tell him where I was going."

"Well, don't you want to have a word with our old priest?"

"Where does he live?"

"Here, with us. Where else should he live? But he's not in either. He's got a funeral."

"Do they still quarrel?"

"Even more now than they used to. Now he's on Ferdinand's side and my husband on John's."

"Please tell him, madam, that I send him my respects."

132

He purposely did not call her mother.

The lady stitched another row and only after a couple of minutes of silence answered: "Well, in that case I'll not delay you, Gergely, my boy. I'll just get you a bite for lunch. I put it aside for you. I didn't want to disturb your rest."

Gergely hung his head. He was probably wondering whether to accept lunch. In the end he decided he would, so as not to offend them.

The lady spread a yellow leather cloth on the table and placed cold roast meat on it and some wine.

Meanwhile Father Bálint also arrived home. Normally only darkness drove him home from his work of mercy, but that day he was worn out by the heat and the work and returned earlier. Cecey limped in after him.

Gergely kissed the priest's hand. Then, after the priest had pushed him back to the table, he answered his questions as he ate.

"How you've grown!" said the priest in amazement. "You're a real man now! Yet it only seems yesterday that you left us." And he looked round. "Where's Evie?"

"At the palace," replied Cecey.

The priest's expression demanded an explanation. Cecey excused himself, saying, "The queen's become very fond of her. She won't let her go."

"Since when?"

"Several days now."

"She's surely not with the *infant?*" snorted the priest.

"Yes, she is!" replied Cecey. "You surely don't think she's a nanny. There are plenty of those there. Evie just happens to be there, that's all."

"Your daughter, with Szapolyai's son?" The priest lost his temper and jumped up.

Cecey stumped the length of the room uneasily.

"Well, what's the matter with that?" he growled, turning round. "Wasn't it you who said 'Better a Hungarian, dog though he is, than an Austrian, angel though he is'?"

"But your daughter rocking Szapolyai's son?"

In a passionate rage he roared at Cecey, "So that's how a man goes soft in the brain when he grows old! Have you forgotten

133

that the father of that boy was an executioner? Have you forgotten that you and I both ate the flesh of György Dózsa?" And he threw the chair to the ground with such force that it snapped in pieces.

The food fell from Gergely's mouth. He ran down the stairs and fetched out his horse. He galloped off without saying good-bye.

14

He dismounted outside the royal palace and led the horse by the bridle.

On the wall of the palace he glanced at a sundial the size of a cartwheel. The sun happened to be clouded over just then, and the gilded gnomon cast only the faintest of shadows towards the figure IV.

Gergely surveyed the windows. He looked at each of them in turn: those on the ground floor, then the first floor and then the windows in the tower.

Soldiers came and went through the gate of the palace. A grey-bearded, crook-backed ancient Hungarian gentleman tottered through it, followed by two secretaries.

"Out of the way!" said the sentry to two little boys, "What are you goggling at here?"

The aged man went tottering on. He must have been some-body important, because everyone greeted him but he never returned the greeting. His secretaries carried scrolls of paper. They had goose-quills stuck into the sides of their cloth caps. From their belts dangled brass inkstands. As the sun shone out on them, even their shadows moved along the palace wall with dignity.

Then Gergely caught sight of a lanky fair-haired soldier. He could only see his legs, those two thin legs in red boots and red trousers, but these marked him out as one of the guards from Szigetvár. His name was Bálint Nagy. Gergely turned round and hurried towards St. George's Square with his horse. He did not want any of Master Bálint's men to catch sight of him.

But even there he once again came across an acquaintance. This was a nimble little man with a round beard: Imre Martonfalvay, Bálint Török's secretary, bailiff, lieutenant—in other words one of his domestic staff who could be put to anything.

Gergely slipped round to the other side of his horse and stayed there to hide his face from him. All the same Imre, ever on the watch and ever curious, caught a glimpse of him.

"Just look!" he shouted. "If it isn't young Gergely!"

Gergely raised his head, blushing to the ears.

"How come you're here? Did you come to see the master? And wherever did you pick up that ox with a horse's head? That's not one of our horses."

Gergely would have liked the earth to swallow him, together with the worthy beast he had called an ox. But he quickly pulled himself together.

"I've come to see the master," he said in embarrassment. "Where is he?"

"I don't know whether he's arrived back yet. He escorted the Austrian prisoners to the sultan. Hey, what a brave man our master is! You should have seen him hacking down the Austrians! A week ago today he came back from the battle with his right hand just one mass of blood. The queen was sitting at her window. As he rode past her he showed her his right hand and his sword too. Have they got cattle-plague at home?"

"No," replied Gergely.

"And have the captives cleaned out the old well?"

"Yes."

"The threshers aren't pinching the corn?"

"No."

"Are the boys in good health?"

"Yes, they are."

"And the mistress?"

"She is too."

"Have you been in Remeteudvar?"

"No."

"Do you know whether they're getting on with the hay harvest?"

"No."

"Well now," says the secretary, fanning himself with his cap, "where are you staying? Have you got lodgings?"

"No."

135

"Well then, come to my place. Have you brought some important news? Or have you brought a letter to the master?"

"No. I just came..."

"Well, wait about here then. I'm going into the palace. Or you come along with me into the courtyard. Then we'll go home and you can change into your best clothes. Or haven't you brought them? Oh well, we'll find some. Then you can talk to the master."

He led the student into the courtyard and found a shady spot for him.

Gergely watched the voluble, lively little man go. He saw him run up the broad red marble staircase. Then he wondered whether to escape from Master Bálint's curses. Ah, but it wouldn't be possible to escape those! Even from a distance his imperious glance rivets one to him. And then one has to tell the truth. To confess that... oh no!, that would be impossible to confess!... He scratched his ear. He thought so hard that his head was boiling, and then just stared at the windows again.

As he was looking around, he saw the trees in the garden showing green through an opening in the courtyard. Suppose he were to slip through there? He might be able to see his little Eva from afar. From afar, because rustic mortals like him were not allowed into the presence of the queen.

Where were they, he wondered. Probably somewhere in the shade on the other side, either in the garden or at some window. He would recognize Eva from a long way off. He would recognize that gentle white face and feline eyes with their sweet smile. He would wave to her with his cap. Then Eva might go on guessing for even a week whether it was Gergely who had been there, or a boy resembling him, or perhaps Gergely's ghost.

The courtyard was full of hay blowing around. The wall contained a long line of big iron rings. They were fixed so that whoever went there might tether his horse to them.

Gergely tied up his own horse there, then quietly strolled off through the soldiers. He slipped into the passage-way where the foliage of the trees peeped out.

*

136

Gergely thought that the entrance to the garden was there. As if they would make an entrance to a large garden in such a narrow passage! There is no trace of any doorway there. One side of the passage is bounded by tall iron railings, the other by a building. Once upon a time King Matthias's scholars and artists lived in that part, then in the time of Wladislas there were Polish priests and servants there, and later women servants.

But Gergely knew nothing of this. He merely looked at the railings. They were white, and the tips of them were gilded. In places the foliage came through the railings.

Gergely kept peering inside. He caught sight of a gravel path and one or two little rustic buildings roofed with green-painted tiles. The railings now and again had iron crows sitting on them, but in some cases only their legs remained. Then he spied a few pink patches through the leaves. Women's dresses! Gergely's heart began to pound like a sledgehammer.

He kept peeping through as he went down the path by the railings. Finally he glimpsed a group of women beneath an old lime tree.

They were sitting round a cradle. They were dressed in light rose-coloured clothes. Only one of them wore black, a long-faced, long-nosed lady with thin arms. Her face was pale, her eyes black and sorrowful. She only smiled when she bent down and looked into the cradle, but even her smile was sad.

Gergely could not see into the cradle. It was hidden from him by the back of a stout woman. She was waving a little branch of lime above the cradle.

Gergely tried to find a better viewpoint through the railings. He now saw that there were altogether four women around the cradle while a fifth one was bending over a big marble vase shaped like a chalice.

He ran down by the railings towards her. It was indeed his own little Eva. But how she had grown! She was picking horse-chestnuts from the ground and putting them in a basket.

"Evie! Eva!" he called softly through the railings.

The girl must have been twenty paces away. She was humming a song. This was why she could not hear Gergely's call.

"Evie! Eva!"

The girl raised her head. She looked towards the railings with grave surprise.

"Evie!" repeaeted Gergely, almost laughing. "Come over here!"

The girl could not see Gergely for the tamarisk leaves, but she recognized his voice. She came along like a young doe. Stopping now and again, starting forward, her great staring eyes not even glancing in her astonishment.

"It's me, Evie," repeated Gergely.

Then the girl suddenly appeared there. She clasped her hands. "Gergő! How ever did you get here?"

She positively radiated joy, and put her face up to the railings for Gergely to kiss it. Meanwhile he caught the scent of some attractive perfume, like the fragrance of the honeysuckle blossom in April.

Then both of them held on to the railings with their hands next to each other. The railings were cold. Their hands hot. The faces of both of them blushed red.

The boy gave a brief account of how he came to be there, and in the meantime examined the girl's face, hands and clothes. How she had grown! How beautiful she was! Only her eyes, those wide-open, innocent cat's eyes were the same.

Others might not have seen her as beautiful. After all, she had reached an age when only hands and feet develop; the face is still immature, the breast still boyish and the hair still short. But to Gergely all this was beautiful all the same. He liked the girl's big hands; he felt them to be white and velvety, and since she was wearing attractive shoes, he cast a long delighted glance at them too.

"I've brought a ring," said Gergely. And he drew the big Turkish ring from his pocket.

"My own dear master left it to me. And I'll give it to you, Evie."

Eva took the ring in her hand and examined the topaz half-moon and diamond stars with delight. Then she put it on her finger and smiled.

"What an enormous ring! But it's lovely!"

And since the ring just hung loose on one finger, she pushed two through it.

"It'll be fine when I grow up," she said. "You keep it till then." Then with childlike frankness she added, "You know, when I'll be your wife."

138

Gergely's face clouded and his eyes became moist. "You'll not be my wife, Evie."

"Why not?" asked the girl indignantly.

"Now you're living among kings and princes. They'll never let you marry such a nobody as me."

"Oh, of course they will," replied the girl. "Do you really think I stand in awe of them? Why, the queen herself told me once just to love the little king, and she'd find me a proper fiancé when I grew up. 'I've already got one,' I replied. And I mentioned your name too, and that Bálint Török was your foster-father."

"You told her that? And what did she say?"

"She laughed so much she almost fell out of her chair."

"Is she here in the garden too?"

"Yes. That one in black."

"That one?"

"Yes, that's her. She's beautiful, isn't she?"

"Yes, but I thought she'd be more beautiful than that."

"More beautiful? Why, isn't she beautiful enough?"

"I haven't seen any crown on her head."

"If you like, you can talk with her. She's a very good mistress. She doesn't understand Hungarian."

"What then?"

"Polish, German, Latin, Italian, French; all sorts of languages, but not Hungarian. She even pronounces your name *Kerkő*.

"Why should I want to talk with her?" said Gergely bashfully. "Though I do know a few words of German. But tell me, Evie, how can I talk to you if I come up to Buda again?"

"How? Why, I'll tell the queen to let you in."

"And will she?"

"Of course. She likes me so much she'll let me do anything. She even gives me her perfume. Just sniff the sleeve of my dress. It smells nice, doesn't it? Queens always smell as nice as that! And then she's showed me her prayer-book. There are lovely pictures in it. There's a Virgin Mary in a blue silk dress, surrounded by roses. You should just see that!"

From under the lime there came a little squeak like a cat's when someone treads on its tail. Eva gave a start.

139

"Oh dear! The little king's woken up. Wait here, Gergő."

"Evie, I can't wait for you, but I'll come along tomorrow."

"All right," replied the girl. "Come here every day at this time."

And she ran off to the little king.

15

Nothing turned out as we expected it to.

When Bálint Török arrived home, it was impossible to get near to him for hours. He shut himself in his room and walked up and down. His heavy, even steps could be heard in the rooms downstairs.

"The master's angry," said Martonfalvay anxiously. "Surely not with me?"

"And suppose he catches sight of me," shuddered Gergely. And he scratched his head.

Martonfalvay went up the stairs three times before he finally dared to open the door.

Bálint Török was standing by the window overlooking the Danube. He was dressed in the same clothes as he had worn for the sultan. He had not even taken off the ceremonial sword in its velvet sheath that hung at his side.

"What's that?" he growled, turning round. "What do you want, Imre? I'm in no mood to talk just now."

Martonfalvay retreated with a humble bow. He stopped in the porch and scratched the lobe of his ear in confusion. For there would be trouble if he opened his mouth. When he was angry, Master Bálint was like a storm-cloud: thunderbolts burst from him all too easily. But suppose there would be trouble if he did not speak? The master was always glad to see anyone from home.

Bálint Török's house leaned up against the Fejérvár Gate. On one side the windows looked out over Pest, on the other to the Gellért Hill. Finally Martonfalvay was rescued from his predicament; as he looked down from the window he saw Werbőczy enter the door of the house. So he hurried back and once again opened the door.

"Sir, Master Werbőczy's coming."

"I'm in," replied Bálint Török.

"Gergely's here too," continued the secretary with a deep breath, "the little Bornemissza boy."

"Gergely? Alone?"

"Yes, alone."

"Why, whatever's he doing here? Let him come in!"

Gergely arrived at the door at the same time as the grey-bearded, crook-backed Werbőczy. As Martonfalvay gave a deep bow, Gergely followed his example.

That was the old gentleman he had just met outside the royal palace. It was he who had been preceded by the secretaries with goose-quills, carrying scrolls of paper. (What a famous man! When he was a lad he had seen King Matthias.)

"Welcome, brother," Bálint Török's deep masculine voice was heard to say from inside the room. He caught sight of Gergely. "Just let me have a word with my adopted son first. Come in, Gergely!"

Gergely did not know whether he was alive or dead. He stood stock-still between the two gentlemen.

Bálint frowned as he looked at him. "Is there something the matter at home?"

"No," said the boy.

"You came with the priest!"

"Yes, I did." And he turned pale.

"And how did you come to be taken captive? After all, the priest died. Were my boys with you?"

"No."

"Then how did you come to be among the Turks?"

The aged Werbőczy spoke up. "Come now, brother Bálint," he said in a kindly, vibrant voice, "don't shout so at that poor lad. Can't you see he's too frightened to speak?" And he sat in a black leather armchair in the middle of the room.

At the word "frightened" the boy recovered his composure, as if water had been dashed in his face.

"Well," he said, suddenly bold, "it was this way. We wanted to blow the Turkish emperor to the skies.".

"Per amorem!" exclaimed the scandalized Werbőczy.

Bálint Török himself was startled.

141

The boy—in for a penny, in for a pound—described how they had carried the gunpowder to the highroad, and how the priest had mistaken the janissary pasha for the sultan.

Werbőczy clasped his hands. "What thoughtlessness! What a stupid thing you dreamt up, my dear boy!"

"That's not where the stupidity was," replied Bálint Török, striking his sword on the floor, "but in the fact that the chaplain didn't recognize the sultan." And the two gentlemen faced each other.

"The sultan's our friend!" said Werbőczy.

"He's our destroyer!" replied Bálint Török.

"He's a man of noble intentions."

"He's a scoundrel in a crown!"

"I know him, you don't! I've visited him in Constantinople..."

"The word of a pagan isn't holy writ. And even if it were, their holy writ isn't ours and ours isn't theirs. Their holy writ says that the Christians must be trampled underfoot!"

"You're wrong."

"God grant I am, brother, but I think this visit stinks. I'm getting out and going home." And he turned to Gergely.

"My boy, you might have saved Hungary!"

And as he said this, his voice was full of pain.

*

Next morning Gergely was woken by Martonfalvay, who laid out on the table a page's red and blue silk uniform from the wardrobe.

"The master's orders are that you are to dress in this and be ready at ten o'clock in the yard. You're going with him to the royal palace."

And he took Gergely in hand like a caring mother. He supervised his washing and dressing. He parted his hair down the middle. He rubbed his gold buttons with a washleather. And he even wanted to pull the cherry-red boots on his legs.

"Now I'm not going to let you do that!" laughed Gergely. "I'm not quite such a helpless babe."

"But aren't you afraid?"

"What should I be afraid of, master secretary? Going to see the queen? My mistress is a greater lady than she is, even if she doesn't wear a crown."

"You're right there," said the secretary, looking the boy up and down with approval, "but, you know, she is a queen all the same."

As he accompanied Bálint Török to the royal palace, one of the royal servants hurried to meet them.

"Sir," he panted, "Her Majesty sent me to tell you to come immediately. Some pasha's coming. They're bringing so many treasures, it's awful."

Bálint Török turned to his retinue of soldiers. "They're not bringing them for nothing, you just wait and see!"

The soldiers remained in the courtyard. Master Bálint and Gergely climbed the broad marble staircase.

The halberdier guarding the doorway raised his battleaxe in salute and pointed to the right. "Her Majesty wishes to see you in the throne-room, gentlemen."

"Then you can come with me," Bálint said over his shoulder to Gergely. "Always stand four or five paces behind me. And stand like a soldier! Don't talk to anyone! Don't cough, spit or yawn, and don't pick your nose."

High-vaulted halls, coloured and carved walls; coats-of-arms everywhere, crowned and sparkling with gold; tall, wide doors, one ceiling studded with silver stars; red carpets that swallowed up the sound of feet. Gergely was stupefied by the splendour. He felt as if there were a crowned ghost in every corner, whispering, "You're treading in the steps of kings! The air here was breathed by kings!"

In the throne-room five brilliantly-dressed gentlemen were standing waiting. Behind them were pages and officials. Beside the throne were a few halberdiers. But the throne was empty as yet.

The room was vaulted like the others, and the stars in the chicory-blue silk covering the ceiling depicted the sky at the hour when the nation elected Matthias as king.

Behind the throne was a great purple tapestry bearing the arms of the country in gold thread. Inside the country's arms there was another smaller coat-of-arms, two white unicorns and

143

two wolves on a shield held by an angel, with a Polish eagle above it. These were the arms of the Szapolyai family.

A lieutenant in the household guard stepped up to Bálint Török. "Her Majesty summons you, sir."

Gergely remained on his own with the pages and secretaries. He turned to two youths who were talking nearby. "My name is Gergely Bornemissza. I'm page to Bálint Török."

One of them, with fair hair and a merry face tanned by the sun, shook hands with him.

"I'm István Zoltay, from Batthyány's troops."

The other was a short-necked, thick-set young man. He merely kept his hands folded and stared over Gergely's shoulder.

Gergely gazed at him indignantly. (This bull-headed young gentleman must surely despise him!)

"My name's Gergely Bornemissza," he repeated, throwing up his head.

The bull-headed youth looked sideways at him.

"That's nothing to do with me. A page's name is *Silence.*"

Gergely reddened. His eyes flashed at the haughty youth.

"I'm not your page! And the master I serve doesn't call me *Silence,* but *Suffer no insults!*"

The bull-headed youth looked him up and down.

"Right. When we get outside in the courtyard, I'll teach you my name." And he raised his hand in an unmistakable gesture.

Zoltay stepped between them.

"Now, now, Mekcsey, just leave this boy alone!"

"I'm not a boy if I'm insulted," fulminated Gergely. "When I was only seven years old István Dobó girded me with a sword and called me a hero."

At the name of Dobó Zoltay turned round and put his hand on Gergely's shoulder.

"Why, in that case," he stared at him, "you must be the boy who captured a janissary's horse."

"Yes, that was me," answered Gergely, proud and glad.

"Somewhere near Pécs, wasn't it?"

"In the Mecsek Hills."

"Well, comrade, give me your hand once more."

He shook Gergely's hand and squeezed it, then drew him to him.

Mekcsey had his back to them.

"Who's that surly character?" asked Gergely.

"He's a good chap," smiled Zoltay, "but a bit prickly at times."

"But I'm not going to leave it at that!" said Gergely wrathfully.

He struck Mekcsey on the shoulder. "Just listen, sir..." Mekcsey turned round. "We can make each other's acquaintance at midnight in St. George's Square." And he slapped his sword.

"I shall be there," replied Mekcsey briefly.

Zoltay shook his head.

Meanwhile more and more gentlemen arrived. A pleasant scent of pomade began to spread. Then it was as if a breeze blew through the room, and there were signs of movement. Two halberdiers, or palace guards as they were called then, came through the doorway. They were followed by a few court dignitaries: the major-domo, chamberlain, a black-robed priest who was presumably the court chaplain, then four little pages, then the queen; then came the Friar, Bálint Török, Werbőczy, Orbán Batthyány and the old Petrovich.

Gergely blushed and gazed at the door. He still waited for someone to come. He must have imagined that just as the men had their boy-pages, such a great lady would also be accompanied by girl-pages. But not one appeared.

The queen was wearing mourning-clothes with a veil. But on her head there glittered a thin, crescent-shaped diamond-studded crown. She sat down on the throne. Two bodyguards stood behind her. The dignitaries beside her.

The queen looked round the room. She quietly asked the Friar something, then settled herself once more on the throne. The Friar nodded to the sentries at the door.

*

In came the Turkish sultan's envoy, a well-built man dressed in white silk fringed with gold. As he came through the door, he bowed to the ground. Then he hurried at a run to the carpet on which the throne stood. There he flung out both arms and lay prostrate.

With him came ten dark-haired Circassian boys like pages in

145

lemon-coloured robes. They too rushed in like their aga. Each pair carried a chest covered in violet-coloured velvet. They set the chests down on each side of the aga, and then prostrated themselves behind them.

"Welcome, Ali aga," the queen spoke for the first time, in Latin.

Her voice trembled weakly. It was impossible to tell whether her chest was weak or whether she was one of those women whose soul trembles like a poplar-leaf.

The Turk rose. Only then could it be seen what a fine-faced Arab he was. He might have been forty.

"Your Majesty," he said in Latin in a gruff morning voice, "I bring to your throne the greetings of the mighty padishah. He asks you to receive them as readily as he sends them."

He nodded and the pages lifted the lids of the chests, and the aga took out one by one the glittering gold chains, bracelets, silks and velvets, a beautiful jewel-studded sword and a mace.

He laid them out on the carpet at the queen's feet.

A faint rosy glow of delight spread over the queen's pale face.

The aga opened a filigree silver-mounted crystal casket and held it out. Rings sparkled in it, some of the finest treasures of the fabulous Orient. The queen surveyed the rings with genuine feminine delight.

"The sword and mace, Your Majesty, are a present from my master to the little king," Ali aga went on. "And down below in the courtyard there are three thoroughbred Arab steeds. Two of them are from the two sons of the sultan. They too have come along, and send fraternal kisses to the little king, John Sigismund. If you would care to glance at them, Your Majesty, I have placed them where they can be seen from the window."

The queen rose and moved with the dignitaries to the window. As she passed by Gergely, he caught the same delicate honeysuckle fragrance that had surrounded Evie. A bodyguard pulled aside the thick tapestry-curtain. Sunlight flooded into the room. The queen shaded her eyes with her hand and looked down into the courtyard. There stood the three lovely little steeds, with rich, gold-studded oriental trappings; around them the courtiers gazed at them.

The queen exchanged a few words with the Friar. The Friar turned to the envoy.

"Her Majesty is deeply touched and thanks His Majesty the Sultan and the two princes for their gifts. Tell your master the sultan to designate an hour for the reception of the envoys of the King and Her Majesty, so that they may convey their thanks to the gracious padishah."

The queen nodded and placed her hands on the two arms of her throne to rise. But the aga had not yet finished.

"All these gifts," he went on with an owlish glance, "are sent by the mighty padishah merely as a token that he regards King John Sigismund as his son and Your Majesty as his daughter. And it would give him the greatest pleasure if he might see the son of his friend the late lamented king and give him a paternal kiss."

The queen turned pale.

"Wherefore," continued the envoy, "the mighty padishah requests Your Majesty to put His Majesty the little king into a carriage with his nurse, and send him to him with an appropriate escort."

He emphasized the words "appropriate escort." At that time nobody understood that. But next day they all did.

The queen was white as a sheet. She lay back on her throne to stop her from fainting away. A murmur of horror ran through the room.

Gergely felt cold.

"What did he say?" asked Mekcsey in a whisper.

"I didn't quite hear," replied Zoltay. And he turned to Gergely. "Did you understand him? You surely know Latin better than we do."

"I did," replied Gergely proudly, "and I'll tell *you*."

But before he could open his mouth, the Turk's voice could be heard once more. "There is no cause for concern. The mighty padishah is fearful only to his enemies; to good friends he too is a good friend. Moreover he would have come in person to express his respects and good will, but this is forbidden by the rules of our religion, Your Majesty."

He paused in his speech. He waited for the Friar or the queen to reply to him. But there was no reply.

"Furthermore," the Turk went on with another owlish glance, "my master and emperor desires that His Majesty John Sigismund be escorted by all those gentlemen who distinguished themselves in the defence of Buda. He desires to make the acquaintance of the Hungarian heroes; he regards them all as his own heroes."

When there was still no reply to this, he made a bow. "That is all the mighty padishah bade me convey to you. I await a gracious reply."

"That will be forthcoming at three o'clock this afternoon," Friar George answered in place of the queen. "His Majesty the Emperor will be satisfied with our reply."

The queen rose. She beckoned to Bálint Török, who stepped up to the throne. She put her arm through his. It was obvious that she hardly had the strength to stand.

16

At noon Ali aga went the rounds of the dignitaries' houses. He visited Friar George, Bálint Török, and Péter Petrovich, who was not only related to the infant king but was also his guardian. He went on to see Werbőczy, Orbán Batthyány and János Podmaniczky as well.

To each he presented a valuable kaftan, accompanying this naturally with honeyed words, assuring them of the sultan's good intentions and generosity.

It was Bálint Török who received the most splendid of the kaftans. It was of ankle-length heavy yellow silk. The others were all alike, purple outside and lined with orange-coloured silk. Just the one was of sunflower-coloured silk with a lining of white watered silk. The belt woven of gold thread was so finely wrought that the maker must have grown old and wrinkled in its making. From neck to waist the buttons on it were of gold encircled by diamonds.

As those in his house assembled to marvel at this present, Bálint Török shook his head with a smile. "It'll make a good bedcover." Then he grew serious. "Get ready to move! This afternoon we're going home!"

At three o'clock he went to the palace again. There the dignitaries were waiting for him in the library.

"The queen won't give in to his request," said Friar George. "Please have a word with her."

Bálint Török gave a shrug. "I've come to say good-bye." The others were taken aback. "Whatever do you mean?" "I can tell which way the wind's blowing. I don't want to be caught outside my own home."

"You're gambling with the fate of the country!" Werbőczy growled at him.

"Would it really change because of me?"

Friar George furrowed his brow. "We mustn't upset the sultan."

"Am I to oblige him with my head?"

"The man's out of his mind," said Werbőczy with an angry shrug. "Why, didn't he send you the finest kaftan? Didn't he give you the warmest embrace?"

Bálint Török leaned on the rim of the great blue globe and nodded as he pondered. "The clever fowler whistles most enchantingly to the bird he most wishes to ensnare."

The sentry at the door opened it to signify that the queen was waiting for the gentlemen.

A lengthy and agonizing dispute arose inside. The queen was fearful for her son. The gentlemen raised the problem of the fate of the country and the nation if she refused to comply with the sultan's request.

"And have you nothing to say?" the queen turned to Bálint Török who was standing against the wall, silent and grim.

Bálint gave a shudder as if he were waking from a dream. "I've only come here to say farewell, Your Majesty."

"Say farewell?" The queen turned her sad eyes on him in astonishment.

"I've got to go home today. Things have happened there that make it impossible for me to stay a moment longer."

The queen wilted visibly. She wrung her hands nervously. "Wait. Sit down if you're not feeling well. Tell me what we should do."

Bálint Török shrugged his shoulders. "I don't trust the Turks. To the Turks all Christians are dogs. We must not hand over the royal infant to them. Say that he's ill."

Werbőczy snarled, "They'll only say, 'We'll wait until he's

better.' And they'll spend weeks here on our backs. We've got to feed the army and the horses..."

The Friar broke in angrily, "And think of the country too! The sultan's here with a large army. It was we who invited him to come. He was a friend of the late lamented king. We must fulfil his wishes. If he sees that we're suspicious of him, who'll guarantee that he won't get angry with us? In that case he'll call His Majesty not his son but his prisoner."

The queen pressed her hands to her brow and collapsed back on her throne. "Oh what an unfortunate woman I am! They say I'm a queen, but even a beggar creeping on the ground has more power! It doesn't hurt a tree when its blossoms are picked, but oh, the Creator moulded the mother's heart out of pain!"

17

While all this was going on inside the room, Gergely was standing waiting in the ante-chamber. As he stood there beside the tall white-tiled stove, he suddenly felt something like a spider run down his face. He snatched at it. And into his hand fell a peacock-feather.

The stove stood between two rooms; it was possible to look alongside it into the next room.

"Gergely!" someone called softly.

Gergely looked round with a thrill of joy. There he saw Eva's face, and her mischievous eyes as she peeped at him from the next room.

"Come out into the corridor," whispered the girl.

Gergely slipped out. The girl was waiting for him in the window-recess. She seized his hand.

"Let's go down into the garden."

And she led him there. They hurried through four or five rooms. All of them had thick carpeting, and every one had the blinds drawn on the side where the sun was shining. On the walls were pictures of kings and saints. In one place there was a cavalry conflict too. There was gilding on the furniture and walls. One room was lobster-red, the next lily-white, the third lavender-blue. All of them were decorated in different colours. And there was little furniture in any of them.

Down a broad staircase, with Eva running ahead, they finally stepped into the garden. Gergely relaxed.

"We're all alone," said Eva.

She was in a white dress of some light summery material that was cut low at the neck. Her hair fell in a single plait down her back. On her feet she wore yellow morocco shoes. She stood on the shady sandy path beside a clump of bushes, smiling as Gergely stared at her.

"Do I look nice?"

"Yes, you do," replied Gergely. "You're always nice. You're a white dove."

"The queen had this dress made for me." And she put her arm through Gergely's. "Come on! Let's go and sit there under the lime trees. I've got a lot to tell you, and no doubt you've got a lot to say to me too. I recognized your voice the minute you spoke to me through the railings, but I just couldn't believe it. I've often thought about you. I dreamt about you last night too. And I told the queen that day that you were here. She said she'd like to see you as soon as the Turks have gone."

They sat down under the lime tree on a marble seat that had two sitting lions as arms. From it there was a view of the Danube below and of Pest on the other side of the river. Pest was a little tiny colourless town, surrounded by a high wall of stone. Inside the stone wall were single-storeyed houses, two little churches, and on the south side a tall wooden tower, obviously a watch-tower. Outside there was a yellow, sandy plain, with an occasional old tree. Gergely, however, had no eyes for either the Danube or Pest; he looked only at Evie. He marvelled at the pure lily-white of her cheeks, her fine teeth, her round chin, her velvet neck and merry, innocent blue eyes.

"Now it's your turn to talk," the girl smiled at him. "How are you getting on at the Töröks? Are you still doing a lot of study? Do you know that I'm now learning to paint as well? Come on, why are you staring like that? You haven't said a word yet!"

"It's you I'm staring at. How you've grown, and how beautiful you are!"

"That's what the queen said too. She said I was growing into

151

a young lady now. My hands and feet won't grow any bigger than they are now. Because with girls, hands and feet stop growing after the age of thirteen. You're good-looking too, Gergely."

Her face was suffused with blushes and she hid her eyes with her hand. "Oh, what silly things I'm saying! Don't look at me. I'm ashamed of myself."

But the boy was confused too. He blushed red up to his ears. They were silent for a moment or two. A swallow perched on the dry branch of the lime tree began to twitter. Perhaps they were listening to it. But no, they heard finer music, the music that rang in their hearts.

"Give me your hand," said the boy.

The girl offered it readily.

The boy took hold of the girl's hand. Eva waited for Gergely to say something. Gergely just remained silent and looked at it. Then he slowly raised the girl's hand and kissed it.

Eva blushed.

"This is a lovely garden," remarked Gergely, simply for something to say.

Once more they fell silent. A lime leaf fell from the tree just in front of them. Both of them watched it, and then the boy spoke once again.

"It's all over."

He said this so sorrowfully that the girl was almost scared when she looked at him. Gergely got up.

"Come along, Evie, in case my foster-father comes."

Eva also got up. Once again she took Gergely's arm and pressed him close. They walked like this in silence for ten paces. Then the girl broke the silence.

"Why did you say that it was all over?"

"Because it is," said Gergely, shaking his head.

They walked on silently. Then Gergely sighed. "I feel it in my bones that you'll not be my wife."

Eva was shocked. "Well, I feel that I shall be."

The boy stopped. He looked into Eva's eyes. "Do you promise?"

"Yes, I promise."

"Hand on heart?"

"Hand on heart."

"And what if your parents want something else? And if the queen does too?"

"I'll tell them that we've already agreed on it."

Gergely shook his head in disbelief. They mounted the steps, and went through all the rooms again. At the door leading out of the corridor, Eva squeezed Gergely's arm.

"So long as the Turks are here we can't meet unless you come with Master Bálint. When you do, just stand here beside the stove. Then I'll come out here for you."

Gergely took the girl's hand. She felt his hand trembling.

"May I kiss you?" asked Gergely.

Before now they had always kissed each other without asking. But Gergely felt that *this* girl was no longer the same as *that* one, the one he had loved like a sister at home in Keresztes. She was more. The girl also sensed something like this, because she blushed at Gergely's question.

"Yes, do kiss me," she said, happy yet serious.

And she offered him not her cheek, as she usually did, but her lips.

18

At four that afternoon the little king was dressed. In the courtyard a golden coach waited to take him down into the valley of Óbuda where the Turks were encamped.

But even at the very last moment the queen was reluctant to let her child go. She took his head in both her hands and wept.

"You haven't got any children!" she moaned. "Neither you, Friar George, nor Podmaniczky. Nor has Petrovich. You don't know what it is to let a baby go into a tiger's lair. Who knows whether he can ever come back again! Bálint Török! You mustn't leave me! I entrust my child to you! You're a father yourself; you know what it is for a parent's heart to tremble for her child. Guard him as if he were your own."

And when she said "You mustn't leave me!" she forgot all her dignity and fell on her knees on the carpet before Bálint Török. She stretched out her hand to him imploringly.

This scene affected everyone deeply.

153

"For the love of God, Your Majesty!" said Friar George, catching her. And he raised the queen from the floor.

"Your Majesty," said Bálint Török with deep emotion. "I will accompany the infant. And I swear that if they touch a hair of his head, my sword will be steeped in the blood of the sultan this very day."

*

The sultan was encamped below Óbuda. His splendid triple tent was constructed where the Császár Baths are today. It was a tent in name only; in reality it was a kind of palace of wood and rich materials. Inside it was divided into rooms and alcoves; outside it gleamed with gold.

With the customary bugle-call, the Hungarian delegation set out at about five o'clock in the afternoon from the courtyard of the royal palace to pay its respects to the sultan.

They were led by a company of hussars, followed by the soldiers belonging to the dignitaries, then the red and white-clad pages bearing gifts. (They carried the treasures belonging to the traitor Tamás Bornemissza, who had dealt with the Austrians, as a gift to the sultan.) Then came another troop of royal soldiers, palace guards, other court servants and then a select group of soldiers. Then came the chief dignitaries themselves with the white-garbed Friar George in their midst on a broad-backed grey horse. His white robe was splendid and dignified, showing up against Bálint Török's blue flower-adorned summer satin uniform. The other great men wore all the colours of the rainbow too, but they all had flat fur caps, yellow high boots and broad swords. At that time broad swords were in fashion, as if by mistake the swordsmith had made them twice as long and had chopped them in two when he was told to hurry. They were curved, broadening out towards the tip. In their caps they wore white ostrich feathers like the Turks, some a single one, others three, but all so long that they reached down at the back almost as far as their saddles. Among the dignitaries was the six-horse golden carriage bearing the little king. There were two ladies-in-waiting in it and his nurse. The little pink-cheeked king, dressed in white silk, danced on her lap.

The horses were each led by a long-haired, silk-capped page. Behind the carriage came the royal bodyguard in silver helmets.

And following them rode a long line of officers who had distinguished themselves in the siege of Buda.

"There'll be something to drink too, you'll see!" said a merry voice.

"Yes, we'll have water to drink," said a bass voice in reply. "Don't you know that the national drink of the Turks is water?"

There was laughter.

Gergely followed behind Bálint Török on a small copper-coloured horse. As his master was out of sorts, he too tried to look solemn as he rode. He only brightened up when he glanced behind and caught sight of old Ceccy. How oddly the old man was sitting on his horse! One leg, the one of wood, was stretched out ahead, while the other, which was only of wood to the knee, was drawn up. And then he held the reins in his right hand and his sword was on his right side too.

Gergely had never seen him on horseback or armed. He broke into a laugh.

In any case the old man looked peculiar in all his finery. The big old-fashioned cloth cap with its eagle feather was stuck sideways on his head, and his moustache—a little white one —was waxed to a sharp point like those of a young Romeo. Since he had no teeth in front and his eyes were deep-set with age, old Cecey might have been a scarecrow in fancy-dress rather than a Hungarian in his best uniform.

So Gergely laughed at him. But immediately afterwards he regretted this, and to make up for his lapse, he waited for him. He greeted him.

"Good afternoon, sir! How is it that I haven't seen you before?"

"I've only just joined the procession here," said the old man, staring at him. "What on earth's that gorgeous outfit you're wearing?"

By this he meant Gergely's splendid red and blue satin page's uniform and expensive mother-of-pearl handled sword.

"My master's made me a page," boasted Gergely. "I go everywhere he goes, I'm often in the royal palace too. Now I'm off with him to the sultan's tent."

He was showing off. He wanted to boast that he was not the nobody that he appeared to be. He was moving in the same circles as Eva.

Crowds thronged St. George's Square. Doors and windows were wide open in the streets. Happy children were sitting on the roofs and in the trees, their mouths wide open. But everyone was looking only at the little king. What a mite, yet already an elected king!

"He holds his head in just the same way as his father did," said a woman who wore a grass-green scarf almost reaching her ankles.

"Oh the little darling!" purred an aristocratic young woman with fiery black eyes. "Oh, how I'd love to kiss him!"

At the gateway the red uniform of Bálint Török's own three hundred soldiers formed a solid block. They were all from Somogy, and one of them stood head and shoulders above the rest like a single rye-stalk that has come up by mistake in a cornfield. When they reached them, Bálint Török turned his horse. His sword flashed skywards and he indicated to the procession to halt.

"Men! My lads!" he said to his soldiers in a deep resonant voice. "Do you recall that scarcely a month ago at this very gate every man and every soldier vowed at my appeal not to surrender the castle of Buda to either Austrian or Turk?"

"We do," muttered the troop.

Master Bálint went on, "We've beaten back the Austrians. Now we're going to the Turkish camp to see the sultan. God is my witness, and you too be my witnesses, that I opposed this delegation in the council."

Then his voice lost its resonance. "My lads, I feel that I'm never going to see you again. God is my witness that it was only for the sake of the country that I obeyed. Heaven bless you, lads!"

He was unable to continue; his voice choked. As he stretched out his hand, the soldiers shook it one by one. Eyes were filled with tears.

Master Bálint put spurs to his horse and galloped through the castle gateway.

"Come now, Bálint my boy," said the aged Werbőczy. "What's the point of all that emotion?"

Bálint Török shrugged. Then he replied with a touch of anger, "I've shown more than once that I'm not made of lead."

"Well, don't shiver if you don't feel the cold."

"Oho, sir, we'll soon see who's the best judge of the weather."

The Friar rode up between them.

"Even if the emperor hadn't said so," he said soothingly, "we should have gone along just the same to pay our respects. If only the queen had come along too with the infant! We mustn't give him the cold shoulder."

Bálint looked grimly at him. "Friar George, you're a clever man, but even you aren't God. Even if one were to carry one's heart on one's sleeve, the emperor would hide it from us."

The Friar shook his head. "If the Austrians were still on our backs, you'd talk differently."

From the gateway to the camp janissaries lined the route. They cheered the Hungarian dignitaries and the little king so wildly that it was impossible to talk any more.

They continued their way through an assortment of soldiers and tents. There was the stench of horses and men and dust. A few minutes later they saw a glittering band of beys and pashas as they wound their way to receive the little king.

Anyone looking down from a height on these two processions might well have thought he was looking at two lines of tulips of all colours approaching each other in a huge field of flowers. When they met, they stopped and bowed, then mingled and continued onwards along the bank of the Danube to the north, where a palatial triple tent stood out green from among the others.

19

The sultan was standing outside his tent. His face was rouged as it always was. He smiled and nodded when Friar George lifted the sturdy little blue eyed boy out of the carriage.

They went into the tent. Gergely also followed his master inside. He was met by a pleasant coolness and the scent of roses. The overpowering stench of the camp, almost intoxicating in the heat, did not penetrate there. The sentry at the door held back the other members of the retinue. The sultan was dressed in an ankle-length cherry-red silk kaftan. A white cord held it together at the waist, but the kaftan was of such transparent loose cambric that the muscles of his arms were visible through it. And it was those thin arms that made Europe quake at that time! Inside, the sultan took the boy in his arms and looked at him with approval. The boy laughed and tugged at his beard. The sultan smiled and kissed the child.

The dignitaries breathed a sigh of relief. Why, this was not the ferocious Suleyman! This was a benevolent father of a family! His glance was clear, his smile genuine. Look! The boy is reaching for the diamond star that twinkles on his turban. He gave it to him.

"Here you are; play with it. It's plain that you were born a king."

Both Bálint and Gergely understood his words.

The sultan looked at his sons behind him. "Give the little Hungarian king a kiss!"

And the two sons of the sultan obeyed. Both of them smiled at him, and the child smiled back.

"Will you adopt him as your brother?" asked the sultan.

"Of course," replied Selim. "Why, this child is as sweet as if he'd been born in Stamboul."

Gergely took a look round the tent. How splendid the blue silk was! And on the floor too there were thick blue carpets patterned with flowers. In the walls of the tent there were round unglazed windows. Through one of them the sultan could look at the Margit Island. Below, along the base of the tent walls, were thick cushions to sit on.

The only people in the tent were the three Hungarian leaders, Friar George, Werbőczy and Bálint Török, not to mention the nurse and Gergely, who in his fine uniform was probably regarded by the sentry as the little king's page. And then there were the two sons of the sultan, two pashas and the interpreter.

The sultan gave the little king back to his nurse and went on looking at him with delight, tapping him on the cheek and stroking his flaxen hair.

"How handsome he is! How healthy!" he kept saying. At which the interpreter said in Latin, "The gracious sultan sees fit to declare that the child is beautiful as the angels and as full of health as an oriental rose that has opened this very dawn."

"I'm glad to see him," the sultan spoke again. "Take him back

158

to the queen and tell her that I will be father to him in place of his real father, and that my sword will keep guard over him and his country for all time."

"His Majesty is as delighted," said the interpreter, "as if he were looking on his own child. He receives him as his own son, and expands the wings of his world-dominating power over him. Tell this to Her Majesty the Queen and convey to her his most gracious greetings."

The sultan took a dark red silk purse from his pocket, and with a gracious gesture slipped it into the hand of the nurse. Then he kissed the boy once more, and waved graciously to him. This was a sign that the sultan regarded his wishes as fulfilled, and that they might leave.

All of them breathed freely and happily. The nurse almost ran as she carried the child outside.

They stepped out of the tent. The pashas took the Hungarian gentlemen by the arm with great courtesy.

"You are the guests of the sultan for the evening, and will dine with us. And let the rest of the escort take back the young king, then return here. The table is already laid."

"And there's wine from Cyprus, waiting for you there too," said an affable young pasha with thick black beard.

"And today we too may drink to your health," added another jolly red-bearded young pasha, whose face was so freckled that it looked as if all the flies in the camp had left their mark there. The fine gold brooch in the shape of a sea-shell that held the feather in his turban did nothing to make his face more attractive.

"Escort the little king back home," Bálint Török said over his shoulder to Gergely. And he disappeared on the arm of a pasha inside the tent.

By now the sun had gone down behind the Buda hills, and the glow of the clouds gave light down below.

The little king was put into the carriage again. He waved goodbye with his right hand to the pashas and Hungarian dignitaries, and the golden carriage set off once more between the two lines of cheering soldiers, up to the castle of Buda.

20

Gergely rode behind the carriage. Cecey with his wooden hand went on ahead with the old men; the young ones rode behind.

"Well, those Turks aren't such a wild lot after all," they said cheerfully. "They do respect the Hungarians. The Austrians are a lower order."

Gergely was riding behind Zoltay and Mekcsey alongside an auburn-haired youth with the first signs of stoutness to whom he had introduced himself when they set out.

"Fürjes, my friend," he said with a respectful glance at this blonde youth, "I've only just come to Buda, so I really don't know anyone."

"What is it you want? I'll be glad to help you if I can." He thought the boy needed money.

"I've got some business to settle at midnight in St. George's Square."

Fürjes gave a smile. "What sort of business?"

He thought the boy had a lovers' meeting in St. George's Square. He shook his long auburn hair and looked at him cheerfully. "Well, whatever next!"

"It's nothing to laugh at exactly," Gergely shook his head. "Nor is it anything serious either."

"In other words, an affair of the heart."

"No, of the sword."

Fürjes's eyes grew large. "You're surely not going to have a fight?"

"I certainly am."

"With whom?"

Gergely pointed at Mekcsey, who was riding ahead of him in his green satin uniform.

Fürjes stared. He grew serious. "Mekcsey?"

"Yes."

"Look here, he's a devil of a lad!"

"Maybe I'm not so soft either."

"He's already slain Austrians."

"Well, I'll do the same to him!"

"Are you good with the sword?"

"I started when I was seven."

"Hm. That's a different matter."

He felt the muscles in Gergely's arm. Then he shook his head. "It would be better if you begged his pardon."

"What, me?"

Fürjes shook his head worriedly. "He'll give you a hiding."

"Me?"

And he threw out his chest and looked at Mekcsey riding there in front of him. Then he turned to Fürjes again.

"You'll be my second, won't you?"

Fürjes shrugged his shoulders. "Well, if that's all you want, I'll gladly be that. But if anything happens..."

"What could happen?"

"Anything. But I'm not going to fight instead of you or because of you."

There was a lot of sudden movement and noise at the head of the procession. Incomprehensible shouts were heard; horses tossed and turned. All the necks seemed to have gone rigid as every eye stared at the castle.

It was then that Gergely also looked up.

And there above the gates of Buda flew three huge horse-tail banners. They were on the churches and towers too. And in the gateway itself Turkish halberdiers with turbans had replaced the Hungarians.

"Buda's fallen!" yelled a ghostly voice.

And at that a shudder went through the Hungarian throng just as a forest shudders when the wind passes over it.

It was the wooden-handed Cecey who had yelled.

There was no answer. Faces grew pale. And the silence was frozen through and through by the chant of a *muezzin* who began to call in a resounding voice from the tower of the Church of Our Lady: *Allahu akbar... Ashadu anna la ilaala ull Allah...*

*

Gergely rushed back at a gallop to the Turkish camp with some of the others in the escort.

"Where are the gentlemen? Sirs! Hungarians! There's been a dastardly piece of treachery!"

But at the sultan's tent red-capped *bostandjis* blocked their way. "Back! You can't come here!"

"We've got to go inside!" roared Mekcsey, almost breathing fire. "Or else send the gentlemen out here!"

The *bostandjis* did not reply. They merely pointed their lances at their breasts. There was merriment throughout the Turkish camp, with pipes and tambourines playing on all sides.

Gergely called to them in Turkish.

"Send Master Bálint Török out here for a word!"

"Impossible!" laughed the bostandjis.

The Hungarians stood there at a loss.

"Gentlemen!", yelled a thick-necked Hungarian. "Come outside! There's trouble!"

No reply.

Gergely made a short tour on his horse. He climbed up the hill amongst the spahis to see whether he could find a way down from there to where the Hungarian dignitaries were being entertained. In front of one tent a Hungarian voice called to him, "Is that you, Gergely?"

Gergely recognized Martonfalvay. He was sitting in front of a spahi tent with two Turks, eating melon.

"What are you doing here?" called Martonfalvay.

"I want to get to the master."

"You can't get in to see him now. Come and join us!" He dug into the melon and offered Gergely a slice.

Gergely shook his head. "No, thank you."

"Oh, come on!" said Martonfalvay encouragingly. "These two Turks are good friends of mine. And then when they've lit the torches, we'll go down there too and join the dignitaries."

"Come, Hungarian brother!" said one of the *spahis* in broken Hungarian, beckoning him across. He was a well-built, broad-shouldered dark man.

"I can't," replied the boy sullenly. And he continued on his way.

He went down the alley between the tents to where the bombardiers, hunters and janissaries were. At last he arrived back at the sultan's tent. The *bostandjis* encircled it on that side too. He could not reach Bálint Török from there either.

The young Hungarians were still shouting where they had been before. From the tent rose the strains of Turkish music: the tinkling of the metal-stringed *kanun,* the gentle murmur of the lutes and the whine of the pipes.

"Swine!" shouted Mekcsey, grinding his teeth.

Fürjes was almost weeping with rage. "If my master had stayed in the castle, none of this would have happened to us." He was the Friar's page. He thought the Friar was omnipotent.

And as the music stopped, they all shouted, "You gentlemen inside there! Come out, sirs! The Turks have occupied the castle!"

But nobody came out. The sky was cloudy. Then suddenly it began to rain, and this went on for almost half an hour before it ceased. In the sky the black clouds raced eastwards like a fleeing army.

At last, around midnight, the party came to an end and the dignitaries emerged. They pressed out of the door of the tent with caps askew and in high spirits. A long line of torches lit their way through the camp. It wound its way up to the gate of Buda like a double fiery serpent. The air had been purified by the rain, and now it was perfumed by the smoke from the oriental torches.

By now Martonfalvay was there as well, and the *bostandjis* allowed those outside to mingle with those who had been in the tent. By the light of the torches they could see how the ruddy faces turned grim and then one by one grew pale.

The Friar with his white habit stood out from them like a ghost. "Don't cry!" he turned on Fürjes who was riding beside him. "Don't let them see us weeping too!"

The gentlemen set off in ones, twos and threes, galloping along the torch-lit track up to the castle of Buda.

Gergely had still not seen Master Bálint. Martonfalvay was standing beside him, also watching with an anxious eye the doorway to the tent from which a reddish glow emerged.

The last to come out was Podmaniczky. He tottered out on the arms of two Turkish officers, and had to be helped on to his horse.

After that only a few Saracens in a variety of coloured clothes emerged; they were the servants.

Then nobody else.

The tapestry covering the door dropped. That shut out the light from the tent too.

"Well, what are you two waiting for?" said an ostrich-plumed fat-bellied Turk.

"We're waiting for our master, Master Bálint Török."

"Oh, hasn't he left yet?"

"No."

"Then he must be the one the Padishah is talking to."

"We'll wait for him," said Martonfalvay.

The Turk shrugged and went away.

"I can't wait for him," said Gergely uncomfortably. "I've got to be up there by midnight."

"Well, get along then, lad," said Martonfalvay benevolently. "And if you find some Turk in my bed, just throw him out of it."

He meant this as a joke, but Gergely did not laugh. He said farewell to Martonfalvay and went galloping up the winding road.

*

By now the moon had emerged from the clouds and lit up the way to Buda.

The Turkish sentries with their lances at the gate took no notice of Gergely. At that stage men might come and go singly as they pleased. Who knew what might happen the next day? Would Hungarians be shut out of the castle then, and for ever?

The horse's steps turned to a clatter on the cobbles inside the gate. Gergely saw janissary lancers in front of the houses too, one in front of each house. On every tower there was a horsetail with a crescent. Only on the Church of Our Lady did the golden cross still stand.

Gergely arrived at St. George's Square. To his great surprise there was no one in sight. He rode round the fountain and the cannon. Not a soul anywhere, apart from a Turk with a spear, presumably on guard over the cannon.

Gergely dismounted and tethered his horse to the wheel of one of the guns.

"What are you doing here?" the Turk shouted at him.

"Waiting," replied Gergely in Turkish. "You surely don't imagine I'm going to slip your gun in my pocket?"

164

"Oh no," replied the topchi amiably. "Are you a Turk, then?"

"No, I haven't that good fortune."

"Well then, get off home."

"But I've got an affair of honour here today. Please bear with me."

The Turk then aimed his spear at the boy. "Get out of my sight!"

Gergely loosed his horse and mounted it. Someone was coming at a run from the Fejérvár Gate. Gergely recognized Fürjes, whose auburn hair almost shone in the darkness. He went to meet him.

"Mekcsey's waiting in Master Bálint's house," he panted. "Come along there, because the janissaries won't let us talk in the street."

Gergely got off his horse and went on foot with Fürjes.

"How did this vile treachery happen?" asked Gergely.

Fürjes gave a shrug. "It was cunning. A piece of pagan trickery. While we were down below in the camp with the little king, the janissaries slowly sauntered through the gateway as if they only wanted to look at the buildings. They just sauntered around and stared. But they grew in numbers. When all the streets were full of them, there was a bugle-call and they drew their weapons and chased everyone into the houses."

"They're devils."

"It's an easy way to occupy a fortress."

"My master said so..."

The windows of the palace were open and lit by candles. Two heads leaned out of one of the upstairs windows.

That was just the time when they were changing the guards at the gate. The foot of the gate was blocked by a big janissary.

"What do you want?" he asked in Hungarian.

"This is where we belong," said Gergely bluntly.

"I've just had orders," said the Turk, "to let no one in or out."

"I belong here, in this house. I'm one of Bálint Török's domestic staff."

"Get back home, lad, to Szigetvár," said the Turk scornfully.

Gergely's eyes opened wide. "Let me in!" And he struck his sword.

The Turk unsheathed his sword. "Wretched little whelp! Are you going?"

165

Gergely released the reins of his horse and also drew his sword. Perhaps he relied on the fact that he was not alone.

The Turk's sword flashed. It struck at Gergely's head.

Gergely caught the blow, and his sword struck sparks in the gloom. At the same instant he slipped forward and stabbed.

"Allah!" the Turk gasped.

His words ended with a choke as he staggered against the wall. The plaster crackled and fell behind his back.

From upstairs a voice cried, "Stab him again!"

Gergely plunged his sword up to the hilt in the Turk's breast. He stared in astonishment at the giant when he saw him let his sword fall and collapse against the wall like a sack.

Gergely looked around. He sought Fürjes. He had run off as fast as he could towards the royal palace. Instead, three janissaries with tall caps ran out of the line of houses on the other side to the aid of their companion.

The boy saw he had no time to lose. He leapt for the gate and opened it. With swift hands he bolted it on the inside.

Excited by the fight, he took a few trembling steps, and then, hearing someone thundering down the wooden steps from inside, he sat down on the bench under the arch of the gate and panted.

It was Zoltay. There was a sword in his hand. On his heels came Mekcsey. He too held a sword. The lamp in the gateway illuminated their astonished faces when they caught sight of him.

"Is that you?" said Zoltay in surprise. "Aren't you wounded?"

Gergely shook his head.

"Did you kill the Turk?"

Gergely nodded.

"Come to my arms, you young hero!" shouted Zoltay enthusiastically. "You caught that blow splendidly!" And he embraced him.

They were hammering on the gate from the outside. "Open up, you dogs, or we'll burn it to ashes!"

"We've got to get away," said Mekcsey. The janissaries had come running up from all sides. "But first, your hand, lad! Don't be angry because I insulted you."

166

Gergely offered his hand. He was in a whirl. He did not know what was happening to him. He said nothing, but let them drag him along through the courtyard, up a flight of stairs and into a windowless room. He only came to his senses when the two young men had twined together a rope of sheets and straps. Mekcsey called him to be the first to drop down it from the window.

Gergely looked down.

In the moonlit depths he saw the royal kitchen-garden beneath him.

21

Next morning Ali aga appeared again before the queen. He spoke thus:

"His Majesty the Padishah thinks it right to put the fortress of Buda under the protection of Turkish troops until your son grows up. The boy cannot defend the fortress of Buda against the Austrians. And the Padishah cannot keep coming here from two or three months' journey away. Until that time comes, retire to Transylvania, Your Majesty. The income from the silver, gold and salt mines there is yours anyway."

The queen was prepared for the worst by now. She listened to the envoy with disdainful calm.

The envoy went on:

"So His Excellency the Padishah will take the castle of Buda and Hungary under his protection, and a few days hence will deliver in writing his royal promise to defend you and your son against all enemies. And as soon as the boy comes of age, he will restore Buda and the kingdom to him."

All the dignitaries were present with the exception of Bálint Török and Podmaniczky. The Friar was even more drained of colour than usual. His face seemed to dissolve into his white cowl.

The envoy continued:

"Thus the castle of Buda together with the Danube and Tisza area will come under the protection of the Padishah. Your Majesties will move to Lippa and from there govern Transylvania and the part of the kingdom beyond the Tisza. In Buda there will be two governors: one Turkish and one Hungarian. The Padishah will nominate István Werbőczy to this latter high office. He will be the governor and judge of the Hungarian inhabitants of the province."

The gentlemen stood there dejected and sad, as if they were standing by a coffin rather than a throne.

When the envoy departed, he left a funereal silence in the room. The queen raised her head and looked at the gentlemen. Werbőczy burst into tears.

A teardrop rolled down the queen's face too. She wiped it away. "Where's Podmaniczky?" she said listlessly.

"He's gone," replied Petrovich, as if in a dream.

"Without saying farewell?"

"He's escaped. He disguised himself as a peasant with a hoe, Your Majesty, and went off today at dawn."

"And Bálint Török still hasn't returned?"

"No."

*

On the next day the Turks threw the bells of the Church of Our Lady into the street. They tore down the altar-painting. They knocked down the statue of St. Stephen the King. They scattered the altars with their gilding and paintings in front of the church, together with the wood-carved statues of angels and the missals. The organ too was destroyed. Two carts carried away the tin pipes to the camp bullet-factory. Three more carts carried the silver pipes, the exquisite gold and silver candlesticks, altar carpets and cloths and vestments down to the sultan's treasurer. The splendid frescoes were whitewashed. The cross was smashed down from the tower and in its place they hoisted up a huge gilded brass crescent and fixed it there.

On 2 September the sultan, accompanied by the pashas, rode up into the castle. His two sons went with him too.

At the Szombati Gate the agas awaited him in their finest robes. They accompanied him into the church to the sound of trumpets.

The sultan prostrated himself in the middle of the church.

"Blessed be thou, oh Allah, that thou hast spread thy powerful hand over the land of the infidels."

22

On 4 September forty ox-carts wound their way down from the royal palace to the bridge of boats across the Danube.

The queen was moving out.

The carriages were also standing in the palace yard, with the dignitaries crowded round them. They were all ready for the journey. Only Werbőczy was staying behind in Buda, accompanied by his favourite officer, Mekcsey.

Gergely glimpsed Fürjes standing behind the gentlemen.

"Well, Gergely," he said with a condescending smile, "aren't you coming with us?"

Gergely looked him up and down contemptuously. "Don't talk to me like that. I don't count rabbits among my friends."

The blonde young man winced. But since he also saw Mekcsey's piercing glance, he shrugged.

Old Cecey was also crouching on horseback behind the officials. Gergely put his hand on his saddle-bow.

"Sir."

"Good day, my boy."

"Are you going as well?"

"Only as far as Hatvan."

"And Eva too?"

"The queen's taking her along too. Go and have lunch today with my wife and comfort her."

"Why are you letting Eva go?"

"Werbőczy encouraged us to. Next year we'll be back with thousands and thousands of troops..."

They had no time to say more. The appearance of the bodyguards was a sign that the queen was coming.

She arrived. In mourning. Among her ladies in waiting there was Eva.

A light hazel-coloured travelling-cloak with a hood was draped over her shoulders, but she had not yet pulled the hood over her head. She kept looking around as if she were searching for someone.

Gergely made his way through the gentlemen and appeared at her side.

"Eva..."

169

"Aren't you coming with us?"

"I'd like to," replied Gergely sadly, "but my master hasn't come back yet."

"Will you follow us?"

"I don't know."

"If you don't follow us, when shall I see you?"

"I don't know." And the boy's eyes filled with tears.

The queen had already taken her seat in the capacious carriage with its leather hood and windows. The boy-king was in it already with his nurse. They were only waiting for a little square basket to be put under the driver's seat.

Eva held out her hand to Gergely. "You won't forget me, will you?"

Gergely wanted to say, "No, Evie, no, not even in the next world either!"

But since he was unable to speak, he just shook his head.

23

Ten days later the sultan also departed.

He took Bálint Török with him. In chains.

PART III

The Captive Lion

1

A cavalryman was standing on the bank of the Berettyó, a soldier in the king's army, in a blue cloak and red cap. He waved from the bank with his cap, and shouted over the willows, "Hey there! There's water here." And he rode down the sun-baked slippery bank among the marsh-marigolds with their vivid yellow blooms.

The horse went up to its knees in the grass, at whose roots the water almost disappeared from sight, and it stretched out its neck to drink.

But it did not drink. As it raised its head again, water ran from its mouth and nostrils. It blew it out and tossed its head.

"What's got into this horse?" muttered the soldier. "Why won't you drink, you wretch?"

The horse lowered its head once again. Once again it shook the water out of its nose and mouth.

Across the fields came another eighteen Hungarian horsemen in different uniforms. Among them was a tall, wiry man with an eagle-feather in his cap and a cherry-coloured short cloth jacket over his shoulder instead of a cloak.

"Sir," said the soldier in the water over his shoulder, "this water's got maggots in it or something; my horse won't drink from it."

The man with the eagle-feather galloped into the water. He examined it. "The water's got blood in it," he said in surprise.

The bank was full of willows, and the bushes were full of yellow catkins. The earth was blue with violets, and the early bees buzzed among the flowers.

The captain struck his horse and splashed upstream a little way. On the bank among the willows he soon came across a young man in shirt-sleeves. The young man was washing his head, standing in the water up to his knees. It was a big stocky head like a bull's. His eyes too were black and strong. His little moustache bristled as sharp as a thistle. His dolman, yellow boots, cherry-coloured cap and sword in its black leather sheath lay on the grass.

173

It was his washing that had made the water of the Berettyó run red.

"Who are you, my lad?" asked the captain in surprise. The youth just replied over his shoulder, "My name's István Mekcsey."

"Mine's István Dobó. What's happened to you?"

"A Turk struck me, damn him." And he held his hand to his head.

Dobó looked around. But all he could see in the fields were willows, poplars and bushes.

"A Turk? Devil take that Turk! He can't be far away. How many are there of them? Hey there, lads!" And he leapt out of the water.

"Don't bother," said Mekcsey shaking his head. "I've killed him. He's lying behind me here."

"Where?"

"Somewhere not far away."

Dobó spoke to his servant from his horse. "Bring some bandages here."

"There are some others a bit further up there," said Mekcsey, once again holding his hand to his head.

"Turks?"

"No! An old nobleman and his wife."

The blood trickled from his head and streaked his forehead and nose. He bent down to the water again.

"Over there in the willow thicket," reported one of the soldiers.

Dobó urged his steed up the bank and came across an old man a few steps away.

He too was sitting in his shirt-sleeves on the bank of the stream. A stout little woman was weeping as she washed the blood from the old man's head.

"Oh dear, oh dear! Why do you have to get involved in something like this at your age! And with your maimed hand too!"

"Stop bleating!" growled the old man.

"Good day!" called Dobó. "Is it a big wound?"

The old man looked up and waved his hand dismissively. "It's a Turkish blow..."

It was then that Dobó saw that the old man had only one hand. "Why, I think I know him!" he muttered, and got off his horse. "My name's István Dobó."

The old man peered up at him. "Dobó? Is it really? Is it you, Pista, my lad? Why, of course you know me! You've been at my house too—old Cecey's house."

"Cecey?..."

"Yes, yes, Cecey. Don't you remember? When you were looking for Móré."

"Of course, now I remember. Well, what's been happening here, sir? How come you to be here instead of in that valley in the Mecsek?"

"Oh the pagan curs..." and the old man again bent his head towards his wife for her to go on washing it, "the pagan curs attacked my carriage. It was lucky for me that this young man caught up with us just when they fell on us. He's a brave lad! He cut down the Turks like pumpkins. And I too was able to lay about me from the carriage. And the driver behaved like a hero too."

"How many were there of them?"

"Ten, the dogs; may they roast in hell! It was lucky that they couldn't get the better of us. I've got about four hundred gold coins with me, if not more." And he shook the purse at his side.

The lady squeezed the red-stained water out of the handkerchief.

"Didn't the young man die?" she asked, looking up.

"No, not a bit of it," replied Dobó. "He's washing himself too, a bit further down there."

He caught sight of a bleeding Turkish corpse nearby.

"I'll just have a look," he said, "to see what sort of folk you encountered." And he rode along the stream and the road.

He discovered seven dead bodies in the willow-thicket, two Hungarians and five Turks; on the road was a waggon and three, which had tipped on its side into the ditch. A young driver was working hard, piling up the boxes from it.

"Don't strain yourself, lad," he said to him. "You'll get some help immediately." And he returned to Mekcsey.

"There are five Turks here, young man, not one," he said to him. "Splendid blows! They do you credit."

175

"There ought to be one more," replied Mekcsey. "Maybe he's in the water. Have you come across my men, Master Dobó?"

"Yes, poor chaps. One had his head split open."

"There were only three of us."

"And the Turks?"

"There were ten of the curs."

"In that case four of them have run away."

"Yes. I wonder whether they'll come back."

"Let them come. Now I'm here too." By now he had dismounted and was examining the wound. "It's a long cut, but not a deep one," he said pressing the gash together. He himself bandaged it up with a pad and a strip of linen.

"Where were you going, young man?"

"To Debrecen."

"Not to the Töröks, by any chance?"

"Indeed, yes."

"Well now, that's where one of my folk is, a particular favourite of mine, Gergely Bornemissza. He must still be a child. Do you know him?"

"It's for him that I'm going there now. He wrote saying that he'd like to join me in the army."

"Is he that old, then?"

"He's eighteen."

"Of course, Master Bálint's folk have scattered far and wide."

"Oh yes. The wind's blown them in all directions since the master's been in prison."

"Has Tinódi gone too?"

"Yes, he's wandering around the country. But maybe he's staying for the time being in Debrecen too."

"Well, give him my respects and greetings—and the two Török boys too..."

While they were chatting, Dobó pulled up the sleeve of his jacket and took up a rag. He washed Mekcsey's face. And one of Dobó's men cleaned the bloodstains from his clothes with a wet rag.

"Is the old man there?" asked Mekcsey, nodding towards the Ceceys.

"Yes. There's nothing much the matter with him. He's got a gash on his head too. Are you hungry, my lad?"

"No. Only thirsty."

Dobó beckoned for the bottle. He sent the other soldiers to help right the waggon.

Then they went to the Ceceys. By now the old couple were sitting on the grass beside the coach. Cecey had a turkey-leg in his hand. He was eating like a wolf.

"Come and join us!" he cried cheerfully. "Thank goodness you're all right, my boy."

Mekcsey shrugged it off, saying that it was nothing.

The soldiers collected the booty: five Turkish horses, the same number of cloaks, and all sorts of weapons.

Mekcsey had a look at the Turkish horses and then at the weapons lying on the ground.

"Make your choice, sir," he said to Cecey. "We'll share the booty."

"What use is it to me?" replied the old man. "I've got enough horses and enough weapons."

"Then I'll offer Master Dobó one of the weapons."

"No, thank you," Dobó said, smiling and shaking his head. "I've no right to choose. I didn't fight for it."

"All the same, do choose something."

Dobó shook his head. "The booty's all yours down to the last button. And how can I accept a gift from you?"

"I'm not giving it to you for nothing."

"Now you're talking," said Dobó. And he looked with interest at a finely-wrought Turkish sword. "What's the price, then?"

"If ever you become commandant of a fortress, call me to your aid if you're in trouble."

Dobó smiled and shook his head. "We're not reckoning on uncertainties."

"All right; I'll fix a different price. Come along with me to Debrecen."

"I can't do that at the moment, my lad. I'm a royal commissioner now. I'm collecting tithes on derelict estates. Unless, of course, I've got time."

"All right then. Just make your choice and give me your friendship in exchange."

"You have that already. But so that we shall remember each

other in friendship, I'll accept a weapon. These were high-ranking Turks; the weapons betray that. One was a bey. I wonder where they came from."

"I think they were from Fehérvár."

Dobó picked up the swords. One was studded with turquoises and had a velvet sheath; its hilt was a gilded snake's head, and the eyes were two diamonds.

"Now that's yours, my lad. I'll not take that. It's worth a fortune."

There were two other swords lying there; they were of Turkish iron and of cheaper workmanship. Dobó picked up one of them and bent it into a hoop.

"This one's of real steel!" he said with delight. "I'd be glad of this, if you'll give it to me."

"Gladly," replied Mekcsey.

"But now, if you're giving me this one, do me the additional favour of taking it with you to Debrecen, and if Tinódi's there, tell him to inscribe some words on it. Whatever he likes. There's a goldsmith there; he'll engrave it."

"I'll be glad to," replied Mekcsey. "I'll get him to write something on this snake's-head sword too."

He flourished the sword once and girded it on beside the other.

"Did you find any money on the Turkish officer?" Dobó asked his soldiers.

"We haven't searched him yet."

"Then search him now."

A soldier soon brought along the dead Turk, dragging him by his feet over the grass. He searched him there. There were no pockets in his baggy trousers of red velvet, but in his belt they found a little purse of gold and all kinds of silver coins.

"They'll be just right for expenses," said Mekcsey cheerfully. "Soldiers can always do with them."

There was also a ruby jewel in his turban, and a gold chain. This the bey wore inside his shirt, and from it hung a parchment talisman round a coconut chip.

Mekcsey put the two gold jewels in his hand and offered them to Cecey.

"Now you must choose between these, sir."

"Put them away too, lad," said the old man with a wave of the hand. "An old horse doesn't need any finery."

But the woman's eyes glittered.

"But you could certainly accept this chain for my daughter, she said. "We've got a beautiful unmarried daughter," she said in explanation, "at the queen's court."

"Come along to the wedding, lad!" croaked Cecey merrily. "I'll dance to my delight just once more before I die!"

Mekcsey let the chain fall into the woman's hand.

"Who's to marry her?"

"The queen's lieutenant, Ádám Fürjes. Do you know him, by any chance?"

Mekcsey's expression grew stern as he shook his head.

"He's a fine young man," boasted the woman. "The queen's giving my daughter away."

"God bless them both," responded Dobó.

Mekcsey presented the Turkish clothes and ordinary weapons to Dobó's soldiers. They got up to go.

Mekcsey picked up his cap and twisted it in his hands with annoyance. It was sliced through and almost fell apart.

"Don't be so angry," said Cecey comfortingly. "If it hadn't been split, it certainly wouldn't fit your head now."

Their clothes were still wet, but they would be dry by evening, thanks to the sun and the breeze.

"Choose two of my men," said Dobó, "to go with you. And Cecey can have two as well."

"I don't know whether we're going on together," Mekcsey said, turning to Cecey. "Shall we?"

"Where to?" said the old man.

"To Debrecen."

"We'll go together."

"Well, in that case three soldiers will be enough."

"Take as many as you want," said Dobó graciously.

While the elderly couple were settling into their coach, the two of them surveyed the dead bodies. Among them was a thirty-year-old well-built Turk lying on the grass with his hands and feet outstretched. He wore blue broadcloth trousers. The blow had caught him across the eyes.

"I seem to know him," said Dobó. "I think I once fought with him."

"He yelled like a jackal," smiled Mekcsey. "By heaven, you're silent now, jackal!"

The two Hungarian soldiers were horribly gashed all over. They covered the head of one of them with a cloth. They stabbed the Turks in the stomach and the soldiers threw them into the Berettyó. They dug a grave for the Hungarians in the soft earth of the bank under an old willow, and laid them in it fully-clad. They covered them with their cloaks and filled in the grave. They thrust their swords into the mound for a cross.

2

On the southern tip of Constantinople there stands an old fortress. It had been built by the Greeks. That was where the southern gate of the walls of the famous Byzantium had been, the splendid white marble Golden Gate, constructed by sculptors and painters in honour of the Emperor Theodosius. The white stones of the gate are still surviving today. The walls are high. Within the walls are seven stumpy towers, like seven giant windmills, situated like this:

```
              *
      *               *
         *       *
      *               *
```

The Sea of Marmara washes its walls on the eastern side; elsewhere it is bordered by wooden houses. This is the famous Yedikule, or the Seven Towers.

The Seven Towers are full to overflowing with all the treasures of the sultan. The middle two contain all the jewels of gold and pearl. Those on the sea side contain siege-weapons, hand arms and silver treasures. In the other two are old weapons, documents and books.

There among the seven towers the royal prisoners were also kept under guard. All of them differently. Some of them in chains and in dark holes, others in comfort and freedom, as if they had been at home; they may have walked in the garden and the kitchen-garden, on the balconies of the towers and in the bath. They may also have had up to three servants with them, written letters, received visitors, made music, eaten and drunk; the only thing they could not do was go outside.

*

Two grey-haired men were sitting in the spring sunshine in the garden of the Yedikule on a bench. Both of them wore light chains on their legs—just to remind them of their status as prisoners. One rested his elbows on his knees. The other leant back with his arms outstretched on the back of the bench and watched the clouds.

The one looking at the sky was greyer than the other. His beard reached the middle of his chest, and his hair was a mane. Both of them were in Hungarian clothes. Alas! Hungarian clothes were wearing threadbare on many prisoners in the Seven Towers!

They sat there in silence.

The spring sunshine flooded the garden with gentle warmth. Among the cedars, thuyas and laurels, tulips and peonies were already flowering. Over their heads an old banana tree drank in the rays of the sun with its long leaves.

The man gazing at the clouds took his muscular arms from the back of the bench and folded them. Meanwhile he looked at his companion.

"What are you thinking about, friend Maylád?"

"My walnut-tree," he replied. "In Fogaras there's an ancient walnut-tree beneath my window."

The two men fell silent again. Then Maylád broke it. "The outside branch was nipped by the frost. I'm wondering whether it's put out new shoots."

"It must have done. A tree catches the frost and grows new shoots. Vines also put out shoots from the stock. Only human beings don't..."

Once again they fell silent for a time. Then it was Maylád who spoke first. "What about you, Bálint? What are you thinking about?"

"About whether the *kapu aga* is just as big a rogue as the rest of them."

"Of course he is..."

181

"They said he was cunning. My wife sent thirty thousand gold pieces to get these chains taken off my legs, and that was three months ago."

They were silent again. Maylád bent down to a dandelion showing yellow in the grass. He broke it off, pulled it to pieces in his hand and let it fall on the ground.

"Last night I was thinking, Bálint, that I still don't know why you're sitting here. You've often told me how they brought you down the Danube, how you struck a guard against the side of the boat, and how they led you here. But the start of it all, the real reason..."

"I've already said I don't know that myself."

"After all, you were sitting tight in your own little nest. They couldn't have suspected you of aspirations to be king or prince. And you were a friend of the Turks. You called them in against Ferdinand."

"Not only me."

"Yet here you are, the only one of them. Of course I know that it wasn't because..."

"I've often thought a lot about that too. I'd like someone to tell me why I'm here."

A troop of sentries crossed the yard to the beat of drums; then they were left once more to themselves.

Bálint shrugged. "All the same, I think that conversation at night was the main reason. The sultan asked me why I'd reported his approach to the Austrians. And he was angry when he asked me. 'The Austrians?' I said in surprise. 'It wasn't the Austrians I told, but Perényi.' 'That's the same thing,' replied the sultan. 'Perényi was in with the Austrians.' And he looked at me with eyes blazing with wrath. 'If you hadn't informed them, we should have overrun the Austrian camp here. We'd have captured every nobleman and I'd have smashed all Ferdinand's power. Vienna would have been mine too!' As that rogue of a Turk growled at me like that, my blood began to boil too. You know I've always been a gentleman my whole life through; I'm not used to hiding my thoughts from other people."

"Did you go for him?"

"I wasn't rude; I simply explained to him that the reason why

182

I told them about the sultan's arrival was because I wanted to spare the Hungarians in the Austrian camp."

"Hm. That was a great mistake!"

"I was still free at the time."

"And what did he say then?"

"Nothing. He walked up and down in front of me. He pondered for a time. Then he suddenly turned to his pasha. He told him to take me to a good tent where I might sleep, and we'd continue our talk the next day."

"Well, what did you talk about next day?"

"Nothing. I didn't see him again. They put me up in a good big tent, but they wouldn't let me out of it. Every time I wanted to go outside, ten spears were fixed at my breast."

"And when did they clap you in chains?"

"Only when the sultan set out on his return home."

"In my case they clapped chains on my leg the minute I was captured. I cried like a child in my rage."

"I can't cry. I've no tears. I didn't even weep when my father died."

"Haven't you wept for your children either?"

Bálint Török went pale. "No. But every time I think of them, it's as if a sword's being turned in my breast." He sighed, and sank his face into his hands. "I'm often reminded of a captive," he said, shaking his head, "a thin, nasty Turk I captured on the bank of the Danube. I kept him in the castle for years. Once he cursed me to my face."

In the distance the sound of trumpets could be heard. They listened to it. Then once again they became immersed in their thoughts.

When the sun had turned the clouds red, the commandant of the castle strolled through the garden and, reaching them, said over his shoulder, "Gentlemen, we're locking up."

Normally the gate was locked half an hour before sunset, and then every prisoner had to be in his own room.

"Kapudji effendi," said Bálint Török to him, "what's happening today, with all that music?"

"The tulip festival," answered the commandant. "They'll not be sleeping tonight in the serail." And he went on his way.

The prisoners already knew about this. The previous spring

there had been a similar festival, and all the sultan's ladies had made merry in the garden of the serail. The sultan had had stalls and tents set up among the tulip-beds. The stallkeepers were the lower ranking women of the serail. They sold all kinds of trinkets, pearls, silks, gloves, stockings, shoes, veils and the like. His own several hundred women might never go out to the bazaar, so once in the year they were delighted to be able to spend their money lavishly.

On such occasions the garden bubbles over with joy. The parrots, blackbirds, nightingales and canaries from the palace are suspended in their cages from the trees and bushes, and try to outdo each other with their singing. Then in the evening the perfumed torches and variegated Japanese lanterns are lit on one of the boats in the Bosphorus, and the harem travels down by boat to the Sea of Marmara to the sound of music.

The two captives shook hands at the foot of the Blood Tower.

"Good night, István."

"Good night, Bálint."

*

For there's no other pleasure there, except a good night. The sleeping prisoner is always at home every night. He continues his work as if it were daytime, and as if his imprisonment were a dream. But Bálint Török was not in the least sleepy. Unusually for him, he had lain down and had a nap after lunch, so he did not feel like sleep that night. He opened the window and sat by it.

He looked at the starry sky.

The boat was gliding past the Yedikule in the Sea of Marmara. The sky was full of stars, but there was no moon. The stars flickered as they gleamed, and the surface of the sea also gleamed with reflected light. The boat, lit with lanterns, hovered there between the stars on high and those down below.

A stone wall hid the boat from the prisoner's eyes, but the sound of the music reached him. The *kanun,* the Turkish dulcimer, tinkled and the tambourine rattled. He would gladly have listened to them in his boredom, but his thoughts strayed elsewhere.

Towards midnight the noisy music grew quieter. The women

184

themselves sang, with different tones and different instruments. But Bálint Török was only dimly conscious of all this too. He was looking at the sky, which was now covered with slowly-moving dark and ragged clouds. The stars kept appearing through the tatters.

"How different even the sky is here," he thought. "It's a Turkish sky, with Turkish clouds."

And then, since there was a long silence on the boat, he went on thinking, "Even the silence is different here; it's Turkish silence."

He thought he would go to bed now, but still made no move.

Then the silence of the night was broken by a harp, and through the foliage Hungarian chords suddenly rose in the dark Turkish sky:

A kind of painfully sweet thrill ran from Bálint Török's heart to his feet. The harp was silent for a minute. Then the trembling chords rose up again, ascending like gentle weeping into the darkness of the night:

Bálint Török raised his head. This is how the captive lion imprisoned in its cage raises its head when the south wind whispers, and stares with a fixed gaze into the far distance.

The chords on the harp faded softly into the calm of the night, then the strings were plucked once more and a thin, sad female voice sang in Hungarian:

Whoever drinks the Tisza's water will
Return there, his heart's longing to fulfil...
Alas! I too have drunk of it...

Bálint Török caught his breath. He looked towards the sound with head upraised and staring eyes. His white locks seemed to stand on end, and his face was like marble.

And as the old lion listened to the song, well-nigh turned to stone, two great teardrops welled up in his eyes and trickled down his cheeks and beard.

3

Round about midnight the servant knocked on the Török boys' door.

"Master Gergely!"

"Well, what's the matter? Come in!"

He was not yet asleep. He was reading Horace by the light of a candle.

In the other two beds the Török boys woke up.

"The watchman sent me," said the servant. "There's a gentleman at the gate."

"What's his name?"

"Something like Kecske or something."

"Kecske? Who on earth can that be?"

"He's come from Győr and he'd like to stay here."

At the word "Győr" Gergely leapt out of bed. Jancsi Török looked at him in wonder.

"Who's that, Gergely?"

"Mekcsey!" shouted Gergely happily. "Let the gentleman in straight away."

The servant ran off.

Gergely pulled on a pair of boots and threw his cloak over his shoulder. The two boys also got out of bed. (Jancsi was now sixteen and Feri fourteen.) They were curious to see the visitor, whom they knew only by name.

"Order some wine and food," Gergely turned round as he reached the door. And then he dashed downstairs.

By the time he got to the bottom, Mekcscy was standing in the courtyard, with the watchman and the commandant of the castle beside him with a lamp.

And from upstairs too the light of a lamp shone down. For a time it swung to and fro over the courtyard and then it stopped on the new arrival, who was just taking leave of Dobó's soldiers, giving them each a thaler.

"Thank goodness I've got here," he said, giving Gergely a hug. "I was just about asleep on my horse. I'm so tired."

"But Pista, what have you got on your head?"

"A turban, damn it! Can't you see I've become a Turk?"

"Don't joke, old chap! That bandage is red with blood."

"Well, just give me a room and a basin of water, and then I'll tell you about the journey from Győr to Debrecen."

A maidservant appeared on the stairs and looked queringly at the newcomer.

Gergely shook his head. The servant disappeared.

He turned to Mekcscy to explain.

"Our mistress doesn't really get much sleep. Even at night she expects her husband to come back, or waits for a letter from him."

*

Mekcsey's wound kept him in bed with fever for three days at the castle. All that time the two Török boys and Gergely sat by his bed. They gave him red wine to drink. And they listened eagerly to his story.

The lady of the house visited him too from time to time. Ill though he was, Mekcsey told her that he had come for Gergely, to take him to join the royal army.

The boys looked at Gergely in astonishment, the lady with a sad, reproachful expression.

187

"So you'd abandon us, would you? Haven't I been like a mother to you? And haven't my boys been brothers to you?" Gergely hung his head and replied, "I'm eighteen now. Am I to live a life of idleness here, when the country needs soldiers?" He certainly looked well-developed for his age. The first signs of a beard were beginning to appear on his delicate, almost girlish, brown face. His gleaming black eyes were intelligent and serious.

"Must it be you?" said Mrs. Török, shaking her head. "Can't you wait for my boys? Everyone's abandoning us!" and she wiped away the tears that were coming to her eyes. "Those whom God has forsaken are forsaken by men too."

Gergely knelt down in front of the lady and kissed her hand.

"My dear mistress and mother, if that's how you take my departure, I'll stay."

Tinódi was also sitting there in the room. He had arrived that day from Érsekújvár. He had come to get news of his master, but of course his questions were stifled when he found the castle without its flag raised and the mistress in mourning.

He was sitting by the window on a bearskin-covered chest, writing something on the blade of a sword.

At Gergely's words he put aside his work.

"Madam, allow me to put in my oar too."

"All right, Sebők, have your say."

"A bird always returns to its nest, wherever it may fly. Gergely too would like to fly around a little. And I say that it would be good for him to see a bit of the world. For as you can see, Master János will be grown up in no time, and it would be better for him too if he had a trained soldier with him."

There was nothing to smile at in these words, but all the same they smiled. For the scholar Sebők was always joking when he was not singing, and when he spoke seriously, they always felt that some merriment was lurking behind his words.

"All right, we'll think about that," the lady nodded.

Then her eyes fell on the work he was doing. "Is the poem ready then?"

"Indeed it is! I don't know how you'll like it." He took up the snake-headed sword and read from it:

The brave man also strong must be,
The strong man conquers easily.
The conqueror leads invincibly,
And from him even death shall flee!

"Put that on my sword too," said Jancsi Török with approval. "No," replied Tinódi, shaking his head. "I'll compose something different for that."

Mekcsey spoke up from his bed. "You ought to get the king's name in too for Dobó's sword, Sebők. Something like *For God, country and king.*"

"That's out of date now," said Tinódi dismissively. "And it's not in fashion since the crown's been on an Austrian head. If he'd wanted that inscribed on his sword, he would have taken it and had it done himself."

"There's something just come to my mind," said Gergely, putting his finger to his forehead. "When I was a child, I heard one of his sayings. That's what you should put on it."

"What was it?"

"The main thing is never to be afraid."

Tinódi shook his head. "The thought's good, but it's got no colour. But wait a moment..."

He rested his chin in his hands and stared ahead. The others were silent. All of a sudden his eyes sparkled.

"If you're afraid, you're better dead."

"That's good," shouted Gergely.

Tinódi stuck the quill into the wooden inkpot and wrote the inscription down.

There was still another sword there without any inscription. It was like Dobó's. Mekcsey had given it to Gergely.

"Well, what shall we put on this one?" asked Tinódi. "Will this do: *Gergely Bornemissza, saddle your horse quicker!*"

They laughed. Gergely shook his head.

"No. I don't want anything like that. Just a thought. And in that thought is all poetry and all thought. Write this, my good Sebők: *'For my Country!'*"

*

189

On the fifth day, Dobó turned up. They were glad to see him. This was the first time in all the years since the master had been taken captive that the table had been set with gold and silver vessels. An unusual atmosphere of joy filled the house.

All the same, the lady appeared at dinner in her normal mourning dress, without any jewels. She sat in her usual place facing the door. Opposite her too there was an armchair and a place laid. Dobó thought at first that this was for the priest, who was a little late, but then he realized that it was for Bálint Török. A place was always laid for the master of the house: every day, morning, noon and night.

Mrs. Török listened with interest to the news that Dobó had brought from Vienna, as well as that from gentry living elsewhere in the country.

In those days there were no newspapers; only through correspondence and from the occasional visitor was it possible to discover what was happening in the world, and which branches of the great families had been cut off and which were flourishing.

There was only one name that did not occur for a long time in the conversation: that of the master of the house. Gergely had warned Dobó not to mention it and not to ask about him.

But when the servants had disappeared from the dining-room, the lady herself brought it up.

"And have you heard any news of my own dear husband?"

And all of a sudden her face was covered in tears.

Dobó shook his head. "Until this sultan's dead..."

The woman's head sagged.

Dobó banged the table angrily.

"But how long does he want to go on living? Tyrants like him don't usually die in honourable old age. So history teaches. All the same... My view is that if some high-ranking pasha were to fall into our hands, they'd exchange him for him."

The lady shook her head sadly.

"I don't think so, Dobó. My husband isn't kept in chains like some acquisition of the treasury; they keep him like a lion, because they're afraid of him. I've already promised everything for him," she went on sorrowfully; "I've told them to take away all our goods, all our gold and silver. The pashas simply pocket the money we send, and the sultan doesn't reply to them."

"Or they don't dare to mention the subject to him."

Mekcsey leaned his elbows on the table. "Couldn't he be freed in some other way..."

Dobó shrugged. "From the Seven Towers? Haven't you ever heard of the Seven Towers, my lad?"

"I have indeed. But I've also heard that nothing's impossible if someone wants it badly."

"My dear Mekcsey," said the lady with a sad smile, "can you possibly imagine that both my husband and his fatherless family don't want that badly? Haven't I been on his behalf to the queen, the Friar and the pasha of Buda? Haven't I crawled on my knees to King Ferdinand too? I didn't even dare write that to my poor husband."

And as her words were stifled by tears, they gazed at her in gloomy silence. However, she wiped away her tears and turned to Tinódi.

"Master Sebők," she said, forcing herself to smile, "are we to entertain our friends here with sadness? Come on, bring out your lute and sing the songs my husband loved to hear, just those, Master Sebők. We'll close our eyes while you're singing and imagine that he's sitting here with us too."

It was three years since Sebők's lute had been heard in the house. The boys brightened up in anticipation of this concession.

Sebők went out to his room and picked up the guitar-like instrument. He recited the *Tale of Lady Judith* in a quiet narrative tone, playing the melody to accompany it.

This was good consolation. Everyone recognized Holofernes as the sultan. But, alas!, where was the Lady Judith who would destroy him utterly from the face of the earth?

But when Tinódi reached the middle of the song, the melody suddenly changed beneath his fingers, and in a deep and resonant, but soft, voice he started on a new song:

> Poor Hungary does penance now with tears,
> All pleasure's gone; no sounds of joy she hears.
> In ruins lies so many a fine estate,
> And many a noble shares the captive's fate.

A painful shudder ran through those who were sitting at the table. Tears trickled from even Dobó's eyes.

"May I go on?" asked Tinódi imploringly.

The lady nodded.

Then Tinódi sang of how the Turks had lured Master Bálint into a trap, and how they led him in captive chains first to Belgrade and then to Constantinople.

His voice turned to a sorrowful whisper when he came to the end of the song:

> Your lady wife, with frequent copious tears,
> And two fine sons offer their frequent prayers;
> Now only of their father's loss they sing,
> And helplessness and grief in everything.
> Your faithful servants too are filled with grief,
> They love you well and pray for your relief,
> While some, confused, in exile seek their peace,
> Yet most remain to welcome your release.

Here the lutenist himself broke down in tears. For after all, he was that confused, exiled servant who most of all lamented for his master.

The two boys wept at their mother's knee, and she embraced both of them. Tinódi threw aside the lute and leaned on the table. A few minutes passed like this in that sad household, and then Dobó broke the silence in a flat, bitter voice.

"Why aren't I a free man? Even if it were to take me a year, I'd go down to that city and at least see whether that prison is really so impregnable."

Mekcsey lept up. "But I'm a free man! And I swear by the Almighty that I'll go there! Yes, I will! And if possible, even at the cost of my own life, I'll set Bálint Török free!"

Gergely jumped up too. "I'll come with you! I'll go with you through every peril for the sake of my master and my father!"

"Mother," said the young János Török, much moved, "am I to stay here at home when there are men ready to go now and free my father?"

"It's madness!" faltered the lady.

"Whether it's madness or not," said Mekcsey, fired with enthusiasm, "I'll do what I've said I'll do."

Tinódi got up. "I'll go with you too! My arm's paralyzed, but maybe my brain will be able to help you."

The lady shook her head. "What are you trying to do? Can you do what two kings and a royal estate have failed to accomplish?"

"You're right, madam," said Dobó, regaining his composure. "Neither money nor artifice will work; only the sultan's goodwill can loose his chains."

"But suppose that goodwill never comes?" retorted Mekcsey.

*

Next morning Dobó went on his way. They did not urge him to stay. They knew that he was pressed for time. Mekcsey remained there. He called Gergely into his room.

"I waited until we'd slept on the conversation we had last night. Not for myself, because however much I sleep on it, I'm still resolved to go down to the Turkish lands."

"I'll come with you," replied Gergely.

"In any case there's no war going on here at home for the moment. And who knows? We might possibly discover some loophole."

"Even if we fail, we shan't have any reason to be ashamed of ourselves. The main thing is to try it. If we try, we may succeed. But if we don't..."

"We've got to try the impossible. But tell me, shall we take Tinódi as well?"

"Whatever you think."

"And what about Jancsi?"

"Our mistress won't let him come."

"Then just the two of us will go. We'll leave Tinódi here."

"As you will."

"We're risking our lives. It would be a pity to involve the old man. He's one of the most worthwhile people now in the land. It's also the Lord's will that he should travel around and fan the dying embers in men's hearts to flame. That man embodies the grief that cries out from the soul of the nation."

The door opened and Jancsi Török came in. He had a riding

193

whip in his hand, and yellow deerskin breeches on his legs. On his head was a broad-brimmed cloth cap from Debrecen, and on his feet yellow boots. Mekcsey pretended to be continuing some tale, and just looked up at Jancsi before smiling and gesturing, "It's the red rabbit. And he's even getting married!"

He turned to Jancsi and said by way of explanation, "You don't know the person we're talking about, though maybe Gergely has mentioned him before."

"Who?" asked Jancsi, displaying no interest.

"Ádám Fürjes."

"And who's he marrying?" asked Gergely with a smile.

"The daughter of an old man with a wooden hand."

Gergely's face was suddenly drained of colour. "Eva Cecey?" he asked, almost shouting.

"Yes, that's the one. Do you know her?"

Gergely gazed at Mekcsey with a frozen stare.

"Oh, stop joking!" broke out Jancsi, striking the whip against his leg. "You weren't talking about this just now. Do you think I'm an infant? I'm no longer a child! I didn't sleep last night. There's one kind of fruit that ripens during the night. I've ripened too; during the night I've become a man!"

Mekcsey looked at him with approval. "But will your mother let you come?"

"I haven't spoken to her, nor shall I say anything about it. There are some repairs to be done to the castle of Hunyad. I'll tell her to leave them to me."

Mekcsey shrugged his shoulders. "In that case we can set out."

"Stop a moment," said Gergely, still very pale. "You mentioned something just now, Pista. Is it true? Or did you just make it up on the spur of the moment?"

"What I was saying about Fürjes?"

"Yes."

"It's true. Her mother herself was boasting that she was giving her daughter in marriage to the queen's lieutenant."

Gergely blushed furiously, and the veins stood out on his forehead.

"What's got into you?" Jancsi stared at him. "Do you happen to know her?"

194

Gergely jumped up almost beside himself. "Of course I know her! Why, she's my own Eva!"

"They're taking your own Eva away from you?"

"Yes, if it's true. I don't believe it." And angrily, almost dancing with fury, he shouted, "I'll kill the villain!"

Mekcsey tried to calm him. "You'll kill him. But suppose the girl loves him?"

"She doesn't love him!"

"So you think she's being forced into it?"

"I'm certain of it! As certain as can be!"

"And has she promised to marry you?"

"She's been my intended ever since I was a child!"

"Well, in that case..." said Mekcsey, "we'd better do something." And leaning on his elbow, he continued. "But even if we do, you won't be able to marry her. And suppose they really have become friends?"

"How can you think of such a thing?" replied Gergely.

Mekcsey shrugged again. "It's a long way off."

"She's always close to me. She's in my heart."

"Do you correspond?"

"How could we? I haven't got a servant. If I had, he'd have been on horseback all the time, taking our letters to and fro."

Mekcsey gave another shrug.

A rapid knocking could be heard from the porch. Jancsi Török leapt for the door and turned the key in it softly. The next moment the handle rattled. Jancsi beckoned for silence. For it was his younger brother knocking. He did not want him to know anything about their project.

4

Queen Isabella spent the winter at Gyalu, and when spring arrived she was still there.

The two young men, Gergely and Mekcsey, arrived in Gyalu on the third day. Jancsi Török did not go with them, in case his mother had got wind of their conversation.

All that Mrs. Török knew was that Gergely had gone with Mekcsey to join Ferdinand's army and would be spending the summer with the forces. He would return by 8 October, St. Demetrius's day.

But the plans of the young men were already laid. They agreed that first of all Gergely was to find out whether the girl loved Fürjes or not. If she did, then Gergely could do nothing but bid farewell to his dreams. But if she did not, Gergely would disappear as if he had never been there, and Mekcsey would make such a laughing-stock of Fürjes that no girl in Transylvania would ever have any desire to marry him.

After they had completed their business in Gyalu, the three youths would meet at Hunyad and set out for Constantinople.

They would go on horseback as far as the frontier. Jancsi would hold on to the money designated for the repairs to the castle, and would get as much extra money as possible so that it might be used, if necessary, to liberate Bálint Török. From the frontier onwards they would continue their journey on foot, disguised as dervishes, traders or beggars, in order to escape the attentions of robbers and roving Turkish military patrols. Whether their attempt to free Master Bálint was successful or not, they would return in the course of two months, if not before, so that Mrs. Török would not be worried about her son.

*

The two young men arrived at Gyalu in the evening. Only one servant accompanied them; Mekcsey had engaged him in Debrecen. The lad was called Mátyás, and he had previously been a horseherd on the Hortobágy. He rode the little Turkish grey that Mekcsey had kept out of the five.

At the very first house they asked a Wallachian if he would give them lodging.

The Wallachian understood Hungarian. He shook his head in surprise, and with it shook the big black cap he was wearing.

"Haven't you come to the wedding?"

"Yes, that's just why we've come."

"Well, if that's why you're here, why aren't you staying in the castle?"

The two youths looked at each other.

"I'm not staying there," said Gergely, "because I fell ill on the way."

And he really was pale enough to be a sick man.

"Only my companion's staying there," he went on. "And if you've got an empty room, I'll pay you for it."

When he heard mention of payment, the Wallachian ceased to be surprised. He readily opened his wicker gate for the riders to enter.

"Aren't we too late for the wedding?" asked Mekcsey.

"How should you be late, young gentlemen?" answered the Wallachian. "Or don't you know that it's fixed for the day after tomorrow?"

When they were alone in the room, Gergely looked despondently at Mekcsey. "We're too late."

"Yes, I think so too."

Gergely sat down on a shaky straw-bottomed chair and gazed ahead in bewilderment. Mekcsey went over to the window and stared at the lilacs that were just turning green.

"I think it would be best if we went back," he said at last. "One dream the less, one experience the more."

Gergely rose. He shook his head. "No. I'm not going to throw my salvation behind my back so easily. One day's a long time. I think I'll stay here, while you go up to the castle and mingle with the guests."

"And if they ask me what I'm doing there?"

"Didn't Cecey invite you? The main thing is to meet the girl and find out whether she chose Fürjes of her own volition. But that's impossible! Impossible! Completely impossible!"

"All right. I'll go up to the castle with Matyi and stay there, if they'll let me."

"You can tell them that Cecey invited you. After all, you did save the old man's life."

"Yes, that's true enough. I too think that whatever reception I get from him, the result will be that they'll put me up in the castle, and I shall be able to speak with the girl. If possible, today; if not, then tomorrow. But couldn't you find some way of coming with me as well? Perhaps you might come as my groom?"

"No. If the girl says she's been forced into it, then it's better if they don't know that I'm here. But then..."

"But then I'll box Fürjes's ears!"

197

"Don't do a thing until you've talked with the girl. Come back here straight away, and we'll see..."

The Wallachian's wife made up a soft bed for Gergely and offered him medicine and a wet compress. But the patient neither lay down nor drank the herbal tea, nor did he put the compress on his forehead. He just stumped up and down in the little room and struck great blows in the air with his fists.

Mekcsey returned in the morning. He discovered Gergely at the table. A nightlight was burning in front of him, and he himself was slumbering with his head on his arms.

"Why didn't you go to bed?"

"I didn't think I should sleep."

"Well, I've had a word with the girl. You were right when you suspected that she's not marrying Fürjes because she loves him."

Gergely shuddered as if he had suddenly been drenched from top to toe. The sparkle of life returned to his eyes. "Did you tell her I was here?"

"Yes. She wanted to rush here immediately, but I restrained her."

"What did you do that for?" Gergely burst out.

"Oho! That's a nice way to thank me."

"Don't be angry, but I feel as if I'm walking on fire."

"Well, the reason I wouldn't let her come to you is because she'd have had the whole household on her heels. For her it would have been disgrace, for us real trouble."

"So what did you say to her?"

"That I'd humiliate Fürjes, and she'd give back the ring."

"And what was her reply to that?" asked Gergely with glowing eyes.

"That the queen had urged her to marry, and her parents were forcing her into it too. It's understandable; the old queen's bored stiff here during the winter, and is amusing herself by arranging marriages. And Fürjes is eager to grab her, of course. And the girl, to win the queen's approval, puts her heart on a plate and offers it to her with fine virgin humility."

"But why should she do that? Oh, she's forgotten! She really has forgotten me!"

"Of course she hasn't. I expressed myself badly. I haven't the faintest idea how it all happened."

198

"Well then, what did she say? Did she say in so many words that she doesn't love Fürjes?"

"She did."

"And does she want to talk to me?"

"Yes, whatever happens. I told her I'd take you along there this evening."

Gergely went round and round the room like a drunken man. Then he collapsed in despair again in the rickety chair.

"What's the use of throwing Fürjes out of the saddle anyway? They still wouldn't let her marry me, even if I could marry her. Who am I? A nobody. I've no father, no mother and no roof over my head. It's true, the Töröks have brought me up as their own son, but I've never been so much their son that I'd have dared to open my mouth on such a subject. And especially now when their own home is so shattered."

Mekcsey stood with his arms folded and his back to the window. He looked with pity at Gergely. "I don't know what you're talking about, but I can see that you're all confused. After all, if you want to marry the girl, you don't need a father or a mother, and only a little place to live. If you'd like it, I've got a tiny house in Zemplén. It's empty. You can live there for ten years or so."

"A man doesn't live on words..."

"You're a scholar, aren't you? You know more than any priest. These days they're falling over themselves to find good scholar-secretaries."

Gergely came to life again. "Thank you, Pista."

"Now the main thing is for Eva not to get married. You'll come with me to the army, and within a year you'll have enough pay to be able to keep her. Until then she'll stay with my sister."

Gergely threw on his cloak, sword and cap. "God bless you, Pista! You're my guardian angel. Now I'm going to her father and mother, and I'll tell them that what they're doing is sacrilege! That..."

Mekcsey pushed him back into the chair so hard that it creaked. "The devil you're going! They'd simply dump you in some lock-up until the wedding's over. I tell you straight: they mustn't see even the tip of your nose!"

Three horsemen rode past the house. The guests were arriving from Kolozsvár.

*

When darkness had descended over the valley, Gergely got into the saddle and went with Mekcsey to the castle.

Nobody asked who they were. The castle was teeming with guests. The windows were all lit up. Torches lit the courtyard and wax candles the corridors. Gentlemen, ladies, pages, servant-girls all came and went and swarmed around and gave themselves airs and graces. Gergely's heart sank: would he be able to speak to the bride with so many people around? Why, she was never alone for one minute. And he was an uninvited guest here. Nobody but the bridegroom knew him.

"Let's go into the kitchen-yard," said Mekcsey.

They made their way to the rear of the castle. There the light was even more brilliant. The leather-aproned kitchen-staff were turning an ox on a huge iron spit, and in the kitchen the white-clad cooks were bustling about.

"Wait here," said Mekcsey. "I'm going to make my way somehow into the women's corridor, and I'll find out from Eva where you can meet."

Gergely joined the group watching the roasting of the ox. They were mainly drivers, of course, but there were one or two pages loitering among them as well. Curiosity had drawn them there. The ordinary people have great dreams about the royal cuisine, and the country gentry themselves like to hear what is cooked and how in the greatest kitchen in the land.

At Gyalu the kitchen building stood between the castle proper and the garden, and at the instructions of the elderly master-chef eleven cooks in stiff white caps and aprons and twenty apprentice-cooks, also in white, were busy there. There was not a single woman among them.

In the kitchen-yard a huge fat ox turned on the spit, filling the air with delicious smells.

The chef superintending this operation indicated simply by pointing his stick where the fire needed attention to keep an even heat.

Behind the hellish fire and heat mortars clacked, chopping-knives clattered, meat-beaters clumped amid all the bubbling and sizzling, the smoke, steam and aroma of food.

A lanky page with a red cloth cap sideways on his head was shouting explanations to the others.

"I've been here from the beginning. And they even roast the fatted ox differently here."

The hot breath of the fire filled the little yard and turned all the faces red. Gergely also quickly turned red as he stood among the others and listened, preoccupied, to the page's tale.

"Why, here," continued the boy, "they sewed an entire calf inside the ox. They stuffed a fat turkey into the calf, and a partridge into the turkey."

"And what went inside the partridge?" inquired a stupid little page with red ears and sparkling eyes.

"Inside that," replied the speaker solemnly, "they put a gander's egg. They'll give that to the youngest page."

They roared with laughter. The little page also laughed, but he blushed and left them.

Half an hour later the master-chef in charge of the roasting got to work. He opened the ox and pulled out of it a half-roasted turkey. The scent of marjoram wafted over the spectators and roused the appetite even of those who were not hungry.

It was not ready yet. They pushed the silver skewers back and pulled the fire together under the ox. They went on turning it.

The noise of the mortars, the clattering and banging, sawing and beating in the kitchen had now reached such a pitch that the red-capped page was unable to continue his explanations. But they did not interest Gergely anyway. His master had once owned a bigger kitchen, indeed six of them, and ox-roastings like this were more frequent in Master Bálint's castles than at the court of the queen in Transylvania.

A servant brought two freshly-baked loaves out of the kitchen. The pages seized them from him and tore them apart, warm as they were. The lanky youth who had just been talking offered Gergely a piece too. He accepted it. He was hungry.

Seeing them eating hungrily, the master-chef stopped the spit. He drew his hone along the chained knife he wore at his waist and sliced off the two ears of the ox for the pages.

They thanked him with loud shouts of "Vivat!"

Gergely ate with a good appetite. At the Wallachian's house he had eaten nothing but gruel at midday. The pages managed to lay hands on a goblet of wine. Gergely drank from it too.

Then he wiped his incipient moustache and offered his hand to the page who had supplied him with food.

"My name's Gergely Bornemissza," he said.

The page mumbled some name or other, but neither of them could hear the other. In the meantime the goblet came back. Gergely was still thirsty, and took a good swig from it. When he took the goblet from his lips, he saw Mekcsey standing in front of him.

Mekcsey beckoned him over. They went down into the garden. There was a mist lying there among the trees and bushes. The noise in the yard could scarcely be heard there. Mekcsey halted underneath an elm.

"Well, I've spoken to the girl. Her eyes are red with weeping. She implored her father and mother not to marry her to anyone except in due course to you. Of course, they're blinded by the light, the kindness of the queen and the generosity of the Friar. They consoled their daughter by saying that theirs hadn't been a marriage of love either, but they'd got used to each other all the same."

Gergely listened with bated breath. His very eyes seemed to drink in the words.

"So that's why the girl was crying," continued Mekcsey. "It's absolutely certain that she loves only you."

"And she's marrying Fürjes?"

"That's hardly likely now. She says she wants to have a word with you anyway, and she'll speak to the queen too."

"Why didn't she speak to her before?"

"She wasn't asked. Queens like that assume that what they think to be good is good for others too, and nobody will contradict them. And you haven't blinked an eyelid in her direction anyway. She didn't know whether you were alive or dead."

"And suppose the queen still insists on Fürjes?"

"In that case she'll say no tomorrow at the altar."

"That's impossible!"

"She'll say no to everything. There'll be a fine old mess. And in that case the least that will happen is that the queen will be angry with her and send her home to Buda. And in time you can marry her."

"Except that they'll certainly not let her marry me then."

"Of course they will. But now don't let's talk about what may happen in four years' time. The girl's coming here at midnight, if not earlier. There's some kind of house here, a greenhouse. She told me you were to wait for her there. She won't go to bed until she's spoken with you."

They soon found the greenhouse in the garden. A lamp was alight in it. Three gardeners were bending down, picking lettuces and leeks. They looked up from time to time, but none of them spoke; they thought they were visitors looking round.

Mekcsey took a good look at everything. "Well, Gergely, I'll leave you here now. Pretend to be ill or drunk. Lie down somewhere and wait for the bride. Maybe I'll come with her too." And he went away.

Gergely really did feel tipsy. Was it the wine that had gone to his head? Or was it just emotion? He felt heat in his heart and his head too, an angry heat that made him clench his fists.

He walked the length of the greenhouse among the lemon-trees, bananas, cacti and fig-trees. He stumped up and down restlessly and at increasing speed. Suddenly he flung out of the greenhouse. He pulled his cap down over his eyes, clapped his hand firmly on his sword, and went rushing up to the castle.

"Which is the bride's parents' room?" he asked in the corridors.

A page carrying a green water-jug at speed to the order of some dignitary directed him. "Over there; that's it."

It was a room with a white door. As on all the doors there was a little black board with the name of the guests in chalk.

The old man with the wooden hand was sitting at the table in shirt-sleeves. Half his face was a mass of shaving-soap. His wife was shaving him. His wooden hand lay before him on the table.

Gergely did not kiss their hands. He merely bowed, and returned the gaze of the two old people as they looked at him with an icy stare.

"Father..." began Gergely. Then since he felt that word to be inappropriate, he began again. "Sir. Don't be angry that I'm here. I haven't come to the wedding. And I shan't get in anyone's way. Nor have I come to remind you of your old promise, when I saved little Eva from the Turks..."

"What do you want?" old Cecey snorted at him.

"I only want to ask you," said Gergely, totally unmoved, "whether you are aware that Evie doesn't love that..."

"What's it to do with you?" burst out the old man. "What are you raving about? Clear out!" And his eyes burned as if his head contained blazing coals instead of a brain.

Gergely folded his arms.

"Do you want to make your own daughter unhappy?"

"How dare you take us to task? You scoundrel! You dog of a peasant!" screamed the old man. "Get out!" And he grabbed the wooden hand from the table to throw it at Gergely. The old lady, however, caught hold of the old man and turned to Gergely.

"Just go away, lad. Don't wreck our daughter's good fortune! With your infant minds you think you're in love with each other, but look, that young man's a lieutenant already..."

"And I shall be too!"

"But he's one now; there's no question of 'shall be.' The queen's in favour of this marriage. Go away, I beg you, for God's sake! Don't upset this celebration!"

"Clear out!" yelled Cecey.

Gergely looked imploringly at the lady. "Fürjes is just a coward and a parasite! Evie loves me! She can only be happy with me! Don't break her heart! Wait until I can marry her! I swear I'll be a worthy match for her!" And tears glistened in his eyes. He knelt before them.

The old man roared at him in a fury, "Get out before I kick you out!"

Gergely rose. He shook his head like someone waking from a bad dream. "Mr. Cecey," he said in an obdurate, stern tone, "from this moment I do not know you. I merely wish to know whether those gold coins which are stained with the blood of my mother are still with you."

"Three hundred and fifteen," croaked the old man. "Pay him, woman! Even if we've nothing left afterwards, pay him!"

So saying, he felt at his waist. He pulled out a narrow leather belt and poured out the golden coins in front of Gergely. The lady counted out Gergely's inheritance on the table—it was really spoils of war—as if she were counting rats' ears. Gergely swept them into his pocket.

He stood there for a moment or two. Was he wondering whether he owed them any thanks? For keeping his money safe? But it was not for him they had kept it, but for their daughter. Without a word he bowed and left them.

*

He wandered down the corridor like a sleep-walker. At the corner he bumped into a stout man.

"I beg your pardon."

He stood against the wall to allow a dignified-looking man and his companion to pass.

Meanwhile his eye fell on the door opposite, where he read Mekcsey's name.

He opened the door. There was nobody in the room. A candle was burning on the table.

Gergely threw himself on the bed and wept. The tears poured from his eyes as if stung by horseradish. Why? He himself did not know. His pocket was full of money. He had become a gentleman and a free man in that hour. Yet he felt a sense of forsakenness and loneliness. How many insults and scornful remarks had he had to endure!

"You old pagan! You've got a heart made of wood too!"

The castle walls shook at the cheerful sound of the bugle. It was the sign for the guests to assemble for dinner.

All along the corridor doors opened and shut. Women's shoes tapped on the marble floor and spurs jingled. They could be heard greeting each other.

"Hello! So you've come too!"

"Hello! I'm delighted to see you!"

A thin, croaking voice shouted "Amalia!" It might well have come from a parrot. Then there was a pause, and during the silence the door opened.

"Mekcsey!" said a woman's voice quietly.

Gergely leapt up. There stood Eva in a rose-coloured silk dress.

A moment of surprise, a soft cry, and then the two young folk were in each other's arms.

"Eva! Oh, my Eva!"

"Gergely!"

"Will you come with me, Eva?"

"Yes, to the end of the world, Gergely!"

*

About seventy guests were sitting at the splendid table in the light of a chandelier the size of a waggon-wheel with its hundred candles. Half of them belonged to the court. The others were the invited relatives of the bridegroom.

The queen sat with her little son at the head of the table, both of them dressed in green velvet. Behind them on the wall were garlands of flowers depicting crowns. On the left of the queen was Friar George, next to the little king the bride, and beside her the bride's mother.

The bridegroom sat opposite the bride.

The dinner began quietly. The guests talked only in whispers. After the third course Friar George rose and proposed the health of the newly-engaged couple. In his speech he called the queen a star of good fortune, the bride a lily and the bridegroom a man favoured by fortune. In his speech he threw everyone a graceful compliment, and even those who opposed him listened to him with pleasure.

By the time the best of the wine had reached the table, general conversation had begun. Naturally this was in undertones, each speaking only to his neighbour.

"Why do they call this the night of laments?" asked a merry-eyed young woman with a smile.

"It's when the bride laments her maidenhood."

"But she's not lamenting. She's so happy she seems to be glad at the ending of it."

"I'm surprised the queen's letting her go."

"She's not. Up to now she's been a maid-in-waiting; now she'll become a lady-in-waiting."

There was to have been no music that evening, but somewhere they had found an Italian singer for the wedding, and the queen gave permission for him to give them a foretaste of his art.

In came the Italian, a thick-set, short-necked dark-haired man in Italian clothes of yellow and blue. With a guitar. He had a good voice, but he sang rather loudly. While he was singing, the bride spoke softly to her mother with a faraway look in her eyes.

"Mother, what would happen if I were to die today?"

Her mother glanced at her in astonishment, but since the girl was smiling, she just rebuked her. "How can you say such a thing, my dear?"

"All the same..."

"Now, now."

"Would you cry for me?"

"We'd follow you to the grave, your father and I."

"But suppose I were to come to life again a month or two later and turn up at your house in Buda?"

The woman just stared at her daughter. Eva continued with a smile, "Well, you see, in that case you'd be sorry in the grave that you'd been in such a hurry to follow me there." And she rose. She got behind the queen, bent down to her ear and whispered something in it.

The queen gave a smile and nodded. The girl hurried out of the room.

The guests were concentrating on the singer. He had a fine baritone voice, and his middle range was beautiful. They liked him and applauded.

"*Encore, encore!*" said the queen. And the singer continued to entertain the host of guests for over half an hour.

Only Eva's mother saw her leave the room, and she pondered what her daughter had been saying with increasing unease.

*

When the Italian came to the end of his programme, the servant at the door called, "A new singer! Anonymous!"

Every eye turned to the door, but all they saw was a slender boy about fifteen years old. He was wearing cherry-red satin, and his coat reached half-way to his knees. At his waist was a little sword with a gilded hilt. He entered with his head down. His long hair covered his face. He made a deep bow to the queen.

Then he stood up and shook his hair to reveal his face. The

guests were totally taken by surprise, because the singer was the bride herself.

One of the queen's pages followed her in with a gilded harp and in the centre of the room handed it to her. The bride ran her fingers over it expertly. And she sang.

Out of respect for the queen, she began with a Polish song, one she had learnt from the queen herself. She had a marvellous silvery voice. The audience held their breath.

Then in turn she sang a Hungarian song, a Wallachian lament, then Italian, French, Croatian and Serbian songs.

After each of them the audience applauded enthusiastically. So did the Italian singer.

"She's fiendishly clever!" Mekcsey's neighbour said; he was a white-moustached court dignitary. "Just you wait and see, my lad, she'll even dance for us too!"

"And is she always so joyful?" asked Mekcsey.

"Always. The queen would have died of grief long ago if that girl hadn't been with her."

"So that Fürjes is making a good match, then."

The speaker shrugged. "He's a mother's boy. You'll see, she'll even join the army in his place. For she's also an expert with weapons."

"Impossible!"

"During the summer she took on Italian fencers and beat them. And how she can shoot and ride! She's got enough in her for seven men, and there'd still be room for a fiery devil too."

The bride whose praises had been sung like this started on another Hungarian song, whose refrain ran like this:

> Quick, my lad, up and away
> On your steed, the iron-grey
> To your dear one!

The guests knew this song, but the bride's version of the refrain ran thus:

> Quick, my lad, up and away
> On your steed, the iron-grey
> To your Gergely!

208

And as the bride sang this, her glance ran over the lines of guests and rested on Mekcsey.

The guests laughed. They thought the last line was a comic variation.

Mekcsey, however, gave a start. When the singer looked towards him again at the end of the second verse, he downed his wine and slipped out.

He ran down the stairs and shouted into the stables, "Matyi! Matyi Balogh!"

Not a soul replied. He had to search among the servants in the kitchen yard. They were drinking from wooden cups, clay pots, caps, boots and horns in the light of two huge torches.

Somehow he managed to pick out his servant. But what a state he was in! While he was sitting at the table he was human, but when he stood up he was no longer a man. About ten of them were lying under the table and by the wall. The ones under the table were just left there, but those who fell backwards off the benches were dragged away and piled into a heap beside the wall.

Matyi got up, or rather tried to get up when he recognized his master, but he quickly sat down again because he felt he too would stumble over the bench and join the rest by the wall.

"Matyi!" roared Mekcsey. "Devil take you! Where's my horse?"

Matyi got up again, but only with his hands on the table.

"Over there, sir... in 'is place."

"But where?"

"Among the 'orses." And raising his eyes, he went on, "An 'orse's place is among the 'orses."

Mekcsey grabbed him by the chest. "Talk sense, or I'll shake the life out of you!"

Much good that would have done. He was half seas over. Mekcsey pushed him away among the others and then hurried to the stalls to find his horse himself.

The stable-groom was tipsy too. Mekcsey could have taken away all the horses as far as he was concerned. So he walked right through the dark stable and gave a great shout of "Musta!"

An answering neigh came from one of the corners. The yellow

horse was feeding there next to Matyi's horse. With the help of a half-drunken servant Mekcsey saddled them both and left without anyone asking him why he was leaving so early, before the end of dinner.

Gergely was already waiting for him in the yard of the Wallachian's house. His own horse, ready saddled, was pawing the ground by the fence. The night was chilly. The clouds seemed to be motionless. But the moon, like half a silver salver climbed slowly from cloud to cloud and filled the countryside with pale light.

"Is that you, Gergely? I've come. I took it that the bride meant me to come here."

"That's right," replied Gergely happily. "We're making our escape tonight."

Scarcely half an hour later a nimble shadowy figure in a cloak appeared in front of the house. It opened the gate quickly and slipped inside.

It was Eva. She had made her escape in the cherry-red satin suit in which she had been singing.

5

The highroad to Adrianople was just as dusty and rutted as that to Gyöngyös or Debrecen. But if all the tears that had trickled on to it were to change into pearls, the world would be filled with them. And they might have been called "Hungarian pearls".

The inns at the end of the little towns were each a Babel in miniature. All sorts of languages were spoken there. But whether they understood each other was a different question. And in particular they could not understand it when a traveller accustomed to the life of a gentleman demanded a room or a clean bed or some such peculiarity.

The inn, or caravanserai as they called it, was the same everywhere in the east. It was a big, shapeless building with a lead roof. Its spacious courtyard was entirely surrounded by a man-high stone wall. Inside this there was another lower, broader wall. One could call this a bed, but it was not that; it was just a broad flat wall. But if I were to call it a wall, it was still more of a bed, because that was where the travellers retired for the night so that frogs did not jump into their pockets. The Turks needed just such a place to rest. They cooked their evening meal on it, they tethered their horses to it, and there they slept too. If they were accompanied by women and children, or if it rained, they threw a rush-mat or canvas on to the upper wall and fastened it below to stakes and they had a shelter. The main thing was to remain next to one's horse. If the horse happened to bump his head into his master's during the night, he slapped its face, but at the same time was comforted to know that his horse was still there. He turned over and went off to sleep again. That, then, was the caravanserai. It smelled of hay, manure, onion and rotten fruit, but all the same it was a good smell for the tired traveller.

One May evening two young Turks on horseback arrived at the Adrianople caravanserai. They were wearing Hungarian-style clothes—tight blue trousers, blue jackets, yellow sashes with Turkish daggers stuck in them, and over their shoulders loose rust-coloured camel-hair cloaks, whose hoods were pulled up over their heads. It was obvious at first sight that they were *deli*s, freebooters who serve the cause of the true faith only in war; at other times they live by robbery. The Hungarian cut of their clothes was in fact just as Turkish as Hungarian. Both peoples come from the east. All the *deli*s were Turks.

Nobody in the caravanserai gave them a second thought. At most their cart was worth looking at, because two good-looking young captives were sitting in it, and two fine coach-horses were harnessed to it. The driver was also a captive, and he was young too. The captives were either Hungarian or Croatian, and their hands and faces betrayed that they were of noble stock. Ah well, wherever those two *deli*s had been plundering, they might make a lot of money from those prisoners!

There were all nationalities teeming in the courtyard of the caravanserai: Turks, Bulgarians, Serbians, Albanians, Greeks and Wallachians, women, children, merchants and soldiers in a confused and noisy mass. That one highroad was like the Danube: everything poured into it. So it was no surprise that the caravanserais along it every evening and morning displayed scenes of Babel, with the crowds and confusion of tongues.

211

The sun was setting. The men were watering the animals, some horses, others camels. And everyone hurried to find a place for himself on the stone wall, spreading a rush-mat or a carpet on it. Those who had neither mat nor carpet threw bundles of hay or straw on it to stop the stone from breaking their backs.

When the two *deli*s had come to a halt in the courtyard, one of them, a bold-looking youth hardly eighteen years old, called for the innkeeper: "Meyhanedji!"

At this a stocky man in a red cap stepped out from under the porch and asked in a bored tone what they wanted.

"Have you a room, meyhanedji? I'll pay for it."

The innkeeper shook his head. "It was taken an hour ago."

"Who took it? I'll pay him too, if he'll let me have it."

"You'd find that difficult. The noble Altin aga has taken it." And he nodded respectfully towards the porch on whose stones a raven-faced dark Turk was sitting on a little carpet. He had his feet drawn up beneath him in Turkish fashion.

His clothes showed that he was indeed a gentleman. There were two white ostrich-feathers in his turban. Beside him was a servant who fanned him. And another was mixing him a drink. In the yard there were another twenty or so soldiers, half in red and half in blue. They were *spahi*s, cavalrymen and fighters for the true faith with their broad swords, bows and arrows. They were drinking and cooking. One was washing the aga's underclothes at the well, another was untying the rug for his bed from the back of a camel. It was a thick, expensive woollen rug.

Yes, it would indeed have been difficult to ask him for his room.

The two *deli*s returned to the cart dejected. The driver rapidly unharnessed it. He took the chains from the captives' hands and watered the horses. Then he too laid a fire on top of the wall and set a pot on it to cook dinner.

The two young prisoners did not appear to be sad at all. True, the two Turks treated them respectfully. They ate together from the pot and drank from the same cup. They must be high-ranking prisoners.

Now the aga too was having his meal. His cook had set a silver plate of mutton and rice before him on the rug. He used only his fingers to eat; eating with a knife and fork was both unnecessary and impolite. Only the unclean dogs of *giaour*s eat with cutlery from a table.

212

On the right of the *deli*s and their company a Greek family was eating. Two men, two children and an old lady. They must have been transporting saffron, because the two men had yellow fingers. On the other side a barefooted, one-eyed dervish settled down on the wall. All he was wearing was a rust-coloured cloak of hide reaching his ankles. This was secured at the waist by a cord, and a string of beads hung from the cord. There was no cap on his head. His long tousled hair was tied in a knot. That did for a cap. In his hand was a long stick with a bronze halfmoon handle. His clothing was grey with dust from the road.

The dervish crouched there. From a rough wooden cup fashioned out of a coconut-shell he picked at some bits of fatty meat, presumably begged from the travellers. That wooden cup was also tied with a string to his waist. So he just sat there, picking at his food. Meanwhile he took stock of the company eating dinner beside him.

"Aren't you followers of the Prophet?" he asked the *deli*s severely.

They looked at him with annoyance.

"Maybe more than you are," replies the younger one, a dark-skinned youth with sparkling black eyes. "After all, there are lots of wandering dervishes who pay respect to the prophet only with their bellies."

The dervish shrugs. "The reason I asked," he says, rubbing his sunken eyes, "is because you're eating with the infidels."

"But now they're true believers too, janissary," replies the *deli* over his shoulder.

The dervish stared at the *deli*. He put down his cup and wiped his greasy fingers down the length of his wispy beard. "How do you know me?"

The *deli* gives a smile.

"How do I know you? I knew you when you were in the army, bearing the *Padishah*'s weapons."

"Why, have you been serving all that long?"

"Five years."

"I don't remember you."

"So why did you abandon the glorious struggle?"

Before the dervish could reply, there came an appalling yell from the porch, so loud that the horses reared and pranced.

213

It was the aga who was yelling. The young men looked with startled faces to see what was happening. Was he being killed? Or what was the matter with him? The only thing they could see was that the aga's face was red and that he was drinking.

"Whatever's got into that man?"

The dervish gave a scornful wave. "Can't you see? He's drinking wine."

"How can I? He's drinking from a flask."

"Maybe you're not a born Muslim?"

"True, my friend. I was born a Dalmatian. It's only five years since I came to know the true faith."

"Ah, now I understand," nodded the dervish. "Well, you must know that the aga shouted like that so that his soul should descend from his head to his feet while he's drinking. For the soul dwells in the head and ascends to the other world when we die. And there, as you know, the true believer is punished for drinking wine."

"But if the soul isn't guilty?"

"Well, the aga too thinks that his soul won't be touched by sin if he scares it away for a minute. But my view is that such tricks don't do any good."

He sighed. "You asked me just now why I'd given up the glorious struggle."

"Indeed I did. After all, you were a brave soldier, and you're still young. You're hardly more than thirty-five, if that."

The dervish gave a satisfied glance, but then his face turned sad again. He waved his hand resignedly.

"Bravery without good fortune isn't worth a thing. I was brave so long as I had my amulet. It came into my possession on the battlefield, from an old bey who was dying. The protecting spirit of some hero's in it. Some hero who fought alongside the Prophet. But now his spirit fights alongside whoever possesses the ring. Then I was taken prisoner and a priest took it from me. So long as that amulet was with me, neither bullet nor sword touched me. As soon as it had left me, I had one wound after another. My officers hated me. My father, the famous Mohamed Yahya-Oglu, Pasha of Buda, drove me out. My elder brother, the famous Arslan Bey, became my enemy. My

214

companions robbed me. I was even taken captive a few times. All good fortune has deserted me." And his head fell.

The *deli* looked at the dervish's left hand, on whose forefinger a great red scar was visible all down it. It looked as though the forefinger had once been cut off right as far as the wrist and stuck back in place again.

"There's a scar on your hand too."

"*Jushallah!* I couldn't move it for a whole year. In the end a holy dervish recommended me to go three times to Mecca. And look, it was cured the first time I went."

"So presumably you'll remain a dervish."

"*Jushallah!* I hope my luck will come back again somehow. And if I make the holy pilgrimage twice more I shall be able to rejoin the army. But nothing's certain, worse luck, until I find my amulet."

"Do you hope to find it, then?"

"Everything's possible once I've completed the thousand and one days."

"You're doing penance for a thousand and one days?"

"Yes, for a thousand and one days."

"And you're visiting the mosques."

"No, I'm just following the road from Pécs to Mecca. And every day I tell my beads and repeat the holy name of Allah a thousand and one times."

"It's astonishing that such a clever man as you..."

"Nobody's clever in the sight of Allah. We're worms."

By now the dervish was holding the long string of ninety-nine beads in his hand and he began his prayers.

The driver cleared away the meal and brought out travelling rugs. He spread two on the wall. The third he threw over the top of the cart. The youngest prisoner occupied the cart for his bed. They pulled the shaft of the cart up to the wall. One *deli* lay down beside the shaft and put a saddle under his head for a pillow. He would remain on watch while the others slept.

The moon flooded the caravanserai with light almost as bright as the daylight. It was possible to see how the travellers found their places on the wall and prepared for their night's rest. Only the stench compounded of horse and onion did not settle, and there was a bat flitting hither and thither above the yard.

215

A servant with red coat-facings ran across the yard and halted in front of the *deli* who was just about to lie down.

"Sir, the aga would like to talk to you."

The other *deli* raised his head apprehensively from his bed and gazed after his companion as he silently obeyed the aga's request. He buckled on the sword that had been lying beside him where he took it off.

The aga was still sitting in the porch. But now he was not yelling. He stared at the moonlight, red-faced.

The *deli* bowed to him.

"Where are you from, my boy?"

"Buda, sir. The pasha doesn't need us any more."

"Those are splendid horses you've brought... Are they for sale?"

"No, sir."

The aga looked as if he had bitten into a lemon. "Have you seen my horses?"

"No, sir, I haven't."

"Well, take a look at them tomorrow. If any of them takes your fancy, we might do an exchange."

"We might, sir. Is there anything else?"

"You may go." And the aga watched the *deli* go with a deep frown.

*

Now everyone was asleep. The aga too had retired to his room and gone to bed behind the white-curtained windows. The inn yard was filled with the sounds of men snoring and horses crunching oats. And every moment a horse moved its foot. All this did not disturb the sleeping folk. The travellers were tired, and they slept as if they were in silken beds and wrapped in silence.

The moon rose slowly in the sky like half of a golden plate that had been divided into two. Sometimes the bat flitted across it.

The older *deli* raised his head. He looked round. The captive youth also stirred. And all three of them put their heads together.

"What did the aga want?" asked the older *deli* in Hungarian.

216

"He liked the look of our horses. He wanted to buy them."

"What did you say to that?"

"That they weren't for sale."

"You surely didn't say it like that? Turks don't say no to a gentleman like that."

"I certainly did. What is he..."

"Well then, how did it end?"

"By saying that we'd exchange them tomorrow with one of his horses."

The rug over the cart was opened and the youngest captive peered out with a white face. "Gergely..."

"Sh!" gestured the third *deli*. "What do you want, Evie? There's nothing the matter. Go to sleep."

"What did the aga want?"

"He was only asking about the horses. Go to sleep, dearest."

And since the two faces were close to each other, they exchanged a soft kiss.

Then the three young men had a few more words.

"There's nothing to worry about," said Gergely encouragingly. We'll start off again as soon as it gets light and leave the aga and his horses here."

"But tomorrow I'm not going to be a captive," said Jancsi Török. "Let Mekcsey be the captive tomorrow. I'm bored with this chain. And all these gold pieces are terribly heavy. It'd be much more sensible to hide them in the cart."

"All right, then," smiled Gergely. "I don't mind being the captive tomorrow, but when shall we change clothes? We can't do it during the night in case the aga wakes up earlier."

"We'll do it tomorrow then, Gergely, on the way. That aga was quartered here by the very devil!"

Mekcsey shook his head. "I don't like it either. Gentlemen like him don't put up with their requests being rejected by any old *deli* in rags."

Gergely put his finger to his lips. "This dervish knows Hungarian."

The dervish was lying beside him. He was curled up like a hedgehog.

*

217

Next morning when the sun shot its first golden rays into the sky, the aga stepped out of the doorway and rid his head of the last traces of sleep with gigantic yawns.

"Where are those two *deli*s?" he said to the servant who bowed to him. "Call them over here."

The dervish was squatting by the door. He rose from his place when he heard the aga speak. "They've gone, sir."

"Gone?" exploded the aga. "Gone??"

"Yes."

"How dare they go?"

"That's why I've been waiting for you, sir. Those two *deli*s are up to no good."

"How do you know?"

"I listened to what they were saying last night."

"What were they talking about?"

"All sorts of thing. But chiefly that it wasn't good for them to meet a man like you."

The aga's gaze stiffened. "Then we'll take away their horses! The captives! The cart! All the lot!" And as he spoke his voice rose with each word until he was roaring when he reached the end.

"They've got money too," continued the dervish. "One of the captives was saying that he couldn't carry all the gold. I suspect they're not really of the true faith."

"Gold? Hey, *spahi*s! On your horses, all of you! Follow those two *deli*s! Bring them back here either dead or alive! But above all bring their cart!"

In the next few minutes twenty-two mounted spahis clattered out of the gateway of the serai. The aga watched them go. Then he turned to the dervish.

"What else did they say?"

"I didn't catch everything. They were talking quietly. What's certain is that they were talking Hungarian, and that one of the captives is a woman."

"A woman? I didn't see her."

"They dressed her in men's clothes."

"Is she beautiful?"

"Beautiful and young. They're going to Stamboul."

The aga's eyes grew twice as large as they had been. "You'll get your share of the booty." And he went inside.

"Aga effendi!" the dervish called after him. "I've been a janissary. Would you let me ride a horse?"

"But I'm coming too!" said the aga in a rage. "Right: saddle a horse for me too!"

A quarter of an hour later, mounted on two fiery steeds, they were on the tracks of the twenty-two *spahis*. The aga waved to them from afar to keep up the chase.

The highroad was covered in white dust from the horses' hooves.

Scarcely two hours later the spahis' yells proclaimed to the aga that they could see the cart. By then the *spahis* were on the top of a hill, and then they disappeared from the aga's sight as the road went down the other side.

The aga could scarcely wait to get to the top of the hill himself. He spurred on his horse to a gallop, fired by the thought of the rich booty. Behind him the dervish sat huddled on his horse like some hairy devil. He gripped his horse hard and beat it. It was not that the horse was a bad one, but he was barefoot and the horse was used to spurs. But the dervish would have liked to fly. If that suspicious crew got into his hands, that would be a sign that his luck had returned. So he flogged his horse. His hair came loose from its knot, and his head turned into a great shaggy mop. He had not yet had time to buckle on the sword he had been given by the aga in the heat of the moment, so he held it in his hand and beat his horse with it, now in front, now behind.

From the hilltop the aga now saw that the quarry was still a long way off, but they had scented danger.

Now the two captives also took to horses and grabbed weapons from the rack of the cart. The driver too snatched some objects from the inside of the cart and distributed them among the riders. They stacked them in the saddle-bow and in front of it. Then the driver crawled under the cart. From beneath it rose white smoke. Then the driver too got on a horse and galloped after the four other riders.

The aga was puzzled.

"Whatever kind of prisoners are they?" he called back to the dervish. "Don't they want to be free?"

"I said they were curs," screamed the dervish.

The flames were now enveloping the cart. The *spahis* stood round it, not knowing what to do.

"The main thing's the cart!" the aga had said to them. So they just stood there, or rather pranced round the fire on their scared horses.

"Put it out!" shouted the aga. "Break up the cart!"

Then he shouted again. "Only three of you stay here. The rest of you go after those dogs."

But which three? And why was the cart blazing? Such a thing had never happened before since the existence of men and carts on the earth.

"What are you still staring at?" exploded the aga. "You lazy dogs!..."

At that moment there was a huge blinding flash and a tremendous explosion. The world was torn asunder by flame in the very eyes of the Turks.

Neither cart nor man was left there, just the single shaggy dervish, deafened by the explosion and the rush of air, looking like a witch's cat on top of a chimney.

"What was that?" bellowed the aga from the middle of the dusty highroad, where his horse had thrown him.

The dervish wanted to go to his aid, but his own horse too was scared. It danced backwards and reared on its hind legs, rolling its eyes to the sky. Then in a mad dash it galloped into the fields. It shot the dervish into the air and leapt away into the distance, scattering white foam from its mouth. But the dervish still clung to it.

The aga scrambled to his feet. He spat out the dust and vented his rage in a fearful curse. He looked round him. The highroad was like a battlefield, with horses writhing and *spahis* sprawling there. Where the cart had been there was a large empty space. Over the road hung a wide nut-brown cloud which had once been the cart.

The aga's horse had run off too. The vulture-faced man did not know where to turn.

In the end he went off limping to his men.

Well, they had certainly been scattered by the explosion. They

220

lay like sacks in the dust. Blood trickled from their noses, mouths and ears. The aga saw that none of them was stirring, so he sat down on the bank of the ditch and gazed ahead stupidly. Maybe he was wondering why bells were ringing so thunderously and where. Of course, there were no bells anywhere; it was only his ears that were ringing.

He was still in this stunned, deaf state when he was found half an hour later by the dervish, who had galloped his wild steed till it was flecked with foam and now returned. He tethered his quivering horse to a beech-tree at the side of the road and hurried across to the aga.

"What's the matter with you, sir?"

The aga shook his head. "Nothing."

"But you must have been hit somewhere."

"On my bottom."

"Blessed be Allah, who has saved us from this peril!"

"Blessed be Allah!" the aga repeated mechanically.

The dervish looked in turn at all the horses lying on and near the road to see whether any of them could be raised to their feet. But there were none. Those which were still alive were such wrecks that only vultures might consider them of any value. He returned to the aga.

"Sir," he said. "Can you get on your feet? Or shall I put you on this horse?"

The aga rubbed his legs and knees. "I'll have revenge for this! I'll have their blood! But where can I find horses and men?" And he stared stupidly at the dervish.

"Curse them! They're certainly on their way to Stamboul. We'll be able to find them there," the dervish said.

The aga stumbled to his feet. He groaned. He felt his brow. "Come on. Help me up on to the horse and take me back to the inn. Enter my employment as a servant. You know how to ride."

The dervish looked at the aga, scandalized. "As a servant?" But then he humbly bowed his head. "As you command."

"What's your name?"

"Yumurdjak."

6

Meanwhile the five Hungarian riders were far away, galloping along the highroad to Constantinople.

The explosion had maddened their horses too, but that only made them fly all the faster. They kept chasing ahead of each other in their mad dash, and other travellers along the road got out of their way in good time. They could not decide whether they were engaged in a race or being pursued.

But how did Eva Cecey come to be among them?

On the evening of the banquet when she met Gergely, the old feeling that she was one with him had reaffirmed itself. She had thought of him before, but with all the pressure on her she had been unable to get free. And Gergely had neither house nor land nor even a table of his own; he was a young lad in the care of a guardian. They could not even correspond with each other. So she had begun to bow to her fate.

But the appearance of Gergely had destroyed all other forces.

"The words in my heart are the words of God!" she said to Gergely. "Even if you can only provide me with a shelter from which we can hide from the rain, I'd sooner be with you than with anyone else, even if they live in a palace."

They escaped over the Gyalu Mountains, and the morning sunlight shone on them by the waters of the Aranyos.

The forest was magnificent in the pale green of new foliage. Violets were open everywhere, and the valley was yellow with dandelion and crocus in bloom. The air was full of the scent of pines.

"Now I know why they call this stream the Aranyos," said Gergely. "Look, Eva, it's just as if its banks were sprinkled with gold everywhere. But you've got something on your mind. What's making you look so sad, dearest?"

Eva gave a rueful smile. "The fact that I'm a girl, after all. What I'm doing isn't right."

Gergely looked at her. "Oh no..."

"Today you're glad that I followed what my heart told me to do, but perhaps years later when we're old it may cross your mind that you led me not out of a church, but out of a banqueting hall."

Mekcsey was leading the way with a Wallachian peasant who had guided them over the mountains. The two of them were riding side by side behind them.

"You're young," continued Eva, "and there isn't a priest in the world who'd marry us."

Gergely became serious and shook his head. "Haven't you always felt that I'm your brother, Eva? Isn't that what you're still feeling now beside me? And if it's the absence of a priest that's upsetting you, won't you trust me to protect you until we can get married? Why, your guardian angel couldn't look after you better! If you so wish, I won't even take you by the hand or kiss your face until the priest gives us his blessing."

Eva smiled. "Take my hand. It's yours. Kiss my face. It's yours." And as they rode there side by side, she offered him her hand and cheek.

"Oh, you did frighten me!" said Gergely, taking a deep breath. "That was the catechism that spoke from you just now. I'm a Catholic too, you know, but my master taught me the knowledge of God not from the catechism but from the stars in the sky."

"Father Gábor?"

"Yes. He was a Lutheran, but he never wanted to force anyone to become a Lutheran. He told me that the true God is not the one of whom pictures and books speak. He's not that flowing-bearded, threatening, hysterical old rabbi in the clouds. We can have no idea of the real nature of God. We can only see his intelligence and love. The real God is with us, Eva. The real God isn't angry with anyone. If you raise your head to the heavens and say, 'My God and Father, I choose this man Gergely as my partner in life', and if I say the same thing with your name, then, my dearest Eva, we're married in the sight of God."

Eva looked happily at Gergely as he spoke softly, half-absorbed in his own thoughts. How soon the child brought up as an orphan grows mature in spirit!

The boy went on: "The ceremony in church, Eva, is only to gain the agreement of the church. It's the proper thing to do. So that the world may have documentary proof that we have become one in accordance with the intentions of our hearts and souls, and not on impulse, for a time or an' occasion, like animals. We were really married, my dearest, when we were little children."

Mekcsey had reached the top of a grassy hill. He stopped and turned round. He waited for them. "A little rest wouldn't come amiss," he said.

"All right," replied Gergely. "Let's dismount. I can see some water down there. The Wallachian can water the horses."

He jumped down from his horse and helped Eva to dismount. He spread his cloak on the ground and they lay on it.

Mekcsey opened the knapsack. He took out bread and salt. Gergely knelt and cut off the dry parts. He offered the bread first to Eva.

But then he put down the bread and looked at Eva.

"Before we share the bread, Eva, wouldn't it be a good thing to confirm the contract we both desire in words and in the sight of God?"

Eva knelt too. She did not know what Gergely wanted, but the resonance of his voice told her that his thoughts were sacred and solemn. She held out her hand to Gergely.

"Am I supposed to marry you?" asked Mekcsey, taken aback.

"No, Pista. He who created our hearts."

He took off his cap and looked up to heaven.

"Our God and Father! We are in thy temple. Not in a building with towers, made by human hands, but beneath the vault of thy heaven, among the splendid columns of thy trees! Thy breath floods over us from the forest. And from the heights thine eye sees us. From the days of my childhood this girl has been my partner, more dear to my heart than all the other girls on earth. She is the only one I love. She is the only one: for all time, till my death and beyond the grave too. The will of men has not allowed us to be married in the normal way. Allow her to be my wife with thy blessing." And he turned his misty eyes towards the girl. "I hereby declare before the face of God that you are my wife from this moment onward."

Eva whispered, with tears in her eyes, "And I declare that you are my husband..." And she rested her head on Gergely's shoulder.

Gergely raised his finger. "I swear that I'll never leave you, in trouble or in adversity. Till your death. Till my death. So help me God!"

"Amen," growled Mekcsey solemnly.

Eva also raised her hand:

"I swear what you have sworn. Till your death. Till my death. So help me God!"

"Amen!" repeated Mekcsey.

And the young couple embraced. They kissed each other with such devotion that they might have felt the hand of God on their heads in blessing.

Mekcsey sat down again by the bread and kept shaking his head. "Well now, I've been to lots of weddings, but never to one like this. I'm absolutely certain that this was a stronger and more sacred marriage than that ceremony at Gyalu in the presence of nine priests, my lady."

They smiled. They sat down and began to eat.

That evening they arrived at the castle of Hunyad. Jancsi was waiting for them with dinner. (He had awaited them every day, either with lunch or with dinner.)

The parish priest was also at the table, a sickly, old man with a drooping moustache who had run to seed in the peace and quiet of the castle like the lime-trees there. He listened with a smile and in silence to the story of the elopement of the young couple.

"I sent for the priest," said Jancsi Török, "so that he could marry you."

"We've got over that already," said Gergely with a happy wave of the hand.

"How's that?"

"We took the sacrament of marriage in the presence of God."

"Where? When?"

"In the forest."

"In the forest?"

"Yes. Just like Adam and Eve. I suppose that might not count as a legal marriage?"

The priest looked at them in horror. "Per amorem..."

"What?" Mekcsey snorted at him. "If God wants to give his blessing, he can do so without the help of a priest."

225

The priest shook his head. "That may be so. But he doesn't give a marriage-certificate."

Gergely shrugged his shoulders. "But we know even without a certificate that we're married."

"That's true too," nodded the priest, "but in due course your grandchildren won't know that."

Eva blushed.

Gergely scratched his ear.

The priest laughed. "So you see there's some point in having the priest at the end of the table after all!"

"Well, would you be able to marry us, sir?"

"Of course."

"Without the consent of her parents?"

"Yes, without it. After all, there's nothing in the Bible to say that parental consent is necessary for a marriage. You're not related, I suppose?"

"Only in spirit, aren't we, Evie? Let's do it then, for the sake of the certificate."

"And straight away," said Jancsi urgently. "We've got to wait a little anyway for the capon."

"Yes, it can be done straight away," said the priest.

They went over to the chapel, and the wedding was over in a few moments. The priest wrote their names in the church register. The witnesses were János Török and Mekcsey.

"I'll send on the document to the parents," the priest said when they had returned to the table. "Make your peace with them."

"The sooner the better," replied Eva, "but it can't be done immediately. It'll take a month or two. Where shall we spend those two months, my dear husband?"

"Well, my dear wife, you here in Hunyad, while I..." And he glanced at his companions.

"We can tell her," said Jancsi with a shrug. "After all, now that you're one, there's no secret between you from now on. And it would be a good thing if our priest knew as well. If anything happens to us, at least he'll be able to tell my mother as well in two months' time."

"All right, then, my dear young wife," said Gergely, "you

226

must know that we were about to set off for Constantinople when I heard you were going to get married. The three of us have sworn a sacred and binding oath to free Bálint Török, our noble father."

"If possible," added Jancsi Török.

The young bride heard her husband with serious attention. Then she tossed her head. "My word, you've got a bad bargain in me, dear husband!" (Sometimes she addressed him in familiar fashion and sometimes she was more formal since they had been married.) "For as for me, I'd gladly cool my heels here in this marvellous castle even for two months, but haven't I sworn today—and in two different places too—that I'll never leave you?"

"You surely don't mean..."

"Can't I ride a horse as well as any of you?"

"But this won't just be riding, my angel. It'll be a dangerous journey."

"I can fence too. I learnt that from an Italian master. I can shoot a rabbit with an arrow. And I've practised rifle-shooting too."

"A pearl of a woman!" said Mekcsey enthusiastically and raised his glass. "I envy you, Gergely!"

"All right, all right," said Gergely anxiously, "but ladies like you generally sleep in lace-frilled beds."

"On the journey I shan't be a lady," replied Eva. "I came this far in men's clothes, and I'll go on in them too. How soon you've come to regret marrying me! Father, divorce us immediately, because this man's making a mockery of me; he's abandoning me on the very first day!"

But the priest was now busy separating the capon-breast from the bone. "The Church doesn't dissolve marriages."

"But after all, you don't even know Turkish," Gergely objected.

"I'll learn it on the way."

"And we'll teach you," said Jancsi. "It's not as difficult as people think."

"Give me a few words," said the hour-old bride.

"Well, for example: *elma* = alma [apple], *benim* = enyim

227

[mine], *baba* = papa, *pabuch* = papucs [slippers], *daduk* = duda [bagpipes], *chagana*..."

"Csákány [axe]!" cried Eva, clapping. "I'd no idea that I knew Turkish too!"

The footman who was waiting on them bent down to Mekcsey. "There's a man here who's determined to see you at all costs. He's told me all I'm to say its that he's here, or rather, that Mátyás is here."

"Mátyás? Mátyás who?"

"He didn't mention any other name."

"Gentry or peasant?"

"A servant, I'd say."

Mekcsey burst out laughing. "It's Matyi, devil take him! All right, let him in. What does he want?"

Matyi, alias Mátyás, appeared with a face as red as a lobster and blinked at Mekcsey. "Here I am, captain, sir, at your service."

"So I see. But where were you last night?"

"I was all right soon enough last night, but you rushed off so quickly that I couldn't catch you up, sir."

"Why, you were drunk as a lord!"

"Not really, begging your pardon."

"And how did you get here? After all, I took your horse."

Matyi raised his shoulders and eyebrows. "There were enough horses there."

"You mean you stole one, you gallows-bird!"

"No, I didn't. But when you left, young sir, I had myself mounted on a horse. The grooms there helped me on it, because I couldn't get on it myself. Can I help it if they didn't put me on my own horse?"

The company had a good laugh at this story, so Matyi was totally forgiven. His drunken escapade particularly appealed to Gergely.

"Where do you come from, Matyi?" he asked, laughing.

"Keresztes," replied the lad.

"And where the hell's Keresztes?"

How odd it would have been if now the driver had replied like this: "Oh, poor Master Gergely, you'll know one day where Keresztes is! When you've grown into a fine bearded man and a gentleman, that's where the wicked Turks will entice you into a trap and clap your hands and feet in irons! And only death will release you from them..."

*

Three days later they set out. Matyi was their driver. The four of them took it in turns to be captives and *deli*s. The cart was also where Eva slept at night.

7

What's that smoke down there in the rock-strewn valley? Is it a camp or a village? A robbers' lair or a leper colony? Is that a funeral or a wedding going on there?

Well, it's neither camp nor village, neither robbers' lair nor leper colony, but a large gypsy caravan.

In the shadow of the rocks, under the cypresses and olive-trees there were tattered sooty tents. Smoke curled up towards the sky. In the clearing violins scraped and drums rattled: the girls were dancing.

So it was neither festival nor wedding. This was their custom: while they were unmarried, the girls danced; when they were married, they told fortunes.

Some of the gypsies were sitting round the dancers. The children, naked as they were, imitated the dancers. Even the two- or three- year-old little children whirled and turned in the grass like dirty little angels. Instead of tambourines they banged coconut-shells, and instead of veils they draped spiders' webs over their arms.

All of a sudden, just like a host of sparrows flying up from a bush, every single child suddenly took flight towards a gap in the forest.

It was our five riders who had arrived there weary, leading their horses. With a great noisy twittering the host of children surrounded them, holding out their hands for *baksheesh*.

"Where's the chief?" asked Gergely in Turkish. "You'll all get baksheesh, but I'm only giving it to the chief."

229

But they certainly did not run off for the chief; they still pressed round the riders and whimpered.

Eva had already put her hand in her pocket for a few coppers to throw among them, but Gergely beckoned to her not to.

"Haydi!" he shouted at them, drawing his sword at the same time. The sparrows scattered in terror.

But the older gypsies also took fright. Some leapt into their tents, others made for the bushes. Only the women stayed there. They stared expectantly at the strangers.

"Don't be frightened," said Gergely in Turkish. "We shan't harm you. I just wanted to scatter the children to stop them making so much noise. Where's the chief?"

An ancient gypsy stepped out of one of the tents. He wore a Turkish kaftan and a high Persian cap on his head. There were big silver buttons on his jacket, and a gold chain round his neck. In his hand was the big stick of a chieftain. He had forgotten to put on any boots, or perhaps the thought had not entered his mind. So he stood there barefoot. And he looked anxiously, expectantly, moving only his white eyebrows. On his silver-buttoned breast a bean stuck there in some yellow stain was proof that he had no liking for insubstantial breakfasts.

"What language do you speak?" Gergely asked in Turkish.

The chief shrugged his shoulders. "Whatever language you ask me in, noble young sir."

"What were your people so scared of?"

"There's a band of Greek robbers raiding these parts. They say they're about fifty in all. Last week they murdered a trader in this forest. It was a good thing they saw them, otherwise they'd have said it was us."

"Well, we're not robbers, only travellers who've lost our way. We're from Albania. We've also heard that story about the robbers; that's why we got off the highroad. All we want is to ask you for a guide who'll accompany us to Stamboul and stay with us for a few days. We'll pay for him."

"You can have ten if you like. After all, it's not far away."

"We only need one. Someone who knows his way around in the capital. Who can deal with horses, if necessary, and mend weapons if they go wrong. He's to bring a hammer and a file too. We'll pay."

The chief looked thoughtful for a moment, then turned towards a smoky tent. "Sárközi!"

The five riders almost started when they heard the Hungarian name. From the tent emerged a grimy gypsy about forty-five years old. He was wearing cowhide trousers and a blue shirt. The Wallachian trousers were patched at the knees with red cloth. Under his arm he had a Hungarian short jacket, which he put on as he came over to them. By the time he had reached the chief, he had buttoned it, beaten the dust out of his trousers and even combed his hair with his ten fingers. He turned his pockmarked face anxiously and queringly to the chief.

"You'll accompany these gentlemen to the City and be their servant there. Put a hammer, pincers and file into your knapsack."

Gergely handed the chief a silver coin. "Divide this among the children, chief. Thank you for your kindness."

The chief put the coin in his pocket. "I'll see to that immediately..."

The gypsy children scattered.

"What do you want me to bring?" Sárközi asked humbly in Turkish.

"What the chief said, in case a horseshoe comes loose or the flintlock on a rifle. And if you've got some good balm for wounds in men and horses, bring that too."

"I'll fetch them, sir." And he ran back to his tent.

"Aren't you tired, young gentlemen?" asked the chief hospitably. "Come inside and have a rest. Have you eaten today?" And he led the way towards his own tent, which stood out red among the rest under the highest rock.

The chief's wife spread three multi-coloured rugs on the grass. Her daughter, still wearing the veil she had used in the dance, went to help her mother.

"We've got cheese, eggs, rice, butter and bread," said the woman. "I can roast a chicken too, if you've time, young sirs."

"We'll wait for that," replied Gergely. "We're really very hungry. Our journey isn't as urgent as all that."

Now they were surrounded by gypsy women, all of them wanting to tell their fortunes. One of them was already squatting there shaking the various coloured beans on the grid.

231

"Please give them this thaler," said Gergely, feeling in his pocket and turning to the chief. "We're not in the least anxious to have our fortunes told."

The chief thrust the thaler into his pocket. "I'll give these women what for..." And he raised his stick. He yelled at them, "Clear out!"

The five travellers were able to settle down on the grass in peace beside the various dishes the chief's wife lay before them.

"You're having a jolly time of it," said Gergely conversationally to the chief, while he took a deep draught from the water-jug. "Is there a festival today, or do the girls always dance like that?"

"It's Friday tomorrow," replied the chief, "and we'll make a little money at the Sweet Waters."

Gergely tried to turn everything he said to their advantage. "We've never been in Constantinople before," he said. "And now we're going there to join the army. What are the Sweet Waters?"

"It's an amusement-place at the end of the Golden Horn. On Fridays all the Turkish families go up there by boat. And a few piastres drop into the hands of gypsies there too. The girls dance. The old women tell fortunes. We've got some good ones..."

"And aren't you worried about your girls?"

"Why?"

"Well, you know, the things that may happen to them..."

The chief shrugged his shoulders. "What might happen to them?"

"Slavery..."

"Slavery? That would only be good for us. We too would make something out of it. Anyway, it's blonde women the Turks want, not gypsies. And on occasions like this our girls even get into the courtyards of the harems. The reason they're dancing in a group today is because tomorrow they'll plead their way into the serail.

Eva turned to Gergely. "What's the Turkish for 'water'?"

"*Su,* dearest."

Eva went into the tent and turned to the chieftain's daughter. "*Su, su,* dear."

232

The gypsy girl pulled aside the sheet at the back of the tent. There was a spacious, cool cavern there. From the rock water trickled down and dripped below. The drops of water had worn away a basin in the rock.

"You can have a bath if you want," indicated the gypsy girl with gestures. And she handed Eva a little cube of clay for soap. Eva looked at her. The gypsy girl returned her gaze through half-closed eyes. Her glance said, "My word, what a fine-looking boy you are!"

Eva smiled and stroked the girl's face. It was smooth and hot. The gypsy girl seized Eva's hand and kissed it. Then she ran out.

*

When they had gone a good way into the forest, Gergely spoke to the gypsy blacksmith.

"Sárközi, my friend, have you ever possessed ten thalers?"

The gypsy looked up in astonishment at being addressed in Hungarian.

"Oh, I've 'ad more than that. But only in me dreams, sir."

"Well then, in real life?"

"In real life I once 'ad two together. I kept one fer two years. I were goin' ter give it ter a little boy. But I bought an 'orse wi' 'it. The 'orse died. Now I've no 'orse, no money."

"Well, if you serve us faithfully, you'll earn ten thalers in a few days."

The gypsy's face shone.

Gergely went on: "Why did you come to Turkey?"

"They brought me. Them Turks. They kept sayin' that the army were the only place fer a strong chap like me."

"You were never a strong chap."

"Not as far as me size goes, kiss yer 'and. But I were great on the piccolo. Once I played the piccolo, then I were a tinker too, kiss yer 'and, and then them Turks kept layin' 'ands on me. They brought me 'ere an' put me to work in a workshop. But I escaped, I did."

"Have you got a wife?"

"Sometimes I 'ave, sometimes I 'aven't. Jes' now I don't really 'ave one."

"Well in that case, if you'd like to, you can come home with us."

233

"What's the point of goin' 'ome, sir? I'll never find me dear old master again. An' the Turks'll capture me agin at 'ome."

"What, have you been in service, then?"

"I 'ave indeed, sir, I served a very great man, the greatest 'Ungarian. 'E gave me roast every day, an' 'e talked to me like a friend. 'E'd say, 'Mend this rifle, Smokey!'"

"And who was this gentleman?"

"Oo else but Master Bálint."

"Bálint who?" asked Jancsi Török.

"Bálint who? Why, Master Bálint Török, of course, sir."

Gergely quickly got in his question before Jancsi.

"What do you know of him?"

And he beckoned to Jancsi to be wary.

The gypsy shrugged his shoulders. "I don't get no letters."

"But you must know something about him."

"Only that 'e's bin taken captive. I don't know if 'e's alive or dead. 'E must be dead, or I'd 'ave 'eard of 'im."

"Where were you in service with him?"

"At Szigetvár."

The two boys looked at each other. Neither of them remembered the gypsy. True, they had not spent much time in gnat-ridden Szigetvár; they had been here and there on Master Bálint's numerous estates, and could not possibly have known every one of his countless servants.

Gergely took a good look at the gypsy's face and then gave a smile. "Yes, I do remember you. Now I remember. Once upon a time you were Yumurdjak's captive, and Dobó released you from him."

The gypsy stared at Gergely. Then he shook his head. "It wasn't Dobó. It was a little seven-year-old boy. Believe it or not, it were a little seven-year-old boy. Or maybe not even that. It were a miracle. 'Is name were Gergely, that I do remember. Devla bless that boy, wherever 'e is! An' 'e put me in the way of an 'orse an' cart. It were for 'im that I were savin' up me thaler. But then I realized 'e were an angel."

"Suppose that angel were me?"

The gypsy blinked disbelievingly at Gergely. "I've never seen an angel wi' a moustache."

"It is me, all the same," smiled Gergely. "And I also remember that you got married that very day. Your wife's name was Böske. It took place in a forest, up above Pécs. And you were given some weapons from the booty."

The gypsy's eyes almost dropped out in his astonishment. "Oh may the Devla up there in paradise bless you, young sir! May 'e multiply all your darling children like the sand! Oh what a lucky day this is!" And he knelt down. He grasped Gergely's leg and kissed it.

"Well now I'm certain that we haven't come in vain," said Gergely happily.

"It's a good omen!" said Mekcsey too.

"Yes, there's a good angel with us," said Jancsi Török joyfully.

They lay in the grass. Gergely told the gypsy why they had come. He asked him how he thought they might reach Master Bálint.

The gypsy listened to Gergely now with shining eyes, now despairingly. He kissed Jancsi's hand. Then he nodded thoughtfully. "We can get into Stamboul. Maybe even into the Seven Towers. But they're not wooden swords that guard the master..." And rocking his head in his hands, he wailed. "Oh poor Master Bálint! In that place! Oh, if only I'd known, I'd 'ave shouted through the window too! I'd 'ave said 'Good day!' to 'im! And I'd 'ave the cards out to tell when the master'd be free!"

Gergely and his friends waited for the gypsy's imagination to run its course, then got him to think seriously.

"Well, there's no problem about getting into the city," said the gypsy. "And especially today. Because today's the Persian day of remembrance, and that brings as many pilgrims 'ere as the Feast of Our Lady at 'ome. But the Seven Towers... not even birds dare fly in there."

"Oh well, we'll have a look at those Seven Towers," said Jancsi enthusiastically. "Just let's get into the city first. Where birds can't fly, mice can creep!"

*

235

The Golden Horn is about as wide as the Danube. It is an inlet from the sea, and reaches up like a horn into the middle of Constantinople and beyond it to the woods.

A roomy fishing-boat took our travellers along its length. In the bows of the boat sat Gergely, whose clothes made him appear the most Turkish of them; in the middle was Mekcsey, who was red enough to be a Turk; the others huddled inside the boat.

In the glow of the setting sun the towers of the minarets reached into the sky like golden pillars, and the gilded domes of the churches simply shone. The sea reflected all this glory.

"It's a dream-world," marvelled Eva, sitting at Gergely's feet.

"It's more beautiful than a dream," replied Gergely. "But it's like a legendary castle, my dear. Outside it looks splendid, but inside it's full of dragons and the damned."

"It's a fairy city!" Mekcsey broke his silence.

Only Jancsi sat quiet and sad in the boat. He seemed almost glad to be able to see a black spot among all the splendour of the buildings.

"What forest is that on the hillside between the houses?" he asked the gypsy. "It looks to me as if there's nothing but poplars there. But how black they are! And they've grown so high."

"They're not poplars, young sir, but cypresses," replied the gypsy. "And it isn't a forest, but a cemetery. That's where the Turks from Pera are buried. If only all the lot of them were there!"

Jancsi closed his eyes. He was wondering whether his father too might not be lying there now under one of the cypresses.

Gergely glanced in that direction and then tried to turn Jancsi's thoughts elsewhere. "This city's like Buda on the bank of the Danube. Except that here there are two Budas, or rather three."

"I hadn't thought that it would be such a hilly city either," added Mekcsey. "I was afraid it would be as flat as Szeged or Debrecen."

"It was easy for them to build such a lovely city," said Eva. "It's a robbers' lair. They've stolen from every part of the world to create it. I wonder which house has our queen's furniture in it?"

"You mean King Matthias's, darling," replied Gergely.

For he had no love for Queen Isabella. And he was right too. The furniture that had been in the castle of Buda had not been brought there from Poland.

The sun had set by the time they got to the bridge. There was a crowd of people milling on it endlessly.

"There'll be a lot of people at the festival today," said the boatman.

"We've come to that too," replied Gergely.

At that Jancsi shuddered. His face drained of colour, he gazed at the teeming throng pushing its way over the bridge into Stamboul.

*

It was the crowd that helped them over the bridge too.

The sentries on guard there looked at nobody. The human tide bore them into the streets of Stamboul.

They themselves did not know where they were going. On its way upwards, the crowd made its way along three streets or so. Then it came to a halt, just like a river in spring when one ice-floe gets stuck and the ones behind it also get caught and build up there. Soldiers broke up the throng. They made way for the Persian pilgrims.

Gergely hugged Eva to him. The others were pressed against the wall of another building. They could only keep each other in sight.

All of a sudden there was light at the end of the street. It was as if the sun had been brought down from the sky and carried along as a lamp. A giant of a flaming, sparking torch appeared, a barrel-sized iron-ribbed basket. A strong Persian carried it on the end of a six-foot pole, and in it were flaming logs the size of human arms. They were presumably soaked in naphtha. In the bright light some ten dark men in mourning walked in stately procession. Their clipped, curled beards and small jaws proclaimed them to be Persians.

Behind them a child led a white horse. On the horse's back was a white sheet. On the sheet was a saddle. On the saddle lay two crossed swords and two white doves.

The two doves were tied by the leg to the saddle. And the horse, doves, sheet and saddle were all sprinkled with blood.

Following the horse came another band of mourners. They

sang a sorrowful litany, whose every line contained the two words *Hussein! Hassan!* and a shout of *Hoo!*, mingled with an odd drumming sound.

As the procession passed the reason for the drumming sound became clear. Two lines of bare-breasted Persians came next. They wore black shifts reaching their ankles. Their heads were surrounded with black kerchiefs, the corner of which dangled behind on their necks. Only their breasts were bare.

And as they moved on, stepping sideways, they waved their hands at the words *Hussein! Hassan!*, and at the shout of *Hoo!* they beat their breasts with their fists close to their heart.

The drumming sound was the beating of breasts. And the bluish-red bruises on their chests were proof that this was no token beating.

The breast-beating Persians may have numbered about three hundred. They stood sideways, and took two or three steps after each beating. Among them were triangular pennants in different colours. Most of them were green, but there were black, yellow and red ones too.

On the poles of the pennants and on the caps of the Persian children too there was a silver hand. This depicted the hand of the Turkish martyr Abbas. His hand was cut off because he offered a drink to Hussein after his capture at the Battle of Kerbela.

And the song grew louder and louder:

Has-san! Hus-sein! Has-san! Hoo!

The torches lit up a new black band surrounding a camel covered with a green rug. On its back was a little tent of leaves, and inside it was a small boy. Only his face was visible, and at times his hand, as through the opening in the tent he threw an occasional handful of something like sawdust over the men in mourning.

After them a curious rattling and clinking was heard from time to time.

The second band of mourners soon arrived. These too moved sideways and were likewise dressed in black shifts. But their shifts were open at the back. In their hands they held whips made of thick chains. They were so heavy that they took two hands to them. As the lines of the chant ended, they scourged themselves on the back, first over one shoulder, then over the other.

When Eva saw the blood and weals on the men's backs, she clung tight to Gergely's arm.

"I'm going to faint, Gergely."

"But there's something much more horrible to come," said Gergely. "One of the Turkish captives told me all about this remembrance festival. I thought it was a fairy-tale."

"They're surely not going to kill that boy, are they?"

"Of course they're not. Those two doves and the child are merely symbolic. At midnight they'll cut the cord on the doves' legs. They're the souls of Hassan and Hussein. A roar of devotion accompanies their flight to heaven."

"And what about the boy?"

"He symbolizes the fatherless Persian people."

"And what comes next?"

"Men with swords, who beat their heads."

And indeed a second bloodstained procession came next: men dressed from head to foot in white linen. All of them had shaven heads. In their right hands they carried a dagger. Each with his left hand clung to his neighbour's belt to prevent him from falling through loss of blood, or to hold his companion upright if he collapsed.

These men too stepped sideways, one or two of them falteringly. All had pale faces. Among them was a boy scarcely ten years old. The chant on their lips became a shriek.

"Hassan! Hussein!..."

At the end of the line each dagger flashed in the torchlight and every one struck his own bare head.

These men were steeped in blood. Some of them had streams of blood trickling down their noses and ears, and their white linen robes were stained red with it. The torches crackled as they burnt in the breeze, and at times sparks fell like rain on the bloodstained heads.

"Hassan! Hussein!"

And the miasma of blood hung heavy in the air.

Eva closed her eyes. "I'm revolted by it."

"I told you, didn't I, to stay at home? A trip like this isn't for womenfolk. Shut your eyes, my lamb."

Eva gave her head a shake and opened her eyes wide. "Just for that I *will* watch them!" And pale but determined, she went on watching the blood-soaked procession.

Gergely was calmer. Even as a child he had become used to the sight of blood. It did not give him much pain. It was more surprising, he thought, that these men voluntarily poured out their blood. And these were the kind of people that the Hungarians had been fighting almost without a break for several decades.

He glanced over the bloodstained throng to the other side of the road.

How strange it is that we feel when someone is staring hard at us!

Gergely looked almost directly over the teeming multitude. The eyes of two men were fixed on him. One had the face of an Armenian. That was the aga from Adrianople, whose soldiers he had blown into the air.

The other was Yumurdjak.

8

One morning during the summer of the previous year Maylád waited for Bálint Török to come out of his door.

"There's great news! Last night some new prisoners arrived."

"Hungarians?" asked Master Bálint eagerly.

"I don't know yet. All I heard was the sound of their chains clanking across the yard this morning when the gates were opened. I know the sound of all the prisoners' chains. Even when I'm lying in bed, I always know who's going past my door."

"So do I."

"This morning I heard a new chain rattling. But it wasn't just one man. There were two, three, possibly four of them. They

240

clanked their way right across the yard. Surely they weren't taken to the *Tas-chukuru?*"

The *Tas-chukuru* is a cavern-like prison in the Seven Towers. It is the condemned cell at the foot of the Tower of Blood. Anyone who is put there soon gets to know the higher secrets of the starry sky.

They strolled down to the garden where they usually sat. But that day they did not examine the growth of the bushes or the clouds on their way towards Hungary. They waited impatiently to see the new prisoners.

There were no chains on their legs now. All the golden treasure that Mrs. Török had sent to the sultan and the pashas had not opened the gates, but it had at least unlocked their chains. In any case, the two men were elderly now, and the castle was guarded by two hundred and fifty soldiers and their families. Nobody had ever yet escaped from it.

The inner guard was changed. A fat-bellied young bey appeared in the yard to give orders to the men who were going off duty.

"Three of you go to the mill," he panted like a fat duck. "Three of you to the mill to hew stones."

He named the three. Then he turned to two short men.

"Come back here in an hour's time. You'll clean out the armoury. And you..."

Bálint Török could hardly wait for the bey to finish. He walked over to meet him. "Good morning, Veli Bey! How did you sleep?"

"Thank you. I slept badly. They got me out of bed early this morning. Three new prisoners arrived from Hungary."

"They surely haven't brought the *Friar* here?"

"No, not the Friar. He's a decidedly aggressive gentleman. But perhaps he isn't a gentleman at all, but a beggar. He hasn't even got a decent shirt. They say he lay in wait for the Pasha of Buda and robbed him."

"The Pasha of Buda?"

"Yes. And they brought in his two sons as well."

"What's his name?"

"I did write it down, but I don't know now. You've all got such peculiar names. Who on earth can remember them?" And

241

then he merely nodded, turned round and walked back, maybe to his bed.

Master Bálint went and sat down again by Maylád in some confusion. "He beat up the Pasha of Buda? Who can that be?" "A beggar?" mused Maylád. "If he were a beggar, they wouldn't bring him here."

"Well, whoever he is, the first thing I'll do is give him some clothes."

They pondered and racked their brains all morning. They listed perhaps a thousand names from Hungary and Transylvania, but none of them seemed at all likely to have treated the Pasha of Buda like that. After all, the pasha travels with a large retinue.

"Who can it be?"

At noon the new prisoner at last made an appearance at the communal table which was laid on the shady side of the inner courtyard.

Both of them looked at him so hard that their eyes almost started out of their heads. They did not recognize him. They noted that he is a short but strong dark man with greying hair, and bald too on top of his head. He was dressed in Hungarian canvas clothes which were in tatters. Beside him were two better-dressed Hungarian youths, twenty to twenty-five years old. Their features revealed that they were brothers and that they were the old man's sons, though they were a head taller than he was.

The old man's legs wore that very same light steel chain that Bálint Török had borne for some two years. It was bright with wear and shone like silver.

Maylád hurried to greet the captive. He did not know who he was, but merely saw that he was Hungarian. Bálint also stood by the table, deeply moved, and stared hard at the old man. Maylád was unable to utter a word. He just embraced the old man. Bálint, however, simply stood there and quivering with excitement called "Who are you?"

The old man bowed his head and muttered almost inaudibly, "László Móré."

Bálint looked as if he had been struck. He turned away. He sat down.

242

Maylád's hand also fell away from the old man. The two young men stood gloomily behind their father.

"This is where you'll eat, gentlemen," said Veli Bey, pointing to the corner of the table opposite where Bálint Török was sitting.

Bálint Török got up. "Well if they're going to eat here, I'm certainly not going to!" And he turned to the servant standing behind him: "Bring my plate up to my room."

Maylád hovered undecided for a moment, then he too spoke to his own servant: "Bring my plate up too." And he set off after Master Bálint.

Veli Bey shrugged his shoulders. But all the same he could not pass this over in silence. He looked at Móré. "Why do those two hate you?"

Móré gave a black glance at the two gentlemen. "Because they're Hungarians."

"Aren't you Hungarian too?"

Móré gave a shrug. "That's the reason why. Two Hungarians can get on all right, but three snipe at each other..."

✳

Bálint Török did not stir from his room for a fortnight. He did not go down to the courtyard. Nor did Maylád. He listened to Master Bálint discoursing on the new faith that the famous John Calvin and Martin Luther were disseminating.

"The faith of Jesus is more genuine than the Latinized Roman one that's proliferated like weeds," Bálint Török would say. In the end Maylád also became converted to that faith. He wrote this in a letter to his son Gábor, encouraging him to think about it too at home.

But they began to get very tired of the four walls of the room. One day Master Bálint said, "We might go down to the garden."

"That brigand's there."

"But suppose he isn't?"

"Suppose he is?"

"Well, if he is, he is. We won't speak to him. But we've just as much right to walk in it as he has."

Maylád smiled. "*Right?* So after all we do have some sort of *right.*"

Bálint's face brightened up for an instant. "Of course we have, for heaven's sake. How long have we been captives? He's only been here a fortnight, after all."

And they went down into the garden.

A Persian prince was sitting there under the plane-tree; like them, he had been a prisoner for a long time. And there was another Asiatic prince there who was almost mouldering with grief and boredom. They were playing chess. They had played chess from morning till night for years, and they never said a word to each other.

To Bálint and his companion the two chess-players were like the marble gate shining white between the Tower of Blood and the Tower of Gold, or that gigantic old Kurdish dignitary who was then wearing the heaviest chains for having cursed the Emperor, and drooping under the weight of iron sat or lay till dusk in the iron-barred prison of the Tower of Blood. Only his eyes moved as he followed the prisoners walking among the bushes.

But they would have had no eyes for the chess-players, except that there was a new figure sitting behind them watching the players, and this struck them.

"Who can that little old Turk in the yellow kaftan be? And why is he bare-headed?" They had never yet seen a Turk without a turban, unless he happened to be washing or shaving.

The man in the yellow kaftan turned as he heard them approach. It was Móré.

He got up and left the chess-players. The weary look that on the first day had made him look ill had disappeared from his face. His tiny black eyes were full of life as they blinked, and his gait was firm, almost youthful.

He went up to the two magnates and folded his arms.

"Why do you hate me?" he burst out, his eyes flashing. "What makes you any better than I am? Are you richer? Here nobody's rich. Are you more noble? My nobility's as old as anyone else's."

"You were a robber!" Bálint Török growled at him.

"Well, weren't you robbers too? Didn't you acquire a fortune wherever your hand reached? Didn't you fight each other too? Didn't you turn like a weathercock now towards John, now towards Ferdinand? You piped the tune of whichever would pay you more."

Maylád grasped Bálint's arm. "Let's get out of here and leave this man to himself!"

"Certainly not!" replied Bálint Török. "I'm not retreating from either dog or man."

And he sat down on the bench. He forced himself to contain his anger, because he saw Veli Bey approaching from the gateway. He was coming with a Turkish priest and the two Móré lads. The two were likewise dressed in Turkish garb, but they had no turban on their heads yet. They went about, like their father, bareheaded.

Maylád also sat down beside Bálint Török.

Móré stood in front of them with legs apart and one hand on his thigh. He went on with the quarrel. "I was in the war when we beat György Dózsa. I was at the Battle of Mohács where the blood of twenty-four thousand Hungarians was spilt for the homeland."

"I was there too," snorted Maylád, "but not simply so that I should have something to boast about."

"Well if you were at that baptism of blood, you must know that those who escaped from there respect each other like brothers."

"But I'm not going to be regarded as a brother by a common highway bandit like you!" thundered Maylád, growing red in the face. "I know very well why the castle at Palota was razed to the ground."

"Maybe you do. But you don't know why they did the same to Nána. You don't know that the whole Hungarian nation bows and scrapes before the feet of the Pasha of Buda, and I, László Móré, I was the only one who shouted at him, 'I'm not taking orders from you with the top-knot!'. For years I fought the Turks with my own little band. It wasn't Ferdinand who fought, or the noble Hungarian nation, but me, László Móré. It was I who scattered his army last year on its way to Belgrade, I, László Móré, whom you call a robber and highwayman."

He panted. Then, waving his fists, he went on: "Suppose I'd had as much money as István Maylád once had! Suppose I'd had as many possessions, castles and servants as Bálint Török! Suppose I'd had as many soldiers as the one who's now wearing the crown merely as an ornament! In that case they would be extolling the name of László Móré today as the liberator of the nation. But since I hadn't sufficient money or troops, the Turks surrounded me in Nána and razed my castle to the ground, curse them!"

Veli Bey reached them with the imam. "I don't know what you're arguing about, but the words of Selim are the truth. For he lives closer to the truth than you infidels do."

"Selim? Who's Selim?" said Bálint Török, astounded.

"Selim," replied Veli Bey, "is the one who a few days ago was called László Móré in the language of the infidels."

Bálint Török leant back and gave a bitter laugh. "Selim! And he's the one who's preaching to us about patriotism! Off with you, pagan, the shame of your father!"

He would certainly have struck him had not Veli Bey stepped between them.

"Pig of an infidel!" roared the bey at Master Bálint. "I'll have you clapped in chains this instant!"

Master Bálint jerked up his head like a steed struck on the nose. His eyes flamed. God knows what might have happened if Maylád had not dragged him away.

The bey gazed contemptuously after them. Presumably he had one eye on his pocket at that moment, and that stopped him from any further offensive remarks. He turned to Móré and spoke to him loudly enough for them to hear too: "His Majesty the Sultan is delighted to learn that you are entering the army of the true believers. He has sent this worthy imam to instruct you in knowledge of the prophet, blessed be his name for ever."

"Let's go back to our room," snorted Bálint Török. "Let's go back, Maylád, old friend."

*

A few days later the two Móré boys were set free. Both of them were given some official post in Constantinople.

Only old Móré remained inside the walls.

Bálint and Maylád exchanged no further words with him, but they often heard him demanding to be set free too.

On one occasion Veli Bey replied to him thus: "I've been once more to the Sublime Porte about your case. The letter has at last arrived from Hungary. The Pasha of Buda's painted you pretty

246

black, I can tell you. Among other things he writes that when they were besieging Nána you scattered money among the Turks behind you to be able to save your own skin!"

And he wagged his head and laughed: "You're a cunning old fox, aren't you."

*

By this time the Turks had occupied Székesfehervar and Esztergom too. The sultan himself led the army to destroy those two fortresses in Transdanubia. It was winter by the time he returned.

Week by week the prisoners in the Seven Towers were kept abreast of the campaign and of his return. They waited for the new prisoners; may God not hold it against them as a sin, but they were even glad to think that new acquaintances, perhaps even good friends, might turn up in the seven-towered prison. How much news they would hear! Perhaps they might hear about their families too.

One morning they happened to be discussing this very thing when their door opened and Veli Bey stepped in. His face was red from his haste to get there. He placed both his hands on his breast and bowed to Master Bálint with a deep and humble bow.

"The gracious padishah summons you, sir. Be so good as to dress immediately. Then we shall be off."

Master Bálint gave a shudder. His glance seemed to stiffen.

"You're free!" stuttered Maylád.

And they grabbed his clothes out of the cupboard. Veli Bey himself dashed off to dress too.

"Remember me!" pleaded Maylád. "Mention me to him, Bálint. After all, you're going to see him face to face. You'll have a talk. You can mention me. You can ask him to set me free as well. Oh God! Oh God! Please don't forget to mention my name, Bálint!"

"I won't forget," stammered Bálint.

And with trembling hand he buttoned up the light blue flowered satin garb in which he had been taken prisoner. His fine winter clothes had worn out by now. He had not worn that blue satin. He had kept it in reserve. He hoped to go home in it some time.

But he could not wear a sword.

"You'll have it for your return," said Maylád encouragingly. And he accompanied him downstairs. "Please don't forget me."

He watched delightedly as he sat in the coach with Veli Bey, and both of them were wrapped in ample Turkish fur-lined coats. How attentively the bey adjusted the coat so that Bálint's feet should not feel the cold, and how humbly he sat beside him, on the left of Master Bálint!

"The angels in heaven are your outriders, Bálint!"

The coach started off. Two guardsmen with pikes rode behind it.

"Oh God! Oh God!" prayed Master Bálint on the way. It seemed like a hundred years before at last they turned in at the gateway of the serail.

They crossed the janissaries' court on foot and went into the palace.

Many stairs, all of white marble; many stalwart bodyguards, all of them slaves; impressive marble columns, soft carpets, gilding, all the splendours of oriental filigree-work everywhere. But Bálint Török saw nothing but the middle of the back of the white-kaftaned servant hurrying ahead of him and the occasional door covered with a thick silk curtain which, he kept thinking, must be the sultan's door.

He was taken into a small room. There was nothing in it except a carpet with a cushion on it. Beside the cushion was a large copper basin like the copper font in the church at Buda, except that it was not supported by a stone pedestal but by a cube of marble, and it contained not water but a glowing fire.

Bálint Török recognized this piece of furniture; it was called a *mangal,* the brazier which acts as a stove in winter in Turkish lands.

There was nobody in the room but three Saracen guards, one at each of the three doors. They stood stock-still with their huge gleaming halberds. Veli Bey also stood there trembling and silent beside the door.

Bálint looked at the window. He had a view below of the green sea as it rose and fell, and over the sea to Scutari; it was like looking from the palace of Buda across to the town of Pest.

He stood there for perhaps five minutes until a Saracen hand pulled aside the curtain of the door at last. Next moment the sultan stepped inside.

There was no retinue either in front or behind him, just a thin sixteen-year-old Saracen boy who stopped beside the guard at the door.

The bey prostrated himself on the carpet. Bálint came to attention and bowed. When he raised his head, the sultan was standing by the *mangal,* holding his two thin hands over it. He was wearing a nut-brown kaftan edged with ermine. It was so long that only the two red toes of his slippers peeped out below it. On his head he wore a light cambric turban. His face was shaven. His thin white moustache drooped even below his chin. For a moment they just stood there in silence. Then the sultan looked at the bey.

"Out!"

The bey got up, bowed and walked backwards to the door. There he bowed once more and disappeared into thin air.

"It's a long time since I've seen you," the sultan began calmly. "You haven't changed a bit. Except that you've turned white."

Bálint thought, "And you haven't grown any younger either, Suleyman." For since he had last seen him the sultan had grown very thin and his great sheeps' eyes were encircled with wrinkles. His nose seemed to have grown longer too. And his face was hideously coloured with rouge.

But Bálint kept silent. He merely waited, waited with an anxious heart to see what would happen next.

The sultan folded his arms. "You may know that Hungary has ceased to exist."

Bálint's colourless face turned even more pale. If the country no longer existed, what could the sultan want of him?

"Those few pockets of resistance that remain," continued the sultan, "are just a matter of time. They too will submit this year." (Master Bálint took a deep breath.) "So I have to find a good pasha for Buda. A pasha who's no stranger to the Hungarians or to me either. You're an outstanding man. I'll return your estates to you. All of your estates."

Bálint just stares. His lips move. But since he does not say anything yet, the sultan continues: "Do you understand what I'm saying? You know Turkish, after all."

"*Evet efendim*," nods Bálint.

"Well, I'm making you the pasha of Buda."

Bálint's shoulders gave a sudden quiver. But his face remained serious and sad. His glance slipped from the sultan to the mangal through whose arabesques the embers were glowing. The sultan was silent for a moment. Perhaps he expected Bálint to fall at his feet, Turkish fashion; or perhaps to kiss his hand like a Hungarian, or at the very least to mutter some words of thanks. But Bálint just stood there. And as if he were not in the presence of a sultan, he too folded his arms.

The sultan's face darkened. He walked up and down the room twice. Then he came to a halt again and looked at Bálint. "Maybe you don't like the proposal?"

Bálint roused himself. For where had his spirit been during those few minutes' silence? It had winged its way to all his fortresses, fields, forests and meadows, it had embraced his wife, kissed his children, delighted in his horses, sheep and cattle and his thousands of servants; it had sat on his favourite steed and breathed the Hungarian air in the Hungarian lands...

He came round at those words like a man waking from sleep.

"Gracious emperor," he said with deep emotion, "if I understand you correctly, you are ordering me to take Werbőczy's place."

The sultan shook his head. "No. Werbőczy's dead. He died in the same year that you came here. We shall not fill his post again. I want you to be a regular pasha. I am giving you the largest pasha's domain in my lands, and the most complete freedom."

Master Bálint merely looked at the sultan in astonishment. "But how can that be, Your Majesty?" he said at last. "A Hungarian pasha..."

"No, a Turkish pasha."

"A Turkish pasha?"

"Yes. I said that Hungary no longer exists. So it follows that there are no more Hungarians either. I thought you had understood what I was saying."

"That I'm to become a Turk?"

"A pasha."

Bálint Török's head fell. He sighed as if his soul had been torn

250

from him. Then he looked the sultan in the face and spoke in a deep, sorrowful voice. "There's no other way?"

"No."

Bálint Török closed his eyes. His breast heaved with the efforts of his panting heart.

"Your Majesty," he said at last. "I know that you are not used to hearing men speak frankly, but that is how I have grown up, and even in my old age I can only say what I think."

"Well then, what do you think?" said the sultan icily.

Master Bálint answered in calm and measured tones. "I think, Your Majesty, that even if the whole of Hungary belongs to you and every Hungarian became a Turk, I shall not... No, I shall not!"

9

Veli Bey was horrified when on the way back he learnt about the secret conversation.

"What a foolish type you are!" he mused, shaking his head. "I'll wager my neck that tonight you'll be sleeping in the Tower of Blood."

And all night he wandered round in the yard waiting for the sultan's decree.

But neither that night nor during the following days did the decree arrive. Neither letter, nor message came; there was just nothing.

A week later the aged Sheikh-ul-Islam, the chief religious leader of the Turks, deigned to visit the Yedikule. And he came alone and unattended like any ordinary priest. This caused Veli Bey almost to collapse on the ground from sheer astonishment.

"You've got some important infidel here," said the mufti. "He's called Bálint Török."

"*Evet,*" replied the bey with a bow.

"The Padishah (May Allah grant him long life!) cherishes the thought that this Hungarian can become the governor of our province of Hungary, but the faithless cur does not want to convert to Islam."

"He's a dog."

"I asked him (May Allah grant him long life!) to let me see the prisoner. Maybe I can do something with him. You know, my son, that I am old and experienced."

"You are the wisest of the wise, sheikh, the Solomon of our age."

"I also think that every knot has a thread that can untie it. All it needs is patience and wisdom. Maybe he will be moved by the fact that I myself am bringing him enlightenment from the Prophet. First he will at least pay attention to me, and then he will hardly realize that the first tiny seed of the true faith is dropping into his heart."

"He's quite an intelligent man."

"And then you'll see, my son; if we convert this wicked infidel, we shall bring joy to the Padishah."

And together they repeated, "May Allah grant him long life!"

*

At the eighth hour of the day, which according to our way of calculating the time is two o'clock in the afternoon, Master Bálint was asleep in his room, when the door suddenly opened and the bey ushered in the Grand Mufti.

Master Bálint raised himself up on his elbow on the divan and rubbed his eyes in puzzlement.

He just looked at the biblical figure with the great beard whom he had never seen before, but whose priestly function he recognized from the black kaftan and white turban.

"Wake up, Master Bálint," the bey commanded him. "You have been granted a great honour. The Sheikh-ul-Islam in person has come to instruct you. Listen carefully to him."

And he pulled the rug behind the bed from off the wall and laid it in the middle of the room. Then he took off his own kaftan, to spread it over the rug, but the old man would not allow this. He sat down and crossed his legs. His beard reached his lap. His intelligent old eyes examined Master Bálint from head to foot. Then he turned the pages of the Koran, a pocket-sized thick little book bound in parchment.

"What do you want?" growled Master Bálint. "I've already told the emperor that I'm not turning into a Turk."

The bey made no reply. He looked at the Grand Mufti.

Instead of answering, the Grand Mufti raised the book to his heart, his forehead and his lips. Then he spoke: "In the name of Allah, the merciful and compassionate. Abdul Kazem Mohamed, the son of Abdullah, the son of Abd el Motalleb, the son of Hazem, the son of Abd Menaf, the son of Kasi, the son of Kaleb, the son of Morra, the son of Lova, the son of Galeb..."

Master Bálint just stared. He put on his jacket. He sat on the chair opposite the old man. He wondered where all this was leading.

The old man went on undisturbed: "The son of Fer, the son of Malck, the son of Madar, the son of Kenana, the son of Kazima..."

Master Bálint yawned.

The old man went on: "The son of Modreka, the son of Elias, the son of Modar, the son of Nazar, the son of Moad..." And he listed a sea of names before he got back to Mohamed and his birth.

By now the bey had left the room. He slipped out silently to resume his duties. In the corridor he came across Maylád who had also just got up from sleeping. He was strolling over to Master Bálint to wake him up.

The bey blocked his way. "Don't disturb him," he said, raising a finger. "There's a priest with him. He's teaching him the true faith."

"The Turkish faith?"

"Yes." And the bey leapt down the stairs in his hurry.

Maylád watched him go, stupefied.

10

Even before the Persian memorial procession had passed by, Gergely seized Eva's hand and set off. He wormed his way through the crowd. On the way he spoke to the gypsy and to Mekcsey.

"Come along! We've got trouble!"

After that it was Mekcsey who took the lead. With his broad shoulders he forced a passage through the dense crowd.

Yumurdjak and the aga were hemmed in on the far side; they could not make their way through the holy procession. Nor would the soldiers on duty have allowed this. And all those daggers that flashed in a religious frenzy would have been turned on them.

The Sunni Moslems and the Shiites detest each other. The Shiites maintain that the modern priests of Mohamed debase their functions, while the Turks think that the Persian people are heretics.

At last, after much pushing and shoving, they emerged from the crowd and came together in a narrow, dark side street. Only then could Gergely speak. "We've got to run! I caught sight of Yumurdjak and the aga too! They've brought soldiers with them!"

And they made off in the darkness. They ran. First the gypsy, though he did not know why they were running away and from whom. He went head over heels into a pack of sleeping dogs. One of the dogs gave a shriek and the others scattered in terror.

For Constantinople is a paradise for dogs. There are no courtyards here, or if there is anything like that, it is on the roof of the house, so there is no room anywhere for dogs. Those red-haired, fox-like creatures swarm in hundreds through the streets in some parts. The Turks do not disturb them; indeed, when one or other of them has a litter of puppies, they throw down rags or a bit of rush-matting by the gate to help them. Those dogs keep Constantinople clean and tidy. Each morning the Turks empty the square tin dustbins beside their gate. The dogs eat the contents. They devour everything except iron and glass. And the dogs are not ugly or wild either. You can pat any of them, and they will wag their tail with delight. There is not one of them that is not glad to be stroked.

When the gypsy fell down, the whole company came to a halt. They were panting. Gergely laughed. "Devil take you, Sárközi! Whatever makes you run so madly?"

"If someone's chasing me," gasped the gypsy, stumbling to his feet.

"Nobody's chasing you here now. Let's listen."

The street was quiet. Only the sound of the Persians chanting could still be heard in the distance. They listened hard.

254

"I'm not running any more," said Mekcsey with annoyance. "If anyone attacks me, I'll stab him with my dagger."

But no one appeared.

"They've lost track of us," Gergely gave his opinion. "Well, Sárközi my friend, where shall we sleep?"

The gypsy looked up into the sky. "The moon'll soon be up. I've got a mate 'ere. We can sleep there. But it's a long way off, by the Yedikule."

Jancsi suddenly came to life. "Are we going past the Yedikule?"

"Yes," replied the gypsy. "The inn's only a stone's throw away from it."

"And you say the moon's coming up?"

"Yes. Can't you see it getting light there, young sir, at the bottom of the sky? We've got to get a move on. The innkeeper's a Greek. 'E's our receiver. And for good money 'e'll sell clothes too."

"Couldn't we just take a look at the Yedikule?" asked Jancsi, his voice trembling. "Maybe..."

"Tonight?"

"Yes, tonight."

"We could, if it's so urgent," shrugged the gypsy. "But they mustn't catch us."

And he led the way. He stepped cautiously over the sleeping dogs and when the moon came out he always kept to the shady side of the road.

Sleeping houses and sleeping streets. Only the dogs barked from time to time. Nowhere a human soul.

The moon cast its light on small wooden houses. They were all alike, two-storeyed, each with two windows with grilles on the upper floor, but the grilles were of wood. They were the windows of the harem. Occasionally there was a stone house to break the endless line of wooden ones.

The gypsy stopped at one of the houses and signalled to them to keep quiet. Inside a child was crying and a man's voice could be heard. Then an angry woman's voice. Of course there was no glass anywhere in the windows. And the woman could be heard shouting, *Sesini kes! Hunyadi geliyor!'* (Keep quiet! Hunyadi's coming!)

255

The child stopped crying. Our travellers hurried on their way. It was not yet midnight when the moonlit, star-studded sea suddenly glistened in front of them at a turn in the road.

The gypsy listened again.

"We'll 'ave to go by boat," he said softly, "if we can find one at all, and go round the Yedikule. The inn's on the other side of it."

"Why, do the Turks drink here too?" smiled Gergely.

"Yes, the Turks drink too in that inn," replied the gypsy with a wave of the hand. "There's an inside room, where only Turks drink."

He walked along the sandy beach with a searching glance until he found a boat beside a stake. The boat had been drawn up out of the water on to the sand, or possibly the tide had left it there as it went out.

At that moment a little female form in a brown dress flitted like a bat out of the street. She made directly for the gypsy on the beach.

The gypsy looked at her in astonishment. "Is that you, Cherhan?"

It was the gypsy chief's daughter.

"Where are the *deli*s?" she asked anxiously.

The gypsy pointed to the shadow of the row of houses, where Gergely and his friends were standing listening.

The girl ran across to them. She grasped Eva's arm. "You're in danger! There's a crow-faced aga on your track with twenty spahis!"

Eva looked at Gergely. She did not understand what the girl was talking about.

"The aga came to our camp," went on the girl, "almost as soon as you'd gone. They searched and ransacked our tents. They beat my father with a sword to make him tell them where you were. They even searched the cave too."

"And did you lead them on our trail?"

"No, of course not! For two reasons. One I'll not tell you", —and here she glanced at Eva. "The other is that Sárközi came with you, and they might have killed him too."

"You're frank," smiled Gergely, "so I'll tell you that we've already come across them."

256

"But they're coming! They're on your track! Come along, quickly! Run!"

Sárközi had untied the boat. "Get in, quickly!"

"The moon's lighting up the sea," said the girl anxiously.

"Never mind," said Gergely. "There aren't any more boats here. Even if they see us, it'll take them some time to get hold of a boat." And he made for the boat.

"Come on!"

The moon illuminated the sea and the high bastion-wall in the middle of which the four towers overlooking the sea loomed like four giants in tall caps in the brightness of the night.

As they got to the boat, the sound of running feet and weapons rattling came from the street.

"Here they come!" said the girl, alarmed.

No frog ever leapt more swiftly into the water than our travellers into the boat.

"The boat's too small!" said Gergely anxiously. But his words were lost in the yells that came from the beach.

Mekcsey seized the two oars from the gypsy and with a single snap broke the straps from them. "Sit down!"

"Push out the boat!", shouted Gergely.

Mekcsey, however, just stood there with legs wide apart, and waited for the Turk who was dashing towards them a hundred paces or so ahead of his companions.

"Come on, dervish!" he shouted angrily, "come on!"

Yumurdjak pulled up suddenly. Only the dagger hung gleaming from his hand.

"Come on, then!" Mekcsey encouraged him.

And instead of pushing out the boat, he jumped out of it and lunged at Yumurdjak with the oar.

The dervish turned round and ran away.

"Oh, come on!" Jancsi Török called impatiently. "They'll be attacking us any minute now!"

Mekcsey strolled calmly back to the boat and with a single push shoved it away from the beach."

But by now the pursuers had arrived, and their angry shouts accompanied the rocking boat on its way.

But the load was certainly heavy. The sides of the boat were hardly a hand's breadth above the water. They had to sit motionless to prevent the boat from rocking.

The *spahi*s rushed up and down the beach trying to find a boat.

Mekcsey turned to the gypsy. "Which way?"

The gypsy was crouching at the far end of the boat, his teeth chattering so much that he could hardly reply.

"Gu-gu-gu-go round the castle, s-s-s-sir."

"What is there on the other side of it?"

"N-n-n-nothing, sir."

"Woods, fields?"

"G-g-g-gardens an' p-p-p-places with shrubs."

Gergely dipped the two blades deeply into the water with all his strength. The gypsy girl suddenly groaned. "They've found a boat!"

And indeed there was a boat setting out from the shore. There were six men in it, but they too had only a single pair of oars.

The other Turks must have run in all directions to get hold of another boat.

"Let's change places," said Mekcsey to Gergely. "I'm stronger than you are. How many are we?"

"Eight," answered the gypsy.

"Only six, because you and the girl aren't fighters."

They rowed on eastwards in silence. The Turkish boat followed them.

"If there aren't any more coming," said Mekcsey, "I'll get to work on them with the oars, and you can fight as best you can."

"We can hardly fight here," said Gergely. "If they catch up with us, both boats will founder. I suggest you row towards Scutari."

"Well, who is there who can't swim?"

"I can't, sir," said the gypsy, trembling.

"In that case hold on to the front of the boat if it should capsize."

"It won't be like that, Pista," said Gergely, shaking his head. "Just make for the opposite shore, so that where the water's only waist-high we can put our feet on the bottom. Use the oar to measure the depth."

"Then what?"

258

"I've got two pounds of gunpowder tied up here. I'll moisten it and set fire to it. As soon as they catch up with us, I'll throw it into the middle of them. At that instant, you jump out of the boat. I'll follow you, then Jancsi and then Matyi. The Turks will be in confusion. We can deal with them one by one."

And he handed the tinder and steel to the gypsy. "Strike a light, Sárközi!"

Without a word Mekcsey made for the Asian shore. But they were still a long way from it: they had to row on for another hour. They sat silently in the boat. Mekcsey and Matyi took it in turns to row. From time to time Mekcsey probed the depth of the water with his blade, even up to his elbow. But as yet he could not touch the bottom.

Meanwhile the Turks chased them with screams and shouts.

"*Perzevenk dinini sikeim!*" roared one, as if he had the barrel of a cannon for a throat.

"*Perzevenk batakdji*" yelled another voice, not so strong, but all the more furious.

Once Jancsi shouted back, "*Perzevenk kenef oglu! Hersiz aga! Batakdji aga!*" And they had a good laugh at that.

Gergely stretched down into the sea and on Sárközi's back kneaded the gunpowder into a black paste about an inch thick.

"Now, Eva, put a little dry powder in the middle of it."

Eva twisted the stopper of the powder-horn and poured dry gunpowder into the middle of the cake.

Gergely folded it over and rolled it into a ball. He wrapped it in his handkerchief. He left just one hole to enable him to set fire to the powder.

"Land!" said Mekcsey suddenly. Yet they were hardly beyond the middle of the strait.

The lad had done well. The distance separating them from the Turks when they set out had hardly diminished. And the Turks' boat must have been about as far away as a strong-armed man could skim a flat stone on the water.

"Is the tinder alight, Sárközi?"

"Yes."

"Keep it going. And you, Mekcsey, row more slowly now. Turn the boat sideways on. But watch out that they don't hit us. Rather let them rush past us, if they come with any speed."

259

"I'll turn in due course, don't you worry."

"When there's only about ten paces between us, the gypsy must slip into the water from the prow of the boat. The gypsy girl too. And maybe you too, Eva, but only at the moment when I've thrown the fireball at them. They mustn't suspect that the water here's only waist-deep. Let them swim!"

He gave another twist to the handkerchief and pulled the knot tight with his teeth. Then he went on: "If the flames throw them out of the boat, you stay here in this boat, Mekcsey, with the oar. Jancsi and I will jump into the water and pick off those who are swimming. If they're in total confusion, then you, Matyi, try to grab hold of their boat and strike any one of them who tries to hold on to it."

"What about me?" asked the gypsy.

"You three hold our boat so that Mekcsey doesn't fall out."

And he bent down to Eva's ear and whispered, "You get into the water on the far side of the boat and put your head down in case the gunpowder strikes your face. After that, pick up the second oar and hit any Turk who comes near you. After all, an oar's longer than a sword."

The Turks saw that the distance between the two boats was shrinking. Their yells of triumph proclaimed that they felt sure of victory.

When they were only about thirty paces apart, Mekcsey probed with his oar. "The water's waist-high."

"In that case, let's stop," said Gergely. And he rose from the bench. "Give me the tinder, Sárközi." And he shouted across to the Turks, "What do you want?"

"You'll know soon enough!" they replied with a guffaw.

Gergely gave the tinder and the handkerchief to Eva, and took up the seat from the boat.

The Turks had swords in their hands and daggers between their teeth. They kept silent. Their oarsman rowed with great splashes.

They were nearly there now. Gergely hurled the seat in front of their boat. It made a big splash. The Turk who was rowing suddenly stopped when he felt water splashing on his neck and looked round to see what it was.

The boat continued under its own momentum.

When there were scarcely fifteen feet between them, Gergely thrust the tinder into the gunpowder. It began to splutter with a red glow. Gergely wasted no time before hurling it into the Turkish boat with a well-directed lob.

The Turks started apart as the fiery monster flew across. The next moment the boat seemed to have turned into a fountain of fire, and then an eighteen-foot tongue of flame shot up among them with a huge explosion.

The Turkish boat capsized. The six Turks plunged into the sea in six different places.

"After them!" shouted Gergely, who was already in the water.

But their eyes were blinded by the brilliant light that had now gone out. None of them could see a thing. It took some time for Gergely to catch sight of the first Turk. He fell into their boat. The great shock of his fall caused Mekcsey to tip out.

Gergely struck him with his sword and felt that he had hit something hard. "Hit them!" he shouted. But his companions were half-blinded too.

By the time they had regained their sight, they saw Mekcsey struggling in the water with a broad-shouldered Turk. Gergely made his way over there and hit him hard on the head. But he had a hard skull. He turned round and struck Gergely so hard on the shoulder that he almost fell. But then Mekcsey caught hold of the Turk. He grasped him by the neck from behind and forced him down into the water.

He held him there until only bubbles rose from him.

11

One afternoon in May three Italian youths in yellow velvet and two Italian girls in short skirts appeared at the gate of the Seven Towers. One of the youths had a lyre; so did one of the girls. The other girl carried a tambourine under her arm.

The guard was standing in the shade of the gate, snatching forty winks as he stood and only opening his eyes when boots clumped past him. All the same, he did catch sight of the strangers, and thrust his lance towards them.

"Halt!"

261

"We're Italian singers. We're going to see the commandant of the castle."

"That's impossible."

"But we must."

"It's impossible!"

"Why?"

"He's moving."

About half a dozen soldiers were standing or squatting in the shadow of the wall. An old gypsy woman was telling their fortunes with coloured beans shaken on a sieve.

One of the girls, the smaller one, stepped boldly over to them and addressed the gypsy woman. "Lalaka. The guard won't let us in. Send someone to Veli Bey to tell him we've brought him a gift."

The gypsy woman had just reached an interesting prediction. She divided the beans into five portions and chattered to the soldier. "I've just cast the shape of your fortune. But I'm not going to tell you what it is until you've been to the bey and reported to him that there are some Italians here; they've brought a present for him."

The soldier she addressed was red in the face with curiosity. He gave the back of his neck a scratch and then got up and hurried inside.

He reappeared in less than ten minutes. He beckoned to the Italians, "Follow me."

And he set off ahead of them. He led the way through a chilly corridor and a warm garden beside a mill with a large wheel, then through another garden which was full of green vegetables with bushy leaves. The soldier broke off a lettuce and began to pull off the leaves and eat them raw. He offered them to the girls too.

"Have some *marul*."

The gypsy girl accepted a leaf and offered it to her companion.

"No, thank you, Cherhan."

"Oh, do have some! It's good."

"I know it's good, but we're not used to it like this."

"How then? with salt?"

"Yes, with salt and roast chicken."

One of the Italians interpreted what they were saying, and

262

since the two girls did nothing but talk while the interpreter kept turning away, one girl kept saying, "Gergely, what's Cherhan saying?"

The garden was between two high brick walls, for the castle had double walls. And two towers in the middle had a separate wall joining them together.

"The towers also have double walls inside," explained the gypsy girl to Gergely. "One of the guards once told us in the inn that these towers are stuffed with gold and silver. He was sweeping there and looked through the keyhole.

"That's why there are so many soldiers on guard," replied Jancsi sadly.

The boy was particularly excited. He went red and pale by turns, and looked and listened all over the place.

They arrived at the bey's lodgings. There were no other houses along the wall on the inside; there were only lots of big guns at intervals of fifty paces. Beside them were piles of rusty cannon-balls the size of medium water-melons.

The bey's courtyard was littered with iron-bound chests, not to mention sections of a tent made of red canvas. There were arms, camp furnishings and rugs scattered on the gravel and the carefully-tended flower-beds. Anyone who leaves here certainly does not meet his successor.

Ten or fifteen soldiers were busy packing the chests. The bey stood there amongst them, and he too was eating lettuce raw, without roast chicken, like a goat.

He beckoned to the Italians and sat down on the wheel of a large cannon pointing outwards. There he continued to munch.

"Well, what is it you want?" he asked genially.

Gergely stepped forward. Holding his hat in his hands, he spoke in Turkish.

"We're Italian singers, sir. Last night we were fishing here underneath the castle. You know, sir, we're poor, so we have to go fishing each night. But last night it wasn't only fish that we caught. As we pulled in the net, something was glistening in it. We looked to see what it was, and it's a splendid golden dish."

"What the devil...?"

"Please take a look at it. Have you ever seen anything finer than this?"

He reached inside his jacket and brought out a little golden dish. In the centre of it were marvellously-fashioned figures of Greek gods in relief.

"*Mashallah!*" stammered the bey. And his eyes grew wide with delight.

"We've never seen anything like it either," Gergely went on. "We wondered what to do with it. If we sell it, they'll accuse us of stealing it, and God knows the trouble we'll get into. If we don't sell it, what's the use of a dish to folk who haven't got anything to eat out of it?"

The bey turned the plate this way and that, and tested its weight. "It's not gold. It's gilded silver, that's all."

"But it's a work of art. And they always make things like this out of silver."

"All right then, so why did you bring this to me?"

"I was just about to explain that, sir. As we were thinking about it, it occurred to us that a benefactor of ours is in captivity in the Seven Towers here. He's a Hungarian gentleman. When my brother and I were tiny, we were that gentleman's prisoners."

The bey surveyed the dish with a smile. "And did he treat you well?"

"He had us taught, and loved us as if we were his own sons. Well, we thought we'd ask you to let us sing him a song."

"And is that why you've brought me this dish?"

"Yes."

The bey smiled once again at the dish. He thrust it in his bosom. "And can you sing well? Let me hear you sing something."

The five Italians immediately formed a circle. Two of them played the lyre, and they struck up:

> Mamma, mamma,
> Ora muoio,
> Ora muoio!
> Desio tal cosa,
> Che all'orto ci sta.

The two girls had voices like violins. Gergely and Jancsi sounded like two flutes and Mekcsey like a cello.

The bey stopped munching the lettuce-leaf. He stared at the dish again and then said, "Are you angels or djinns?"

Instead of answering him, they broke into a merry jig. The gypsy girl whirled out into the middle and spun round and round in front of the bey, rattling her tambourine.

The bey rose. "I'd gladly watch you three days and three nights. But tomorrow morning I have to start out for Hungary. Join me. You can either join me here or do so on the way. So long as you're with me, I'll look after you well. I'll give you money too. You'll not have any more cares in this life."

The five Italians glanced at each other questioningly.

"Sir," said Gergely, "we shall have to consider that. But in the meantime, if you'll allow us to do what we asked you..."

"Gladly; but who is it that you want to see?"

"Master Bálint Török."

The bey spread his hands deprecatingly.

"Török? That'll be difficult. At the moment he's in the *Hundredweight.*"

"What's the hundredweight?"

The bey made an angry gesture. "He was very rude to the Grand Mufti..."

*

All the same, he fulfilled the wishes of the Italians. He entrusted them to one of his soldiers.

"Put Master Bálint outside in the yard. These Italians are going to sing for him. Whether he wants to hear them or not, just put him outside."

The gate of the inner fortress was also opened. The courtyard behind it is no bigger than the Elizabeth Square in Pest. The two chess-players were there as usual under the plane-tree. Móré too stood behind them, looking bored. A few Croatian and Albanian gentlemen were yawning their heads off there too. They took no notice whatsoever of the game; they were there simply because man is a social animal, just like the ant, the goose or the sheep.

Maylád was sitting on a camp-chair in front of the iron-barred prison so that if Bálint happened to say anything he could make a reply. But they had nothing new now to say to each other. Only one or the other broke the silence.

265

"What are you thinking about?"

The five Italians were kept in the gateway until Master Bálint had been brought out. He was dragged out from behind the iron grille. Two soldiers lifted his chain so that he could walk. They set a hard wooden seat in the middle of the yard and sat him down there. It was kind of them to put him in the shade. He could settle there quite comfortably. But he could not have moved in the iron chain that was as thick as his arm. So he sat there. He did not know why they had settled him there. He was wearing his summer clothes of hemp-linen. There was no cap on his head; but his white hair had grown there into a mane. The chains dragged his hands down each side of the chair. Those two chains weighed fifty pounds. His weak old arms could not lift them. And his face was as drained of colour as if he had just been taken down from the scaffold.

"You may come in now," the soldier gestured to the singers.

And now they came forward from the gateway. They stopped side by side in a line, scarcely five paces in front of Master Bálint.

The captive watched with weary indifference. How ever did these strangers get there?

Even the chess-players abandoned their game. What was going on here? Why, this was splendid entertainment—Italian singers in the Seven Towers! They ranged themselves behind Master Bálint and waited for them to sing, and particularly for the two girls to dance.

"The younger one isn't Italian," thought the Duke.

"You can tell she's a gypsy; she stands out a mile," replied Maylád.

"But the rest are Italians."

Quite by chance all of them were indeed dark-skinned. Mekcsey had the broadest shoulders, Gergely was the lankiest, Jancsi had the most lively eyes. Eva had darkened her skin with hazelnut-oil. Her hair was covered by a red Phrygian cap like all the rest.

The five Italians just stood there.

"Come on, then. Sing!" the soldier urged them.

But they just stood there looking pale and stupid.

Tears ran down the face of the youngest Italian. And on the next one too.

"Sing, you damned troupe of comedians, sing!" the Turk grew impatient.

At this the youngest of them staggered forward and collapsed at the feet of the captive sitting in the chair and embraced his legs. "Father! Dear, dear father!"

12

An arrow-shot away from the Yedikule, behind the Armenian hospital, there stands a solitary inn frequented by day-labourers. Once upon a time it must have been a summer residence of fine marble standing in a garden, dating from the time when Constantinople was known as Byzantium. But alas! time and earthquake loosen even marble blocks. They break down the alabaster balustrades of the terraces and the carved stone flowers round the windows. They push the steps askew and plant weeds where the columns are cracked.

The summer residence had become a wayside inn. All kinds of riff-raff frequented it. And the owner, whose first name was Miltiades, supplemented his income by dealing in stolen goods.

It was Miltiades who gave our young friends their Italian get-up and the golden dish—at a good price, of course—not to mention lodging too.

The fiasco of their performance in the Seven Towers almost landed them in serious trouble. The soldier immediately reported to the bey that the Italians must be some sort of relatives of the prisoner, because they were weeping round him. But by then the bey was not particularly concerned with the Yedikule. All his thoughts were concentrated on Hungary and the *vilayet* there. In the Yedikule he too was no more than a prisoner. He had to live within its walls and might go outside only once a year to pray in the mosque of Aya Sofia.

"You idiot!" he roared at the soldier. "Those Italians were once prisoners of that gentleman, but now they're mine."

He was just putting his pen-case into his chest—a fine porphyry pen-case. He drew a reed-pen from its side and pressed it into the ink-sponge. He wrote a few lines on a piece of parchment the size of a hand, and held it out to the astonished soldier.

267

"Here you are. Give it to the Italians and see them out of the gate. Don't let them come to any harm!"

Gergely of course read the script straight away, as soon as it was put into his hand. This is what it said:

These five Italian singers are attached to my army. I have given them this temessük *in order that no one shall do them harm when they are not with me. Veli Bey.*

Gergely joyfully put the note away. He looked at the soldier. Where had he seen that owlish face before? Where?

At last it occurred to him that he was drinking the previous evening in the Greek tavern among all the day-labourers and boatmen. It was obvious from the redness of his nose that he would be in dock when once he came before the Prophet Mohamed.

"Are you coming with the bey as well?" asked Gergely as they went out of the gateway. And he thrust a silver thaler into his hand.

"No," replied the soldier, recovering his spirits quickly at the sight of the money. "The bey's only taking mine-layers and *deli*s with him. From tomorrow onwards, my master's Ismail Bey."

"But he's not living here yet?"

"No. He lives over there in that house covered with vines."

And he pointed to a house covered with wild vines, with its back joined on to the wall of old Byzantium. Maybe the stones with which it was built had come from the wall too.

By that evening the owl-faced soldier had drunk away the silver thaler at the Greek's inn.

Our youthful travellers dined that evening in an attractive little marble room. They ate mutton with rice, and during the meal discussed whether they should return home with the bey or make their own way back. For it was absolutely certain that danger was on their heels. It was even more certain that they could not release Master Bálint.

"We must go back with the bey," said Gergely. "That's the most sensible thing we can do."

"Well, I'm not going to sing for him," growled Mekcsey. "Thunder and lightning can do that!"

"In that case you can pretend to have a bad throat," shrugged

Gergely. "Why shouldn't I sing to him? Doesn't the proverb say, 'Sing the song of the man in whose cart you've got a lift?'"

"If they ever get to know back home that we've entertained a Turk..."

"Why not? Here we'll sing to him, there we'll make him dance."

Jancsi took no part in their conversation. He just stared blankly, and tears welled up in his eyes from time to time.

Gergely put his hand on his shoulder. "Don't cry, Jancsi. That big chain won't last for ever, after all. Maybe they'll take it off tomorrow morning."

"I couldn't even have a talk with my father. I only had time to answer him when he asked about Feri. I told him he'd stayed at home, so that if I lost my life on this trip mother would still have one son."

They said nothing, but looked pityingly at him.

"Oh, what an idiot I am!" Jancsi went on. "To dress up in disguise and creep in to see him when I might have visited him in the normal way! Can I get in after what's happened? After all, they'll know straight away that we're not Italian singers. The safe-conduct from the bey won't be any protection. At least I might have handed the money over to him."

The gypsy girl took the plate and carried it out. The moon shone into the room and made the light from the little lamp seem pale.

"There's still something we might try," Gergely said suddenly. "We've still got all our money, more or less. You've got a thousand, Jancsi, and I've got three hundred gold pieces. Mekcsey's got enough for us to get home with and so has Eva."

The gypsy girl returned. "Go and have a look at that owl-faced Turk, will you? He's so drunk that he's fallen off his chair. Sárközi's drinking at the Turk's expense, but he's not yet drunk. They're playing dice with Matyi."

But since she was the only one who laughed at this, she gave it up. She sat down on the matting with the others and rested her chin on her hands. She stared at Eva.

"The new bey," went on Gergely, "will certainly jump at the money. He'll jump at it like all the others. Suppose we can do something through him? Money has always been the key to every lock."

"I'll give all I've got," said Jancsi eagerly. "I'd even give my life too!"

"In that case, let's make a final attempt."

"How can you get to see the bey by night?"

"He'll arrest you," interposed Mekcsey. "He'll listen to what you've got to say, take the money and—you'll stay there."

Gergely smiled. "I'm not quite such a nitwit. I'm not going to see him as myself."

"How then?"

"I'll dress as a Turkish soldier."

Jancsi seized Gergely's hand. "Would you do that, Gergely? Would you really?"

"Yes, I'll do it now," replied Gergely.

He rose and called in Miltiades the innkeeper.

"Mine host," said he, "I need a Turkish soldier's uniform. The sort the soldiers in the Seven Towers wear."

The Greek stroked the length of his bushy black beard. By now he was used to these guests who wore disguises, but he was also used to receiving two or three gold pieces from them every day. Devil take them! Whether they were robbers or thieves, the chief thing was that they should pay him well! He had already suggested that they should live in the underground room.

"Well, I don't happen to have such a uniform at the moment," he said with a smile and a wink," but there's a drunken Turk here; we could strip him of his turban and cloak."

"That will do well enough. But I've got to have a beard as well."

"I've got plenty of those."

"But I must have one exactly like that Turk's."

"I can find you one like that too." And he went out. Hardly five minutes had passed before he returned with a variety of ready-made beards, black stubble and glue. "Shall I stick it on for you?"

"Yes, please. Make me up a face like that Turk's."

He sat down. Miltiades got to work. Meanwhile they chatted.

"Do you know the new bey who's coming to the Seven Towers?"

"Of course I do," replied the Greek disparagingly. "He was a gunner."

"What do you know about him?"

"He's as dumb as they come. He drinks water, and his brain's water too. He can't even write."

"Nor can the other officers. The most they can do is read."

"But this one prances around like the sultan's horse, though that knows more than he does. But you should see him when he sees someone even greater than he is; he keeps bowing like flax in the wind."

"Has he seen active service?"

"Yes, last year. He was with the emperor. And he was flogged below Esztergom."

"In other words, he's a coward?"

"A coward and a fool. That's why they posted him here. Can someone brought up on water be anything else?"

Gergely twisted his face to right and left to get away from the glue. But by then he was so changed that Mekcsey almost collapsed with laughter.

The Greek got hold of the turban, the dagger and the cloak too.

"*Allaha emanet olun!*" said Gergely, bowing jokingly.

They wanted to accompany him, but he would only allow Jancsi and Mekcsey to go with him. On the way, Jancsi handed his gold coins to him. Gergely pondered for a moment and then sent Jancsi back too. Only Mekcsey stayed with him.

"You too," he said. "Don't keep so close to me. Don't let them suspect that we're together."

Within half an hour he was standing in front of the bey's house. He rattled the brass plate on the door. An ancient capon-face appeared at the spyhole in the gate.

"What do you want?"

"Send the bey immediately to the Seven Towers. There's trouble!"

The capon-face disappeared. Gergely withdrew. He knew that the man would reappear. But he also knew that if he found nobody at the door, he could not pass on to anyone the bey's queries. He would be compelled to return to the bey and explain that the soldier had already left. The bey would toss and turn and grumble, but in the end he would get up and go to the Seven Towers.

Gergely strolled off towards the Seven Towers. At the Adrianople Gate, as they called the northern gate of the Seven Towers, he halted. The gate was locked. The sentry was squatting beside the gate, asleep. Above his head burned a feeble oil lamp on an iron pole projecting from the wall.

All around there was silence and the smell of wheat. Presumably they had been carrying wheat to the mill and one of the sacks had sprung a hole.

Mekcsey was following Gergely about thirty or forty paces behind, and when Gergely halted, so did he. Perhaps Gergely had stopped in the light of the lamp so that Mekcsey would be able to see him.

The minutes went slowly by. Gergely inwardly cursed Turkish time for going so slowly.

And since man and insect alike are attracted by light in darkness, Gergely too turned his eyes to the light of the oil lamp.

"Oh! I'll be grey by the time that bey gets out of bed!" he muttered impatiently.

Poor young hero! You bright star of the Hungarian galaxy, you will never turn grey on this earth! With what expression, I wonder, would you look into the mirror of the future if some divine hand displayed it before you, and you were to see yourself in captive's chains in this very spot, and you were to see the Turkish hangman knotting the rope for you round that rusty lamp-bracket!...

*

The banging of a door broke the silence of the street. Gergely jumped. He set off swiftly in the direction of the noise. The bey was coming.

He came alone. He was wrapped in his cloak and a high-crowned turban showed white on his head.

Gergely stopped for a minute. He listened in case anyone was coming with the bey.

There was no one else.

Then he hurried to meet the bey.

272

"Good evening, sir," he said, giving a Turkish salute. "It's not Veli Bey who's summoned you. It was I who got you out on a very important matter."

The bey suddenly recoiled. He grabbed at his sword. "Who are you?"

Gergely also reached for his sword. He drew it out, reversed it and offered the hilt to the bey. "Take it, if you think you've got to be afraid of me."

The bey thrust his own sword back into its scabbard. So did Gergely.

"I bring you more good than you might imagine," said Gergely.

He lifted up the money-bag, taking it from the inner pocket of his cloak. And he rattled the coins in it. "Accept this to begin with."

The bey took the weighty bag in his palm, but then returned it. "First of all I've got to know who you are and what you want." And he too stepped into the shadow of the house, where a stone bench glimmered white. He sat down on it and gazed intently at Gergely's face.

Gergely also sat down on the bench. He folded his arms and, scratching the stinging false beard from time to time, spoke softly and cautiously.

"My name is *A Hundred Thousand Gold Pieces*. That sounds quite good, I think."

The bey gave a smile. "Isn't that a pseudonym?"

"You can soon see for yourself. But your name is *Poor Man*, though there's no doubt that you're a fine warrior. Everyone knows that you were in the victorious campaign in Hungary."

"I can see that you know me."

"Well, to come to the point, from tomorrow morning onwards you're in command of the Yedikule. In other words, you'll be a captive too, except that you'll be paid for it. You may go into the city once a year. And if Allah grants you a long life, well, you'll be able to visit Constantinople twenty or thirty times in all. You'll grow nice and fat like Veli Bey."

"Go on."

"It's up to you to choose for yourself a greater and freer fate."

"I'm listening."

273

"In the Yedikule there's a certain prisoner, a very rich Hungarian gentleman called Bálint Török."

"And you want to set him free, I suppose?"

"As you say. I agree that that's what I want."

"I'm listening."

"Some new soldiers will be coming with you—your own servants, if no one else. What would happen if, for example, tomorrow evening you were to bring Master Bálint outside, as if the sultan were summoning him?"

"Not even the commandant may come out after sunset."

"He can if the sultan commands it. But anyway, let's say that he comes out by day, with you and two soldiers. By then the streets round here are deserted. You'll send the two soldiers back and stroll onwards with Master Bálint. But instead of going to the serail, you'll lead the captive I've mentioned to a boat. A boat drawn up on the shore, flying an orange-coloured flag. That boat might be a grain-carrier, a barque, or even a rowing-boat. There's not much of a choice round here. So, as I say, at most you'll change clothes and cloaks and both of you make your way down to the boat."

"Is that all?"

"Not quite. As soon as the boat sets out, three hundred gold pieces will be counted into your hand; that's to say in Turkish, three thousand kurush or piastres. After that we shall go either by sea or by land to Tekirdagh. There one of our men will be waiting with good horses and five hundred gold pieces for you. That's another five thousand kurush. We shall go down to Athens, and from there to Italy; as soon as we step on to Italian soil another five hundred gold coins will be given to you."

"That's thirteen hundred."

"So far. Ten years' pay for you, I think. But just consider this too: the man who calls Debrecen, Szigetvár and Vajdahunyad Castle his own, and who on top of that is lord of a royal a estate, almost the whole of Transdanubia, will have no problem whatever is paying you the extra ninety-nine thousand gold coins, even if he has to part with half his fortune."

"And suppose I don't see the colour of the first thousand?"

"I'll give it to you this very moment, if that's what you want."

The bey stared ahead, deep in thought.

Gergely shrugged his shoulders. "If you see that we're cheating you—though you've never yet seen a Hungarian who'd do that—well, you'll still have plenty of time to accuse Bálint Török of escaping; you can say that you followed him by yourself and arrested him on the boat. Whether you bring him back from the boat or from the land, they'll take your word for it, because you'll have got him back."

The boy thought it over. "All right, then," he said at last. "Tomorrow, an hour before sunset, have that boat with a yellow flag an arrow-shot away from the Seven Towers. But you be waiting on the shore. How shall I recognize you?"

"If you can't recognize my face—though take a good look at it now, for the moon's shining—my turban will also be yellow, sulphur-yellow. You'll be able to recognize me."

"An hour before sunset."

"At eleven precisely," replied Gergely.

For according to Turkish time the sun sets at twelve o'clock.

*

It was midnight when Gergely returned with Mekcsey.

"Is that owl-faced Turk still here?" he asked as he stepped inside the inn.

"He's asleep," replied Miltiades.

"Can you arrange for him to sleep until eleven o'clock tomorrow?"

"Yes," answered the innkeeper. And he took down a glass. He poured water into it and stirred some kind of powder into it. The powder dissolved like salt. He shook the Turk awake. "Hey there, Bayguk! Time to go home!"

The Turk raised his head and stared in confusion. He yawned.

"Just drink this glass of water, and then be off with you."

The Turk did not give the glass a glance. He simply stretched out his hand. He drank it up. Then he stared again. He made a move to get up, but once more slumped down.

Gergely pressed five gold ducats into the innkeeper's hand.

"You've no need to worry," winked Miltiades. "He won't move from here, right till tomorrow evening."

*

It was easy for them to hire a boat. They chose a four-oared Greek boat in the Golden Horn and hired it to go as far as Tekirdagh, a day's journey from Constantinople. They produced an orange-coloured flag for it, and paid two ducats deposit. Early in the afternoon the boat was lying where Gergely directed it. Two hours before sunset he ran up the flag.

Next Gergely hurried to the inn. They shook the Turk out of his dreams. They told him that the aga had ordered him to go to meet the boat with the orange flag; he was to stand there on the shore.

The Turk was still fuddled. Sárközi had to guide him. He tottered along, poor chap, in his yellow turban. He did not know whether it was morning or evening. All he knew was that the bey had ordered him to meet some boat on the shore.

Gergely and his friends, well separated, strolled after him at a distance.

If the bey accepted the offer, they would materialize on the boat the minute he stepped on to it. But if the bey dare not or could not act, then let him see how he would get on with his compatriot in the yellow turban.

The first question was whether the bey would bring Bálint Török with him.

This task they entrusted to Cherhan. They did not tell her that Master Bálint was going to escape, but merely that he was being taken to the sultan and they wanted to see him once again. The signal was that when she caught sight of the bey, the two soldiers and Master Bálint, she would stretch up to the wild vine on the corner of the street as if she was going to break off a leaf. Mekcsey would be able to see this from about a thousand paces away and beckon to his companions.

They were another thousand or so paces away, walking towards the shore. Gergely was dressed as a dervish, Eva as a gypsy girl, Jancsi as a Persian merchant, Matyi as a Kurdish biscuit-seller and Mekcsey as a fishmonger.

Eva squatted down next to Matyi, eating one of his biscuits. Exactly at the appointed time Mekcsey raised the wooden plate of fish, put it on his head and set off towards the shore. This was the signal.

Jancsi turned pale. His eyes were filled with tears of joy. Gergely went red; his heart seemed to be beating hard in his mouth. And they set out a couple of hundred paces apart down to the shore.

The boat stood there. The wind merrily fluttered the orange-coloured flag. The owner of the boat, a young Greek onion-merchant, was counting his day's takings by the rudder.

And in front of the boat the owl-faced Turk stood, looking stupid. On his head was a yellow turban. Behind him Sárközi was sitting on the beach washing his feet in the green water of the sea.

"Here he comes!" murmured Jancsi to Gergely, hurrying across to him. "God help us!"

And even his legs trembled.

Gergely looked behind. He saw the bey approaching on foot with the white-haired Hungarian gentleman. Behind them were two soldiers in white turbans, armed with spears.

The bey turned round and said something to the soldiers. The soldiers returned to the Seven Towers.

Jancsi set off towards the boat with swift steps, but as he passed close to Gergely, the latter seized him by the cloak.

"Wait!"

The bey strolled calmly down to the beach with Master Bálint.

They passed the Kurdish biscuit-seller without so much as a glance at him or at the gypsy-girl sitting beside him. It was obvious that Master Bálint was dazed and astonished. The bey was happy. He kept chatting. They avoided a dog that was lying in their way and settled down on the shore.

The Turk in the yellow turban came to attention.

At that moment the bey suddenly turned round. His sword flashed. He beckoned behind with it. Then he thrust his sword into the scabbard and hurled himself like an eagle on to the soldier in the yellow turban. He threw him to the ground. Meanwhile some fifty soldiers broke out of the bushes and houses.

First of all they tied up the soldier in the turban, and then the gypsy. Then they leapt on board the boat and swept the young Greek from his feet. They tied up everyone on the boat.

In all the noise and bustle Cherhan suddenly appeared and pleaded, screaming, for Sárközi. She too was seized and her hands tied with cord.

*

The sun was just going down behind the Christian quarter of the city when Gergely turned round beside the Column of Constantine. His companions were all panting in his wake. They were dusty and pale, almost staggering with weariness.

Gergely wiped his brow. He looked at Jancsi. "Well, now you know that 'Slow but sure' is best." And they mingled with the crowds in the street.

13

Around the middle of July Veli Bey reached Mohács with his *silahtars* and fifty mine-layers.

Every time a Turkish army went to Buda or Transdanubia, the field of Mohács was their main staging-post. They liked the place, calling it the Field of Fortune. Suleyman himself always rested there the longest. He had his tent erected on the hill where it had stood that memorable day.

The bey's tent was ready for him when the troop arrived there tired out in the evening.

First of all the bey bathed in the Danube, then he had a capon killed and when the sun went down he sat outside his tent. He had certainly lost much of his stoutness since he had left the Yedikule.

The field was still white with the myriads of bones of horses. The soldiers rested their wooden plates on horse-heads and ate from them. They were merry.

The agas, some fifteen in all, stood round the bey and presented their daily report. As each one came to the end of his report he sat in front of the bey on the rush-matting. The officers normally dined together at Mohács, and there even enemies were reconciled.

That evening a mounted despatch-carrier arrived and went to the bey. He had been sent to the sultan with the news that

278

Visegrád was now in the hands of the Turks. Nor had they won it in battle; they had wrecked the defenders' water-supply, and thirst had forced them to surrender. They had awaited help from King Ferdinand, but he was the kind of Hungarian king who entrusted his fortresses to God. So Amade had given up the keys. His only condition was that they might withdraw unmolested. The Pasha of Buda swore that they would not be harmed. But unfortunately his people did not take such an oath. As soon as the Hungarians piled their weapons in the middle of the fortress and set out from it unarmed, the Turks overran them and chopped them to pieces.

"Well now, we'll rest here for a couple of days!" said Veli Bey jovially. "Today we'll sleep, tomorrow we'll enjoy ourselves, and the day after that we'll set out for Nógrád."

For after Visegrád that was the next fortress that was scheduled for occupation.

The Turkish messenger continued his way to Constantinople. Veli Bey's army lay down to sleep.

At noon next day the bey gave just one single command to his officers: "This evening all of you will dine with me. There's wine, and it's good wine too! The Italians will sing."

The bey was a jolly man. He loved eating and drinking. And every time the Turks stepped on to Hungarian soil they immediately forgot the prophet Mohamed's prohibition of wine.

"One of the rank-and-file soldiers has something secret to report. Will you see him?" asked one of the agas.

"Let him come." replied the bey good-humouredly.

A short, foxy-eyed *silahtar* stepped forward. His clothing was as tattered as the others'. His turban was hardly larger than a handkerchief. He bowed.

"Your servant has something to report about the Italians."

"I'm listening," replied the bey.

"Those five men have long been suspect to the dust of your feet. My first suspicions were roused when I saw one of the Italians cleaning the others' swords with pieces of paper."

"You're a fool," retorted the bey. "You must know that they are giaours. We pick up paper, because it is possible that the name of Allah may be on one of the pieces, but those pigs live without Allah; their wits are dim and they are lower than animals."

279

The *silahtar* stood his ground, unmoved.

"My second doubts arose around Sofia. You may remember, noble bey, that we came across carts laden with loot and one of them lay on its side by the road."

"Yes, I remember."

"The chicken-cage had burst open, and the chickens were running all over the place. An ancient woman kept calling them, *polatyi, polatyi!* Neither the chickens nor the hens took the slightest heed of her. She was a Greek woman. A Turk tried to help and he called *Gak-gak-gak!* They still did not run up at this. Then one of the young Italians, the one with the girlish face, took the basket of grain from him and shouted to the hens, *Pi-pi-pi! Pitye-pitye-pitye, pityikém, pityikém!* At that all the chickens rushed towards him. He even got hold of a hen and kissed it."

"Well, what's odd about that?"

"The fact, sir, that the hens and chickens understood Hungarian. And the person who called them!"

The bey hummed and hawed. "Suppose 'chicken' is *pipi* in Italian too? Do you know Italian?"

"Italian? No."

"Then stop talking, you camel!"

The *silahtar* acknowledged the title of *camel* with a submissive bow.

He went on calmly: "And what about when one of the silahtars exchanged a foal near Belgrade? His name's Kereledje. It was a peasant who sold it to him and he paid ten *aspers* for it. But the foal was so wild that nobody could stay on its back. Then that Italian with the broad shoulders leapt on it like a panther and galloped off. The foal almost collapsed. How on earth should an Italian singer know how to ride like that?"

The bey shrugged. "Perhaps he was a rider when he was a child."

"Please allow me to go on, sir."

"Carry on."

"Last night an aga came to join us, the biggest aga I've ever seen in my life."

"Manda aga."

"Yes. As he went past the Italians, he stopped in front of the

280

lanky one and said to him, 'Why, if it isn't Bornemisszza!' He gave a start and replied, 'No, I'm not.' 'But I swear you are!' said the aga, 'Gergely Bornemisszza.' And he went on, 'Don't you recognize me? Have you still got that fine ring? And the advice you gave me, that's certainly been useful. As you see, I'm now an aga. But now my name isn't Hayvan any more, but Manda. Bullets don't touch me.'"

"And what did the Italian reply?"

"He said, 'I don't know what you're talking about. But I do know that there's someone who resembles me. How do you know that Hungarian's name?' 'I got to know it in Buda,' replied the aga, 'when Bálint Török was captured. He was among his retinue. What a pity you aren't him. You're very much like him. You've missed out on ten gold ducats by not being him!'"

"Well, there you are then, you elephant! He's not Hungarian, is he?"

"Oh but he is!" replied the *silahtar* triumphantly. "Last night I had proof that not only he, but all of them, are Hungarians. When they set up a pot to cook dinner, one of them took hold of a hemlock and pulled it up by the roots to make a place for the fire. A skull came out of the ground with the roots. All five of them looked at it and discussed whether it was Turkish or Hungarian. Your servant was lying near to them and pretended to be asleep. Your servant understands Hungarian."

The bey snorted like a horse.

"What? Were they talking Hungarian? What were they talking about, the dogs?"

"The young, lanky one said that it must have been a Hungarian, because the Turks buried their dead. Then the other one took the skull in his hands and said, 'Whoever you were in life, you died for the homeland: to me you're a saint!' And he kissed the skull, and they dug it into the ground again."

The bey struck his sword. "Good-for-nothing dogs of giaours! Why on earth didn't you report this to me immediately, you dolt?"

"You were asleep, sir."

"Bring chains for the dirty spies! Bring them here!"

The *silahtar* rushed off, his face shining with delight. With

281

grim contemplation the bey watched from the hill as the *silah-tar*s ran in all directions among the tents.

Two hours elapsed before the silahtar returned. Sweat poured from his brow. "Sir, the Italians..."

"Well, where are they?"

"They've escaped, the dogs, they've escaped!"

PART IV

Eger in Peril

1

If there is a register in heaven recording the history of the Hungarians, the next eight years were entered like this:

1545: The Turks possess Buda, Esztergom, Fejérvár, Szeged, Nógrád, Hatvan, Veszprém, and Pécs—almost the whole of the country.

1546: The Turks divide Hungary into fifteen *sanjaks.* The Hungarians retain only Upper Hungary and one or two counties bordering Austria.

1547: The Hungarians are harassed not only by the Turks, but also by the Austrians.

1548: The faith of Luther and Calvin spreads throughout the country. The Turks and Austrians are not the only enemies; Hungarians become hostile to each other.

1549: Under the pretext of collecting tax, the Turks seize everything, including children.

1550: A Wallachian and Turkish army sets out against Transylvania. Friar George raises an army of 50,000 in a matter of days. They defeat the Wallachians. The Turks withdraw.

1551: Queen Isabella leaves Transylvania. Friar George is assassinated.

*

Then came the year 1552.

*

In Sopron the plums were turning purple and the sunflowers were in bloom as one sunny, windy day Mistress Eva stood on the veranda of a house in the town. She was selecting some of her husband's clothes for a young man about to travel abroad.

Since we last saw her she has developed the stature and limbs of a full-grown wife. The tender white velvet of her face is still girlish, but the old impishness has gone from those lovely catlike eyes. Her face radiates calm, gentle intelligence.

"Well, Miklós," she says to the student, "there are two suits

285

here too," and she spreads out on the table a worn cherry-red damask suit and an everyday one of hemp.

"This damask one's still a bit big for you. But maybe you'll grow into it in a couple of months."

"Thank you, madam, thank you very much," stuttered the student. And his face grew pink with delight.

"And it's certainly got a bit frayed," said the lady, examining the suit. "But you'll be resting until this evening, so I'll stitch it up." Then she picked up the hemp suit. "This one will be just right. My husband wore it when he was in Buda. When the Turks occupied Buda and we moved to Lippa with the queen."

"Thank you," said the student happily. "I'll wear that one to go on in. It won't collect the dust."

The lady felt in every pocket. They were all empty. But all the same she felt something hard in the corner of the jacket. The pocket had a hole in it. Eva put her finger through it and discovered a tightly-folded thin piece of parchment in the lining. She looked at it, unfolded it and spread it out. It was a kind of five-sided sketch with all sorts of lines and dots.

"What can it be, Miklós? A sort of tortoise, isn't it?"

The student put it in his hand. Soon he turned it round and examined it for a long time. "It's not a tortoise," he shook his head, "though it's the same kind of shape."

At this moment a little black-eyed boy of six came galloping out of the room. At his side was a splendid little sword with a gilded hilt. The scabbard was of worn red velvet.

"Mummy," piped the boy, "you promised you'd buy a trumpet too, a golden trumpet."

"Don't bother me just now, Jancsi", replied his mother, pushing him aside. "Go out into the garden, dear, to Luca."

"But you will buy the golden trumpet?"

"Yes, yes."

The boy held the sword between his legs and trotted down into the yard and from there into the garden.

"Well now," said the student, looking closely at the parchment, "this is a sketch of a fortress, and the fortress is Eger."

"The fortress of Eger?"

"Yes, indeed it is. Just look: this tortoise is outlined with a double line. That double line is a wall. The head of the tortoise

286

and the four legs are five projecting bastions. The little squares with thin lines inside it are the buildings."

"And what about this sickle-shaped thing here beside the tortoise?"

"The outer fortress. There aren't any buildings in it like you'd find in other outer fortresses, only two bastions and two towers on them."

"And these two black hooks that link the middle of the sickle with the tortoise?"

"That's the Dark Gate."

"Why is it Dark?"

"Because it's under the ground."

"And this here beside the gate?"

"A stable."

"Such a big one?"

"They need a big one there, madam. And there must be a cart-shed there too and places for the horsemen to live. The steward lives there too."

"And this dotted line by the gate?"

"That was a church. The church that the King, St. Stephen, had built. They pulled half of it down not long ago, in fact just ten years ago."

"What a pity!"

"Indeed it was a pity. But they brought the new big moat through the nave of the church and built that outer fortress. It was necessary, because that was the weak side of the fortress, the eastern side."

"But how do you know all this, Miklós?"

"There's nothing odd about that. I was at school there for two years. Everyone talked about it there. It was then that they built the Dark Gate."

"And there's another gate here on the west side, beside the brook."

"And another one here too, on the south side. There are three gates to the fortress."

"And what about these red lines everywhere?"

The student looked at them and followed the lettering. He shook his head. "They're underground passages."

"All those passages underground?"

"There are lots, but you can't get through all of them now."

"And these squares that look like rooms?"

"Underground chambers. This one here's a reservoir. And this over here's a burial-place."

"A burial-place? Among the underground passages?"

"It must be, because you can see written along this underground passage 'The Road of the Dead'."

The woman shuddered. "It's strange that they bury the dead here."

"Only when there's cholera," replied the student. "I've just remembered that that's what I was told."

"Oh what a pity that you didn't come at least a fortnight earlier, Miklós!"

"Why, madam?"

"If you'd come earlier, I'd have given you the suit earlier. And if I'd done that, I'd have found this sketch in it earlier. It's there that my poor husband has just gone, to Eger."

"I heard the Turks were making in that direction."

"And that's just why my husband's gone to Eger. If only my poor father hadn't gone with him! Just imagine: he's a man of seventy. He's got a wooden hand and legs. And he's gone off with my husband!"

"To fight?"

"Well, yes, that too. But also because he's got a good old friend, Father Bálint. A year ago they had a quarrel about something. My poor mother was still alive then. After that the priest left for Eger to go to Dobó. So my father's gone off there to make peace with him. They're very fond of each other."

While she was speaking, the lady opened a green-painted chest with flowers on it, and took out a little book. It was her prayer-book. She slipped the sketch of the fortress into it. And she glanced out into the garden at her son who was running around near the maid as she watered the flowers.

"Someone's bound to come soon from Eger," she said thoughtfully. "Gáspár Pető's elder brother lives here. He's on the king's side. He sent a cartload of gunpowder to the fortress, and bullets, since his brother's there. If a messenger comes to him from Eger, I'll give him this sketch to take to my husband."

And she picked up her needle and cotton. She took the hemp

suit on her lap. As they went on talking, a man in a dark blue short jacket stepped through the gate, and as he turned to close it, he spoke to someone.

"Don't come any further," he said. "I'll find my way inside."

Eva got up. She did not recognize the voice. Or the man. There were three steps up to the veranda. There the stranger raised his head. He was a corpulent, dark man with one eye. He had a hussar's moustache. In his hand he carried the kind of stick village mayors have.

"Good day to you!" he greeted the lady. "I'm told that Captain Gergely Bornemissza lives here."

"Yes, he does," replied the lady. "But he's not in."

"Oh, so he really has gone already?"

"Yes, to Eger."

"Oh dear, oh dear," the man shook his head. "What a pity! I wanted a word with him... But perhaps his wife..."

"I'm his wife. Come in."

The man walked up the stairs. He took off his cap and gave a deep bow. "My name's Tamás Balogh," he said. "I'm a nobleman from Révfalu."

The way he bowed showed that he was no peasant.

The lady's expression was friendly as she drew a chair from under the table and introduced the student at the same time. "This is Miklós Réz, a student. He's on his way to study abroad. His elder brother's serving in the royal army and knows my husband, so he came this way in a market cart and came in to have a rest."

"Good day to you, lad," the one-eyed man gave him a cursory nod over his shoulder and sat down, repeating "What a pity!"

"I came to the horse-fair," he said, slapping his knee, "and there are lots of things I'd like to have seen him about. And among other things, I've brought some money for him."

"Money?" said Eva in surprise.

"They said he needed money to go to Eger, and was selling some of his gold and silver."

"We don't really have any of that."

"I'm particularly fond of rings." And he held out his hand. On his left hand gleamed ten of the most beautiful rings. There might have been some on his right hand too, but that was

289

covered by a greyish leather glove. He went on: "And they said
he had a superb ring, among other things."

"Yes, he has," said the lady, smiling.

"With a moon on it."

"And stars."

"The moon's a topaz."

"The stars are diamonds. But how do you know this, my
friend?"

"Could I have a look at that ring?" His voice trembled.

"No," replied the lady. "He always carries it in his pocket. It's
a sort of lucky talisman. It belonged to a Turk."

Little Jancsi was galloping round the yard again. With one
leap he turned up on the steps and, seeing a stranger, he gazed
at him fixedly as children do.

"Say hello to the gentleman," smiled the lady.

"Are you the captain's boy, maybe?", asked the stranger.
"But I've no need to ask. He's the very image of him!" And he
drew the child to him. He gave him a kiss.

A wave of unpleasant sensations enveloped Mistress Eva, but
only for an instant. The next moment she had forgotten them.

"Aren't we going to buy that trumpet?" insisted the boy.

"I'll buy him one," said the student, eagerly. "In any case, I'm
going to take a turn in the market. I'll take Jancsi to see my cart
too, and show him the little foal."

"All right," agreed the lady. "Here's a dinar. Buy him a
trumpet; but do look after him, Miklós. And you too, Jancsi...
You remember what your father said!" And she turned to
Master Tamás with a sad smile. "He was very insistent that we
should take care of the boy."

Jancsi danced about in his glee. And off he went with the
student. His mother called after them, "Keep near the church,
Miklós. We'll come out directly."

For she had already prepared to go out to the market. There
were odds and ends she wanted to buy from the Viennese
merchants who came down to the fair.

Master Tamás Balogh twisted his cap in his hands absent-
mindedly, and stared moodily ahead.

"What news have you of Szolnok?" asked the woman
anxiously. "It's too big a task for the Turks, isn't it?"

"That's my view too," replied Tamás Balogh absently.
"When my husband left me, he said the Turks were hardly likely to get to Eger this year. The fortifications at Szolnok were strengthened very much last year. It's stronger than Eger."

"Much stronger."

"And even if it does surrender, Eger's protected by the whole of Upper Hungary."

Master Tamás Balogh gave a wry smile. "Do you happen to have a picture of the captain here in the house?"

"Of course," replied the lady. "It was painted last year by a German artist."

"Could you show it to me, madam? I've heard a lot of nice things about the captain, and I'd like to know him."

"What? Don't you know each other, then?" said Eva in surprise.

"Once upon a time we did, but it's a long time since I've talked to him."

The lady led the guest into the room. It was dark and filled with the scent of lavender. Mistress Eva opened the shutters. It was obviously the guest-room. On the floor there were Turkish carpets. Beside the wall was a divan with a bearskin on it. A writing-desk and bookcase stood by the window. There might have been a hundred parchment-covered books in it. On the walls were portraits. One of old Cecey in a helmet, in the days when his hair was dark. Mrs Cecey, looking slightly cross-eyed, wearing a head-scarf worked in gold thread. And then a yellowing picture of Christ in a walnut frame, an impish girl's face resembling Mrs. Bornemissza, and next to it the portrait of her husband. A young, thin-faced, dark-skinned man, dark enough to be a gypsy. His candid eyes radiate blithe intelligence. His moustache is twisted. A soft little beard surrounds his chin. His hair is shoulder-length.

Master Tamás examined the picture with interest. He nodded. "A fine figure of a man. How old may he be?"

"Twenty-six."

"And your son is as big as that?"

"We've been married now for eight years," smiled the young wife. "We were children when we got married."

Master Tamás took another look at the picture. "And is it true that the captain's even been in Constantinople?"

"Indeed it is. And I was with him there too."

"I've a Turkish acquaintance who mentioned him, Manda Bey. A giant of a man. Once upon a time the captain was very kind to him."

"Manda Bey? I've never heard that name before."

"Perhaps he mentioned him under the name of Hayvan. That was his original name."

Eva smiled. "Hayvan? Of course we know him. I've seen him too."

Master Tamás took yet another look at the picture and stared at it for a long time in silence, frowning. He nodded to it as if in greeting, then bowed to the lady and backed out through the door.

Once again the lady was overcome by that sensation of unease that had seized her when Master Tamás bent down to her son. All the same, she accompanied him to the veranda-steps. The man kept to her right. That was like a peasant. He said farewell with a bow. That was like a gentleman. He backed out through the door. That was like a Turk.

Something disturbed the woman. But she quickly reproached herself for it. "It's wrong to think evil of that unfortunate man. He's only got one eye, and that's why he's got the glance of a snake."

She went back to her sewing and began to sing to banish the unease from her mind. The servant was singing in the garden, and she joined in the song; with nimble fingers she sewed the loose buttons one by one on to the cherry-red damask suit. In one place it was frayed too. She looked for red silk thread to mend it.

But she could not get the visitor out of her mind.

"Who is that man?" she wondered, dropping the suit on to her knees. The ring... the way he kept looking at the portrait... his mention of Hayvan... that Turkish way of taking leave...

Who was that man?

Her face drained of colour, she stared at the locked gate and strove hard for enlightenment to dawn on her. That face seemed familiar to her now, so did that voice. But she could not place them. Then she thought of the ring. Gergely had said that he was taking it with him. He said it jokingly and put it in his everyday jacket. Had he taken the jacket with him? The woman hurried to the wardrobe and turned out the clothes in it. The jacket was there. She felt it; there was something hard in it. The ring! The ring!! He had not even wrapped it in paper.

And then, like lightning flashing through a cloud, a name pierced through her brain. She clutched at her brow.

"Yumurdjak!"

*

At that moment the maid returned from the garden. She saw her mistress collapse among the clothes scattered in front of the wardrobe. Her face was white and she had dark rings round her eyes.

"Madam!"

There was no reply.

The servant looked round. She ran into the other room too. Had a robber been here? Last Saturday Bota the gingerbread-man had been robbed in broad daylight, and even today they did not know who had done it.

She picked up the vinegar bottle, held it to her mistress's nose and rubbed her skin with it.

"My husband's in danger," were Eva's first words. "Where's the boy? Oh yes, I sent him out. Quick, get my cloak, Luca! Let's go and fetch Jancsi!"

"But you're ill, madam."

"No, I'm not. Come on."

Yet she was as white as a corpse. And dressed as she was, she got up and hurried out of the gate. Her sense of peril gave strength to her muscles. She went off at a run straight to the church.

The streets were teeming with market-folk coming and going. Carts, cows, pigs limping on the end of a rope, and among the animals village-folk laden with tubs and barrels. All the noise of the fair, dust and the smell of onions.

She reached the church before the maid caught up with her and threw her cloak over her.

Then all of a sudden the student emerged from the crowd. He

293

was running, pushing people aside as he made for them, shouting, "The Turks have occupied Szolnok! They've just announced it outside the church. How can I go now..."

"My son!" Eva shouted to him. "Where have you left him?"

"Mr. Balogh took him into the church. He said I was to bring you the news while he said his prayers. Oh God! Oh God! The county's done for! If Szolnok's fallen to the Turks, there's no hope for Eger!"

"My boy!... My boy!" panted Eva. And she dashed up the steps, through the crowds and in at the main door.

"My son!" she shouted, her voice failing, "My son!"

Inside the litany was in progress and the German-speaking peasants from the neighbourhood were chanting. *"Christus, höre uns! Christus erhöre uns! Herr erbarme Dich unser!"*

The lady dashed through them, shrieking.

"Jancsi, Jancsi, my son!"

But there was no reply from little Jancsi in any of the pews.

2

On the fifth of September Gergely welcomed the rising sun beneath the castle of Sirok. The sun shone straight into his eyes, and into those of his 250 merry infantrymen. Nor was it the sun that he welcomed, but the approach of another brigade along the road. That was why he held his cap in front of his eyes. But the brigade was coming the wrong way.

He alone was on horseback at the head of his troops, so he was the first to catch sight of the disorderly band armed with swords and pikes as it swarmed along.

"What on earth is all this?" he muttered to himself. They certainly weren't Turks. And if they were Hungarians, they couldn't be coming away from Eger.

And the awful thought occured to him that Dobó had abandoned Eger...

For alas! All that King Ferdinand did was to promise help, and not put his words into action. That was how Lippa and Temesvár had been lost that year. And who knew whether Szolnok could hold out? Dobó was a clever and calculating

294

man, and he would soon put two and two together and realize that one Hungarian could not cope with a hundred Turks.

On their way they had seen nothing but priests sitting in carts. All of them coming from Eger! And all of them surrounded by big chests, cupboards and sacks. At first he had simply greeted them, but later, dispirited at the sight of them, he did not get out of the way for them.

So he was startled for a moment by the thought that Dobó had abandoned the fortress of Eger. But only for a moment. The next instant he dismissed the idea from his mind. He wasn't that kind of man! Whoever was coming along the road, it was not Dobó. And if they were Dobó's troops after all, then Dobó wasn't with them. He would remain there alone and die alone, but history could never record that he had abandoned the fortress entrusted to him. For after all, Eger was the gateway to Upper Hungary.

The approaching troops were not carrying any banners. There were about two hundred of them. And they were hurrying along in small groups.

Gergely beckoned to Cecey. The old man was riding in the rear of the detachment, talking with an elderly soldier. The old man was always talking. As his son-in-law beckoned, he spurred his horse on to join him.

"I'm going to have a look a bit further ahead," said Gergely. "You take the lead while I'm away, father."

He put spurs to his horse and galloped to meet the approaching brigade. His eyes sought out the leader. None of them was wearing a feathered cap. So he stopped in front of them and raised his arm for them to halt.

"Are you from Kassa?"

Not one of them replied. They looked at him in confusion. Some of them even blushed.

"Where have you come from?"

That brought no response either.

"Well then," shouted Gergely angrily, "perhaps you all belong to an order that's taken a vow of silence?"

In the end a large man with a big chin raised his head and broke the silence, a wry look on his face. "Well, yes, we are from Kassa, Captain, and we've come from where you're going."

"Eger?"

"Yes. And it would be a good thing, sir, for you not to go there either. It's not worthwhile. You'll have to turn back anyway."

"Why? What's happened?"

"What? Why, simply that it would be mad to put one's head into the lion's den."

"What lion's den?"

"Do you know what happened at Temesvár?"

"Yes, I do."

"Do you know that they cut down Losonczi and slaughtered his folk?"

"I've told you so."

"And do you know that the Turks number a couple of hundred thousand?"

"Yes, I know that too."

"Well, do you also know that Master Dobó doesn't have even a thousand men?"

"There may be more than that."

"And do you know that Szolnok has been in Turkish hands since the day before yesterday?"

Gergely looked at him. He turned pale. "Now I know that too. And I also know that if you had been there, it would have fallen sooner. Well, just get back to your mother's apron-strings. And so that you won't go back empty-handed, take that—and that goes for all of you rats!"

And he hit the big-jawed man such a blow on the face that he staggered back into his neighbour. The next moment he had drawn his sword and would certainly have slashed his way through them if they had not leapt out of his way.

"My respects to György Serédi!" he called after them. "I wish him better soldiers than you, you rats!" And he spat after them.

The troops from Kassa left the road and scattered over the fields, grumbling. Gergely did not give them another glance. He set off again, and from the pressure of his spurs his horse felt his master quivering with anger.

It was a good thing he found a gypsy caravan there on the road. Whether it was the troops from Kassa who had overturned one of their carts or whether it had tipped over into the ditch of its own accord, the gypsies were busy trying to right it. Gergely glanced over his shoulder to see whether his men were far away. Then he halted in front of the gypsies to wait for them. He watched them to overcome his annoyance.

"Why, if it isn't my friend Sárközi!" he called suddenly in delight.

One of the tousled gypsies started in surprise, then gave a broad grin at this kindly greeting. He took off his cap. He approached, bowing profusely while he peered curiously at Gergely's face with his cunning eyes.

"Don't you recognize me, then?"

"Of course I recognize you sir, kiss yer 'ands an' feet, I recognized you instantly. But I can't remember what they call you."

"Never mind, you'll remember it soon enough. What are you doing here? You're as ragged as a scarecrow."

The gypsy took a scared look at himself. He was indeed in rags. All he wore was a shirt and a pair of leather trousers patched with bits of cloth, or rather a pair of cloth trousers patched with leather. His legs showed red through them. He had nothing at all on his feet.

"And have you still got a horse?"

"No I 'aven't, kiss yer boots, sir, I certainly 'aven't. I'll never 'ave one again!"

"Come with me to Eger, old chap. I'll pay you the same wages as any other gunsmith. You'll get a horse too, if you serve there for a month. And I'll give you on top of that such a pair of red trousers that all the gypsies will go green with envy."

The gypsy grinned. He took a look at his own ragged clothes and then looked again into the soldier's face. He scratched his head. "Eger? It'll be 'ot there, sir."

"Don't worry about that. You can work under the coolest of the bastions. You'll be my armourer." And he went on in Turkish, *"Allah işini rast getirzün!"* (May God help you in your work).

The gypsy leapt in the air. "Gergely Bornemissza, captain, sir!" he shouted, his words almost quivering with joy. "Kiss the feet of yer 'orse too! Oh, it weren't fer nothing that I dreamt about a golden oriole last night!"

"So you've recognized me at last."

"Yes! Yes! Of course I recognized you, kiss yer feet. I knew you immediately, but I couldn't make out 'oo you were."

"Well, will you come with me?"

The gypsy was startled. He scratched his head. "I'll come, so 'elp me God, I'll come..."

"Well, come on then."

"Only those damn' Turks..."—and by now he was scratching his head with both hands—"may God make 'em lame in both feet!"

"But there aren't any there yet."

"Ah, but they'll be there, the dogs. Where them soldiers keep coming and going, it's not an 'ealthy place to be."

"I shall be there too, Sárközi. So long as you can see me, there's no need to be afraid. And if we're really in a tight corner, there's a secret way out of the fortress to Miskolc."

Gergely said this without thinking. For after all, every fortress has a secret tunnel, but the first to discover it is the enemy. All he knew of the fortress of Eger was that Dobó was the commander there and his deputy was Mekcsey, and for them he would go to the end of the world.

Was it mention of the underground passage that persuaded the gypsy? Or the horse? Or the red trousers? Or that he liked Gergely? Anyway, he agreed.

"Well then, I'll enlist, captain, sir. I'd do it for nothing; if you'd throw in a pair o' yellow boots and spurs as well, I'd be grateful. It don't matter if there are 'oles in them, sir, so long as they've got spurs."

By now Gergely's brigade had arrived. They laughed as they listened to this conversation. Their merriment grew when Gergely offered his hand to the gypsy, who gave it a great slap.

"Right," said Gergely, reaching into his pocket. "Here's a dinar to confirm your engagement. As far as Eger you can ride my second horse. And once there, as soon as any horse goes blind, you can have first choice. You'll get the boots too, but only after the siege."

The gypsy jumped joyfully on to the horse and beat its flanks with his bare feet.

The gypsy caravan shouted farewell to him. He shouted something back in Romany. Then he stuck his cap on one side and sticking out his chest rode proudly on beside Gergely.

"Eh! But the Lord's sent me up in the world!"

*

A few hours later high up on the Bakta road, between the green trees and the hills, they caught the gleam of the huge towers of the fortress at Eger with their green-enamelled tiled roofs. There were national flags on the towers, and the red and blue ones of the town. The walls were massive and white.

What a beautiful castle! And all round it were hills clad in red and yellowing vines and trees. Behind it in the distance was a high bluish hill six times the height of St. Gellért's Hill.

Gergely raised his cap and turned to his brigade. "Take a look at that, lads! For the good God himself also looks on it with delight from heaven."

With that, he spurred on his horse and galloped ahead.

The gypsy pondered for a moment whether to stay at the head of the troops or to gallop on with the captain. He suddenly realized that he would look a fool if he were to lead the brigade, so he smacked the horse's haunches with his hand and drummed with his heels below its belly. "Gee up there, gee up!"

The horse gave huge leaps and threw the gypsy into the air. But not for nothing had the gypsy done some horse-trading in addition to his craft; he always fell back cleverly on to its back.

A cloud of warm dust spread over the highroad. It was raised by refugees. Women, children and old men were sitting in carts or walking, driving cows beside the carts and waggons loaded with furniture and fowls. Some carts even carried calves standing there mooing, while in others pigs grunted.

Turks do not eat pork, but who knows when they might ever return? A little girl in red boots carried a tit in a cage beside the cart, while one woman had a rose-bush in bloom in a pot on her back. There were many carts and a great exodus. Some of them surely would never return, especially those who down there in the valley were disappearing through the Ornamented Gate in the direction of Felnémet, the cotters and widows. They would stay in Upper Hungary, where no Turkish horse had left traces so far. The main route of the refugees led towards Putnok and Kassa.

Gergely, however, was not interested in them now. Before a quarter of an hour had passed, he galloped through the Bakta Gate, the western entrance in the town wall. Then, glancing upwards from time to time, he rode past the episcopal church with its single tower, through the market-place and wound his way up to the gate of the fortress.

There the wall was white and almost smelt of lime, it was so new.

The drawbridge was down. Gergely flew like a bird into the fortress. He looked about for the commander.

There stood the tall, lean man, his back straight as a ramrod, in the main square of the fortress in front of some two hundred men. He was wearing a violet-coloured velvet jacket, a broad-bladed sword at his side, tall red boots and a red velvet cap with eagle's feathers in it, which he was holding in his hand. Beside him was a sunburnt fair page holding two flags in his hand, one in the national colours and the other blue and red. On the other side of Dobó stood old Father Bálint wearing a white surplice over his broad shoulders. In his hands he held a silver crucifix. With his long white beard he looked like a biblical prophet.

They had just finished swearing in the soldiers. Dobó rasped out the closing words of his address to them, then put on his cap. He turned towards the galloping steed.

Gergely jumped down from his horse and with gleaming eyes flashed his sword in salute. "Beg to report my arrival, sir."

Dobó just stared. He stroked his round grey moustache and long drooping beard and resumed his stare.

"Don't you recognize me, commander? It's eight years since we saw each other. I'm your most devoted soldier, Gergely Bornemissza."

"Gergely, my boy!" shouted Dobó, opening his arms wide. "I knew you wouldn't desert me!"

And with joy in his eyes he embraced Gergely and kissed him.

"But have you come all alone?"

At that moment Sárközi pranced in on his steed. The horse tossed the ragged, barefooted gypsy three feet into the air.

The soldiers roared with laughter. Dobó smiled too. "Surely this isn't your army?"

"Of course not," laughed Gergely. "He's only my armourer, a gypsy. Have I done right to bring him along?"

"Every man's worth his weight in gold here, my boy."

And he snatched his hand away from the gypsy in case he kissed it. But the gypsy was not to be outdone. He kissed the leg of the commander's boots.

"So how many of you have come, then?" asked Dobó anxiously.

"Not many," replied Gergely, ill at ease. "I've only been given command of 250 infantrymen in all."

Dobó's eyes shone. "Two hundred and fifty? My lad, if as many soldiers as that had come from everywhere, I'd go out to meet the Turks on the plain of Maklár."

"Why, haven't you got any aid coming?"

Instead of replying, Dobó waved his hand dismissively in the air. Then he turned to the officers standing round him. He introduced Gergely to them. From the royal army Zoltay was among them, whose acquaintance Gergely had made eleven years before in Buda. He was still just as blonde and lanky, a jolly man without a beard, so he was unmarried. And then there was Gáspár Pető, a little man whose moustache was waxed flat and pointed; he was also from the royal army and had a title. A wiry-haired, blue-eyed young man was standing beside Pető. He too clasped Gergely's hand warmly.

"János Fügedi's my name, captain to the chapter."

Gergely looked at him. "Oh, but I know you, young man!"

He shrugged his shoulders and smiled. "I don't remember..."

"Wasn't it you who gave me an ox-ear in Transylvania?"

"An ox-ear?"

"Yes. At what was to have been Fürjes's wedding, in the back courtyard."

"Maybe. It was certainly I who distributed all kinds of food there to the pages."

"I hope I can return your kindness now."

"How do you mean?"

"I'll give you a pasha's ear in return."

301

Then Gergely turned to Pető. "And why are you so down-hearted?"

Pető shrugged. "I've every reason to be downhearted. Twenty of my cavalrymen slipped off on the way here. If ever they cross my path again!..."

"Never mind," said Dobó deprecatingly, "the gate's open. Those who fear for their lives can go. It's not lizards that I need on these walls!"

Only now did Gergely glance at Father Bálint. It was a year since he had seen him. He embraced the old man and kissed him.

"So you didn't go away with the priests then, Father?"

"Somebody's got to stay behind," grumbled the old man. "What's Cecey doing?"

"He's coming!" replied Gergely, almost shouting. "The young men escape, the old ones come and bring swords. Just see how my father can wield a sword with his wooden hand!"

A short-necked stocky man stepped out of the shadow of the church. He wore a dark-blue pelisse and cherry-red trousers. A sword with a blade as broad as a hand knocked against his yellow-booted leg. He approached with an old man wearing glasses who walked rapidly, and waved and laughed at Gergely from a distance. It was Mekcsey.

Since Gergely had last seen him, he had grown a beard and looked even more like a bull. The ground seemed to quiver beneath his footsteps.

"So you're married, then?" said Gergely happily, after embracing him at least three times.

"What do you mean?" replied Mekcsey. "Why, I've got a little girl called Sárika too."

"Who was it you married?"

"The angel with the bluest eyes in heaven."

"Come on! Who was she?"

"Eszter Szunyogh."

"Good for her! What about that fine serpent-headed sword you had?"

"I've still got it, but I don't wear it out in everyday use."

"And where's your family?"

"I sent them to the castle of Budetin until we've beaten the Turks." Glancing at Dobó, he went on, "I did tell the old man

302

not to send the wives away, but he's so fearful for his own Sara...
He's hardly been married for a year."

Their conversation was interrupted by the steward's report.
The old man in glasses who had come with Mekcsey opened the
sheet of grey paper he had brought in his hand as he stood in
front of Dobó; holding it a long way from his glasses, he read
out:

"So there are: lambs 8050; oxen, cows, calves, in other words
animals for slaughter 486; wheat, rye and flour together 11,671
bushels; barley and oats 1540 bushels."

Dobó shook his head. "That's not enough, Sukán."

"That's what I think too, commander."

"If the Turks bottle us up here for the winter, what can we
give the horses?"

The old man shrugged his shoulders. "Well, commander, it'll
most likely be bread, like the soldiers."

"How much wine is there?"

"2215 casks."

"That's not enough either."

"But at least it's vintage wine. This year's vintage has been
devoured completely by dogs. There are also a few barrels of
beer."

"Pigs?"

"139 living. Bacon, 215 sides."

Only then did Bornemissza have a better look around him. To
the north was a line of palaces and to the east a large building
like a monastery, now almost certainly barracks. Beside it was
a building like a church, but the squat square tower had a flat
top, and on it gabions to protect guns showed up brown. There
was a great bustle everywhere—masons, carpenters, barrows,
workmen, clattering and banging.

He would have gone on listening with interest to the old
steward's report, but he thought of his brigade. He returned to
his horse, jumped in the saddle and galloped through the gate
in order to lead them in. He did so, and paraded them. Dobó
shook hands with the standard-bearer. He handed them over to
Mekcsey to swear them in, show them their quarters and give
them breakfast.

303

"You go along too, to my house. That yellow one over there, the two-storeyed one. Get a bite to eat."

After taking the oath Gergely set off there, but all the same, he was more interested in the fortress; he went its rounds on horseback.

"It's a splendid fortress!" he said enthusiastically when he returned to Dobó. "If ever I command a fortress, God grant me to settle in this one."

Dobó smiled with pleasure. "You've not seen anything yet. Come with me and I'll show you."

And as Bornemissza dismounted, he beckoned to the fair page, "Kristóf, bring the horses after us!"

He took Gergely by the arm and led him to the south gate. There a strong palisade extended far to the left and right, creating a path along the bottom of the wall. Clearly Dobó intended it to defend those going alongside the wall from the expected hail of bullets from the north.

"There you are, then," he said, halting there. "To get your bearings quickly, just imagine a big tortoise facing south, towards Füzesabony. The place we're now standing is its head. Its four feet and tail are the bastions. Its two sides are two pedestrian gates."

And he called up into the gate-tower, "Are you on watch up there?"

The guard leaned out of the tower-window and pushed aside the horn that was hanging at his side.

"Yes sir, there are two of us on watch."

"Let's go up," said Dobó, beckoning Gergely on. "This is the side from which the Turks will come today or tomorrow, so have a look at this too."

He motioned with his hand for Gergely to go first, but he moved back. "I've already taken the oath, commander." By which he meant, "I'm not a guest."

So Dobó went first. There were four guards sitting in the tower. They saluted. "Meet Captain Gergely Bornemissza," said Dobó. At this the guards saluted once again, and Gergely likewise raised his hand to his cap.

From the gallery of the tower two little villages and a mill could be seen to the south. One was an arrow-shot away from the fortress, the other a further arrow-shot away from that. Beyond the two villages lay a bluish-green plain with a chain of hills opening out on either side of it.

"That's where the Great Plain begins," said Dobó, describing the scene.

"And these two little villages below us?"

"The nearer one with five houses is Almagyar. The far one with thirty or thirty-five houses is Tihamér."

"And this stream?"

"Eger Brook."

"There's a little lake over there."

"That's simply called 'Warm Lake'."

"To the right of the lake that gate has a stone wall, and there are lots of trees..."

"It's a game-reserve. It belongs to the bishop."

"Are these walls here round the gate new?"

"Yes. I had them built."

"They're a good height. The Turks are hardly likely to attack here."

"That's why I had them built. As you can see, there's a cannon defending the gate on the left, and up above there are loopholes."

"Every fortress has its defence on the left. Approaching attackers don't carry shields on their right arm."

"Here it would have been impossible on the right anyway. As you can see, the brook flows past the west flank of the fortress. I had the sluices closed up there by the mill to give us water. We've also raised the level of the bed there."

They went over to the west side overlooking the town.

"It's a dizzy height, this wall," said Gergely in amazement. "It must be all of sixty feet."

"Perhaps even more. The Turks really can't launch any attack on this side. It's stone outside and earth inside. But now let's ride. We're unlikely to have any trouble with the Turks on this flank."

They mounted and continued their way on horseback.

Down below the town was quiet and deserted. The episcopal church and palace rose high above the houses. On the far hillside towards the west was the church of St. Nicholas, which belonged

to the Augustinian friars. On the west side the town was bounded by a solid level flank of a hill, and beyond that the peaks of
the Mátra appeared blue.

There were also two bastions on the west side of the fortress,
with a small fortified gate in the middle. The soldiers were just
leading horses down to the brook. Beyond the brook in the town
market-place a few people were lounging around a herd of pigs.

"Are there still people here?" asked Gergely in astonishment.

"Yes," replied Dobó, "though every day I keep sending instructions to them to clear out. They all want to sell their pigs
and small animals."

Inside the gate of the fortress a lean-faced lieutenant with a
fierce glance was instructing some fifty men.

They had swords. On their heads were rusty helmets with
visors let down, and there was armour on their shoulders. Two
were standing in the middle. The lieutenant kept shouting:

"Back! Back! Back! I'm telling you, you idiot, to whip back
your sword the minute you've struck."

The man under instruction had obviously never been a
soldier. He was a stocky, powerful little peasant youth, and
Dobó had assigned him to the troops from Kassa simply
because youthful energy was wasted on the guns.

"Who's that lieutenant?" asked Gergely.

"Hegedűs," replied Dobó, "the captain of the men from
Kassa. He's a tough man."

And he spoke down to the group. "If there's anything you
don't understand, just ask the lieutenant."

At this the youth dropped his sword and looked at Dobó.
"Well, I don't understand, commander, why I've got to whip
back my sword."

"The lieutenant will tell you."

"So that you can defend yourself with it, you nitwit," said the
lieutenant angrily, "and so that you can strike again."

"But sir!" said the lad, spitting to one side, "anyone I strike
once isn't going to strike me in return!"

Dobó flicked his horse with his whip and gave a smile.

"He's a lad from Eger. What he says is good."

They rode the length of the wall to the north. Two palaces
stood there, both with wooden shingles, but the shingles were

painted green. The smaller one was more ornate, with leaded lights in its glass windows. The larger one, looking something like a granary on a large estate, was called the monastery. In Dobó's time it had once been possessed by the chapter in the fortress; it was where the officers of the fortress lived and had only parchment-windows. Behind the smaller palace was a flower-garden with a green fence; in it were benches and an arbour of vines. A late tortoise-shell butterfly was fluttering above the asters.

As Gergely's eyes rested on the asters, Dobó looked that way too. "My poor wife planted all those flowers for nothing, didn't she?"

"Where is she?"

"I sent her home to my sisters. A woman's eye makes a man weak."

They crossed the garden to the north-western corner. There too the wall was immensely high. Beneath it part of a stony hill projected to where it had been cut away steeply down to the level of the town.

"Look here," said Dobó. "This is the earth-bastion. Its only purpose is to defend this corner from shots and to protect that other bastion over there. That's the prison bastion." And he pointed to the bastion rising at the rear of the fortress, the tail of the tortoise.

From there once again there was a fine panorama of the town and of the valley of poplars stretching northwards along the brook. At the end of the valley was a beautiful tree-lined village, Felnémet. It was a large village. Beyond it wooded hills hemmed in the broad valley on all sides.

But Gergely did not spend long admiring the view. The rear of the fortress claimed his attention. There high hills rose up behind the fortress, and only a deeply-dug ditch separated them from it.

"This is where we can expect to be attacked," he said, surveying the hills.

"Yes," replied Dobó, "and from the east, but here's where the wall is strongest and four of the biggest guns are trained this way."

At the prison bastion he dismounted and threw the reins to his page Kristóf. "You can take him to the stables."

They went up the prison bastion, where a large cannon, four mortars and about twenty falconets yawned towards the hill. Beside the guns a fair, curly-haired German artilleryman was instructing the peasants.

"When I say *bor!* give me *bor!** When I say *düss!* give me *düss!* (Fire!)"

The peasants listened to the artillery instructor with serious faces.

Dobó smiled.

"Guten Tag, Meister Fayrich! Wenn Sie sangs *bor,* dann bekommen Sie keine Pulver, weil das *Bor* keine Pulver ist, sondern Wein."

He spoke German just as badly as the artilleryman spoke Hungarian, but they understood each other. The latter began again: "When I say *por,* then don't bring me *wine* but *powder,* Krucifix Donnerwetter!"

In the end it had to be explained to the peasants that when Master Fayrich asked for wine, they had to open a pouch of gunpowder for him, but when he asked for powder, they had to fetch him wine.

There were five Austrian bombardiers in the fortress. Dobó had them sent from Vienna.

"Look at this marvellous gun," said Dobó, stroking it. It's called 'Frog'. When it croaks, the Turks will feel the rain!"

The gun was of bronze, and had been polished till it shone. Together with its strong iron-bound oak cradle it did indeed look like a squatting frog.

They walked on eastwards, where on the corner another strong bastion jutted out, looming high up. That was the left hind leg of the tortoise.

"This is the Sándor Bastion," said Dobó.

Gergely stopped and stared.

From this bastion, the eastern side of the fortress was enclosed by a strong, high section of wall shaped like a sickle broken into three sections like this:

* In Hungarian *bor* = wine; *por* = powder.

308

Both outside it and inside there was a ditch, sixty to seventy feet deep. Only across the middle of it was a narrow embankment, obviously thrown up so that soldiers might cross it.

"This is the outer fortress," explained Dobó. "You can see that on the eastern side there's a mound about the size of a hill rising beside it; that's the King's Seat. It's called so because it was from there that the king, St. Stephen, watched the building of the church as he sat outside his tent. This hill down below here had to be cut in two."

"I see," nodded Gergely. "The man who did that had some sense."

"It was Perényi who did it ten years ago. At the far end there's another bastion, the Bebek Bastion. And that tower at the corner is so that we can see the enemy down as far as the gate and up to here, and of course fire at him too."

There the wall was raised by a palisade of wattle, as indeed it was all around. In some places the mud on it was still moist. The reason for the palisade was so that if the defenders walked along the top of the wall they might not be seen from outside.

"Well, now let's go to the Church Bastion," said Dobó, again taking Gergely by the arm.

Only a few paces from the Sándor Bastion two huge buildings confronted Gergely. One was like a monastery, with half of a very large church built on to it. One tower still survived. (Previously it had had four.) The door itself was carved, and above it were gigantic flowers sculpted in stone and saints with mutilated faces. But what sort of a church was this, filled not with worshippers but with earth? Instead of bells cannon were sited on the roof, and instead of an organ the roar of cannon sounded from it, the organ of death.

The side of the church was piled up with earth. On the top of the pile grazed a goat. There was a vaulted entrance in the side. Its stones were blackened.

"Is this perhaps where the gunpowder store is?" asked Gergely.

"Yes. Come and see the potentiality we've got stored there."

"This was the sacristy."

"Yes. It's a nice dry place for gunpowder."

"Well, it was a great crime that this church..."

"I regret it too. But maybe it will mean that we can save the fortress. Rather that than hear the praise of Allah sung in it." They went inside. The place resembled a wine-cellar more than a sacristy. It was full to the ceiling with black barrels.

"How many are there?" Gergely wondered.

"A lot," smiled Dobó. "More than two hundred barrels. This is where I keep all my gunpowder."

"In one place? Suppose it blows up?"

"That's impossible. There's a guard on the door. Nobody has a key to it but me. Nobody but Mekcsey or old Sukán may go inside. From sunset to sunrise I never give the key to anyone."

Gergely glanced up at the window. It was of glass, with small circular leaded lights in it, protected by a triple iron grille. Opposite the door, where the light came in slantwise, stood a big round vat. It was full to the brim with gunpowder.

Gergely took a handful of it and let it trickle back.

"This is for cannon," he said. "It's nice and dry."

"I keep the rifle-powder in small tuns," replied Dobó.

"Is it made here or in Vienna?"

"Both here and in Vienna, too."

"And what's the composition you use here?"

"Three quarters saltpetre, the other quarter sulphur and charcoal."

"Soft charcoal or hard?"

"Soft."

"That's the best. But I mix in one or two more spoonfuls of charcoal than others usually do."

On the wall above the vat could be seen a big dirt-stained and tattered painting. Only two heads could be seen in it. One was of a bearded man with a sad face. The other showed a youth who was bending over the man's breast. Both figures had haloes glowing yellow round their heads. From their necks downwards the canvas was split, showing the white of the wall beneath.

"That was probably the altar-painting from the church," said Dobó. "Perhaps even St. Stephen had it painted."

In front of the sacristy two powder-mills were operating. Both

310

were worked by horses. At the side of the church beneath some vaulting soldiers were making hand-grenades. Two bombardiers were supervising their work.

Gergely halted. He looked at the gunpowder and the fuse and shook his head.

"Aren't they any good?" asked Dobó.

"They're all right," said Gergely with a shrug, "but I'd like your permission to have my own grenades made in whichever bastion I'm stationed."

"Tell me if you can do a better job. You're an educated man, and the main thing is to defend the fortress; other considerations are subsidiary."

"Well, I can do something better. These old grenades splutter, jump about and burst, and that's all. I'll put a core in them."

"What sort of a core?"

"A little bomb, oily tow mixed with bronze-dust, iron filings and a bit of sulphur. My bomb will begin to work only when it has exploded."

Dobó called back to the grenade-makers, "Stop working! Captain Bornemissza will come back here. Work under his instructions."

They went up to the roof of the bastion transformed from the church. On top it was surrounded with wicker-framed gabions filled with earth. Among the gabions were guns in stone-vaulted niches. In the middle was a pile of cannonballs and a pit full of gunpowder.

From there there was a view of the whole of the outer fortress, which enclosed the eastern side of the inner one in the shape of a huge semi-circle. There were two bastions in it, and two round towers on them. But also visible facing the wall was the great hillside which was half as high again as the fortress itself.

"Well, the siege will be fierce here on the eastern side," was Gergely's view. "And in the mornings the sun will shine in our eyes too. We need a real man here."

"I'd got you in mind."

"Thank you. I'll stand firm."

And the two men shook hands.

Among the guns there squatted a large fat bronze cannon. In

its big mouth it would take a cannon-ball the size of a human head. The lettering and decorations on it gleamed like gold.

"This is *Baba*," said Dobó. "Read the inscription."

On the barrel of the gun, between two palm-leaves curled to form a wreath, there gleamed this sentence:

A safe stronghold our God is still!

3

On 9 September the sun did not shine. The sky was covered in dark clouds. The peaks of the Mátra seemed to have disappeared. The weather was like the face of a spoilt child who wants to cry but still has to discover something to cry about.

Inside the fortress there was much activity and a lot of hammering. In the lower square carpenters were hammering flat the ends of three-foot stakes. Beside each of them a soldier bored a hole in the flattened end and formed a cross out of it. A third group of soldiers bound oily tow dipped in pitch to the crosses. The name given to them was *Bludgeon*. There was already a heap of them there.

Beside the sacristy old Sukán was measuring out gunpowder by the bushel. Peasants were filling small leather pouches with it. These were carried to the bombardiers.

Also beside the sacristy Master Bombardier János was supervising the filling of earthenware bombs with gunpowder. These were the *Balls*. An inch of wick dipped in gunpowder hung out of them. When they want to ignite them, they attach them to a wire frame like an English racket. But they hurl them by hand too, and those with loops they throw from pikes. There were about a thousand of these in stock.

Towards the old gate, where two long lines of houses divided by the lower square formed the barracks, there was the squeal of grinding and the banging of fitters. Their job was to repair the weapons of those who brought them along.

Beside the Dark Gate the cattle were munching hay in the spacious underground stalls. The butchers slaughter them there beside the wall, and the blood drips into the moat through a hole. Four or five cattle are slaughtered each day for the defenders.

Gergely happened to be standing on the Sándor Bastion. There they had constructed a platform of beams and planks so that detachments of men might come out on to the walls together. The stone stairways of the bastions were not suited for a simultaneous charge of defenders if they were summoned urgently.

Every bastion now had such a platform, but the one at the Sándor Bastion had to be reconstructed, because one of the piles had not been dug in properly and moved.

Dobó climbed up with his officers and kept testing the piles for movement.

"This has got to stand so firmly," he said, "that it will take the weight of a hundred men even if all the piles are shot away. Nail supports to each pile, and put a thick coat of lime-wash on them." He turned to the page. "Go to the women and tell them to bring lime-wash and brushes."

The watchman on the church-tower gave a long fierce blast on his horn.

"What's all that?" Mekcsey shouted up to him. "Here we are!"

"They're coming!"

Those few words told the officers all they needed to know.

"Here's the advance-guard!"

For days now a long line of guards had been set up as far as Maklár. It was a living telescope stretching as distant as the plain of Abony and kept watch day and night for the arrival of the Turks. There were also spies in civilian clothes who circulated as far as Vámosgyörk and Hatvan. They had already informed Dobó of the Turkish advance. Lieutenant Lukács Nagy had asked permission for this very reason to take twenty-four of his good cavalrymen out to harass the Turkish advance troops. But the arrival of the first detachments at Abony only became public news now. It was certain now that they were making for Eger and not elsewhere. That was what "They're coming!" meant.

Mekcsey leapt on to the top of the wall and hurried off to the south gate. Dobó too. The officers followed. Then they stopped at the south bastion and, shading their eyes, looked at the road which leads from the distant plains through the hamlets of Almagyar and Tihamér straight to the gate of the fortress.

Along the road from Almagyar a rider was approaching at a swift gallop, carrying with him the cloud of dust that his horse kicked up. He wore no cap. His red jacket fluttered behind him on a strap.

"That's my man!" thought Gergely. "It's Bakocsai."

For Bakocsai was an excellent horseman, but fate had made him an infantryman, so he was always pleading to be allowed to ride. That was how he came to be on watch that day.

As he arrived beneath the fortress, his face was seen to be covered in blood, and his horse had a lump on its flank the size of a melon.

"It is my man!" said Gergely, full of joy. "It's Bakocsai. That's him, Bakocsai."

"He's been in a fight!" muttered Dobó.

"He's a lad from Eger," Mekcsey praised him.

"But he's my man!" retorted Gergely joyfully. "He's learnt it from me!"

Another three guards kicked up the dust in his wake. Maybe the rest had been killed.

So the Turks were here!

What were Dobó's feelings at the news? This was the Turkish army that during the summer had overwhelmed the two strongest fortresses in the country, Temesvár and Szolnok; it had occupied Drégely, Hollókő, Salgó, Buják, Ság, Balassagyarmat... anywhere it wanted. For the Turkish army had set out with the object of forcing what remained of Hungary to submit to the power of the sultan.

Well, now they were here. They came as a raging tempest, a world-shattering storm of fire and blood. A hundred and fifty thousand tigers with human faces, destructive wild beasts. Or maybe even two hundred thousand. Most of them had been trained from early childhood in archery, shooting, climbing walls and military life. Their swords had been made in Damascus, their armour was of Derbend steel, their lances wrought by master craftsmen in Hindustan, their cannon cast by the finest gunsmiths in Europe; they had immeasurable

314

quantities of gunpowder, cannon-balls, guns and arms. Their lust for blood was devilish.

And to oppose them?

Here was this small fortress with a mere six old, shoddy cannon, and a few iron tubes—falconets masquerading as guns.

What were Dobó's feelings?

István Bakocsai the messenger galloped up into the fortress and leapt from his horse. He halted, covered in blood, sweat and dust, in front of Dobó. On a thong from his saddle hung a dark Turkish head with a curled moustache. His own left cheek was entirely black with congealed blood.

"Beg to report, sir," he said, clicking his heels, "the Turks are here, damn them!"

"Only the advance-guard," said Dobó calmly.

"The first of them, sir! We couldn't see the main army because of the forest at Abony, but they were making good speed, damn them! As soon as they got wind of us, they captured two of us, and they chased me too for a bit: the last was this romany, damn him!"

"Where are your mates?"

The soldier glanced towards the gate. "They're washing in the brook, damn them."

"Well now," said Dobó. "From today you're a corporal. Get along and drink a quart of wine—damn you!" he added with a smile.

Everyone crowded into the courtyard of the fortress to look at the severed head. There was a long lock of hair in the middle of the shaven head. Bakocsai held it by this lock and displayed it proudly.

*

At the news of the arrival of the Turks the fortress became like a disturbed beehive.

Everyone gathered round Bakocsai to hear what he had to say and see the head. Even the women ran to him from the ovens and kitchens. Standing on tiptoe behind the crowd they listened to the soldier's words and shuddered at the pagan head from which blood was still dripping.

All this, of course, happened only when Dobó had left the

square and retired with the officers to the palace. There they halted and consulted each other.

The soldier hung the Turkish head on a lime-tree and sat on a chair to let the barber-surgeons look at his head.

There were thirteen barbers in the fortress, four masters and nine assistants. They were not there to shave and cut hair. Their job was to wash wounds, dust them with alum and sew them up. Doctors? In the whole of the country there were fewer than would be found today in a small country town. The barber was the doctor everywhere—and the good God too, of course.

Well, all thirteen barbers fell on Bakocsai, just to hear what he was saying. The first thing they did was to pull off his jacket and shirt.

The eldest of them was Master Peter, so he settled down to clean him up first. They held a big earthenware dish in front of him and a pot of water above him. They washed him well and truly.

The soldier allowed himself to be washed and dusted with alum too, but when they began to sew up the long wound on his head, he kicked aside the chair, the dish, the barbers and their assistants and with a storm of fearful curses went into the barracks.

"I'm not a pair of trousers, damn you!"

He pulled a big spider's web down from the edge of the window and put it on his head. He bound up his head himself. He sat down, had a hearty meal of bacon, then rolled over on to a palliasse and fell asleep immediately.

*

At about the same time as Bakocsai arrived at the fortress, a peasant on a horse also rode up there. He wore a frieze coat and a black hat with a turned-up brim. In his hand he held a cudgel as tall as he was.

When Dobó had finished talking to the soldier, the man spoke to a woman from his horse, "Which is the commander?"

"That's him, there," said the woman, "that big tall man walking past the barbers. You can tell which one he is from the feather on his cap."

The man glanced where she pointed. He saw the barbers

straight away. All thirteen of them were cutting hair. The officers had their heads shorn almost totally, with the five-toothed comb of their fingers and a couple of snips of the scissors. Shoulder-length hair can easily catch fire. And there would be no time to comb it while the siege was on.

The man got off his horse. He tied it to a tree. He reached inside his knapsack and took out of it a letter with a large seal. He ran after Dobó.

"I've brought a letter, sir!"

"From whom?"

"The Turks."

Dobó's face darkened. "How dare you bring it!" he thundered at the man. "Or are you a Turk?"

The man sagged. "No, certainly not, begging your pardon. I come from Kál."

"Do you know it's a crime for a Hungarian to carry a letter from the enemy?" And he turned to the soldiers. "Put him under armed guard!"

Two lancers stepped up each side of the peasant.

"Sir!" the man pleaded. "They compelled me!"

"They only compelled you to take it in your hand, not to bring it here." And he looked at the soldiers. "Stand here!"

He had the trumpeters summon the defenders and waited with folded arms by the lime-tree from which the Turkish head was dangling.

Then Dobó opened his mouth.

"The reason I have called you all together is that the Turks have sent a letter. I do not correspond with the enemy. If the enemy writes me a letter, I throw it back. Or else I ram it down the throat of whoever dares to bring it to me. Only I shall have this first letter read out and send it immediately to the king. Let him see with his own eyes that the Turks are here and that we need help. In any case I know what's in the letter: threats and negotiations. We are not afraid of threats. We do not enter into negotiations. Our homeland is not for sale at any price. But so that you may hear with your own ears how the enemy normally talks, I shall have it read."

He handed the letter to Gergely. He already knew that he

could read any kind of script at the first glance. He was the most educated of all the folk in the fortress.

"Read it out aloud."

Gergely went and stood on a stone. He broke the seal and shook the sand out of the paper. He glanced at the bottom of the letter and read it out:

"From Ahmed Pasha in Kaál.

Greetings to István Dobó, Commander of Eger.

I, Ahmed Pasha from Anatolia, the chief counsellor to the powerful and invincible Emperor, the captain-in-chief of an army without number that tramples every power under its feet, hereby inform you in writing that this spring the mighty Emperor sent two armies to Hungary. One army occupied Lippa, Temesvár, Csanád and Szolnok and all the castles and fortresses in the region of the rivers Kőrös, Maros, Tisza and Danube. The second army occupied Veszprém, Drégely, Szécsén and the whole length of the River Ipoly, and defeated two Hungarian armies on the way. There is no power that can withstand us!

And now these two victorious armies are uniting beneath the fortress of Eger.

In accordance with the wishes of the all-powerful and invincible Emperor I warn you not to dare resist his Majesty but bow obediently to his will and admit the pasha I shall send, and surrender the fortress of Eger and the town to him.

"Not on your life!" came cries from all directions. "Don't read any more! Let the dogs hear it!"

But Dobó motioned them to be silent.

"Just listen to the music of the Turks. It's very fine when it sounds so loud. Go on reading."

If you are obedient, by my faith I declare that neither you nor your possessions will suffer any harm. You shall obtain all that is good from the Emperor, and I will maintain you in the same freedom you enjoyed under your kings of old.

"We don't want Turkish freedom!" interrupted Cecey, shouting loudly. "Hungarian freedom's good enough for us!"

318

That made them all smile.

Gergely went on:

And I shall protect you from all harm...

"So that's why they're coming, to protect us!" shouted Gás-pár Pető.

Everyone laughed, including the reader of the letter.

The ordinary folk already knew how the Turks behaved when any fortress submitted to them.

Only Dobó stood with a grim face.

Gergely continued reading:

To this I set my official seal. If, however, you do not submit, you will bring the wrath of the powerful Emperor on your heads, and then both you and your children shall all perish by death. Therefore reply to me immediately!"

The reply was an angry roar.

"Devil take the all-powerful Emperor! Just let him come here!..."

Faces grew red. Even the mildest folk's eyes flamed.

Gergely offered the letter back to the commander. The noise subsided.

Dobó had no need to stand on a stone to be seen above the crowd. He could see over all their heads.

"There you are," he said in a steely but sad voice, "this is the first and last letter from a Turk that has come into this fortress and been read out. You can gather from it why they are coming. They are bringing freedom with sword and gun. It is the pagan emperor steeped in the blood of Christians who brings us this freedom. Don't we want it? If we don't, he'll cut off our heads. Well, let's reply to it. This is my reply!"

He crumpled up the letter and threw it into the peasant's face.

"How dare you bring it here, you rogue!"

And he turned to the soldiers.

"Put his legs in irons! To prison with the rascal!"

4

After the Turkish letter that had roused all their passion, Dobó summoned his officers to the palace.

"All of you be there in half an hour."

The room was full before that. Those who arrived late did so only because they were putting on their best uniform. Everyone felt that the letter was the first peal of the alarm-bell.

Dobó was still waiting for Bakocsai's companions. And for Lukács Nagy too, and his twenty-four cavalrymen. Surely the Turks had not surrounded them? That really would be a thoroughly depressing piece of bad news...

He stood by the window with his arms folded, and his glance strayed over the town spread out below. What beautiful buildings, and what fine white houses! And the town was empty. Only under the palace were there people busy by the brook. Soldiers watering horses, people carrying water. Further down in the town a woman in a yellow head-scarf was just stepping out of the gateway. On her back a big bundle. And she hurried towards the fortress, making two little children run by her side.

"She's coming into the fortress too," murmured Dobó without enthusiasm.

The page was standing beside Dobó. He was wearing a flax-coloured velvet jacket. With his long hair and girlish face he looked like a girl dressed as a boy. But a glance at his hands revealed the strength in them. Every day the boy practised pike-throwing.

Dobó turned to him. He ran his hand down the boy's shoulder-length hair. "What did you dream about, Kristóf? Did you dream you were at home?"

The boy blinked. "I'd be ashamed to dream anything like that, sir."

"You'd do well to get your hair cut."

He was the only page remaining in the fortress. And that was only because his father had written to the commander asking him not to send him home. The boy had a stepmother who did not look kindly on him. Dobó regarded him as his own son.

Dobó had sent all the other pages home. They were boys

fourteen to sixteen years old. Dobó's court was for them a military academy. Dobó had not yet put them to the test.

Among them was another favourite page, Balázs Balogh, the son of a lieutenant in the army of Friar George who had been killed the previous year. He was a year younger even than Kristóf, and an excellent rider. He had left in tears in August, grieved because Kristóf could stay in the fortress while he could not.

"They're sacking me as if I were a cobbler's apprentice," he complained. "What's so special about you," he rounded on Kristóf, "that you're being allowed to stay? Just you wait! When I come back I'll break a pike over you!"

"You surely don't imagine that I'm responsible for sending you away?" said Kristóf unhappily. And he himself pleaded with Dobó. "Please let Balázs stay too, sir!"

Dobó waved him aside. "No, he can't stay. His mother's a widow. He's an only child. He mustn't even climb a tree. Away you go!"

It was Lukács Nagy who took Balázs with him to restore him to his mother on his way.

"You know, that Lukács is taking his time out there!" Dobó glanced at Mekcsey. "I'm afraid he's got himself into trouble." And he shook his head.

"I don't think so," smiled Mekcsey. "I don't worry about small men. I've a peculiar superstition that small men are lucky in war."

"Just the opposite!" said Gergely, highly amused. "Small men never sit a horse as firmly as tall men do. A small man is carried in battle by his horse, while a tall one guides his horse in it."

"Of course, that's because you're tall."

The sentry announced that the guards had arrived. Dobó's expression grew serious.

"Let them in."

Seven soldiers in yellow boots and spurs clicked their heels in the centre of the room. Two of them had wet hair. So it was true, they had been washing. One of the wet-haired ones stepped forward.

"Beg to report, sir, the enemy's here, below Abony."

"I know," replied Dobó. "And the first Turk's already got here. Bakocsai brought him along."

He said this in a tone of reproof. The soldier was wearing the blue and red colours of the town. He took a deep breath and threw back his head.

"Commander, sir, I could have done the same; three of them, if you like."

"Then why didn't you?"

"Well, sir, simply because I split the heads of all three of them."

A ripple of amusement went round the room. Four of the seven soldiers wore bandages. Dobó himself gave a smile.

"Well, Komlósi, my lad," he said, "it's not the Turk's head that's at fault, but yours. Your duty was to bring news, not to fight. It was Captain Bornemissza's man who brought the news. But for you it was more important first to wash, comb your hair, change your shirt and wax your moustache. What sort of a soldier are you, Antal Komlósi?"

Komlósi gave a dejected stare. He realized that Dobó was right. But he raised his head. "Well, sir, you'll soon see what sort of a soldier I am!"

Two other guards should have reported, but they were missing. The Turks had seized them, so they could report only in the next world.

Dobó gave orders for new guards to be sent out. He ordered them not to clash with the Turkish sentries, but to report their approach hourly to the duty officer. Then he dismissed them and sat down to the table.

By now all the lieutenants and officers in the fortress had crowded into the room, together with the five Austrian master bombardiers too. The priest was there too, so was old Cecey. They were talking quietly. Some were looking at the pictures: the one of Bishop Miklós Oláh looking to one side with those two great owl's eyes beneath a wrinkled forehead. In his hand was a little book and behind him the fortress of Eger when it had only one tower. On the wall in the shadow was a picture of King John, but only his beard showed yellow. And the other picture was entirely black except for a hint of light on the nose and one cheek, and the name on it was *Perényi*.

"My friends," Dobó broke the solemn silence at last, "you have heard that what we have been expecting for years has now caught up with us."

His voice was like a great bell. He was silent for a moment. Perhaps he was suppressing a thought. Then, as if he wanted to keep short what he had to say, he continued in an ordinary tone: "My fellow-commander Mekcsey has just handed me a complete inventory of the forces in the fortress. You know more or less what they are, but all the same I regard it necessary to read them out. Listen and take note. Gergely, please."

He handed the document to Gergely, who could do this more easily and quickly than old Sukán. Gergely read it gladly.

"The strength of the fortress of Eger, 9 September 1552."

"In other words, today," said Dobó.

"Today the fortress contains 200 regular cavalrymen and a like number of regular infantrymen, 875 riflemen conscripted from Eger and its environs. Ferenc Perényi has supplied 25 men, György Scrédy some 200."

Mekcsey shook his head. "There aren't more than fifty of those." And he glanced at a shifty-eyed, extremely gaunt-faced lieutenant.

"I can't help it," he muttered. "At least I'm here." And he rattled his sword.

Dobó said in a conciliatory tone, "Hegedűs, my friend, who's talking about you? Hunyadi had poor soldiers too. True, they were Wallachians."

Gergely continued reading: "Likewise 210 volunteers from Kassa. So here we are," he glanced at Hegedűs. "There are soldiers in Kassa too."

And he went on: "The 'silent monks' have sent four infantrymen, the chapter of Eger nine."

"Nine?" growled Tamás Bolyky, the lieutenant of the Borsod riflemen, "Why, they've got over a hundred soldiers!"

"They wouldn't supply any more, even though I offered to pay them," said Dobó dismissively.

Fügedi, the lieutenant from the chapter, got up. But Dobó waved him to his seat again. "Another time, if you please. Nobody touches the chapter. The town of Eger is in Heves, the fortress in Borsod county. Beyond the stream is Heves, this side is Borsod. Carry on, Gergely, my boy; make it as brief and quick as you can."

So Gergely went on reading in a fast monotone. The list of soldiers was quite lengthy. The counties of Sáros, Gömör, Szepes and Ung, and the free cities had all sent a small troop of infantrymen. The Provost of Jászó alone had sent 40 men. And he was cheered. At last Gergely raised his voice again: "So in all we number a hundred short of two thousand."

Dobó glanced at all who were sitting at the table, and stopped at Hegedűs. Looking at the lieutenant from Kassa, he went on, "To this we can add those men I have called in to serve inside the fortress, the thirteen barbers, eight butchers, three fitters, four blacksmiths, five carpenters, nine millers and 34 peasants who will assist with the guns. In time of siege all of them can take up arms. Then we must include Lukács Nagy, whom I despatched with 24 cavalry to Szolnok on 29 August, the Beheading of St. John the Baptist." "They may arrive at any moment," he said, turning towards Mekcsey. And he continued, "Well, that's about the sum of it, but I'm expecting the main help to come from His Majesty."

Old Cecey beat the air and muttered.

"Oho, friend Cecey," Dobó looked at him, "things aren't what they used to be. The king knows very well that if Eger falls, well, he can put the Holy Crown into store."

"And then that'll be the end of Hungary," added Mekcsey darkly. He was standing beside Dobó.

"There'll be the Austrians," grumbled the old man.

"The king's army is coming in two large forces," continued Dobó, "forty or sixty thousand, maybe a hundred thousand well-nourished and well-paid soldiers. One of them is led by Moritz, Prince of Saxony and the other by Prince Maximilian. The king will surely instruct them not to waste time but to hurry. And Eger is the goal of both armies."

"Nobody's going to believe that!" muttered Cecey.

"Well, I do," growled Dobó at him. "And please stop interrupting what I'm trying to say. My envoy Miklós Vas will set out even today once again for Vienna, and if he does not meet the royal army on the way, he will deliver news of the arrival of the Turks." He turned to Gergely. "Immediately after the meet-

324

ing you will write the request to His Majesty, enclosing the letter from the Turks. Draft it in such a way that the very rocks will roll up here below Eger."

"I will," replied Gergely.

"We have no cause to await the Turks with heavy hearts. The walls are strong. There's plenty of gunpowder and food. We have four thousand tithe-lambs in the fortress, and most of them are already smoked. There are 456 beef-cattle, and most of those are smoked too. As for corn, there are 835 bushels of it, most of it made into flour. There's plenty of everything. We can hold out for a year if necessary. Even if the king only despatches his Transylvanian army here, every Turk will leave Eger to join the Prophet. So now read out the second list too," he said to Gergely.

Gergely read, "A large cannon, another large cannon, named Frog and Baba respectively, two. Three cannon from the king, four from Gábor Perényi, one from Benedek Serédy."

"We haven't calculated how much gunpowder there is, because that's impossible," interrupted Dobó. "There was some from last year, and the king has sent more. The floor of the sacristy is full to the brim with gunpowder ready for use. And on top of that we've got saltpetre and a grinding mill so that if necessary we can make our own gunpowder. Go on."

Gergely read, "A large cannon, another large cannon, named guns, five. Bronze siege-guns from His Majesty, four. Bullet-moulds for the siege-guns and falconets, 25. Double-barrelled falconets from Prague, two. Batteries of falconets, five."

"So we can reply to the Turks. But that's nothing. Read on."

"Bronze and iron falconets from Prague and Csetnek, 300. Rifles, 93. German rifles, 194."

"They're worth nothing!" croaked Cecey. "A good bow is worth more than any rifle."

This caused a small controversy. The older ones approved of Cecey's words. The younger ones were for the rifles.

In the end Dobó put an end to the argument by saying that rifles were good and so were bows, but best of all were cannon.

Kristóf the page placed a superbly-crafted gilded helmet and a small silver crucifix on the table. And over his arm he had a cloak like a cope as well. He went and stood behind Dobó, and held it in silence.

Gergely went on reading for quite a time. The list contained every sort of weapon: pikes, spears, shields, various kinds of cannon-ball and bullet, grappling-irons, picks, clubs, fuses, lances and all military equipment that had not been brought in by the troops sent to their aid.

And then Dobó rose. He put the gilded helmet on his head and donned the red velvet commander's cloak. And resting his left hand on the hilt of his sword, he spoke:

"My good friends and fellow-defenders, you have seen the walls, and now you know the strength inside the walls too. It is in this fortress now that the fate of the remnant of the country lies."

There was silence in the room. Every eye was fixed on Dobó.

"If Eger falls, then neither Miskolc nor Kassa can stand. The Turks will shake down the smaller castles like nuts. There will be no further resistance. And then history will be able to inscribe Hungary in the book of the dead."

He looked around grimly and continued: "The fortress of Eger is strong, but we have the example of Szolnok to prove that the strength of the walls lies not in stone, but in the spirit of the defenders. There they employed foreign mercenaries for money. They did not go there to defend the fortress but to receive payment. Here only the five bombardiers are Austrian, but they are all good men. Here everyone is defending his homeland. If necessary, with blood. If necessary, with his life. But never let the next generation say of us that those Hungarians who lived here in 1552 did not deserve the name of Hungarian."

The sun shone in through the window and lit up the arms hanging on the wall and the suits of armour on poles beside the walls. The commander's gilded helmet gleamed in its light too. Gergely was standing beside him. He glanced at the window, then lifted his hand to his eyes so that he could see the commander.

"I have summoned you together," continued Dobó, "in order that you may all take stock of yourselves. For anyone who puts a higher price on his skin than on the future of the nation, the gate still stands open. Men are what I need. Better a few lions than a lot of rabbits. Let anyone who trembles at the approaching storm leave the room before I say any more, for we must swear to defend the fortress with an oath so binding that anyone who breaks it will be unable, after his death, to stand before the eyes of the eternal God."

He looked away and waited to see whether anyone stirred. The room was silent. Nobody moved.

Beside the crucifix stood two wax candles. The page lit them.

Dobó continued his address: "We must swear an oath to each other in the holy name of the eternal God to agree to these conditions..." He picked up a sheet of paper from the table and read out: "First: whatever kind of letter comes henceforth from the Turks, we shall not accept it, but burn it unread in the presence of the defenders of the fortress."

"So be it!" they cried. "We agree!"

"Secondly: when the Turks surround the fortress, nobody is to shout out to them; whatever they may shout to us, there is to be no reply of any kind to it, neither good nor bad."

"We agree!"

"Thirdly: after the siege has begun, there is to be no talking in groups outside or inside, and no whispering in twos or threes."

"We agree!"

"Fourthly: subordinate officers will not give orders to their troops without the knowledge of the captains, nor the captains without the orders of the two commanders."

"We agree!"

A hoarse voice spoke up beside Fügedy. "I should like to add something here."

The speaker was Hegedűs, Serédy's lieutenant. His face had turned red.

"Go on, then!" said those sitting at the table.

"I propose that the two commanders always act together with the captains whenever it happens that in defence or in some other important matter even one of the captains wishes to consult with them."

"I'll accept that when there is a pause in the siege," said Dobó.

"We agree!" they all cried.

Dobó went on: "Finally: Anyone who talks of surrendering

the fortress, asks or answers questions about it or in any other way wishes to surrender the fortress, shall die!"

"Let him die!" they shouted with blazing eyes. "We'll not surrender the fortress! We're not mercenaries! We're not from Szolnok!" came shouts from every corner.

Dobó took off the gilded helmet. He stroked his long grey hair. He nodded to the priest.

Father Bálint got up. He picked up the small silver crucifix that was standing on the table.

"Take the oath with me," said Dobó.

Everyone in the room stretched out a raised hand towards the crucifix.

"I swear by the one living God..."

"I swear by the one living God," came the muted sound of solemn voices.

"That I dedicate my blood and my life to the homeland, the king and the defence of the fortress of Eger. Neither force nor stratagem shall make me afraid. Neither money nor promises shall make me waver. I shall not talk of surrendering the fortress, nor shall I listen to such talk. I shall not surrender myself alive either within the fortress or outside it. In the defence of the fortress, from beginning to end I submit myself and my will to the commands of my superiors. So help me God!"

"So help me God!" they declared with one voice.

"And now I take the oath myself," thundered Dobó with blazing eyes. He raised two fingers to the crucifix. "I swear that to the defence of the fortress and the country I will devote all my strength, my every thought and every drop of my blood. I swear that I will be with you in every peril. I swear that I will not allow the fortress to fall into pagan hands. I will not surrender the fortress or myself alive. So may earth receive my body and heaven my soul. May the eternal God cast me away if I break my oath!"

Every sword flashed. With united breath they shouted, "We swear! We swear! We also swear the same!"

Dobó replaced his helmet and sat down.

"Well now, brethren," he said, picking up a sheaf of paper, "let's discuss where to station the guards on the walls. To defend the walls, we don't need them to be distributed equally, because on the town side and by the new bastion the land is flat and low. It's by the eastern and northern bastions that there are hills and mountains. They're certainly going to site their guns there and batter the walls there to make a charge on the fortress."

"They'll never make a breakthrough," said Cecey dismissively.

"Now, now!" replied Dobó. And he went on: "The reason why I have summoned a good number of carpenters and stonemasons into the fortress is so that they can repair by night any damage caused by the Turks. That's where the greatest work will be. And even if we decide now on the positioning of the guards, that will change during the course of the siege."

"You decide, commander! We'll accept that," they called from all directions.

"Well, I think we'll divide the defenders into four contingents. One at the main gate, a second along the section as far as the corner tower, a third in the outer fortress and the fourth on the north side around the prison bastion. The reserve troops inside will be divided similarly, corresponding to these four contingents. My fellow-commander Mekcsey will be in charge of the reserve troops. During the siege, he will decide how the troops are to be relieved and will be responsible for the defence of the inner fortress too."

"What about the side overlooking the town?" asked Hegedűs.

"We'll only post single sentries there. Twenty men will be sufficient at the gate. In any case it's a narrow entrance for pedestrians only, and the Turks can't attempt an attack there."

He took up another sheet of paper.

"I've divided the forces roughly as follows: at the Old Gate, that is the main gate, and as far as the new bastion one hundred infantrymen are to be on duty at all times. At the Prison Bastion 140, together with one officer, making 141. Along the Sándor Bastion 120, not counting the gate. From there back to the gate 105."

"That's 466," said Gergely.

"Ten infantrymen on each of the two towers of the church. So much for the defence of the inner fortress."

"486," Gergely calculated aloud.

Dobó continued: "Now comes the outer fortress. 90 men from the Csabi Bastion to the Bebek Bastion. From there to the corner tower 130. From the Old Gate to the corner, 58. And at that point there's still a narrow stone wall connecting the inner fortress with the outer one. That's a place for observation rather than arms, so 38 men will be enough there."

Glancing at Mekcsey, he went on:

"We'll post the weaker ones there, and if there's an attack, the walking wounded too."

"799," said Gergely.

"Now how shall we assign the officers? To begin with myself, I want to be available everywhere."

There were enthusiastic cheers.

"We already know my fellow-commander Mekcsey's duties. Of the four captains, one will be at the Old Gate. That's where we need strength and a resolute spirit. For it's to be expected that the Turks will try to break in there. That's where death must be looked boldly in the face."

Gáspár Pető rose and struck his breast. "I'd like that assignment, please!"

Amid the cheering only Dobó's nod of agreement could be seen. Old Cecey offered Pető his left hand.

"Apart from that," he said, "the outer fortress is the most dangerous side. The Turks will try to fill in the moat there. There too we need officers in command who are brave and patriotic and who scorn death."

The other three captains all leapt to their feet.

"I'm ready!" said Bornemissza.

"I'm ready!" said Fügedy.

"I'm ready!" said Zoltay.

"Well, to stop you quarrelling over it," smiled Dobó, "you'll all three be there."

The bombardiers had already been posted. But Dobó still needed someone to command them. Who should it be?

The only officer with any knowledge of cannon was Dobó. So he undertook this duty.

At this a new bout of cheering shook the walls of the room, and they looked at the bombardiers, who asked anxiously, *"Was ist das? Was sagt er?"*

Bornemissza turned to them and explained to the five

330

Austrians, *"Meine Herrn. Kapitany Dobó wird sein der Haupt Bum-bum! Verstanden?"*

Next Dobó had the trumpeters summon the troops. In the yard of the fortress he also read out to them the five points to which those inside had sworn their agreement. He told any who were afraid to lay down their arms rather than scare the rest too. "For," he said, "fear is just as infectious a disease as the plague. Indeed it is worse, for it is transferred to the next man in an instant. Well, in the difficult days that lie ahead for us, we need men whose spirits are strong."

Then he unfurled the blue and red banner of the fortress and joined it with the national colours.

"Take the oath!"

At these words the bell of the cathedral in the town rang out. It pealed just once, and no more.

Everyone looked towards the town. The peal was like a cry for help. Just one. And after it an expectant silence fell on the fortress, the town and the surrounding countryside.

5

That evening Dobó entertained all who in the morning had taken the oath in that room.

Dobó sat at one end of the table, Mekcsey at the other. On Dobó's right was Father Bálint, on his left Cecey. Next to the priest was Pető, a hail-fellow-well-met man with his stubbly moustache waxed almost flat. In any case Pető was to be honoured with this high place. His elder brother János Pető was a court dignitary, the king's chief cup-bearer. It was through him that he had come to the fortress, and it was he who had sent the gunpowder and the five bombardiers from Vienna. Only after him were the others seated according to age or rank, beginning from either Mekcsey or Dobó: Zoltay, the fair-haired lanky man whose eyes were apparently aiming at hurling a lance, but whose lips were always smiling. Bornemissza; Fügedy, the stocky man with a wolf's forelock. Then Farkas Koron, lieutenant of the Abaúj county infantrymen, a young dark man with jaws of steel. Bálint Kendy and István Hegedűs, György

331

Serédy's lieutenants who had brought along along fifty infantrymen. Lőrinc Fekete, who had brought fourteen men from Regéc, a jaunty red-faced man whose hair, greying early, had been hideously cropped by the barber. Mihály Lőkös, despatched with a hundred infantry by the free cities, a big man with the face of a child. Pál Nagy, who commanded György Bátori's thirty footsoldiers, a bold man with the strength of a bull. Márton Jászay, the lieutenant in charge of the forty infantrymen sent by the Provost of Jászó, resembled a tranquil young clerk, with his black hair parted in the middle. Márton Szency, a lieutenant from Szepes who had brought forty foot-soldiers, was a thickset, rather stout man in a blue jacket, and had piercing eyes. Mihály Bor, an excellent marksman, had been despatched there with 76 infantrymen from the county of Sáros; he had a dreamy expression and a thin blonde moustache, as if his coat of arms depicted moonlight and a musical clock. From Ugocsa came György Szalacsky, a sturdy-legged man with double chin and stern gaze, and Imre Nagy, a genial and well-mannered young man who respected everybody. He had been sent with eighteen infantrymen by Mrs. Gábor Homonnay. From Eperjes Antal Blaskó had come, a strong man with a curly beard and a petulant expression, wearing a blue hussar's jacket with a big, heavy sword at his side.

All these were lieutenants. After them in rank came Jób Paksy, the tallest officer in the royal army, whose warm glance radiated affection and whose long moustache was waxed stiff. Then there was Tamás Bolyky, in charge of fifty riflemen from Borsod; though his hair and beard were grey, his movements were those of a young man. They arrived late, so they were seated among the officials belonging to the fortress: János Sukán, the elderly steward, Imre the clerk and supervisor of the wine-cellar, Mihály, another clerk and catering officer, or "loaf-distributor", as they called them in those days, Mátyás Gyöngyösy, the bishop's secretary (the fortress was part of the bishop's estate), Boldizsár, another secretary, and one or two others. For Dobó had invited not only the officers, but also a corporal, a private, a nobleman from Eger and a peasant also from the town, in order to show his respect for all the defenders of the fortress.

Serving the meal was the duty of the four or five servants in Dobó's house, but to lighten their burden, the chief officers sent their own servants along too. Behind Dobó stood Kristóf Tarjáni the page. It was he who served Dobó, setting the food in front of him and refilling his glass whenever it was empty.

That day was a Friday, so the meal began with pike and horseradish, then continued with fried pike-perch, sheat-fish and sturgeon; it ended with noodles and cheese and dried fruit stewed with cinnamon. But the table was also well supplied with cow's cheese, grapes, apples, pears and melons.

Why did the frugal Dobó give this dinner? Was it to end the meeting where the oath had been sworn? Or so that the officers who had not known each other beforehand might become better acquainted? Or was he examining the strength of their spirits in the light of the wine, maybe? At first the atmosphere was solemn, almost church-like. The great and sacred seriousness of the oath-taking still clouded their brows. The snow-white tablecloths, the silver cutlery bearing Dobó's coat of arms, the carved barrel hanging on a chain above the table and the posies of autumn flowers all helped to increase their sense of occasion.

Even after the pike, when fine garnet-coloured wine was poured from the barrel into the glasses, none of their hands grew warm. Dobó's noble speech still vibrated in their spirits, just as after the peal of a bell we can still hear the silence resonating for a long time.

The servants changed the plates after the fried fish. Everyone waited for Dobó to toast his guests. But he just sat with a weary expression in his brown leather armchair. Perhaps he thought that this was no name-day, no wedding-feast; after the oath he was their commanding officer, and he was merely sitting at dinner with his subordinates. All the same, they expected him to say something.

The great silence was suddenly broken by the sound of the cooks singing happily:

I live at the end of the village. And why?
To water his horse there my darling rides by:
To water his horse and to strut round the place
Till I plant a big kiss on his merry red face.

333

The clouds dispersed immediately. The sky grew bright. Could the men remain solemn and serious when the women awaited the oncoming peril with a song? Mekcsey picked up the silver goblet in front of him and rose. "My good friends!" he said. "Great days are ahead of us. The good God himself is sitting at the window of heaven to see how two thousand men here will fight against two hundred thousand. And yet I do not despair. There is not a single coward among us. Why, even the women down there are singing happily, as we can hear. But even if this were not so, there are amongst us two men at whose side not even the blind or lame can despair. I've known both of them from early youth. One was created by God to be an example of Hungarian bravery. He has the strength of iron in him. He is like a gilded sword. He is all strength and nobility. And the other, whom I have also known since my youth, is a master of intelligence and boldness, presence of mind and inventiveness. Where these two men are present, I feel myself to be confident in the presence of strength and ingenuity. Where they are, Hungarian bravery, Hungarian intelligence and Hungarian glory go with them. One cannot fear any peril. My wish is that you should know them as I do, István Dobó, our commander and Gergely Bornemissza, our captain."

Dobó stood to receive the toast, then stayed on his feet. And he replied: "My dear brothers! Even if I were as scared as a deer and started quivering at the barking of any pack of dogs, I stop and resist when the fate of my nation is at stake. The example of Jurisics proves what strength lies in the most ill-favoured fortress if there are real men in it. Our fortress is stronger than Kőszeg was, and we too must be stronger. I know the Turkish army. When I had hardly begun to grow a moustache I was there on the field of Mohács and saw Suleyman's wild host. Believe me, those 28,000 Hungarians would have overrun that mob of 100,000 if there had been a single man there who knew how to direct the battle. There was no one to direct or give orders there. The troops were deployed not in accordance with the disposition of the enemy, but just arbitrarily. Poor Tomory was a heroic figure of noble memory, but no leader. He thought that the science of leadership consisted of the one command, "Follow me!" So he said a prayer, then gave a curse and said "Follow me!" And with that our army set off like a whirlwind into the middle of the Turkish horde. And the Turks scattered at our approach like a flock of geese. And we dashed blindly forward on our frantic steeds with the old Hungarian fire straight into the line of cannon. Naturally the cannon, the chain-shot, did what human strength could not do. Of the 28,000, only 4000 of us remained alive. But this appalling tragedy has provided two great lessons. One is that the Turkish army is not a mass of soldiers but an assortment of riff-raff. They assemble together all sorts of men and animals simply to scare chicken-hearted folk with their numbers. The other lesson is that however few the Hungarians are in number, they can confuse and conquer the Turks if alongside their bravery they take intelligence with them as a shield."

Those sitting at the table listened to the commander with puckered brows.

Dobó went on: "In our situation, intelligence demands that our feet be of iron until the king's army arrives. The Turks will bombard the fortress and wreck it; maybe they will destroy the walls which give us some protection. But then is the time we shall have to stand our ground. And as the walls have defended us, we shall have to defend the walls. The enemy scaling the walls will find us in every breach. We will never allow the fate of the Hungarian nation to be wrenched out of our hands!"

"Never! No! No! We'll not allow it!" they all shouted, leaping up.

"Thank you for coming," Dobó continued. "Thank you for bringing your swords and hearts to defend the country. I have a very strong feeling that God is stretching his hand over the fortress of Eger and saying to the sea of pagans, "Thus far and no further!" Let this feeling strengthen you too, and then I shall believe for certain that in this same place we shall also celebrate our victory with a feast."

"So be it!" came shouts from all sides and the clink of silver and zinc goblets.

Dobó was followed by Pető, the captain whose movements were so brisk. He jerked his head to right and left and twirled his moustache. He smiled into his cup and then grew serious again. In the end he spoke: "Friend Mekcsey trusts in Dobó and

335

Bornemissza. And they trust in us and in the walls. Well, I too shall declare what I believe in."

"Tell us! Tell us!"

"Two strong fortresses have fallen this year among the rest, Temesvár and Szolnok."

"And Veszprém?"

"There were no men in Veszprém. Why did those two strong fortresses fall? In due course they'll say that they fell because the Turks were stronger, but that's not so. They fell because Temesvár was defended by Spanish mercenaries, Szolnok by Spaniards, Czechs and Germans. And now I'll tell you what I believe in. In the fact that Eger is not defended by Spaniards, Czechs or Germans. Here, apart from the five bombardiers, everyone is Hungarian, and most of them are from Eger. Lions defending their own den! I trust in Hungarian blood!"

By now every face was warm and cups were raised. Pető might well have ended his speech here, but with the verbosity of a demagogue he went on: "And the Hungarian is like flint. The more he is struck, the better he sparks. So as for that water-drinking riff-raff plucked from Mohamed's shacks and dropped from fig-trees, surely these two thousand soldiers born of Hungarian mothers to be heroes, reared on horseback, fortified by Hungarian corn and draughts of Eger Bull's Blood can deal with them!"

His words were drowned in a storm of cheering, rattling of swords and laughter, but once again he merely twirled his moustache, gave a sideways glance and finished his speech: "Up to now Eger has simply been a noble town, the town of the Hungarians of the counties of Heves and Borsod. God grant that henceforth it may be the town of Hungarian glory. Let us inscribe on the walls in pagan blood, 'Hands off the Hungarian!' And when with the passage of centuries the moss of eternal peace on earth covers the remains of this fortress with green, may the sons of future generations be able to walk here with heads bare and say with a sense of pride, 'It was our fathers who fought here; blessed be their ashes'!"

At this there was such a disturbance and the speaker was covered in such embraces that he could not continue. Nor did he want to. He sat down and offered his hand to Tamás Bolyky, the lieutenant of the troops from Borsod.

"Tamás," he said, "may the Turks' heads be addled where the two of us shall be!"

"You spoke so splendidly," replied Tamás with a nod, "that I'd like to charge a hundred Turks this very instant!"

After Pető nobody felt strong enough to propose a toast. They kept asking Gergely, but he was a scholar and not used to public speaking. So everyone just talked to his neighbour and the happy buzz of dinner-time conversation filled the room. Dobó also relaxed in the warmth and raised his cup to first one, then another of his neighbours. At one point he held it out towards Gergely, and as the priest went to sit beside Pető and talk, he beckoned him over.

"Come and sit here, my boy."

Then, when Gergely had sat down by him, he went on:

"I want to talk to you about the Török boys. I wrote to them too, but there's no point in it, is there?"

"You're right," said Gergely, setting down his cup in front of him. "I don't think we shall see them. Jancsi prefers to fight the Turks in the open, and Feri won't come as far as this. He won't leave Transdanubia."

"Is it true that Master Bálint is dead?"

"Yes, poor man. He died a couple of months ago. Only death released him from his chains."

"How long did he survive his wife?"

"A good few years. His wife, you may know, died when we came back from Constantinople. Her funeral was just when we arrived in Debrecen."

"She was a good woman," nodded Dobó, deep in thought. And he reached for his cup as if to drink to her.

"True, there aren't many like her in the world," sighed Gergely. And he too reached for his cup. They touched them silently. Perhaps the thought crossed both their minds that the good lady saw from up there the cups raised in her honour.

"What about Zrínyi then?" Dobó began again. "I wrote to him too, asking him to come to Eger."

"And he would have come too, but for months now he's kept hearing reports that the Pasha of Bosnia is preparing to attack

337

him. I talked with Uncle Miklós at Csáktornya in February. He knew then that the Turks were marching on Temesvár, Szolnok and Eger with a large army. He had me write the letter to the king."

"I don't understand that Lukács either. He should be here by now!" and his face darkened. "And there's Varsányi too, my spy... He should have reported..."

The sound of pipes and trumpets arose outside the door:

> Mishka in his yellow boots walks the muddy lane,
> At the brook his Annie waits for him again.

It was like an infusion of new blood. At a nod from Dobó the page let the players in. There were three pipers and two trumpeters. Among them was the gypsy too, with a huge rusty helmet on his head and three cock feathers stuck in it. At his side was a naked sword on a piece of string, and there were enormous spurs on his bare feet. His cheeks were puffed out as he blew his wooden pipe.

They were all glad to listen to them. When they had repeated their tune, a deep baritone voice rose from among the lieutenants:

> Heaven deck the willows quickly now with green!
> Once again my saddle on my steed be seen,
> Let me try my waiting weapons once again;
> Let the Turks lament if e'er they hear my name.

The singer was a well-built young man with a curling moustache. This moustache always lay horizontally beneath his nose in such a way that he was recognizable from behind too.

"Who's that lieutenant?" asked Gergely, leaning towards Dobó.

"Jób Paksy, the younger brother of the commander of Komárom."

"He's got a good voice."

"And he's undoubtedly a brave lad. Men who are good at singing always make good soldiers."

"And that fiery-eyed young man with a curling moustache?"

"Pista Budaházy; in the cavalry."

"He looks a born fighter. What about that one lower down, with a dense beard? He's just reaching for his cup."

"Ferenc Bay, also in the cavalry. Likewise a good fellow."

"And that jaunty young man with a silk scarf next to the civilian from Eger?"

"Pista Fekete, cavalry officer."

"Yes, of course; I've had a talk with him."

Lieutenant Paksy wanted to sing another verse of his song, but could not remember the words. The players were also waiting to begin. In the momentary pause someone suddenly shouted out, "Hurrah for the priest!"

"Hurrah for the old man among us!" called Zoltay.

Cecey responded jovially, "Old man, my aunt!"

"Hurrah for the youngest defender of the fortress!" shouted Pető. At this Kristóf Tarjáni also reached for a cup and blushed as he touched it with those of the guests.

"Hurrah for the first Turk whose teeth we knock out!" shouted Gergely. There was no one to respond to this toast. Everyone laughed and touched his neighbour's cup.

The red-faced nobleman from Eger rose from his seat. He threw his blue collared cloak over his right shoulder. He gave his moustache a wipe on both sides and then stroked back his hair. And he spoke: "Hurrah for the first man to die for Eger!"

He looked around proudly and seriously, and without clinking his cup with anyone drained it to the last drop.

He hardly realized that he was toasting himself.

*

The hand of the tall clock pointed to eleven when in stepped a sentry and halted in the doorway. He reported:

"Commander, the Turks have reached Maklár."

"Only the advance-guards, my lad."

"More than that, sir. They're flooding in by moonlight like the tide. You can see lots of tents and fires."

"Then they'll be here tomorrow," nodded Dobó. And he dismissed the sentry, saying that there was no need for them to bring any further reports till morning.

Then he rose. That was the signal for them to disperse.

Mekcsey drew Gergely aside into one corner of the room, together with Fügedy, Pető and Zoltay. He exchanged a few words with them, then hurried over to Dobó. He clicked his heels.

"Commander, we'd like to go out tonight, about two hundred of us."

"Where the hell to?"

"Maklár."

"Maklár?"

"To say good-evening to the Turks."

Dobó gave his moustache a good-humoured twist. Then he went over to the window-recess. Mekcsey had to follow him.

"All right, Pista!" he said. "I've no objection. A charge like that will put new heart into the defenders."

"That was what I thought too."

"If there's a strong fighting spirit around the sword does its work better. But I'm not allowing you to go."

Mekcsey showed his disappointment. Dobó looked at him calmly.

"You're like a bull. You charge every tree and all of a sudden you'll be unable to withdraw your horns. And you're the one to look after your head, so that if mine falls, yours will still be there. I'm not saying that to anyone else. But Bornemissza and the others may go. Gergely is a more cautious man, so let him be the one to harass the Turkish vanguard. Call him over here."

Gergely came immediately.

"Well, you may go out, Gergely," said Dobó, "but not with two hundred men. You can take eighty or ninety. That will be plenty. You'll make a charge, harry them a bit and return. And there are to be no casualties."

But by this time the other officers were there too. "Do let me go as well, sir."

"You can't all go. I've put Bornemissza in charge. He may choose three of you. Let those he doesn't choose remember their oath: total obedience!"

"Pető, Zoltay, Fügedy," ordered Gergely.

The silk-scarfed Pista Fekete looked so pleadingly that Gergely included him too. "I've already had a word with Pista Fekete."

340

"Sir," pleaded the young page Tarjáni, "let me go with them too!"

Dobó gave his moustache another stroke. "All right. I've no objection. But you must always keep behind Captain Gergely. And if they happen to strike you dead, don't you dare come into my presence again. That's all I have to say."

6

Gergely almost ran to the monastery where the cavalry were quartered. Instead of a bugle-call, he fired a pistol-shot in the broad corridor.

The men leapt out of their beds.

"To me, quickly now!" shouted Gergely.

He chose the nimblest of them for his company.

"One, two, three! Get dressed! By the time I've counted three I want you at the gate, on horseback and armed with swords. You there, run to the commander's deputy and collect a mantrap from him. Bring it with you. Everyone carry a small rifle across your saddle."

"Small rifle" was the term they used then for pistol.

Gergely ran down the steps and hurried down to the stables. By the light of a red lamp shining from one of the arches he caught sight of a man in a helmet and yellow jacket. He was sitting on an upturned wooden tub with a water-melon on his knee. He was scooping it out.

The man was barefooted.

Gergely shouted at him, "Sárközi!"

"Sir?" replied the gypsy eagerly.

"If you come with me, you can get hold of a horse today, and a fine one at that!"

The gypsy put the water-melon on the ground.

"I'm coming. Where to?"

"To the Turks," replied Gergely merrily. "They're asleep now. We'll give them a surprise."

The gypsy scratched his head. He looked at the melon. He sat down again on the tub.

"No, I can't come after all," he said seriously.

"Why not?"

"Because I took the oath today with the rest of them that I wouldn't leave the fortress."

"But that's not what we swore. We swore to defend it."

"Maybe that's what the others swore," replied the gypsy, raising his shoulder almost up to his ear. "What I swore was that I'd be struck dead if I left the fortress, so 'elp me God." And with that he picked up the melon and put it in his lap. He wagged his head and went on eating.

*

Gergely was soon riding outside on the road to Maklár with Pető, Fügedy and Zoltay under a moonlit starry sky. About fifty paces ahead of them rode the corporal, Pista Fekete, and Péter Bódogfalvi, a private from Eger who knew the way. Beyond the Warm Lake they turned off into the fields. There the sound of the horses' hooves was swallowed up by the soft earth. The hundred riders resembled a hundred fleeting shadows.

They caught sight of the first watchfires in the willows at Andornak. Péter halted. So did the rest.

The sickle of the moon among the clouds gave just enough light for the shapes of trees and men to stand out like black shadows in the night.

Gergely rode over to Bódogfalvi.

"Dismount. Go along as far as the first sentry, keeping low and crawling like a snake. If he's got a dog with him and it barks at you, come back just as silently and close to the ground as when you went. If he hasn't got a dog, creep round behind him and stab him. Then take a look at the fire. If there are no other guards beside it, wrap a pinch of gunpowder in a tree or burdock leaf and throw it on it. But get down that instant so that nobody catches sight of you."

"What about my horse?"

"Tie your horse to this tree. You'll find it here when you get back."

"And if there are guards at the fire?"

"Have a good look round to see where and how they are lying and where most of them are. Then come back here quickly."

They stood for a good half hour by the banks of the stream beside the willows. Gergely gave his orders.

"So long as you see them running, hit them and strike them. Nobody is to go further than a hundred paces from his neighbour in case he takes a tumble. As soon as you hear the sound of the bugle, we turn and gallop back home. Until the bugle sounds, you're free to enjoy yourselves."

The men stood round in a circle, drinking in every word.

Gergely went on: "They'll take fright and won't think of resisting. But if they do, keep striking where they are closest together until they fall apart. Learn once and for all that anyone fighting on horseback must strike so swiftly that the enemy hasn't time to strike back. The blow must fall like hail."

"Like lightning in a thunderstorm," added Pető.

Gergely fell silent. He listened for the Turks. Then he turned to the men again. "Where's the mantrap?"

"Here it is, captain," replied a jolly voice from the lines. And a tall young man came forward.

"Have you got it with you?"

"Yes, sir." And he raised aloft a long, fork-shaped instrument.

"Do you know how to use it?"

"The captain taught me."

"Well then, just grab the neck of one of them with it and bring the dog down. It would be splendid, lads, if we could capture one of their high-ranking officers. They usually have the finest tents. And they're most likely to be sleeping in only a nightshirt. Let's grab one of them if we can."

He listened again. Then he continued: "The prisoner must be tied up, but only his hands. And those behind his back. If we can get hold of a horse too, we'll set him on it. And in that case you, Kristóf, and you little man there put him between you, tie his horse's reins to yours and fetch him along. If he tries to escape or talk or shout out, or slip off backwards, hit him immediately!"

"Suppose we can't get hold of a horse?" asked Kristóf.

"Then make him run beside your horses and get off home as quickly as you can. Don't wait for us."

They fell silent. The night was quiet. Only the mournful drone of the cricket could be heard from the vineyards, and the occasional soft noise of horses pawing the ground.

"It's flared up," a voice said at long last. They all saw the sudden flare of the fire.

"He's coming!" said several voices after a pause. And every hand gripped the reins.

The figure of Péter broke out of the darkness of the bushes. He arrived at a run.

"I stabbed the sentry," he panted. "He didn't utter a sound, but just fell over like a sack. The fire's burning in the middle of the tents. There's just one Turkish servant sitting beside it. He's got yellow slippers in his hands and yellow paint on his knees."

"He's a batman," smiled Gergely. "Go on."

"The rest are lying on the grass in their hundreds, on blankets, all together to the left of the fire."

"Are they sleeping?"

"Like logs."

Gergely tightened the string of his cap under his chin.

"Right then, lads, keep well apart, at least ten paces. We'll make a circle round them. When I fire my pistol, you all fire yours into the middle of them and fall on them like wolves. Shout, scream and strike with all your might!"

"Shout as if there were a thousand of us!" added Pető.

Meanwhile Bódogfalvi had also mounted his horse. They scattered towards the east.

Pető was right on the wing. The three eagle's feathers in his helmet made him easily recognizable from a distance. He led the long line of cavalry in a semicircle and adapted his speed to that of Gergely's trot.

Now Gergely was in command. For a while he trotted gently along the line of the bushes, then he suddenly broke into a swift gallop.

The wild cry of the first Turk shrilled into the night. He fired his pistol at Gergely. Gergely returned the fire. The next minute all the pistols fired and the hundred cavalrymen swept like a whirlwind from hell on to the sleeping Turkish troops, shouting at the tops of their voices.

At that instant the forest of tents came alive with creaks and cries. The shouts of Turks and Hungarians mingled into a single

344

tempest of sound. Those sleeping on the ground lost their heads, started up, leaping, running and pushing their way through the tents hard on each other's heels.

"Forward! Forward!" shouts Gergely.

"Allah! Allah akbar!" scream the Turks.

"Curse you!" cries a hoarse voice.

"Strike the dog!" thunders Gáspár Pető somewhere among the tents.

Turkish shouts, Hungarian curses. Shadows dodge, leap and mingle. Swords glint and swish, clubs thud, horses clatter and snort, tents creak, dogs whimper. The ground trembles beneath the galloping of the hundred cavalry.

Gergely gallops into a pack of pagans squeezed in between two tents. He slashes them right and left. He feels his sword pierce flesh each time; they fall in front of him, parting aside like corn in June when a hound gallops through it.

"Allah! Allah!"

"Damn your eyes, you pagan cur! Take that!"

All the Turkish horses are grazing together in a herd. The fleeing Turks slash the hobbles with *yataghans* and leap on to them.

"Follow me, lads!" cries Gergely.

And they assail the riders too. They cut and stab men and horses alike. Swords rattle and lances clash.

"Allah! Allah!"

"Christ, help us! There you are, you dog!"

Hatchets rain down too. The Turks jump on horseback in sheer terror. Sometimes there are two to a horse. All who can escape on horseback. Those who cannot reach a horse slip away on foot in the darkness.

Gergely, however, does not pursue them. He halts and has the bugler summon his men together. They gallop towards him from all directions through the tents.

"The Turks are on the run!" shouts Gergely. "Seize everything you can carry! Nobody let go of his horse! Wherever there's a fire in front of a tent, kick the fire on to it!"

The men all disperse. Gergely shakes the blood off his sword and plunges it about three times into the canvas of a tent to clean it.

"Ugh! What a filthy business!" he pants to Zoltay, who is wiping his sword in a similar way. Then when there were no more Turks left moving anywhere there, he called Fügedy to come.

"Let's have a look at all the tents in turn."

In the feeble light of the moon it was impossible to tell which belonged to the commanding officer. The tents were all different. One was circular, the next square. And if a tent was more showy than the rest, that was merely because it had been set up in advance. Ordinary soldiers slept in it.

From one of the tents Gergely picked up a horse-tailed banner, and seeing Kristóf he called to him, "Well, lad, did you strike any of them?"

"Two," panted the boy.

"Only two?"

"The rest ran away from me!"

The men rounded up a few carts and waggons too. They threw on to them what they could not find room for on their horses: carpets, gilded horse-tails, horse-collars with precious stones decorating them, riding equipment, clothes-chests, helmets, arms, cooking vessels and everything else they could lay hands on. They even dismantled a tent or two and threw them into a cart.

Dawn was breaking when they arrived back at the fortress.

Dobó was waiting impatiently for them on the bastion. If the raid had been unsuccessful, the defenders would despair. And he was particularly worried that Gergely had taken three of the chief officers with him. But when he caught sight of the page galloping ahead, then after a pause the loaded horses, waggons and carts and Gergely brandishing the horse-tail banner in the distance, his face lit up with delight.

When the soldiers thundered through the gate the defenders were all waiting for them and cheered them heartily.

The soldiers had not only survived intact, but increased in number. The tall private brought along a Turk with a gag in his mouth. A Turk in a short blue waistcoat, yellow trousers and sandals. He had no turban on his head, so it was seen that his head was shaven and his mouth was hidden by a bushy grey moustache. He was still rolling his bloodshot eyes angrily. The soldier dragged him straight to Dobó. There he pulled the turban-gag out of his mouth.

"Beg to report, sir, we've brought in a tongue too."

"Idiot!" the Turk, fierce as a tiger, roared in his face.

Dobó was not a man to laugh, but at that moment he laughed so much that the tears rolled down his cheeks.

"Varsányi," he said to the prisoner, "you play the Turk very well, don't you?" And he turned to the soldier. "You can release him. After all, he's one of our spies."

"I wanted to tell the fool that I was Hungarian," complained Varsányi, "but every time I opened my mouth he hit me on the head, and then he even gagged me."

And he raised his hand to hit him. The soldier got out of his way in embarrassment.

*

Dobó beckoned Gergely and Mekcsey to him. And he also spoke to the spy.

"Come along."

He went into the tower that stood at the inner gate and entered the guardroom.

He sat down in a wicker armchair and nodded to Varsányi to report.

"Well, sir," began the spy, rubbing his forearm, "the entire army's on its way. Ahmed Pasha is leading. Last night the army slept at Abony. They sent the vanguard as far as Maklár with Manda Bey. Damnation!..." he added in a different tone.

The "Damnation!" was for the soldier who had dragged him off to Eger. The cord had left deep furrows on his hands, and a couple of blows still ached on his head.

"What? Was there a bey with you?" Gergely asked in surprise. "Why, we might have captured him!"

"Not very likely," replied the spy. "He's as fat as a pig. He weighs 300 pounds, if not more."

"What did you say his name was?"

"Manda. Bullets don't touch him. He's not been a bey very long. It was only in the summer that he was promoted after the battle at Temesvár. The soldiers, by the way, call him *Hayvan*."

Gergely shook his head with a smile. "He's the one I was

347

talking about the other evening," he said to the two commanders. "Well, here bullets will touch him."

"Tell us more," said Dobó to the spy.

"Then there's the beylerbey, Mehmed Sokolovich. He's a good shot. He is the one who sites the guns and gives the first order to fire. They say his eyes are so keen he can even see through walls. Myself, I don't believe it."

"How many big guns have they got?"

"Old siege guns, sixteen. Other big guns, eighty-five. Smaller cannon, 150. A very great number of mortars. They're bringing 140 cartloads of cannon-balls and bullets, and I've seen 200 camels carrying gunpowder. In one waggon drawn by four oxen, there's nothing but marble cannon-balls, the size of the biggest water-melon."

"Has the army got good supplies of food?"

"There's not a lot of rice. That's only being distributed to the officers now. But they steal flour, sheep and cattle wherever they go."

"Is there any disease in the army?"

"None. Only Kason Bey fell sick at Hatvan, and that was through eating cucumber."

"Who else is coming?"

"Arslan Bey."

"The son of the former Pasha of Buda?"

"Yes."

"And who else?"

"Mustafa Bey, Kamber Bey, the Bey of Belgrade, the Bey of Szendrő, Dervish Bey, Veli Bey..."

"Confound that Veli Bey!" exploded Mekcsey. "I'll make him sing!"

"Yes, and we'll make him dance too," said Gergely.

"What about that Dervish Bey?" went on Dobó. "What sort of a chap is he?"

Varsányi shook his head. "He's very odd. A normal bey like the rest, but when he's in battle he takes off his bey's uniform and puts on a hair-shirt. That's why they call him Dervish Bey."

And he looked uncomfortably at Dobó, because he realized from the question that another of Dobó's spies had got there before him.

"What sort of a man is he?" Dobó continued his questioning. "What troops does he command?"

"I saw him with the cavalry. He's only got one eye. Earlier he was a janissary aga and his real name is Yumurdjak."

At this name Gergely's hand came to life and slid down to his sword. "Yumurdjak," he repeated. "Do you remember him, sir? Why, it was from him that I was set free when I was a child."

Dobó shook his head. "In my lifetime I've crossed swords with so many Turks that it's no surprise at all if I forget one or two of them." He clutched his forehead. "But of course I know him. He's Arslan Bey's younger brother. And a damned cruel man!" And he turned again to the spy. "What were you in the army?"

"Most recently I was Manda Bey's servant. Devil take that bull of a man who captured me! I might have brought you news of all their intentions."

"And how did you get alongside the bey?"

"I made friends with his servant and kept hanging around his tent. Beneath Hatvan the bey flew into a rage against him and beat him. Since he had seen me around a lot, he simply called me over, because by then I too knew how to boil ink."

"What?"

"Ink. He drinks ink like we do wine, sir. Morning, noon and night he drinks nothing but ink."

"Come off it! It can't be ink."

"Oh but it is ink, sir, good genuine black ink. They make it out of some kind of bean, and it's so bitter that I was still spitting it out the day after when I tasted it. And in Turkish the name of the bean is *kahve*."

The officers looked at one another. Not one of them had yet heard of coffee.

"Anyway, it's a good thing you got thus far," Dobó was thinking aloud. "What do they say in the army about Eger? Do they talk of it as strong, or do they think it will be an easy task?"

The spy shrugged.

"After the fall of Szolnok, sir, they think the whole world's theirs. They say that Ali Pasha wrote to Ahmed that Eger's only a tumbledown sheepfold."

"You mean they haven't linked up yet?"

349

"Not yet."

Dobó looked at Mekcsey, who smiled and gave a shrug. "Ah well, they'll soon discover what sharp teeth the sheep have in this tumbledown sheepfold."

The spy went on: "There are a lot of riff-raff in the camp. The army's accompanied by all sorts of Greek merchants, rope-dancers, Armenians, horse-traders and gypsies. They've got prisoners too: several hundred of them, mainly women from Temesvár. They're all divided up among the officers."

"The rascals!" exploded Mekcsey.

The spy continued: "As for male prisoners, I've seen only boys, and of course the drivers who transport the cannon-balls. At least ten times every day Arslan Bey says that as soon as the folk in Eger catch a glimpse of the countless host they'll run away just like those of Szolnok."

"What's the main strength of the army?"

"All the janissaries, and the even greater number of *müsellem* cavalry. There are also sappers with them. They're called *lagumdjis*. And there are also *kumbaradjis*, who toss shrapnel-bombs into the fortress with pikes and slings."

Dobó got up.

"All right. Now just go and get some rest. Show yourself to the defenders, particularly to the sentries in the watch-towers, so that they'll recognize you if they don't know you already. Tonight you'll return to the Turkish camp. If you've got anything to report, come below the wall on the town side and give a whistle. After all, the guards at the gate know your whistle by now."

7

In the market-place the auction began immediately. There were five loaded carts and eight small Turkish horses.

They dragged the clerk in charge of provisioning out of his bed. He had a table in front of him and a drum at his side. They made Bódogfalvi the auctioneer.

"Let's begin with the horses," said Pető.

"One fine Arab horse," began Bódogfalvi.

350

"Put the two together," said Mekcsey, for there were two identical little piebald horses in the loot.

Well, nobody made a bid for them, but they went all the same. Dobó had asked Mekcsey to buy the two fine horses for the pages. So Mekcsey waited to see whether anyone would bid. But everyone was keeping hold of his money, waiting for the arms and clothing. Mekcsey bought all eight horses for four forints and led them off to the stables.

Next came the carts. There were plenty of fine weapons in them. Swords set with precious stones and rifles with ivory butts could be bought for one or two dinars. The women bargained for the clothes. Fügedy bought a twenty-pound mace, Jób Paksy a velvet saddle-cloth, and Zoltay a silver helmet with a nose-piece. Money fell on clerk Mihály's table, and he kept a careful note of who bought what and how much he gave for it.

When they had got to the bottom of the first cartload, Bódog-falvi called out merrily, "And the next item is the treasure chest belonging to the famous King Darius!"

And with the help of a soldier with large hands he lifted a fine calf-hide chest on to the tail of the cart. The chest was shut, but there was no obvious lock or padlock on it. They had to use a hatchet to break it open.

The assembled crowd jostled each other to see what was in it. Even if it was not the treasure of Darius, there must surely be some valuable things in it.

Even the two innkeepers were standing there, Laci Nagy and Gyuri Debrőy, both wearing blue aprons.

"I'd like to buy a couple of silver goblets," said Debrőy, "so that if any gentlemen drop in for a drink they can do so in style."

"I'd like a nice silk scarf," said a pasty-faced young woman in red boots. And she glanced at a dark young soldier. The lad immediately felt in his pocket.

For since they had now thrown a pile of women's clothes and a few flower-pots out of the cart it was plain that some Turkish officers had brought their wives along too.

"I'd just like a pair of slippers," said an elderly woman long-ingly. "They've always told me that the Turks make good slippers."

The chest sprang open. To the considerable astonishment of

the onlookers, a little boy six or seven years old rose out of it. A white-faced, scared little Turkish boy with hazel eyes. His hair was cropped short. A little shirt covered his body. Round his neck hung a little gold coin.

Bódogfalvi cursed. "Damn and blast those pigtailed barbarians!" And feigning disgust he wrinkled his nose. They all laughed.

"Strike the child dead!" shouted a soldier from the next cart.

"Destroy him root and branch!" called another one.

The boy burst into tears.

"Get out of it then, for goodness' sake!" Bódogfalvi roared at him. And he grasped him by the shoulder. He raised him out of the chest and threw him on to the grass so that he fell over.

The child screamed.

Everyone looked at him as if he were some kind of toad.

"Oh, what an ugly child!" said one woman.

"No, he's not," retorted another.

Meanwhile the boy stood there with tearful, scared eyes and drooping mouth. He kept wiping his eyes all the time. He looked in terror from one woman to another. He dare not cry aloud, so he just whimpered.

"Go on! Strike him dead!" The soldier who was unfolding a tent gave a shake of his fist.

The boy took fright at the sound of his voice, ran to a woman and buried his face in her skirt. It happened to be the one who had said how ugly he was. An old woman, thin and hawk-nosed, who was one of the cooks. Even then her sleeves were rolled up, and she wore a head-scarf knotted at the back.

"Oh no! How could we?" she said, putting her hand on the boy's head. "Suppose he isn't Turkish after all? You're not a Turk, are you, my boy?"

The child raised his face but did not speak.

"What else could he be?" said Bódogfalvi. "Here are his clothes too. Here's his cap, a red one; here's his jacket, that's red too. And whoever's seen trousers like these? There's a cord at the bottom to tie them up like a sack."

And he threw down the boy's clothes.

"*Annem,*" the child spoke out, "*nerede?*"

"There you are! He's Hungarian!" the woman shouted in triumph. He's saying, *"Anyám, gyer ide!"* [Mother, come here!]

"Of course he isn't Hungarian, Mrs. Vas," smiled Pető. "He's not saying *gyer ide* but *nerede*. He's asking where his mother is." And he turned to the boy, *"Yok burada annen."* [Your mother isn't here.]

The boy burst into tears again. *"Medet! Medet!"* [Help! Help!]

Mrs. Vas knelt down and without saying a word dressed the boy. Red trousers, red cap, red sandals, violet-coloured velvet jacket. The little jacket was patched, it was true, and the red sandals faded. She wiped the boy's face on her apron.

"We must let him go back," she said decisively.

Pető himself did not know what to do.

"Hey!" roared Bódogfalvi, pulling out his sword. "Don't the dogs slay our children? They don't even spare babies!"

"Stab him!" called the soldier with the tent.

Mrs. Vas pulled the boy aside and held up her hand to prevent the soldier from striking him.

"Don't touch him!" And by then three women were holding the boy. By the time the soldier had sheathed his sword, he had disappeared so completely among the skirts and aprons that not even a bloodhound could have found him.

*

After the night skirmish Gergely galloped down to the Warm Lake. He bathed, then returned quickly. In front of the palace he met a stocky lad in a blue waistcoat.

The lad was carrying an iron ramrod over his shoulder. At the end of it there was tow dipped in pitch. He greeted Gergely.

As he turned to face him, Gergely came to an astonished halt. "That blonde lad in a blue waistcoat, that boyish little nose, those two bold eyes..."

There are faces that remain in our memory like portraits in oil on the wall. They never change. That face and that build remained alive in Gergely's memory. When he was taken captive as a child and was sitting in the lap of that peasant girl on the cart... that was when he had seen that face. The lad was in chains and cursed the Turks.

Gergely called to him, "Gáspár!"

"That's my name," said the lad in surprise. "How come that you know me, sir?" And he took off his hat.

Gergely simply stared at him. "This is quite stupid," he mused. "After all, it can't possibly be *him*. It's twenty years since I saw him. What's your father's name?"

"The same as mine, sir, Gáspár Kocsis."

"And your mother's Margit somebody or other, isn't she?"

"Yes."

"Didn't they get married in Baranya?"

"Indeed they did."

"They were in Turkish captivity."

"The Turks carried them off."

"But they were freed."

"That's right."

"It was Dobó who freed them."

"And a little boy."

Gergely blushed to the roots of his hair.

"Is your mother here?"

"Yes, she came here because my father's here too, sir. He's with me; we're in the same gun-crew."

"And where's your mother?"

"That's her, coming now!"

A stout, round-faced woman was walking slowly from the gate. In her hands were two pots of milk and on her back a wooden carrier. Her apron too was full of carrots.

Gergely ran towards her.

"My dear Auntie Margit! Dear, dear Aunt Margit! Here, let me give you a kiss." And before the woman could recover herself he planted a resounding kiss on both cheeks.

The woman just stared at him in amazement.

"My dear, I'm that little boy you took in your lap on the Pécs road," said Gergely effusively.

"What?" said the woman, startled. "Would that be you, sir?" Her voice was as deep as a bassoon.

"Yes, it's me, my dear," Gergely replied joyfully. "Oh, how often I've been reminded of that kind face of yours when you were a girl! And how you mothered us and looked after us on the top of the cart!"

354

Mistress Margit's eyes filled with tears of joy.

"Just take this pot," she said to her son. "Or else I'm sure I'll drop it. And what about that tiny little girl? Is she still alive?"

"Oh yes, she's alive all right. She's my wife now. She's back home in Sopron. I've a little boy too. He's called Jancsi. I'll write and tell them that I've seen dear Auntie Margit. Yes, I'll write to them."

But where is your little son, bold warrior Gergely? And where is your beautiful wife?

8

That day Gergely slept late on his bearskin-covered bed. He was woken by an enormous noise of crashing and crackling, as if a thousand doors were being broken down in the fortress.

He stretched and got up. He opened the shutters to see that the town was in flames. The wonderful big cathedral, the bishop's palace, St. Nicholas Church, the tile-roofed canons' row, the Cifra Mill, the two towers of the Cifra Gate and all the houses everywhere were engulfed in a sea of leaping flame and billowing smoke. The crashing above him and everywhere in the fortress was hellish.

He opened the inner window, and there a hail of roof-tiles shot past his nose. They were tearing apart the roof of the monastery and the fine new roof of the church too. All the green glazed tiles, wooden shingles, laths and horizontal beams were flying down from every side.

He opened the third window; from that one too he saw nothing but roofs being torn off. There was no one in the square or among the houses, but the walls were crowded with people.

He looked at the position of the sun. It was past noon. He called for his batman. He was not there. He reached for the water and washed quickly. The next minute he was fully dressed, with his sword and eagle-feathered cap too. He plunged down the stairs. He snatched up a shield and under its protection hurried out through the falling tiles on to the bastion.

The Turks were pouring out of the valley like a multi-coloured flood to engulf the whole world. They were approaching with

355

great clanging and banging, the beating of drums and the braying of trumpets. Waves of red, white and blue colour intermingled as they came on.

Almagyar and Tihamér, the two pretty little villages by the Warm Lake were in flames. Every house was burning.

On the Maklár road the long line of oxen and buffaloes extended to infinity. They were all pulling guns.

On the hillside there was a mass of *djebedjis* in gleaming armour and down below in the game reserve another mass of red-capped mounted *akindjis*. And what more was there to come behind them?

"Where's the commander?"

"On the church tower."

Gergely glanced up there. The roof of the church was flat. Dobó was standing there in his everyday cap made of cloth. Beside him stood Mekcsey with his thick neck, the blonde Zoltay, Pető, the priest, Cecey and old Sukán.

Gergely hurried to join them.

A wooden staircase led up the tower. Gergely leapt up it three at a time. On one corner he bumped into Fügedy.

"Why is the town burning?" he asked, panting.

"It was on the orders of the commander."

"And what's all this dismantling going on here?"

"We're knocking down the roofs so that the Turks won't have anything to set fire to, and so that there's nothing to hide them."

"Where are you going?"

"To get more water carried to the reservoir. Just go up there. Dobó's been asking for you."

There was an even better view of the Turkish army from the tower. It stretched away in various colours as far as Abony, like some forest on the move.

"Here you are then, Gergely!" Mekcsey welcomed him on the tower. "I was just asking Kristóf whether this was how you killed the Turks last night."

"They've risen again, the dogs!" Gergely continued his jest. "Look, there's the one whose head Bakocsai brought in."

Dobó was shaking his head.

"Lukács Nagy is lost," he said to Cecey. "That's a great pity. My best twenty-five cavalrymen."

356

Gergely saluted Dobó. "Shouldn't we fire off a volley to give them a good solid welcome?"

Dobó shook his head. "No." Then, as Gergely looked obliquely at him, he nodded in the direction of the Turks. "It's up to the visitor to say good-day first."

Beneath the wall surrounding the town the army was spreading out towards the game-reserve just like a flood that finds a stone in its way and flows round it.

9

That night once again a few men from Upper Hungary disappeared. Others came in their place. From Felnémet about thirty peasants came in, all bearing scythes that had been straightened. One even brought a flail. Of course this was studded with nails. They were led by a stocky man in a leather apron. On his shoulder he carried a sledge-hammer.

When they came to a halt in front of Dobó, he lowered the sledge-hammer and dropped it to the ground. He took off his cap.

"We're from Felnémet. We've come inside. My name's Gergely. I'm a blacksmith. If necessary, I'll beat iron, or if necessary, I'll beat Turks."

Dobó offered him his hand.

That day folk came from Almagyar, Tihamér and Abony too. They were mainly peasants and their wives, the latter with bundles. The men had well-filled knapsacks, horses and carts as well.

There was also an ox-cart that wound its way up to the fortress. In the cart there was a bell, so large that on each side the wheels grazed against it.

In front of the cart walked an elderly gentleman, and beside him two young men in blue cloth jackets and red boots. One was twenty, with an upturned moustache, the other sixteen and still a boy.

Their faces were both round and dark. Their necks were equally short. The old man, however, had a deeply furrowed, careworn brow. At his side hung a broad sword in a black velvet sheath; the two young men had slender swords in red velvet scabbards. All three of them had red faces from the warm sunshine.

The old man was wearing black. His boots were black too.

Dobó had noticed this mourning garb from a distance. But since he was occupied with the people from Felnémet, he only caught sight of the old man again when he came up. It was the mayor of Eger.

"Why, if it isn't András!" said Dobó, holding out his hand to welcome him.

"Yes, it's me," replied the mayor of Eger. "I've brought the old bell along. I've had the others buried."

"And these two fine lads?"

"They're my sons."

Dobó offered his hand to them too. And he turned to the ox-drover. "Put the bell down by the Church bastion. Kristóf," he beckoned to his page, "tell Master Mekcsey to have the bell buried deep enough to escape damage from any cannon-balls."

His glance fell on the mayor's boots. "Who are you mourning, sir?"

The mayor of Eger gazed at the ground. "My town." And when he raised his head, his eyes were full of tears.

Then a man dressed in grey cloth arrived, and two women, each of whom was leading a child. Dobó turned a welcoming gaze on the man and spoke to him.

"You're a miller, aren't you?"

"Yes, I'm a miller from Maklár," he replied, his eyes reflecting his pleasure at this friendly welcome. "My name's János Bódy, at your service, sir. I slept the night here in the Cifra Mill."

"And these two women?"

"One's my wife, the other's my daughter. And those are my two little boys. They didn't want to leave me, so I said there'd probably be room here for them too."

"Well, there's certainly room. That's no problem, but I think we've got too many women already." And he turned to Sukán. "How many women are there in the fortress?"

"Forty-five up to now," replied Sukán.

Dobó shook his head.

Then another three men arrived, together with a priest, a thin

358

man with a sunken face. He carried no sword, but only a stick, and he had a knapsack of fox-hide over his shoulder. Dobó was glad to see him, at any rate. There was always need for a priest in the fortress, indeed many of them. They were needed so that the defenders might always feel the nearness of God, and so that they might preach too. And naturally so that the dying might be given the last sacraments and the dead buried.

"Welcome!" said Dobó, stretching out his hand. "I won't even ask your name, for you have come from God; it was He who sent you to us."

"Are priest in fort?" asked the man of God. "How much priest?"

"Only one," answered Dobó, disheartened. For he realized from the priest's pronunciation that he would not be able to preach to the soldiers.

*

And as the Turks poured from the south and spread out in horseshoe formation around the town, the remaining inhabitants withdrew inside the fortress, all of them. Most of them were peasants and artisans, and they brought their wives and children with them too.

In every occupied town there remain those who doubt and say, "It's not true that the Turks are coming. Every year we get scares like this, and we grow old and die without having as much trouble from Turks as we do from cockchafers." They are the ones who are most overwhelmed by floods and destroyed by war. The descendants of the family whose motto runs "We've all the time in the world" never die out.

Dobó was not worried by their arrival. The more men the better. True, he did not welcome women and children inside the fortress, but now he could not get rid of them. And in any case so many soldiers needed a woman's hand, so they might as well come.

The women were divided up among the kitchens and baking-ovens. Old Sukán showed each family their place. Some of them found themselves ten or twenty in a room. After all, what they needed was only a place to sleep at night and somewhere to put their belongings.

The men, however, were assembled by Mekcsey in the angle of the bastion and not allowed to go further inside until they had taken the oath like the soldiers.

"Well," said one of the Eger vineyard-owners after taking the oath, "that's why we've come here, to defend the fortress."

To which another added, "We're not going to surrender our birthplace to the Turks! Certainly not!"

Mekcsey distributed arms among them then and there. There were piles of swords, spears, shields and helmets lying beneath the vaulting of the bastion. Of course they were not the work of craftsmen from Damascus, Hindustan or Derbend, only the everyday, rusty equipment that gets left behind in fortresses from century to century. Each could select what he wanted.

A bushy-moustached cobbler whose eyebrows themselves would have made good moustaches spoke up with great confidence, "Well, sir, all these weapons are quite good, but I've brought along my shoe-knife. Just look!" And he drew a gleaming paring-knife from the breast pocket of his apron. "If I'm attacked by any Turk, why, I'll slit his belly with this!"

A few of them tried on helmets too, but finding those iron hats heavy and more like cooking-pots than fine, shining soldiers' helmets they left them there. "What's the point of them?"

Well, you'll soon find that out!

As dusk fell, the sentries on the tower reported that an aristocratic carriage and four was approaching at speed in a cloud of dust on the road from Felnémet.

Nobody could imagine who it was. The bishop usually went around in a four-horse carriage. Other gentlemen rode in carriages only when they were ill. But no sick man would come here.

The captains themselves went to the bastion and surveyed the four-horse carriage flying along like a kite.

"You'll see, it's the bishop who's coming," rejoiced Fügedy, the lieutenant from the chapter. And since nobody believed him, he produced some examples from history.

"Weren't they there at every battle until now? Weren't almost all of them at Mohács? After all, the office of bishop isn't only an ecclesiastical post, but a military one too. Every bishop has his own troops. And every bishop is also a captain."

"If only every captain could be a bishop too," replied Dobó. Perhaps he was thinking that in that case he might have been able to deploy more soldiers against the Turks.

"Suppose it's someone carrying despatches from the king to say that he has indeed fallen ill on the way," said Mekcsey.

Dobó's face lit up. "The king can't leave us in the lurch!" And impatiently he set off down the steps and crossed the square to the Old Gate, which was the access to the fortress for vehicles.

The carriage was painted yellow and had a leather hood, like any aristocratic one. It came round the corner up to the southern gate and drove beneath it into the main square of the fortress.

Then out of it stepped a tall woman dressed in black. "The commander?" were her first words.

As she caught sight of Dobó, she threw back her veil. She was about forty years old. Her clothes betrayed that she was a widow.

"Mrs. Balogh!" said Dobó in surprise. And he took off his cap and bowed. The lady who had arrived was the mother of the page whom Dobó had sent home with Lukács Nagy.

"My son..." said the woman with trembling lips. "Where's Balázs?"

"I sent him home," said Dobó in surprise. "It's over a month ago that I sent him home."

"I know, but he's come back here."

"No, he hasn't."

"He left a letter to say that he was coming here."

"He hasn't come."

"He slipped out after Lukács Nagy."

"He hasn't returned either."

The widow pressed her hand to her forehead.

"Oh! My only son! Has he perished too?"

"That's not yet certain."

"I swore to my husband on his deathbed that I wouldn't let him go into danger until he married. He's the last of the family."

Dobó raised his shoulders.

"I know, madam. And that is why I sent him home, after all. Now please return home before the Turkish army closes the ring

361

round us." And he ordered a company of cavalry to escort the lady.

The lady clasped her hands and looked pleadingly at Dobó.

"If he were to come back..."

"He can't get back now. The town's been completely surrounded during the night. Only the royal army can break through now."

"Well, suppose he comes back with them..."

"I'll lock the rascal up in my house!"

The woman got back into her carriage. There were fifty cavalry in front and fifty behind. The four horses took the carriage back towards the Cifra Gate as if it were a feather. By now that was the only gate of the four left open. That was the only way towards Szarvaskő or Tárkány.

A quarter of an hour later the sentries at the gate reported that the northernmost flank of the Turkish army had reached the Cifra Gate. A cavalryman came dashing back from the lady's escort.

"Lieutenant Fekete wants to know whether he's to carve a way for the lady through the Turkish lines."

Dobó climbed up the bastion. He saw the mass of Turkish armed troops around the gate and the *asabs* behind them.

"No!"

And he stayed there on the bastion. Shading his eyes with his hand, he looked towards the north.

"Lads!" he said to the soldiers standing on the bastion. "Which of you has got good eyesight? Just look over there towards Felnémet."

"A few cavalrymen are coming along there," replied one of the soldiers.

"Twenty," thought another.

"Twenty-five," said the first one.

"Here comes Lukács Nagy!" shouted Mekcsey from the Church Bastion.

And it really was Lukács Nagy, the lieutenant who had been hanging around, looking out for Turks. Where the devil had he been for such a long time? And how was he to get in? They were galloping as if driven on by a fierce wind. It's too late now, Lukács Nagy! The Turks have blocked the gateway.

Lukács Nagy knows nothing of this yet. He wheels down from the hill to the Cifra Gate. There he catches sight of the Turkish cavalry. He jerks his horse's bridle and the little band circles round swiftly and makes for the Bakta Gate. There are even more Turks there.

"Now you can scratch, Lukács, where it doesn't even itch!" laughs Zoltay.

"But if only there weren't any cavalry at the gate," booms Dobó, his eyes flashing, "then Lukács could cut his way through them."

Lukács halts there and looks towards the fortress. He scratches. The soldiers standing on the wall keep waving their caps at him. "Come on, Lukács, if you dare!"

The Turkish horses in the distance suddenly become speckled with colour as some hundred or so *akindjis* mount them. They set off in pursuit of Lukács Nagy. He is no sluggard either. He sets off with his twenty-four cavalry, and the contest begins. At first it is possible to see the horses too, but later there are only two clouds of dust rising to the tops of the poplar trees and spreading swiftly towards Felnémet.

10

Next day was Sunday, but the bells of Eger were silent. The fortress and the town were surrounded by a sea of Turks.

Everywhere on the hills and slopes there were thousands of different-coloured tents: red and white tents, in places blue, green, yellow and light red ones. The men's tents were like playing-cards bent in two. The officers' tents were tall, decorated octagonal constructions. The sun gleams on the golden ball surmounting the horse-tail banners, and the flags with the crescent on them flutter in the breeze. In the pastures of Felnémet and the fields of Kistálya and everywhere where there is grass thousands of horses graze. All the way along the brook men and buffaloes are bathing. Out of the noisy flood of people the occasional camel rears its head, and the turbans of officers on horseback flash white from time to time.

In this swirling torrent of colours the fortress of Eger stands out like an island, together with the little town of Eger within its stockade, and the King's Seat, that hillside towards the east opposite which the highest wall has been built.

Dobó and his officers were standing once again on the roofless tower. It was a good thing that St. Stephen had had those two towers built; they offered a good view of how the Turks were siting their cannon.

Behind the fortress is a large grassy area, circular in shape; it is half as big as the Vérmező in Buda. Beyond it is a lovely little vineyard on a hillside, glowing red. It was there that the Turks had dragged their big cannon.

They had not even bothered to shield them with gabions. Nor had the thirty buffaloes been driven far off; they were on the grass below the hill, grazing there. Now only camels were visible by the guns. Their backs were loaded with black sacks.

"They're leather sacks," explains Dobó. "That's where they keep their gunpowder."

The small red-turbaned *topchis* are busy there in full view of the defenders. For the moment the black mouths of the cannon gape silently towards the fortress. The *topchi pasha* keeps squatting down to look along them. He adjusts them right and left, up and down.

One of the cannon points at the tower, the second is aimed at the middle bastion on the north side, which covers the palace.

"Do you see how he's aiming them?" says Dobó. "It's not with the top of the barrel, but from the rear."

One of the bombardiers puts his head round the door of the tower and says, "Commander, sir!"

"Come here," replies Dobó.

The soldier climbs up. He looks anxiously at the Turkish cannon, then comes to attention. "Sir," he says, "Master Balázs wants to know whether he should fire at them."

"Tell him not to fire until I give the order. Then come back here."

The *topchis* went on loading the three cannon. They pushed the gunpowder into their fat barrels with club-headed iron ramrods.

"I'd like to fire into the middle of them," said Mekcsey,

becoming excited. "By the time they're ready, we could scatter them."

"Just let them enjoy themselves," replied Dobó calmly.

"Let's at least make a raid on them!" said Jób Paksy, the brother of the captain of Komárom, beginning to fidget.

"I've got an itching hand too," grumbled Bornemissza.

Dobó smiled. "Let's just see how they fire."

By now the *topchi*s had stuffed the wadding into the mouth of the cannon. Four men were handling the ramrod, thrusting it into the barrel at words of command.

"Hell and damnation!" Cecey also bursts out. "Commandant, my boy, what's our gun for?"

"My dear chap, are you too getting angry with me? You'll find out tomorrow why I'm not firing."

The *topchi*s were pulling hides out of another sack. Two of them held them while another smeared them with tallow. Then they turned them over and wrapped the cannon-ball in the ungreased side.

"Maybe they're firing eggs!" said Zoltay scornfully.

At that moment the bombardier arrived back.

"Come and stand in front of me," said Dobó. "I noticed just now that you were afraid. Well, look; they're going to fire here, at me. Stand right in front of me!"

The soldier blushed as he stood in front of Dobó.

Dobó looked down from the tower and caught sight of Pető. He called down to him, "Gáspár, my lad! You've got a good voice. Shout as loud as you can that the Turks are going to fire any minute now. Nobody's to be scared. If the women are frightened, they can walk on the sunny side."

By now the topchis had rammed the cannon-balls into all three guns. The three bombardiers held lighted fuses in their hands. One topchi at the back spat on his palm and, stroking the back of his neck upwards, looked towards the fortress.

The gunpowder flashed, the guns sent out smoke and flames, and nine booms shook the ground in succession. The fortress trembled with the blast. Then followed silence.

"It was nothing," Dobó smiled dismissively. And then he sent the soldier down again.

The smoke drifted lazily upwards above the cannon. But how the devil did three cannon cause nine explosions?

It was simply that the hills around Eger echoed the noise of the shots, three times for each gun.

So there'll certainly be plenty of music here if the three or four hundred Turkish guns all fire together!

A quarter of an hour later Pető ran up the tower. A butcher's boy plodded up behind him too. In his two strong arms he lugged a stinking, steaming cannon-ball up to Dobó.

"Beg to report, sir, here's a cannon-ball," said Pető. "It fell into the brook. The water-carriers brought it up here in a vat."

"Tell them to go on carrying water. We'll not shut the fortress gate."

"Aren't we going to fire?" asked Pető too.

"Today's Sunday," smiled Dobó. "How should we fire?"

And he went on watching the *topchi*s cool the cannon and reload.

11

Next morning the three siege-guns were squatting in the middle of the open space, half the distance away. They had also been doubled in number.

The nine shots of the previous day had been wasted. They had not even produced a reply from the fortress. So they sited the guns closer, near enough for a good arrow-shot to reach them from the fortress.

Dobó knew that this would happen. Why should he have startled them away? And what point would there have been in shaking the confidence of the defenders with a few empty shots in reply?

He was up at daybreak and himself prepared the guns on that side to reply. He did not wrap the cannon-balls in hides, but merely greased them. And it was he who carefully measured out the gunpowder with a measuring-spoon.

"Now let's have the wadding. Ram it well in with the rod. Now in with the cannon-ball..." And he took aim carefully, taking his time over it.

He waited until the Turks were all prepared behind the gabions. Then when the first Turkish gun thundered, he called, "In the name of God, *fire!*"

The fuses were raised all together to the twelve Hungarian guns and they fired simultaneously.

The Turkish gabions and gun-carriages fell over and broke apart. Two Turkish guns turned over. One was smashed to pieces. The furious cries and scurrying of the *topchis* behind the gabions brought laughter from the defenders.

"Well now," said Dobó merrily to old Cecey. "Do you see why we didn't fire yesterday?"

And he stood on the wall with legs planted firmly apart. He twirled his long moustache with both hands.

*

The defenders were not as scared as Dobó feared they might be. Ever since the discovery of gunpowder, Eger more than any other place in the world had resounded to the noise of firing. Even today spring festivals, firemen's parties, elections, choir celebrations, garden parties and public performances are inconceivable without being preceded by gunfire. The gun is a substitute for the poster. Sometimes there are posters too, but all the same they do not dispense with the gun. In the fortress there are always a few mortars lying around in the grass. Anyone who likes fires them. So how could the folk of Eger feel afraid?

There was only one man in the fortress who at the first shot fell off his chair and cried out in alarm. Even if I do not mention his name, you can easily guess it.

But the soldiers got hold of him and pulled him out of his corner. Just as he was, in his yellow jacket, red trousers, helmet and bare feet, he was dragged to the bastion. There two of them held his arms outstretched, and two held his legs, and one supported his back with his own. And they shouted to the Turks, "Aim here!"

The gypsy put up with it while they were loading, but when the gun fired again, he jerked himself out of their hands and with a hair-raising twelve-foot leap landed below the platforms. There the first thing he did was to feel himself all over to see that the cannon-ball had not taken any bit of him away, then he ran like a greyhound to the Old Gate.

"Dear, oh dear, oh dear!" he bawled, holding his hands to his head. "If only the cramps had got me feet when I set out 'ere! Dear, oh dear, oh dear! If only that stinkin' 'orse 'ad gone blind that brought me 'ere!"

*

That day Dobó shot all the King's Seat guns to bits.

The topchis ran away shouting and raging. Two *topchi* agas died. The third officer was carried off on a stretcher from the guns. All that was left in the open space were overturned and splintered gabions, three dead camels, wrecked guns, chests and bits of wheels lying around.

And as if that were not enough, Gergely launched a midnight raid on them and brought back twenty steeds and a mule.

But the Turks had so many horses, men and guns that by dawn the wickerwork gabions filled with earth were in place again. Naturally they were sited rather further back, and a fairly high rampart of earth was raised in front of the cannon. In the gaps between the gabions were twelve new guns. And around the guns new topchis and new agas.

The sun had hardly risen before the fortress was rocked with fearful blasts, and dull thuds made them realize that cannon-balls were pounding the walls.

Once more Dobó fired his guns and once more the gabions fell over, as did the guns. But behind the fallen gabions there were new ones, and beside them new guns. And the topchis did not run off in all directions. Behind them sat a brigade of armoured djebedjis with nail-studded whips. "Here you can only fire and die!"

"Oh well, just let them fire," Dobó shrugged. "We've got to save our gunpowder."

And he only fired off a few falconets from time to time to harass them in their work.

That day the Turks had not yet occupied the town. The Hungarian infantry were guarding the fortress gates and the cavalry the town gates.

The Turks made no attempt to engage them. The town was nothing urgent as far as they were concerned. There was nothing in the deserted houses for them to steal. And the weather was still so summer-like that they all preferred to sleep in tents or even under the open sky.

For two days the Turkish commanders had been riding on horseback over all the neighbouring hills in order to see inside the fortress. But only the birds can do that. The towers alone stand out. The wickerwork, clay-filled stockade that crowns the walls and bastions also hides the interior.

So where were they to aim?

They fired at the wall and at the stockade.

Yet there were some fine buildings lurking inside. The enormous church, even the half of it that remained standing, was an architectural marvel. Next to it the old monastery was also built of sculpted stone. (Not even since that time have Hungarian soldiers had such splendid barracks!) And as for the commander's palace, Dobó had improved it when he got married. An Italian master-builder had done the carving. And the windows were of glass, while down below in the town even the bishop's palace had only parchment ones. The old bishop's palace still stood in the fortress, from the time when the church there was still the cathedral. There stood the deputy commander's house, Mekcsey's, and at that time it too was called a palace. The permanent fortress officials—the royal inspector, steward and episcopal lawyer—all lived in a row of houses along the north wall.

So the Turks just went on firing. Their guns boomed and bellowed from dawn till dusk. They broke the wall and splintered the woven palisade on the top of it. And when the sun went down behind the Bakta hill, they fired off all their guns at once and the chaplains' devotional chant of *Allahu akbar* rose on all sides in the camp.

The whole Turkish army knelt to pray. The *topchi*s too.

Meanwhile Dobó's masons got out their trowels and began their work while it was still light, filling the breaches with stone.

The two pashas shook their heads. Both of them had grown old in war. Wherever they went, they left ruins behind them and the empire of the sultan was extended.

"Let's penetrate into the town too, and fire at the walls from that side as well."

So on the fourth day they broke into the town. That was child's play for such an army. A thousand ladders and a thousand young warriors, and only a stockade plastered with mud...

The Hungarian sentries had been given orders to retreat the minute the Turks appeared on the walls. So they abandoned the gates. They returned to the fortress in fine array with drums beating.

Then Arslan Bey had four large siege-guns brought alongside the Church of Our Lady and trained them on those bastions where the Hungarian guns stood silent.

Arslan's aim was better.

His cannon-balls smashed the walls and the palisade on the town side. His particular target was the Earth Bastion. One or two of his shots landed inside the fortress too, causing some confusion until they learnt by experience beside which walls to walk to avoid the range of the guns.

That day the Turks removed the cross from the two churches in the town and replaced it with the crescent. They threw out the altars and burned the pictures. And at noonday the muezzins chanted in a long drawn-out wail: *Allahu akbar! Ashadu anna la ilaha ill Allah! Ashadu anna Mohammed arrasulu Allah! Heya alassalah! Heya alalfalah! Allahu akbar! La ilaha ill Allah!* (God is the all-highest. There is truly no god except God. Truly Mohamed is his prophet. Come and pray. Come and worship God. God is the all-highest. There is no god except God.)

When they were eating lunch together at noon, Dobó was silent and gloomy. Still there was no message from the king. The spy had returned in the night from the Bishop of Eger. The bishop replied that he had no money and no troops, but he would pray for the defenders.

Dobó moved not a muscle of his face as he received this message. Only his brows were knit even closer.

He was also grieved about Lukács Nagy. He was a bold officer, who always liked to snap at the heels of the Turks. He had taken a bite at the Turkish main army and slipped away. And now how was he to get back, with the fortress entirely surrounded and the tents dotting the ground as far as Felnémet? Or had they perhaps caught up with him?...

At lunch it was reported that Antal Nagy had been struck by a shot. Bornemissza leapt up: "Sir, let me make a raid on the Turks! I feel ashamed that we abandoned the town gates without exchanging a single blow!"

Budaházy, the officer with the moustache like a ring, also spoke up. "Sir, let the Turks see that it's not only by night that we dare to raid them, but by day too."

And Pető thrust out his chest too. "Even though there are only a few of us, a hundred of us will take on a hundred thousand."

Dobó's eyes lit up. "I won't say no. But all the same, there's no point in leaving your lunch uneaten."

Then he talked no more about the Turks until after lunch.

"You'll attack the infantry by the great church. You'll charge straight through them in one sweep and wheel round to gallop straight back here immediately. And I mean immediately. As for fighting, keep it to a minimum, as opportunity arises. No rallying-cries, no waiting for orders from the commander during the attack, or you will lose your heads. Just a quick strike and back! You can take a hundred men."

The officers rapidly seize weapons and armour and leap on their horses. All the men are eager to go with them, but Gergely halts them. "The only ones to come will be those that I choose."

The asabs, lagumdjis and plyades are having lunch on the grass in front of the church. Today all they have is soup, and they have stuck their spoons back in their belts and sashes. Now they are eating bread and onions. Some eat water-melons, some cucumber and other greenstuff after the soup. All this is clearly visible from the fortress. The only things that divide them are the brook and the market-place. A squadron of janissaries has also settled down beside the houses in the square. They are in

371

a happy mood now. One agile soldier throws a dagger and a melon into the air. First he catches the dagger, then the melon on the tip of the dagger. It is obvious that he is doing this for a bet. For there comes a janissary to him with a water-melon. They chat for a while, then the janissary throws up the water-melon and the other the dagger. A third janissary jerks the exhibitionist from behind. The melon drops to the ground and bursts, to the great amusement of the soldiers. They roar with laughter, scratch themselves and eat melons.

The gate of the fortress is still open, and the peasants from there are busy carrying up water. Yesterday they were still driving cattle and sheep down there, but today it is only the horses. What would the Turks gain by throwing a bridge over the brook and storming the gate? A few bullets in their sides. The Turks know this; even if the gate is open, it is like the open mouth of a lion, and has teeth in it. And what if they fire at them? It's not usual to fire on unarmed men, but if they were to shoot, then the defenders would also fire from above on to the men watering animals in the brook and at the horses and camels too.

The janissaries scarcely notice that there is a sudden pause in the watering down at the brook and water-carrying stops.

It lasts only for two or three minutes, so how should it be noticeable? Nor do they observe the increase of men on the walls, particularly archers and riflemen. But what does make them stir is a great thundering of hooves. As they turn towards the fortress, the mortars on the walls blast off, hurling all kinds of nails, bullets and shrapnel into their faces. A long line of horses and riders gallops out of the fortress gateway. Bornemiszsza is lightly dressed, wearing little more than a thin leather jerkin. Zoltay waves his fist threateningly, Pető spurs on his horse, Budaházy has his cap over one ear. But Fügedy too is dashing along there with his wolf's mane of hair, and all of them are fired with enthusiasm.

They leap over the brook like a whirlwind and by the time the Turks hear a word of command they are slashing and striking them.

"Allah! Allah!"

They charge through them and appear on the great knot-grass

covered square where the episcopal church casts its shadow every afternoon. The Turkish infantry jump up in alarm and look towards the market-place. Some of them run away, some stand there and draw their swords.

The galloping company of cavalry suddenly appear there. Their steeds are spurred on like fire-breathing dragons. The thousands of Turks flee like a flock of sheep scared by wolves. The Hungarians at their heels.

"Take that, curse you!"

But now aid arrives from the streets, mounted *akindjis* and *gönöllüs,* janissaries with rifles and spears.

One white-capped janissary aims his spear at Gergely, intending to strike him down from his horse. Gergely's sword flashes twice: after the first flash the spear breaks in two and after the second the Turk goes sprawling.

"Jesus! Jesus!" they shout from the bastions too. "Jesus, help!"

"Allah! Allah!" scream the Turks.

The Hungarians spread out further as they wheel amongst them. Their swords gleam and flash. Mihály Horváth's horse is stabbed in the breast by a janissary. The horse falls down. Horváth jumps off it and strikes the janissary, then strikes another, breaking his sword on him. As for the third, he simply delivers a blow with his fist on his nose, then he sets off at a run across the empty space left by the cavalry charge back to the fortress.

The rest of them are still advancing. The horses' legs trample men down. Budaházy raises his arm to deliver a fearful blow when the janissaries forced against the side of a house fire a rifle at him. The sword falls from Budaházy's hand. Four janissaries hurl themselves at him with swords and spears. One blue-jacketed Hungarian soldier immediately strikes to defend him, but he is stabbed.

"Who's that?" ask the watchers on the wall.

"Gábor Oroszy," says Mekcsey sorrowfully.

But Budaházy finds space to escape. He turns his horse and, keeping well down on its neck, gallops back. At this the others also turn round.

Along the main street a thousand *akindji*s dash like a whirlwind to aid their fellows.

Allah! Allah! Yazik sana!

Gergely just has enough time to escape them. He wheels round in a big S towards the Canons' Row. There is a mass of seething Turks there too. But there are more infantry than cavalry, and as the former flee madly, they only throw the cavalry into confusion—for they now have to watch out for their own troops as well. All the same, a fearsome number of Persian *gureba*s come galloping towards them. But their charge against the inflamed Hungarian squadron is all in vain. A street full of blood opens in their midst and they stagger to right and left like stooks scattered by a whirlwind.

Only now does it become clear how weak the small oriental horse is alongside the large, strong Hungarian type. Ten Hungarian men on horseback can scatter a hundred Turkish cavalry when they charge them. And if a Hungarian has a tussle with a Turk, the latter is never going to be an officer in the fortress of Eger.

Now they are galloping homewards. "Get away from the gate!"

The shouting of the cheering crowds on the fortress walls mingles with the noise of the returning fighters.

Dobó is alarmed at the sight of the *akindjis* and *djebedjis* still pouring out of the side streets to the aid of the other Turks. He orders his men to fire. On the wall the rifles crack and arrows hiss. The vanguard of the Turkish troops comes to a sudden halt and crowds together.

At this moment an appalling animal screech is heard on the wall—as horrible as the braying of a donkey. Everybody looks towards it. It is the gypsy screaming there. Leaping around in a rage he shakes his sword towards the Turks.

"*Vaj sana!* [Woe to you!], wicked Turkish curs!"

The Hungarian troops cheerfully speed out of the confused mass of Turks and gallop on their foaming, bloodstained, sweating horses through the gateway to the defenders' shouts of victory.

The raid had lasted less than a quarter of an hour. But the church square, the market-place and the Canons' Row were left full of wounded men and limping horses. The surprised Turks retreated seething with rage, and in the distance kept turning round and shaking their fists.

*

Even on that day Dobó did not have the gate to the brook shut. Let the defenders go out from morning till night! And let the Turks see that Eger is facing the siege with calm.

The gate was wide open. No armed sentries were visible around it. True, further inside there were 120 infantrymen in line. It was also true that the guard was sitting in the window of the tower, and at a single movement of his hand the organ, that portcullis made of iron rods like organ-pipes, would come crashing down to defend the gate at the bottom. A mortar also stands guard deeper under the gate. And the drawbridge could also be pulled up even when it was full of men.

So men and horses and water-carriers came and went. The men watered their horses, and the water-carriers fetched water to the stone-lined reservoirs inside the fortress. Of course, there was a well in the fortress too, but two thousand defenders and all the horses, cattle and sheep could not be supplied with water by just one well. So water had to be brought from the brook, and as much as possible.

On the far side of the brook it was the Turks who were watering horses. And some of the infantry also went there to drink the water.

There was plenty of water in the brook since Dobó had dammed it. In the middle it was waist-high. The Turks had not touched the dam; they needed even more water, and every day too. Not only for the huge number of animals, but also for their countless troops. There was no well in the town, and only two springs on the hillside.

Well, as the peasants of Eger became used to the Turks and had also seen how they had been put to flight and trampled down by the raid from the fortress, one of the water-carriers could not resist calling across to a Turk as he was filling his tub, "Come over, old chap, if you dare!"

Even if the Turk could not understand what he was saying, he could see the movement of the head. "You come over here!"

A second Turk smiled, and he too beckoned. Next minute five or six Turks and the same number of Hungarians were calling to each other.

A gigantic Kurd in a dirty turban was washing his wounded leg on the far bank. His leg was bare to the knee. He got up and stepped into the brook. He thrust his big face with its blonde moustache towards the Hungarians.

"Here I am, then. What do you want?"

The Hungarian peasants however did not jump out of his way. They too were standing with rolled-up trouser-legs in the water. One of them seized the Turk's arm like lightning and jerked him across to them.

By the time the other Turks had recovered their senses, four peasants were pushing and pulling the Kurd among the water-carts. The others brandished pikes towards the Turks as they jumped into the water.

The Kurd roared. He squirmed and wriggled. But strong hands held him. His jacket, buttons and piping were torn from him. His turban rolled off his head. His nose bled. He shouted *Yetishin!* (Help!) and threw himself on the ground. But no help arrived. They dragged him by his feet so swiftly that he was unable to get up until he had slid through the fortress gate.

They took him to Dobó.

By now the Turk was not so proud. He dusted himself down and crossed his arms on his chest. He made a deep bow. But his legs were trembling. Dobó had him taken to the commander's room. He called Bornemissza to act as interpreter. He sat down beside a suit of armour hung on a pole. He did not have the Turk put in chains yet.

"What's your name?"

"Djekidj," panted the Turk, blinking his bloodshot eyes.

"Whose army are you in?"

"Ahmed Pasha's."

"What are you?"

"A *piyad*."

"You mean you're an infantryman?"

"Yes, sir."

"Were you at the siege of Temesvár?"

The Turk pointed to his foot; on his calf there was a red scar four fingers wide. "Yes, I was, sir."

"Why did that fortress of ours fall?"

"It was the will of Allah."

"Talk to me in the knowledge that if I find you lying you'll meet your end." And he raised his pistol.

The Turk bowed. His eyes indicated that he had understood. Dobó was not fully informed about the siege of Temesvár. All he knew was that Temesvár was better fortified than Eger, and that only half of the army gathered below Eger had been there, yet they had occupied it.

Also present in the room to hear the interrogation were several officers off duty at that time: Pető, Zoltay, Hegedűs, Tamás Bolyky, Kristóf the page and András, the mayor of Eger. They were sitting around Dobó. Only the page stood behind Dobó, leaning on the back of the armchair, while the prisoner stood barefoot and bald four paces in front of Dobó. And behind the prisoner were two pikemen.

"When did you arrive beneath Temesvár?"

"On the fifth day of the month of Redjep (27 June)."

"How many siege-guns did you have?"

"The pasha brought up twelve of them."

Bolyky muttered, "He's lying!"

"He's not lying," replied Dobó. "After all, Ali was in Upper Hungary with the rest." And he went on questioning the Turk.

"How many siege-guns did Ali bring when he joined you?"

"Four," replied the Turk.

"My own spy reported that there were sixteen siege-guns too." And he turned to the Turk again.

"Tell me how the siege of that fortress proceeded. I'll make no secret of the fact that I'm asking you this to help our own defence. If you try to deceive me with only a single word, you're a dead man. If you tell the truth, I'll set you free after the siege."

He said this in such a decisive tone that every word could have been engraved in brass.

"Sir!" said the Turk in a voice of grateful thanks, "the salvation of my soul be dependent on my tongue!" And then he spoke boldly and fluently. "There, just as here, the pasha searched out the weakest walls and points in them, and kept firing at them and breaking them down until they could easily be climbed."

"What was the weakest point?"

"The water-tower, sir. We had a great struggle to occupy it. Men fell like grass beneath the sickle. That's where I got this wound from an arrow in my leg. After the fall of the water-tower, the Germans and Spaniards sent a message from the fortress saying that they would surrender if they might leave unmolested. So the pasha promised on his word of honour that they would not be harmed."

While the Kurd was speaking there was the continuous sound of gunfire outside, and just as he reached this point there was a fearful crash as the ceiling of the palace cracked open. A cannon-ball the size of a human head brought down whitewash and plaster debris with it as it fell between Dobó and the Turk. And it spun round and round.

The Turk started back. Dobó, however, merely glanced at the cannon-ball as it gave off the stench of gunpowder, and nodded calmly as if nothing had happened, "Go on."

"The people in the town..." the Turk went on, "the people in the town..."

Unable to get his breath, he could not continue.

The page Kristóf took an embroidered handkerchief out of his pocket and dusted the powdery plaster off the commander's face, cap and clothing. This gave the Turk a chance to get his breath back.

"Go on!" said Dobó.

"The people wanted to take all their things with them. And that was their mistake. Losonczy asked for a day's grace to make preparations. The soldiers saw that they were being deprived of their chance of plundering the place and the following morning watched angrily as the procession of giaours set off. "What? Have we been fighting here for twenty-five days," they said, "so that they can take everything away now?" And they kept grabbing things from the carts. The Christians did not defend themselves, so they grew greedier and greedier. They were particularly eager to get hold of children and younger women. You won't find more beautiful girls for sale in Stamboul, sir, than they were."

378

"But didn't the pasha give them any protection?"

"Yes, he did, but it was no use. When the Christian soldiers trooped out, they even seized one of them, a good-looking young page belonging to Losonczy. The page called out. Losonczy flared up. The Hungarians all became enraged. They pulled out swords and charged us. It was lucky for us that the armoured *djebedji*s happened to be standing there, otherwise they'd have slashed their way through the whole army."

Dobó shrugged. "The *djebedji*s? Do you think that anyone who's wearing a bit of tin is automatically invincible? It wasn't the armour that did it, but only because there were few of them."

Another cannon-ball crashed into the room. It tore through the old faded banners that decorated the wall and smashed the floor too.

All those sitting there got up. Hegedűs went out. The others, seeing Dobó still sitting where he was, remained waiting.

"Where is Ahmed Pasha encamped?" he asked the Turk.

"By the Warm Lake, in the game reserve."

"I thought so," nodded Dobó, glancing towards his officers. And he turned again towards the Turk. "Now tell me where the greatest strength of this army is." He looked hard at him.

"In the janissaries, the artillery and in its size. Ali Pasha's a skilled leader. In one hand he holds a rich reward, in the other a scourge. For anyone who does not advance when he gives the order is beaten from behind by *yasavuls* with scourges."

"And where's its weakness?"

The Kurd pondered, then shrugged his shoulders. Dobó's eyes were fixed on him like two daggers.

"Well," said the Kurd, "the only answer I can give, even if I bare my soul like an unrolled scroll before your feet, sir, is that up to now the army was strong even while it was divided in two. After all, it's destroyed about thirty fortresses, sir, and it's never suffered defeat, so what can I call weakness in it?"

Dobó beckoned to the two soldiers standing behind the captive. "Tie him up and throw him into the prison." And he got up.

A third cannon-ball crashed into his chair. It splintered the finely-carved armchair into matchwood and went on spinning by the pillar.

Dobó did not even turn round. He took his everyday steel helmet from Kristóf and put it on. He went out to the top of the Prison Bastion and from there watched to see which gun was wrecking the palace. He soon spotted it. He aimed three of his guns at it, and fired them all at once.

The gabions turned over. The *topchi*s rushed around in confusion. The gun fell silent. Dobó did not waste any more gunpowder on it.

"A splendid shot!" Gergely shouted for joy too. And as they went down the bastion steps he smiled at Dobó and drew him aside into a niche.

"Sir, when you made the Turk swear to tell the truth, you forgot to do the same for the interpreter."

"You don't mean to say you've distorted his evidence?"

"Indeed I do. When you asked, sir, what was the greatest strength of the army, I left something out. The Turk said that Ali was able to do more damage with his four guns than Ahmed with his twelve. So it's predictable that Ali will keep shelling the fortress until all the walls collapse."

Dobó shrugged. "Good luck to him."

"That's the only thing I kept back," Bornemissza said finally. "If you think fit, sir, tell the other officers too."

Dobó held out his hand. "You did well. We mustn't overburden the defenders with worries. But now I've something to tell you, something that the Kurdish *piyad* didn't know—what the weakness of the army is."

He leaned back against the wall of the bastion and folded his arms. "The sixteen siege-guns," he went on, "may well be operating together tomorrow. And together they'll fire some hundred or two hundred guns. They'll break down gates in the walls and smash down the towers. But that will take time— weeks, probably. Meanwhile this enormous army's got to be fed. Do you think they've been able to bring enough food to satisfy all this army? Do you think they'll be able to produce, and go on producing, what else is needed? And do you think that if the frosts of October catch them here, men who've grown up in a warm climate are going to scale these walls with empty stomachs and shivering skins?"

A cannon-ball dropped beside them and made a hole in the

ground. Dobó merely glanced up at the bombardiers and went on: "The folk here will be brave as long as they see us to be brave. The main thing is for us to maintain the fortress so long as we've got something to eat, so long as the weather holds, and so long as the royal army's on its way to our aid."

"And what happens if they've got enough food? And if there isn't any frost in October? And if the royal army stays at Győr?"

If Gergely had asked these questions with the kind of emphasis that suggested a fourth question to follow, maybe Dobó would have clapped him in irons immediately. But Gergely spoke with an open expression, almost with a smile. Perhaps he did not expect an answer from Dobó, but since they were talking confidentially he may have thought that Dobó had some trust in something beyond what he had already said.

Dobó shrugged his shoulders. "Didn't the Bishop of Eger send to say that he would offer a mass for us?"

*

That day towards evening a woman wrapped in a black *feradje* hurried across the market-place. She was accompanied only by a Saracen boy of about fifteen and a big spotted dog from the camp. At the brook the dog ran down to the water, while the woman walked up and down the bank wringing her hands. She kept looking towards the gate. At dusk the gate was shut and locked from inside; it was also bolted with iron bolts as thick as a man's arm. Perhaps the woman was waiting for this. And as the gate was closed, she waded through the brook without raising her skirts.

"My son!" she called towards the gate, almost screaming. "My own son!"

They reported to Dobó that the little Turkish boy's mother was at the gate.

"Let her in, if she wants to come," replied Dobó.

The portcullis, which also acted as the gate, had a little narrow iron door in it. They opened it for the woman.

But the woman started back in terror. The dog barked.

"My son!" she pleaded again.

And she lifted up something like a purse. She poured gold coins from it into her other hand.

The door shut again.

The woman walked up and down outside the gate wringing her hands. She raised her veil and wiped the tears from her eyes with a white handkerchief. And all the time she kept shrieking, "Selim! My own dear son!"

In the end she rattled the iron door too.

The door opened again, but the woman backed away again.

Then Gergely appeared above the gateway on the bastion, holding the boy by the hand.

"Selim!" screamed the Turkish woman as if her soul were rent asunder by the cry. She stretched out her hands towards the child. "Selim! Selim!"

"Anam!" wept the boy too.

The dog jumped up whimpering, and then barked.

Gergely might not speak from the fortress, but the boy could. And the boy shouted this down to his mother: "You can exchange a Christian captive for me, mother. After the siege."

The woman knelt down, stretching out her hands as if to embrace him through the air. As the child disappeared, she sent a shower of kisses after him.

*

That night darkness covered the fortress, the town, the hills, the sky, the whole world.

Dobó went to bed late, but at midnight he did the rounds of the bastions once again. He was wearing a thick broadcloth jacket of considerable length and on his head he had a black velvet kalpak. In his hand was the guards' duty-roster.

At that hour Zoltay was the officer on duty. He too wore a similar jacket, since it was a chilly night. As he noticed Dobó on the Sándor Bastion, he saluted him with his sword in silence.

"Have you anything to report?" asked Dobó.

"I have just had a look round," replied Zoltay. "All the men are at their posts."

"The masons?"

"They're working."

"Come with me. I trust you, but the guards have got to see that I'm on the alert too. Take this list."

They set off along the bastions. Zoltay read out the names

everywhere. Darkness covered the guns on each bastion. The guards on them were black shadows. Before the arches of the bastions and walls there was a fire burning by each watch. That was where the relief-guards warmed themselves.

There was silence in the fortress apart from the soft tapping and knocking of the masons as they plastered the walls.

Dobó stood out on the edge of the bastion. Every five minutes a lamp flashed out from the loopholes. The lamp was fixed to a pike and threw a hundred-foot swathe of light over the wall and beyond the moat. Then the pike was drawn in again and another ray of light shot out into the night from the next bastion.

Dobó stopped at the west gate. The guard saluted. Dobó relieved him of his pike and sent the man for the gatekeeper.

The guard charged up the stairs. He could be heard waking the gatekeeper.

"Oy there, Mike, old chap!"

"Eh?"

"Come down quick!"

"What for?"

"The commander's here."

A thump. (He's just jumped out of bed.) Two thuds. (Now he's pulling on his boots.) A rattle. (Now he's grasping his sword.) A clatter. (He's running down the wooden stairway.) And now the man with his big moustache, wrapped in a heavy cloak, comes to a halt before Dobó. One side of his moustache points upwards, the other downwards.

"First of all," says Dobó, returning the pike to the guard, "if you're a soldier, don't say *'Mike, old chap!'* to the corporal, or *'Come down quick'* either. Say this: *'The commander wants you, corporal.'* That's the correct way. And especially in time of siege. Worse still, you're right. Anyone who's asleep in his shirt and trousers isn't 'Corporal' but only 'Mike, old chap'. How the hell can a corporal who's supposed to be keeping the gate dare to sleep undressed in a fortress under siege?"

At this angry question even the upturned point of Mihály's moustache drooped downwards. Dobó went on: "From today onwards, you will sleep here each night on the ground under the gate. Is that understood?"

"Understood, sir."

"The other thing I want to say is that we're not going to let the gate down any more in the mornings. Instead, we'll drop the portcullis, except for one bar, and as soon as there's any attack, you will drop that one too without any separate orders."

"Understood, sir."

Before five minutes had passed, the thick, pointed iron poles had shot down one by one on the inside of the gateway, cutting off the entrance like a row of organ pipes. Only one pole remained aloft, just sufficient for a single person to go in and out.

Dobó clambered up the Church Bastion. There too he examined the guns and the bombardiers, asleep and on guard. Then he folded his arms and looked around in the night at the distant scene.

The sky was black, but the earth as far as the eye could see was sparkling with thousands of stars. They were the Turkish camp fires.

He stood and looked.

And then in the quiet night a penetrating male voice rose on the eastern side not far from the fortress, calling from the depths of the blackness: "Gergely Bornemissza! Captain in the royal army! Can you hear me?"

Silence, a long silence.

The voice calls again: "You have a Turkish ring. I have a Hungarian child. That ring is mine. This child is yours."

Silence.

Again the voice calls: "If you want your son, come to the market gate. Give me my ring. I'll give you your child. Answer me, Gergely Bornemissza."

Dobó saw all the guards' faces turn towards the voice, though in the darkness surrounding the fortress it was impossible to see anything.

"Keep your mouths shut!" he muttered, rattling his sword.

Nor did anyone reply.

The voice went on: "If you don't believe what I'm saying, you will when I have your boy's head thrown over the wall to you."

Dobó looked to left and right and again rattled his sword. "Don't you dare to say anything to Captain Bornemissza! If anyone dares to tell him about this, or tell anyone else, for that matter, I swear I'll have him given twenty-five strokes of the lash!"

"Thank you, commander," replied a hoarse voice behind Dobó. It was Bornemissza.

He was tying black tow to an arrow, and coated it with pitch as he went on: "Every night they shout out stupid things like that. Last night they called out to Mekcsey that his wife sent her respects—from Arslan Bey's tent."

He dipped the arrow in a pot of oil and went on: "My wife and boy are in Sopron. They'll not stir from there either in winter or in summer."

The voice shouted once again: "Listen to me, Bornemissza! Your son's here with me. Come to the gate in an hour's time, and you can see him for yourself."

Gergely put the arrow to the bow. He touched it to the fire and raised it, then shot it towards the voice.

The fiery arrow flew through the darkness like a comet, and for a moment lit up the hillside behind which the sun usually rose.

On the hill stood two Turks in kaftans. One held a loud-hailer in his hand. The other one had one eye covered by a white kerchief.

There was no boy with them.

*

Something else happened that night too.

Varsányi demanded to be let in at the gate. The guards had already been told to wake Dobó if any of his spies turned up.

Then Dobó was still standing on the church Bastion. He was warming his hands by the fire.

"Well, what news?"

"Beg to report, sir, that all the siege-guns are in position. They've also sited three in Hécey's courtyard. And all the other cannon and mortars will fire. On the town side there are two places and on the hills three from which the siege-guns will bombard the wall; and there are fifty emplacements from which other guns will pump in cannon-balls. At noonday prayers the *kumbaradji*s will charge out and launch thousands of fire-bombs with pikes and catapults. Oh, oh!" He rocked his head, almost in tears.

"Which means," said Dobó calmly, "that they will be aiming at the Prison Bastion, the outer fortress and the Old Gate—and what else?"

"Everything, sir!"

"Have you anything else to report?"

"No, sir, nothing else, except... wouldn't it be better... seeing that there are so few of us... and the danger's so great..."

He was unable to continue, because Zoltay struck him such a blow on the face that blood from his nose spurted on to the wall.

Dobó put out his hand to keep them apart. "Don't touch him."

And as Varsányi wiped his nose and looked sourly at Zoltay, Dobó said in a conciliatory tone, "Surely you know that anyone who even dares to mention surrendering the fortress is as good as dead?"

"I'm a spy," raged Varsányi. "I get paid for telling you everything."

"That's enough," said Dobó. "This very night you'll take the oath too. Then I'll see to it that you'll be able to wipe your nose on gold. Come with me."

They went past the wall, where Gergely, the gypsy and four peasants were making bombs. There were five men there day and night engaged on making bombs. Gergely was their instructor, and they had to work at night as well in case an unexpected attack led to a last-minute rush for them.

Dobó called Gergely over. All three of them went up to the palace. There Dobó opened the drawer in his desk and turned to Gergely.

"Write a letter to Szalkay, saying that up to now no aid has come from the king and the bishop, and telling him to urge the counties and towns to send us help."

While Gergely was writing the letter, Dobó swore in Varsányi in the next room.

"Sir," said Varsányi after taking the oath, "I know whom I'm serving. If this fortress survives, I shan't have to put on this disguise any more."

"Well said," replied Dobó. "But even if you expected no reward, you still ought to be serving your country for its own sake."

There was a jug of wine standing on the table. He set it in front of the spy. "Drink, Imre."

The spy was thirsty. He drained the jug.

When he wiped his moustache, his eyes betrayed that he was pondering how to thank Dobó. But the latter anticipated him.

"There's no need now to return to the Turks. You must take this letter to Szarvaskő this very night. Then you'll wait there until Miklós Vas returns from the king and the bishop. If possible, you'll bring him in too. If it's not possible, then come back by yourself. Does the Turkish army use passwords?"

"No, certainly not, sir. If anyone dresses like a Turk and knows a couple of words of Turkish too, he can go about among them as if he's come with them. But if only they hadn't given me such a blow on the face!..."

In the next room Gergely's spurs clanked. Dobó got up to listen to the letter.

13

And next day, 16 September, the sun rose from behind the hills to the thunder and boom of the guns.

The earth shook. From the gun-sites brown clouds of smoke rose among the clouds in the sky, blotting out the sun and the blue ocean of the sky within the first hour. The bastions and walls rumbled and cracked. A mixture of large cannon-balls and bullets rained down on the inner fortress. There were showers of fiery arrows and fire-bombs. Cannon-balls crashed down and rolled around in all directions. The lives of both man and beast were no longer secure.

But the defenders were ready to meet this peril too. Dobó had ordered the soldiers up before dawn. Some of them raised the height of the stockade in the areas where missiles were expected the next day, particularly on the side where Provost Hécey's house stood. Others, at his command, brought out the animal hides left over from the great slaughter before the siege and soaked them in tubs of water.

Others carried beams, barrels and sacks filled with earth to the outer fortress, the Prison Bastion and the gates, so that all kinds of material might be at hand in time to fill any breach.

Every empty pail and pot in the fortress had to be filled with water. Every superfluous item was carried out of the ground-level and underground premises and beds were stored in them. Things like carrots, pumpkins, cabbage and salt, which could not be harmed by cannon-balls, were all brought up above and their place taken by men working and resting.

The horses and cows were tethered further inside the large underground chambers.

The northern and eastern sides of the houses were covered with earth. Where shots fell in the square, they dug trenches and raised a rampart of earth in front of them. The missiles fell into this soft earth.

The only things in the fortress left to burn were the roof of the peace-time cattleshed and a hayrick in front of the shed, together with a small corn stack and a pile of straw for bedding. Dobó had the roof of the cattleshed dismantled too. The two stacks were covered with wet cow-hides, and there were plenty left for the straw too.

He had soaked hides scattered around the fortress to quench anything that might still catch fire, such as lofts in the houses and the wooden siege-positions.

It was while this work was going on that the guns found their target in the fortress. The first half-hundredweight cannon-ball struck the kitchen and smashed a pile of dishes.

The women were just lighting the fire and getting flour, fat and bacon to cook for the soldiers.

They were scared when the big cannon-ball landed. They rushed helter-skelter out of the kitchen shouting "Jesus Christ! Help!" And those who could not get through the door climbed out of the window.

Meanwhile the cannon-ball went on spinning there in the middle of a heap of broken dishes and wooden platters and splinters of earthenware.

Mekcsey had seen the cannon-ball land from the stables. He ran up. "What's all this?" he roared at them, his hands outstretched to stop them.

"A cannon-ball's fallen!"

"Back! Back! Come along after me!"

And he hurried into the kitchen. He grabbed up a bucket by its two handles and poured it over the ball.

"There you are," he said, kicking the cannon-ball into the corner. "Just go on cooking. The ball landed from the left, so work on the left-hand side of the kitchen. Collect up all the pots from the other side, and don't let anyone go over there. Here on the left-hand side of the kitchen there's no danger."

"Oh dear, captain," wailed a woman with a furrowed brow, "last night my hen crowed like a cock. It's all up with us!"

"That was a cock," Mekcsey dismissed the incident.

"Oh, but I swear it was a hen, sir."

"All right. If it was a hen, just you cook it for me for lunch. That'll stop it crowing!"

The women still went on crossing themselves for a few more minutes. But when the second cannon-ball broke through the roof they themselves poured water on it and rolled it beside the other one.

"Ugh, how it stinks!"

And they went on working.

All the same the hail of bullets and cannon-balls did upset the defenders. Up to then the guns had roared in only one place, and even if an occasional cannon-ball landed inside, they knew they must avoid the walls on which only the morning sun shone and those where it never shone. But now that missiles of all sizes, from water-melon to hazel-nut, were rolling, whistling, crackling, rattling and leaping around from all sides, they did not know where to find refuge.

Now there was certainly a rush for all kinds of decrepit helmets and armour. Until now only the gypsy had worn a helmet and breastplate, even though he was also barefooted; now, however, with the rattle, bang and thud of bullets everywhere and the barbers having to sew up and disinfect the wounds of ten victims in the first hour, everyone rushed to the armoury to put on the thickest possible suit of armour.

The two commanders and the six captains visited every part of the fortress in the first quarter of an hour.

"Don't be afraid!" thundered Dobó.

And the captains echoed his words everywhere: "Don't be afraid! The hail of bullets won't change direction. Don't go where they have once landed!"

But they themselves went everywhere.

And indeed hardly an hour had passed before the missiles themselves indicated which buildings and walls were perilous. The cannon-balls brought the mortar down, and where the buildings were of sandstone, their walls turned black with the number of balls lodged in them.

On the other hand there were some walls that remained white and untouched. Even if an occasional cannon-ball fell on them, they were only ricochets from another wall.

Every such wall was at the same time a protection, where the craftsman could work and the soldiers rest. True, there were not many of these in the fortress.

*

And in this raging tempest of death Dobó appeared first on one bastion, then on another.

Now he wore a gleaming steel helmet on his head, and a breastplate and protective armour on his legs and arms. On his hands he had gauntlets.

Here he adjusted the position of the gabions, there the gun itself.

"We're firing only at definite targets," he roared. "Spare the gunpowder, men!"

This one order they could not understand in the fortress.

"Damn him and his gunpowder!" the peasants muttered. "What's it for if not to use?"

And there was not a man in the fortress whose hand did not itch to fire. After all, it was only too plain that the Turks were here under their noses; the evil brigands were to be destroyed or at least scared away from the fortress.

But they did not dare to speak to Dobó. The more tempestuous the siege became, the more he assumed personal charge of all arrangements.

By now the Turks had swarmed all over the King's Seat too. There were tents and horse-tail banners, and among them the attacking army in all its many colours thronged and pressed around the fortress on all sides.

Turkish military bands struck up first here, then there. The music of pipes, trumpets and cymbals accompanied the ceaseless thundering of the guns.

Where the cannon had not smashed the walls, the *kumbaradjis* hurled bombs and the janissary archers shot fiery arrows. A hail of cannon-balls and a rain of fire. Naturally the arrows and exploding bombs caused more confusion among the defenders than the cannon-balls. But the experienced officers showed them how to deal with these too.

When the first bombs fell inside and hissing and leaping spewed out red fire and sparks, Dobó himself seized a wet hide and threw himself down on it with the hide. The people were astonished to see that the bomb not only did not blow the commander to bits but merely pattered a little, then was extinguished beneath the hide.

The next bombs were extinguished by the soldiers. They were made of earthenware and glass.

"We'll soon show the Turks we can do better than that," cried Gergely. And he sent for his own bombs, the ones he had been busy with for the whole week.

Dobó put his hand on Gergely's shoulder.

"Not just yet!"

*

And from morning till night the cannon roared unceasingly and the rain of death poured down.

The half-hundredweight cannon-balls from the siege-guns blasted gaps in the walls the size of gates. The falconets and mortars sent their heavy small bullets into the splendid carvings on the church and brought them down; they tore at the back wall of the commander's palace. A long straight wall protects it on the north side, and this was the wall where the guns did most damage.

"Bring earth along!" ordered Dobó, "and pile it inside and outside the back rooms of the palaces."

But Mekcsey had already arranged barrows and handcarts to bring it along by devious routes. The dangerous streets and corners were barricaded with barrels and gabions filled with earth.

"Bring a big barrel over here!" shouted Lieutenant Balázs Nagy. And as if he had been snatched away, he rolled off the mound of earth, struck down by a cannon-ball.

Then the officers ordered digging and filling in to begin in other parts of the fortress too; they set up gabions and barrels to protect them from the cannon-balls. The big bastion by the Old Gate required a particularly large earth-filled gabion.

When the troops on guard at the Sándor Bastion took up their position at dawn behind the palisade, a hail of bullets from the Turkish falconets rained on them from behind.

"Get down!" shouted Gergely. The hundred and fifty men dropped flat on their faces. Gergely pressed himself against the wall.

The bullets whistled over their heads and struck the wall of the fortress. The palisade on the wall was riddled like a sieve.

Then came a pause at that gun-site. The Turks had fired all their guns, and had to reload them.

"Up!" called Gergely. Five men remained on the ground.

"Take them in front of the church," said Gergely, shaking his head. "Are any of you wounded?" Fifteen men with bloodstains on them stepped silently out of the ranks. "All right. You go off to the barbers."

He clenched his fists and swore. "Lads," he said. "We can't lie flat here until nightfall. Bring spades and we'll dig a trench."

Some ten of them ran off for spades, and soon all the soldiers were digging. In less than an hour the soldiers had dug a trench deep enough to stand in waist-high.

Gergely waited for the Turks to fire again, then jumped out of the trench and hurried to the inner fortress to report on the trench-digging to Dobó.

Beside the monastery he came across the little Turkish boy playing on the dry ground under the eaves. He was digging out a smouldering cannon-ball from the wall with a spoon. The boy must have escaped from the kitchen, and was standing in a place where ever more cannon-balls were falling.

"*Haydi!*" (Get away!) Gergely shouted at him.

The boy was scared and turned towards Gergely. He leaned

against the wall and with pale and terrified eyes looked at Gergely, running his two hands along the wall as if to feel for his mother's skirts.

Fresh missiles smashed into the wall and battered the plaster. A black cannon-ball the size of a fist struck the wall just above the boy's shoulder, leaving a dirty ring round it. Gergely jumped over to the boy, pulled him away and carried him in his arms into the palace.

*

That evening the sun sank towards Bakta behind ashen clouds. Only for a moment did it flash a gleaming golden ray across the middle of the sky before disappearing among blood-red clouds to give light to those in a happier part of the world who that very evening were retiring to their beds to the peaceful droning of the cockchafer.

It was now that work began in the fortress of Eger.

As the last shots of the *topchis* died away, the masons picked up their trowels and the peasants carried stone, earth, beams, water and sand, and began to fill in the breaches. And axes rang everywhere too. Dobó ordered the stone projections on the towers to be broken off, since the cannon-balls had knocked many of the stones out of them, wounding defenders walking or standing in protected areas.

So the work continued even by night. Riflemen lay prone on the edges of the walls, and in the breaches men were at work. From time to time a mortar-shot was heard from one or other bastion. The missile that was launched exploded high in the sky and for an instant lit up the ground in front of the fortress in a red glow. These were flares. And they were needed now to keep an eye on any Turkish trickery.

"Just keep working, men! Keep at it!" The officers' words of encouragement could be heard here and there.

One mason was let down on a rope from the top of the wall on the outside in order to fix the beam across the breach with clamps to the outside of the wall. From below there was the flash of rifle-fire. A hail of bullets fell on the workmen. And after that many more rifles flashed and crackled. The light from the Turkish rifles revealed two companies of janissaries prone on the ground.

A volley of shots replied to them from the walls.
But the mason had fallen into the depths outside.
"Only work on the inside!" Pető's instruction rang out.
And the workmen carried on to renewed fusillades from the
tüfekchis.
At midnight the sentry on the gate blew his horn.
Dobó was sitting on a barrel of gunpowder. He pricked up
his ears.
"Why, here's the letter from the king!" Pető thrilled with joy.
And indeed within five minutes two men, panting and blood-
stained, were standing before Dobó.
Both of them were dressed as Turks. The bloodstained swords
in their hands were proof that it was not easy to reach the
fortress of Eger.
"Well now," said Dobó, "let's hear what you've got to
report."
One of them was Varsányi, who had gone out the previous
night. The other was Miklós Vas, who had taken Ahmed
Pasha's letter to the king. Varsányi was panting. "They almost
killed us!"
Miklós Vas thrust his bloodstained sword into the scabbard
and sat down on the ground that was covered with stone-dust.
He was wearing yellow boots. He pulled them off. He pulled out
a knife and prized open the sole. There was a letter inside. He
offered it to Dobó.
Only then did he find his voice.
"I was in the presence of the bishop. He sends his regards to
you, sir. The bishop himself took the letter to the king. Here's
the reply."
"The third man was killed," said Varsányi.
"What third man?" Pető turned on him.
"István Szűrszabó, one of our soldiers. He too was unable to
get into the fortress. He came with us. He was felled by a lance
here below the gate."
He took a deep breath and went on, "We didn't think we
should find Turks here at the entrance-gate. As we approached,
I blew my whistle. The minute I did that, why, ten Turks fell on
us just by the gate. It's a good thing it was dark, and that the

394

gate was opened immediately. István was struck down right in front of me, and we could scarcely get inside."

Dobó had broken the seal, which in any case had crumbled to dust inside the boot, and bent over to a lamp. He read the letter. His face grew darker as he read. His two eyebrows almost met. When he reached the end of it he jerked his head once and thrust it into his pocket.

Pető dearly wanted to ask him what the king had written. But Dobó glanced grimly around and turned to Varsányi.

"Did you give the letter to Master Szalkay?"

"I did, sir. He sends his regards. He spent the whole morning writing, and sent off each one by a mounted despatch-rider to different places before noon."

"Have you anything else to report?"

"I haven't," said Miklós Vas. "The bishop received me most graciously. And everyone at the king's court received me well, but I've got a cut on my head. I'd like to go and see the barbers now..."

"Pető, my lad," said Dobó, "don't forget tomorrow to tell Sukán to include the names of these two men on the list of those for whom we're going to ask the king for a reward after the siege."

"Sir," said Varsányi, scratching the back of his neck, "I've still got something to report."

Dobó looked at him.

"It's this," went on Varsányi. "Lukács Nagy requests you to have some torches waiting at the main gate. He wants to return tonight..."

"Oh, does he indeed?" Dobó burst out angrily. "I'll teach him what's what!"

A man with a barrel hurried past them with mortar for the masons. Dobó stood to one side and called to the latter, "Put that beam crosswise, not lengthwise."

Then he turned again to Varsányi. "Maybe that Lukács thinks... Oh well, just let me catch sight of him!" And he snorted with rage just like a bull getting ready to charge.

Varsányi rubbed his chin and looked imploringly at Dobó.

"He's very upset, sir, that he's been forced to stay outside. He's so miserable, he doesn't know what to do."

Dobó walked up and down under the lamp.

"It would be madness! Whatever's he thinking of? Anyway, whatever messages he may send, he's not going to avoid punishment. You must both go back this night. You'll take another letter to the bishop and the king. Can you manage to do that, Miklós?"

Miklós was holding a handkerchief to his head. The blood was streaming down his young face on the left side, and his handkerchief was already red with blood.

"Yes," he replied with alacrity. "In that case I'll get a stitch put in my head at Szarvaskő."

14

Each day the destruction of the walls extended further. Quite a number of men were now helping the masons in their work, including the guards for some nights. The following day when the Turkish cannon boomed out again the mortar spurted out of the walls some sixty feet up, and the cannon-ball remained stuck there.

"Just go on firing!" cackled old Cecey. "Reinforce our walls with iron!"

But on the tenth day the Turks woke up to ruins that had not been repaired. They could not repair all the breaches in the night.

At the end of the second week all the Turkish guns were silent. The defenders looked around to see what had happened. Nothing.

"Here comes a country fellow," they said at the market gate. "That's odd!"

And indeed an elderly peasant in a frieze coat walked up and announced himself. It's not a local coat he was wearing. All the same they let him in.

Dobó received him in the square. He knew that the Turks had sent another letter.

"Where do you come from?" he turned on the man.

"From Csábrág, sir, that's where I live."

"And what has Csábrág to do with Eger?"

"Well... I brought flour, sir, to the Turks."

"How much?"

"Well... Sixteen cartloads."

"Who sent you?"

"The bailiff."

"Bailiff? He's no bailiff; He's a filthy rascal!"

"But sir... we had to give in... in case we should share the same fate as our neighbour."

"And who's your neighbour?"

"The fortress of Drégely, sir."

"You've brought a letter, haven't you?"

"Well... er... yes, I have."

"From the Turks?"

"Yes, sir."

"Did your conscience tell you you were committing a crime when you brought the letter?"

"Well... I haven't any idea what's in it."

"Can there be anything good in a letter from a Turk?"

The man made no reply.

"Can you read?"

"No."

Dobó turned to the women. "Bring a pan of charcoal out here."

They brought it and tipped it on to the ground. Dobó threw the letter on it.

"Take this old traitor and hold him in the smoke. At least smell it, you rogue, even if you can't read it!"

Then he had him put in the stocks in the square. Let the defenders see what happens to anyone who accepts a letter from the Turks.

*

The officers also witnessed this scene. And the defenders crowded round. They laughed and jeered at the man who was weeping copiously as a result of the smoke and his own rage.

"There you are, you see!" said the gypsy to him. "Why ever did you agree to be a postman?"

The letter disintegrated in the embers into red and black leaves. When it was red, the lines of writing appeared on it like black decorations. And when the pages turned black, the letters for a moment snaked across them glowing red.

Gergely was standing there too.

When the peasant stepped inside the gateway, all the guns fell silent.

The Turks were waiting for the reply.

"Commander," said Gergely when they had stepped out of the group. "Whether I liked it or not, I did read one line of that letter."

Dobó shrugged.

"What did you do that for? I didn't read it, but all the same I know what it says."

"It wouldn't really be worth mentioning," Gergely went on, "but since that one line was so truly heathen, I can't resist telling you what it said."

Dobó said neither "Tell me", nor "Don't tell me." So Gergely continued. "The line was this: 'Or have you got your coffin all ready, István Dobó'?"

Dobó grunted.

"It is ready, as a matter of fact. And if by that they mean am I ready for death, well, I'll give them a reply to that one point."

A quarter of an hour later a black coffin appeared on the wall of the fortress. It was held at each end by a chain attached to a pike. The soldiers stuck the shafts of the two pikes into the loopholes.

At that the Turkish guns thundered out once again.

15

On the evening of Michaelmas Day there were some fifteen huge breaches yawning in the walls.

Most of them were in the outer fortress. The second big breach was by the corner tower on the south-eastern side. The third and fourth were on the south, where the gate had been smashed. The tall watch-tower was so shot to pieces, with great holes in its side, that it was almost impossible to comprehend what was holding it up and why it did not collapse.

The defenders by now were quite unable to keep up with the

infilling and repair of the walls. It was to be anticipated that even if all of them were engaged on this work half of the damage would still go unrepaired.

"All the same, men, just go on working!"

At midnight Dobó called his officers to the Church Bastion and had flares fired high in the sky towards the east.

"Have a look," he said. "Those mounds of earth coming in this direction like molehills when the moles are burrowing underground—those trenches are all full of Turks."

And indeed that night the Turks all withdrew from the hills and came close to the walls. By the occasional light of the flares the proximity of the mass of tents was revealed. And in all directions the yellow and red banners of the janissaries were to be seen nearby, as were the siege-ladders lying among the tents and the sackcloth tents of the janissaries in which maybe ten or twenty men could sleep. The inner line of the besieging troops had moved closer round the fortress.

"Lads," said Dobó, "they're beginning their attack tomorrow. Everyone is to sleep outside here."

He placed mortars and riflemen in the breaches. He also aimed the cannon to face the breaches. All round the walls the whole stock of arms in the fortress was ranged—pikes, lances, bombs, pickaxes and clubs.

He shook hands with each officer.

"You all know what you have to do, lads. Sleep as long as you can. We have to repel the attack."

The words were still on his lips when he turned his head towards the town. A strange rumbling could be heard rising from below. A gradually increasing clatter of hooves.

They all looked in that direction.

Varsányi's whistle pierced the air at the gate by the brook.

"Open the gate!" shouted Dobó.

The rumbling down below in the town grew louder. Horses galloping. Arms clashing and clattering. Urgent cries on the walls.

"Open the gate! Here comes Lukács!"

Lieutenant János Vajda of the watch at the gate ordered a torch to be lit immediately and had it held out. And there was the long line of Lukács Nagy's cavalrymen, galloping through and over the slumbering *djebedji*s in the market-place on their way to the fortress.

"Down with the torch!" shouted Vajda. "Hold it under the gateway!" For he realized immediately that it would be better for them to come on in darkness.

The drawbridge was let down instantly and the portcullis raised.

"Riflemen, get above the gate! Lancers, to the gate!"

The Hungarians followed each other in at a gallop, with the Turks pressing and leaping at their heels, yelling.

"Allah! *Sana yazik! Vay sana!* Allah! Allah!"

And a bloody struggle began beneath the gateway.

One barefooted *piyad* ran like a cat up the cain of the drawbridge. In his mouth he gripped a dagger. The guard with the torch caught sight of him. For a moment they glowered at each other. Then the guard hurled the lighted end of the torch in his face so hard that the Turk toppled over backwards into the darkness.

With unceasing cries of *Allah akbar* and *sana yazik* the other Turks piled in beneath the gateway.

"Up with the drawbridge!" shouted Dobó.

The sound of his voice was drowned by rifle shots.

"It's impossible to pull the bridge up!" the gateman called down.

And it was seen to be full of Turks.

At that moment Gergely arrived there. He seized a torch from one of the guards and rushed with it to the mortar. The next moment the mortar detonated with a belch of flames and cleared a path among the Turks swarming on the drawbridge.

The bridge rose creaking and cracking on the pulleys which were as big as barrow-wheels. The Turks rose with it.

On the near side the portcullis dropped, on the far side the bridge closed up with a screech and a dull thud.

Some fifty Turks were caught in between them in the gateway. They twisted and turned in their fury until they were felled by shots and pike-thrusts. A few minutes later only a pile of panting, twitching bodies remained beneath the darkened gate.

By now Dobó was in the square. By torchlight twenty-two bare-headed cavalrymen dismounted and stood in line before him, holding their horses by the bridle. The foam on the horses was white and red. The riders were panting. Some of them had bloodstained faces. The shirt of one of them showed white through the shoulder of his jacket which was slashed in two. A stocky little man stepped forward and came to a halt in front of Dobó.

"Beg to report, sir," he panted, "I've arrived!"

"Lukács, my lad!" replied Dobó with emotion, "you deserve to be clapped in irons, you scamp, you vagabond! And a gold chain round your neck, you fine upstanding hero!" And he embraced his soldier. "Well, how did you manage to get in?"

"We had to wait, sir, until we'd killed enough Turks for each of us to have a turban and a cloak. We kept making raids from Szarvaskő, and this evening we only needed two more turbans. Varsányi gave me his whistle. And we'd have got here easily enough, sir, if there'd been cavalry too in the market-place. But the infantry suspected that we didn't belong to them and attacked us."

"Who's missing?"

The soldiers looked at one another. Only half of their faces were illuminated by the lighting there. All of them were bleeding. Blood shone red on their clothes and horses too.

"Gábor," said a quiet voice.

"Bicskey," came another.

"Balkányi..."

"Gyuri Soós..."

Dobó's glance lighted on a little lad with the hair of a girl. He was standing well back from the line, hiding his face in his horse's neck.

"Balázs!" he shouted, his heart leaping. "Is it you?"

The boy stepped forward. He knelt down. He placed his bloodstained sword at Dobó's feet and bowed his head in silence.

It was Balázs Balogh, his own youngest page.

16

That night every man was able to sleep except for eighty riflemen. They slept beside the walls just as they were, in their cloaks, and in the trenches. Their arms were on them and beside them: swords and pikes. Up above beside the palisade the riflemen had their weapons resting on the wall, loaded and ready to fire; they were covered with rags and tow to protect them from the dew.

Sentries stood every ten or twenty paces among the sleepers. By the guns and on the towers it was the same. They were fewest on the side overlooking the town.

All those who were not soldiers were awake and at work. Dobó ordered all the peasants in the fortress to help the masons —the butchers, millers, mechanics, carpenters, the four black-smiths and two flayers and even the gypsy.

He had the longest beams set up in the breaches. Earth, planks, mortar and as much stone as possible in all the con-fusion of urgent work were poured into the holes. The gate that had been knocked down had to be replaced with earth, stone, sand and filled barrels; mortars were sited in front and above it, smaller ones at the side and as many falconets as were available.

Down below the *tüfekchi*s were stationed in the deep trenches; they fired every time one of the workmen appeared in the breach. And however much they tried to hide what was happening behind gabions, every now and then workmen did appear there.

At the corner tower Tamás Bolyky superintended the repairs. Since the collapsed wall there had left a hole eighteen feet wide, the lieutenant from Borsod had the beams secured with ropes and chains. It was difficult work, and meant occasional work outside too; every time this happened the janissaries down below opened fired.

In vain was the fire returned and in vain were the bombs tossed down on them. They had so covered their position with earthen ramparts and wicker palisades that only the tips of their rifles protruded. And of course the moving lamps of the masons illuminated their targets.

"Raise the beams!" shouted Tamás Bolyky. The peasants were standing there with the beams, but that night three of them too were numbered among the wounded. "Raise the beams!" repeated Tamás Bolyky. The peasants were reluctant to move. The lieutenant stepped right up to the breach and shouted once more, "Get moving there, for heaven's sake! This way! This way!"

And the beams rose up swiftly. From below came the crackle of Turkish rifles. Up above the hammers banged and the six-inch iron nails with which the chain was fastened to the beams clattered and rattled on the chains.

"Don't be afraid!" the lieutenant from Borsod encouraged them. And nobody dared to be afraid.

A bullet struck the lieutenant's helmet and knocked the silver clasp holding the plume from it.

"Quickly, there! Quickly!"

He seized hold of a log and himself chained it to the next beam.

"Tamás!" called Mekcsey. "Come away from there!"

For now a hail of bullets was raining on the tower, and down below the Turkish rifles were crackling ever more frequently.

"I'm coming," replied Tamás Bolyky. And he bent down for the next beam, to help hoist it up. "Bring rope here!"

He stayed there, bent down as if he had turned to stone.

"Tamás!" shouted Mekcsey, shocked.

Tamás remained there on one knee. The helmet fell from his head, and his long grey hair fell forward.

Mekcsey dashed up and embraced Tamás, dragging him from the breach in the wall. He laid him down in the inner angle of the bastion wall.

"Bring a lamp here!"

Tamás Bolyky's face was waxen-white. Blood trickled right down his grey beard and dripped on the white lime-dust on the ground.

"Tamás!" Mekcsey said in a trembling voice, "can you speak?"

"Yes," murmured Tamás. "Fight on... for Hungary..."

*

All over the fortress lamps and pitch-torches were burning as they hung from hooks. Dobó rode on horseback from one breach to another.

The tower above the old gate gave him most cause for concern. The Turkish guns had both smashed the gate to pieces and wrecked the tower too. On the south side the spiral staircase loomed black out of it, and that too had four broken steps.

They could patch up the gate somehow, but there was no time to rebuild the tower now. What would happen if they fired at the tower tomorrow too? That was the tower which watched over the southern approaches and was also a rifle-position. If it collapsed the fortress lost an important strong point.

He ordered up forty good riflemen. They had to sleep there with rifles ready primed and prepared for battle.

"Get some sleep!" he called towards them. "It's sufficient for two men to keep watch by the outer window."

And he turned his horse. He trotted over to the corner tower. "What's going on here? Why aren't you working?"

"Sir," said one of the workmen in a trembling voice, "Lieutenant Bolyky's just been shot, this very minute."

Just then they brought him down the steps on a stone-carrier's stretcher. His legs were dangling from it. His two hands were clasped, gloveless, over his breastplate. Mekcsey carried his helmet after him. Their shadows moved like a gigantic funeral procession along the bastion wall.

Dobó was appalled. "Is he dead?"

"Yes," replied Mekcsey sadly.

"Keep on working!" shouted Dobó towards the bastion. And he got off his horse. He took off his cap. He stepped up to the dead man and gazed at him sorrowfully in silence.

"My dear Tamás Bolyky... Stand before God. Show him your bleeding wounds, and point him to this fortress too."

Bareheaded and sorrowful, he gazed after them until the lamp disappeared by the corner of the stables. Then he mounted his horse again and hurried to the other breach behind the palace.

There Zoltay was wrestling with a big coil of rope, tying beams together to fill in the breach. He himself gives a hand in pulling on the rope, and meanwhile shouts to the workmen: "Don't be frightened of the rope. It's not a sausage! Grab it,

Jancsi, for goodness' sake! Pull on it as if you're hoisting the Turkish emperor on to the scaffold!"

And the beams creak as they are pulled together. The carpenters and smiths hammer in the clamps, and earth, stones and gravel pour down to fill in the hole torn by the Turkish cannon.

Dobó calls up to Zoltay, "Come down!"

Zoltay lets go of the rope but calls back once more, "Iron clamps here, as many as you can bring!"

Dobó puts his hand on his shoulder. "Go off and get some sleep, lad. You need strength for tomorrow."

"Just another couple of barrels..."

"Go away and sleep!" Dobó roared at him. "Left, right'!"

Zoltay raised his hand in salute and went off without a word. Dobó would allow nobody to gainsay him.

Next Dobó sent in Fügedy and Pető, then himself dismounted in front of the palace. He handed his horse over to the sentry at the door and went into his room.

The little ground-floor room where he had made his quarters since the shelling was lit by a green earthenware hanging lamp. On the table there were cold meat, wine and bread. Dobó merely picked up the bread as he stood there and broke off a piece of it.

The door from the next room opened and a white-haired lady in mourning appeared to Dobó. She had a candle in her hand. When she caught sight of him, she stepped into the room. It was Mrs. Balogh, the mother of the page Balázs.

The courageous little gentlewoman, unable to leave the fortress, had immediately found her place there. She took over the duties of the steward's wife and it was she who cooked for Dobó and took charge of everything.

"How is your son?" asked Dobó.

"He's asleep now," replied the lady. "He's wounded in six places. On his chest, head and arm. But you, sir, aren't eating by day or sleeping by night. You can't go on like this. If you don't come in to lunch tomorrow either, I myself will bring it out after you and wait till you've eaten it up."

"I just haven't the time," replied Dobó, sipping from his cup. "Is my bed ready for me?"

"Yes, and it has been for three days now, day and night."

"All right, then I'll lie down today." And he did indeed sit down. "Your boy's wounds, they're not large ones, I hope?"

"Well, the cut on his head's a long one. The others, thank God, were diminished by his leather jacket. He's got no trouble in moving all his limbs."

"How's Budaházy?"

"The barber took the bone out of his shoulder in five pieces."

"Will he survive?"

"The barber said so."

"Now you go to bed too, madam. I'm going to do the same today. I've got to get some rest. Good-night."

He looked up into the air and once more hurried out of the room.

His long night cloak was hanging in the hall. He seized it. He buttoned it up as he went out. He hastened to the Sándor Bastion. There he found Gergely ordering a soldier to take a big leather pouch up the stairs.

"What's going on?" he rounded on him angrily. "Why are you out of bed? Didn't I order you to get some sleep?"

"I've already carried out that order, sir," replied Gergely. "I have slept. But it occurred to me that dew might fall on the guns. I'm having dry powder taken everywhere."

Dobó spoke down to the flare-gun.

"Fire!"

The gun crackled and exploded. The missile threw out a flame six hundred feet above them, lighting up the surroundings of the fortress.

There was no sign of movement in the Turkish camp surrounding the fortress. Only the sentries were sitting, heads buried in their collars, in their places in front of the troops.

Dobó followed Bornemissza to the Church Bastion and watched how he blew the damp powder out of the touch-holes, carefully replacing it with dry gunpowder. And how he looked to see whether the fuse was in place, and the ramrod, and the spoon for the gunpowder, and the cannon-balls. The bombardiers were asleep beside the gun, wrapped in their cloaks.

"Get along and sleep," said Dobó.

He himself stayed there. He stood with folded arms on the top of the bastion beside the gun called Baba. And in the great silence all around him he raised his eyes to the heavens. It was a cold, cloudy night with no moon. Only a few white stars gleamed in a little patch of clear sky.

Dobó took off his cap and went down on his knees. He raised his eyes to heaven.

"Oh my God," he murmured, placing his hands together in prayer, "You can see this countless host of robbers and murderers. You can see our tiny, crumbling fortress and this handful of determined defenders in it... In Your great universe this earth of ours is a tiny nothing. Oh, but for us this is our universe! If our lives are needed, then take them from us, Lord! Let us fall like grass beneath the reaper's scythe! Only let this country survive... this little Hungary..."

His face was pale. Tears welled up in his eyes. And with tearful face he went on, "Mary, mother of Jesus, patron saint of Hungary! It is your likeness we carry on our banners! It is your name that millions of lips sing in Hungarian! Pray for us!"

And again he continued, "Stephen, King and Saint! Look down from heaven! Look on your country as it is laid waste, your nation as it perishes! Look upon Eger, where the walls of your church still stand and where the people still praise the Almighty in your language and in your faith. Arise in your heavenly dwelling, King and Saint Stephen! Oh, prostrate yourself before the feet of God! Oh, God, God! May Your heart be ours!"

That little patch of clear sky seemed to be a window in heaven, and the stars in it white candles...

Dobó wiped his tears away and sat down on the gun-cradle. Deep in thought, he gazed motionlessly into the darkness below the fortress.

There was a gentle murmur as the Turkish camp slept. The air quivered with the breath of a hundred thousand men.

Dobó leaned back with his elbows on the barrel of the gun. His head drooped, then bent towards his arm. He went off to sleep.

17

From near the stables came a thin, immature cock-crow, followed by a full-blooded one. A pale grey band divided the black sky from the hills towards the east.

Day began to dawn. Down below it was as if the clods of earth had been stirring. A gentle rattling arose in the far distance. The face of the earth moved in black waves and the rattle and rumbling grew ever louder. Now the sound of an occasional bell mingled with the noise, and now a soft whistle or two. The grey band at the base of the horizon grew broader, and the darkness of night in the heavens was now a transparent veil.

Now the banners could be seen moving down there below. And now the whitish groups of turbans and the thin ladders pointing to the sky as they made their way unsteadily towards the fortress.

The sky towards the east quickly grew light. The general greyness was replaced by rose-colouring and the cold darkness dispersed to reveal the roofless towers and ruined walls looming out of the fortress.

"Sir!" said Bornemissza. And he put his hand on Dobó's shoulder.

Dobó started up. "Is it you, Gergely?" And he glanced down at the seething mass of Turks. "Sound the reveille!"

The bastion bugle sounded. Eight bugles replied immediately. Weapons rattled. Suddenly the sounds of clattering and men's voices arose on all sides. The trenches in the outer fortress also came alive. The soldiers lined up on the bastions and walls.

Dobó leapt on his horse and in the light of dawn surveyed where and how the Turkish brigades were positioned. Most of them were behind the palaces.

"As soon as they storm the wall, hurl down the fireballs," was Dobó's order everywhere.

The page Kristóf met the commander in the square. He was riding.

"Good morning, sir. Shall I bring out your armour?"

"No. I'll come in in a minute." But he did not do so. He

dashed from bastion to bastion to see what preparations were being made.

"Only shoot where they are massed together," he said to the bombardiers. "The most important weapons now are the fireballs."

Then he called out again, "Don't climb up on to the walls until the Turks have fired their cannon."

There were huge piles of fireballs near the breaches. They had been making them for weeks. Gergely Bornemissza had a little extra charge inserted in them, and this gave them double power. They exploded first when they were thrown down, and a second time when the charge fell out of them. Then huge white sparks that burnt for minutes on end leapt out of them in all directions, presumably from porcelain ground to dust; anyone whose clothing or face was struck by them leapt out of the way.

The Turks were unable to make anything like them.

Kristóf the page waited a while for his master in front of the palace door. Then when he saw him galloping ever faster from one bastion to another, he went into the room and fetched out the armour, and put it on his horse—the breastplate, greaves and gauntlets. He put the helmet under his arm and caught up with Dobó at the corner tower.

Dobó proceeded to put on his armour on horseback. Sitting on his horse, Kristóf put on his breastplate, arm-guards and gauntlets. Then he jumped from his horse and strapped on his greaves. Finally he offered him the gilded helmet.

"Bring me the other one," said Dobó. "The steel one."

By now it was light enough to be able to see the Turkish troops clearly down below. Below the walls to the north and east there was a sea of turbans surging white in the trenches together with the silvery glint of helmets. As yet, however, they had not moved. They were waiting for the signal to start the attack.

They had not long to wait. As soon as there was enough light to see the ramparts, the projecting stones and lines of beams, the muezzins' devotional chanting was heard rising from a hundred places in the Turkish army around the fortress. The vast army fell on its face with a far-resounding clatter, and rose again to its knees.

409

The huge heathen army murmured the prayer like the rumble of an approaching storm.

"...Allah... Mohammed our Prophet... strengthen our hearts... Extend your invincible arms over us... Stop the throats of their fire-spitting weapons... Change the infidel madmen into dogs that they may bite each other to death... Send a whirlwind on their lands so that their eyes may be filled with dust and they may be struck to the ground... Smash the bones of their legs so that they may not be able to stand before us... Put them to shame, glorious Prophet, that we may shine above them and your kingdom flourish for ever!"

And with a great clatter they leapt up.

"Bismillah!" (In the name of God!)

The Turkish cannon and rifles thundered out together. The walls of the fortress trembled and the ramparts cracked apart from the countless cannon-balls that burst on them. Arrows and rifle-bullets rained down on the palisades protecting the bastions. The air became filled with the stench of gunpowder. And mingled with the earth-shattering thunder came the clamour of drums, bugles and trumpets and the screams of "Allah!" from a hundred thousand Turks.

The *asab*s, janissaries, *deli*s, *djebedji*s and all kinds of Turkish infantry leapt out of the trenches like a swarm of locusts as the smoke from the rifles billowed up in clouds above them. A forest of siege-ladders floated towards the wrecked walls and bastions, and behind them a hail of arrows whistled in a high curve on to the walls. And on all sides the Turkish military bands struck up.

But a reply came hurtling down from above too. The cannon, aimed downwards, spewed out flame, iron, lead and fragments of glass where the Turks were massed most closely. Hundreds were covered in blood and wavered and fell. But at the same moment hundreds pressed forward over the fallen.

The stench of sulphur spread inside the fortress too in swirling clouds.

The iron hooks of the Turkish siege-ladders crashed into the stone, iron and beams of the walls, and the mob rose up them almost at a run, shield over their heads, a barbed lance in one hand and a dagger held horizontally in their mouths.

410

Twenty-seven red Turkish banners wove and fluttered, leading the army up the ladders over the ruins behind the palaces.

"Allah akbar! La illa il Allah! Ya kerim! Ya rahim! Ya fetih!" raged the ceaseless cry.

"To the walls! To the walls!" came the cries from up above. And the walls filled with defenders. Only now did the rain of bombs begn. They were simply thrown by hand: first they spluttered, then they burst into flame and finally they exploded down below. A thousand rumbling, crackling sparks of lightning rained down. Shouts, cries, smoke, explosions, the smell of sulphur, hell. Axes, matchets and cleavers clanged on the grappling-irons of the ladders. Some ladders had twenty men on them when they fell.

"Allah! Ya kerim!"

They crashed down on each other and cut a path through the swarm of men below.

"Ya rahim! Allah!"

But a minute later their places were taken by a new wave of armed attackers, and a new host of ladders rose beside those that have fallen.

"Allah! Allah akbar! Allah!"

On the corner bastion, which since yesterday evening had been named the Bolyky Bastion, Gergely and Zoltay were in charge. Gergely kept an eye on everything, while Zoltay was on the wall.

That is where the tempestuous attack raged more fiercely than at the other three breaches. The breach was larger there, and the attacking troops were more numerous.

"Allah akbar!" yelled a sonorous voice, as if coming from a gigantic copper cauldron, drowning all other voices.

They beat off the climbing soldiers with hundreds of bombs and shot at them from the flank. But when they were so numerous, lives counted nothing to the Turks. If only ten of them could force their way in! Pressing on behind them, the whole army would surge in like a giant flood.

So it needs a man to meet the challenge.

For an hour now the bombs had been beating back the continuous stream of attackers. The double-exploding bombs were something new to the Turks. As each one exploded, a dance of woe surrounded it, but a couple of minutes later the pressure of the mass of soldiers closed up the gap. New ladders and new fighters stormed the walls. However much the fire swept them off, there were always ladders in place and men on the ladders; as soon as the first long ladder was fixed firmly to the wall, smaller ones were passed from hand to hand to be propped in the breaches and the upper parapet.

"Grab the ladder and pull it up!" Gergely shouted.

And to the great astonishment of the Turks the ladders are not smashed; indeed, as they are raised aloft they are neatly snatched and jerked upwards.

They had pulled up some five ladders when a Turkish officer in brass armour hardly waited for his ladder to grip the wall before he started climbing.

"Pull!" shouted Gergely. And he stuck the end of his pike between the rungs and pressed on it.

"Help me!"

The ladder stood out from the wall like a bridge. The brass-clad Turk hung on the end of it. In his hand was a long lance with a tassel. But as he rose into the air he dropped both shield and lance and held on to the bottom rung with both hands. He swung in the air.

Below the army yelled *"Allah! Allah!"*

Gergely would have liked to drag the Turk inside, but there was no time for that. An *asab* in a fur cap ran up the next little ladder and he had to deal with him.

"Turn it over!" he shouted with perspiring face to the four soldiers pulling on the ladder.

One of his men collapsed in front of him. It was Gyuri Gyulai. Gergely jumped over him with his pike and struck the asab on the shoulder. The *asab* wavers for a minute as his arm is covered in blood. Then he falls head over heels, bringing another ten or so of the climbing soldiers down with him.

Now the soldiers act on Gergely's orders, and turn the ladder over. The armoured Turk has to choose between a twisted arm and a flight through the air of over a hundred feet. He chooses the latter.

A Turkish drummer, beating a loaf-shaped drum down below, about sixty feet away from the wall, catches the ar-

412

moured man on his head and both of them roll away among the Killed.

But what is this among thousands?

A crocodile-skin shield rises up at a run, as if carried by a man with wings. The Turk beneath it is invisible. The tip of a pike simply slithers off its smooth surface. The cunning Turk has probably fastened the centre of the shield to the top of his helmet. From whatever side the pike-thrusts come, the shield merely tips and the pike stabs air.

With a bound Gergely appears there.

"Here's how you do it!"

He reverses his pike and with the thick end scrapes it across the crocodile shield. The Turk falls back head first. And all the while there are unceasing yells of *"Allah akbar! Ya kerim! Ya fetih!"*

And sometimes in Hungarian too: "Surrender the fortress!"

"Take that!" bawls Zoltay. And with a fearful blow of his axe he perforates shield, helmet and skull alike.

At the far side of the breach he uses no other weapon but an axe. The wall protects him up to his waist. He has left his soldiers to fight with pikes. He himself stands above a wall of beams where it is easy to hook ladders and there is a line of them there. The armed multitudes swarm up them *en masse.*

One or two ladders are smashed, but he gives a great yell:

"Aim at their heads, lads, nothing else!"

And he stands out ahead of them to receive the new arrivals in person. His armour is of steel. The blade of his axe is as long as a cudgel. His face is bathed in perspiration but brimming with life. He keeps spitting in his two hands and shouts:

"Come on then, you gypsy, come on! I'll make a meal of that fine calf's face of yours!" he encourages a black-faced Saracen who with a light round shield of wickerwork is leaping up into the billowing clouds of smoke from the bombs and flashing the whites of his eyes from behind it. As he gets within six feet of him, he curls up into a ball and carries on. His intention is suddenly to uncurl on the topmost rung and hurl his lance into Zoltay, then reach the top of the wall.

The post of Pasha of Eger is promised to the first man to raise the standard of victory. The defenders know this too. So the black panther scampers on upwards. In his wake a *djebedji* with a big beard and foaming mouth yells "Allah akbar!" Stuck in the back of his belt is a horse-tail banner with a short staff. He grips the broad naked blade of his yataghan between his teeth.

"*Allah akbar! Ya kerim! Ya rahim!*"

Zoltay pulls down the visor of his helmet. And just in time. The Saracen suddenly straightens up and thrusts his lance upwards, breaking its tip on the button of the visor.

At that instant the axe clangs down on him and the Saracen falls head first from the ladder through the air.

There comes the bearded soldier who was beneath him. He carries not a lance but a mace on a chain; it is the head of it that dangles on the chain. He pants like the blacksmith's bellows.

Zoltay snatches his head away from the blow and strikes him so hard with his axe that the hand of the bearded Turk is broken and hangs to one side.

For a while the Turk hangs on with one hand, bellowing "Allah!", but a second blow silences him. And his great body rolls down the ladder, sweeping the living out of its way.

"My respects to your sultan!" Zoltay shouts after him. And he glances to his side through the smoke.

"Strike him, János lad!" he shouts to one of his men. "Strike him as if you were a fiery thunderbolt! Puff! He's not going to be Pasha of Eger either!"

"What are you waiting for?" he yells at another. "For him to give you a kiss? Puff! For heaven's sake!"

Then as a *gureba* wearing a shirt of mail and a turban rushes towards him, he calls to the men beside him, "This is the way to do it!"

He aims at his neck. The blood spurts out on to the wall, and the gureba turns on his side and drops below.

"Fall to the bottom of hell!" he laughs merrily.

But then he looks down in astonishment at his leg. There is a foot-long tear in his trousers, and his thigh shows red through it. But there is no time even to wonder why; another heathen is approaching...

"Come along, old chap!"

The sun has broken through now, as far as can be seen through the smoke of cannon and bombs. But from time to time

414

as the breeze blows away the smoke there is a glimpse of the enemy with their gold-tipped pennants and steel shields swarming below in a blinding dazzle of light. And there is no pause in the thundering, exploding rain of missiles, the shaking of the ground and shouts of "Jesus" and "Allah", mingling in a hellish din. Dobó gallops on horseback from one danger-spot to another. Here he directs a cannon, there he sees that the wounded are taken away. He speeds up the loading and firing. He has new supplies of pikes and lances delivered to places where weapons are scarce. He encourages, praises, reproves and curses; he keeps his two pages busy with orders to the reserves in the inner fortress under Mekcsey's command.

"A hundred men to the palaces! Fifty to the Bolyky Bastion! Fifty to the Old Gate!"

The troops are relieved after half an hour's fighting. Sweating, dirty and smelling of gunpowder, but with undiminished enthusiasm they retire to rest in front of the two inns inside the fortress, boasting of their heroic deeds to those who have not yet been in the battle.

These latter are burning impatiently with a desire to fight. Secretly Mekcsey too is furious that he is not allowed to fight, but only wait around in the square; he has to content himself with despatching troops on Dobó's orders and giving them a word or two of encouragement.

"Fight like heroes, lads! Every weapon defends Hungary too!"

And they hasten off to the raging battle with faces aflame.

The siege-ladders are now slippery with blood. And the wall round the tops of them is purple-coloured. Down below there are bloodstained, twitching heaps of dead and dying. But there too ever more regiments of fresh troops press on over the dead, leaping and yelling. Bugles sound, drums roll, military bands bray, and the unceasing shouts of "Allah!" mingle with the battle-cries from above, the shouted orders of the *yasavul*s on horse-back down below, the roar of cannon, the crack of rifles, exploding bombs, whinnying of horses, groans of the dying and the creaking and snapping of ladders.

"Come on pasha, come on! Puff!"

"Tell your sultan it was Zoltay who delivered this blow!"
comes a cry from the smoke enveloping the bastion.
The shouts of the captain are drowned by animal screams and
mortar fire. But the swift movements of the figures around him
and the rapid thrusts of the weapons there show that the men
are hard at work too. The sun is blotted out by smoke. The environs of the fortress
are enveloped in it too; now and then there is a momentary
glimpse of a Turkish corps in helmets or a line of powder-carry-
ing camels, all brown; and banners and horse-tail pennants
suddenly appear.
The bastion at the Old Gate requires the most relief troops.
Gáspár Pető is in command there. The Turks are pounding the
wall and palisade there with hundred-pound cannon-balls whenever the forest of ladders leaves a gap.
The Turks are destroying the barricaded gate with axes and
spades; they have already broken three shafts of the portcullis.
"Five hundred men!" Dobó shouts to Kristóf.
And Kristóf turns his horse and dashes off to fetch five
hundred soldiers. That is almost all the reserves.
Mekcsey straps on his helmet and runs with nine others to the
Old Gate. If they succeed in breaking through, he will have his
own work to do—defending the inner fortress.
And the Turks fall like flies under the gateway and on the
bastion above it. The Hungarian riflemen keep up a hail of shots
from the tower and fell them in droves. The thundering voice
of Gáspár Pető can be heard all the time:
"Follow me, lads! Don't retreat! Use both your hands, for
heaven's sake!"
And he himself, stained with blood to the waist, whirls now
his axe, now his pike, delivering huge blows.
"Jesus help us!"
"Allah! Allah!"
When there is a gap in the attackers on the ladders, the cry
of "Water! Water!" goes up on all sides.
The women carry the water beneath the bastion in jugs and
wooden cups.
Pető snatches up a wooden cup. He pushes up his visor. He
drinks so greedily that the water runs in two streams down his

416

armour, then continues towards his elbows, knees and heels as if from a fountain. But he has no time to worry about that in his rage and thirst.

As he puts down the cup, still panting, he sees a Turk leap up on the wall. In one hand he carries a horse-tail pennant. With the other he slashes like a madman. And after him there bobs up a second Turkish head, then a third.

"Hey there! Damn and blast you!"

And he grabs the ankle of the Turk with the horse-tail and drags him down. He rolls with him on the steps. When they stop he grasps his neck and smashes his gauntleted fist into his face.

"Take that, you dog!"

Then he leaps up again. Panting, he leaves the half-strangled Turk to the peasants down below. He himself hurries back to the bastion, striking and slashing with his hands in six directions at once.

"*Allah akbar!*"

There is a swarm of Turks on the wall. The Hungarians too are falling and dying, covered in blood. One *akindji* dashes up the tower like a cat. He gets to the top and plants the banner firmly there. Down below the Turkish troops greet this with a roar of victory.

"Jesus help us!"

The flag does not survive for two minutes. The Hungarian soldiers rush there and rain blows on the heads of the ascending Turks. One of the Hungarians in a rusty helmet climbs swiftly up the tower after the akindji. He wedges his heel in the stonework and aims a terrible blow at him. The Turk's arm, still gripping the banner, falls down from the heights.

"What's your name?" shouts Pető joyfully beneath the wall.

"Antal Komlósi."

The young page Balázs comes at a gallop from the palaces. One side of his head is hidden beneath a white bandage, but he dashes along as if nothing were the matter.

"The repairs by the palace!" he shouts. "They've been smashed!"

"A hundred men!" orders Dobó.

And while the lad gallops off to Mekcsey, he rides off even faster to the palace, crouched over the neck of his horse.

The Turks have broken the repairs apart. The beams stick out of the wall like the backbone of a fried fish. The Turks swarming up the wall are as densely-packed as an army of red ants. Dobó jumps up on to the top of the wall. He splits the head of a Turk in two, and pushes another down with his foot. And he shouts down, "Knock that beam down on the outside!"

Until now they have been pulling it in with grappling-irons. But at Dobó's command they suddenly push it out.

The beams themselves sweep the yelling heathens off the ladders and take the ladders with them too. And in the noise old Cecey can be heard yelling, "To hell with them!"

After the Turks have been swept down, a huge hole is left gaping in the wall. It makes no difference: the attackers still have to be fought off, whether from a few feet higher up or from lower down.

One shot strikes the Hungarian flag from the wall. It falls among the Turks. And now the large breach comes into its own: a Hungarian soldier jumps out on it, strikes an advancing Turk and seizes the flag before they can reach him.

"I saw that, László Török, my lad," calls Dobó with joy.

A cannon-ball hits the wall and fills the eyes of the soldiers with stone-dust. In front of Dobó a heavily-built elderly man collapses against the wall and falls along it. The helmet falls from his head and rolls to Dobó's feet.

Dobó wipes his eyes and looks at him. It is András who lies there, the Mayor of Eger, with his care-worn brow. He clutches his sword stubbornly in his hand. And from his neck the blood flows in a long stream as if it were an unwinding cravat.

But now both of his pages are running from the Old Gate. A single glance at its tower reveals the horse-tailed Turkish banner fluttering up there. One, two, five, ten—they keep increasing in number.

And through the loopholes in the tower rifles fire inwards at the defenders. The janissaries are scrambling up it on the outside. One carries a big fluttering red flag between his teeth to site it on the top of the tower.

Terror begins to spread inside the fortress. All round it the air is shattered by the shouts of victory from a hundred thousand Turks.

"Allah! Ya kerim!"

The faces of the Hungarians grow pale. Swords droop as if every arm has been paralysed.

Dobó jumps on horseback and dashes to the Church Bastion. He trains the guns on the middle of the tower. And while the janissaries, some three hundred of them, swarm all over the tower in their victory, he has three guns fired simultaneously.

The tower sways like some drunken giant. And it falls. With a great explosion it falls lengthwise along the ground. Clouds of lime-dust rise from the ruins, and Turkish blood trickles from the stones like wine from the wine-press during the grape-harvest.

The others who have crowded into the gateway and on to the walls turn their backs in terror at the earth-shattering explosion. Hardly have five minutes past when the siege-ladders there are empty. The Old Gate and its surroundings are covered with a bleeding mass of dead and dying men, inside and out.

Towards noon the battle slowly dies down in other places too. The smoke disperses. The sunshine breaks through. Beneath the walls lie thousands of dead and wounded Turks, blackened and bloodstained. The air is intoxicated with the cries of the wounded. They sound like bleating sheep.

The yasavuls have lost their authority; that day they cannot compel the men to continue the attack.

But the square inside the fortress is also full of standing, sitting and lying wounded men covered in blood. All the barbers and women are there, carrying bowls of water, linen, bandages, alum and arnica among the wounded. Some of them groan, others sway and grind their teeth.

And they are still bringing men out of the ruins of the tower, some in handcarts, others in blankets.

From time to time all faces turn to see who is coming. And the names are passed from mouth to mouth, "Péter Görgey... Jancsi Pozsgay... Jakab Zirka... Gyuri Urbán..."

"Is he still alive?"

"Yes. He was shot through the shoulder."

The barbers deal first with those whose arms and legs have been shot away. They bind them up as best they can. For the time being the rest have to content themselves with having their wounds cleaned by the women. Most of them bear their suffering in silence and wait their turn. But some moan pitifully at the pain of their wounds.

"Oh God! Oh God!" weeps one young soldier, a rifleman from Eger called Mihály Arany, "they've shot out one of my eyes." And he presses the singed sleeve of his shirt to his bloodstained face.

Pető sits there too among the rest on a wicker chair covered with a peasant frieze-coat. The wound on his ankle is so large that there is a puddle of blood under the chair. And it was caused not by a weapon, but by a falling stone.

"Stop moaning, Miska!" he says over his shoulder to the soldier. "Better be alive in the fortress of Eger with one eye than be hanged with two eyes by the Turks!"

And clenching his teeth he bears the pain of the barber washing his fearful wound with arnica.

Those with light wounds do not bother to go to the barbers. They clean them themselves. Many of them change their shirts there in the square, since the sweat-soaked shirts are more uncomfortable to them than their wounds.

"Well, I..."

"And as for me, I..."

The dead are laid out in lines by the church door. They are bloodstained, ragged, blackened, burned and motionless. One of them has lost his head. There is also an arm lying there still covered by the sleeve of a jacket; it has been torn off somehow at the shoulder.

A woman weeps and wails as she makes her way from the square to the church.

Dobó dismounts and takes off his helmet, making his way past the dead grimly and wearily.

The Mayor of Eger is lying there too. His white hair is reddened with blood. His dust-covered black boot also carries a bloodstain from a shot. His two sons kneel beside him.

Dobó turns to his page Balázs. "Bring the town flag here!"

And he pulls the blue and red flag of the town from the flagstaff and drapes it over the Mayor of Eger, as his shroud.

PART V

Eclipse of the Moon

1

The commander of Szarvaskő stood in the tower of his fortress till sunset listening to the thunder of the cannon from Eger. The autumn sun shone benignly on Szarvaskő. Only a day or two earlier the forest had begun to turn yellow and since up to then there was rain every day and the sky had been clear at night. There were new signs of green round the foot of the trees and along the bank of the stream. It was more like spring than autumn.

The distance from Szarvaskő to Eger is not much more than six miles, but it is surrounded by hills. From Felnémet northwards hills rise ever more frequently as if a great hand had pushed them all together; they are hills the size of the Gellért Hill in Buda. Only one narrow twisting road leads along the bottom of the valley to Szarvaskő.

Each morning as the guns roared the clouds piled up, the sky grew dark and within an hour it began to rain. Sometimes the rain carried dirt in it. The wind carried the mixture of smoke and cloud that far, and it was as if some heavenly sweeps were pouring away the water they had washed in, so filthy was the rain that sometimes fell on the walls, courtyard, rocks and the commander's asters in Szarvaskő.

The fortress there is a small one like that of Drégely. It was built on a high cliff of slate. At first sight it looked as if the towering cliffs had been carved at the top to create a fortress. So it was tiny. There was room for only three buildings there, and the courtyard was just big enough for a cart to turn in it. It was more of a hunting-lodge. It was useful as a refuge only before the invention of cannon. At the time of our story troops on the way to Eger might rest there, and it could also be used as a postal halt if Eger were occupied.

If Eger were to fall, Master Balázs Szalkay, the commander, could only leap on his horse and take his forty-nine men to his relatives in Upper Hungary, unless, of course, he wished to follow the example of the infuriated Szondy at Drégely or

Lőrinc Nyári, commander of Szolnok, who on the fourth of that month had stood alone in the gateway of the fortress, faced by a hundred thousand Turks.

"Come on then; at least I've not fled!"

So there stood good Master Szalkay in the tower. He was wearing an ankle-length, mushroom-coloured fur-lined coat and a cap of fox-fur. Filled with anxiety, he fixed his watery blue eyes on the high hill that blocked his view of Eger. He could not see the fortress there, so he gazed at the hill. If he had looked anywhere else, he would still have seen hills, because they are so close that a good rifle-shot would bring down a deer grazing on any hillside.

Below the fortress were a few small houses and the Eger Brook. And a stone cart-track alongside the brook.

Master Szalkay stood in the tower and gazed at nothing.

Silence enveloped him. It was no surprise, then, that he almost fell down when all of a sudden the sentry behind him blew his bugle.

"There's someone coming," the sentry excused himself, when he saw his master jump at the unexpected call and raise his hand to strike him.

"Idiot!" roared Master Balázs. "Why blow that thing in my ear when I'm here? You fool!"

He glanced down at the track winding among the crags and saw two riders beneath him. They looked like gentry. The smaller one might be a page. They must have come some distance, because their saddles were piled with baggage. They had short rifles slung over their shoulders. Both of them wore stirrup-length hazel-coloured fur-lined coats.

"They're not coming from Eger," mused Szalkay aloud.

"Maybe it's Miklós Vas," said the sentry.

He seized on his master's words to obliterate the memory of his previous stupidity. But it was not his day. Master Balázs flared up again.

"How on earth could it be Miklós Vas, you double-dyed clot, you stupid mutt! Do you think Vienna's only as far away as Apátfalva? You numbskull! You great ass!"

The good commander had been on edge ever since the Turks

had besieged Eger. And now, since he was ashamed of being scared by the bugle in front of his man, he almost devoured him. The sentry went bright red with embarrassment. He dare not open his mouth again. Master Szalkay grasped his sword in the middle and set off down the spiral staircase to see what the wind had blown in. For two days people had only gone from here. Nobody at all had come.

In the yard of the fortress stood a young man with bold eyes and a pale face. He had neither moustache nor beard. The two horses were held behind him by the boy who looked like a page. As soon as the young man caught sight of the commander, he went to meet him. He took off his cap with a flourish and bowed.

"I'm the younger brother of Captain Bornemissza of Eger. My name's János. And this boy here is a student, Miklós Réz. His elder brother's in the fortress too."

Szalkay offered his hand to János Bornemissza, but not to his companion. His practised eye told him he was not a gentleman.

"Welcome," he said without emotion. "I don't know your brother. But if I meet him, I'll embrace him. Be my guest."

Glancing at the visitor's hand, he was astonished to see that it was gloved. What an effeminate young man he was! And with a welcoming gesture he nodded towards the door.

"Thank you," said the youth with a bow. "I've not come to stay. I only want to ask a couple of questions. I'd like to know what news you have of Eger."

Szalkay shrugged and beckoned in the direction of Eger. "You can hear that."

"I can hear the guns."

"For nineteen days now."

"Is the fortress a strong one?"

Szalkay shrugged again. "The Turks are strong too."

"Are there enough defenders?"

"On the tenth there were 1935 of them. They've been firing at them continually since then."

"Hasn't the king sent any assistance?"

"Not so far."

"And the bishop?"

"Neither has he."

"But they're expecting aid?"

"Oh yes, they're expecting it, all right. But don't let's talk so much, my boy. Come in and rest your weary bones. I can tell from your horse that you started out early this morning."

Master Balázs made it plain that he did not like answering his visitor's numerous questions there in the courtyard. He himself had long wanted to sit down and eat, and only the distant rumble of the siege had kept him up there. The time was approaching noon and he had not yet even breakfasted.

"Sir," said the visitor pleadingly when they reached the doorway, "that boy who came with me is a theological student."

"A student? Oh well, in that case... Hi there, student!" he called over his shoulder.

He gave his guests a room and perfumed water to wash in. (Varsányi had brought him some rose-water from the Turkish camp, and he wanted to show off with it.)

By the time the guests arrived in the dining-room the table was laid and roast rabbit was steaming there.

"Rabbit again?" growled Master Balázs at his cook. And as the two youths entered, he excused himself.

"We're always having rabbit nowadays. All the rabbits from Eger have retreated up here from the noise."

Bornemissza had taken off his long coat and appeared in the dining-room in a close-fitting cherry-coloured damask jacket. The student wore only a suit made of flax. Both of them had similar belts with curved Hungarian swords.

The only eating implements on the table were spoons. In those days everyone used his own knife. And forks were known only out in the kitchen. The two guests reached for their knives. The older one produced a knife with a handle of mother-of-pearl and gilded. The student's was the sort of wooden-handled knife that came from Fehérvár.

"For myself, I like rabbit," smiled János Bornemissza. "And this is beautifully cooked. In our part of the world they cook it differently. I wonder if you know anything about my brother, commander?"

"Differently, you say?" asked Szalkay. "Differently?"

"Yes," replied János Bornemissza. "There they soak the rabbit in wine, then put it on the flame with a little water. They also put a slice of bread in it and cook it like that. But they watch to see that the juices don't boil away. When it comes to the boil they take it off the flame, remove the meat and strain the liquid. Then they put camomile, pepper, saffron and ginger into the strained liquid. But do you think we can get to know today what's been happening inside the fortress? Is my poor brother still alive, I wonder?"

And his eyes filled with tears.

"What, don't you put any vinegar into the liquid?" asked Szalkay, surprised. And he looked at the speaker's hands.

"Yes, of course," he replied eagerly, "but only at the end, when the rabbit is put for the second time into the juices. We've got to get to Eger this very day."

Szalkay sucked the thighbone of the rabbit clean, then clinked goblets with his guests. They did not drink wine.

"Hm," said Szalkay. He wiped his moustache on the tablecloth, looked at them again, and once again said, "Hm."

He was silent for a time. Then he leant on the table and broke the silence. "To the fortress of Eger?"

"Yes, yes," said János Bornemissza impatiently, his face drained of colour. "This very evening."

"Hm. I'd like to know how. Like a bird, perhaps? Or like a ghost, through the keyhole?"

"Like a mole, my dear fellow."

"A mole?"

"There are underground passages to the fortress too."

"Underground passages?"

He shook his head.

János Bornemissza reached inside his jacket and drew out a piece of parchment. He set it in front of Szalkay.

"Here we are: these red lines."

"I know," nodded Szalkay, glancing at the sketch. "These here did exist, but they don't now. They destroyed them with shot in Perényi's time."

"Destroyed them?"

"Oh yes. When Perényi demolished half of the church built by St. Stephen, they came across the underground passages and fired shot into all of them. They all fell in. It wasn't Hungarians who excavated them. Hungarians don't think about escaping when they build fortresses."

"Are you certain?"

"As certain as I'm sitting here with you."

"But is it absolutely certain? How do you know? What makes you so sure?"

Szalkay shrugged.

"Dobó's envoys come here. They come and go through the Turkish camp. Naturally, in Turkish dress. The other day they killed one of them. If even one of those underground passages existed, don't you think they'd use it?"

Young Bornemissza fell silent and pondered. In the end he raised his head.

"And when is an envoy coming or going?"

"Well, there are two of them outside at the moment. Miklós Vas is one, the other's Imre Szabó. Dobó sent them to Vienna to the king."

"And when are they coming back? When are they going to the fortress?"

"Miklós Vas may be here in a week's time, Szabó in two weeks, perhaps. An envoy leaves here each week."

The questioner's eyes were filled with tears. He stared ahead, pale and tearful.

Szalkay drained his goblet. He gave another "Hm!" Then he leaned back in his chair and watching out of the corner of his eye spoke quietly: "Listen to me, János Bornemissza! You're no more János than I'm Abraham. And you're no more Bornemisz-sza's younger brother than I'm the Bishop of Eger. You're a woman, my dear, whatever you're wearing. You can't deceive me!"

The visitor rose.

"Forgive me, Mr Szalkay. It wasn't my intention to mislead you, nor is it that I don't trust you as I would my own father, but I didn't want you to delay me on my journey. I'm Gergely Bornemissza's wife."

Szalkay got up and bowed.

"I'm at your service, dear lady."

"Thank you. Well, now I'll tell you why I've come. My dear husband has a Turkish talisman. The man it belonged to stole away our little son and brought him here to Eger. He thought my husband had the talisman with him. Look, here it is."

And the lady reached into her bosom and drew out the marvellous Turkish ring on a cord. Szalkay stared at the ring. The lady went on: "For a time I got the soldiers in Sopron to look for the Turk, but when they couldn't find him, I came after him myself. The Turk is superstitious. That talisman is everything to him. If he can, he'll kill my husband. If he can't he'll kill my son. For if my husband had this ring with him, they might be able to talk to each other. My husband would give him the ring, and the Turk would return the boy."

Szalkay shook his head.

"My dear lady, the defenders of Eger have sworn not to speak to the Turks and not to receive any messages from them. Anyone who speaks with a Turk or exchanges messages with them, whether he be officer or common soldier, is as good as dead."

Scratching his head, he went on, "If only you'd got here yesterday... but who knows whether they managed to get inside?" The commander was thinking of Lukács Nagy.

"Well, anyway," replied the lady, "I've got to get inside, and what's more, today! I've taken no oath not to speak to the Turks."

"But how do you think you'll do that? After all, you two can't fight your way through the camp."

"We'll go in disguise."

"If you go in disguise, they'll shoot you dead from the fortress."

"We'll call out to them."

"In that case you'll fall into Turkish hands outside the fortress. The gates are barricaded. Maybe by now they're blocked up with stone."

"Well, how is Dobó's envoy to get in in five days' time?"

"Only by risking his life. He must know which gate they're expecting him to arrive at. He's got a whistle and a password. He knows Turkish. You'll have to wait for him if you're absolutely determined to rush into peril at all costs."

"And suppose I go with a white kerchief? If I say that I'm looking for an officer called Yumurdjak?"

"You're good-looking and young. Even if you look like a boy, you are just as valuable to them as if you were recognized as a woman. The first soldier to arrest you will tie you up in his tent."

"But suppose I appeal to a distinguished officer?"

"There are a couple of hundred thousand troops out there. Not all of them know even the names of the officers. Nor do they all speak the same language. There are Persians, Arabs, Egyptians, Kurds, Tatars, Serbs, Albanians, Croats, Greeks, Armenians—a thousand nationalities. And the names of the officers are known only to their own battalions. And even those are not their real names; the men make them up. If, for example, there's an officer with a big nose, whether his real name is Ahmed or Hassan, the men will call him Bignose or Elephant. If he's got red hair, it'll be Squirrel or Copper. If he's thin and has long legs, he'll be known as Stork. And so on and so forth. There each one's name is something by which he can easily be recognized when they look at him. One of their officers is called Belcher, because he always belches when he talks."

The woman hung her head.

"Well then, give me some advice, Master Szalkay."

"My advice is to wait for someone going there. Whether it's Miklós Vas or someone else, you can give him the ring and he'll take it in. Then Master Bornemissza will work out how to talk with the Turk."

This was really sound advice. But alas! The heart of an anxious mother does not know the word "will". She sees only the sword hanging over her loved ones. She must raise a shield as soon as possible to protect them from it.

Eva spread out the sketch of the fortress and studied it long and intensely.

"If the fortress was built before the arrival of the Hungarians," she said at last, raising her head, "the present generation can't know what's underneath it. Look, here's the church with three underground passages branching out from it. They may well have wrecked those. But here's a fourth passage, a long way away from the others, and that goes underneath the present palace. They can't have discovered that when they were building the Sándor Bastion. Either they knew of it, or they did not. Where's the entrance to it, Miklós?"

She pushed the sketch over to the boy.

"By the brick-kilns," replied the boy after studying it for a minute.

"Are there any there?" the lady asked Szalkay.

"Yes," replied Szalkay. "They're to the north-east of the fortress."

The boy read out the tiny little words: *A brick-kiln to the north-east. Flat round stone, ten paces to the south of a walnut-tree. Entrance here.*

"Is there a walnut-tree there?" asked the lady.

"I'm sure I can't remember," replied Szalkay. "I've only been there once, in Perényi's time."

"And is the brick-kiln far from the fortress?"

"No, not far away. A quarter of an hour away, maybe, or even less."

"Then there are Turks there too."

"Yes, there must be. Camp-followers at the very least, shepherds and folk like that, if there aren't any troops there."

"Could you give me some Turkish clothes?"

"Yes."

"Have you a *deli*'s cloak too?"

"Yes, but I've only got one. And even that's torn right to the bottom."

"I'll sew it up," replied the lady. "I once travelled dressed as a *deli*. I never thought I'd ever profit by that experience."

She rested her forehead on her hand and went on thinking.

"You're not certain that the spy you mentioned will be here in five days' time. Suppose he's late? Suppose they kill him?"

"It's true that spies and the like always walk in the shadow of death."

The lady jumped up. "No, I shan't stay even as long as it takes for me to sew up the cloak. It'll be better like this anyway. Thank you for your hospitality." And she offered her hand to the commander.

"But surely you're not..."

"We're going this very moment."

The commander rose and blocked the doorway.

"I can't allow that! Only flies walk so blindly into danger... I'd never forgive myself for that."

Eva collapsed into the chair again.

431

"You're right," she sighed. "We've got to try some other way. We've got to devise something to avoid being captured."

"That's just it," replied Master Balázs, and also sat down. "If there's even the least possibility, I'll let you go."

2

To the north-east of the fortress of Eger there stands a high hill called Eged. Its real name is St. Egid or St. Egyed (Giles), but since the name *Egyed* never appealed to Hungarians, it is still called *Eged*. It is only a mile or two from Eger, but quite high and massive.

If a well-trained archer were to discharge a goose-quilled arrow in the direction of that hill from the fortress at Eger, it would sail over that hill where one group of Turkish cannon thunders out and fall into the valley where the riff-raff of the camp-followers are quartered. The traders, horse-dealers, dervishes, quacks, knife-grinders, sellers of sherbet and *halva,* rope-dancers, slave-merchants, sellers of bric-a-brac, gypsies and the like have taken over the valley. From there they go each day to the army camp to trade, barter, collect waste, entertain the troops, tell fortunes, steal and cheat—in other words *live* among the soldiers.

On the second day of October, three days after the Michaelmas attack, a young *deli* arrived there from the direction of the Tárkány Forest. He was riding a horse. He was wearing a braided tunic, close-fitting trousers, yellow boots and a camelhair cloak. Instead of a turban, the hood of his cloak covered his head, as was the custom among delis. There were daggers in his belt, and over his shoulder a bow and quiver. He was driving a Hungarian boy with chains on his legs in front of him. And the boy was driving an ox. It was obvious that the *deli* had captured boy and ox as his plunder.

There are vineyards in that area. That autumn the Hungarians had not harvested the grapes. And the vineyards were full of Turks anyway. Wherever one looked there were Turks in turbans or fur caps moving up and down among the vines.

432

Some of them called out to the young *deli,* "Wherever did you pick up that marvellous prize?"

But that was when they happened to be driving the ox most furiously. They made no reply.

The *deli* was Eva, the prisoner Miklós.

There were no sentries in those parts. Or if there were, they too were looking for grapes in the vineyard. Why post sentries if there's no enemy? Mrs. Bornemissza reached the brick-kilns in the valley without being stopped. There they were swallowed up in the confusion of squalid and magnificent tents and the din of dogs and gypsy children thronging around. Then the merchants broke through the crowd.

"How much do you want for the boy?"

"I'll give you fifty piastres for him."

"I'll give you sixty kurush for him."

"I'll give you seventy."

"That ox—I'll give twenty piastres for it."

"I'll give you thirty."

"Forty."

The *deli* did not exchange words with them. He guarded now the ox, now his captive with his spear. And a whip cracked in the captive's hand.

They wound their way down from the vine-clad hill to the brick-kiln. There the scene was even more colourful. The gypsies had improvised houses out of the bricks. They were covered with boughs or canvas instead of roofs. Some gypsy families had even camped inside the brick-kilns. They baked, cooked or lay around in the autumn sunshine.

The ancient walnut-tree still stood there, and was living. A horse-trader had settled down under it. Eva had eyes only for a spot ten paces to the south of it. That was where the horses were corralled. Beside it was the trader's tent with its four tent-poles, and a quotation hung on it in Turkish script from the Koran: *Fakri, fahri* (My poverty, my pride). For Turkish traders never put their own names on their shops, but only a few words from the Koran.

Eva caught sight of the stone. At some time it had been a millstone. It must have been lying there for a long time. It was so deeply sunk into the earth that only half of it was above ground. Grass grew tall out of the middle of it and moss and stonecrop had taken root on it.

Eva drove the ox and the captive in between the horses. She thrust her spear into the middle of the millstone.

The trader came out with deep bows.

"How much for the prisoner?" he asked, stroking his beard.

Eva pretended to be dumb. She pointed to her lips and nodded "no".

Dumb soldiers were by no means rare. If a man is dumb and has neither beard nor moustache, the Turk immediately realizes that he is in the presence of a creature who, if not a *deli*, makes his living out of what he does not possess.

So the Greek spoke. "Thirty piastres."

Eva indicated that only the ox was for sale.

The Greek examined the ox in front and behind. He gauged the size of its breast with a lifting motion and offered a new price, "Twenty piastres."

Eva shook her head.

The trader offered thirty, then thirty-five piastres.

Meanwhile Eva sat down on the stone and felt her ankle painfully. Raw meat was tied to it, and its juice showed through the blue cloth.

When the Greek promised her thirty-five piastres, Eva indicated with signs and the tip of her spear that she wanted a tent, and it was to be erected on that spot.

The Greek saw that the *deli* was wounded, pale and tired to death. He understood that the *deli* wanted to rest until his wound was healed. That was obviously why he needed a tent too. He sent his servant to bring out three or four disgracefully tattered tents.

"Here you are. Make your choice."

Eva chose the largest of them, which was also the most patched, and indicated that the ox could be led away. The trader thought the price too small, so Eva added the horse too, provided that the tent was also erected above the stone.

The trader agreed. With his two Saracen servants he put the tent up over Eva.

Well, all that went smoothly enough.

434

"God help us!" whispered Eva when she remained alone with Miklós inside the tent.

Now the only problem was how and when to raise the stone. Somehow they had to get hold of a pole. They would fix it into the hole in the millstone and tip it over. It would not be too difficult to get a pole either. They simply had to remove one from the barrier-rail where the horses were. They would do that by night.

Over the hill the guns thundered unceasingly, and the slender falconets in the fortress kept up a constant reply. The stench of the smoke reached them from time to time. They could also see one of the towers of the fortress through the foliage. It was wrecked, and looked like a mouse-eaten candle. All the same, they were glad to see it. The tower showed where they were to go that very night.

People of all kinds thronged around them. Sometimes soldiers also appeared among them, mostly leading horses or looking for fortune-tellers. There was a good trade in gypsy talismans. They did not really trust in them, but bought them all the same. A line of tiny talismans hung like a garland round the hairy chest of one asab.

Eva lay down on her cloak.

"What do you think, Miklós? Wouldn't it be possible for me to go and look for my boy? Having got as far as this, I can get further inside too."

"Are you still worrying your head about that plan?"

"In this disguise, nobody's going to stop me. I can go and look for him in the army camp and find him too. I'll face Yumurdjak and say to him, 'Look, here's the ring. Give me my son'!"

"Then he'll take the ring and not give you your son."

"Oh, the heathen beast!"

"If only he weren't... But even if he were an honest man, what would happen if some officer in the camp were to give you an order? There may be some troops with whom delis are not allowed to mingle. The gun sites too are bound to be forbidden areas. They'd know immediately that you were a stranger in the camp."

"They'd arrest me..."

435

"And even if they don't do that, Yumurdjak would never let you out of his clutches."

Eva sighed. She opened her knapsack. She took out bread and cold chicken, and set them out on the millstone.

"Let's have something to eat, Miklós."

At last darkness fell. The noise of the guns subsided. In the dark everyone soon went to bed.

Eva produced a taper from the knapsack. They lit it with flint. Round about midnight Miklós crept out of the tent and returned a few minutes later with a pole as thick as an arm.

They stuck it through the hole in the millstone.

"Now heaven help us!"

The stone moved. Under it there was nothing but damp black clay soil and a few black beetles.

Eva tapped with her foot where the stone had been. This was a query to the earth: "Are you hollow?"

The earth gave a dull thud. "Yes, I'm hollow."

Eva took a spade from the knapsack. She fixed it to the shaft of her spear and dug. Miklós scratched the earth away with his hands. About eighteen inches down the spade hit wood. It was a nine-inch thick oak beam, but had rotted away. They dug it out and pulled it up. Below it yawned a dark stone-lined hole big enough to take a man.

There were about ten small steps to go down. There the hole grew wider. It was lined like a cellar, and they could walk upright in it.

The air was rank and the tunnel dark. In places the walls glimmered white with saltpetre. The stones exuded damp and cold.

Miklós went first, carrying the taper. In some places they walked through ankle-deep water, and sometimes they stumbled into stones that had dropped out of the vaulting.

Sometimes Miklós said over his shoulder, "Look out! There's a stone in the way."

Sometimes the earth echoed under their footsteps. Presumably there were other tunnels there. What people could have built them? When the fortress was first constructed, there were no historical records. Who knows what sort of folk lived in that part of the world before the Hungarians?

Miklós turned again and said, "Be careful! We've got to bend down."

The passage sloped downwards for some distance and the vaulting grew lower and lower; then the passage went upwards again but the vaulting did not.

Now Miklós was on all fours. Eva stopped.

"Just go on ahead, Miklós," she said. "If the tunnel is blocked, we'll have to go back for the spade."

Miklós crawled on. The light of the taper grew smaller and finally disappeared. Eva remained alone in the darkness.

She knelt down and prayed.

"Oh God! Father of my poor wandering soul! Can You see me here even in these blind depths? Only a couple of steps separate me from my own Gergely... Did You bring us together only for us to be torn apart so miserably?... I turn my face and trembling heart to You... Oh God, here beneath the feet of the enemy, in the black depths of the earth I implore You: let me get to him!"

The light showed red once again. Miklós too soon made an appearance. He was crawling on his stomach, and then he emerged from the darkness still bent over.

"The passage gets narrow for twenty paces, then it's wide again for ten more. There the way divides into two. But both of them have caved in."

"Go back for the spade, Miklós. We'll have to dig till morning. But every hour, Miklós, you'll have to appear in front of the tent so as not to arouse suspicion."

The boy obeyed in silence.

"If I get to my husband, Miklós," said Eva, "we'll reward you for your kindness. My husband's like a younger brother to Dobó. He'll get you a job as secretary to Dobó."

"I can't take it," replied Miklós. "It was my fault that the boy was lost, and I must help to find him again. As soon as he's found, I'll take up the pilgrim's staff and go off to school."

Poor good Miklós! You'll never get to school again!

3

The Michaelmas attack went raging on till noon. In the after-noon the cannon on both sides cooled down. In the fortress the funeral chant *Circumdederunt* rose in mournful strains. Below the fortress the camp dervishes and priests collected the dead in carts together with the wounded who had not sufficient strength to walk.

The fortress was black with blood, both outside and inside. On the bastions and in the four areas that had been attacked the women sprinkled ashes and stone-dust on the pools of blood. The executioner in the fortress threw down the janissaries who had fallen when the corner tower collapsed. Their banners were brought into the hall of the knights and their weapons scattered around for the soldiers to choose any they wanted for nothing. And they did seize them eagerly, but the weapon most in demand was the axe.

Hundreds of them assembled outside the blacksmith's.

"An axe for me too! I want an axe!"

Mekcsey immediately gave orders for the smiths to make axes. So they chopped nine-inch pieces from iron bars and threw them into the fire. They beat one side to a point and the other flat, and bored a hole through the middle. For any soldier who offered a dinar or two to promote his chances, they would file his axe too and on the pointed side gouge out so called "blood-channels". The handles were fashioned by the soldiers them-selves.

"Now let's see you, you with the pigtails!"

On Dobó's orders, the soldiers who had been least in battle went to repair the walls immediately after lunch. First of all they carried stones from the collapsed tower to the breaches. Till nightfall they kept pulling crushed Turkish bodies from among the stones, and doubtless there were Hungarians there too.

So there was work for everyone. Even the children were given a task to do.

"Collect together the cannon-balls lying all over the place. Carry the big ones to the big guns and the little ones to the smaller guns below the bastions."

That night Lieutenant Hegedűs was sleeping outside on the Sándor Bastion with Gergely. The night was chilly. The white sickle of the moon shone white among the stars. The weary defenders lay all over the square and around it. The sentries too paced sleepily along. If they stopped, they fell asleep as they stood there.

Gergely had palliasses put under an arch for himself and his two companions, both lieutenants. A fire was burning under the arch. And as they lay there in the gentle warmth of the fire, Hegedűs spoke:

"Gergely, you're a scholar. I too trained for the priesthood, but they threw me out. Today I've brought down forty Turks single-handed. So you can't say that I'm lacking in courage."

Gergely was weary and sleepy. But Hegedűs's voice had a strange resonance in it. He looked at him. The lieutenant was sitting on his palliasse. The light from the fire illuminated his face and the blue cloak that reached his ankles.

He went on: "All the same, I often find myself thinking that a man's only a man, after all, whether his head's shaven or not. And what we're doing is... murder."

"Yes, that's so..." murmured Gergely sleepily.

"And they're killing us too."

"Of course they are. If instead of weapons they climbed the walls with bottles of wine, we'd also meet them with bottles of wine. Wine would flow instead of blood. But now let's get some sleep."

Hegedűs glanced sideways at the fire, as if undecided whether to say anything or not. In the end he said, "What is courage?"

"You said just now that you brought down forty Turks single-handed, and you want to know what courage is? Lie down and go to sleep! You're tired too."

Hegedűs shrugged his shoulders.

"If there were one clever man among us who had as much intelligence as all of us put together, or let's say, as much intelligence as all the people in the world, my view is that he wouldn't be a courageous man."

He looked at Gergely. The firelight was shining in Gergely's face, but only the outlines of the bones in Hegedűs's face were visible.

Gergely shut his eyes and replied sleepily. "On the contrary, he's the one who'd be most full of courage."

"But look, Gergely, he'd be better able to put a value on human life. For one thing's certain—we're here on this earth; but if the Turks chop off our heads it's not certain that we shall live on. A man of such intelligence won't easily throw away what exists simply in order to be called a brave man."

Gergely yawned. He answered, "Do you want to philosophize? A man of weak intellect is brave because he doesn't understand death. And a man of strong intellect is brave because he does."

"Death?"

Gergely turned over on his side. He had already shut his eyes to go to sleep. He mumbled in reply, "Yes. The man of weak intellect lives the life of an animal. Animals don't know death. Look at the hen and see how she protects her chickens. But as soon as one of them dies, she abandons it without regret. If she understood death like a fairly well educated man, she'd weep and cry over it, wouldn't she? She'd know that her child had lost its life. But those who have no idea of death haven't any idea of life either. Then look at a man with a clear mind. He's brave precisely because he knows that the body isn't all he's got. He senses that he is soul and not body. The more spiritual a man is, the less his body means to him. The heroes, the great heroes of history, were all spiritual men. Every single one of them. And now do let's go to sleep."

But to put Hegedűs's mind at rest he went on thoughtfully, "Where we were before we were alive, and where we shall be when our lives end, we don't know in this earthly body. And what would become of us if we did know? For in that case we shouldn't be concerned about what we're doing now, but about what this acquaintance of ours or that is doing in the next world, and about how the affairs from which we've been cut off are continuing there."

"All right, all right!" Hegedűs answered. "I've often heard priests say things like that. But this life here on earth must surely have some value; it isn't just meant for any old heathen to have someone to kill."

The fire crackled as it burned, transforming the armour and

swords lying by the palliasse to gold. Gergely had a leather shield as his pillow. He straightened it under his head and replied dreamily, "You're talking nonsense, my dear Hegedűs. The subhuman man sometimes does good unconsciously, the man of intellect always does it knowingly. You know very well what a great and sacred thing it is to defend one's homeland; it's just like children protecting their mother."

And he pulled his cloak up to his ears. "Where is it written, which law decrees, that anyone should defend his mother? Defend her, if necessary, even at the cost of his own life? Animals certainly don't do that. But man, from the most stupid to the most intelligent, pitches into anyone who attacks his mother, and even if he dies he feels he could not have done anything else."

And he continued drowsily, "Sometimes divine laws stir the will. Love is a divine law. Love for one's mother and love for the homeland are the same. The Turks can't destroy the soul. Now for heaven's sake let me go to sleep! Philosophy at this time of night? I've a good mind to hurl this rotten shield at you!"

Hegedűs said no more. He too lay down on his bed.

The fortress was silent except for the measured tread of the sentries and a distant clanging—someone was beating iron with iron; there was also a gentle rumble from one of the mills and the clip-clop of the horse's feet in front of it.

*

Next morning the guns were silent. But behind the Turkish earth-ramparts the camp was alive with sound.

"The Turks are writing another letter," said Dobó.

He held a sheet of paper in his hand. He had the buglers summon the troops on parade. In two minutes the off-duty soldiers were on parade in battle-order. There were many bandaged heads, eyes and hands. All the same they were in good spirits.

Dobó spoke: "Men! I have summoned you here to express my praise for you. You repelled the first attack on the fortress as firmly as Hungarian soldiers should. I saw not a single coward among you. You well deserve the name of heroes. After the Turks have retreated I shall go in person to His Majesty the

King and myself ask him to reward you. But until I can do that, let us give particular honour to those great heroes who without regard for their own lives have excelled themselves in repelling the attack. Stand forward István Bakocsai, László Török, Antal Komlósi and Szaniszló Soncy."

The four men stepped out of the ranks and stood in front of Dobó. All of them had bandaged heads.

Dobó went on: "The enemy succeeded in climbing the wall of the outer fortress and hoisted the first flag. Private István Bakocsai dashed alone into the janissaries' battalion, seized the flag from the hands of the Turks and flung it back. So even before I can put his name before the king, I promote him to corporal and award him fifty silver dinars and a new suit of clothes."

In the midst of the cheers of the defenders, Sukán the steward counted out the fifty silver pieces into the soldier's hand.

Dobó continued: "A cannon-ball brought down the flag of the fortress together with the wall. It fell among the Turks. László Török jumped alone into the breach and brought it back at the risk of a thousand deaths. While he waits for his reward from the king, he is to receive one forint from the funds of the fortress and a suit of broadcloth."

The soldier looked triumphantly round at the applauding defenders, and Sukán put the money in his hand.

Dobó went on: "They also hoisted a flag at the Old Gate. Antal Komlósi rushed up the wall and cut it down, together with the Turk's right hand. While I am waiting to recommend him for an award to the king, he is to receive two forints and a suit of clothes."

Only the fourth soldier was left.

"Szaniszló Soncy," said Dobó, "when the repairs to the breach were smashed and hundreds of Turks might have poured through, you jumped down there alone and taking no account of their numbers struck the invaders right and left until help arrived. Apart from the king's reward, you are to have two yards of fine cloth and one forint."

Dobó also had this to say: "I fixed these amounts not as a measure of your bravery, but in line with the funds of the fortress. There are many in the army apart from you whose merits are almost as great as yours. I myself have seen how some of you have slain as many as fifty Turks. To mention only one example, here are Lukács Nagy and his troop. You know what he has done! So please understand that it was only the most outstanding men that I wanted to praise, those who risked their lives for their country in the midst of the peril of certain death."

A bugle sounded from the gate, and immediately afterwards an unknown peasant ambled across the square towards Dobó. He held a letter in his hand. He took off his cap as he approached.

"Back to your duties!" said Dobó to his men.

He exchanged a word with Mekcsey, and when the peasant reached him looked him up and down with disgust. He mounted his horse and rode away.

The officers received the peasant. And that was just his bad luck. They did not even open the letter, but tore it in half. One half they threw into the fire and the other they stuffed in his mouth.

"Eat up what you've brought, you cur!"

Then he too was thrown into prison, where he had time to think that no good whatever came out of serving the Turks. The name of the man was András Sári, and the Turks had brought him with them from Fehérvár.

The pagan host waited a whole hour to see whether he emerged again from the gateway or not. When they saw that the defenders of Eger were not replying, the guns all thundered out once more around the walls. And the trenches dug below the fortress filled up with Turkish warriors.

Until now only cries of "Allah!" and mocking comments had been heard from the Turkish camp, but this time there were shouts on all sides in Hungarian: "Give yourselves up! If you don't, you'll come to a horrible end!"

Another voice: "Do you think you can go on beating off attacks for ever? This was only a trial run! We'll have no mercy, even for babies!"

And another: "Abandon Dobó! Dobó's mad! If he wants to die, then let him die alone! Anyone who comes out of the gateway will suffer no harm! He can take his money and arms with him!"

"Anyone who wants to come out has only to put a white handkerchief on his spear!" roared a *spahi* in a pointed helmet from the trench.

"A thousand gold pieces to anyone who lets us in!" thundered a janissary aga sporting an ostrich feather.

At that three defenders fired at him, but he ducked in time.

"Dobó's gone mad!" came another cry from the other side.

"Don't you follow his example! The first man to come out of the fortress will get a reward of a hundred gold pieces, and the next twenty to follow him will get ten each, and they can go unmolested."

"The others will be impaled!" added another voice.

It was the Turkish troops who knew Hungarian shouting from the enemy camp. But they also shouted in Slovak, German, Spanish and Italian.

The defenders, however, made no reply in either Hungarian, Slovak, German, Spanish or Italian.

The shouting grew more intense. Promises grew more alluring and threats more appalling. In the end Gergely placed his drummers, trumpeters and buglers on his section of the wall and every time a Turk down below began shouting, drums rolled, bugles brayed mockingly and trumpets drowned the noise.

The defenders were amused by this. Drummers and buglers were positioned on the other sides too, and even the three pipers in the fortress found work to do. And those soldiers who had iron shields rattled them. All further shouts were drowned in the hellish din.

Jób Paksy the cavalry lieutenant asked Dobó for permission to lead a raid on those who kept shouting.

He was the officer with the good singing voice, the younger brother of the commander of Komárom, a fine figure of a young man with the strength of Hercules. When he pulled his moustache full out in the mornings it reached his ears. During the attack he used a broadsword. With a single stroke he struck a helmeted Turkish head so hard that the helmet itself fell in two pieces.

He asked for only a hundred men.

"Don't argue, Jób, my boy," said Dobó with a shake of his head. "Suppose you run into trouble?"

444

But Jób Paksy could not keep still: it was as if he had eaten a plate of hot ashes for breakfast. He kept reducing his demands, like Abraham on the road to Sodom.

"Only fifty! Only twenty!"

In the end he asked for only ten men to make a sally.

Perhaps Dobó would not have permitted even that number, but by then there was a crowd of soldiers crowding round Paksy, all itching to go. With eager faces they called, "Commander, sir!"

Dobó was afraid that if he continued to resist they would put it down not to his well-advised caution but to the fact that he considered the defenders to be too few in number now. So he simply said, "All right, if you really want to kill yourselves, carry on."

"How many of us?" shouted Paksy gleefully.

"Two hundred," replied Dobó.

The gateway leading to the brook was still intact. Paksy chose his two hundred men and charged out.

This occurred around noon.

All the way along the brook there were crowds of Turks watering horses and camels. To the right of the gate these were mainly *akindji*s.

The two hundred soldiers swept down on them like a whirlwind. The akindjis fell in droves. As Paksy led the way, he chopped a path through them, and his armour and horse were red with blood on the right side. The rest followed his example, and the host of *akindji*s, screaming with terror, scrambled over each other as they turned their backs. Then from two sides janissaries in their thousands rushed to attack them.

Dobó had the retreat sounded. But down below they could not hear it. Roused to fury in the struggle, they slew and cut down the janissaries.

Suddenly Paksy's horse was startled by a camel and jumped to one side. At that very moment Paksy was delivering a huge blow on a *spahi* in a shirt of mail. He fell from the horse as it veered. The horse was stabbed in the chest, and fell. Paksy too was left there.

Seeing this the other soldiers formed a group round him and brandished their swords to give him time to get up again. But

Paksy did not get up. His leg was either sprained or broken. Even as he sat there he whirled his sword angrily, slashing and striking around him. The helmet fell from his head. A janissary struck him there.

The bugles on the fortress walls loudly sounded the retreat. The soldiers wheeled and broke through the mob of Turks. Only ten men remained there round Paksy. They were suddenly surrounded by a forest of spears.

"Surrender yourselves!" cried the Turks.

One after another the ten soldiers dropped their swords.

"Cowards!" came angry shouts from the fortress.

Mekcsey could hardly be restrained from charging out.

*

An hour later a high circular platform was constructed by carpenters on the King's Seat.

There on the hill, in full view of the defenders, the wounded soldiers from the fortress were broken on the wheel. All of them, except Paksy.

4

Until then the defenders had merely hated the Turks; but after that they abominated them. The women wept. The soldiers were all ready to charge down on them without waiting for permission. But Dobó had the gate locked.

After this shameful act of cruelty Ali Pasha shouted into the fortress, "Know that we have scattered the royal army that was sent to your aid! From now on there's no mercy! If you don't surrender, you'll all share the fate of these men here."

The defenders turned pale when they heard this. Even the drummers had been so stunned by the perfidy of the Turks that they forgot to interrupt the shouting.

"They're lying, the rogues!" said Gergely contemptuously to the men standing around him. "They're lying in the same way that they keep shouting every night that our wives, fiancées and children are in captivity. The royal army is on its way. We can expect it at any minute."

"But suppose they're not lying?" said a harsh voice behind him.

Gergely's face was already drained of colour. But at this remark he went so white that every single hair in his beard and moustache seemed to stand out separately.

Lieutenant Hegedűs was the speaker. Gergely looked at him with a glance that seemed to pierce right through him. Gripping the hilt of his sword, he answered, "Oh come, lieutenant! You ought to know enough of military customs to realize that the enemy normally captures the banners of a defeated army. If they really had done that, wouldn't they have displayed their banners?"

And he looked him up and down.

This occurred on the Church Bastion. Dobó was standing there too, a little way off, with Cecey beside him, leaning on his stick. Zoltay stood there too, with Fügedy and Father Márton, the latter in a white cassock and surplice. (He had just taken the funeral of a soldier who had died of his wounds.)

Gergely's words made Dobó take notice of them. He looked at Hegedűs in amazement. Cecey also turned round.

"Stupid talk!" he croaked at Hegedűs. "Do you want to scare our folk?"

Hegedűs looked back at Gergely in a fury.

"I've been longer in the army than you have, you puppy! How dare you try to teach me? How dare you look at me like that?" And all of a sudden his sword slipped out of its scabbard.

Gergely also drew his sword.

Dobó stepped between them.

"You can finish your business after the siege. So long as the fortress is surrounded, don't dare to draw swords on each other!"

The two furious officers replaced their swords. In a cold voice Dobó gave out his orders: Hegedűs was to go on duty with Mekcsey's troops at the Old Gate, while Gergely was forbidden to leave the outer fortress without urgent cause.

"After the siege!..." repeated Hegedűs with a threatening glance.

"I shan't shrink from it," replied Gergely contemptuously.

*

Dobó was upset by this altercation. As the two officers went away in different directions he turned to Cecey.

"What will happen to us," he said, "if officers are at each others' throats too? How can they fight together? We ought to make peace between them."

"Devil take those men from Kassa!" said Cecey wrathfully. "My boy spoke well."

He accompanied Dobó on foot to the square. The sound of singing came from the inn, and three soldiers lurched out of the door just as they arrived there. They clung to each others' necks. They snaked their way unsteadily towards the barracks, still singing. The middle one was Bakocsai. At the end of the song he gave a great yell, "We'll never die!"

When the revellers saw Dobó they let go of each other and stood like towers of Pisa. They fell silent, blinking. Dobó walked past them without saying a word and stopped in front of the door of the inn.

There was singing inside too. László Török was waving the bandage for his wound. Komlósi was banging the table with his tin cup. Szaniszló Soncy was shouting merrily for the pipers. Beside them another three privates were helping them to drink away their reward for bravery.

Dobó turned to his page: "Call the two innkeepers out here."

A minute later the two men were standing there, György Debrőy with his shirt sleeves rolled up, László Nagy in a blue apron. Both of them stood ill at ease before the angry gaze of the commander.

"Innkeepers!" Dobó thundered at them. "If ever I see another drunken soldier in the fortress, I'll have the keeper of the inn where he got drunk hanged!"

And he turned round and went on his way.

*

That night once again they repaired and filled in the walls that had been bombarded by day. Dobó slept only an hour or two. Night and day he was to be seen now here, now there, and the calm determined sound of his voice was heard giving orders.

On the third night after the attack a loud voice was heard once again calling from the hill to the east: "Listen, István Dobó!

Arslan Bey, your old enemy greets you! My honour is as undefiled as my sword. You can never have heard any evil of my name."

After a minute's pause: "Don't take the death of good István Losonczy to be an example to follow. He himself brought it about. But if you happen not to trust us, I'll offer myself as a hostage. I'm not afraid to enter the fortress alone if you put out the white flag. Keep me under arrest while you retreat from the fortress, and kill me instantly if so much as a hair of the head of one of your men is touched as he goes. It is I, Arslan Bey, who speak, the son of the famous Mohammed Yahya Pasha Oglu."

There followed a silence, as if the speaker were waiting for an answer. But at the very first words Dobó had mounted his horse and ridden to the next bastion. That was how he showed how deaf he was whenever the Turks talked.

Only the soldiers heard the continuation of the message:

"I know that my person is sufficient safeguard for you. But if that is not enough for your people, we shall also arrange for our army to withdraw totally a distance of three miles away. Not a single Turk shall appear until you too have gone three miles in the opposite direction. Answer me, brave István Dobó!"

The fortress was silent.

5

At midnight Dobó observed a soldier in front of the door of the gunpowder-store; he was carrying a pile of large dishes on his head—ten or so peasant dishes.

"What's that?"

"Captain Gergely ordered me to bring dishes from the kitchen."

"Where is the captain?"

"On the Bolyky Bastion."

Dobó rode there. He dismounted and hurried along in the pale light of the lamps. He found Gergely under the wall, with a lamp. He was on his knees, bending over a large bowl of water, motionless, pale and grim.

"Gergely!"

Gergely got up.

"I didn't know you were still up, commander. In any case, I've reported to Mekcsey that I was having bowls watched."

"Are they mining?"

"It's only a thought. Since we repelled the attack, it's certain that they'll start mining."

"Good," replied Dobó. "Get the drummers to put their drums on the ground too and spread peas on them."

"And small shot."

Dobó called down from the bastion to the page Kristóf.

"Go round all the sentries and tell them to examine the drums and dishes each time they pass them. As soon as there's any movement of water in the dishes or peas and shot on the drums, they're to report it immediately."

And taking Gergely by the arm, he drew him inside the fortress. "My dear boy Gergely," he said in the paternal tone he normally used only to his pages, "I've been watching you for a week now. What's the matter? You're not usually like this."

"Sir," replied Gergely, and his voice quivered, "I didn't want to bother you with it. But since you've asked me, I'll tell you. Ever since they've surrounded the fortress, they've been shouting every night that my little boy's in their hands."

"They're lying!"

"That's what I thought too. At first I didn't take any notice. But a week ago today they tossed a little sword into the fortress. It belongs to my little boy."

So saying, he took a little sword in a velvet scabbard out of his jacket.

"Here it is, sir. I know you won't remember it, but in fact it was you who gave it to me when we first met. Then I gave it to my boy when I left him to come here. How did it get into the hands of the Turks?"

Dobó stared at the sword. Gergely went on: "I left my wife and boy in Sopron. No Turks ever go there. If they did, they'd be beaten to death. And my wife won't stir from there, because there's nobody for her to go to."

Dobó shook his head. "I don't understand it. Maybe they stole the sword? Did it get into the hands of dealers or soldiers?"

"In that case, how did they know that it belonged to my boy?
And there is a possible link in the affair that keeps gnawing at
my heart like a serpent. This Yumurdjak, alias Dervish Bey, had
a talisman. Father Gábor, my dear tutor, God rest his soul!,
took it from him. And he left it to me. Since then that mad Turk
hasn't stopped searching for it. How did he know that it had
come to me? That I can't understand. But he did get to know,
that's certain, because he wants it from me."

"And do you think he's really got your son? If so, devil take
the ring! Throw it to him!"

"But that's what's so odd," replied Gergely, removing his helmet. "I haven't got the ring with me. I left it at home."

Dobó said, "Hm. I'm at a loss. Even if one supposes that a
few Turks may possibly have ventured as far as Sopron... hm...
The bey would have stolen the ring and not the boy."

"That's what's driving me mad too," replied Gergely.

"And do you think that your boy really is here?"

"Since the little sword got here from Sopron, I'm bound now
to think that my little son may have got here too."

They had reached the palace. Dobó sat down on the marble
bench outside it, beneath the palace lamp. "You sit down too,"
he said.

He rested his elbows on his knees and stared ahead. They did
not speak.

At last Dobó slapped his knee and broke the silence.

"Well then, we'll find out this very night whether the Turks
are telling the truth or not."

He called to the sentry on his rounds in front of the palace:
"Miska, go to the prison. Bring back that Kurd who was captured in the brook."

Mrs. Balogh called through the window, "Commander, your
long cloak..." For Dobó was wearing only a short jacket of grey
deerskin, and the night air was more than chilly.

"Thank you," replied Dobó. "I'm going to bed soon. How's
Pető?"

"Raving and groaning."

"Who's staying up with him?"

"I got Gáspár Kocsis's wife to come in. But I'm watching him
until he settles down."

451

"There's no need for that," replied Dobó. "I've seen his wound. It'll heal. You get some rest!"

The sentry clattered up with the Kurd.

"Take the chains off him," ordered Dobó.

The Kurd crossed his hands on his breast, gave a deep bow and waited expectantly.

"Now, you heathen," said Dobó, with Gergely translating all he said, "tell me, do you know Dervish Bey?"

"Yes, I do."

"What does he look like?"

"He's got one eye. He goes around in the garb of a dervish, but wears armour under it."

"That's him. Where do you come from?"

"Bitlis, sir."

"Is your mother living?"

"Yes, sir."

"Have you a family?"

"I've got two children." And his eyes grew moist.

Dobó went on, "I'm letting you out of the fortress. But you must faithfully fulfil a duty I've got for you."

"I'm your slave, sir, to my dying day."

"You'll go to Dervish Bey. There's a little boy captive with him. Tell the bey to bring that little boy tomorrow morning to the gate by the brook, the place where you were captured, and he'll get for him what he desires. You're to show a white handkerchief when you come."

"I understand, sir."

"One of our men will come out of the gate for the boy, carrying the bey's talisman. And you will fetch the boy from the bey and hand him over to our man. You'll see to it that our man suffers no harm."

"I'll answer for that with my life, sir."

"That's not enough. You must swear here, by your mother's heart and your children's happiness, that you'll do what we desire."

"I swear to, sir."

Kristóf had arrived now and was standing beside them. Dobó turned to him.

"Kristóf go to the Hall of Knights. In the corner you'll find a pile of Turkish things and among them a little Turkish book. Bring me that book."

That book was the Koran, which literate Turkish warriors carry with them. It was bound in parchment and had a steel ring in one corner. In that ring was a cord. That was how the Turks who could read carried it on their breasts. The Kurd laid his hand on the Koran and took the oath. Then he knelt at Dobó's feet. He kissed the ground and went joyfully and briskly away.

"But sir," said Gergely in a trembling voice, "if the Turk sees that we're deceiving him..."

"If he had the child with him, he would have displayed him before now. All Turks tell lies. It was only your mind I wanted to put at rest."

*

With beating heart Gergely hurried off to the bastion to get a little rest before dawn. As he passed the mills he heard someone say "Psst!" out of the shadows, though it sounded more like "Psht".

Gergely turned to look. He saw the gypsy. He was kneeling on some straw and beckoning to him.

"Well, what is it?" asked Gergely with bad grace.

The gypsy got up and whispered, "There's a snake in the grass, Master Gergely!"

"What?"

"Last evening I were mending the visor o' one o' them Kassa men's 'elmets. Lieutenant 'Egedűs were sayin' that when there's an attack, there should be double pay. The men are grumbling about Mr. Dobó. They're sayin' them Turks are promisin' everythin' and 'e's promisin' nothin'."

Gergely caught his breath.

"And they said this in front of you?"

"In front of all the soldiers. I wouldn't 'ave said that. But if I've got to be afraid, I'm more afraid of the Turks than of that there lieutenant from Kassa."

"Come with me," said Gergely. He looked for Mekcsey, and found him supervising repairs to the breaches.

"Pista," he said, "Sárközi's got something to tell you." And he left them there.

6

When Dobó stepped out of the palace next morning, Hegedűs was waiting for him at the door.

"Sir!" he said, raising his arm in salute. "I've got something to report."

"Is it important?"

"Not really."

"Come along with me, and tell me what it is when we're on top of the gateway."

Gergely was already standing there with Mekcsey and Fügedy. The wicker palisade hid them from the Turks thronging the banks of the brook. Dobó looked down through the palisade and then turned to Gergely.

"Nobody yet?"

"Nobody," replied Gergely. And he glanced at Hegedűs.

Hegedűs raised a finger to his cap. So did Gergely. But they glanced coldly at each other.

Dobó looked at Hegedűs, waiting for him to report.

"Sir," said Hegedűs, "I have to tell you that I'm finding some discontent among the men."

Dobó's eyes grew wide.

"Unfortunately," Hegedűs shrugged his shoulders and looked away from him, "there are among them old soldiers who know about, er, siege-pay. Yesterday they were all expecting to get it, as was the custom elsewhere and at other times. By evening they were fuming. I thought it would only make matters worse if I read the riot act, so I let them talk. They asked me to tell you, sir, what they wanted."

Dobó's face grew stern.

"First and foremost, you should not have forgotten, lieutenant, that there is no place in this fortress for murmuring and whispering. Secondly, as far as siege-pay is concerned, anyone who is fighting here just for siege-pay and not for his country has only to report to me: he'll get it."

And he walked away from the lieutenant and leaned over the palisade.

"He's coming," said Gergely, as if his heart were beating in his mouth.

The Kurd could be seen picking his way through the Turks. He was now fully armed. He was leading two Hungarian boys. Both of them were peasant-boys in waistcoats and trousers and barefooted. The Kurd took big strides, and the two children had to run to keep up with him.

The one-eyed dervish could be seen about a hundred steps away from them. He was following the Kurd on horseback, but stopped when he reached firing-range and straightening up in his stirrups looked towards the fortress.

"Neither of them's mine," exulted Gergely.

And indeed both boys were older than his little Jancsi. One was about ten, the other twelve.

The Kurd stopped in front of the gate and cried, "Instead of one boy the bey sends you two. Give me the ring, and he'll send the third one too."

Dobó spoke up to the sentry on the tower.

"Bend down and wave your hand to that Kurd; tell him to go away."

*

That day the Turks pounded and wrecked the walls as before. The big siege-guns worked slowly but with terrible force. Each detonation made the wall crack, and from time to time the rumble of falling stones could be heard.

But also on that day there was a change, and the sentries reported it early in the morning. The cavalry withdrew from the fortress. There was no sign anywhere of the red-capped *akindjis*, the spahis in their gleaming armour, the varied garb of the beshlis, the delis in their hoods, the *gönüllüs* on their little horses or *gurebas*, *müsellems* and *silahtars*. And even the nine hundred camels with the army were absent.

What had happened?

Joy showed in the faces of the defenders as they went about their duties. Even the gypsy appeared among the peasants who were grinding arms and had a long rusty sword sharpened till it gleamed bright. The women at the ovens sang as they baked. The children played on the grassy hillside by the ovens, the boys playing soldiers and the girls dancing round to a song:

Little Katy, so I'm told,
Wears a skirt all fringed with gold.
Oats, oats, oats for her charger,
Pearls, pearls, pearls for her mother,
Pearls in a great big string for her daughter!

Mrs. Balogh's maid led the little Turkish boy to them too. He stared at them as they played.

"Let him play with you," she implored the boys.

"No, we won't," they answered.

But the girls did. The little Turkish boy did not understand what they were singing, but he whirled around with them with such an expression of devotion that he might have been taking part in some sacred ritual.

But what was the cause of all this merriment and gaiety?

The Turkish cavalry had disappeared. It was certain that the army sent to help them was approaching. The royal army! Where else would the Turkish cavalry have gone if not to encounter them?

And the drummers drowned the shouts of the Turks with even more zest. The drum-major himself kept leaping on the wall, where the shouts from below were lost in yells and tattoos from his drum.

But leaflets also fell inside the fortress. They were shot in on arrows. Nobody read them. They picked them up and threw them into the fire, while the arrows were taken off to Cecey. The old man sat on the Prison Bastion till sunset, aiming at any Turk who appeared near him.

Only Dobó's expression remained serious.

He climbed one tower, then another to keep watch on the enemy. Sometimes he gazed long and hard at the Eged hill, sometimes he shook his head.

Suddenly he called Mekcsey into the palace.

"My dear Pista," he said, sinking into his chair, "that man Hegedűs, I don't like the look of him. Have him watched."

"I've done that already."

"Report to me every hour who he talks to, where he's looking, where he goes."

"We'll find that out."

456

"But he mustn't get wind of this, or he'll spring a surprise on us."

"He won't know."

"If there were a revolt in the fortress, that would be the end of us. I could have him locked up, but we've got to know who else and how many are on his side. We've got to cut out the part that's rotten so as to leave none of it behind. Who's watching him for you?"

"The gypsy."

"Can you trust him?"

"He feels safer among us here since we beat back the attack; he'll not trust his skin to the promises of the Turks. He was working among the men from Kassa yesterday, and he'll find something to do there again today. I've told him he'll get a good horse complete with trappings if he proves his usefulness in this business. He can pretend to be on their side."

"Have you any other man you can trust?"

"Yes, I have, but the Kassa troops wouldn't trust him. They think so little of the gypsy that they won't mind their words in front of him."

"He's only got to discover who the ringleaders are."

"That's what I've told him too."

"That's all right then. Let's go."

"Commander," said Mekcsey in a different, warmer tone, "there are all the signs that the king's army is on its way."

Dobó shrugged. "Maybe it is," he replied sadly. "But the signs that indicate that to you don't mean the approach of the king's army to me."

Mekcsey stopped dead in his tracks.

Dobó spread his hands. "The *yasavul*s in charge of operations are all here. I saw the two commanders on horseback on the Almagyar hill. They haven't removed a single gun. And their two bands are still here."

"Well what does it mean?" said Mekcsey, looking uncomfortable.

Dobó shrugged once again. "It can only mean, my boy, that they've gone out into the forest."

"The forest?"

"Yes, and into the vineyards. They're carrying twigs and

457

earth. They're going to fill in our moat and build a rampart where the breaches are. But that's only for your ears, Pista. Let the defenders be glad that the relief army's on its way."

He offered his hand to his co-commander and looked at him with confidence. Then he went into the room where Pető and Budaházy were lying.

*

As dusk fell the Turkish cavalry reappeared. The light of a flare revealed that each rider was leading his horse, and that each horse was loaded with twigs and vines in bundles.

A long line of camels carried full sacks. They approached in single file, winding their way down the Bajusz Hill.

Dobó aimed the falconets and mortars downwards and opened fire on them. But the night grew darker and the cavalry still came on. So Dobó stopped bombarding them and merely had the riflemen fire at them from time to time.

Meanwhile the Turks bustled about their work down below. The bundles of twigs and vines crackled as they were piled up. The cries of the *yasavul*s could be heard giving orders.

Dobó had most of the lamps in the fortress taken to the breaches and holes in the walls. They were arranged to shed light outside, but without making it easy for arrows or bullets to be shot from below.

Inside the fortress was in darkness. Very few lights were burning. The surroundings of the Old Gate were lit up by the light from the ovens. Even then the women were still singing as they worked.

"Let them sing," said Dobó. "Where there's singing, there's always good fortune."

Round about midnight Mekcsey was keeping watch in the tower of the Bolyky Bastion for any sign of movement among the Turks that might lead to a sudden night attack. Most of the officers too were keeping watch, scattered all over the fortress.

Mekcsey held both hands to his ears as he leant down and his glance tried to penetrate the darkness. Someone tugged his jacket from behind. It was the gypsy.

He had come upstairs in his janissary boots. On his head was

458

a helmet decorated with cock-feathers. On one side of him was a sword, on the other a Turkish *yataghan* with a white hilt.

"Pssht!..." he said mysteriously, "Pssht!...

"What is it?"

"Please Mr. Captain, I can feel the reins of a good 'orse in me 'and."

"Do you know anything?"

"Aah, aah!"

"Have you proof as well?"

"Aye, I 'ave, but 'e's got ter be caught."

"Well, catch him then, you idiot!"

"Me catch 'im? Jes' come wi' me, an' it's done. But this very minute."

"Where to?"

"The reservoir. That's where 'Egedűs went down. Aah!"

"Alone?"

"Three of 'is men are on guard by the door to the reservoir."

Mekcsey went rushing down the steps, almost falling over in his haste. At the base of the tower he called for six men to accompany him.

"Don't bring any weapons with you. Take your boots off. Bring a belt or some cord with you."

The soldiers obeyed in silence.

When they had got down from the bastion, Mekcsey stopped them again.

"We're going to the reservoir. There are three soldiers sitting there, or maybe they're standing or lying down. Charge them from behind and tie them up. Take them off to the prison and hand them over to the warder for him to lock them up. No shouting and no sound!"

It was dark round the reservoir. The light shone only on the top of a broken pillar. From there the soldiers continued on all fours. The gypsy crossed himself unceasingly.

A few minutes later the silence round the reservoir was broken by the sound of rattles, thuds and oaths. At that Mekcsey appeared on the scene.

The three soldiers were overcome. Both trapdoors to the reservoir were wide open. Mekcsey bent down and looked inside. Down below there was darkness and silence.

He turned round.

"Is he here?" he asked the gypsy quietly.

"I saw 'im go down meself."

"Lieutenant Hegedűs? You're quite sure?"

"Yes, yes."

"Run to the commander. You'll find him on the new bastion. Tell him that I'd like him to come here. On the way tell Captain Gergely to send five infantrymen immediately."

The gypsy cantered off.

Mekcsey drew his sword and sat on the steps leading up from the reservoir. At that moment he seemed to hear voices down below. He got up and closed the side of the trapdoor that covered the steps.

Up above he heard the five infantrymen arriving, and Dobó and the page Kristóf came up at almost the same time. The page was carrying a lantern in his hand, lighting the way for Dobó. Mekcsey beckoned to them to hurry. By now the sounds down below in the reservoir were getting louder.

"This way! This way!" a muffled voice said in the depths.

Dobó ordered the infantrymen to cock their rifles. They had to hold them on the edge of the reservoir with barrels pointing downwards. Then he said, "Kristóf, bring another twenty men from Master Gergely."

He took the lantern from him and set it down beside the pillar, but so that it did not shine into the reservoir.

Down below the rattle of weapòns and the clatter of footsteps.

"This way! Along here!" The shouts grew louder.

A big splash... then another splash... Cries of *"Ey va! Meded!"*... More splashes.

The trapdoor over the steps gave a thud. Someone rose out of it. Dobó seized the lantern and shone it in his face.

It was Lieutenant Hegedűs, his face pale and wan.

Mekcsey grabbed his collar.

"Seize him!" cried Dobó. Strong hands grasped the lieutenant. They pulled him up out of the depths.

"Take away his weapons!"

Down below the noise of splashing and confused cries of *Yetishin! Yetishin!* (Help, help!) grew louder.

Dobó looked down by the light of the lantern. And there in

the great black reservoir a crowd of armed Turks in turbans was thrashing around, while from a hole in one side the rest were pouring out on each other's heels.

"Fire!" shouted Dobó.

The five riflemen fired into the hole. The hollow cavern of the reservoir resounded like a siege-gun. There was a furious roar in reply.

"Stay here!" Dobó said to Mekcsey. "There's a tunnel here. I didn't know of it. Have it examined, and take a look at it yourself too. Go as far as you can along it. If it goes outside the boundary of the fortress, we'll bring down the roof and wall it up. Post a sentry at all times down beside the wall."

And he turned to the soldiers. He pointed to Hegedűs and his companions.

"Put them in irons! Lock them up separately!"

And he went back to the bastion.

Mekcsey heard a Hungarian voice coming from down below.

"Help! Is there anyone there?"

He held the lantern down. A leather-capped Turk was struggling among the drowning men. It was he who was shouting.

"Let down a rope," he said. "Perhaps he's one of the defenders too."

The rope for the water-bucket was lying there. They let it down, bucket and all. The drowning man clung to the bucket. Three men pulled him up.

When he got to the surface, he kept opening his mouth like a pike tossed on to the bank. Mekcsey held the lantern up to his face. He was an *akindji* with a big moustache. The water dripped from his moustache and clothing.

"Are you a Hungarian?" asked Mekcsey.

The man went down on his knees. "Have pity on me, Sir!"

The way he addressed Mekcsey made it plain that he was a Turk. Mekcsey almost threw him back again. But all the same he thought he would make a useful witness.

"Take his arms from him," he ordered the soldiers, "and lock him up with the peasants who brought letters."

461

7

Next day, 4 October, the rising sun shone on newly-erected wooden ramparts around the fortress. The deep gully on the north side had been partly filled in. The new mounds rose opposite the breaches. The base was of twigs, dried scrub from the forest and bundles of vines; all this was covered by earth. The Turks were obviously going to carry on with this work. In one or two places they would raise it high enough to enable them to fire over it and launch an attack on the fortress without using ladders.

Dobó watched their work closely. He examined it from all sides, saying nothing and preserving an unruffled expression. Then he turned to Guthay the treasurer who was waiting to report. Dobó had given him the task of cross-examining Hegedűs and his accomplices, since he himself could not spend much time on hearing the case.

"We've finished, sir. The men confessed that they wanted to let the Turks in. But we had to work hard on Hegedűs. And even then he shouted, 'I confess, I confess, but I'll declare to Dobó that you tortured me and that's why I confessed'."

Dobó sent for the officers. He called the four captains into the hall of the knights, then added a lieutenant, a sergeant, a corporal and a private to their number, together with the clerk in charge of rations, Mihály.

The table was covered with green baize. On it stood a crucifix, with two candles burning beside it. In the corner of the room was the executioner dressed in red broadcloth. Beside him was a pan of burning coal, and in his hand he had a pair of bellows. Beside the pan were pieces of lead and pincers.

Dobó was dressed in a suit of black broadcloth. On the tip of his helmet was the eagle's feather denoting his rank of commander. Before him was a clean sheet of paper.

"Comrades!" he said in a stern voice. "We have assembled to examine the case of Lieutenant Hegedűs and his companions. Their acts suggest that they are traitors."

He beckoned for the prisoners to be brought in.

Gergely got up.

"Gentlemen," he said, "I cannot be judge in this affair. I have a quarrel with the accused. I ask to be relieved of this duty."

Mekcsey also got up.

"I can only be a witness," he said. "Nobody can be both judge and witness."

"Then be a witness," said the men seated at the table.

Gergely left the room. Mekcsey went out into the anteroom. The guards brought in Hegedűs and his three companions. And the Turk too.

Hegedűs was pale. His eyes were ringed with blue circles. He dare not lift his head.

Dobó allowed only him to stay there; he sent the others out. "Let's hear your defence," he said. "What did you mean by leading in those Turks?"

Hegedűs pulled himself together and made some incoherent excuses:

"I only intended to lure the Turks as far as the reservoir. I didn't want to surrender the fortress. The reservoir's big. We found a narrow entrance to it. I thought it would be to my credit if I alone destroyed a thousand Turks."

Dobó listened to all this without stirring. Nor did the officers ask him any questions. When he had no more to say, Dobó had him stand aside, and brought in the men one by one.

The first one, a wan-faced man of about forty whose coat was covered in mud, shrugged his shoulders. "We couldn't do anything except what the lieutenant ordered us to do. We have to obey orders when they're given."

"What did he order you to do?"

"He ordered us to stand at the edge of the reservoir, while he led in a couple of Turks."

"Did he say why?"

"To discuss the surrender of the fortress."

Dobó looked at the lieutenant. Hegedűs shook his head.

"That's not true. He's lying."

"What, me?" the soldier winced, offended. "Why, didn't you say, sir, that the Turks have got plenty of good things to say, and Dobó hasn't any? Not even siege-pay..."

"He's lying," repeated Hegedűs.

They led in the second soldier. He too was scared. There were bits of mud in his long black hair. He stood there blinking.

"Why were you at the well?"

"We were waiting for the Turks," he replied, still blinking. "Lieutenant Hegedűs said the fortress would fall into Turkish hands sooner or later, so it was certain we'd die if we didn't surrender the fortress."

Dobó had the third soldier brought in too. He was a young lad whose face was almost smooth. His faded red trousers were in holes at the knee.

"I don't know anything," he stammered. "I was simply ordered to go to the well, but I don't know why."

"Didn't Lieutenant Hegedűs say that it would be a good idea to come to an agreement with the Turks?"

"Yes, he did."

"When did he say it first?"

"On the evening after the big attack."

"And how did he put it?"

"Well, he said, er... He said there are only a few of us and a lot of them, and, er... the other fortresses couldn't hold out though then the Turkish army was divided, going in two directions."

"Did Lieutenant Hegedűs say anything about siege-pay?"

"Yes, he did. He said that they pay double money in other fortresses at times like this."

"And what did he have to say about surrendering the fortress?"

"Well, he said, er... he said the Turks'll take it anyway, so it'd be better if they paid us rather than us paying the price with our heads."

"And what did the men have to say to that?"

"Nothing. We only happened to be chatting round the fire when the Turks shouted to the fortress."

"And didn't you shout back?"

"No. Only the lieutenant talked with them in the night."

"How did he talk with them?"

"Through a crack at the Old Gate. He went there and talked three times."

"With Turks?"

"Yes, with Turks."

"And what did he say when he came back?"

"That the Turks would allow everyone to go out unharmed; they wouldn't kill anyone. And they'd give each man from Kassa ten pieces of gold too, and the two pashas would send a letter with a seal promising to keep their word."

"How many of the soldiers heard all this?"

"About ten."

"Then why didn't you report it to me? Didn't you take an oath that you wouldn't talk of surrendering the fortress?"

The soldier was silent.

"Wasn't it your duty to report what the lieutenant said immediately?"

"We daren't."

"In other words you determined to play into the hands of the Turks and surrender the fortress. Who agreed to it?"

The lad mentioned another seven names from memory. Then he began to make excuses. "Sir, we didn't make any agreement. We just obeyed. Only the lieutenant spoke and he gave the orders."

The wall shuddered as a cannon-ball struck it. The suits of armour on their poles clattered. A piece of plaster broke on the floor.

Dobó looked at the judges.

"Have any of you any questions?"

The judges were almost frozen to their seats at the table. At last the private broke the silence. "Did the ten privates all agree that the fortress should belong to the Turks?"

The accused shrugged his shoulders wanly. "The private can't want anything except what his officer wants."

There were no further questions.

"There's still the Turk to come," said Dobó. "Bring him in."

The Turk bowed three times before reaching the table. There he remained bent, his hands crossed on his breast.

"Do you understand Hungarian?"

"Yes, sir."

"What's your name?" asked Dobó.

"Yusuf."

"Yusuf, that's József in Hungarian. Stand straight!"

465

The Turk straightened up. He was an *akindji,* about thirty years old, a thick-set, muscular little man. His flattened nose and a red wound-scar on his head indicated that he had been in battle before. His eyes betrayed that he had not slept at all during the night.

In answer to questions he explained that he had been coming to Hungary for ten years, and that he was by the wall when Hegedűs spoke through the crack, saying "Hi there, you Turks! Which of you understands Hungarian?"

"He's lying," growled Hegedűs, white as a sheet. "Zoltay was always talking to the Turks too."

"Me?" exploded Zoltay.

"Yes indeed, you spoke to them. Every time there's an attack you're always shouting at them."

Pale with fury, Zoltay leapt out of his seat. "I demand an examination into my conduct!" he said. "I can't sit in judgement any longer. Maybe I do give a shout every time I deliver a blow. But that's only swearing. That's no crime! What sort of talk is this?"

Dobó calmed him down. "We all know that habit of yours. Others also swear in the heat of battle. But since you have flared up in anger against the accused, we relieve you of your duties as a judge."

Zoltay bowed and left the room.

Dobó turned his gaze on the Turk again. In broken Hungarian the Turk explained how Hegedűs had spoken at the Old Gate with an aga and then with Arslan Bey. As an assurance he asked the bey for his word of honour and a hundred gold coins. He said he would let the Turkish army into the fortress at night; all they had to do was dig by the gate where the big brass drum was usually beaten. He—and here he pointed at Hegedűs—said that one night he had been down to the reservoir and came across a tunnel which, however, had collapsed by the gate. At that place he had heard the sound of the brass drum above his head; there were also soldiers marching there, and this meant that there was no need to dig very far. He would expect them at midnight precisely. But they must also guarantee that no harm would come to the soldiers from Kassa on duty at the Old Gate. They agreed. At midnight Hegedűs guided them with a lamp. The janissaries, *asabs* and *piyads* all came in a mixed troop. There were three thousand of them who set off along the tunnel. The rest of the army, God knows how many thousands, were waiting for the two gates to be opened. But what happened was that Hegedűs's lantern struck the wall at the corner of the reservoir and went out. He led the vanguard onwards in darkness. He knew where to go, but the side of the great cistern was narrow. He was able to manage there even though it was dark, but as the leading troops pressed hard on each other, they slipped into the water.

"Do you happen to know," asked Dobó, "that Dervish Bey has stolen away the son of one of our captains?"

"Indeed I do," replied the Turk. "They've been looking for the boy in every tent for a couple of weeks or so. The bey's trying to find him. Either they stole him from him or he escaped three days after our arrival here."

Dobó looked at Hegedűs. "Scoundrel!" he said.

Hegedűs went down on his knees. "Have mercy on me! Pity me!" he wept. "I was wrong. I lost my senses."

"Do you too confess that you wanted to surrender the fortress to the Turks?"

"Yes, I confess. Just have pity on me! I've got a family... You can understand that..." And his words died away.

The discussion of the case lasted less than an hour.

The next hour saw Lieutenant Hegedűs in the square of the fortress, hanging from a hastily improvised gallows made of beams. And Fügedy proclaimed to the defenders: "That's the death that waits for anyone who breaks his oath, be he private or officer, and wants to surrender the fortress to the Turks!"

They cut off the ears of the three privates beneath the gallows. The other seven were put in leg-irons and sent to work inside the fortress.

The Turk was thrown over the high wall on the west side. His neck was broken when he fell among his companions.

The defenders had visible proof that Dobó meant what he said.

8

There is no stronger power on earth than motherly love. It is sunlight in human form, a holy flame from the heart of God, a powerful gentleness that has no fear of death. You who have abandoned your safe home, soft pillows and all your treasures to make your way in disguise through the forest of death to reach your loved ones in peril, you who descend into the depths of earth, you who wish to break through that wall with feeble arms, that wall at which armed beasts in their myriads have been yelling impotently, you who do not know the meaning of the word "impossible" if the one you love is concerned, even if you have to suffer and die with him—I marvel at you, and at your heart of a wife!

*

For two whole nights and days they dug their way again and again through falls of earth in the tunnel, in damp and cold under the loose vaulting. In some places the falls were only a few feet long, and they were able to struggle through them after only an hour's work. But in other places they had to cope with stones, and neither the powerless arms of the lady nor the undeveloped muscles of the fifteen-year-old youth were used to such heavy work.

On the evening of 3 October, hardly waiting for the camp to quieten down and go to sleep, they collected up all the food they had. According to their calculations they were only a hundred paces from the fortress. They hoped there would be no need for them to return again.

And they worked all night long.

There under the earth they did not know when it was still dark or when the sun rose. All they heard was the noise of the horses' hooves as they carried the earth and twigs, and the thunder of the cannon and mortars from the fortress too. They thought down there that there was a night attack and worked all the harder to gain entrance.

Outside, however, the night passed, dawn broke, morning came and the sun rose behind the Borsod hills. The Turkish horse-trader's servants saw that the tent was deserted and had a look inside it. They were taken aback when they saw the stone moved aside and the broad hole. As the cavalry were once again busy collecting twigs everywhere, the merchant himself hurried off to a *deli aga* and quivering with delight declared, "Sir! I myself will deliver the fortress into the hands of the army! I've discovered a tunnel in the night!"

All the *deli*s, *akindji*s, *beshli*s, *gönüllü*s and *gureba*s suddenly left the twigs and the horses as they were, in the open. Whistles and trumpets sounded to assemble them. All types of soldiers swarmed together and poured in a noisy throng through the entrance to the hole in the ground. They were led by the merchant with a torch.

*

Meanwhile the two poor souls were struggling onwards, hidden away, drenched to the skin and pushing stones aside.

At one point the passage again began to slope. There the stones were dry and the tunnel grew wider. They reached a large triangular underground chamber that felt damp.

"We must be under the moat of the fortress," said Miklós.

"No, this is inside the wall. It might have been stables at one time, or maybe a corn-store," said Mrs. Bornemissza thoughtfully.

But there were two roof-falls in two corners of the chamber. Which of them was their route?

One was a pile with a little hole at the top of it. It was only big enough to take a human fist. Beside the other fall there was the black outline of a narrow opening.

"The passage divides here into two," said Miklós. "The question now is which one to work on."

He climbed over the stones and held his candle up to the holes. At the first, the candle flickered. He did the same at the hole on the left-hand side. There the flame burned steadily.

He stuck the candle into the side of his fur cap and stretched up to grip the topmost stone. Eva helped. The stone came bumping and rolling down over the others.

"Another one!" said Miklós.

Once again the two of them strained hard. But that stone refused to move.

"We'll have to pull the little stones out from round about it."
He took the spade and poked all round it. Then he grasped
it again. The stone began to rock.
Miklós took a deep breath and wiped his face.

"I'm tired!"

"Let's have a rest," panted Eva.

And they sat down on a stone. Miklós sank down against the
wall and instantly fell asleep. Eva herself was dizzy and desperately tired. Her clothes were wet to the knee and covered in
mud; her hands were stained with blood. Her hair had come
down with all the stooping, and she had caught half of it inside
her jacket, while the rest fell in waves around her neck.

She picked up the candle and looked into both holes. They
might go either way now, if only they could get through this
obstacle.

"We'll have a little rest," she said, fixing the candle to a stone,
"but I'm not going to sleep. I'll just rest."

And as she leaned back, she heard a low rumble from the
direction in which they had come. She frowned and listened.
Was the noise coming from up above or down below?

A red streak of light suddenly appeared from the depths of
the tunnel.

"Miklós!" shrieked Eva, shaking the boy. "They're coming!"

The boy raised his eyelids listlessly.

"They're coming!" repeated Eva in desperation. And she
reached for her sword.

Only the sheath was still there. The sword had been left
behind at one of the obstacles where they had moved a stone.
Moreover the *yataghan*s in her belt had all been broken during
their work; so had her pocket-knife. They had no weapons at
all.

The light grew stronger as it approached.

Eva gathered all her strength and grasped the stone. So did
Miklós. Their candle went out. The stone stirred, but refused to
move out of the way.

Frozen to the spot with terror, they watched the merchant
holding the torch emerge from the darkness. Beside him was a
well-built aga with a drooping moustache and daggers glinting
in his belt. The next minute hands reached up to them and they
were prisoners.

470

The aga took in the work they had begun at a glance, and made a swift decision.

"Hold the torch, you whelp!" he ordered Miklós. "You know which way to go."

Miklós did not understand what he was saying. All he saw was the torch being pressed into his hand.

It took the soldiers only a minute to pull the heavy stones apart. The passage was wide enough to take two men side by side. By now the chamber was full of armed soldiers.

"You lead," said the aga to Miklós. "And the other one," he went on, pointing at Eva, "stays here. If you take us on the wrong track, I'll throw that woman among the common soldiers."

A janissary interpreted his words. Eva shut her eyes.

The aga glanced back. "One *deli* to guard her!" And he poked Miklós to lead the way.

The *deli* stood beside Eva. The rest set off. But since the aga had not said which of them was to guard the prisoner, he quickly gave up his post to another *deli*.

"You guard her!"

He too stood there for a time, but perhaps it occurred to him that those who first entered the fortress would be rewarded with high rank to their dying day, so he offered the prisoner to a *müsellem*.

"I'm not going to guard her," said the *müsellem* dismissively. And he left them.

"I'll do it. Just get along," said an elderly asab in a beaver-fur cap. And he drew his dagger and stood over by the woman.

Eva leant against the wall, half-dead. Beside her there went a pack of dirty soldiers in various garbs, smelling of gunpowder and sweat. All of them now carried bare swords in their hands, and the eyes of all of them were lit by the glorious hope of being among the first. Sometimes a torchbearer came to light the way for a particular group. At others they groped their way along in darkness. Their weapons clattered and rattled. One of them carried a rolled-up red banner over his shoulder.

All of a sudden there was a deep dull roar, like thunder coming from the depths of the earth. The tunnel back from the entrance to the chamber caved in all the way along. The roaring went on for minutes. Stones fell down and thudded on the ground. After the leading troops had gone, nobody else could follow.

From where the fall had taken place there were muffled cries and pants. In the other direction the receding rattle of weapons grew faint.

The asab on guard suddenly spoke in Hungarian: "Don't be afraid!" And he grasped the lady's hand. "Who are you?"

The lady was unable to speak.

"Are you Hungarian?"

The lady nodded.

"Come along," said the *asab*. "The passage divides here. If I can open out the other hole, we're free. But if it caves in here too…"

Eva felt a current of life surge through her once again.

"Who are you?" she asked, recovering her senses.

"My name's Varsányi. I'm on your side."

He took flint and steel from his belt and struck a spark.

The tinder quickly caught light. Perfumed smoke mingled with the rank air of the tunnel. He held it to a wax candle and blew it. The candle burst into light.

"Hold this candle, my dear."

He stepped over to the fall on the left and loosened the stones with one or two tugs.

He was a little man, but a strong one. He rolled the big stone blocks away, some outwards, others inwards. Soon there was an opening big enough for a man to get through.

He took the candle from the lady and crawled ahead. He held his hand in front of the candle. He was in such a hurry that Eva found it difficult to keep up with him. Now the passage was clearer, but they still found themselves going downhill.

Varsányi turned round at one point. "Are you perhaps a spy? Maybe you've got a message from the king?"

"Yes," agreed Eva, as if she were talking in her sleep.

"Is the king's army on the way?"

"I don't know."

"Ah well, never mind. If only I knew where we were! Let's hurry to get there before the Turks."

472

The passage started rising at last. There were occasional niches that showed up black in the walls. The stones were brown, and the damp glistened like dew on them.

"We're inside the fortress now," said Varsányi. "We'll probably come out by the reservoir."

A pile of white plaster blocked their way. A strong smell of lime seeped through it.

Varsányi scratched his head.

"Pooh! To hell with this awful world!"

"What is it?"

"Oh, nothing. I'll crawl ahead. Hold this candle."

He threw himself face down on the pile and crawled over it. Eva handed him the candle.

Varsányi was now standing on the other side. He took the candle and hummed and hawed. He offered his hand to Eva, helping her to slither over the pile and stand up again.

They were in a spacious chamber which even in the darkness glimmered white. From up above came the sound of a funeral chant, *In paradisum deducant te angeli.* The light of day filtered down from far above that.

The chamber was full of white coffins piled on top of each other, and scattered all round them was wet lime, which had dried on the sides of the coffins in clods. On one side on the coffins a dead man in a shirt, with a moustache and a bony face, rose sideways out of the sea of lime. The light from above illuminated his face. From his neck dangled a noose.

Varsányi stared in astonishment at the corpse. Then he looked round.

Eva lay on the ground behind him in a dead faint.

*

Meanwhile the boy was guiding the Turkish troops.

At first his steps were leaden with terror, but then he thought that when they emerged into the fortress he would give such a big shout...

The thought encouraged him. Without faltering he carried the torch, sometimes ahead of the aga, sometimes beside him.

Soon they too began to wind their way upwards. Up and up they went, higher and higher. In the end they came up against

473

a wall built of the sandstone typical of buildings all over Eger; the mortar revealed that it had been built long ago.

"Demolish it!" ordered the aga.

The mortar quickly fell beneath the blows of *yataghans* and lances. Only the first two or three stones were difficult to dislodge; the rest moved more easily in those hands with muscles of steel. All the same, they had to work at them for over an hour.

When the hole was big enough to take a man, the aga made Miklós go first.

They arrived in a spacious cellar-like building, with barrels and barrels everywhere. The only odd thing was that the place was more like a large room than a cellar. On the wall too there was a tattered picture, a large one, and under this was a round tub. Two heads could be seen in the picture. One was a sad face with a beard, the other a young man, also looking sad, leaning on the breast of the bearded man. Round their heads was a halo. Under the head of the young man the wall glimmered white through the tears in the canvas.

And the defenders could be heard walking about.

"Arms at the ready!" said the aga softly, turning round. "Assemble quietly. Quiet! Quiet!... When we break open the door, no shouting! If we see nobody, we'll wait for those who are following us. Standard-bearers, run to the wall immediately!"

Two standard-bearers stepped forward.

The aga continued, "The rest of you follow me to the gate. No mercy! The first task is to disarm the guard there and get the gate open. Is that understood?"

"Understood," came the soft murmur of the soldiers in reply.

The aga stepped forward and caught sight of the huge vat of gunpowder in front of the iron door. He started in surprise.

They were in the gunpowder-store. It was not wine in those barrels, but powder.

But Miklós had also realized where they had arrived.

As he stood there beside the great vat, he turned round. He took a long glance at the armed mob of soldiers pouring in. His face was pale and his spirits high. He raised the burning torch and plunged it into the gunpowder.

9

When they had let down the coffin, Varsányi called up to the men, "Hi there!"

At this shout startled faces appeared up above in the trapdoor of the burial-vault. One was bare-headed, the other wore a rusty old helmet with a chin-strap.

Varsányi shouted again, "It's me here, Varsányi! Pull me up!"

He raised Eva in his arms and stepped from coffin to coffin as far as the ropes. He grasped the two ropes and sat in them. The men pulled him up. At the entrance to the vault there were only the two priests and the two peasants with the ropes. They just stared at Eva who lay like a corpse on the grass where Varsányi had put her down.

"Bring some water," said Varsányi to the peasants.

At that moment there was an earth-shattering explosion and roar of flame that deafened and blinded everything. A red tower of flame shot up from the Church bastion. It hurtled to the heavens, with black planks, beams, stones, pieces of wood and men whirling round in it.

The explosion so shook the fortress that everyone staggered and collapsed as if struck by an invisible hand of immense power.

From the air a hail of stones, blood, weapons, wood and barrel-staves rained down.

This explosion was followed by deathly silence lasting for several minutes, a silence both inside the fortress and in the Turkish camp outside it. Everyone stared in a daze.

Had the heavens fallen? Or had the earth opened up to cover the whole world in a terrifying flood of flame spouting from a hellish volcano? Nobody could fathom it.

"It's a Turkish trick!" That was the only immediate thought of everyone in the fortress.

"The fortress is doomed!" That was the only sensation, and it turned all hearts, already stunned by the explosion, to stone.

Gergely was at the foot of the Sándor Bastion, tying up pots filled with explosives. The blast of the explosion hurled him against the shields that hung from the wall on hooks and covered it. When he raised his head, the pillar of flame up above had become funnel-shaped and glowed red in the sky. In it he saw a black mill-wheel, and around it men on their backs, spinning as they fell, and a complete human leg from the thigh downwards falling separately. He had sufficient presence of mind to leap under the arches of the bastion, but he too just stared for the first minute, deprived of thought, with a stunned expression.

But next minute there was a stirring among the defenders. Men ran up and down, soldiers threw down their weapons, women wailed and maddened horses broke away from their tethers and plunged in all directions.

Down below in the Turkish camp there was a roar of triumph, siege-ladders were raised and thousands of armed men surged towards the fortress.

"We're done for!" was the cry everywhere in the fortress, amidst the moans and groans. Women gripping children by the hand or carrying them ran aimlessly over the blackened stones and beams and smouldering embers. Everyone was fleeing, but nobody knew where to.

And it seemed as if the heavens were also playing their part in the utter confusion. Thick black snow began to fall. Black snow! It kept falling. It was so thick that it was impossible to see more than ten paces ahead. These were ashes, and they covered the whole fortress, as if enveloping it in mourning.

And disfigured bodies and bleeding human limbs lay everywhere on the scattered stones and beams.

Dobó, bareheaded, tugged at his steed and galloped to the site of the explosion. He ordered the soldiers to the wall.

"There's nothing to worry about!" he shouted left and right. "There were only twenty-four tons of gunpowder in the sacristy."

The officers too jumped on horseback and calmed the defenders everywhere with Dobó's words.

"Back to your posts, everyone! It was only twenty-four tons of gunpowder!"...

In his fury Mekcsey thrust a broken lance at the stunned and mutinous soldiers. "Pick up your arms, damn you! Get to the wall!" And he jumped from his horse. He grabbed a six-foot pike and rushed to the top of the wall. "Follow me, lads! Follow me, if you're a man!"

476

The Turks were met by a long line of fire as they climbed the wall. Even without anyone to lead them, the soldiers ran from the inner part of the fortress to the wall and got to work with pike, sword and axe.

The Turks likewise pressed each other forwards and backwards in confusion, which was just as great outside the walls as inside them.

Most of them thronged to the site of the explosion.

From his own bastion Gergely could see the mixed mob of Turks pouring towards the Church Bastion in the gradually thinning clouds of black ash.

"Stay here!" he shouted to Zoltay, as he drew his sword and ran to the Church Bastion.

"Korcsolás!" he called to a corporal who was going inside. "Come with me!"

The man was only five paces away from him. He took no notice.

"Máté Korcsolás! For goodness' sake!"

The man just stared straight ahead and walked on calmly.

Gergely leapt after him. He grabbed his shoulder.

"What? Can't you hear me!"

The man seemed to start out of sleep, and looked at Bornemissza. It was only then that Gergely saw blood dripping from both ears. He had indeed been deafened.

Gergely left him and hurried on.

On the way his glance fell on the cooking pots. They contained the soup for the men who were on duty at noonday and were now due to come to lunch. In the eight large pots hot soup with pieces of meat chopped small in it was steaming and bubbling.

Gergely stopped. He got hold of the carrying-pole and pushed it through the handle of one of the pots. He shouted to the peasant who carried the dishes, "Get hold of it! Bring the other ones up to the bastion too!"

And when they got up there, he tipped the boiling soup on to the Turks who were swarming up the ladders.

*

When Varsányi recovered, he saw the woman on the ground in front of him. The two priests, still in cassock and surplice, ran to the walls and seized weapons, while the two peasants hurried off in different directions, probably to the cannon.

Varsányi raised Eva to his shoulder like a sack and carried her into the palace. He thought that was the place for her if she were a spy from the king; she must have brought a letter. And he entrusted her to Mrs. Balogh to bring her round.

*

It was only after driving off the attack that they surveyed the damage caused by the explosion.

The right side of the Church Bastion and the sacristy were a gaping black hole. The wall of the fortress and the repairs completed at night had collapsed at that spot, and of the two horse-driven mills that had been at work there only wreckage remained. Thirty cattle for slaughtering had been standing down below at the side of the sacristy. They lay there dead in their own blood.

The eight men on watch were found torn to shreds. A lieutenant died there too, Pál Nagy, who had been sent by György Bátory with thirty infantrymen from the castle of Erdőd.

Many of the soldiers who were standing nearby were wounded. A stone from the explosion had struck a soldier called Gergely Horváth on the shoulder and severed his arm. He died the same day, and was lowered into the burial-pit that day too.

The defenders recovered their senses completely only when they saw that the Turks were not able to get inside the fortress.

"God defends Eger too!" shouted Dobó, smoothing back his hair and looking up into the sky. "Trust in God, men!"

Actually it was the soup that beat off the attack. The Turks had got used to fire, sword and pike, but knew hot soup only in spoons. As the boiling paprika-spiced liquid poured down the first ladder, the men seemed to be swept off it. The swarm of men at the foot of the ladders also jumped away. Some clutched at their hands, others their faces, others their necks. Covering their heads with their shields they backed away from the walls cursing.

The defenders breathed a sigh of relief. Dobó summoned the millers and carpenters.

"Collect together the bits of the mills as quickly as you can, and out of the two of them make one spoked mill to make gunpowder. Whatever else you need is to be made by the carpenters immediately."

And he looked round. "Where's the steward?"

A soot-blackened figure stepped out of the walls of the monastery. Blowing the dirt from his moustache and beating his beard, he came and stood before Dobó.

It was old Sukán.

"Sukán, old chap," said Dobó. "Release saltpetre, sulphur and charcoal from your store. As soon as the mill is working, the millers are to grind gunpowder."

Only then did he think of going to wash himself. He too was as black as a chimneysweep.

*

A soot-blackened man was standing in the doorway of the palace. He was partly dressed like a Turk. In his hand he held a big piece of baked pumpkin. He was eating it with a spoon.

He got up when Dobó caught sight of him.

"Is that you, Varsányi?"

"Yes, sir, it's me."

"What news have you brought?"

"I've brought an envoy from the king into the fortress. A woman."

Dobó hurried off with long strides to Mrs. Balogh.

"Where's the envoy?"

The lady was sitting by Pető's bed. She was lining a helmet with red silk—her son's helmet.

"Envoy?" she stared at Dobó. "It's only a woman they brought here."

"Well, where's that woman?"

Mrs. Balogh opened the door into the next room and closed it again. "She's asleep," she said. "Don't let's disturb her. She's worn out, poor soul."

Dobó looked inside.

Eva lay in the bed, a clean white bed. Only her head was

479

visible; her pale face with the brown hair in disarray encircling it was sunk deep in the pillow. Dobó looked with astonishment at that deadly pale female face, suffering even in sleep. He did not recognize it.

He went back.

"Did she bring a letter of any kind?"

"No."

"Bring me the woman's clothes. Who can she be?"

Mrs. Balogh shrugged her shoulders, then looked imploringly at Dobó.

"She said we weren't to ask her name. She's afraid you won't be pleased to see her."

"Bring me that woman's clothes!"

Mrs. Balogh carried in a mud-stained, lime-covered Turkish military jacket from the corridor. The little boots of yellow morocco had spurs on them. In the belt were over fifty Hungarian gold pieces, the scabbard of a sword and two Turkish *yataghan*s.

"Feel the pockets."

In one of the pockets some paper rustled.

"That's it," Dobó seized it. And with his sooty hands he immediately unfolded the tightly crumpled piece of parchment.

It was a sketch of the fortress.

The only other things in the pockets were a handkerchief and a pair of crumpled gloves. They felt the seams of the jacket too and unpicked them. They even took the boots apart. There was nothing.

"Hasn't she got it with her in bed?"

"No," replied Mrs. Balogh, "I gave the poor thing a night-dress too. Oh, how tired out she is! She can't have slept for ages. She came underground, along the Way of the Dead."

Dobó summoned Varsányi.

"You said she was an envoy."

"So I understood."

"Why, didn't she say so in so many words?"

"We didn't talk, sir. We came through the tunnel almost at a run."

"What tunnel?"

"Under the burial-vault."

480

"What, is there a tunnel there too?"

"Not any longer, sir."

"Have the Turks got provisions?"

"Occasionally ten to twenty cartloads of flour come, and the odd herd of sheep. God alone knows where they get them! Their rice has run out long ago."

"Which means that they're not starving yet?"

"Not really up to now."

"What other news have you from the army?"

"Only that they're digging a mine from the King's Seat."

"Into the fortress?"

"Certainly; they've got sappers working on it."

"Why didn't you come in earlier? You ought to have reported about them transporting all that wood."

"It was impossible. They've stationed the strongest janissaries in front of the gates, and I hadn't got a janissary outfit. It would have roused suspicion if I'd wanted to pass through them."

"All right. Now stay inside the fortress. Report to Gergely Bornemissza and tell him the direction from which they're mining. Then come back here and stay close to the door."

The sketch was still in his hands. He sent for Mekcsey.

"Take this sketch," he said to him. "The underground passages are marked on it. I had no idea that such a drawing existed anywhere in the world. Summon the stonemasons immediately and block up any that aren't blocked already. And the first task of all is to wall up that lower passage by the burial-vault."

He gave the two pages a few further orders, then asked for two buckets of water for his bath. After bathing he changed his clothes. He also put on his greaves, then stretched out on the bearskin-covered bench.

This was how he always slept, wherever sleep overtook him by day or night for an hour or so. The soldiers in the fortress declared that he never slept.

10

It was only that evening that Dobó was able to speak with Eva.
By then Mrs. Bornemissza was up and about. She was wearing a light house-coat. Presumably she had picked it out of the women's clothes that had come into her husband's hands as loot from that first raid. Those were the ones that could not find buyers at the auction, so they had been hung up in one of the empty rooms of the palace. They would come in useful for the poor after the siege.

Dobó summoned her at dinner-time.

"Who are you, madam?" were his first words to her. He realized immediately that she was a woman of quality.

The page Balázs was standing behind Dobó. Mrs. Balogh was also busy in the room. At that moment she was setting out red wine to go with the mutton stew. She lit a third wax candle to go with the two already alight.

"I don't know whether I can tell you that unless it is in private," replied Eva listlessly. "Not because of Mrs. Balogh, but because I don't know whether you, sir, will allow my name to become publicly known."

At Dobó's gesture the page left the room. Mrs. Balogh also went out.

Eva spoke. "I'm the wife of Gergely Bornemissza." And tears rolled down her cheeks.

Dobó's knife fell from his hand.

Eva continued with anxious eyes, "I know that it's not good for a woman to be present in such a place and in such an affair. But believe me, sir, I haven't come to make trouble or to try to get my husband out of the battle with my complaints."

Dobó nodded towards a chair. "Please sit down. Please forgive me for receiving you while I'm eating. Help yourself..." But his words were cold.

"No, thank you," said Eva, brushing aside his invitation. And she sat down wearily.

There was silence for some minutes. Then Dobó broke it.

"Does Gergely know that you're here?"

"No. And I'm sure it's as well that he doesn't know."

"Well, my dear," said Dobó, now with a warm glance, "you

did well to keep quiet about your name. Gergely must not know that you're here. I'm adamant about that. The siege can't go on for much longer. The relief army must arrive soon. And why did you come here?"

Eva's eyes filled with tears. "My son..."

"So it's true that he was stolen?"

"Yes."

"And the ring?"

"Here it is," replied Eva, and pulled out the cord round her neck.

Dobó simply gave a glance at the ring. He drank a draught of wine and got up.

"What guarantee will you give me that you won't talk to Gergely?"

"I'll obey all your commands, commander. I know that..."

"Do you really understand, madam, why you must not talk with him?"

"I think so."

"Gergely is the brains of this fortress. His mind mustn't be diverted for a single minute from the defence of it. Who else do you know here?"

"Mekcsey, Fügedy, Zoltay. My father's here too, and old Bálint, our priest."

"You mustn't be seen outside. You must keep yourself hidden in Mrs. Balogh's room. Promise me that on your honour."

"I promise."

"Swear to it!"

"I swear it."

"There's a crucifix on the wall there. Please bring it here. Swear with a strong and sacred oath."

"I swear by the life of my son, the life of my father, the life of my husband."

"Thank you. And I promise in return that I will do all I can to find your child. Give me that talisman, please."

Eva handed it to him.

Dobó buckled on his helmet, and before pulling on his gauntlets offered his hand to the lady.

"Please forgive me for being so blunt. It's the only way. Have a look at my wife's room and the things she left behind: regard them as yours."

"One more thing, commander. What am I to say to Mrs. Balogh about who I am?"

"Say what you like. Only Gergely mustn't get to know."

"He won't."

Dobó said farewell, went through the doorway and called for his horse.

*

Towards evening the wind rose. It blew away the soot and ash from the fortress. There had certainly been no sweeping done there since the siege. Rubbish and the smell of corpses were everywhere. Not to mention outside the fortress!

Dobó called the masons and peasants to the debris left after the explosion.

"Collect up all the scattered stones. Build up the wall so that you are always protected by stones."

Then he turned to his page.

"Balázs, go and fetch me the sealing-wax. And a candle too."

He went up to the cannon called Baba, sat down on it and wrote on a slip of paper with a lead pencil:

"Take notice, Dervish Bey! As soon as you have found Bornemisz-sza's boy, let me know by hoisting a blue and red flag on the poplar tree that stands by the brook to the north of the fortress. The impression of your ring is on this letter. An envoy with a white flag may bring the boy. I will give you not only the ring for him, but also a Turkish boy we have in captivity.

He called Mekcsey over. Covering what he had written with his hand, he said to him, "Sign your name here, Pista."

Mekcsey signed without saying a word.

Balázs was standing there now with the sealing-wax and candle.

Dobó bent down from the gun and dropped the molten wax on to the letter beside Mekcsey's signature. Mekcsey pressed his ring into the wax, then hurried on without asking who it was for and why.

Dobó folded up the letter and sealed it on the outside with the Turkish ring. The crescent and stars were clearly visible on the seal.

Then he called for Varsányi.

"Varsányi, my friend," he smiled. "Now I understand why you don't come inside the fortress. Why should you, when we're always sending you out again. Do you know Dervish Bey?"

"Like the back of my hand," replied Varsányi cheerfully.

"Well, here's this letter. Slip it into his tent or his clothes or his drinking cup, whichever you can manage."

"I see."

"Then go to Szarvaskő and wait for Miklós Vas. He must be on his way now."

"And how are we to get into the fortress?"

"Tell the guards on the gate to let down a rope each night. The rope's to ring a bell up above."

Varsányi wrapped the letter in a handkerchief and hid it in his breast.

Cannon-balls were thundering down on the Sándor Bastion. Dobó saw that there was trouble there. The soldiers were jumping away from it in disorder.

Somehow the Turks had got to know that the outer fortress wall was joined to the inner one by a little gateway. (The passage between them was like the tongue of a buckle.) How could they have found that out? The Turks had put together and tied two tall ladders; these stood on the King's Seat like a reversed letter V. A Turk ran up it and saw how the soldiers went in and out of the little doorway. Thereupon they dragged a cannon up to the hill and were bombarding the gateway fiercely.

Before an hour was out, Hungarians were being wounded in droves near the gateway and five of them were dead.

"Bring up planking!" called Dobó. "Raise the palisade higher!"

But it was no use. The Turkish guns were so sited that their cannon-balls pierced both planking and palisade and reached the gateway.

"This'll cost me a hundredweight of gunpowder," grumbled Dobó. "And now, of all times!"

Gergely came running from the corner tower.

"Sir," he panted. "We can't leave the gate like this! My best men are being shot down!"

"We'll do something about it," replied Dobó. Then in a quiet

485

voice he went on, "We've got to wait. We can't fire until they start making gunpowder."

Cannon-balls were falling like hail on the gateway.

"Give me permission, sir, to make another opening or to dig one from below."

"You don't need to get special permission, Gergely. Go ahead and do it!"

Gergely had a hole cut in the wall and made his men use that.

Meanwhile the Turks went on shelling the empty gateway so frequently that the cannon-balls could be swept up at the bottom of it.

*

That night once again the Turks were transporting earth and twigs.

The moon gave them a little light. There was sporadic firing from the fortress.

"Don't fire!" said Dobó.

As the defenders grew quiet, the sounds of Turks swarming around, horses' hooves and crackling of wood grew stronger and stronger.

There were more of them now. Dobó ordered every rifleman to the four breaches. One line lay prone; the next knelt above them and a third line bent forward above them.

The lamps were extinguished.

The Turks increased in number and were more exposed. Their work was lit by tiny hand-lamps.

When the Turkish soldiers rose higher and higher and their turbans began to appear in front of the breach, Dobó ordered the riflemen to fire.

The volley was followed by cries and confusion. Running and galloping bands proved that the volley had not been in vain. One or two *tüfekchi*s returned the fire, but nobody was hit. They went on with their work but only at the foot of the wall and with great caution, keeping under cover.

11

The mill pounded away day and night. Twelve spokes broke up the saltpetre and charcoal efficiently and swiftly. The fresh gunpowder trickled black into the tub. The defenders recovered their confidence.

The Turks threw up a new earthwork, and at the crack of dawn three siege-guns thundered out by the provost's house. The new target was the north-western tower. Though it would have been difficult to start an attack from that direction, the aim might well have been to draw the defenders away from the other sides of the fortress.

The big black cannon-balls fell nearer to the tower. The infantry quarters lay in the line of fire, all the way along the wall overlooking the town. It was these that caught the cannon-balls that fell short.

The western side of the commander's palace began to crumble. Mrs. Balogh rushed in terror into the room where she had made Dobó's bed.

The commander was sitting by the bed in his armchair. He was in armour, as he usually was outside, but he was not wearing his helmet. He was sleeping peacefully with his hands on the arms of the chair. In front of him was a burning candle. Over his head was a faded oil-painting of St. Stephen offering the crown to the Virgin Mary. Some good Catholic had rescued it from the church when it was transformed into a bastion and hung it there, though it was now so faded that the eyes of the figures appeared like brown spots.

That was where Dobó usually slept.

That day he had only returned home towards dawn. Perhaps he was expecting a sudden attack in the early hours, and that was why he had not undressed.

They were firing at the side where he slept. The cannon-balls were shaking the house so that the beams creaked. In one wall of the room was a crack almost four inches wide, giving a glimpse of the palisade through it.

"Commander!" shrieked Mrs. Balogh. A new shot brought plaster down on the lady's head. She ran to the commander and shook him.

"What's the matter now?" Dobó looked up.

"They're shooting at the palace! Get up, for heaven's sake!"

Dobó looked around. He saw the crack. He got up.

"In that case we'll get my bed taken down to one of the downstairs rooms near the door," he said. "I'll be back immediately."

"I'll be back immediately" was a saying of Dobó's that never came to pass. So even in this time of peril Mrs. Balogh had to smile.

"At least wait while I mull a little wine."

"That'll be nice. Thank you," replied Dobó, beating the plaster-dust out of his hair. "My stomach's empty. I'd like a few cloves in it too."

"Where shall I send it?"

"I'll look in and get it."

"No, you won't, commander. I'll send my son with it."

There was always a horse at the door saddled and bridled, and either one or other of the two pages on his own small horse. Dobó mounted and set off to inspect the fortress.

Some of the soldiers were pouring out of the little barrack-rooms undressed, carrying their weapons and outer clothing over their shoulders or under their arms. Some even had their trousers round their necks. They were cursing.

"Go to the monastery," said Dobó. "They're not firing at that. Take your palliasses there too. There's room in the corridors."

Mekcsey hurried across the square with another detachment. The men were carrying spades, hoes and axes. Mekcsey was carrying a big flintlock rifle in his hand.

As he caught sight of Dobó, he raised his rifle and beckoned to him. Dobó sped over to him on his horse.

"They're digging a mine from the King's Seat," reported Mekcsey. "We're going to counter them."

"Good," said Dobó approvingly. "Just take them out to work then. Let them dig. Then come and see me immediately."

He hurried off to the Bolyky Bastion. In front of the stables at the foot of it sat five men with helmets on their heads. Their faces were red in the firelight. They were making small rings of straw. Pitch was simmering in pots beside them.

Under the bastion he watched Gergely as he bent over the drum. He looked at the peas. Seeing Dobó, he rose.

"The Turks have started mining. We've already got wind of one today. Mekcsey himself has gone to deal with them."

"Yes, I know," replied Dobó.

"All the drums have gone soft and aren't any use, but the quivering of the water gives them away."

Dobó went and stood by the palisade and peered out through a hole. The rampart built by the Turks was about six feet high at the breaches. The dervishes happened to be carrying a dead akindji away from the brushwood on two pikes. He had fallen during the previous night's firing.

Opposite the walls trenches and plank-fences could be seen in all directions. The Turks too were taking cover.

"They're up to something again," Dobó shook his head. "There's no sign of the yasavuls and janissaries anywhere."

It was then that Mekcsey arrived on the bastion.

"They're mining," he reported briefly.

His face betrayed that he had not slept a wink during that night. His eyes were red and colourless. His hair was tousled. His jacket had shoulders stained with lime and mud. Presumably he had been helping the masons to raise the beams.

"Fellow-commander," said Dobó in a peremptory tone. "Go and get some sleep this instant."

It was then that the page Balázs got to the top of the steps. In his hand was a silver tray, and on that a silver goblet. The goblet was steaming white in the cold air of dawn.

Mekcsey saluted and set off down the steps.

Dobó called after him in a voice now mild and gentle, "Pista!"

Mekcsey turned round.

"Take that goblet from Balázs and drink it up, my dear chap."

12

The next night they discovered what the janissaries had been up to that day. They had been constructing canopies rather like those beneath which priests carry the sacrament in processions

489

—except that the top was of strong wooden planking and the four poles supporting it were pikes.

From that day onwards they would transport the earth and brush-wood under such mobile shelters.

The Hungarians of those days called them "objects".

That afternoon the chief officers had a good sleep. They mostly slept in the afternoons, because attacks were to be feared only in the mornings, and it was then that the Turks' intentions for the day came to be known. They were up and about again at night, which was when half the men went to bed. Dobó agreed with Mekcsey that they would not share a regular time for sleep, but when one of them had managed to rest for a time the other would immediately retire to do the same. In practice neither of them really slept. Only here and there in corners of the bastions and on earthworks they managed to scrape an hour or so of sleep as they were sitting there; sometimes in the afternoon they slept for two whole hours. Dobó's eyes looked as if they had been circled with red lace.

The riflemen were furious at the multitude of "objects" that hid the Turks. They had collected whatever wood remained in the ceilings of the houses in the town, in the fences and pigsties. They realized that the only way to succeed was to erect a wall themselves.

At the Sándor Bastion they had now raised the rampart so high that it was level with the breach; in other words it had reached the bottom of the hole made by the cannon-balls in the fortress wall.

The objects covered the Turks and the twigs covered the heads of those who were raising the earthwork. There were always twenty riflemen on watch around the breach, together with a mortar ready loaded. There were also weapons on the wall. But it was no use: the darkness also served to hide the Turks as they worked by night.

Gergely himself was on constant watch beside the largest breach.

All of a sudden some twenty Turks appeared, moving forwards. Each carried a bundle of vines on his head. Of course they were merely shadows in the darkness of the night.

Gergely called down from the wall, "Gasparics!"

"Sir!" answered a man's voice.

"Are you itching to have a go at them?"

"Of course we are, sir! Let's knock them for six, sir!"

"Go on then! Only be careful! Jump back as soon as you've landed your blow."

"I understand, sir."

The masons were working on the breach, but the gap there was still big enough for a cart to go through it.

At Gergely's orders Gasparics leapt out, stabbed in the breast a janissary bristling with *yataghan*s and jumped back again. The Turk fell. The rest went on with their work.

Seeing Gasparics's heroic deed, three men leapt into the breach and each killed a Turk with his lance before springing back again. The Turks cursed and stumbled in confusion. But the rest were pushing forward from below.

Now ten men sprang out into the gap, some with swords, others with lances. They stab and chop at the wood-carriers. Then they turn round and leap back one by one into the breach. The Turks scatter the twigs, and thirty of them go for the three who are left behind.

Gergely orders his men to fire from the wall. The Turks fall head over heels on each other. But Corporal Kálmán returns with a great lance-wound in his breast.

"You down there, fire as well!" Gergely shouts down.

And now death flashes out on the rest of the Turks from the lowest loopholes. By the light of the flash about forty Turks are seen lying bleeding in front of the breach. The other Turks rush the breach in a single detachment with lances and swords.

"Fire!" shouts Gergely to the men up above on the wall. At that moment Dobó arrives.

Kálmán lies in front of the breach, sprawling in his own blood. A janissary pokes his lance through the gap and, finding nobody there, leaps through it with a yell.

Dobó happens to be standing beside the breach. He hits him with his naked fist, striking his nose so hard that blood spatters out of it. At the same moment Gasparics thrusts his lance into him.

The other Turks dare not follow him. They turn their backs and leap in all directions on the pile of brushwood.

491

"Throw the cur outside!" Dobó tells the masons. And he goes up on to the wall.

"The Turks have given up mining," he says to Gergely.

"I thought so," replies Gergely.

"Have you anything to report?"

"Come and look at our pots."

In the lower vault of the bastion five soldiers are at work by the light of an oil lamp suspended there; the gypsy is also with them. Several hundred earthenware pots are lying there, and they are filling them.

One puts gunpowder in them, just a handful. The second man stuffs rags and stones on top of that. The third again puts a handful of gunpowder into the pot. The fourth sits beside a pile of rusty and broken rifle-barrels chopped into small pieces and fills them with gunpowder. He plugs them on both sides with wood. The fifth man secures the two plugs to the barrel with wire. The gypsy coats them with mud.

"We've already got three hundred pots in store," reports Gergely.

"Put some sulphur in as well," says Dobó, "good big pieces of it."

"That's a good idea," agrees Gergely.

Balázs the page ran off for the sulphur.

For a short time Dobó watched this operation with a smile of satisfaction, then he looked around.

"Is Gasparics here?"

"Yes, sir," replied the soldier from down below.

"Come up here."

The man jumped up and clicked his heels in front of Dobó.

"Were you the first to jump into the breach?"

"Yes, I was, sir."

"From today you're promoted to corporal."

*

Next day the defenders can see what good defence the objects provided that first night: from Provost Hecey's house a great earth rampart extends as far as the south-west wall of the fortress, where the modern gate now stands.

By the wall a pile of barrels begins to rise quickly from the moat, with thousands and thousands of hands carrying and piling the empty barrels.

The Turks had broken open the wine-cellars in the town. They had let the wine out of the barrels and carried them and the vats for pressing the grapes under the fortress.

So on that side a huge wall of barrels is being constructed. The barrels are passed from hand to hand and stood on end. The hill of barrels is completed that same day. It leans up against the fortress wall. On the far side steps are made of sacks filled with earth.

The defenders fire rifle-shots at them from dawn till dusk, but the barrels shield the Turks. They work hard. And the bangs and thuds of all those barrels and vats go on well into the night.

The majority of the riflemen are now concentrated on that side. The mortars too squat on the wall there. A few falconets are aimed at the pile of barrels from the side.

"The Turks are mad," says Fügedy.

But they are not mad. For very early in the morning while it is still dark one or two very wide objects move forward at the bottom of the pile of barrels. They are held up by eight pikes, and have room enough under them for twenty or thirty Turks.

"Fire and water!" orders Dobó. "Bring straw, grappling-irons, hooks and clamps, lots of them!"

For he saw not only the movement of the objects, but also torches being lit in the moat down below by the Turks.

Yesterday the Bebek Bastion had been shelled too, and there too they had made steps out of sacks filled with earth. Dobó surveys the scene there also.

He finds Gergely ready with all kinds of grappling-irons and hooks on chains. A fire is burning on the bastion. Next to it fat is melting in cauldrons. The pitch-dipped straw rings glimmer black in their neat piles around the fire. There too the Turks are setting out to attack the fortress under the protection of large objects.

Mekcsey is at the Old Gate, supervising the filling of breaches. The Turks will attack there too. But the greatest threat is still on the south-west corner where the barrels are piled. That is where Fügedy is standing.

Dobó puts on his steel helmet and gallops there accompanied

by the page Balázs. By now the palisade is burning in a mass of flames. Somehow the Turks have set it alight.

Now the Turks do not yell. Huddled under the objects they fire cautiously at the defenders.

From above it is impossible to fire on them. They shoot at them from the bottom of the burning palisade, and with axes cut holes between the stones through which they can fire under the objects.

"Throw straw on them!" shouts Dobó.

On one side water splashes on to the palisade burning up above, while on the other burning rings of straw dipped in oil and fat fly over the objects.

Any object that reaches the wall they upturn with their hooks or push it aside. Any one whose roof has caught fire they leave to its own devices. One after another the Turks throw away their burning shelter and escape with shouts from the hail of fire.

The barrels wobble beneath them. One man in a red jacket carries a flaming straw ring on his back. The defenders roar with laughter.

"Straw, that's all you want, straw!" shouts Dobó.

Once again oil-dipped straw rings fly down in flaming wisps on to the roofs of the objects. The pike-bearers throw aside their weapons and run helter-skelter downwards out of the hail of bullets.

"Have a good trip!" yell the defenders.

But this was only a short pause. When they had beaten back the first attackers, the Turkish cannon began to rip up the palisade.

Dobó made the men lie prone to protect them from the missiles. The Turkish guns succeeded in shooting away two of the supports of the palisade. The palisade swayed and a length of some 250 feet keeled over outwards with cracks and creaks. It only needed one more support to break and the whole length would fall down completely.

"Bring hooks!" shouts Fügedy. "And chains! And ropes!"

Fifty hooks grip the outward-leaning palisade. Iron chains and ropes, new piles and cross-pieces are produced, and the palisade soon stands again where it had done before.

By that time Dobó was in the vicinity of the Bolyky Tower,

where Gergely was bearing the brunt of an attack with the stench of pitch, gunpowder and burning fat all round him. The Turks had high hopes with that corner tower which was shattered in the middle. Temesvár too had fallen into Turkish hands by means of one single tower, so they regarded this as a lucky corner, although in the first attack they had not succeeded in gaining a foothold there.

Now that they had brought nothing but earth to pile against the wall, the defenders could not do them any harm from within.

"Here they come! They're coming!" shout the defenders excitedly.

The Turks swarm hard on each other's heels upwards under the broad objects. A rain of burning straw-rings dipped in pitch and tallow drenches them, but somehow they manage to make their way up to the tower.

"Allah akbar!"

"Strike them! Hit them!"

And on the flank of the King's Seat thousands and thousands of Turks assemble to climb the wall. At the foot of the tower along the wall grappling-irons and pikes reach down. They push, drag, chop and scar the objects.

But the Turks get to work too. The tüfekchis snipe from below the objects. Lances and grenades and arrows fly at the defenders from down below. One armoured spahi defies death to leap on to the wall; whirling his two iron-clad hands he smashes the hooks and pikes. A second, then a third follows in his wake.

While these three are beaten down with axes and maces, the rest clamber forward over them.

"Allah! Aferin!"

Within a minute they have pushed a cowhide-covered object to the top of the tower; beneath it thirty or forty janissaries kneeling and lying prone fire on the soldiers fighting on the bastion.

"Allah! Allah!" yell a thousand Turkish voices down below to encourage them.

"Victory's in our grasp!" roar the yasavuls.

Dobó's helmet falls from his head. He dashes to the cannon barcheaded.

The Hungarian soldiers stationed inside the tower still cannot attack the throng of janissaries swarming above them, because the top of the tower is floored with planks, and these cannot be tipped down because of the janissaries treading on them up there.

"Come on out!" shouts Gergely as he sees Dobó re-positioning the guns. And taking no heed of the janissaries' rifles, he seizes an axe. He hooks it round one of the pikes holding up the object and pulls it away.

The defenders standing on the bastion are astounded to see the occupation of the tower. They all reach for the fireballs and rings and cover the janissaries making their way up the wall in flame. Dobó sees a gap in the line of janissaries.

"Down with the gun! Fire at them!"

The gun turns down. Flame and thunder envelop the throng of janissaries on the earth-rampart.

Janissaries are not really scared of guns. Two cannon-balls from two guns do little damage. They are already well used to explosions. But Dobó's guns are loaded with shrapnel. Tens of Turks fall in its wake. The janissaries start back in horror.

"Fire on them! Fire!" Gergely's voice is heard from above. And the rings of pitch fly upwards on the janissaries caught on the roof of the tower. The Turks dodge right and left, but they have fired their rifles and have no time to reload. The fire and flames grow more intense. They hurl themselves off the tower with yells. And those who fell outside had the better fate. They broke their necks with a single crack. But those who leapt down inside the fortress had not long to dance; they were beaten to death with such fury that not a bone in their bodies remained intact.

*

That evening and night the Turks continued the battle at the Earth Bastion.

The Earth Bastion is an extension of the stone bastion on the north-west corner of the fortress. They had probed the earth there all over the place to try to make a hole under the bastion, but the wall of the fortress was not founded on earth there on the hill. Wall stands on wall to a depth of 120 feet, as if in times unknown the fortress had been built up from the valley and the people of the next period had filled the old one with earth and constructed its own fortress on top of it, until in the end King and Saint Stephen's people had arrived and raised the great fortress walls of today on these earlier foundations.

Dobó quickly realized that the Turks were creating a noisy night-attack to draw attention away from the building of the wood and earth rampart. He despatched a lieutenant and two hundred men to the Earth Bastion and left the normal numbers of troops in their positions elsewhere. There was no sign of Turkish cavalry either at the mound of barrels or during the attack on the tower. It was to be presumed that they would continue carrying wood at night. Now instead of twigs they were carrying thick pieces of wood. All the camels, horses, buffaloes, oxen and mules available in the camp returned by dusk beneath the walls, loaded with logs and planks. An endless procession of carts and waggons creaked under their load of wood from Almagyar and Eged.

At first they simply threw the wood at random out of the earthen ramparts opposite the walls; then when the pile of wood was high enough to protect them, they began to tidy it up. Thousands of hands moved and threw the logs and planks into place. The quiet work of the previous nights gave place to thuds and bangs on all sides.

The wood was fastened with iron clamps and chains.

It was in front of Gergely's bastion that a huge wooden bastion was constructed; the top of it was hardly eighteen feet away.

The Turks went cleverly to work. They piled up the wood so that it always sheltered them, and from behind the six-foot high cover they threw the thick logs into the empty ground too. The space there visibly filled up and the pile of wood grew beside the stone wall. And it grew ever closer to the fortress wall. It was obvious that if they could add much more to its height it would fall of its own weight on to the wall.

Gergely kept looking through one loophole after another to examine the enemy's work. Last of all he went up to the palisade. There he found Dobó with Balázs the clerk. The commander was standing there in his usual knee-length coat and a light-black steel helmet on his head. He was listening with half an ear to some complaint made by the clerk.

"Sir," said Gergely, "may I have those piles of wooden slates that we had taken off the roofs?"

"Yes. Have them taken away."

"And then I'd like tallow, pitch and oil."

"Order as much as you need. How much tallow have we got, Balázs?"

"About ten hundredweight."

"I'd like all of it," said Gergely. "If only there were more! But perhaps we can make up for it with bacon. So I'd like bacon too, and lots of it."

"Bacon?"

"As much as you can let me have."

Dobó spoke over his shoulder to Kristóf. "Go and wake up Sukán. Tell him to release tallow and forty sides of bacon from the stores. They're to be brought here at once." And only afterwards did he ask what they were for.

Well, Gergely's plan was to drop bacon, tallow and wooden shingles between the logs and twigs while the Turks were throwing the wood on to the pile there. The Turks took no notice of him. They were always throwing things at them from the fortress —stones, pots, cracked pots, dead cats and things of that sort flew down among them every minute. The two or three-inch chunks of bacon were not obvious among all the other things. If anyone happened to notice them, either he did not recognize them or if he did, he looked at them with disgust.

Gergely had all the bacon cut into strips and thrown down from time to time into the wood. And meanwhile there was a rain of shingles painted with oil, tallow, straw, with a few earthenware pots from time to time; these were wrapped up in straw, sealed up with mud and twisted around with wire. Inside them were gunpowder, loaded bits of rifle-barrel and inch-long bits of sulphur.

Dobó examined the scene below.

"It will be morning," he said, "before they've finished. Kristóf, go and see whether Mekcsey's awake. If he is, tell him I'm going to lie down. If he isn't, let him go on sleeping. Then go round the sentries. Tell them that as soon as they see any signs of an attack beginning, they're to come and report at the corner tower. Aren't you going to get some sleep, Gergely?"

Gergely shook his head. "I'll wait till morning."

"And Zoltay?"

"I sent him off to bed, so that there should be somebody with a bit of strength on the bastion in the morning."

"Wake me up as soon as the wooden bastion is complete."

He went up the corner tower and lay down on a military mattress. The page Kristóf stood with drawn sword in front of the door of the tower.

This was his duty as a page. He guarded the sleeping lion.

13

By dawn the Turks' wooden bastion was almost as high as the wall of the fortress. The difference between them was only about nine feet.

Gergely had another two big pieces of gun-barrel packed with explosives. They were plugged firmly with wood.

"Eh, but this gun 'ere never thought it'd fire agin!" said the gypsy.

"A new gun from an old one," said one of the soldiers.

"Well, if it's a new one, let's give it a name," said the gypsy. "One can be *Rajkó*, the other *Dove*."

For every cannon had its own name.

Gergely took a lead bullet out of his pocket and wrote on the smaller piece: *János*, and on the larger one: *Eva*. He picked up both bits of cannon under his arm and climbed up to the bastion.

Dawn swiftly spread light in the sky. Down below the camp was stirring; the clatter of troops approaching was heard on all sides. A soldier ran up to Gergely. "They're coming, captain!"

"So I see, my lad. Run to the commander in the corner tower and tell his page to wake him."

His men were ready with pikes and grappling irons on the wall. The riflemen grasped newly-loaded rifles on the stones that were white with frost. The three cannon in the bastion were trained downwards and the two in the Dark Gate upwards on the walls.

"Light the straw rings and the burning clubs and throw them down!" ordered Gergely.

The men got to work immediately.

By the time Ḍobó arrived the Turks were swarming over the hills like ants. They were still piling up wood and hammering it. It was as high now as the inner bastion. From time to time they pushed some of the logs across to fill up the space between the two walls. There was an enormous amount of wood there. A whole forest of it. And the wooden fortification was strong. On top of it swayed objects carefully covered with damp cowhide.

The straw rings make no impression on the wet cowhide, and those that fall elsewhere are kicked aside by the Turks.

At the sound of a shrill whistle thousands of them yell *"Bismillah!"* and the air quivers. The Turkish bands strike up noisily. And the gigantic wooden structure thunders to the clatter of feet rushing up it.

"Allah! Allah!"

"Jesus! Mary!"

From under the objects short siege-ladders are quickly pushed out to span the gap between the wooden and stone bastions. But by now the defenders are up there too. All of a sudden hundreds of blazing straw rings fly down on the Turks. Burning bundles of straw and sulphur envelop the ladders and on top of them fall pitch-dipped shingles.

The first group of Turks trying to burst through the blazing fires runs into the points of hooks and pikes. The rest are received with sword, axe, burning clubs and flailing maces. One full-faced Turk in a green turban raises high some huge horse-tail standards as he suddenly appears on the pile of wood some eighteen feet from Gergely. As he roars "Allah!" his head seems to change into a huge mouth, and Gergely picks up the smaller piece of cannon and hurls it into his face. The larger piece of cannon he throws into the fire raging down below.

"Allah! Allah! *Bismillah! Ileri!"*

And the Turks throng together in the huge wooden edifice like ants whose nest has been disturbed. They would certainly have charged through the blazing fire too, had they not suddenly been taken aback by rifles and guns exploding from down below as well. The earthenware pots began to crack and hurl burning sulphur all around. It was like a hill spouting flame that opened up beneath them.

"*Ya kerim! Ya rahim! Meded! Ey va! Yetishin!*" they shout in confusion. And they leap in all directions.

But the *yasavuls* will not let them come down.

"We're winning! This is the hour of triumph!" they shout in reply. And they send those at the bottom for water.

"Water! Water! Buckets!" And they try to save the huge wooden structure that had taken days and nights to build with water, weapons and clothing. But by now the tallow and bacon had begun to melt among the logs. The pots were exploding all the more rapidly and shooting sulphur everywhere, setting light to the big logs.

"*Ya kerim! Ya rahim!* Through the flames and into the fortress!" They could not believe that those great pieces of wood would catch light everywhere.

Now water is rushed to the place in leather buckets, pots and all kinds of vessels on poles. They dash with it wherever the fire spurts up like a horse-tail from the pile of wood. They douse it furiously, leaping about in terror.

"*Bre, bre! Ya hu!*" they keep shouting to the water-carriers. But by now the structure had become an immense pyre. Only now do the rifle-barrels begin to burst. The fat, with its spitting blue flame, spurts into the eyes of the fire-fighters. With an enormous explosion the two pieces of cannon fired in succession, scattering wood and Turks as they did so.

Hellish terror, fury and yelling! With renewed efforts the janissaries who are unable to retreat because of the explosions and fire behind them press forward through the sea of smoke and islands of flame over the bridge of siege-ladders. One or two of them leap desperately and cling to the wall, only to fall down at the same moment with bleeding heads. The rest dance with fury on top of the pyre and keep hitting the ends of the blazing logs with their weapons. But their labour is in vain. It is a tempest of flame, beginning by the wall; and the roar of the tempest inside it comes from all the explosions. The Turks are fiendish shadows leaping in all directions in the flames. Their clothes are ablaze, so are their beards, and their turbans are on fire too. Through the horrors of hell they go wailing to the paradise of Mohammed.

Even on the walls of the fortress the heat is so great that the guns have to be withdrawn and the men have to drench the siege-positions to prevent the wood inside them from catching fire.

And in the infernal heat the doomed Turkish wounded scream, while the wrathful shouts of the *yasavul*s can be heard over the flames, and jets of steam can be seen spurting up as the fire-fighters make their last efforts to extinguish the flames.

The two armies are separated by a sea of flame and smoke that reaches the sky.

14

"If we can't get anywhere with wood, we'll certainly do so with earth," thought the Turks.

They trained cannon on the outer fortress, which was most under threat from the moving of earth, and kept up their fire by day, while at night they had twigs and earth brought up. They also kept these damp.

Gergely watched anxiously as the new road towards the bastion, one that could not be fired, grew day by day. That was the way to be used by hundreds, thousands, indeed the whole army. He walked up and down in the fortress, lost in thought. He gazed and peered from every pile of ruins, stones, from stables, pits and heaps of cannon-balls. And he kept scratching and shaking his head.

He also took a turn among the ruins of the sacristy. In the end he stopped by the corner where the mechanics were. There in front of the countless Hungarian and Turkish weapons thrown into a pile was the black outline of a great wooden wheel. Gergely recognized it as the wheel of one of the wrecked powder-mills.

The gypsy was sitting on the wheel, spooning stewed meat from a big earthenware bowl with a hearty appetite. He was fearfully and wonderfully armed. On his feet were red leather janissaries' boots. In his belt shone *yataghan*s. On his head there was a bronze helmet with holes in it that must also have belonged to a Turk.

502

The gypsy now regarded himself as a soldier, so he got up. He grasped the dish under his left arm and saluted with his right. Then he sat down again and continued his meal.

"Just get up a minute, old chap," said Gergely. "Let me have a look at that wheel."

The gypsy stood to one side. The wheel was certainly smashed. Gergely stood on it and tested the spokes one by one. Only one creaked out of its place.

"Hm," he said, putting a finger to his chin.

The gypsy spoke up. "Are we goin' to grind Turks, Mister Captain, sir?"

"Yes," said Gergely. "Nail the loose bits up firmly and do it quickly."

The mechanics put down their plates and picked up hammers.

Gergely asked where Dobó was. Where had he been seen?

"He's been this way today at least ten times," replied one of the mechanics, "but we haven't seen him for half an hour now."

Gergely went off to find him. But on the way he kept looking at everything lying around on the ground in all directions. He went towards the Earth Bastion. As he was making his way there uncertainly, he caught sight of a pair of female eyes in the open window of the palace. Those eyes were gazing at him out of the darkness of the room.

He was astounded. He stopped. He blinked in an effort to see more clearly. But the woman's eyes had disappeared.

Gergely stared rigidly at the window-opening. Some peculiar warm emotion ran right through him when he caught sight of those two eyes, and he was unable to move for a minute.

"Oh, what nonsense!" he muttered, shaking his head. "How could I imagine such a thing?" But all the same he looked up again. By then he saw the face of the little Turkish boy in the window.

Dobó came from the Earth Bastion. Gergely hurried to meet him. "I'd like that mill-wheel, sir." And he raised his hand to his helmet.

"Take it," replied Dobó shortly, and went into the palace.

Gergely hurried off past the kitchens where a long line of soldiers was sitting on the ground in a strong smell of vinegar. They were lunching on lentil soup. There was plenty of meat,

503

but as for wine, it was watered. Dobó would not allow anything else.

He called out ten of them, and had the wheel rolled to his own bastion.

*

There were plenty of rusty and damaged rifle-barrels in the fortress. Once again he had them filled. He had them bound with wire to the wheel so that the mouths pointed outwards. The spaces between the barrels he had filled with shavings, sulphur, tallow and pitch. He had the two sides of the wheel boarded in with planking. Finally he had a wide wooden track of planks fitted to the rim of the wheel so that it would not tip over.

The defenders all looked at the fearsome machine with amazement. Dobó himself examined it more than once. He gave Gergely a mortar to site in the middle of it.

"Fix this, Gergely, so that it is the last to detonate."

"I will, commander."

"Do you need anything else, Gergely, my lad?"

"Well, if possible, I'd like the empty barrels."

"From the cellar?"

"Yes."

"There are plenty of them. Just have them brought out."

Down below the hill grew and grew. Inside the fortress the barrels filled with shavings, sulphur, tallow and pitch multiplied. They were as cunning in the filling of these as they had been with the wheel. They even put stones in them below, above and at the sides. They sealed them in firmly, just leaving a hole for the fuse to enter.

Dobó had a large number—three hundred—of so-called "bearded guns". These were really large rifles whose barrel rested on the wall, taking bullets no larger than a walnut. The "beard" was an iron projection pointing downwards from the mouth of the barrel. Its purpose was to hold the gun in place as it recoiled after firing. Dobó also let them have some of the old rusty "bearded guns" for the larger barrels.

They filled some fifty barrels like this. They put good hoops on them and bound them with wire too—after all, iron hoops were unknown in those days. They wired them and nailed them up. They smiled on them as a mother does on her baby.

Meanwhile the Turks were busy building, each night piling up the earthwork towards the wall to make a good route for the troops to march along.

15

One morning Gergely was asleep among his men when all of a sudden a report came to Zoltay that in the bottom corner of the stables the water was quivering and the peas rattling. So the wicked Turks were not only building an earthwork, but also mining!

Zoltay would not let them wake Gergely. He sent for Mekcsey, who quickly arrived on the spot.

He had the dish and the drum moved from place to place until he finally found the spot to begin digging. Ten men got to work. From time to time they paused and set down the dish to watch it. Round about noon Gergely woke up too and immediately made for the dig.

A stifling smell of dung. The men were already working eighteen feet down. The dull thuds of the *lagumdji*s announced their approach.

"Oho, commander!" he said to Mekcsey. "This is my bastion! You don't give orders here."

"You mean I've not done things properly?"

"We'll give up digging."

"So that they'll take the wall?"

"So that they won't get any hint of the work we're doing."

Only then did Mekcsey realize the sense of this. "Right then; you give the orders."

Gergely had a large musket brought along. He himself loaded it with gunpowder and primed it. He called over ten riflemen, and had the lamps extinguished. They remained in darkness.

The rumbling grew louder. Sometimes the voice of the officer leading them could be heard.

From time to time Gergely put his hand to the wall. He felt where the earth was trembling most obviously.

"Psst!" he said quietly to the men. "They'll break through any minute now." And his eyes gleamed.

At that moment one of the axes broke through and the earth rolled down at Gergely's feet. A man-sized hole opened up. The *lagumdji* stopped and sniffed the air. He could not see anything in the darkness. As he turned round, on the other side of the hole two lamps appeared, with a white-turbaned, gold-braided pot-bellied aga standing between them.

The *lagumdji* called out that he had reached a hole. The aga turned towards it. Gergely took aim. His musket flared and detonated. The aga grabbed at his stomach and collapsed. Gergely leapt back: "Fire!"

The ten men aimed their rifles into the hole. Bang! Bang! They fired at the *lagumdji*s as they fled helter-skelter.

The men returned with thirty axes and the dead body of the aga. But one stayed there with arms at the ready and a lamp in front of him to illuminate the mouth of the tunnel.

*

The aga was laid out in the square of the fortress. They did not make a good job of this; his head bumped on the cobbles and his turban rolled off when they put him down. But that did not worry him now.

He was a fat man with a grey beard. Three long scars on his bald head proved that he had worked hard for his rank. Gergely's shot and charge had landed in his stomach. A smaller bullet had caught him in the breast, presumably when the men fired.

Sukán the steward ordered a thorough search of his turban, belt and pocket. He noted down the amounts of money, rings and arms found on him. These would go to the men who had been engaged on digging. Then he left the body to the curiosity of the onlookers. And it was the women, of course, who first surrounded it.

"Do they go around in red slippers like these?"

"They tie the bottoms of those baggy trousers with laces."

"He must have been a rich man."

"A lieutenant or a captain."

"I wonder if he had a wife?"

"Oh, maybe ten of them."

"He wasn't at all a bad-looking man," said Mrs. Bódy, the wife of the Maklár miller, pityingly. "It's a pity he was a Turk." Zoltay also went and had a look at him. "This one aga at any rate got into the fortress!"

All of a sudden the little Turkish boy slipped through the women's skirts and bent down over the dead man with a cry of delight: *"Baba! Babadjizim! Baba! Babatatli babadjizi!"* (Father! Daddy! Father! Dear daddy!)

And he bent over his chest, embracing and kissing him. He put his face against the man's. He shook him and laughed at him. *"Baba! Babadjizim!"*

The women's eyes filled with tears. Mrs. Balogh took the boy by the hand. "Come along, Selim. Father's asleep."

16

When once again the enormous Turkish army sets out along the valley at dawn to attack the fortress, the men watch them moving along with the furious joy of the well-prepared. The thrill of revenge tightens their muscles like a spring that has been wound up. There is no holding them back now. A stocky little man jumps through the breach on to the earthwork, facing the Turks as they swarm along yelling, and threatens them with his sword. Naturally the soldiers on the wall roar with laughter.

"Who's that?" asks Zoltay, also laughing.

"Little Varga," they say. "János Varga."

The man jumps back again, but seeing all the laughter leaps out into the breach for a second time and threatens the huge Turkish army. By now the *tüfekchis* are firing at him, and he jumps back from the rifle-fire more quickly than he did before. At this the laughter increases.

Dobó sees this too and gives him an approving nod.

János Varga, seeing Dobó's glance of approval, jumps out a third time and taking no account of the bullets boldly threatens the vengeful Turks as they come up towards him.

"You'll all die here, you dogs, every one of you! Just keep coming!"

Bullets, grenades and javelins fly towards him. Not one of

507

them hits him. He jumps around mockingly, sticking his tongue out at them. Indeed he even makes a quick turn and gives himself a very unseemly, but in the circumstances appropriate, slap. Then once more he darts in through the breach. And all this under the Turks' noses! In front of a hundred thousand armed Turks!

"You're a man, Varga!" Dobó shouts down to him. "You deserve a reward!" And seeing that everything is under control, he hurries to his horse and gallops to the Old Gate. For the Turks are concentrating their forces on the east and south sides of the fortress, and directing the main thrust of their attack on two points.

Gergely stands on his bastion fully armoured. There is still protection there from the wickerwork palisade. Behind him are the barrels and the giant wheel. He stands calmly like a rock on the shore of an angry sea.

Down below the Turks are swarming to attack. They fire all their siege-guns at the fortress. An infernal tempest of yells breaks out: *Bismillah! Bismillah!*

For a few minutes the battle-cry drowns the braying and tinkling sounds of the military band. But then the band halts in a trench on the King's Seat and plays without interruption.

"And very soon you'll dance too!" shouts Zoltay.

The Turkish army teems below. The horse-tail banners with their crescents flutter. In front is the janissaries' banner of dull red. Further back is the green and white striped banner of the ulufedjis. The *spahi*s thunder out in iron armour, protected by shields that reach their knees.

"Allah! Allah!"

They have lances or pikes in their hands, and naked swords dangling from straps on their wrists. Another sword hangs from their waists. They set off at a run from the trenches and make for the bastion in a great mass.

"Allah akbar! La illah! il Allah! Ya fettah!"

In reply a black barrel crashes down and rolls into them, spouting flame and leaping about. A spahi thrusts his pike into the ground to stop it, and a second and third do the same.

"Allah! Allah!"

The fourth *spahi* catches hold of it to throw it down into the

508

moat. At that moment the barrel explodes and scatters the vanguard in bursts of flame.

"Allah Akbar!"

By the time they can look up again, the second barrel is on them, spitting flame and shooting it in all directions. It comes to a halt among the men in armour and scatters them.

"Allah! Allah!"

But they cannot turn back. They are pressed forward by thousand upon thousand of troops advancing from below. All that can be seen is a lot of leaping and cowering against the wall, together with the sudden flinching of those further back and flames leaping up sixty feet in the air. Those with shields squat down in sheer terror at the force of the fire.

"Forward, pagans, forward! On through the fire!" And the densely-packed troop of *spahis* swarms upwards. But the fiery barrels roll down in succession too.

"*Ileri! Ileri! Allah! Allah!*"

And the flood of Turks advances into the jaws of hell. But now the palisade on the bastions parts and a gigantic smoking wooden wheel appears high up above. The centre of the wheel emits smoke and crackling sounds. It comes over the edge and crashes down from the stone wall, then rolls towards the massed ranks of the Turkish troops.

"*Ileri! Ileri!*" (Forward!) cry the agas and yasavuls on all sides. But their words are contradicted by the appearance of the wheel to the bold troops in front.

It has hardly reached them when the first flash explodes from it and with it a jet of fire shoots three hundred feet into the air; every particle of it goes on burning with a blue flame, falling on live and dead alike.

"*Gözünü ach! Sakin!*" (Look out! Beware!)

The vanguard of the Turkish forces hurl themselves to the ground in terror to let the infernal wheel roll down over their backs. But it changes into a wheel of sparks and fire among them. It shoots out flames, spits burning oil and scatters violet-coloured tulips of fire on the cropped heads and battle array. Sizzling, crackling, exploding and banging, it leaps on its way over them. From its spokes in snaking coils it scatters, spatters and fires red, blue and yellow stars.

509

"Meded! Allah!"

Even the bravest of the troops recoil in horror to escape on top of each other from this infernal and perilous wonder. And the wheel seems to have a mind and will of its own. It follows the fleeing men, sweeping them off their feet and spraying them with living fire, burning oil and sulphur. It causes their rifles to fire at each other. It fills their eyes, mouths, ears and necks with fire, so that even the dying turn head over heels to get away. And the wheel of fire goes rolling on. Long, fiery thunderbolts fly out of it, striking down the *yasavul*s and their horses too. The long flames burn to the bone and the smoke is stifling. The explosions are deafening. The troops it passes on its headlong way are clothed in flames. And all it leaves in its wake is hundreds of dead men burning and tortured by flames, and living men alight, leaping and twitching like madmen.

And now the wheel rumbles on enveloped in a cloud, ejecting thousand of flashes.

"Yetishin! Yetishin! Allah! Meded!...."

The fury of the *yasavul*s, the knotted whips and slaps in the face for fleeing men are now all in vain. There are no men left to storm the outer fortress. And on top of all this the Hungarians charge out through the breach; with the fury of lions and utterly mercilessly they beat, strike and slay any who lie in the path of the wheel or are rooted there by terror.

"Back! Back!" the bugle inside sounds the retreat.

Gergely can scarcely get his men to obey his command to return.

"Fetch barrels to the wall! Barrels!"

And they roll and set up the barrels. But even the remnant of the Turkish army disperses from there with a great clattering and rumbling. Only the guns remain along with the camels rearing with fear and the stunned bombardiers.

*

It was as well that Mekcsey abandoned the mine, because there were three places where they might have broken in underground at his own post, the Old Gate.

While the fiery wheel was at work on this side, at the Old Gate the struggle continued under the earth. There the wall was so

510

ruinous that the Turks kept poking in through the stones and the Hungarians outwards until Mekcsey dug beneath the ground opposite them and in three places chased them off in succession. In the end the Turks set fire to the gate and attempted to break in through it, but of course they found a thick strong wall behind it; this had been erected in advance by Mekcsey.

As soon as Gergely had seen his men charge out around his own bastion and the mad flight of the Turks, he had damp hides brought to cover the guns and boxes of gunpowder. He left ten men on guard and took the rest off to the Old Gate to help Mekcsey.

There was nothing there that needed his help. The terror in the Turkish army had spread to the area of that gate too. Of the brigades ordered there only the *tüfekchis* stood their ground. They were spread out around the gate, firing and reloading without a pause.

There were sentries standing under the palisade on top of the walls. Only at the base of the wall under the vaulting crouched a troop of men poking their weapons out through the gaps in the wall.

Gergely ran up to the top of the wall. Protected by his shield he looked down. He saw a band of Turks moving at the base of the wall in a place where they were safe from attack from above or from the side.

The Hungarians try to reach them through the gaps. But either they crouch where there are no holes or they bend down. Some have sacks, others stones. With these they try to fill up the holes to prevent the Hungarians firing at them. The defenders keep pushing them out again from inside, and they make thrusts at the Turks too. And when Hungarian lances peep out of the wall, the Turks seize them. Sometimes two or three of them cling to them. For a time they tug them to and fro, then jerk them free. The Hungarians curse.

"For heaven's sake!" Gergely shouts down to the men. "You've got a fire there! Hold the lance in it!"

The fire is burning beside the wall. Twenty men rush over to it and hold the tips of their lances in the embers till they glow red.

The Turks grin as they lie in wait for the next lances. Then all of a sudden twenty lances poke out of the wall. The Turks snatch at them. But their hands burn on them. Their angry curses are answered by the laughter of the Hungarian soldiers inside.

17

Wednesday, 12 October.

On this day the fortress is like a sieve. For thirty-two days it had been shelled in front, behind, on one side or the other. There were now so many Turkish cannon-balls in the fortress that the defenders were always stumbling over them. The peasants used birch-brooms to sweep the smaller ones out of the way in case they caused defenders to trip up during an attack. The large ones were carried off to the cannon and on to the walls.

Between the New Bastion and the Earth Bastion a V-shaped gap yawns in the wall. A large piece of the side of the Prison Bastion has collapsed into the depths. The Earth Bastion is as full of holes as a wasps' nest. Only two walls of the Bolyky Bastion remain standing. The corner tower is like a tree rotten from top to bottom. Only bits of the palisade remain in place. The buildings inside too are simply roofless walls caving inwards and outwards. In the palace only three rooms are still habitable, and even those let in the rain. And the square is spoilt, with deep trenches criss-crossing it. They are used when the Turks start firing; at other times they walk on the bridges and walk-ways across it.

And outside the angry wolves are baying.

Now work on patching the walls carries on by day too. The holes are filled with beams and planks—as far as possible. The stone merely acts as a support behind them.

At the Old Gate Mekcsey himself carries stones. He encourages the weary and calls on God to aid them. It is predictable that there will be a fierce attack there. The wall is examined by Dobó, then Gergely, then Mekcsey. All three of them realize that the corner tower no longer defends the gate, and what is needed there is grenades. So the wooden platforms are stocked with them. Experienced riflemen are posted at the breaches.

512

Gergely manufactures pitch-rings, fire-balls and bombs and has them rapidly taken to all parts.

Zoltay is busy building at the Sándor Bastion. Fügedy has the breaches in the New Bastion held together with chains.

Dobó dashes around on horseback. There is room left for horses all round the wall of the fortress beneath the wooden platforms. But all the same he frequently has to run the risk of flying bullets in the open. He supervises and gives orders to ensure that the work goes on at the same rate everywhere. The page Balázs follows him on the last little Turkish horse in order to carry his master's commands. The other seven horses have been shot away beneath the two pages.

On that day even Pető was on horseback. His leg was bandaged up to the knee. He was pale, but his moustache was twirled jauntily. Mekcsey was now replacing him at the Old Gate, so he took Mekcsey's place with the reserve troops.

He encourages his troops in a deep, resonant voice: "The Turks have been struggling hard here for thirty-two days! If only all the lot of them were here until we despatch the last one of them to hell! The royal army's delayed, but can't fail to arrive. All the world talks of our bravery. Even a hundred years from now 'Eger' will be synonymous with 'courage'."

Seeing the great crowd around the soldier-orator, Dobó stops there for a moment to listen to him. He gives a smile at that last sentence and says to Cecey, who has also stopped beside him, "A hundred years from now? What does the world care about us and the shape of our noses?"

He speaks to himself rather than to Cecey. And as if regretting speaking aloud, he shrugs his shoulders. "It's not the nose, but the spirit that's the main thing. And not the reward, but duty to the nation." And he gallops off to the Sándor Bastion.

The men take heart from the encouraging words. They would have stood their ground even without them, but fine words are like good wine.

Pető tilts his helmet to one side and goes on: "The king himself will come here too. He'll line up the heroes of Eger and shake hands with each of them. 'What's your name?' he'll say. 'My name's János Nagy, Your Majesty.' 'Mihály Szabó Nagy,

Your Majesty.' 'God bless you, my son.' That's what the king will say with joy and gladness. And you deserve that too. I've also heard that in future he'll choose his officers only from privates who've served here. Every private soldier will be a lieutenant after the siege, so I'm told. And they may be captains too! After all, as far as he's concerned the best soldiers are the ones who've proved themselves in battle."

He glances to one side and notices the gypsy who leaps like a goat into the air to escape a shot that lands in front of him.

"Well, gypsy, how many Turks have you killed?"

"Well, devil take 'em," replies the gypsy. "Not one of 'em dares to come where I'm standing, honourable Mister Soldier!"

*

As dusk falls a Turk with a white handkerchief appeared at one of the breaches. They recognized him: it was Miklós Vas.

They pulled him inside and took him off to Dobó. As they went, hundreds asked him, "What news?"

"The army's coming!" shouted Miklós in all directions. The glad news spread like wildfire through the fortress: "The royal army's on its way."

But Dobó had ordered Miklós Vas to say this when he arrived. So the army was on its way! And what Captain Pető had said was right after all!

Miklós Vas took off his turban in Dobó's presence and extricated the letter from its folds. He offered it to him.

Dobó examined the seal. It was from the bishop. He tore it open beside the seal and unfolded the letter with a steady hand. He was on his horse. The defenders crowded round him. While he was reading the letter the onlookers tried to guess its contents from his expression. But that face was like iron. It was as expressionless when he finished reading as it had been when he began. He folded up the letter and put it in his pocket, then glanced around as if surprised to see so many folk standing there.

Of the captains, only Pető was standing there. He spoke to him so that others might hear. "I'll call the captains together this evening. I have some good news for them."

514

He went into his room and shut the door behind him. He collapsed into the chair. His calm, rigid features relaxed into sadness. He gazed ahead bitterly and hopelessly.

*

Another letter arrived that day for Dobó. A peasant brought it to the fortress. As it lay white in his hand it could be seen that it was from the Turks.

That was the fourth letter from Ali Pasha.

The defenders knew by now that Dobó had a short way with postmen from the Turks, so let him receive him in the square. They took the man there.

The evenings were chilly, and the resting soldiers had lit a fire in the square. Some of them were roasting bacon and drinking a cup or two of watered wine with it.

"It'll be better for you if you burn it before the commander catches sight of it," said a soldier helpfully. "Or else you're in for it!"

"But how can I burn it?" replied the man. "It's not mine."

"But you're bringing it from the enemy."

"I'm bringing it from the one who sent it."

"They'll hang you."

"What? Me?"

"Yes, you. The commander even had one of our lieutenants hanged. And he was a gentleman, not a bulge-purse peasant like you."

The gallows still stood there in the square. The soldier pointed at it. "Over there, look. The gallows is still there."

The man blanched. Sweat broke out on his face. He scratched his head. He reached into his knapsack.

At that moment Dobó rode up. "What's all this?" he asked. "Who is this man? What does he want?"

The peasant pushed his knapsack under his cloak. "My name's István Kovács, sir," he replied, twisting his fur cap in confusion.

"What do you want?"

"Me? Nothing."

"Then what have you come here for?"

"Well... I just came in... I mean, I thought I'd come and see how you were doing in all this danger..."

"You've brought a letter!"

"Me? No, I've brought no letter. Not one."

At this Dobó's glance pierced him, and wiping his forehead he repeated, "So help me! I haven't brought one!"

"Search him!"

The man gave in, his face drained of colour. From his knapsack emerged the parchment-letter with the big seal.

"Put it on the fire!" cried Dobó.

The soldier threw the letter into it.

The man was quivering.

"I don't know how it came to be on me," he excused himself, scratching his head. "Someone put it inside..."

"Clap him in irons!" said Dobó. "Then dump the scoundrel in with the rest!"

18

All the cannon-fire caused the rain to fall that day too (12 October). Only in the evening did the clouds part as the biting autumn wind whistled through the countryside.

The defenders saw the Turks assembling on the earthworks. Dobó allowed only three hundred soldiers to rest. The others had to remain in readiness around the breaches.

Towards eleven o'clock the wind blew the last clouds from the sky. The full moon flooded Eger with light almost as bright as daylight.

"To arms!" came the sudden command everywhere in the fortress. "To arms, those of you who aren't soldiers as well!"

And the alarm was sounded on the drums and the bugles brayed.

"There's going to be a night-attack. On your feet, all of you who are able-bodied!"

And among the moonlit ruins helmeted figures with lances emerged on all sides.

Father Bálint, dressed in armour, also joins the reserves in the square. The pike he holds in his hand is big enough to be the side of a cart. The two innkeepers line up there too. All the

516

millers, carpenters, butchers and peasant-labourers await orders, fully armed. The defenders sense that they are facing the last great trial of strength.

"Oh Lord, please help us now!" some of them pray.

Outside the Turkish bronze drums rattle. The Turkish troops pour into the trenches of the earthworks like water after a cloudburst. Horse-tail banners flutter over the human flood. Beyond the earthworks Turkish officers in pointed caps keep appearing on their nimble horses. The jewels and silver rings of their equipment glint in the light of the moon. Many of them wear turbans wound round gleaming helmets.

The *yasavul*s in their tall turbans gallop around, organizing the troops for the attack.

At midnight the Turkish guns round the fortress suddenly flare out and pour cannon-balls into the fortress in thunder that lasts for minutes. Then yells of *Bismillah* and *Allah* rise all round from a hundred thousand throats, and the horse-tail banners seem to fly towards the walls.

In front of the Old Gate and on top of the wall fires are kindled in thirty places. The bombs, grenades and straw-rings crackle as they burst into flame. Hundreds of fiery rainbows fall in great, sparkling curves.

But the attackers move forward with determination, climbing, pressing and pushing their way up on to the walls. The siege-ladders quickly grip. The janissaries, *asab*s and cavalry now turned into infantry run up the ladders like squirrels. Up above the axes clang on the hooks of the ladders. And there is a rain of fire and stones.

"Allah akbar! Ya kerim! Ya fettah!"

The horse-tail banners keep falling back, but there are always new hands to pick them up. New ladders replace the broken ones. New troops swarm to the ladders over the twitching bodies of the fallen.

The wall is so thickly packed with bodies that they hide it. Where Hungarian lances prod through the loopholes the Turks fall from the ladders, but they are quickly followed by others. They do not bother to avoid the dangerous rungs, but trust to fate as to whether the lance-thrust will enter their stomachs or slip past their arms to meet nothing but air.

Now there are no gates to the fortress. The wooden beams covering the gaps in the wall are systematically smashed down by Turks with axes on siege-ladders. Those who fall from above sometimes pull down the axemen too, and they roll around in fire and blood until next minute they are buried under the bodies of the attackers as they press forward.

"Allah akbar! Ya kerim! Ya rahim!"

"Jesus, help us!"

The fiery missiles rain down, axes clang, bombs explode, ladders creak, hatchets whirl and all are enveloped in a raging sea of blood.

Fifty attackers have succeeded in reaching the palisade together. The palisade creaks and bends outwards. Mekcsey seizes a battleaxe from one of the men and aims a blow at one of the ropes securing it. The palisade and the Turkish armed troops clinging on to it turn over and fall down, sweeping hundreds off the wall as it does so.

"To the wall! To the wall!" cries Mekcsey, himself leaping on to it and brandishing a nine-foot pike.

Huge squared stones and iron cannon-balls fired into the fortress by the Turkish siege-guns rain down on to the heap of Turks as they roll on the ground. But arrows and stones fly upwards too. Mekcsey has blood streaming from the visor of his helmet. "Commander!" they call to him to warn him.

"Fire! Fire!" yells Mekcsey. And with his iron-booted leg he sweeps the embers from a fire on to the Turks wallowing on the ground.

Hungarians also fall from the walls, some into the fortress, others outside. But there is no time now to see who has died. As one falls, another leaps into his place there and hurls stones and cannon-balls down by hand, until the siege-ladders fill again and the desperate defenders receive the Turks who reach the wall with axes and pikes.

The struggle at the Earth Bastion in just as fierce. There Dobó is in charge of the defence. When the Turkish troops have penetrated the inferno of bombs and burning rings he has beams brought up and laid on the wall. He uses these to sweep the Turks off it.

This causes a short pause, and he uses it to jump on his horse and gallop over to the Old Gate to see how they are coping with the battle there. Then as he passes the Prison Bastion on his way back he sees that the attack there has ceased and summons the defenders from there to the Earth Bastion. In any case their attention was fixed on what was happening over there. They were all eager to use their weapons. Standing on the palisade, leaning over the wall and high on the guns they watched the struggle at the neighbouring bastion. So at Dobó's command they dashed across to the Earth Bastion.

But now it so happens that the Turks once more set ladders up the Prison Bastion too, at first just one or two, then ten or fifteen. Since neither fire nor stone falls on them from that position they start climbing with all speed. By the time old Sukán who is on guard there has turned round, the panting face of a helmeted Turk has appeared over the top.

"What the devil!" shouts the old man.

He makes a sudden lunge with his pike and, whirling its blunt end into the sky, strikes at him. The Turk and nine of his companions fall off the ladder.

"Over here! Quick!" roars Sukán, thrusting at the Turks on the second ladder. János Pribék is the first to run to his aid; he hurls the cobbler's stool used by the master-bombardier into the face of a Turk bearing a flag as he comes into view. The soldier on sentry-duty below them runs for help. Within two minutes Pető is on the scene with a detachment of his reserves, and there too a hail of burning missiles, bombs, stones and grenades flies down on the attackers.

Dobó's attention is drawn there too. He sees that the national flag is snapped from its staff by a bullet and orders the banner of the standing army to be brought along. He gives it to István Nagy. Now dawn is breaking.

István Nagy runs up with the banner in the red glow of dawn. He has neither armour nor helmet, but nevertheless climbs right to the top of the bastion and looks for the iron clamp which holds the flagstaff.

"Don't unfurl it!" shouts Dobó. "They might capture it!"

At that moment István Nagy clutches at his heart. He turns round once and slumps on the wall like a sack beside the cannon.

Dobó seizes the banner as it flies towards him like a bird and gives it to Bocskai. "Hold it, my lad!"

In the light of dawn an attack begins at the Bolyky Bastion too. Eight flags wave over them as they make their way there. The red light of the rising sun turns the golden decorations of the horse-tails into giant rubies.

They have suffered so much at that bastion that only the janissaries are prepared to make another charge—the oldest and most battle-tested tigers in the army. They have helmets on their heads; their faces and necks are veiled in steel-mesh; they wear armour on their breasts and arms and light morocco boots on their feet.

Gergely and Zoltay are on watch there. All night long they have been on duty with nothing to do except listen without stirring to the turmoil and firing coming from the attacks at the three other bastions. All the same, it is better when daylight comes.

About two hundred *asab*s line up in front of the bastion with skins filled with water. Just let them come! Fire must be doused as soon as it touches a head. There the Turks do not launch the attack with siege-ladders. As the defenders assemble on the wall there is a sudden movement down below and a thousand hands release stones and arrows to envelop them. One stone caught Zoltay on the head, but fortunately he was wearing a helmet. Only the hinge of his visor was broken. Zoltay swore.

"You just wait, you dogs!" he roared, breaking off his visor. "For that I'll put a hole through a hundred heads of yours!"

And before a quarter of an hour had passed he could be heard shouting, "Take that, you heathen, for my helmet!" And again, "There's a little taste of Eger for you!"

A huge object covered in cowhide rose up out of the Turkish troops. It was a remarkable sight. It needed fifty *asab*s to carry it, and there was room for two hundred janissaries under it.

Gergely called for a powder-filled barrel, and lit the oily tow wound round an iron core. The gigantic covering looked like a turtle as it approached the wall. Even if the hide was torn from it with grapnels it would reach the wall by the time they had set fire to it. And there was still doubt whether they could set fire to it anyway. Not only the hide was dripping with water but the wood too. The Turks were learning their lesson.

The sun shone out from behind the hills to the east and blinded the defenders on the Sándor Bastion. The sun was helping the Turks too.

As the siege-object reached the slope of the bastion, Gergely gave a great shout: "Get down flat!"

The men could not understand why. The great hail of rifle fire answered their question. The Turks had devised the cunning plan of surrounding the cover of the large object with rifle-barrels. They stood up like organ-pipes, directed towards the defenders. They were what Gergely had noticed.

"On your feet!" he shouted after the volley of shots. "Bring me a barrel!" He rolled down the burning barrel. Now the Turks did not fall to the ground in front of the barrel. They either leapt aside or jumped over it, so it did not stop them in their advance.

"Two barrels!" shouted Gergely.

He himself positioned the third one and lit the fuse to ignite it. The two burning barrels once again swept a path through the swarming mass down below. The third was seized by a sturdy janissary who knocked it into a hole in the road and covered it with earth. When he trod the earth down the barrel exploded, hurling the janissary and the earth into the sky, and laid low some twenty men standing nearby.

This brought the attacking troops to a surprised halt. But the yasavuls in the rear shouted "Forward!" and the water-filled skins hissed as they quenched the scattered fires in clouds of steam.

"Now just throw stones!" shouted Gergely. He planned to wait until they were densely-packed on the road and the walls. And the army advanced again to the yells of "Allah!" like a hundred thousand roaring tigers, the braying of trumpets and rattle of drums. A forest of ladders approached the walls. One janissary threw a rope with a hook on it over the wall and, gripping his *yataghan* in his teeth scrambled up it with the agility of a monkey. A stone fell on his head, knocking his helmet off. His bald head with all the scars of sword-strokes looked like a melon. He continued to climb.

Gergely picked up a lance to stab him.

When the Turk was only six feet away from Gergely he raised his face. It was covered in perspiration and his lips were panting. Gergely was so startled that he seemed to have been struck in the breast. That face! It was Father Gábor, his old tutor! The same grey eyes, the same thin moustache, the same projecting forehead!

"You're Father Gábor's young brother!" he called to the Turk.

The Turk stared at him uncomprehendingly.

"Kill him!" shouted Gergely, turning away. "He's forgotten his Hungarian."

*

The great struggle raged on till dusk. Then on all sides the Turks withdrew wearily from beneath the walls. There were thousands of dead and wounded lying all round the fortress. From all directions came the cries and whimpers of dying men with broken bones.

But the fortress itself was filled with dead and wounded, and the walls and platforms were red with blood inside. Everyone was stained with blood, perspiring, dirty, ragged and red-eyed. Women carried the dead and wounded.

The officers went to wash. Dobó himself was so black, his beard and moustache so singed that if he had not been wearing his commander's helmet nobody could have recognized his features. And dirty as he was, he received reports by the gun called Baba.

"I've got 65 dead and 78 seriously wounded. We've used five hundredweight of gunpowder," reported Mekcsey.

"Thirty dead and 110 wounded. Eight hundredweight of gunpowder," reported Gergely Bornemissza. "We'll have to set men to work on repairing the breach this night."

"Three hundredweight of gunpowder, 25 dead and 50 wounded," reported Fügedy. And he put his hand to his face.

"Are you wounded too?" asked Dobó.

"No," replied Fügedy. "But I've got such an attack of toothache that it's like a burning lance turning in my face."

Among those waiting to report Dobó caught sight of Varsányi too. The spy was in dervish outfit and looked as if he had a red apron on top of it, bloodstained from the chest right down to his feet.

"Varsányi!" said Dobó, interrupting the reports. "Come here! Are you wounded?"

"No," replied Varsányi. "I had to carry the dead down there among the Turks until I could get inside."

"Well, what news?"

"Master Szalkay has written for a second time all over the place, to counties and towns."

"And hasn't anyone turned up so far?"

"From here and there," replied Varsányi reluctantly. "But they're waiting for each other before they can make an attack on the Turks."

Dobó understood this to mean that Szalkay had not received any replies at all.

"What news have you of the Turks?"

"I've been wandering among them for four days, so I know that they're terribly depressed."

"Louder!" said Dobó, his eyes lighting up.

And the spy repeated so loudly that the bystanders could all hear him: "The Turks are terribly depressed, commander. The weather's too cold for them. They're out of food. I saw with my own eyes how a man from Nógrád brought five cartloads of flour yesterday, and they snatched it all up in dishes and caps. They didn't even wait to bake it; they ate it by the handful as it was, just as they got it out of the sacks. But what was that among so many men?"

"Kristóf," said Dobó to his page. "Go off to the butchers and tell them to slaughter the best cattle for the men. There's to be beef stew for everyone."

And once more he turned to the spy.

"The janissaries were very rebellious yesterday," continued the spy.

"Louder!"

"The janissaries were rebellious," went on Varsányi in a loud voice. "They said that God was on the side of the Hungarians. And they also said that they're used to all kinds of weapons of war, but not to fire from the devil. They've never seen such fiery devices as those they're trying to fight against."

Dobó was silent for a minute as he stared ahead. "Be in front of the palace in an hour from now," he said. "You're to accompany Miklós Vas to Szarvaskő once more."

Then he turned to Sukán. The old man's head was so swathed in bandages that only his eyes and moustache were visible. All the same he reported in a harsh croaking voice: "Today we have used up twenty hundredweight of gunpowder."

19

The rising sun, as it peered over the mist, looked down on a sorry wreck of a fortress, spattered with blood and filth. In places burning beams were still smouldering, and smoke rose from some of the hoops of sulphur and oil-filled barrels. The stench of dead and living men and rubbish filled the air.

The defenders took cautious looks from the walls and breaches. But all they could see was the dervishes collecting the dead bodies. There were so many of them that the dervishes could not carry them away.

The guns were silent. The very sun in the sky rose shivering in the cold and the town and valleys lay covered in fog as high as a tower. It was around eight o'clock when the fog lifted. Then the sun, apparently trying to charm the spring back again, shone gently from a clear blue sky.

The defenders also cleared away the dead bodies. The peasants and women collected them in stretchers and waggons from the Old Gate. Father Bálint conducted burials. Father Márton gave the last rites to the dying.

But there was some movement among the Turks after all. They were assembling to storm the fortress. The various Turkish brigades came down again from the distant hills.

It was plain that they were concentrating all their forces now. As soon as they were all assembled, they would storm the totally wrecked fortress with all their military might.

After the big battle the men slept long and deep that night. Dobó permitted this, except that they had to take their rest round the bastions. Only a single sentry was on duty on each bastion. And the officers also slept so deeply they might have been dead. Even at eight o'clock Bornemissza was sleeping so soundly under the gun named Frog that he was undisturbed by the sound of the bugle or by the noise of passers-by. He was swathed in a thick woollen blanket and his long brown hair glistened with frost. His face was black with soot.

Mekcsey spread a handkerchief over his head and covered him with his own cloak too.

Dobó had the large-bore cannon and mortars loaded with tiny iron nails. He had cartloads of stone brought to cover the breaches in some places, while in others he had them filled with barrels, planks, hides and other such materials. The masons smoothed down the parapet of the walls in various places so that the siege-ladders might not be able to grip them. All the cauldrons and saucepans were carried from the kitchens and filled with water. All the pitch that was available in the fortress was taken to the bastions and placed beside the cauldrons. The old lead guttering from the palace was broken in pieces and divided among the guns. The butchers were ordered to roast an ox on a spit for the midday meal. The bread was carried out into the square where the off-duty soldiers and those in reserve normally gathered together. The loaves were piled up there. Mihály the officer in charge of provisions was not concerned now about rations: anyone could have as much as he liked. He appeared in his fine brown jacket and yellow boots among the bakers in the square and merely noted down on his piece of paper: "14 October. 700 loaves."

The Turks continued to assemble. A motley flood of men surged down from the hills. At ten o'clock the bugler in the square of the fortress summoned the troops on parade. The defenders assembled. They all had bandaged heads or arms. If nothing else, one finger on the right hand was bandaged. But anyone who could move had to take his place on the wall.

In the middle of the square ecclesiastical banners of silk were fluttering. One of them depicted Mary, another King Stephen the Saint, and the third St. John. The banners were worn and faded; originally they had hung in the church. The priests stood at an altar improvised out of a table. They were wearing purple vestments. There was a monstrance on the table.

The defenders had been aware that there would be a mass.

525

There should have been before the earlier attacks. But Dobó would not allow the last sacraments to be mentioned.

"These are only preliminary trials!" he would say. "By the time the full attack comes the royal army will be here." But now it was plain that the end had come.

Everyone had been washed, spruce and smart in his finest clothes. The officers appeared in all the colours of the rainbow, with red boots and spurs; their moustaches were twirled and there were feathers in their helmets. Mekcsey had a new close-fitting suit of steel armour. There were two swords at his side: one of them was the snake-headed sword that he used only for ceremonial occasions.

Gergely Bornemissza came forward in a pointed helmet of steel. There were three white crane-feathers in its peak, held there by a silver bird's foot. He wore a breastplate. A red leather jacket hung from his arms. On his hands he had silk gloves covered on the outside with fine steel mesh. The collar that stood up round his neck was embroidered with gold thread. Zoltay could not let this pass.

"What a bridegroom's collar you're wearing!"

"My wife made it," replied Gergely without smiling. "And I didn't put it on out of respect for the Turks..." What he left unsaid was plain: "out of respect for death."

Zoltay too was wearing a light brown leather jacket and two swords rattled at his side. His helmet had no visor, but a steel projection covered his nose to its tip. All round it a veil of chain-mail fell to his neck. That helmet might once have belonged to some spahi officer. He bought it at the auction that followed their first raid.

Fügedy was armoured from head to toe. His eyes were clouded and he complained of toothache. "I really am ashamed, but it hurts like hell."

"That'll make you strike the Turks all the harder!" Zoltay comforted him. "It's good for a soldier to be furious at times like this."

"I'm furious enough without this as well!" grumbled Fügedy.

Pető wore only a helmet and a jacket of deerskin. He was on horseback, since he still could not walk. He was at the back of the parade and saluted the commanding officers with his sword.

The others too were in their best clothes. This was not for the sake of the mass, because not everybody had known then that there would be one, but because everyone felt somehow that this would be the final day. And however grimly death is painted, he is a great lord and worthy of all respect. Those who had no other clothes but their everyday ones had at least waxed and twisted their moustaches. But almost every eye was red with loss of sleep and the caustic effect of smoke. And every face was pale. There were faces showing wounds, fresh ones, wounds just healing and scars where wounds had healed on faces and hands.

Now only Dobó was missing.

He stepped forward in a gleaming suit of armour. On his head was a gilded helmet, with a long eagle-feather in the crown. At his side was a broad jewelled sword. The gloves he wore were partly laminated and partly of silver mesh. In his hand he grasped a gold-tipped lance with a red velvet grip.

The two pages behind him were likewise in armour from head to foot. They had short swords at their sides, and their hair fell in waves from their helmets on to their shoulders.

Dobó halted in front of the altar and removed his helmet.

The two priests were unable to speak, so Mekcsey addressed the defenders.

"Brothers!" he said, putting his helmet on his arm. "After yesterday's attack we can see that the Turks are concentrating all their forces. This day all the forces of the enemy will measure up against our own forces. But where God is present, all the heathen forces in the world will strive in vain against his will. In the sacred elements we see here we know that the living Christ is present. He is with us! Let us kneel and pray."

There was a clatter of arms as the defenders all knelt together. Mekcsey began the prayer instead of the priest.

"Our Father..."

They repeated it quietly, sentence by sentence. The Amen was followed by a long, solemn silence.

Father Márton leant over to Mekcsey and told him what to say next. Mekcsey got to his feet and spoke again.

"These two faithful servants of God now hold aloft the sacrament in order to give all of us total absolution. We have no time for confession. At such a time the Church gives absolution without confession. Repent of your sins to yourselves." And he knelt again.

The server rang the bell. Father Bálint raised the sacrament. The people listened with bowed heads as the aged priest murmured the words of absolution. When they raised their faces again the monstrance was back on the table and the priest, his two hands wide apart in blessing, gazed with tearful eyes into the clear blue sky as he stood there motionless.

After the ceremony Dobó replaced his helmet. He stood on a stone and spoke solemnly: "After God, I too have something to say to you. Thirty-four days ago we swore not to surrender the fortress. We have kept our word. So far the fortress has defied the siege like a rock in the middle of a world-shaking tempest. Now comes the last trial. We have called on God to help us. With souls free from sin and ready for death we fight to save the fortress and our homeland. The heroism with which you have maintained the fortress till now is unparallelled, as is the defeat suffered here by the Turks. I have faith in our arms! I have faith in the strength of our spirits! I have faith in the Virgin Mary, the patron saint of Hungary. I have faith in the King, St. Stephen, whose spirit is always present with the Hungarian nation. And most of all I have faith in God himself. Let us go forward, my brothers, with all the strength we possess, ready to do or die!"

The drum beat and the bugle sounded.

The men seized their lances with the strength of desperation and dispersed in troops. Dobó mounted his horse. His two pages likewise followed him on horseback. Up above, Dobó looked in all directions. He saw the Turkish horses grazing unattended in large herds in the fields and on the far hills. All around was a moving forest of lances. The Turks were flooding round the fortress like the sea.

And now the two pashas could be seen on the King's Seat. Ali Pasha wore a huge melon-shaped turban; his face was yellowish, like that of an old woman. The other pasha was a giant with a big white beard. Both were wearing blue silk kaftans, but Ali's was lighter-coloured. The diamonds in the weapons thrust into their belts sparkled white with their every movement.

The beys were mounted on splendid horses as they directed

the troops. Apart from them, only the agas and *yasavuls* were on horseback. The rest were all on foot. Among the military banners of the Turks a huge black flag was conspicuous. The defenders had not seen it yet. Only the officers understood its significance: "No mercy! Death to every soul in the fortress!"

About noonday the Turkish cannon thundered out and the two Turkish military bands struck up. The fortress was enveloped in clouds of smoke. And the walls themselves trembled at the cries of *Allah akbar!*

The fires inside were also lit.

*

Dobó ordered all the peasants, women and other refugees to the cauldrons and the walls. But even the sick struggled out too. All who were able to stand up left their beds; if nothing else, they could pass on shouted orders and calls. Some of them had both arms bandaged, yet they went out. They stood by a pile of wood and pushed pieces of it under the cauldrons from time to time with their feet.

Nobody remained inside the houses except the children, and the two women in the palace.

Mrs. Balogh... Poor Mrs. Balogh... She had sent her son to learn the military arts, and dare not ask Dobó to excuse him from service during the siege. The boy was still immature: how would he stand up to the weapons of the heathen brutes? But only her pallor betrayed her fear for her son. Dobó's iron will disarmed even her fears. She dare not take a breath when Dobó looked at her. She was like the soldiers: at Dobó's command everything moved with mechanical obedience. It was his will that pervaded everyone. Nor did he need to speak: a gesture was enough for men's limbs to obey automatically.

What would have happened in the fortress if a single hair of Dobó's head had quivered with fear? He instilled caution into them all. He made them all don armour, breastplate and helmet. But when death appeared on the wall, he led the defenders against it without fear or favour. Nobody was of more value than the homeland.

Poor Mrs. Balogh spent the days of attack in torment. She trembled every morning when her son joined Dobó. She watched every hour with anxiety in case he was struck by a bullet. And what joy it was for her when the page Kristóf relieved him and her son walked into the palace weary and dirty with gunpowder! She always received him with open arms and a kiss. He might have returned from a distant land. She washed and bathed him. She brushed and combed his long silken hair. And she set before him all the good things the kitchen had to offer.

"Who's died? Which of the *officers* has been wounded?" These were always the first questions from the two ladies.

The boy did not know who Eva was. He thought she must be a gentlewoman from Eger, whom his mother had taken into the palace to help her. So he simply told them the news. The news always began with a list of the dead, and always ended with praise of Gergely. What inventions had Gergely come up with! His spirit was full of admiration for Gergely. He described how he had fought with Turks and how many he had engaged, and with what cunning tricks he had despatched each separate one.

Eva listened to him with wide eyes, pale and proud. She gave a smile only when the boy reached the point in his account where the Turks could do nothing against the miraculous Gergely.

While the attacks were raging, the two ladies stood near the window weeping and trembling. All they could see through the tiny opening was people dashing up and down, the smoke, the red flames that kept leaping up, and then the barbers carrying out the linen bandages, which they piled in a heap. Next they fetched bowls of water—clean water. And after that the wounded were brought along one by one, in ever increasing numbers and with greater wounds.

All their attention then was devoted to the wounded. Look! They're bringing another one along! It's not Balázs. It's not Gergely. Thank God! There comes another... But suppose they're not bringing either of them because they've been taken to the burial-pit... Or maybe they've been trampled down in the struggle.

And Eva's aged, crippled father was here too. She often saw him stump along the road past the palace, with a bow on his shoulder as big as he was. Sometimes the quiver was empty, sometimes it was full of arrows. She would have loved to call out, "Father! Dear father! Do look after yourself!"

When that day the cannon thundered, the two ladies embraced each other tearfully. "Let's say our prayers!" And they knelt down, bowed their faces low and prayed. And they were joined in prayer by fifteen hundred wives from all over Upper Hungary, every day and every night. And little children put their hands together in distant places of refuge, innocent children praying for their dear fathers in Eger.

"Dear Lord, keep father alive! Bring father back home to us!"

Infernal roaring and booming, cannon-fire, bugles braying, cries of "Jesus!", yells of "Allah!" Heavy clouds of smoke billowing inside the fortress.

They are bringing in the first wounded now. The first comes on a stretcher blackened with blood. He is a pale young soldier, with his leg shot away at the knee. The barbers bandage him up more or less. Why waste time on him? The bandages will give him an hour or two of hope, but after that he will bleed to death anyway.

Then they bring in a second, a third and a fourth. The face of one of them is an ugly mass of bleeding flesh. Both eyes are missing, and his teeth are visible. The next has an arrow in his neck. It has to be cut out. The third holds his hand to his right side. It is a mass of blood, as if he is wearing a red glove. His blood spurts in great threads through his fingers. He sits on the ground and waits silently for death to close his eyes.

Dobó rushes past the palace on his galloping steed. In his wake, but a long way behind, comes the page Kristóf.

"Where's the other one?" his mother's tortured glance enquires.

"Over there! He too is rushing towards the Sándor Bastion. He must be taking a message." Thank God! And also "Poor boy!"

Now there are so many wounded that all thirteen barbers are busy. They have brought in three Turkish banners with the wounded. The yells of the Turks grow increasingly desperate. The smoke from the gunpowder obscures the surroundings of the bastions on the east and north and descends on the palace too. It is like a winter fog, so thick that it is impossible to see three steps ahead.

"Merciful God!" sighs Mrs. Balogh. "What will become of us if the Turks break in?"

"Then I'll die!" replies Eva, whiter than the wall.

And she goes into the armoury. She takes down a sword, Dobó's everyday sword, and lays it thoughtfully on the table. The moans and cries of the wounded can be heard through the open window.

"Oh, my eyes, my eyes!" cries one of them. "I'll never see God's beautiful world again!"

"I can beg for my living!" moans another. "They've chopped off both my hands."

There are too many wounded for the barbers to keep up the pace of bandaging. Yet now many women are helping them, bustling around with pale faces, washing, dusting with alum, and bandaging like the barbers.

"Only God preserve us!" sighs a young lad sitting there in a bloodstained shirt and holding his stomach with both hands. An upward lance-thrust has split it open.

Mrs. Balogh trembles.

"We've got to go outside!" she says, her face racked with torment. "We've got to go and help the barbers."

"Shall I go too? Yes, I shall. My feeling is that neither word of honour nor command forbids me to care for the wounded."

A breeze disperses the smoke. Mrs. Balogh opens the door and gazes into the distance, towards the Prison Bastion. There she sees Dobó in a cloud of smoke, just as he aims a fearsome sword-blow at the head of a Turk stepping on to the top of the wall; then he pushes the dead man back again.

Balázs the page stands behind him in a steel helmet with the visor down. He holds his master's lance, mace and another sword under his arm.

The sun keeps shining through the clouds and smoke. The weather was chilly and autumnal, but to the fighters it was like a heat-wave. With one jerk Dobó unbuckles his helmet and tosses it to Balázs. Then he pulls a handkerchief out of his belt and wipes the sweat from his face. He goes on fighting bareheaded.

The page Balázs does not know where to hold the golden helmet and puts it on his own head. Smoke envelops them.

Blow away, smoke, blow away!

The smoke-cloud seems to hear the cry from the mother's heart and disperses. Balázs stands there on the wall, watching Dobó fighting. His mother calls, "Get back! Lower down!" As if the boy could hear her in all that infernal din!

And as she raises her hand to wave to her son, the boy drops Dobó's weapons. With a languid movement he reaches for his neck. He staggers and turns round once. The golden helmet falls from his head and rolls away. The boy slumps down on the ground without moving a hand to break his fall. With a piercing shriek his mother flings open the door and dashes over to him. She embraces her son, moans over him, falls on him and puts her arms round him.

"Balázs, Balázs!"

Dobó glances at them and retrieves the helmet that has rolled away. He beckons to a soldier and points to the boy. The soldier picks up the boy, carries him into the palace and into his mother's room.

The boy lies there with his neck bleeding, like a wounded pigeon, drained of life.

"Now I haven't got a son either!" wails the grey-haired widow.

"Maybe he's just fainted," says the soldier. "But I've got to go now."

"Poor Balázs!" Eva weeps for him too.

And she unbuckles the helmet and visor from the page's head, then takes off his breastplate and other armour.

But a huge shot-wound gapes in the boy's neck. The bullet did not enter there, but at his waist; his neck was where it came out.

The widow's face is twisted with pain. Her eyes are bloodshot. She seizes the sword lying on the table, the one Eva has just brought out of the room, and rushes out with it into the smoke, the confused mass of people, up to the Prison Bastion. There are several women up there already. Down below they boil the water, pitch and lead. They carry them swiftly to the soldiers as they boil.

"Bring some cold water too, water to drink!" shout the soldiers when there is a brief pause in the attack. "Water! Water!"

"Go to the cellar, ladies!" Dobó shouts down. "Tap all the wine-barrels! Bring it up in cups to the men!"

Those women who can hear his call run off with billowing skirts for the wine.

Imre the clerk, fully armed, paces up and down at the entrance to the cellar. When all the women rush towards him, he thrusts the key into the cellar door.

"It's for the officers, isn't it?" he asks Mrs. Kocsis.

"It's for everybody, Master clerk, everybody! The commander said so."

Imre pushes the door open. "The best's at the back." And he shuts down his visor and draws his sword. He too runs to the gap-toothed walls of the Prison Bastion.

An ever-increasing mob of Turks climbs up the bastion. Now they leap to the top of it. There murderous hand-to-hand struggles ensue. Dobó himself grabs one of them by the throat, a giant whose bones alone weigh a hundred pounds. He tries to push him backwards. The Turk digs his feet in. For a minute both of them pant with staring eyes. Then Dobó gathers his strength and with a single twist jerks him inside. He throws him down from the top of the platform into the yard.

The Turk's helmet falls off, and he himself falls among stones. But he struggles up again and turns to see whether his companions are following.

That is when Mrs. Balogh arrives there. With a scream she whisks her sword in the air and the Turk's head breaks away from his shoulders under its terrible blow. Now the other women are busy on the bastion. In all the fighting the soldiers cannot take from them the blazing pitch, stones, and lead, so they carry these up themselves and in the smoke, dust and flames keep tipping them on to the Turks as they climb up.

The dead fall down and the living keep coming on in ever larger numbers. The occasional rolling stone and shower of pitch and lead clear a path on the crowded wall, but the mound of dead bodies simply makes it easier for the rested brigades to climb up there. The living snatch the horse-tails from the dead as they fall backwards and once again these banners dance there on the ladders.

"Allah! Allah! We're winning! Victory's ours now!"

"Jesus, help us!"

Dobó casts an astonished glance at Mrs. Balogh fighting at his side, but he has no time to speak. He too fights. The blood runs down his gleaming armour from shoulder to heel.

The lady rains blow after blow upon the advancing Turks until at last a lance-thrust catches her and she falls from the bastion on to the platform. Now there is no one to pull her away. The battle is raging on the top of the wall. The living trample over the dead and the dying. Dobó jumps on to a projecting gable and looks down.

Now the agas also are at the foot of the wall. Veli Bey brings a big red velvet banner on horseback. At the sight of it the Turkish warriors break into renewed yelling.

"Allah is helping us! The moment of victory's here!"

The banner is the flag of victory belonging to Ali Pasha. That summer alone it has flown from the summit of thirty fortresses and castles proclaiming a Turkish victory. Nothing has touched it save the lustre of glory.

Veli Bey reaches the Earth Bastion with the banner. There the defence appears to be most precarious, since even women are fighting there. Dobó catches sight of the broad ceremonial banner glittering with gold script. He sends a message to Pető and himself runs to the Earth Bastion. There is hand-to-hand fighting there. Now and then a Turk with a flag appears and disappears again into the depths. The warriors struggle in a mist of rising dust and smoke. The rings of pitch and fire-balls fly through the smoke-clouds like comets.

"Jesus, help me!" shrieks a woman.

At the moment when Dobó arrives there a stone falls inwards from above on the head of Mátyás Szőr, the second miller from Maklár. The miller collapses, but before he can fall a broad-shouldered Turk on his way up plunges his *yataghan* up to the hilt in his breast. A woman charges the Turk, shrieking. She has grabbed her husband's sword... Dobó beckons upwards, "Charge! Charge! Help's on its way!"

At the sound of his voice new power fills the men. They continue stabbing the attackers climbing the wall in a hail of curses that cannot be considered sinful.

Two Turks are struggling on one side. Dobó recognizes the one in armour as the murderer of the miller and turns towards him. He sees that the Turk is wearing Derbend steel armour from head to foot. Swords merely glance off it. With swift resolve he hurls himself on him and presses him down on the dead miller. But the Turk is a muscular man with broad shoulders. He wriggles beneath Dobó like a man-sized pike. In helpless rage he bites the armour on Dobó's arm, then suddenly drops to the ground and turns his face upwards. But that is death for him. Dobó finds his bare neck and squeezes it mercilessly.

He hardly has time to rise before a Turkish lance falls from above and clatters on to his leg, splitting open the leather thong and coming to rest in his calf. In his pain Dobó gives a roar like a lion. Falling on his knee, he clasps his leg and his eyes grow moist with tears of agony.

"Sir!" says the page Kristóf in terror. "Are you wounded?"

Dobó makes no reply. He pulls the lance out of his leg and throws it away. For a moment he stands with clenched fists and sucks his teeth, waiting for the first surge of pain to pass. Then he gives a kick to see whether his leg is broken. It is not; it is only bleeding. As the pain leaves it, he picks up his sword again and hurls himself like a tiger on a Turk pushing his way through the breach. Woe to anyone who gets in his path now!

While there they are almost tearing at each other with their teeth, a mere twenty yards away the enemy are gathering in large numbers at the second breach. The beams across it are breaking under the weight of hundreds, and the Turks burst in with a shout of triumph, glad not to have to scale a wall. They push and tumble over each other. Weapons in the right hand and horse-tails in the left. The first there jump on to the bastions with the horse-tail banners. The later arrivals charge the wounded waiting under the platforms and the women. Meanwhile one of them kicks the fire and the wooden logs burning in it towards the leg of the platform with his armoured leg. The fire begins to lick the post with tall tongues of flame.

The wounded they dispose of easily, but the womenfolk seize the cauldrons and pots with angry shouts. Mrs. Gáspár Kocsis, a sturdy figure, drenches an approaching aga with a long beard so thoroughly with boiling water that when he makes a grab at his beard it comes away in his hand. Another woman seizes a flaming log from the nearby fire and strikes a Turk in the face with it so that sparks fly from it in all directions like stars. The other women repulse the pagans with weapons.

"Jesus, help us!"

"Strike them! Strike them!" roars the smith from Felnémet. He rushes with his hammer in among the women. Three Turks are fighting there back to back. He strikes one so hard on the head that his brains spatter out of his nose and ears. The second Turk drops to his knees from some blow, but all the same his yataghan flashes in his hand as he plunges it to the hilt in the smith's stomach.

"You're coming with me to the next world, you dog!" roars the smith. And once more he whirls the fifty-pound hammer over his head and only sits on the ground and holds his hand over his stomach when he sees his enemy collapse among the dead, his helmet flattened to a pancake from the fearful blow.

By now all the women have picked up the weapons lying around and engage the Turks with screams of rage and fury. Their head-scarves fall off, their hair comes down, their skirts flutter and twist in the struggle. But they are not concerned that they are women now; they fall on the Turks with shouts. Their swords do not parry any blow. What falls on them is theirs, but what they give is the Turks'.

"Hurrah for the women!" Pető shouts behind them. Then as he notices the flames licking the post supporting the platform, he reaches for a bucket and drenches the post with water. The captain had brought up a troop of rested soldiers. He flashes his sword and falls on an *akindji* who is scrambling up like a cat. The akindji drops among the beams. His soldiers scatter the Turkish intruders like chaff. Indeed, they even charge through the hole.

Dobó kneels on the wall and looks down with heaving breast and staring eyes while the blood drips from his sword and beard. More and more often the infuriated defenders charge out of the breaches in the fortress wall and fight the Turks under the bastion among the dead.

"Get back!" shouts Dobó at the top of his voice. "Get back!" But in the noise of battle they cannot even hear their own voices.

A private named László Tóth catches sight of the bey with the red velvet banner. He leaps at him. In his hand he has a musket. He fires it at the bey's breast. He makes a grab at the banner; his next movement is to hurl the musket into the bey's face. Then he jumps back with his prize while the janissaries chop his five companions to pieces.

Dobó only sees that Veli Bey falls from his horse and that a Hungarian has seized the pasha's flag of victory. He indicates where the rested troops are to fight. He gives a twist to the bloodstained rags on his left arm and dashes down to the breach. Pető has already got there on foot and raises a burning piece of wood to the mortar sited in front of the breach. This shot hurls back the janissaries who are pressing in after the banner.

"Load!" calls Dobó to Fayrich the bombardier. "Four of you stay here. Bring stones and beams here! If you've time!"

20

Eva remained alone with the dead page.

She looked thoughtfully at him. Then she moved. She put his helmet on her head, his armour on her body and the gauntlets on her arms. The boy was about her size. She put on his clothes. She thought his sword too short. She went into Dobó's room and took down from the wall a long, straight-bladed Italian dagger and fixed the strap from its hilt on to her wrist. She left the scabbard behind.

She rushed through the doorway with the naked dagger. She ran, but did not know where. All she knew was that her husband and Zoltay were defending the outer fortress. But she did not know which way it lay from the palace.

The sun was beginning to sink now, but through all the billowing smoke it merely looked like a fiery cannon-ball that had remained suspended in the air. She remembered from the sketch of the fortress that the outer fortress was on the east side, like a sickle beside the tortoise. The sun was setting on the right, so it must be towards the left.

Ten grubby, smoke-grimed soldiers came clattering along in the opposite direction. They came at a run with a corporal leading them. Their right arms and sides were black with blood.

They had lances over their shoulders and were charging towards the Prison Bastion. Then came a soldier staggering... Blood poured from his face. He was trying to reach the barbers. Another couple of uncertain steps and he collapsed on the ground. Eva made a move to lift him up. But a second and a third body, dead or fainting, also lay there. The third one was the elder son of the Mayor of Eger; she recognized him from looking out of the window. An arrow stuck from his breast.

Women come panting from the cellar. On their heads they carry wooden mugs, and in their hands they have pails or pots with handles. They too make for the east side. Eva joins them. As they run past the stables, they disappear into a little tunnel sloping downwards. Two lamps are alight inside the tunnel. This is the Dark Gate, which links the outer fortress with the upper wall.

Eva follows the women. The dust and stench of smoke grow denser. The bustle and shouting in Hungarian and Turkish alike grow more and more diabolical. There are dead bodies scattered around, mainly face downwards, up on the steps and on the platforms. One of them Eva recognizes as Father Bálint. He lies on his back. His helmet is missing, and his long white beard is red with blood. Even now he still grips his sword in his hand.

Eva stumbles over a long-handled club. She picks it up and rushes up the steps. A hand-to-hand struggle is going on there. The soldiers on the wall stand and push the Turks back again. One woman hurls the stump of a burning log down from above. Another one whirls a blazing fireball and hits a Turk on the neck with it. Cursing, cries of "Jesus", yells of "Allah", the clatter of feet, crashing and banging fill the air.

On the bastion two cannon fire in succession. Eva glances up at the sound. She sees her husband holding the smoking fuse; then he fixes his gaze downwards to see the range of the shot.

Five or six Turks remain on the parapet. They strike them down. There follows a minute's pause. All the soldiers turn round and shout at the tops of their voices, "Water! Water!"

An old soldier in a helmet just by Eva shouts from a stone projecting from the ruins of the wall. Blood and sweat roll down his cheeks. His eyes can hardly be seen for blood. Eva recognizes her father.

She seizes a mug from one of the women and offers it to him, holding it and helping him to drink. The old man drinks greedily. It is not water, but mellow red Eger wine.

The old man takes a great draught of it. The wine drips from his moustache when he takes the mug from his lips, and he catches his breath for an instant. Eva notices that the old man's right hand is ablaze. That is no surprise; it is wooden to the wrist, and presumably had been caught by one of the burning straw-rings. The old man had not seen it.

Eva tosses aside the mug and the club and graps the old man's arm. She knows where the wooden hand is fastened. With nimble fingers she undoes the buckle and the wooden hand flies among the Turks.

As for the old man, he grasps his sword and, leaning out over the bastion wall, once again aims a left-handed blow at a shield of reeds decorated with bronze crescents.

Eva dashes on towards her husband. She jumps over dead bodies here and there. Burning sheaves fly across her path, and bullets strike the wall in front and behind. But the soldiers are all drinking. Water is all they ask for, and that would have been nectar to them. But wine—that seems to give them the strength of the gods.

Zoltay's shouts mingle with the din and yells of the Turks swarming down below. "Come on you dogs! Come on! Let me send a message to Mohammed in paradise!" And a minute later simply, "Good night!"

The Turk to whom this was addressed doubtless forgot to return his greeting.

"*Ileri, ileri!*" shout the *yasavul*s unceasingly. "We've won! Victory is ours!"

And new multitudes, new ladders, new shields swarm over the pile of dead bodies. "Allah! Allah!"

Eva discovers Gergely at last. He is setting alight a barrel full of gunpowder and tosses it down from the heights. Then he throws his helmet to the ground. He springs over to one woman, seizes the mug from her and drinks so greedily that the red wine trickles from his mouth on both sides.

Eva offers her own wine to another soldier. And she leaves it in his hand. She turns to pick up the helmet, but as she bends down pitch-smoke gets into her eyes. By the time she has cleared away her tears, Gergely is nowhere to be seen. As she is looking right and left, the soldiers around her suddenly crouch down. Down below the *tüfekchis* fire a volley scarcely sixty feet from the wall. One bullet strikes Eva's helmet and cracks it open. Eva staggers. It takes time for her to regain her strength.

Down below there is a burst of infernal music: the rattle of drums and the braying of trumpets. A long-necked *yasavul* with a rasping voice yells below the wall "This way! This way!" The troops down there are a confused mass. To replace the janissaries, leather-capped *asabs* and red-capped *akindjis* are driven forward.

One white-robed dervish, wearing a helmet instead of a camel-hair cap, grabs a banner and with yells of *"Ileri! Ileri!"* sets out with an entourage of ten elderly janissaries to attack the walls. The Hungarians do not normally fire at dervishes, but since this one has a helmet on his head and a sword in his hand they do. He attracts Eva's attention too. For a moment a breeze clears away the smoke and flutters the horse-tail banner with its triple ball in the dervish's hand. As he turns towards the fortress, Eva sees that he has one eye bandaged.

"Yumurdjak!" she shrieks with the wrath of a tiger. And she hurls her club like a flash of yellow lightning down from the wall. The club flies over the dervish's head and catches a janissary in the breast. The dervish has heard the shriek, and looks up. At the same time the cannon thunders out from the bastion into the Turkish troops and the dervish and his entourage are enveloped in flames and smoke.

By the time the smoke clears from the moat, there is no trace there of the dervish. But all the same the walls are filled with new bands of climbing Turks.

And now they are not confined to ladders. A white-capped janissary sets off without a ladder up the rubble of stones torn from the wall. He steps from stone to stone, always finding a grip for his hands and a hole for his feet. And it is easy enough to climb up among the beams. A second, then a third, ten, twenty, a hundred men follow in his wake. They are like those little red insects that swarm on the sunny side of walls in spring. And all the way along the wall of the outer fortress they clamber and climb upwards with glinting eyes and panting lips. One or two of them bring rope-ladders too. They hook them on to suitable stones and those standing below immediately start to climb up them.

Gergely runs from the bastion to the breach. He is bareheaded. In his hand is a lance. His face is black with gunpowder.

"Sukán!" he yells to someone fighting with a bloodstained pike, "is there any more pitch in the store?" His voice is hoarse. He bends almost to the old man's ear with his question.

"No," replies Sukán. "But there's still one barrel of resin there."

"Have it brought immediately to the Perényi gun."

Imre the clerk in charge of rations is fighting alongside the old man. He puts down his pike and dashes off.

"Men!" shouts Gergely. "Let's give them all we've got!" And like an echo comes Zoltay's call from the other side: "They'll never come again if we beat them back now!"

"Fire! Fire!" shouts rise elsewhere.

The women carry boiling lead, boiling oil and boiling water in pots hung from poles. Mrs. Ferenc Vas runs on to the wall with a great iron shovel full of embers and tips them on to the Turks. But at the same time the shovel falls from her hands as she is struck on the forehead by a piece of stone dislodged by a bullet. She falls backwards against a post and sinks down. A smoke-blackened sturdy woman bends down to her. One glance is enough; she is dead. Her next glance falls on a stone from the bastion lying beside Mrs. Vas. She seizes it and runs on to the wall with it. A bullet hits her in the breast and she falls.

"Mother!" screams a girl in a red skirt. But she does not lean down to her. First she grasps the stone she has dropped and hurls it down where her mother had intended it to go. The stone strikes two Turks dead. Only when she sees this does she turn back to her mother and embrace her; weeping, she carries her down the steps of the platform.

In the sea of smoke down below a tortoise-formation of shields is approaching. The *akindjis* beneath them are invisible, so closely are they packed together.

"Watch out, men!" Gergely's voice rings out.

"Water! Fire!" calls Zoltay. "Over there, over there!" They're climbing the walls without ladders!"

An object covered with tin rises from the moat. Four piyads run up to the wall with it. It is taken by men on the ladder and held over their heads. Then more objects arrive. All of them are covered in tin to prevent the defenders from tearing up the roof with grapnels.

"Boiling water!" calls Gergely over his shoulder. "Plenty of it!"

Eva leaps to him and puts his helmet on his head.

"Thanks, Balázs," says Gergely. "Did Dobó send you?"

Eva makes no reply. She rushes down from the bastion for boiling water.

"Water! Boiling water, ladies!" she shouts at the top of her voice.

Meanwhile up above the tin-covered objects close in on each other. The climbers beneath them are lightly-dressed. Some are half-naked, but even so the sweat pours from them. Their heads are unencumbered by helmets. They have thrown aside all the heavier weapons from their belts. The only thing they carry is a sharp sabre dangling on a strap from their arm.

The mass of joined objects has become a broad metal roof. Some of the agas have also leapt under it. Dervish Bey also runs across the trench, bringing crescent-tipped horse-tail banners.

By the time Eva returns to join Gergely, all the smoke prevents her from seeing anyone; there are only great red tongues of flame and white flashes from swords in the flames and smoke.

"Allah! Allah!"

"Boom, boom, boom!" from the cannon inside.

The smoke is even denser, but it suddenly blows up above the heads of the defenders like a white bed-canopy picked apart into little round waves. And there is a clear view of the Turkish weapons glinting upwards and the Hungarian ones pointing down.

"Water! Water!" cries Gergely.

Down below the metal covering is seen rising. Huge stones rain down from the wall. The metal covering opens to swallow up the stones. Then it closes again.

543

"Boiling water!" shouts Zoltay too as he rushes to the spot. As soon as Gergely catches sight of Zoltay, he leaps for the cannon. There the resin is waiting for him in an open barrel. Gergely turns it up and says to the gunners, "Pack this into the cannon above the gunpowder, as much as you can get in! Hammer it in to break it up! And only put a little wadding on top of it!"

It was then that they tipped the boiling water over the wall. It penetrated where stones could not. The objects suddenly begin to waver and separate. Beneath them the Turks leap aside with cries of *"Ey va!"* and *"Meded!"*

The red insects are still on the wall. Gergely fires a mortar at them. But they still stay there. Gergely rushes towards them with the ramrod.

"Gergely!" calls Pető.

"Here I am," replies Gergely hoarsely.

"I've brought fifty men. Is that enough?"

"Fetch as many more as you can! Get them to lay a fire down below and keep on bringing up boiling water!"

A new volley from the *tüfekchis* mingles with the smoke from the mortar and obscures the wall for a minute. This minute is used by the lightly-clad climbers to overrun the ladders once more.

Gergely dashes back to the cannon. "Have you loaded it yet?" he asks.

"Yes," says old Gáspár Kocsis.

"Fire!"

The cannon emits flame, then detonates.

The resin shoots downwards in a hundred-foot jet of flame. Even those Turks who have only been caught by the edge of it leap down from the wall. Furious yells from the yasavuls and officers follow the clearance of the wall.

From the bastion there is a good view of all the soldiers running away from the wall. *Asabs, piyads, müsellems, delis, spahis, akindjis*—all of them in a confused mass run in terror towards the trenches, some shaking their hands, others their feet. They are bloodstained, angry and hardly human any more. It takes much shouting from all the *yasavuls* and agas to stem the tide. Now they use not whips but swords to turn back the mass of fleeing men.

"If you're a brave man, follow me!" Dervish Bey yells at them.

And new spirit pervades the blood-stained forces. Once more they pick up the siege-ladders and with blood-spattered heads and foaming with rage they charge straight at the wall where the Hungarian cannon are. They are led by the dervish. He flits along in front of them. His white robe is scarlet with blood. Gripping the precious horse-tails in his teeth, he dashes upwards without even a shield. On the ladder next to his an aga leads the way, a giant of a man. His turban is the size of a stork's nest and his sword like an executioner's.

Gergely looks around and once more sees beside him the page lifting a stone in a flurry of furious activity. He raises a big building-stone and hurls it down.

"Balázs!" Gergely turns on him. "Get out of here!" And when he reaches the last few words his hoarse voice has a ring in it. Balázs does not answer. In his hand he has the Italian dagger he brought out of the room. He suddenly makes a dash for the ladder on which the dervish is climbing up.

Gergely glances down.

"Hayvan!" he calls to the panting giant as his head appears. "Oh you idiot! You great jackass!" he goes on in Turkish. "And you really believe no weapon can harm you?"

The Turk comes to a sudden halt. His big wide face stares at Gergely expressionlessly. That instant is enough for Gergely. He thrusts his lance into the Turk's breast. The Turk grasps the lance with one hand and with the other aims a tremendous blow at Gergely. But the blow only cuts the air, and the great body falls on its back on to one of the tin-roofed objects.

Meanwhile the dervish has reached the top. Eva ducks her head away from the thrust of his lance. The next instant she makes a cut at the dervish and catches the left arm which is holding on to the ladder. The woollen robe splits apart on the dervish's arm, but beneath it is the glint of his shirt of mail.

With one leap he reaches the top of the wall. Gripping the sword that hangs on a strap he charges at Eva, panting angrily. Eva leaps two paces back. She holds the dagger rigidly in front of her, and awaits his attack with eyes wide open. But the Turk is an old hand at this game. He sees that a dagger and not a sword faces him, and knows that it is unwise to charge a long extended dagger. He stops himself abruptly and strikes the dagger to hit it aside so that with a second blow he can despatch this lad who looks like a page into the world of the spirits.

But Eva also knows that trick. With a swift circling movement she whisks the dagger upwards and avoids the Turk's sword. By the time he is ready to strike a second time, Eva's dagger has slipped beneath his arm.

It was the shirt of mail that saved the Turk's life. The steel links cracked, but the dervish struck at the same moment and his sword caught Eva on the head. Eva felt as if her head had split open. The world went dark before her eyes. The ground seemed to slip away from her feet. She raised her arm in front of her eyes and fell sideways like a sack beside the cannon.

21

When Eva came to her senses, there was silence all around her. Where was she? She had no idea. She opens her eyes and takes stock. A tumbledown building of logs... Between the logs a clear moonlit sky and stars gleaming white... Something hard presses painfully on her back. And her head rests in some cold moisture...

With a weary hand she feels under her back. She touches stone-dust and a cold cannon-ball the size of an apple.

Then suddenly everything becomes clear to her.

There is silence, so the battle is over. Who, she wonders, is in command of the fortress? The Turks or the Hungarians? Up on the platform she hears the slow, measured steps of a sentry: one, two, three, four...

Eva wants to get up, but her head is like lead. But as she tries to rise she sees that she is close to the bastion, and that next to her a woman lies face downwards and there is also a blue-coated soldier without a head.

Merciful God! If the Turks have conquered...

Lamplight glows red through the logs. Footsteps approach. A hoarse male voice says: "Shall we take the page first or the woman?"

Oh, thank God! They're talking Hungarian.

"Both of them," replies another voice.

"All the same, the page..."

"All right, let's take the page. The commander's still up." And they stop by Eva.

"Shall we take him to the palace, or where the rest are?"

"Where the rest are. He's just as dead as the others."

One of them grasps her legs, the other her shoulders, and they lift her on to a stretcher.

Eva speaks. "Men!"

"What? Are you alive then, young man? Thank God, Master Balázs! Then we'll take you to the palace."

"Men," murmurs Eva. "Is my lord alive?"

"Alive? Of course he is! The barbers are bandaging the commander's leg this very moment."

"I mean Captain Gergely."

"Master Gergely?" And he nudged his companion. "He's off his head."

The man spits into his palm. They get hold of the two ends of the stretcher and raise it.

"Men!" says Eva, almost shouting. "Give me an answer! Is Captain Gergely Bornemissza alive?"

She spoke in such a peremptory tone that the two men answer almost together: "Yes, he's alive."

"Is he wounded?"

"In the hand and foot."

"Take me to him!"

The two peasants stop. "To him?" One calls out to the sentry: "Hey, soldier! Where's Captain Gergely?"

"What do you want?" comes Gergely's voice from above.

"Young Master Balázs is here, sir. He'd like to have a word with you."

The sound of slow footsteps coming down the stairs. Gergely came in limping, a lantern in his hand. A candle was alight in the lantern. At the foot of the stairs he stopped and spoke to someone.

"Impossible! There are so many dead it'll take more than two days to clear them all."

"More than four," says a hoarse voice.

547

The lantern approaches.

"Take off my helmet," says Eva.

The peasant reached for the buckle under the woman's chin. Just then Gergely arrived there.

"Poor little Balázs!" he says. "But at least you're alive."

The peasant unbuckled the helmet and pulled it off. A burning stab of pain shooted through Eva's head.

"Oh!" she cries, almost shrieking.

For the blood has congealed on the lining of the helmet and her hair is stuck to it. The peasant certainly did not know that the wound was in her head as she lay there.

Gergely put down the lantern and bended over the woman.

The woman saw that Gergely's face is still just as dirty as it was. His moustache, beard and eyebrows were singed. His right hand was in a thick bandage. But her own face too was unrecognizable, there was so much blood and dirt on it. Only the whites of her eyes could be seen in that bloodstained, smoke-blackened face.

Gergely felt that same warm current surge through his veins as when he went after the mill-wheel and glimpsed those same eyes through the palace window. And the two pairs of eyes have met for an instant.

"Gergely!" Eva breaks the silence.

"Eva! Eva! How do you come to be here?"

And since at that moment there flashed through his brain all he had heard about his son and all he had seen of the behaviour of the woman he assumed to be the page, he realized the worst as soon as he asked the question. Tears welled into both his eyes and ran down his gunpowder-blackened face.

22

After that fearful attack, three days followed when the dead were cleared away. The dervishes and unarmed asabs carried the bodies. They were piled in heaps at the foot of the walls. The blood in the ditches had turned them to mud so deep that in places they threw log bridges over them to enable them to walk there. And around the dead there lay scattered and wrecked shields, horse-tail banners, swords, spears, bows and rifles everywhere. And a fearful stench of corpses.

The Turks bore off the dead day and night. From below the walls of the outer fortress alone they had to carry eight thousand bodies. Only on the third day was the last of them taken away, and by then the persistent flocks of ravens had to be scared away with rifle-fire.

But inside the fortress too there were great losses. The morning after the attack Father Márton sang the *Absolve Domine* over three hundred dead defenders at once. They lay in long lines around the common burial pit. In their midst was Father Bálint in his surplice and stole with a crucifix on his breast. Beside him Cecey, whose head was missing. Eight lieutenants. The page Balázs with his mother. Máté Szőr the miller from Maklár, Gergely the smith from Felnémet, Gasparics, Mrs. Ferenc Vas, women and girls in a great and silent multitude of unrecognizable, maimed and blood-stained corpses. In places there was only a head, in others only an arm and in others just a blood-stained suit of clothes and a booted leg in it.

The surviving officers were present at the funeral. Dobó himself was bareheaded, holding in his hand the flag of the fortress. When the priest had said the last rites, Dobó broke the silence and spoke sadly in a voice that kept breaking.

"I take off my helmet and stand before you, my brave companions who have died a holy death in blood and fire. Your souls are now far beyond the stars in the eternal homeland, and both present and future bless your mortal remains. I raise the flag of the fortress to salute you, glorious heroes. You have died for your homeland. You will receive your reward from God. Farewell to you! We shall meet again in the brightness of eternity, before the face of our king, St. Stephen."

The dead were lowered into the common grave without coffins, on a single plank.

The snow began to fall from the sky in white flakes.

*

On Sunday, 16 October Dobó slept for an hour in the afternoon, then rubbing the sleep from his eyes he got on his horse and rode to the Sándor Bastion.

The defenders were not engaged in building there now. They were standing and sitting about on the breaches.

The weather was cold and overcast.

The Turkish guns continued to fire unceasingly.

"Go along, Kristóf, my boy," said Dobó to his page, "and take a look at what's happening at the Bolyky Bastion. I'm going from here to the Old Gate."

Kristóf, who himself had a bandage over one eye, mounted his horse. At the Dark Gate he tethered the horse to a post and ran inside on foot, then continued along the wall to Bornemiszsza.

A rifle-bullet struck him through one of the gaps. He just turned and fell from the wall on to the rubble-covered platform. The sentry called to Zoltay: "Captain, sir! The little page has fallen!"

Zoltay climbed the wall dumbfounded. He saw the big red stain on the boy's breast. The soldier knelt beside him, and unbuckled his helmet as his head fell forward on his breast.

"Go immediately to the commander," said Zoltay, clasping the boy to him. "Report it to him."

The boy was still alive. His face was waxen and white. With glazed eyes he looked at Zoltay and murmured, "Report that I've died."

He gave a sigh and did indeed die.

*

The following day they did not awake to the sound of cannon. The tents stood white on the hillocks and hillsides, but there were no Turks to be seen.

"Careful!" said Dobó anxiously. "They may have set a trap for us." And he ordered sentries to the tunnels down below and the breaches up above. For now it was virtually impossible to stand anywhere on the parapet of the wall. The fortress was like a mouse-gnawed currant cake. In places the wall collapsed of itself if anyone stood on it.

As they were watching the peculiar silence and emptiness of the Turkish tents, someone suddenly said, merely as an opinion, "They've gone..."

Like fire racing through dry stubble the words were re-echoed throughout the fortress: "They've gone! They've gone!" And with increasing joy, "They've gone! They've gone!"

But the officers would not allow anyone outside the walls.

A quarter of an hour after sunrise the sentries reported the arrival of a woman. The black silk *feradje* that covered her head proclaimed that she was Turkish. She came from the direction of Maklár, riding on a mule. In front of her in the high saddle was a little Hungarian boy. A fifteen-year-old Saracen boy was leading the mule by the bridle.

They did not open the gate to the woman. How could they have done so? There was no gate there now. She rode through the gap beside the gate. She knew no Hungarian, so she simply called out "Dobó! Dobó!"

Dobó was standing on the ruins of the gate looking towards Füzesabony. He had seen the Turkish woman coming. And he also concluded immediately that she was the mother of the little Selim. All the same, as the woman called out his name, he limped down from the ruins.

The woman prostrated herself at his feet. Then she lifted her head again and, remaining on her knees, held out the little Hungarian boy to him.

"Selim! Selim!" she pleaded, putting her hands together.

The Hungarian boy was about six years old. He had a brown face and an intelligent expression. He was holding a little wooden horse in his hand. Dobó put his hand on the boy's head. "What's your name, my boy?"

"Jancsi."

"And your other name?"

"Bornemissza."

With a thrill of joy Dobó turned towards the Sándor Bastion. "Gergely! Gergely!" he shouted. "Quick! Go and get Captain Gergely!"

But by then Gergely was hurtling down from the bastion.

"Jancsi! My little Jancsi!" he shouted, his eyes full of tears. And he almost devoured the boy. "Come along to your mother!"

The Turkish woman held him tight with all ten fingers. She grasped the boy like an eagle with a lamb.

"Selim!" she called with black-ringed eyes, "Selim!"

551

It was obvious that she was ready to tear the boy to pieces if she did not get her own son back.

A minute later Eva hurried out of the palace in a billowing underskirt. She wore a white bandage round her forehead, but her face was radiant with joy. She held the little Turkish boy by the hand, making him run beside her. Little Selim was in his usual Turkish clothes, and held a big piece of cake in his hand as he ran.

Both mothers flew to their children with arms wide open. One called, "Selim!" The other called, "Jancsi!" And they knelt down to meet their sons. They hugged them, kissed them, devoured them. And as the two women knelt there opposite each other, their eyes met and they offered each other their hand.

23

It was true. The Turks had fled.

Varsányi, who followed the woman into the fortress, related how the pashas had wanted to make another attack, but when the janissaries were informed of this they threw down their weapons in front of the pashas' tent. And they shouted angrily: "We're not fighting any more! Even if you hang the lot of us, we're not fighting. Allah's not on our side! Allah's on the side of the Hungarians! We're not fighting against God!"

Ahmed Pasha wept in full view of the army and cursed Ali Pasha, tearing his beard: "Vile wretch!" he yelled in his face. "You told me Eger fortress was a tumbledown sheepfold and the defenders in it were sheep! Now you can take this disgrace to the emperor on your own!" And only the intervention of the beys prevented the two pashas from fighting each other in front of the whole army.

There were many officers missing too. Veli Bey had been carried from the battlefield on a stretcher. And Dervish Bey had been discovered half beaten to death that night under the walls.

Such despair had pervaded the Turkish army and so many had received wounds that the men had begun to withdraw even before the pashas had time to give the order. Those encamped below Felnémet had set light to the village and set off by the light of the fire. Nor did the rest wait for morning. They abandoned their tents and equipment and started out.

At Varsányi's words the defenders were possessed by ethereal joy. The people danced. They threw their caps to the ground. They ran up the Turkish flags. Father Márton took the crucifix that always accompanied him and raised it to the sky, shouting in a voice ringing with joy, "Te Deum laudamus!" And he fell to his knees, bowed to the ground and kissed the crucifix. He wept.

They dug the bell out of the ground and hoisted the beam from which it hung on to two poles. They tolled the bell.

"Bim, bam, bim, bam!" the bell rang merrily, and as Father Márton held up the cross in the centre of the square and sang, the people, including Dobó, knelt round him.

Even the wounded crept out of the corners and underground chambers and knelt behind the others.

But Lukács Nagy suddenly gave a great yell: "After them! Devil take the Sultan and all his works!"

The eyes of the armed men flashed towards Dobó. Dobó nodded his agreement.

The men leapt on to all the horses available in the fortress. Out they went at a gallop towards Maklár, after the Turks.

The infantrymen also went out of the fortress to the abandoned tents. And they brought them back in carts.

By evening every mounted soldier had returned to the fortress laden with booty.

Of the defenders three hundred were now at rest in the common grave below, and two hundred lay severely wounded on hay or straw all over the inner parts of the fortress; there was no knowing whether they would survive their appalling injuries.

All the commanding officers were wounded too, Dobó and Bornemissza in the hand and foot; Zoltay was on his back, Mekcsey was a mass of wounds and bruises from head to foot. His hair, beard, moustache and eyebrows were singed like those of Dobó and Bornemissza and most of the fighters. Fügedy's head was so swathed in bandages that only his eyes and ears were visible. Three of his teeth were missing too. A Turk had struck him with a club. But he bore his suffering happily, because one of those teeth was the one that had ached.

And not a man or woman among the defenders was without wounds. But rather there was one: the gypsy.

Sukán's last report went thus: "Commander, sir, I have to report that we have collected up all the larger cannon-balls that were fired into the fortress and counted them."

"How many?"

"Well, if we take no account of the several hundred that are still in the walls, there are five short of twelve thousand."

EPILOGUE

Any reader who wishes to know what happened after the siege can discover that in history books. They are my source for the following brief summary:

When before the siege Dobó asked the assembly at Szikszó for aid, he, or rather Mekcsey who represented him, was told, "If there aren't enough of you, why have you continued to be in command? You've made your bed: now lie on it!" To which both commanders gave an identical reply: after the siege they both resigned their command.

The news of the victory quickly spread westward. Europe applauded and rejoiced. In Rome the Pope celebrated a mass of thanksgiving. The king was bombarded with letters of congratulation. The people of Vienna marvelled at the flags seized from the Turks and sent there. (Doubtless Ali Pasha's velvet banner can still be seen there among the Habsburgs' spoils of victory.)

The king despatched Captain Matthias Sforzia to Eger to persuade Dobó and Mekcsey to stay, but they were adamant.

"We have done our duty," replied Dobó. "If only *others* had done so too! Please convey our respects and homage to His Majesty."

Then the king appointed Gergely Bornemissza to be commander of the fortress of Eger instead of Dobó.

GÁRDONYI'S NOTES TO THE TEXT

Page 40   The rifle and pistol were still such unreliable weapons in those days that it was possible to get within fifty paces of them.

Page 238   I myself noted down this song in Stamboul, where I witnessed this ceremony on 19 May 1899. I have recorded it as faithfully as possible.

Page 303   The cask contained 22.5 litres.

Page 442   In those days fine cloth was very expensive and available only in Vienna. The soldiers did not wear uniform. One suit of fine cloth would last a lifetime.

As far as money was concerned, Dobó's salary as commander was 600 forints, Sukán's 50 forints, the clerk Boldizsár's only 20 forints, Dobó's cook's 10 forints and his gardener's 6 forints—for a whole year. What Dobó called the "funds of the fortress" most probably came from his own pocket.

GLOSSARY

Aga   Turkish officer or court official of middle rank.

Akindji   Volunteer (irregular) Turkish cavalryman, serving only in time of war.

Asab   Turkish militiaman, usually locally-recruited for service in the infantry. In Hungary often dressed in Hungarian garb.

Asper   Turkish coin of small value.

Beshli   Turkish irregular cavalryman.

Bey   Senior Turkish officer and administrator of a province.

Beylerbey   "Bey of beys", governor of a conquered large province or *vilayet*.

Bostandji   Member of the Sultan's bodyguard.

Börek   Fritter made with minced meat or cheese.

"Brass pudding" (p. 27)   Misheard for "rice pudding", a dish unknown to the speaker.

Chavish   Turkish mounted gendarme.

Cheshnidji   "Food-sampler", hence steward, butler.

Datura stramonium   Thorn-apple.

Defterdar   Turkish Minister of Finance.

Deli   "Crazy"; irregular freebooter loosely attached to the Turkish cavalry on campaigns.

Dervish   Moslem religious man dedicated to poverty and austerity.

Devla   God (Gypsy).

Dinar   Silver coin.

Djebedji   Armourer to the janissaries, armoured Turkish infantryman.

Dózsa, György   (?1470–1514), leader of the Hungarian peasants' revolt of 1514. Defeated by Szapolyai at Temesvár, he was tortured and burnt to death. Tradition has it that his followers were compelled to eat his flesh.

Falconet   Light cannon.

Feradje   Cloak worn by Turkish women outside the house.

Ferdinand Ferdinand I, King of Hungary, 1526–1564. After the death of Lajos II at Mohács, he was elected king by those Hungarian magnates who opposed the already-crowned John Szapolyai. The latter, aided by the Turks, managed to retain much of the country. Despite the agreement of 1538 between the rival kings, Ferdinand was never able to establish his authority over the whole country; in 1547 he was compalled to cede Buda and the central region to the Turks.

Feri Familiar form of Ferenc (Francis).

Friar George (1482–1551), George Martinuzzi, Pauline monk, statesman and archbishop. Advisor to the Szapolyai family and guardian of the infant King John Sigismund, he tried to secure the independence of Hungary by playing off the Turks and Austrians against each other. The imperial general Castaldo, suspecting him of treachery, had him assassinated in 1551.

Gabion A cylinder of wicker filled with earth or stones, used to protect gun-sites.

Gergely Hungarian form of Gregory.

Gergő Familiar form of Gergely.

Giaour Turkish derogatory name for non-Moslem; infidel.

Gönüllü Irregular (volunteer) Turkish cavalryman, mainly recruited from Turkish-occupied territories.

Gureba Cavalryman of Arabian, Egyptian or Persian origin serving in the Turkish army.

Ileri! Advance! Forward!

Jancsi Familiar form of János (John).

Janissary Turkish *yeni çeri* "new troops"; the élite troops of the Turkish army, composed mainly of highly-trained foreigners captured or stolen by the Turks when children and educated in infantry barracks.

Kapudji "Doorkeeper": Turkish palace guard.

Kazai asker Judge-Advocate in the Turkish army.

Kinizsi, Pál (?–1494) Hungarian army captain renowned for his physical strength and courage in numerous expeditions against the Turks.

559

Kumbaradji   Turkish artificer, manufacturer of bombs and grenades.
Kurush   Turkish gold coin.

Lajos   Lajos II (1506–1526), King of Hungary (1516–1626) who died while attempting to flee from the Turks after the Battle of Mohács which signalled the beginning of the long Turkish occupation of Hungary.
Lagumdji   Turkish sapper, mine-layer.
Losonczy, István   (?–1552), Hungarian commander of the fortress of Temesvár. After a siege lasting a month he surrendered it to Ahmed Pasha, mainly in response to the demands of the German and Spanish mercenaries who were defending it. As they left the fortress, the Turks attacked them; Losonczy was wounded and captured, then beheaded by the pasha.

Martonfalvay, Imre   (1510–?1591) Secretary and steward to Bálint Török and two further generations of the Török family.
Matthias   (Corvinus) (1443–1490), King Matthias I of Hungary, 1458–1490 and one of her most eminent rulers.
Matyi   Familiar form of Mátyás (Matthias).
Mohács   Town in Southern Hungary, the scene of the disastrous defeat of the Hungarians under Lajos II by the Turks in 1526, leading to the Turkish conquest of most of Hungary.
Meyhanedji   Turkish innkeeper.
Müsellem   Irregular cavalryman in the Turkish army, mainly from Turkey proper.

Nishandji bey   The Turkish royal scribe.

Padishah   The Great King, a title of the Sultan.
Pasha   The highest civilian and military rank under the Turkish Sultan.
Piyad   Foot-soldier, infantryman.

Rajkó   Gypsy child.

Sanjak   District, subdivision of a Turkish province.
Silahtar   Turkish squire, cavalryman who carried and looked after the weapons of a senior officer.
Solak   Bowman in the Sultan's bodyguard.

Spahi (Turkish *sipahi*) Irregular member of the Turkish cavalry, usually a landowner whose duty was to serve on horseback. The spahis formed the backbone of the Turkish army.

Stephen I, King and Saint (?977–1038), the first king of Hungary, crowned in 1000, canonized in 1083.

Szapolyai (Zápolya), John (1487–1540), King John I of Hungary (1526–1540), crowned after the death of Lajos II at Mohács but opposed by the rival Ferdinand I. With Turkish aid he managed to secure Buda and most of Hungary, but thus paved the way for the Turkish conquest of central Hungary. Although he entered into an agreement with Ferdinand in 1538 that the latter should succeed him, he broke this in favour of his son John Sigismund (1540–1571), who was duly elected king.

Temessük "title-deed"; here "pass".

Thuya An ornamental coniferous tree, otherwise known as *Arbor vitae,* the tree of life.

Tinódi, Sebestyén (died 1556), Hungarian lutenist and chronicler. An itinerant minstrel, he recorded and published verse-epics on the struggle against the Turks, including the siege of Eger.

Topchi Turkish artilleryman, bombardier.

Tüfekchi "Musketeer", an ex-janissary in the retinue of a pasha, also serving as a member of a gun-crew.

Ulufedji Turkish mercenary serving with the cavalry and military police.

Werbőczy, István (1458–1541), Hungarian statesman and legal expert, codifier of the Hungarian legal system. He was John Szapolyai's chancellor and envoy to the Sultan, who after the Turkish occupation of Buda in 1541 appointed him chief justice; he died shortly after this, probably by poison.

Yasavul Turkish military policeman.

Yataghan Heavy Turkish sabre.

Yumurdjak The nickname means "plague, pest".

Zrínyi, Miklós (1508–1566), Bán (Governor) of Croatia and commander of the fortress of Szigetvár, South-west Hungary from 1561. He was renowned for his exploits against the Turks, and in particular for his heroic defence of Szigetvár in 1566, when he met his death.

Printed in Hungary, 2005
Szekszárdi Printing House